MAN'S BOOK

VILLA MIMOSA
Jerrard Tickell

*

SUBSMASH!
J. E. Macdonnell

*

DEADLY WELCOME
John D. MacDonald

ODHAMS PRESS LIMITED

LONG ACRE, LONDON

CONTENTS

S.1161.SA.
MADE AND PRINTED IN
GREAT BRITAIN BY ODHAMS (WATFORD) LTD.
WATFORD, HERTS

VILLA MIMOSA

Jerrard Tickell

An hour of good fortune is worth more indeed to us as soldiers
than if a letter from Venus recommended us to Mars.

Juvenal, *Satires*, 16, 4.

*"Villa Mimosa" is published by
Hodder and Stoughton Ltd.*

The Author

Jerrard Tickell was born in Ireland and was educated at Highgate School; he is married and has three sons. In 1939 he went into the army as a private; by the time he was demobilized he had reached the rank of major, and had seen service in every theatre of war except the Far East. With his first book, *See How They Run*, he achieved success: it was a Book Society Choice. His first major biography was that of the famous Odette; the novel *Appointment with Venus* was filmed, so was *A Day to Remember*; his other books include *Soldier from the Wars Returning*, *Miss May* and *The Hero of Saint Roger*. Novelist, biographer, lecturer and wit, Jerrard Tickell is all of these. For good measure, he has the unusual honour of being a "blood-brother" to an African king.

FOR RENEE ORIANA

WHO PUT UP WITH IT

Acknowledgments

It was on a sunny morning in Saint John's Wood that I found myself with my old friend Willi Frischauer, to whom I always turn for scholarly guidance on German modes, motives and manners. During that morning the—alas—imaginary ladies of the Villa Mimosa swam gracefully upwards to the brims of our wine glasses. This visionary establishment became solid in our minds and I acknowledge with gratitude the idea as well as many of the technical details concerning the German Army.

During the writing of the book many of my friends—still serving, retired or civilian—helped to plan operations "Firefly" and "Sabine". In particular, I would like to thank Major-General T. W. Richardson, O.B.E.; Brigadier Godfrey Hobbs, C.B.E., and Commander F. E. Sanders, O.B.E., R.N., both of the Ministry of Defence; Colonel L. B. B. Beuttler, O.B.E., of Amphibious Warfare H/Q, and Commander John Eardley Wilmot, M.V.O., D.S.C., R.N., of the Admiralty; Wing-Commander John ("Whippy") Nesbitt-Dufort, D.S.O., Croix de Guerre, R.A.F.; Miss Vera Atkins, Croix de Guerre, W.A.A.F., Mrs. "Schnipe" Malinska, R.C.A.F., and Mademoiselle Marguerite ("Quita") de Mortemart. Geoffrey Snell should possibly have headed this list.

To all of them and to others whose names I may have unintentionally omitted, I am profoundly grateful.   JERRARD TICKELL

1: SAINT VALENTINE'S EVE

AT nine o'clock exactly on the 13th of February, 1944, Madame came out of her room on the first-floor landing of the Villa Mimosa and entered the candle-lit Salon. Her six *pensionnaires* stood up, presenting themselves for inspection.

"Bon soir, mes filles."

"Bon soir, Madame."

Madame inclined her head and looked at each of the six girls with critical affection.

"Ah, Lucille, I see that you have washed your hair. It looks very pretty, but it will be even prettier tomorrow when it has had time to settle down." She passed on. Elsa was wearing threadbare bedroom slippers and Madame frowned. But there was, alas, nothing to be done about it. Madame's little stock of coupons had long been exhausted and in any case the shops of Coville were bare of all but the necessities of living. She stopped opposite Wanda, between whose fingers a cigarette smouldered. She said evenly:

"Where did you get that cigarette, Wanda?"

Wanda answered with a pout.

"Captain Paul gave it to me last night, Madame."

"How many cigarettes did he give you?"

"A few. I cannot remember how many, Madame."

"And have you shared them with the other girls?"

"There were only a few, Madame—and Captain Paul gave them to *me*."

"Nevertheless, you should have shared them. I will not tolerate selfishness in this house. Do not let it happen again."

She transferred her gaze to Monique. Monique was not quite so young as the others and recently the extra years had begun to reveal themselves in many ways. Tonight she already looked tired and dispirited and the corners of her painted mouth were slightly down-drawn. Madame suppressed a sigh. As in the case of Elsa's bedroom slippers, there was nothing to be done about it. She gave Monique a friendly nod and looked at Magda. After a moment, she said:

"Please come and see me in my room."

"Certainly, Madame."

There was no need for Madame to look at Golden Mouse except for the pleasure that she always derived from the contemplation of the immaculate. She dismissed the girls and returned to her room where Magda awaited her in some apprehension.

Madame sat down at her desk. She said after a moment:

"Please show me your nails."

Reluctantly Magda stretched out her two hands. Madame shook her head.

"I asked you to come in here because I was unwilling to reprove you in front of the others. Yours is a sin of omission—unlike Wanda whose selfishness was deliberate. No woman, no matter what her station in life, should ever neglect her hands. I know that soap is scarce but that is no excuse. I have spoken to you about this before, Magda. Please do not make it necessary for me to do so again. Now go to your room and see to it."

"I offer you my apologies, Madame."

"And I accept them. Believe me when I tell you, child, that what I have said is in your own interests. I have known a happy marriage break up from inattention to detail. You may yourself marry one day and cleanliness is largely a matter of habit."

"Shall I show you my hands when I come down, Madame?"

"No. I know that you will do what I ask you. Now hurry. Our guests will be arriving shortly."

*   *   *

Outside the curtained windows of the Villa Mimosa, a thin wind, bringing the rain with it, was sweeping over the Pas de Calais from the English Channel.

General Wolf von Wolfram, Commander of a Panzer Corps in Rommel's XVth Army, sat stiffly in his staff car as it splashed its way with hooded lights from the coast to his headquarters. The day's inspection had brought little joy to the General. Work on the Atlantic Wall and on Hitler's new V-weapon sites had continuously been interrupted by Allied aircraft insolently bombing, machine-gunning and ripping up the railway lines with cannon. The British and American Air Forces were more closely interlocked than ever and merely took over from each other. Four times in one short February day, the General had found himself making for the shelters, a pretty place for one who wore on his breast the Knight's Cross of the Iron Cross with Swords.

Tall, lean and stern, the General stared straight ahead. He had not spoken for over half an hour. He did not see the rhythmic swing of the wind-screen wipers lifting segments of rain off the streaming glass. He was staring into the past and into the future.

He saw Germany aggressive, Germany marching, Germany triumphant; he saw Germany halted, Germany "regrouping", Germany on the defensive; now, with a sense of foreboding as chill as the wind that came from England, he saw Germany in defeat.

The General stirred uneasily. The Fuehrer, whom he had sworn to serve, had boasted that the German Reich would last for a thousand years. To an honourable soldier, even to harbour doubt was in itself an inner act of treachery. The words of the oath he and every other fighting man had been forced to take were clear and unequivocal. He knew every syllable of them by heart. *"I swear by God this holy oath that I will render unconditional obedience to the Fuehrer of the German Reich and people, Supreme Commander of the German Armed Forces, Adolf Hitler, and that, as a brave soldier, I will be prepared at all times to give my life for this oath."*

To give one's life for Germany was the accepted lot of a soldier; to die for a single despot who had already dragged Germany to the brink of the inferno was surely a travesty of patriotism. The General's mind, freed by reality from the control of his will, flowed along the channels of his emotions. Fuehrer or no Fuehrer, he longed passionately to save the Germany he loved from the doom to come.

At General von Wolfram's side in the car sat his Staff Officer, Major Hans Ramberg.

Aged thirty-three, Hans was a rare combination of scholar, soldier, patriot and *bon viveur*. The first three characteristics endeared him to the General and the last was a vicarious compensation for his master's austerity. Hans, too, had taken the oath. Of more flexible fibre than his master, he had come to regard as ludicrous a wordy formula extracted from him by an Austrian Lance-Corporal whose own record of promise-breaking was unequalled since the days of Genghis Khan.

Muscular, fair-haired and with eyes of light, almost metallic, blue, Hans Ramberg was seen to possess all the physical attributes of the pure Nordic. It was, therefore, to the disappointment of Hitler's eugenically-minded experts—always on the look-out for promising stud-farm material—that he remained a bachelor. He treated with politeness the flaxen fillies and brood mares who were led to him for his consideration, remarking to his friends how completely he agreed with Montaigne's comment that *"a good marriage would be between a blind wife and a deaf husband"*. Hans' own hearing was particularly acute.

The General spoke suddenly, sharply.

"Hans, what is the time?"

Hans flashed a pocket torch on his wrist-watch.

"Twenty past eight, Herr General." He rubbed the clouded window and peered out into the rainy dark. "As far as I can judge, we should be at the Manoir at a quarter to nine."

"We cannot arrive too early for me." He went on with a touch of irritation: "When is my watch to be returned? I have been without it for a week and you know that it was a birthday present from my wife."

"I do indeed, Herr General. It was on Monday last that I gave it to Charles Bertin, watchmaker of Coville. He informed me that the balance staff was broken and that it would be necessary to make a new one on a lathe. He had promised to deliver it tomorrow. Bertin is a very reliable fellow and I am sure that he will keep his word."

"If your friend is reliable, he is the only one in Coville who is. The town is a hive of spies. The people watch all our comings and goings with eyes like photographic film, recording everything. When Field-Marshal Rommel ordered the evacuation of all French civilians from the coastal belt, he should have included that thrice-damned town."

"As you say, Herr General." Hans coughed. He knew General von Wolfram in all his moods and this was a moment when he could permit himself a pleasantry. "But consider, Herr General, that if the good Field-Marshal *had* turned all the French out of Coville, there would be nobody left to mend your watch."

General von Wolfram grunted. "You have an answer to everything, Hans. One day, it will be your undoing." He leaned forward and felt with his fingers to make sure the glass partition separating the interior of the car from the driver was securely shut and soundproof. Corporal Mueller was not of his choosing. He had been posted as driver to the General a few days ago and could quite easily be a Gestapo man with orders to report all his master's conversation. Such things happened more and more frequently as the breach between Party and Army widened. Nowadays Himmler's men were everywhere. Their unidentifiable presence was not exactly flattering to a Corps Commander who had been decorated for gallantry with the Knight's Cross of the Iron Cross with Swords. It was galling indeed for an honourable man to be regarded as a potential traitor.

He sat well back in the car and said in a low voice:

"I would like to hear your confidential opinion of the Anglo-Saxons."

"With great pleasure, Herr General."

*   *   *

Hans Ramberg was regarded as an expert on England and the English.

After leaving Heidelberg, he had gone up to Oxford as a Rhodes Scholar and read English. His first year had been dedicated to college ties, scarves, blazers, cuff-links and tobacco jars while he observed his fellow undergraduates with Teutonic thoroughness. During this year, he found much cause to despise the English. They were foul-mouthed, virginal, insular and yet loud in the disparagement of their own country. If a German were to describe Hitler's Reich in similar terms, he would either find himself in Buchenwald—or even dangling at the end of a rope. Yet when the English belittled their own glory, people only laughed. He had returned in disgust to a strenuous, awakened Germany and used words like "effete" and "decadent", convinced that from England nothing was to be feared.

At the beginning of his second year, he had disposed of his multi-coloured college haberdashery to a dewy-eyed freshman, only keeping the cuff-links. He had worn them throughout the Russian campaign. He was wearing them now. During this year, he began slowly, and at first unwillingly, to moderate his views. He pondered the words of Carlyle: *"Of all the nations in the world, the English are the stupidest in speech, the wisest in action."* Could it be that Carlyle was right and he—and Ribbentrop—wrong? For three terms, he had vacillated, keeping stiffly aloof, and, during the long vacation in the Black Forest, was dismayed to find himself counting the days until he could return to the sound of the sprinkling bells.

With his third year came love, love for his friends, love for the lawns and the cloisters and the laughter. He even came to love his bicycle and his shabby gown, attributing lives to these inanimate things because they were part of his own life. He had rowed in his college eight, and taken to accompanying himself on the mandolin while he sang sentimental or bawdy songs. A keen mountaineer, he had climbed the roof of one of the women's colleges and broken both his ankle and his heart. On Guy Fawkes Night, he had got drunk, been arrested and charged with assault and battery on the person of P.C. O'Connell—a frolic that cost him five pounds and a gating for the rest of the term. He had finally got a Second in Schools and when he left Oxford for ever, he saw little of the countryside from the windows of the train that took him to Paddington *en route* for home.

Hans Ramberg, B.A. (Oxon), had been an automatic object of suspicion to the dozen or more competing security services that squabbled incessantly within the Nazi framework. He proved himself "a good German" by joining the Army in 1937, and his various dossiers were closed. He had served in Norway and in Russia as a fighting soldier before being posted to the staff. Throughout the war, he had always joined lustily in the chorus of *"Wir fahren gegen Enge-land"*—only murmuring *sotto voce* and nostalgically: "if only I could. . . ."

Disillusionment had come to him after Stalingrad. His head was already forfeit.

*   *   *

"Come out of your reverie, Hans. I asked you a question."

"I beg your pardon, Herr General." He coughed. "It would be a presumption on my part to offer an opinion. It has already been established that the English are a decadent race. We have it on the authority of no less a person than——"

"Yes. I know. Ribbentrop." He was unable to control the lengthening of his upper lip. "But you forget that I have myself had some experience of the decadent English—at Saint Nazaire. Now you, Hans, were at the University of Cambridge for——"

"*Not* Cambridge. Oxford."

The General snapped his fingers impatiently.

"Oxford, Cambridge—they are the same thing. What I wish to know is——"

"With the greatest possible respect for your rank, Herr General, Oxford and Cambridge are by no means the same thing. As in the case of Yale and Harvard, there is a fierce and lasting rivalry between them. To illustrate this, I remember that during the Boat Race in 1935, the Oxford——"

"The devil take your Boat Race. I care nothing for your infantile memories of a regatta. In the strictest confidence, I want your considered views on two questions. The Western Allies will launch their armies against the Atlantic Wall this year. That we know. But when will they strike, Hans—and where?"

"Surely, Herr General, neither point is in dispute. Our Fuehrer himself has decreed that the landings will take place in early summer and that the attack will be against the Pas de Calais. He bases his strategy on the fact that a horse, when confronted by a water jump, always takes the shortest stretch."

"If my memory serves me correctly," said the General acidly, "our Fuehrer served in the Infantry—*not* the Cavalry. My experience is that a horse jumps where he knows that his foothold will be secure." Again he leaned forward and tested the panel between himself and the driver. One never knew nowadays. "I have been much concerned about this," he said in a low voice, "and attempting to put myself into the mind of my enemies. Montgomery had a photograph of Field-Marshal Rommel in his caravan and he studied it intently, seeking to enter Rommel's mind. The measure of his success was the elimination of the Afrika Korps. I do not, alas, know the English. But you do."

"A few drunken rowing men and one or two troubadours," said Hans deprecatingly.

"Nonsense. I rely on your judgement. The Pas de Calais is more strongly fortified than any other sector on the French Coast. Our powerful XVth Army is concentrated and ready and the ground has been cleared for battle. Our enemies are aware of these facts. Yet they continue to mass their shipping opposite the Pas de Calais, the most elaborately defended lodgement since Stalingrad. It is either the act of fools—or of men full of guile. Churchill, Eisenhower and Montgomery are not fools."

"You interest me very much, Herr General."

He lied. He was only listening with half an ear, for his thoughts were elsewhere. This was the first occasion when the General had become articulate on the subject of Hitler's strategy. He had dared to express a doubt. Great events had small beginnings and Hans proposed to exploit this confidence to the full, underlining that doubt, relating it subtly to catastrophe and to carnage. He would have much to tell his friends—later tonight.

"Now, Hans, I want you to gaze in your mind's eye at the map of northern France."

"Certainly, Herr General."

The map at which Hans Ramberg gazed was far from the fields of war. It was a map of a narrow, unfrequented road that led from the stables at the back of Corps Headquarters to a certain house. In less than an hour, Hans would travel that road and enter that house.

"The bay of the Seine," said General von Wolfram in guarded tones, "has a large port on either flank. The Cotentin Peninsula protects it from the prevailing westerly winds. The two rivers Seine and Loire enclose, as it were, a vast quadrilateral of land, bounded on the north-west by the sea. Broadly speaking, the topography is angular. Have you this angular picture clear in your mind, Hans?"

"It is crystal clear, Herr General."

Again he lied. The picture in Hans' mind was by no means angular. In thinking of that certain house and of those who dwelled there, the image that formed was tenderly curved—and the curves could either be those of Lucille, Elsa, Wanda, Monique, Magda or Golden Mouse. He only wished that the dolt of a driver would go faster.

"By bombing the bridges over these two rivers, Eisenhower could isolate our whole VIIth Army. . . ."

The General talked on, developing his theory. Now and again Hans interjected a respectful word. The wind was rising and the rain came gustily, darting in little erratic streamlets down the misted windows of the car. At a familiar bend in the road, he rubbed a clear space with his gloved hand and peered out. Good. Only five more minutes to go and the General had just reached his peroration.

". . . Is it not possible, therefore, that our Fuehrer has made a miscalculation? Could not the threat to the Pas de Calais be a gigantic bluff devised by that arch-schemer Winston Churchill? If so, it means that we in the XVth Army will be left twiddling our thumbs while the Allies over-run Normandy." He glanced again at the driver's uncompromising back and further lowered his voice. "I need hardly emphasize, Hans, that what I have just said is in no sense a criticism of our Fuehrer. Far from it. I would not like it to be known that I ever even indulged in . . . er . . . academic speculation."

"I am honoured by the confidence you repose in me, Herr General—honoured and encouraged." This was neither the time nor the place for discussion. But a hint could be dropped. He went on deliberately. "It is possible that in the near future I may offer *you* a far more grave confidence—and an opportunity."

"A confidence and an opportunity! You sound positively con-spiratorial." He added jocularly: "Remember your oath."

"The terms of it are clearly in my mind, Herr General. It is binding unto death, that is to say, either Hitler's death or mine. I profoundly hope to be predeceased by the Fuehrer."

"Hans!"

"All men are mortal, Herr General. It is the final debt that all must pay—and my oath is to one who owes millions. I would not like to stand in his shoes before God."

The wheels of the car squelched to a halt outside an elaborately wrought iron gate. Three steel-helmeted sentries, their capes gleaming with rain, squinted into the car and saluted. General von Wolfram wound down the window and a flurry of drops spattered the inside of the car.

"A dirty night, Sergeant. Arrange for a special issue of grog for all sentries when they come off duty."

The gate swung open and the car, followed by a benediction, splashed up the drive and stopped outside the nail-studded oak door of the Manoir.

* * *

Field-Marshal Rommel's anti-invasion plan was a simple one. It was to hurl the Allies back into the sea before they could get a foothold in the Pas de Calais. With nostalgic visions of the wide spaces of the desert, he decided to clear the ground for action—while there was still time. He wanted room for the battle, room in which his Panzers could swing and manœuvre and fight. He therefore ordered the evacuation of all French civilians from a coastal belt some twenty-five kilometres in depth, extending from the fringe of the waves to the outskirts of Coville. French farms and houses that had weathered the centuries were bull-dozed into rubble and their owners conscripted for forced labour in the Reich. The Manoir remained.

Once the residence of the infamous Duc de Coville, eighteenth-century poet and libertine, the old house had been chosen as Panzer Korps headquarters for several reasons. Sheltered and half-hidden by the enclosing wing of a beech wood, it was reasonably safe from air attack. Its many-turreted roof had been most skilfully camouflaged and the huddle of stables, seen from the sky, had a deserted appearance. The huge dining-room, ancient scene of many a carouse, now served General von Wolfram very well as a conference chamber, and a labyrinth of bedrooms on the upper floors was occupied by his staff. The wine-cellars, designed for a more genial purpose, had become admirable air-raid shelters.

Road communications were good and Field-Marshal Rommel frequently paid unannounced calls on his journeys to and from the coast.

General von Wolfram strode into the flagged hall of the Manoir, the steel-rimmed heels of his boots echoing. His servant Ernst took his wet cap and greatcoat and he himself unbuckled his belt. He stood with his back to the old-fashioned stove, warming his chilled hands. His Signals Officer came running with a sheaf of messages and the General skimmed them, dictating terse replies while his servant waited out of earshot. Then, in answer to a snap of the fingers, Ernst stepped forward and bowed obsequiously.

"Draw me a hot bath and serve dinner in thirty-five minutes exactly. What has the cook in mind?"

"Asparagus soup, Herr General, followed by *coq au vin.*"

"A pretty choice. Such a meal deserves a good bottle. Let me think. Hm." It had been a long, cold, wet and humiliating day and what could be more pleasant than to relax and to continue his discussion with Hans in private. He had been both shocked and puzzled by his Staff Officer's last comment and did not want to go to bed with his curiosity unsatisfied. "Tonight I have decided to give myself a treat. Decant a bottle of the Mouton-Rothschild 1933 and put it on the chimney piece." He turned to Hans Ramberg with a smile. "I hope you will give me the pleasure of your company at dinner tonight, Hans. The Mouton-Rothschild '33 is one of the noblest spoils of war. It is unique. The French do not describe it as a wine but as an Act of God. For once they do not exaggerate."

Hans was wholly at his ease. He had had a premonition of this invitation some minutes ago and his agile brain had already considered and rejected half a dozen plausible excuses, finally settling on the one which he knew his host would instantly accept. In the General's mind, a plea of duty would overwhelm every social engagement no matter how attractive.

"You honour me greatly, Herr General," he said apologetically, "but with the greatest regret I am going to ask your permission to say 'no'. Upon reflection, I consider it my duty to study and to consider at once the tactical point we discussed in the car this evening. It has the widest implications and demands my immediate attention. Though it would give me far greater pleasure to dine with you, I am called to a cup of coffee, a sandwich—and the map of northern France."

"Of course, Hans. Duty comes first, always." Though his eyes showed his disappointment, it did not occur to General von Wolfram to doubt the word or the good faith of an officer. Again he snapped his fingers and his hovering servant sprang to attention.

"Tell the cook I shall only require an omelette, some bread and butter and a glass of Moselle. And you, Hans, don't work too hard. You have had a long day and deserve an early night."

"I promise you to be between the sheets as soon as my task is done." He clicked his heels. "Goodnight, Herr General."

"Goodnight, Hans. Sleep well."

Hans looked directly at General von Wolfram. There was the ghost of a smile behind his eyes as he went through the verbal ritual. He said meaningly:

"Er . . . *Heil Hitler!*"

"*Heil Hitler!*"

*　　*　　*

Hans Ramberg walked quickly up the wide staircase and along a corridor to his bedroom. That had been a near thing, a damned near thing. But, thank the Lord, the General had only issued an invitation. He had not given a command—or he would indeed, he thought humorously, have been in the asparagus soup. He rang for his servant and ordered coffee and sandwiches to be brought up as quickly as possible. While he waited, he opened and spread out a map of northern France on his desk. Then he stripped to the waist and washed, besprinkling himself liberally with eau de Cologne. In deference to English tradition, he had reluctantly given up the use of eau de Cologne while he was at Oxford—but this was the more elegant continent of Europe. He brushed his thick, fair hair and put on a new tunic. A glance in the looking-glass pleased him. The sense of elation within him was reflected in his eager eyes. When his servant arrived with coffee and sandwiches on a tray, Hans addressed him genially.

"Thank you, my friend. On the desk, please. I have some very important work to do tonight and I do not want to be disturbed. Not in any circumstances. Is that clearly understood?"

"It is understood. Goodnight, Herr Major."

"Goodnight, Konrad."

When the sound of Konrad's footsteps had died away, Hans

poured the coffee down his wash-basin. A careful man, he
scattered a few crumbs on the plate before wrapping up the sandwiches in paper and putting them in his pocket. He would give
them to old Marie, the housemaid at the Villa Mimosa. Over his
uniform he put on a mackintosh that bore no badges of rank.
Now for his forage cap and he was ready. As always, he left the
light on. Silently he left his room, locking the door behind him,
and tip-toed along the corridor to the back stairs. He met nobody.

He crossed the cobbled courtyard, walking very slowly until his
eyes should become accustomed to the rainy dark. He arrived at
the building he sought, the musty and rat-infested loose-box
where he kept his bicycle. The half-door opened with a rusty
whine and, for the hundredth time, he cursed himself for forgetting to oil that hinge. Wheeling the bicycle and keeping close
to the stable wall, he groped towards the barred gate that led to
the apple orchard with its leafless trees, blackened by rain and
creaking in the eddies of the wind. There was a rickety wooden
bridge over the trout-stream. One dark night last week, he had
missed his footing and fallen into the stream up to his waist and
arrived back at the Manoir sodden and blue with cold. Tonight
he crossed it safely. Next came half an acre of squelching beets
and then, at last, the hard narrow road.

He lit the hooded bicycle lamp which only gave a feeble
glimmer. It was enough for one who knew the way so well.
Weaving round the puddles towards the long hill, Hans began
to sing. His visits to the Villa Mimosa always gave him a feeling
of excited anticipation and, to add a spice of danger, he sang in
English.

> "Oh, I love to climb a mountain
> And to reach the highest peak.
> But it doesn't srill me half as much
> As dancing sheek to sheek. . . ."

Now started the slight gradient that climbed between sentinel
poplars. Hans fell silent, saving his breath for the ascent. Arrived
at the top, he paused for a moment to wipe the rain and sweat
from his face. He knew that there was a flat, ten-acre field of
stubble to his right that ought to be spiked against parachutists.
On the other hand the last thing he wanted to do was to direct
attention to anywhere in the vicinity of the Villa. Let it remain!
He mounted his bicycle again and began to free-wheel down.

"Heaven! I'm in heaven,
And my heart beats so sat I can hardly speak,
And I seem to find the happiness I seek
Ven we're out togezzer
Dancing sheek to sheek. . . ."

Less than a kilometre more. Soon Hans slowed down, peering to the left. He saw the dim shape of a farm cart resting on its shafts alongside a mouldy hay-cock. To the right a tall house was jet black against the racing dark grey of the sky. He dismounted and listened intently, his head on one side and a smile at the corners of his mouth. He heard the rippling notes of a piano played softly by a hunchback within the curtained windows of that tall house. He leaned his bicycle against the dripping hedge and opened the garden gate and walked lightly up the path to the front door. He knew where the bell-push was and he pressed it, giving a private signal. While he waited, he flashed his torch upwards towards the cracked fan-light over the door and his smile widened. Painted in thin, spidery letters was the name of the house.

It was a name that always evoked images and scents that were far away from the war and the wind and the rain of the Pas de Calais. It smelled of the South and of the sun and of a tideless sea, blue as a peacock's neck; it smelled of spring and of feathery clusters, yellower than a day-old chick; it smelled of sun-steeped hillsides where lizards watched from cracks in the rocks; it smelled of conspiracy and of delight.

The door of the Villa Mimosa opened and Hans Ramberg stepped inside.

2: THE VILLA MIMOSA

As soon as Hans entered the dim hall, the door was immediately closed, shutting out the night. The music was clearer now and came from the first floor. Gaston, the hunchback, was playing Debussy's *L'après-midi d'un faune,* and playing it very well, too. Marie, the old housemaid, took Hans' soaked mackintosh and hung it up. He gave her the sandwiches. He was very much at home as he walked upstairs towards the beckoning music.

He paused on the landing and bowed. A statuesque figure in black silk awaited him. Black silk was, he thought cynically, as much a uniform as his own field grey.

"Good evening, Madame."

"Good evening, Major. Might I have a word with you before you join your friends?"

"With pleasure, Madame."

She led the way into a small room and sat down. He looked at her with curiosity. Her face was thin and ageless and the colour of parchment. Her eyes were dark and unfathomable and he had never known her to smile. Her vocabulary was that of a highly educated woman and her diction immaculate. He knew nothing of her birth or background. Even her name was unknown to him. She was "Madame".

She began at once, speaking to him as an equal.

"It always causes me distress to appear in the role of supplicant. You will know that I do not ask on my own behalf—but for those for whom I have made myself responsible. May I have your assurance that you understand this?"

"Of course, Madame."

"Good. We in the Villa Mimosa would very much welcome a sack of flour. Magda—you know Magda—used to be a very good pastry-cook in Budapest and I am anxious that she should continue to practise this art—for art it is. Good pastry-cooks are rare, the war will not last for ever and Magda may one day wish to marry. Few men can resist a first-class pastry-cook."

"I agree, Madame. I will arrange for a sack of flour."

"You are very kind, Major. Flour is of little use, however, without butter and sugar. May I therefore suggest . . . ?"

"Both are scarce, but I will do what I can."

"I have every confidence in you. We also require meat and, if possible, some green vegetables. There are nine of us under this roof. Old Marie, my housemaid, *mes filles*"—she used the word with affection—"Gaston my pianist and I myself. The last delivery of meat," she said reprovingly as if talking to her butcher, "was tough and far from satisfactory."

"I will see that your complaint reaches the N.C.O. who was responsible," he said humbly. "In the meantime, please accept my apologies."

Madame inclined her head.

"My next request is for some more champagne. We are down to our last case—of which there are only eight bottles left." From the Salon next door there was a loud and unmistakable pop. Madame said without the glimmer of a smile: "Permit me to revise that figure. There are now *seven* bottles left."

Hans clicked his tongue in sympathy. "This is a very serious matter. For the Villa Mimosa to be even temporarily reduced to seven bottles of champagne is unthinkable." He smiled. "For tonight champagne will have to be rationed but six cases will be delivered tomorrow."

"Thank you. I have one last request which for once does not concern the Commissariat. You are aware that the future of my girls is my constant preoccupation. I have discovered that Lucille does the most exquisite needlework. During the day she has a lot of time on her hands which she could very usefully employ in making . . . certain garments both for herself and for my other *pensionnaires*. She would thus keep her undoubted talent in practice and at the same time supplement the somewhat meagre wardrobes of her sisters. Elsa, for example, urgently needs a pair of house-shoes. Just as few men can resist a good pastry-cook, a first-class needlewoman has rarely to look far for a husband."

Needlework was a talent that Lucille had failed to bring to his attention. Hans smiled.

"Forgive me, Madame, but I fail to see of what assistance I can be to Lucille in her needlework."

"I will explain. The shops in Coville are bare. The shops in Paris have at least a limited choice of silks, chiffons—and shoes. For Lucille to travel from this, the evacuated area, to Paris without a *permis* would be impossible. Is it within your power to issue such a *permis* for one day? I personally would guarantee Lucille's return."

Hans frowned. In the granting of this last request he saw difficulty and danger. He said slowly:

"All civilian movement is controlled not by the Army but by the S.S. Up to now the existence of the Villa Mimosa is unknown to these . . . er . . . gentlemen in black. I would not wish to draw the attention of the S.S. either to the Villa or to any of its occupants. On the other hand . . ." He drummed with his fingers on the table and suddenly brightened. "On the other hand, I shall myself be going to Paris by car during the next few days. My business in von Rundstedt's headquarters in Saint Germain won't take very long and I will then be free for forty-eight hours." He chuckled. "I can think of no more charming companion than your delicious seamstress Lucille—"

Madame stood up. Until this moment, Hans had not realized how tall she was. She said icily:

"Consider my last request cancelled. And now, Major, I expect you would like to join your friends."

*   *   *

Hans Ramberg opened the double doors of the Salon, stepped inside and closed them behind him, leaning against the panels, smiling.

He saw a long, dim, candle-lit room with a high and ornate ceiling. The candles were placed at some distance from each other, giving pools of light alternating with gloom. Rifts of cigarette smoke stirred as he closed the double doors. There were ten persons in the room, nine of whom looked round at his entry. Only Gaston the little hunchback who played the piano paid no attention to the newcomer. Now he was playing Mozart's Sonata in C major as if for his own private pleasure, not caring who listened.

Of the nine, four were brother officers and five were girls. As his eyes flickered from one to the other, a tiny dossier of each man steadied and focused instantly in his brain, clear, deep-etched and detailed. His knowledge of the girls was less and he was content that it should remain so. He had implicit confidence in Madame and was not at all worried by the fact that each and every one of her *pensionnaires*—he smiled at the word—carried the lives of at least a dozen officers in her slim fingers. The girls were diverse and charming—and silent. The secrets of the Villa Mimosa were safe in their keeping.

Now then, who made up the gay company on this wet and windy night? Hans looked first at the sofa.

Nearest him was Elsa, the blonde from Strasbourg whose French was thick with Teutonic gutturals. She wore a house-coat, her slippers were indeed shabby and she was gazing at her neighbour Gerhard with a curious intensity. Hans had seen that look on her pretty, rather heavy-featured face before and had been slightly shocked by it. Women looked like that when they were in love and love—real love—could have no place in the Villa Mimosa.

The object of her gaze was Gerhard. It was a rule of the house that surnames were never used in the Villa Mimosa. It was safer thus. Gerhard's military dossier clicked open in Hans' photographic memory: *rank*—major; *arm*—infantry; *age*—thirty-six; *born*—Rudesheim-am-Rhein; *religion*—Roman Catholic; "this officer graduated with high honours in Geopolitik from War Academy, 1935".

So much for the dossier. Now for the man.

Gerhard was dark and smaller in stature than most officers. He had all the liveliness of the Rhineland and spoke in its flat accents. A widower, his wife had died of pneumonia in 1942 and his children, a boy and a girl, lived with grand-parents. He carried photographs of the two everywhere and was continually exhibiting them. He had, of course, shown them to Elsa—not once but several times. Could it be that she had the presumption to see herself in the role of step-mother? Gerhard was an anti-Nazi both by faith and by conviction. Though he sprang from another social stratum, Hans liked and trusted him. He was a man who could carry a bomb. . . .

Ignoring Elsa now, Gerhard was deep in conversation with Stefan. Again the dossier clicked open.

Stefan. *Rank*—Colonel; *arm*—cavalry; *age*—thirty-nine; *born* —Vienna; *religion*—Roman Catholic; "this officer had been attached to Logistics Branch, Ministry of War, where he had helped to prepare plans for the invasion of Russia".

A *Bendlerstrasse* type. It was significant how many of these Ministry of War (or *Bendlerstrasse*) types were concerned in this affair. Light-hearted and handsome, Stefan was married to a woman who was reputed to have ample private means and who was some years older than he himself. He did not carry her photograph. General von Wolfram regarded him as a brilliant Staff Officer. His were liaison duties between Division, Corps and Rommel's Headquarters—which involved frequent visits to La Roche-Guyon and to Paris. Stefan was openly contemptuous of his compatriot Hitler but technically amused by defence plans for the Pas de Calais. He was not a man who could be trusted to carry a bomb. If his eye happened to alight on an attractive girl, the bomb would be forgotten. A Viennese to his finger-tips.

Magda, bored by Stefan's inattention, was plucking his sleeve and Hans allowed a tolerant smile to expand on his lips. These Magyar women, with their incurving spines, ran true to type. They demanded notice and they had every reason for doing so. It was difficult to imagine any Magyar as a pastry-cook and Hans did not propose to try. He preferred to see Magda as she was. Black-haired, brown-eyed and lissom, her kimono was barbaric with its great splashes of coloured hand-embroidery, each silken stitch drawn by peasant fingers, emerald, rose, gentian and crimson, the red, white and green of Hungary, moon flowers beyond compare. Nobody other than Magda could wear a creation—the literal word—like that. Nobody would dare. Yet it reflected her temperament to perfection. She was proud, wilful, capricious and explosive. She was Hungarian.

Hans' analysis of the four persons on the sofa had flashed across the screen of his mind at lightning speed. He was about to consider the other two couples in the room when he was interrupted in a manner that was wholly to his liking.

From a far corner of the Salon, where she had been sitting alone and gazing humbly at the floor, a girl rose. She wore a long, concealing coat of golden brocade that flowed from her throat to her toes. It was fastened by innumerable tiny pearl buttons, enclosing her body completely. She glided rather than walked. In every fluid movement there was obedience. She was aware of her status and she accepted it. She was performing an impersonal duty with grace and with elegance.

Hans watched her come, marvelling as always at her effortless progression. She stopped and, for the first time, looked up. There was timidity in her glance.

She had almond eyes, long lashed under thin eyebrows that slanted slightly upwards. The bones of her oval face were small and delicate and her hair was jet-black and shining, fitting her head as tightly as a skull cap. It was extraordinary for Hans to remember that her hair could fall in a black cascade beyond her waist. In the candle-light her skin seemed to glow with the warmth of the sun.

She—a woman—waited with humility for a man to speak first. Hans smiled at her.

"Good evening, Golden Mouse."

*   *   *

Hans knew that he ought to despise Golden Mouse because nobody could possibly be less Aryan than she. Her father was reputed to be an American casket salesman in a land where there was little demand for caskets and her mother was certainly an Indo-Chinese lady of the honourable house of Li. When Golden Mouse's parents parted after a few tempestuous months, the unwanted girl child was left to starve and to die.

The missionaries found her and fed her and taught her to sing hymns. She escaped from them because no descendant of the honourable house of Li should accept charity. That had been written.

She was only sixteen when a French N.C.O. had seen her,

moving among the tables in a water-front café in Saigon, putting
down her tray of cracked cups to pluck at a one-stringed instrument and to sing in a reedy falsetto. The songs she sang were not
hymns. Later that night, he had followed her stealthily to her
habitation, a rat-ridden heap of rotting planks under which she
slept on a sugar-sack. He had asked her to come with him and she
had obeyed. Anything was better than the hands of the Lascars.
The N.C.O. had taken her to a hut behind the barracks where
she could hear the flaring of the bugles. He had bought her some
sort of coat in the Indian market and called her by her Chinese
name. He was a kind man and she made allowances for his
crudities because his ancestors had not been noble. The N.C.O.'s
Captain had seen her and, by making ignoble use of his rank, had
filched her from his Sergeant. These things—the importance and
power of military rank—were hidden from her and she was
unable to understand why the N.C.O. had yielded her up and
bidden her to go to the Captain.

He, the Captain, had bought her nothing. He had boasted
about the possession of her. Though men were gods who kept
hunger and public nakedness at bay, she had calmly decided to
kill this god when the Captain's Colonel saw her.

He had been much disturbed by her dignity and quiet and she,
for her part, knew at once that his ancestors must be noble. When
he left after dinner, she was waiting for him by the garden gate.
She had wrapped all her worldly possessions—the coat the N.C.O.
had given her and a comb—into a neat parcel, and she bowed
with formality.

"Is it your wish that I should come with you?"

"Yes. It is my wish."

"I am very happy." She inclined her head towards the Captain's
bungalow. "Tonight I was going to kill him."

She had begun to walk behind him as the Captain had made her
do, but he had taken her arm and they had walked side by side.
He had called her Golden Mouse and had given her a splendid
coat of brocade and a woman to serve her, to braid her black hair
and to wash her feet.

Soldiers are restless. They are for ever on the move.

War became certain and the Colonel's regiment was posted to
the Levant. Golden Mouse was in Beirut when France fell.
Though her Colonel had come to love her deeply, he loved his
country even more and made his tortuous way to England to
continue the struggle under General de Gaulle. He left Golden

Mouse behind. To be nearer to him—as was her duty and her wish—she stowed away in a Greek freighter bound for Marseilles. A German Major of the Panzer Grenadiers helped her on her way from Vieux Port to Paris. For his pains, for disgracing Hitler by associating with a woman of impure blood, the S.S. sent him to the Russian front where he was rapidly killed.

One night Golden Mouse made a parcel of her brocade coat and set out for the north, for the forbidden coast of France which was nearest to England. In the town of Coville, she got into touch with a tall lady in black silk who indicated that in an establishment called the Villa Mimosa she could be closer in spirit—if not in body—to her Colonel. Golden Mouse had long ago relegated her body to a lowly place in her order of things. It had been fashioned to bring delight and contentment to her Colonel. Until such time as it could be given to that purpose again, its lending to others was a matter of utter indifference to her.

Golden Mouse inclined her head at Hans Ramberg's greeting. She spoke in French.

"Good evening, Major Hans. We were not sure, any of us, if you would come." She described the night with a slow movement of her long-nailed fingers. "In all this wind and rain."

"It would take more than a typhoon to keep me away from you," he said gallantly. "But I had a long and weary day with my General. We were at the coast."

His eyes saw Fritz at a table for two.

Rank—Colonel; *arm*—artillery; *age*—forty-one; *born*—Munich; *religion*—Roman Catholic; "this officer served with distinction in the Balkan theatre and is recommended for staff duties".

Fritz was with Monique. Hans' brow furrowed. There was something very odd about Monique, so odd that he had once asked Madame about her. Madame had answered him sharply with another question. Did he wish to make a complaint? Certainly not. Monique was charming in every way and a well-chosen blossom in Madame's *bouquet des fleurs*. But who was she? Where did she come from? Her French vocabulary was limited and her accent terrible. She spoke no German. "I confess to curiosity," he had said, "about this girl."

"Your curiosity will have to remain unsatisfied, Major. I am aware of the issues at stake under this roof and I would not give shelter to anybody who was unsuitable. I do not propose to answer any questions about Monique or any other of *mes filles*."

So Monique remained a mystery. He had sought to solve it in intimacy—and failed. Short, auburn-haired and lithe like a dancer, she had gone on talking in her execrable French, telling him nothing. Now she was with Fritz. Paul could not be far away. He wasn't!

Paul was the baby of the group.

Rank—Captain; *arm*—cavalry; *age*—twenty-six; *born*—Hanover; *religion*—none; "this officer has played the role of distinguished officer with distinction".

Tall, slim and blond, Paul looked exactly what he was, the elder son of a land-owning family—very glad to be posted to staff duties, which he considered to be his *métier*. He was a close friend and admirer of Fritz, from whom he was inseparable. His companion was Lucille. Almost as tall, as slim and as blonde as Paul was himself, there appeared to be little mystery about Lucille. She was a Parisian. The bottle of champagne which Hans had heard "pop" was, of course, on her table. She lived in an aura of champagne and her hair was its colour. Her story was a simple one, but Madame, who distrusted simplicity, had accepted it. The war, about which she claimed to care or understand nothing, had shattered her career as an actress with a future in light comedy. The Villa Mimosa provided her with an admirable stage on which to keep her hand in—as an exponent of bedroom farce.

Gerhard, Stefan, Fritz and Paul were all here. Only one officer was missing. Colonel Rupprecht, nicknamed "Johnny", was a personal friend of Rommel and therefore a key man. He had spent the last three days at La Roche-Guyon and could have much to tell. A feather of fear fluttered around Hans' heart. Suppose something had gone wrong. . . .

He spoke as easily as he could:

"I expected Colonel Johnny by now."

"Colonel Johnny is here. He came more than an hour ago."

The hovering quill of the feather of fear was whisked away. Hans glanced meaningly towards the ornate ceiling.

Golden Mouse nodded her sleek head and spoke with detachment.

"Yes. He is upstairs. He arrived in his staff car, which was foolish because who can tell if the driver is discreet? Colonel Johnny was a little drunk and very happy. He sat for a while with Magda. Then Wanda came down. There is hatred and jealousy between Magda and Wanda and she set out to take Colonel Johnny from Magda. She did not want him for herself. All men

are one to Wanda. She wanted to take him because she is Czech
and Magda is Hungarian and between these two races there is
strong, bad blood. She was very clever and patient, doing all
things to entice Colonel Johnny. Magda was unwise and allowed
herself to show anger. Because of that, because of Magda's anger,
Colonel Johnny went with Wanda. He is with her now." Golden
Mouse paused. She said slowly: "One day Wanda will provoke
big trouble for herself."

The personal antagonisms of the ladies of the Villa Mimosa
were of little interest to Hans Ramberg. He laughed.

"So we are all here."

"Yes. You are all here. Is it your wish that I should sit with
you until Colonel Johnny comes down?"

Hans bowed.

"I would be most honoured. There are still seven bottles of
champagne in the cellar. Please share one of them with me."

"If it will give you pleasure," said Golden Mouse meekly.

Soon Colonel Johnny came into the Salon. He was no longer
drunk and he greeted Hans boisterously. He was followed, after a
discreet interval, by Wanda. Even Hans could not fail to see that
she was brimming with triumph and that she was careful to sit as
far away as possible from Magda. Golden Mouse was right.
Trouble was not far distant.

The six men gathered together. They were bound not only by
the traditional relationship which obtained among Staff Officers
of the German Army—that fertile breeding-ground of deep and
soulful friendships—but also by a common purpose. All of them
had come to combine a detestation for the Nazi régime with a
loathing for the S.S. and the Gestapo. They saw Germany as an
occupied country, ruled by sadistic tyrants who had at their
disposal every bestial weapon devised by twentieth-century tech-
nology. Their own land was enslaved and in the deliberate
destruction of freedom in Germany they foresaw the universal
destruction of freedom. Others regarded Hitler as a mountebank,
a genius or a fool. Not so the Ramberg Group. As Christian men,
they believed him to be the incarnation of evil and their purpose
was the assassination of the anti-Christ and of the lewd disciples
who carried out his will.

The killing of Hitler was no simple matter of a pistol shot, a
dagger thrust or of a phial of poison. The Fuehrer's personal
bodyguard numbered over three thousand armed fanatics; his diet

of vegetables and cream buns was prepared by his own chef. The forging of a plot was rendered well-nigh impossible by distance, by the constant tapping of telephone calls and by the unrecognizable presence of informers everywhere and in every stratum of society. Only within the walls of the Villa Mimosa were the plotters safe.

Here they were completely removed from the rigidity, the discipline and the eternal guardedness of the Mess. There were no hidden detectors behind the curtains or under the pillows. Under this roof was a microcosm of the Europe they loved, the Europe they had dedicated their lives to save. They believed that no S.D. or Gestapo man could ever penetrate this haven of freedom, made infinitely the more real by wine, women and song.

Colonel Johnny spoke earnestly of his visit to Rommel's Headquarters. The Field-Marshal, he said, was already beset by doubt and the tactical conflict between him and his master von Rundstedt was now common knowledge. It could be put to good purpose by the plotters. His eyes gleamed. With Rommel on their side, all things were possible. It was a glittering prospect.

He turned to Hans.

"And you. What news?"

"I spent a long boring day in and out of the coastal air-raid shelters. Then, coming home, General Wolf began to talk. My friends, if the Field-Marshal is indeed beset by doubt, my man is his brother. . . ."

Hans went on to recount his conversation while the girls, each with her acknowledged escort, sat around and half-listened, stifling yawns and waiting impatiently for the moment when one of the officers would stand up and clap his hands and order Gaston the hunchback to set everybody's feet tapping with a Viennese waltz.

It was—inevitably—Paul who broke up the conference. He bowed with formality to Fritz, his superior and friend, and got to his feet. Lucille, the blonde Parisian, jumped up with alacrity. Paul said, laughing:

"The ladies are becoming bored, Colonel. Have I your permission——?"

"Of course, Paul."

"What tune would you like, Colonel?"

"Tell him to play *Tales from the Vienna Woods.*"

"My own choice exactly." He spoke to Gaston and the little hunchback's fingers tripped along the keys.

Everybody stood up. The girls opened their arms and uni-
formed sleeves slid round their waists. The flames of the candles
wavered in the swinging measure.

"Would you care to dance, Golden Mouse, or shall we sit and
drink champagne and talk?"

"I am your servant, Major Hans."

"Then we will sit and talk—for a little while."

The couples wove in and out. Suddenly there was a shrill cry
of pain. Magda, dancing with Stefan, had jabbed with the high
heel of her sandal at Wanda's slippered foot as she passed
languorously by. Magda laughed. She said:

"I'm so very sorry."

* * *

There was a direct telephone line between the Manoir and
Field-Marshal Rommel's Headquarters at La Roche-Guyon.
When General von Wolfram went to bed, this line was always
plugged in to his room.

The General had dined alone and taken a cognac and a cigar
with his coffee while he read the day's intelligence reports. Just
before half past eleven, he had retired to his room and put the
light out at once. He was just sinking into his first sleep when the
telephone whirred by his bed. With a muttered oath, he sat up,
switched on the light again and took the receiver.

"Herr General von Wolfram?"

"Yes."

"One moment, Herr General. Field-Marshal Rommel wishes
personally to speak to you."

Rommel's voice was sharp and incisive. Tomorrow he proposed
to visit the Manoir. He would arrive at eleven o'clock. There
were several matters for discussion arising out of General von
Wolfram's inspection of the coastal area today. An agenda should
be prepared dealing with the following points. He gave them in
order and, military affairs concluded, his voice became warm and
genial.

"And how are you, my old friend?"

"Very well. And you?" The two officers, who had served
together and who knew each other very well, chatted for a few
moments, using the "Du" or intimate form of address. Then with
a perfunctory *"Heil Hitler"* Rommel hung up.

General von Wolfram got out of bed and put on a dressing-
gown. He glanced automatically at his wrist where his watch

should be. Of course. It was being mended in Coville and coming back tomorrow—or was it already "today"? He had decided that Hans Ramberg must be told at once of the Field-Marshal's impending visit so that the agenda could be worked out first thing in the morning. As he made his way upstairs, he looked at the clock on the landing. Five minutes to midnight. It was unlikely that his hard-working Staff Officer and Aide would be asleep yet.

There was a line of light under Hans' bedroom door. The General tapped lightly with his knuckles. There was no reply. He tapped a little louder. The only sound was the clock ticking on the landing. The third time he knocked really loudly and called out, "Hans!" The ticking of the clock seemed to make the silence more profound. He seized the handle and turned it. The door was locked.

The General stepped back. His heart had begun to thump uncomfortably and he had difficulty in breathing. Nobody knew better than he of the tide of suicides that mounted daily as the Allied invasion drew nearer, and how nerve-racked men, fearful of the Allies in front and of the S.S. behind, could endure no longer and snatched desperately at oblivion. He seemed to see Hans crouched over his desk, his fair, handsome head shattered by a Lueger bullet and his blood soaking into a map of the invasion coast. With all his strength he flung himself against the door. The flimsy lock splintered out of its socket and the door burst open.

The room was empty.

General von Wolfram sat down heavily on Hans' bed. His knees were shaking and, though the February night was raw, there was sweat on his forehead. That had been a terrible moment and the General found himself muttering aloud, using words that had not come into his mind or his mouth since he had been a frightened subaltern in the First World War. The little twisting wire of anger that followed fear had turned into fury as he remembered that Hans had refused a dinner invitation on the plea of work. What was it they were going to have? Oh yes. *Coq au vin* and a bottle of the ... the ... *Mouton-Rothschild,* that was it—instead of a wet omelette and a glass of thin Moselle.

Work, indeed! The ungrateful cur. The most vicious punishment that could be meted out to any German officer—a posting into the carnage of Russia—would not be too heavy for such discourtesy and deceit.

The General's fury began to subside. Hans' bed had not been

slept in. On the other hand, his coffee cup was ringed with grounds and there were crumbs on his plate. Perhaps he had done some work first—and then gone out. But where?

There could only be one place. Coville. Coville was outside the military zone. But what German officer would dare venture alone at night into that cursed nest of spies and saboteurs? There could be nowhere else within this arid armed camp, from which the French had been rooted out, man, woman and child.

A certain memory, never far distant, came back to the General, and he chuckled. Years ago in the First World War, when Germany confronted defeat as she did today, he too had behaved exactly as Hans was behaving now. There had been a small town well behind the firing line in Picardy and in that town had lived a girl called Arlette who had a milk-white skin and freckled arms and whom he had taught to say *"Ich liebe Dich"*. He saw himself as he had been then, a character from the pages of Erich Remarque a Lieutenant with a bicycle, passionately wanting to squeeze the last drop from the fleeting, doom-laden hours. He had been caught red-handed by his General, who had done—precisely nothing. This General of his had been one of the old school, a *"korrekt"* man who believed in the superiority of officers and their absolute right to privilege. He had always turned a blind, monocled eye to bad behaviour, provided that it was, in his opinion, bad behaviour of the right sort. His officers had loved him.

General von Wolfram decided to follow an excellent example. He stood up and went to Hans' desk. On a slip of paper he wrote:

Midnight, Feb. 13th, 1944
Dear Hans:
    Please be good enough to call on me and, if necessary, to waken me on your return.   *W. von W.*
    P.S. You are a fly-by-night!

Hans Ramberg squelched through the beets, crossed the rickety bridge and wheeled his bicycle carefully between the trees of the apple-orchard. The wind had dropped and the rain would certainly be over by dawn. In the darkness he had some difficulty in finding the barred gate, but he located it at last. The Manoir was very silent and the hinge of the loose-box half-door screeched. He stood stock still. Tomorrow morning his first act would be to oil that damned hinge. It was always by the neglect of such trivial things that one got caught out. When he had leaned his bicycle against the cobwebbed wall, he flashed his torch on his watch and whistled. Ten past three! It was always the same. In the Villa Mimosa, the rose-winged hours passed at the speed of a bee's flight. He tip-toed into the Manoir by the back door and up the servants' stairs to his room. The door opened to the gentle insertion of his key and he saw, to his horror, that the lock had been deliberately broken. He said aloud in English:

"Oh, my God."

He picked up the General's note and read it and felt slightly sick. He took his tooth-glass and went to the cupboard and poured himself out a liberal measure of cognac, drinking it in one gulp. It burned pleasantly in his throat, steadying him.

He sat down and re-read the note. He began to take comfort. He had been addressed by his Christian name, as Hans, and that was a good sign. The postscript was an even better sign. If the old boy were really angry, he would never have used the word "fly-by-night". Things might be all right yet.

He took off his muddy boots and changed his tunic, smoothing it down over his hips. He stared into the looking-glass and said to his own reflection: "My dear chap, you look awful." He sprayed his face with a little eau de Cologne and brushed his hair. That was a lot better. Now for it. . . .

Hans walked very quietly down the wide, creaking staircase and stopped outside the General's bedroom door. He drew a deep breath—and tapped boldly. A gruff voice spoke sleepily.

"Herein."

General von Wolfram sat up in bed, switched on the light and blinked. He was as lean as a heron and Hans felt very like a frog at that moment.

"Good morning, Hans."

"Good morning, Herr General." First blood to the old boy. . . .

"Thank you for coming to see me. I have some urgent orders for you. Field-Marshal Rommel telephoned shortly before midnight. He is coming to see us in the Manoir tomorrow at eleven a.m.—I beg your pardon, Hans—I should have said *today* at eleven a.m." Second blood to the old boy. . . . "I require an agenda by ten o'clock. The following are the main points the Field-Marshal wishes to discuss." He rapped out a list. "Right. Any questions?"

"No, none, Herr General."

"You show a remarkable grasp of military matters. I, however, have a question." The heron's beak opened, ready for the kill. "What is the time, Hans?"

Hans coughed.

"The time, Herr General? My watch is not very reliable, alas, but it certainly must be after midnight. Er . . . well after."

"What does your unreliable watch say, Hans?"

Hans drew his sleeve back and smiled tolerantly as if at the vagaries of his watch.

"It says twenty past three, but——"

"I venture to suspect, Hans, that your watch is a great deal more reliable than you are yourself. Er . . . blonde or brunette?"

A warm wave of relief flowed over Hans Ramberg's body. He gave the General a schoolboy grin.

"Brunette, Herr General." This was a moment of friendship between men, a moment when he might well dare to speak.

"I am glad she was brunette, Hans. I have invariably found fair-haired women—and men—to be frivolous. Now go to bed and get some sleep."

"Herr General," Hans began with diffidence, "you will remember that, in the car, you spoke of certain matters. If I might seize this opportunity——"

"You may *not*. I also remember that I invited you to dine with me in order that we might continue our talk—and that you refused. You will now await *my* convenience. I order you to go to bed at once."

Hans bowed.

"Goodnight, Herr General."

3: SAINT VALENTINE'S DAY

COVILLE, that thrice-accursed nest of spies and saboteurs, had been a town of some ten thousand inhabitants at the outbreak of war. Its population was now very much reduced. The odious Sauckel, Minister for the recruitment of forced labour for the Third Reich, had been over the area with a fine-tooth comb and there was hardly a household which had not sullenly yielded up its able-bodied men for work in Germany. It was a community of the old and disabled and of women and children, all of whom lived in the shadow both of starvation and of Notre Dame de Coville, the town's seventeenth-century church. No single move made by the enemy escaped the unblinking eyes of this silent hostile host.

Sauckel's fine-tooth comb had failed to reveal one able-bodied man. This was Charles Addison, seconded from the Coldstream Guards for special duties with the French Section of the War Office, London. His alias was Charles Bertin, watchmaker, and it was into his hands that the unsuspecting Major Hans Ramberg had given his Corps Commander's precious timepiece for repairs.

It was to prove a most inauspicious commission.

At exactly six o'clock on the morning of Saint Valentine's Day, 1944, Charles woke up to a knock on his bedroom door. His right hand shot like lightning under the pillow and his finger slid back the safety catch of a ·38 Colt revolver before he answered the knock.

"Entrez."

It was—of course—Aunt Marguerite. Every morning at six o'clock during the five months that he had lived in Coville, it had been Aunt Marguerite. But there was always the chance that one morning it might not be this adopted aunt of his. It might be the bastards of the *Milice* or the Gestapo, and Charles was not prepared to take that chance.

"Put that foolish thing away, Charles. You are a watchmaker—not a cowboy."

He answered with a slightly shame-faced look.

"I know. I never carry it during the day, but I have a rooted objection to being arrested in bed."

"You will never be arrested in bed. They would have to get past me first. I have told you so a hundred times. Here is your coffee."

She put the tray with its single cup of acorn coffee and its butterless hunk of black bread on his dressing-table and sat down in the only chair. Charles shivered and pulled on a thick fisherman's jersey. It was bitterly cold in the room, which served him both as dormitory and work-shop. As he sipped his coffee and munched his bread, he talked to her at intervals.

"What's the weather like, Aunt Marguerite?"

"It rained heavily until after midnight. Then it began to clear. The day will be fine and cold." She said significantly: "It will also be clear."

"That means air-raids."

"Yes." She shrugged. "It means air-raids. But the more air-raids we have, the sooner it will all be over."

"They should leave the job of destruction to men on the

ground." He ran his fingers through his thick dark hair. "To men like me. The bomb doesn't give a damn who it kills."

Aunt Marguerite had heard this before, not only from Charles but from the many "nephews and nieces" whom she had sheltered. In the secret archives of Baker Street, London, Aunt Marguerite was described as "loyal and trustworthy" and her address, 34 Rue de Voltaire, Coville, Pas de Calais, as a "safe house".

She had been widowed in the last days of the last war and for over a quarter of a century had nourished an implacable hatred for the Germans who had killed her man. British agents in trouble, women as well as men, had confidently made their way to the Rue de Voltaire, sure of a welcome from this elderly, dumpy, ugly Frenchwoman, who took them in, protected them and asked no questions. Usually their stay was brief and they vanished as mysteriously as they had come. Charles had turned up one moonlight night last October with a sprained ankle and a set of watch-making instruments. He had been tossed in the slipstream of an R.A.F. Hudson, the lift webs of his parachute had twisted and he landed heavily on an outcrop of rock. He had stayed ever since.

Aunt Marguerite said casually:

"I have a scrap of news for you. Rommel, the great man himself, is going to the Manoir at eleven o'clock this morning."

Charles looked at her, his coffee cup halfway to his lips. He asked sharply: "How do you know?"

"André was tapping the telephone line from La Roche-Guyon all night. He will be lucky if he fails to get pneumonia, that one. Rommel telephoned at ten to twelve and talked with General von"—she lifted one hand, let it fall—"I cannot pronounce his name but the two talked for five minutes. Rommel will be at the Manoir at eleven."

"You are sure of this, Aunt Marguerite?"

"Certain."

Charles lay back on the pillow, clasped his hands behind his head and laughed softly.

"How damn funny!"

"You find it amusing that these Boches should confer. Me, I would be happy to attend the meeting—with a bomb under my skirt."

"You are a dangerous woman, Aunt Marguerite. I would not like to be your enemy." He sat up in bed, clasping his knees. His blue eyes were dancing. "*Ecoutez*. A week ago, General von

Wolfram had the misfortune to drop his watch and to break the balance staff. His Staff Officer and Aide, Major Hans Ramberg, brought it to me to be mended. Me—of all people! I finished it last night. I was going to deliver it to the Manoir this afternoon. Now I shall deliver it this morning—and hope for a glimpse of the Desert Fox."

She considered his proposal. She loved this man as if he were her own son. She said at last:

"You are mad, Charles. How will you, who are believed to be a Frenchman, contrive to enter the evacuated area? Above all, how will you get near the Manoir? Before Rommel comes, it will be ringed with sentries. I repeat that you are mad."

"With respect, I must disagree with you. I am not mad and no extra sentries will be posted at the Manoir. Because they will not wish to draw attention to Rommel's visit, everything will be normal. Perhaps a little extra whitewash on the gateposts, but nothing else. As for entering the evacuated area and the Manoir, nothing could be more simple. Aunt Marguerite, be kind enough to give me my wallet. It is in the inside pocket of my jacket. Thank you." He drew out a stamped slip of paper. "Listen to this: *'Permission is hereby granted to Charles Bertin, watchmaker, of 34 Rue de Voltaire, Coville, to enter the Military Zone and to report to the undersigned at Corps Headquarters. This pass is valid for one journey only. Hans Ramberg, Major. Dated February 7th, 1944.'* What do you say to that?"

"Show it to me."

She read it slowly. She said:

"It is extraordinary, but true. This Major Hans Ramberg must be an imbecile."

"No. That he is not. But he is a little naïve."

"You are determined on this . . . this folly?"

"Absolutely. I have long wanted to visit the evacuated area by daylight. I have a feeling in my bones that I may happen on some interesting and unexpected things." He laughed. "As well as that, this is the 14th of February, the Feast of Saint Valentine, patron saint of lovers."

"You will find no love up there, but only hatred and war." She stood up. "Now it is time for you to get up. Soon it will be light."

With the first, false dawn, convoys of lorries jolted over the cobbles of the Rue de Voltaire on their way to the coast. They were packed with slave workers from Russia and the Ukraine and

Poland and from every other country where the Swastika flag still waved. The lorries were guarded by S.S. men with automatic rifles who did not hesitate to fire if one or more of the human scarecrows made a desperate, hopeless dash for freedom. Many died that way. Those who lived toiled till dusk pouring concrete into the Atlantic Wall that was to protect the Fortress of Europe, building those mysterious, sinister ramps that were sighted towards London, sinking spikes into the sea bed at low tide, strengthening the gun posts, unrolling the barbed wire.

Charles watched the lorries pass, saddened as always by this prodigal, useless expenditure of so much human misery and sweat. When the last of them had gone, he drew the chair to his workbench and picked up the General's watch, checking it with his own. It was synchronized to the second. He was aware of the craftsman's satisfaction at a job well done.

*   *   *

Charles Addison was twenty-eight, the son of an English solicitor and a French mother, the vivacious Yvonne Duveau of Bethune. He had spent much of his boyhood in France with his grand-parents, and his French was immaculate. Visits to France continued during the holidays from Crécy College and during the long vacation from Oxford, where he had read law, hunted with the Christ Church and New College beagles, played the piano and dabbled in horology. He had come down with a good Second that should have been a First, and entered his father's firm, Addison and Gale of New Square, Lincoln's Inn.

On September the 6th, 1939, he had attended a most memorable party in the Café Royal and, together with his hangover, joined the army the following morning. He was posted to the Foot Guards. He was as strong as a lion and triumphed over both Caterham and Pirbright. Commissioned into the Coldstream after Dunkirk, he landed in North Africa as a major and was hit in the left shoulder by a Schmeisser bullet. It was a clean through-and-through wound. After that, for him, the war began in earnest.

The man in the next bed to his in hospital was a curious person. Somehow he and Charles had found themselves talking French, and this man, who was vastly inquisitive, had asked a great many questions. He was discharged the following morning and Charles never found out his name, rank or regiment.

On convalescent leave in Sussex, he saw a lissom and lovely girl at a party. He enquired her name and was told "Verity Gale".

Charles said: "Rubbish. What's her real name?" The Verity Gale he had known and not seen for some years was a skinny child, all eyes and legs, with cotton stockings and torn bloomers, who kept a jam-jar full of tadpoles. It was ridiculous to suppose that . . . that shrimp could have matured into this radiant creature—ridiculous but true. He went to her and said: "Hullo, Verity. I'm Charles Addison. How are the tadpoles doing?"

She saw a tall, lean man with black hair and blue eyes. He wore a civilian suit and he was taller and leaner and more sunburned than any civilian had the right to be in 1943. She said: "Nonsense. The Charles Addison I know—or used to know—is a horrid little stinker who never washed but who did join the Army. And who told you about my tadpoles?"

Three weeks later, after a breathless courtship, she wore his ring.

The wound in his shoulder healed quickly. Charles reported back to the Battalion. His Regimental Lieutenant-Colonel gave him a basilisk look and said: "Morning, Charles. I've had an impudent request that you should attend an interview in room 057 at the War Office at three this afternoon. I don't know what the devil it's all about, but if the War House think I'm going to let one of my officers polish his pants on an office stool, they'd better think again. Tell them that with my compliments."

"I will, sir." He coughed. "And I'd like to ask your permission to announce my engagement. . . ."

"Would you, b'God! Who's the victim?"

"Girl called Verity Gale."

"Tell me about her at dinner. And tell the War Office to go to hell."

"Certainly, sir."

Charles didn't tell the War Office to go to hell. Neither did he dine with his Colonel. At dinner-time he was sitting in a train in civilian clothes on his way to a country house in Surrey. For training purposes, he had been given the code name of "Martin" and he was about to be instructed in the art of sabotage behind the enemy lines in occupied France. No telephone calls or letters were allowed from this house and Verity was distraught.

From the country house in Surrey, he went on to the Highlands of Scotland. He was allowed at last to write to Verity. He gave no address and explained somewhat lamely that he had all of a sudden been sent on a musketry course. He was unaware that his

letter was censored and posted in Darlington. He did five terrifying parachute jumps at Ringway, Manchester, and after a week's
halcyon leave, during which he lied flagrantly to Verity about his
activities and movements, he went to the New Forest for the final
burnishing.

It was immediately after that that Charles Addison died and
was cremated.

The phoenix that rose from his ashes was Charles Bertin, watchmaker, late of Diego Suarez, Madagascar, now of Coville, Pas de
Calais. He was given beautifully forged papers and written
instructions which he learned by heart and then burned. The last
thing he was handed in Baker Street was a lethal tablet, just in
case. . . . He promptly threw it into the Thames. That was a way
out of trouble which he would never take. He spent many hours
writing a series of letters to be posted at intervals to Verity. He
told her that he had been posted to a boring Staff job overseas and
that it might be some time before he came home. She was his love
and his joy.

The same night he was airborne in a Hudson from Tempsford
and jumped in clear moonlight into the Pas de Calais.

                    *   *   *

At nine o'clock Aunt Marguerite waddled once again into
Charles' room. She put a jug of hot water on his dressing-table and
a clean white shirt on his bed. On top of the shirt she tenderly
laid a hideous, multi-coloured, made-up bow-tie.

"If you insist on visiting these assassins," she said curtly, "I
demand that you shave and look respectable. *Enfin,* you are a
British officer *en civile* and it is correct that you should look like
one. The tie is the property of my nephew who was acknowledged
by all to be the best-dressed man in Lille. I lend it to you for the
day."

"You are more than kind, Aunt Marguerite." He winced. "And
I promise to take the greatest care of it." He noticed with surprise
that she was wearing her only hat, a venerable black straw reserved
for Sundays. He asked with a touch of apprehension: "Er . . . you
are not thinking of accompanying me to the Manoir, I suppose?"

"Certainly not. I have no taste for pigsties. Me, I am on my way
to Notre Dame de Coville. I am going to light a candle for you,
mon cher fils."

Half an hour later Charles was dressed and ready to start. He
wore a dark blue suit that had been run up by a tailor's apprentice

in Amiens, his clean white shirt and Aunt Marguerite's nephew's bow-tie. He pulled on a beret and stared into the looking-glass.

He was profoundly grateful that the Regimental Lieutenant-Colonel could not see him now.

* * *

Charles carefully wrapped up General von Wolfram's watch in tissue paper and put it in his pocket. He went downstairs, wheeled his bicycle out of the hall and set off blithely through the wakened streets of Coville, making for the German control post at the fringe of the town. As Aunt Marguerite had prophesied, the day was clear with a pale sky and little sunshine. After twenty minutes, he saw the heavy red and white striped bar across the road and the forbidding notices: ZONE INTERDITE. EINTRITT VERBOTEN. He dismounted, swept off his beret to the German sentry and produced Major Ramberg's pass. A Sergeant came out of the hut, read the words on the pass and grunted.

"Your papers."

Charles handed him his identity card and work certificate. Both were scrutinized in silence and handed back to him.

"You know your way to Panzer Korps Headquarters?"

"Yes, Monsieur. I know my way."

He scowled. "You damned French know too much."

The heavy bar lifted and Charles rode on. He was well over the first fence. Now for the Manoir.

On either side of the road he saw desolation. There were mounds of bricks where houses had stood and the fields were scarred with the teeth-marks of Panzers. Once a convoy of half-tracks overtook him and he stood humbly in the ditch, his beret in his hand, while they rattled past. On the left, a hundred yards from the road, the burned-out skeleton of a British fighter-bomber cocked its tail obscenely upwards and he saw the remnants of R.A.F. roundels on its broken wings. Poor devils.

As he drew nearer to Corps Headquarters, traffic increased. Motor-cyclists roared past and the occupants of one or two staff cars looked back in curiosity at the sight of a civilian in this armed camp. He should be nearly there by now. He rode more slowly, aware of a slight increase in the beating of his heart and of the fact that his hands had begun to sweat. He was Daniel, Daniel in a made-up bow-tie, about to enter the lion's den.

At a bend of the road beyond a beech wood he saw the Manoir gates and chuckled in spite of his nervousness. Soldiers were the same in Coville or Caterham, and two orderlies were hurriedly adding an extra touch of whitewash to the posts—in honour of the Field-Marshal's visit. He dismounted and began to walk forward.

"Halt!"

He stopped dead as a Sergeant strode towards him, automatic rifle at the ready.

"You, there, what do you want?"

Charles bared his head and bowed. He handed over Major Ramberg's pass. The Sergeant read it and shouted:

"You are insolent. How dare you approach the front gate! To the back door with you. Schmidt, escort this fellow to the back door. And you, lout, if I see you here again, you will feel my boot. *Schnell, schnell.*"

Wheeling his bicycle, Charles walked in front of the sentry. They rounded the Manoir. He saw an orchard and a field of— what were they?—ah yes, beets, and then a narrow road struggling uphill and lined with poplars. He wondered where it went. After handing over the General's watch, he would make it his business to find out.

They entered the kitchen. The sentry said, "Wait," and Charles sat down on a wooden chair, obsequiously twisting his beret in his fingers. The smell of cooking was tantalizing to a degree and his mouth began to water. One of the cooks opened a huge copper, fished out a pair of Frankfurter sausages and gave them to Charles with a friendly grin. They were hot and delicious and he thanked the cook with heart-felt sincerity. The kitchen door was open and all at once he heard the thin wailing of air-raid sirens from the direction of the coast. Blast the R.A.F. They *would* come at a moment like this.

The friendly cook spoke to him in reasonable French, and jerked a thumb towards the sound.

"We pay no attention to that. If they come nearer, then whistles will be blown and we go to the wine cellar. *Verstanden?*"

"*Oui, Monsieur. Je comprends. Merci.*"

An officious Staff Sergeant cocked his head in at the kitchen door.

"Bertin."

"*Oui, Monsieur.*"

"Lift your hands above your head. *Schnell, schnell.*"

He ran his hands over Charles' pockets.

"You are unarmed. It is well for you. The Major will see you.

Do not speak to the Major unless he addresses you first. Now follow me."

Charles walked up the wide staircase. The Staff Sergeant said, "Wait," while he knocked deferentially and announced:

"The Frenchman, sir."

As Charles walked in to the room, Major Hans Ramberg gave him a slightly worried smile.

"Ah. Good morning, Monsieur Bertin. I'm afraid you've happened to come at a very busy moment. You have finished the job? Excellent." He held the General's watch to his ear. "Yes, I can hear it ticking. The General will be very pleased. And now, how much may I pay you for your task?"

"It has been an honour to work for the General, Monsieur." He lifted one eyebrow. "Possibly, as I leave, a pair of sausages from the kitchen?"

"No. That would be niggardly. A dozen pairs at least and a few francs. Shall we say——"

In the last half minute, the distant drone of aircraft had become perceptibly louder. As the drone became a snarl, whistles shrilled all over the Manoir. An inner door was flung open and Hans Ramberg leapt to attention. Looking neither to the right nor the left, Field-Marshal Rommel marched through the room. Followed by General von Wolfram, he was gone in an instant. Hans Ramberg hesitated, then he said: "You'd better come with me."

The wide staircase again, with officers clattering down; a heavy, iron-bound door and stone steps; the smell in the wine cellar redolent of two hundred years of libation. Charles leaned against a bin that had once contained an astronomical number of bottles of claret and closed his eyes. This, all this, would make interesting reading in London.

From the Burgundy bin opposite, he heard a voice ask sharply in German:

"Who is that, the civilian? The one wearing the bow-tie."

Hans Ramberg's voice answered smoothly, apologetically. The sharp voice commanded:

"Bring him to me."

Hans crossed the dim passage.

"The Field-Marshal wishes to speak to you. Come at once."

Good God! Charles automatically stiffened to attention. Thumbs in line with the seams of his trousers, he marched across the passage and halted as if he were on King's Guard. He was a shade taller than Rommel and the two looked at each other directly.

"Do you speak German?"

"*Non, Monsieur le Maréchal. Je regrette infiniement.*"

Rommel turned grimly to Hans.

"Ask him how he enjoys being bombed by his ex-allies, the British?"

The answer came pat.

"Not at all, sir."

A fighter-bomber dived down the sky and screamed over the Manoir roof, skimming the slates. Out of the heel of his eyes Charles saw Hans bend double. Neither he nor Rommel moved a muscle. He heard a muffled, harmless burst of cannon fire in the distant field and then the whine of the aircraft climbing. The beginning of a smile flickered over the corners of Rommel's mouth.

"Tell him that I notice his soldierly bearing. Tell him that I could do with men like him—on our side."

He nodded. Charles stepped back to the other side of the passage. Though his forehead was sweating, he realized with a shiver how nearly he had betrayed himself by his own reflexes. Still, made-up bow-tie or no made-up bow-tie, he wished that the Regimental Lieutenant-Colonel could see him now. . . .

Within five minutes, the Manoir whistles shrilled the all-clear. Hans accompanied Charles to the kitchen. He thrust an uncounted bundle of franc notes into Charles' hand and instructed the Sergeant cook to give this Frenchman a parcel of sausages, a dozen pairs. He said quickly:

"You have had a rare honour, to be spoken to by the Field-Marshal. Now I must hurry back. Thank you again. *Au revoir.*"

"*Au revoir, mon Commandant.*"

Their next meeting was to be sooner than either of them expected.

And now to explore that narrow road.

With Major Ramberg's pass still in his pocket, Charles had nothing to fear. Without knowing he was doing so, he took the exact path followed by Hans last night. At the edge of the beets, he wiped the mud off his shoes and began to wheel his bicycle up the hill. He rested for five minutes at the top, mentally mapping the countryside as he had been trained to do. Beyond the Manoir's beech wood, and sheltered by it, there was a flat field of stubble, big enough to take a whole battalion of parachutists. He made a mental note of it. And there, far away to the left, was the railway line, which was destined for sabotage at three points. The plastic explosive was already in position, only waiting for the detonators —when the time came.

It had been a tremendous morning and now he was glad to be alone and to remember. He went between the poplars, laid his bicycle on the ground and sat down and lit a rare Gauloise. It was damn cold and he wouldn't stay long.

Business first, pleasure afterwards.

This evening at half past four he had a rendezvous with his wireless operator "Georges". Georges was a Captain in the Royal Corps of Signals and the two met at a different place and time twice a week. This evening's meeting was to take place in Coville's cemetery, a somewhat macabre spot, but one in which they were unlikely to be interrupted and were certain not to be overheard. Charles had already written his report for Baker Street but now he could add on a lively description of the morning. Thank God that blasted fighter-bomber had missed the Manoir.

And now—Verity. He gave himself the rare luxury of thinking about her. With pain and pleasure, he traced all that they had done since the blessed moment he had seen her at that party in Sussex. A telephone call next morning that she had pretended not to expect and then the formal round of lunch, dinner, the Crazy Gang, the 400—with both of them acutely aware that they were wasting time. He had asked her to marry him, in a pub at Strand-on-the-Green it had been, and she had said absently, "Of course I will," and that night and for the nights left to them they had walked on a thousand egg-shells, not breaking one. He wondered where she was at this moment and if she were thinking of him with equal tenderness. He smiled and said aloud, "Major and Mrs. Charles Addison," delighting in the words.

The cold of that Saint Valentine's Day gripped his flesh. He stamped the end of his Gauloise into the earth and rubbed his chilled fingers together. Suddenly he was motionless. From the direction of the Manoir, he heard the approach of a lorry coming up the hill in second gear.

He stood screened behind one of the poplars as the lorry passed. It was a small supply vehicle, driven by a private soldier with a Corporal beside him in the cabin. The driver changed gear on the hill's crest and it bumped on downwards. Now where the hell could that lorry be going—and why? Charles jumped on his bicycle and followed.

The road swung to the right and became a cattle-track. Hardly had the lorry vanished from his sight when he heard the driver change down and the engine stop. Charles put on his brakes and slipped off the saddle. Just beyond the bend of the road on the left an old muck-cart rested on its shafts. Charles crouched behind it and watched.

The lorry was drawn up beside the wall of a tall house. Though it looked deserted and shabby, he saw with amazement that a blue thread of wood smoke curled upwards from the chimney. The Corporal and the driver let down the back of the lorry and began to carry its contents into the house. He noted the various items. A sack of flour—butter—sugar—meat—a wooden crate of vegetables. But there was something else to come. The private clambered into the vehicle and pushed out a large oblong case which the Corporal lifted on to his shoulder.

Charles had excellent eyesight. The case was marked CHAMPAGNE and diagonally across it was stamped RESERVIERT FUER DIE WEHRMACHT.

Well, well, well. . . .

A tall woman in black came to the back door of the house and initialled a sheet of paper. Charles rightly assumed it to be some form of receipt. The two soldiers saluted her, put up the lorry's tailboard and drove back at high speed towards the Manoir. The whole incident had taken less than five minutes.

From behind the wheel of the muck-cart, Charles examined the house. There was a name on the fanlight over the hall door but he couldn't quite read it from here. Villa something or other. He would take a closer look in a minute or two. His eyes wandered to the angle of the wall and he saw something which drove the breath from his body.

A clothesline ran from a back first-floor window to the branch of a tree. On it, five—no, six—sets of women's panties and a row of silk stockings danced derisively in the breeze, mocking war. At the end, all by itself and as if contemptuous of this frippery, hung an old-fashioned pair of whalebone stays—quite clearly the property of the woman in black. Charles shook his head in unbelief and, at that moment, he heard the tinny whine of a gramophone from an upstairs room. The song was *Parlez-moi d'amour.*

On this dedicated day, he had happened on a fitting shrine to Saint Valentine.

Charles wheeled his bicycle back on to the road and started to walk towards the house. He glanced at the fanlight. VILLA MIMOSA. How very apt! A first-floor window flew open and a remarkably pretty blonde girl looked out. She laughed and waved a bare arm.

"Bonjour, mon petit."

Charles swept off his beret and bowed.

"Bonjour, ma petite."

She turned her head and called excitedly into the room.

"Come quick and look, *mes filles*. I have found a new man, a Frenchman, a real Frenchman!"

The song on the gramophone stopped with a rending scratch. Four other heads appeared at the windows. Charles bowed again. The first girl spoke.

"What's your name!"

"Charles. And yours?"

"Lucille."

A dark girl laughed and waved a handkerchief.

"Me, I am Magda."

"And I Wanda," came swiftly.

"And I Monique."

"I am Elsa. What do you do here?"

"Good day to all of you, my pretty posy of flowers. I——"

The front door opened. The woman in black came out. The five girls' heads vanished and the windows slammed. The woman said sternly:

"You, what do you want?"

"Madame, I happened to be passing and——"

"Please do not pass again. The Villa is not for a Frenchman. *Adieu, monsieur.*"

"Au revoir, Madame."

Hans Ramberg's pass was far too precious a document to be yielded up lightly. From the Villa Mimosa, Charles broke out over the fields, working round in a vast semi-circle towards Coville, avoiding the roads. He met nobody. A sluggish, ice-cold stream some four feet deep marked the boundary of the military zone and Charles contemplated it with extreme distaste, shivering on the bank. The longer he stayed looking at it, the worse it would be. He unclipped Aunt Marguerite's nephew's bow-tie and, holding it, the sausages, and the bicycle high above his head, waded in. Three minutes later, saturated to the armpits, he half-ran, sobbing and swearing, towards the main road. He was on the safe side of the German control post.

Aunt Marguerite was waiting for him. She crossed herself when she heard the rattle of his key in the lock. He put the sausages and the bow-tie in her lap and dashed upstairs, his teeth chattering. When he came down again in dry clothes, she had poured him out a large glass of cognac. He drank it in one swallow and kissed her on her two puffy cheeks.

"You are mad to cross rivers in February, quite mad. I told you this morning that you are mad and it is true. So the candle I lit for you prevailed. My prayer was heard."

"The prayer, the candle and your nephew's bow-tie. The three together were invincible." He laughed. "It was much admired by Field-Marshal Rommel himself. I give you my word of honour."

"Recount me everything—from the beginning."

He told her everything—up to the point when the supply lorry had passed him on the hill's crest. He did not speak of the Villa Mimosa. In his opinion, Aunt Marguerite would have been profoundly shocked.

Then he went upstairs to finish his report for Baker Street. For possible future use, he gave the exact map reference of the flat field he had found beyond the Manoir's wood and suggested that it be given the code name "Orange Blossom".

*   *   *

At half past four exactly, Charles Addison was waiting at the gate of Coville cemetery. In one hand he held a small sheaf of flowers and in the other a newspaper, between the pages of which his finished report was folded, ready for coding and transmission to England. He was joined at once by Georges. The two raised their berets to each other and shook hands. They looked as undistinguished a pair of Frenchmen as ever trod the pavements of a provincial town. They walked in solemn silence to a deserted corner of the cemetery and Charles reverently laid his sheaf of flowers on the grave of a complete stranger. Darkness was falling as they sat side by side on a bench. They talked in low tones in English.

"I've had a hell of a day," said Charles. "And I've written it all down. You'll see it when you start coding so I won't bother you with it now." He handed over the newspaper. "It's all in there and, by the way, here are four pairs of sausages—with the compliments of Major Hans Ramberg, A.D.C. to the General."

"May God bless you and the General and the Major. I'm ravenous."

"Thought you would be. Now I'll tell you something I haven't written down."

He described the supply lorry, his pursuit of it and his discovery of the Villa Mimosa.

"There they were," he said, "five fantastic popsies and an old battle-axe in black silk." He shook his head. "Brings the war home to you."

"Some people have all the luck," said Georges. "Five of them!"

"There must be six," said Charles sagely, "because I saw six pairs of thingamajigs on the line—plus the old battle-axe's stays. But number six didn't appear at the window. Possibly a shy type. . . ."

"And you haven't told Baker Street?"

"No fear. I don't want a kick in the pants for levity."

"Listen Charles," said Georges earnestly, "you and I know damn well the Baker Street boys never read a bloody word of the stuff we collect"—he coughed modestly—"at the risk of our lives. Well, here's a chance to prove it. Tell 'em about this place and if you get a rocket, at least we'll know that the stuff is read."

"Damn good idea. I will. Got a pencil and a note-book? Right. Add to report from 'Charles—personal to Squadron Officer A'. She's a friend of mine," he explained. "Message begins. *Have today located in evacuated area interesting going concern stop this is love-nest villa mimosa provisioned and frequented by panzer corps headquarters staff stop isn't nature wonderful query love charles stop message ends*."

"That should get you promotion," said Georges cheerfully, "or even a bowler hat if you're lucky. Where shall we meet on the day after tomorrow?"

"In the Café Saint Hubert at six."

"O.K. And in the meantime, keep away from the Villa."

"I have no intention whatsoever of going there. My name's Addison—not Samson."

They walked out of the darkening cemetery, raised their berets and shook hands, taking leave of each other with the time-honoured French Section salutation.

"*Merde*," said Charles.

"*Merde*," said Georges.

4: GASTON

AT three-fifteen next morning, promptly to schedule, Charles message was received in a house near Sevenoaks in Kent. Reception happened to be unusually good and the coded groups of letters were distinct. Their deciphering gave little trouble and the report in clear was rushed to Baker Street and dropped into Squadron Officer A's in-tray.

She read it very slowly and carefully, smiling at the last light-hearted paragraph. Having distributed the various points he had raised to those concerned, she re-read the personal paragraph. This time, she did not smile. She put it down on her desk and gazed into the far corner of the room, sitting motionless for a long time. People came and went but she only paid absent-minded attention to them. All at once, her mind was made up. She lifted the telephone receiver and asked to speak to a friend of hers who had the ear of the Chiefs of Staff Committee.

They arranged to meet for luncheon.

* * *

During the next forty-eight hours the weather was fine and Allied air-raids increased in the Pas de Calais. More slave workers died under the bullets of the S.S., and in the Army the suicide figures mounted again. Charles went quietly about his business. A new series of pylons, as well as telephone and railway lines, were chosen as sabotage targets and the plastic explosive distributed. Twelve containers full of Sten guns were successfully dropped and the contents hidden in barns under sacking and artificial cobwebs spun by a most ingenious machine.

All went well.

The streets of Coville were dark when Charles entered the Café Saint Hubert at six o'clock. He saw Georges sitting in the corner reading a newspaper. Charles ordered a glass of red wine and waited. Soon Georges yawned, folded up his paper and put it on the table. Charles crossed the room and stopped at Georges' table. He said with a smile:

"*Vous permettez?*"

"With pleasure, Monsieur."

Charles picked up the paper and put it in his pocket.

"I will read it later if I may."

"Do." Georges giggled. "You will find it most interesting—Samson."

Charles sat down. He said in an undertone:

"What the hell do you mean—'Samson'?"

"You'll see. Six of 'em—oh my! I told you the day before yesterday that some people have all the luck." He sighed and stood up. "Things are warming up. We'd better meet again tomorrow. Where and when?"

"Let me think. Inside Notre Dame de Coville, by the statue of Saint Thérèse of Lisieux near the first confession box on the left—at eleven a.m."

"You couldn't chose a more suitable place. I'll be there." He winked. "For all I know, you may have something to confess by then."

They bowed and shook hands.

"*Merde*," said Georges.

"And *merde* to you," said Charles. "This time I mean it."

Charles finished his wine and walked quickly back to the Rue de Voltaire. He was consumed with curiosity and more than a little apprehensive. He knew damn well that it had been a mistake to add that paragraph about the Villa Mimosa. The Baker Street boys and girls were good types in their own way but they had no sense of humour. Took the war too damn seriously.

He went to his room and extracted the message from between the pages of Georges' newspaper. He read it standing up.

> *For charles most urgent stop message begins stop landing ground quote orange blossom unquote approved stop you are required immediately to subordinate all activities to detailed investigation into villa mimosas occupants and visitors stop when this mission complete stand by for lysander pick-up from field quote orange blossom unquote stop bbc message will be quote the snipe will lay an egg unquote stop on arrival in london be prepared to give fullest possible report on villa at highest level stop personal to charles from squadron officer a stop let this be a lesson to you stop message ends.*

Charles sat down heavily on his bed.

Supper at 34 Rue de Voltaire was a meagre and preoccupied affair. For Charles to consult Aunt Marguerite about the Villa Mimosa was rather like asking his Regimental Lieutenant-Colonel about the goings on in a suburban palais de dance and he baulked it. He cleared his throat several times and lamely changed what he was going to say at the last split second.

When the plates were cleared and washed up, Aunt Marguerite fetched a sock of his with a hole in it and began leisurely to darn.

"En effet," she said, "all night you have been as restless as a dog with fleas. What is troubling you, *mon fils?"*

He looked at her. She was engrossed in her darning, placid, patient and implacable. He saw her as Marianne. He saw her as France.

He lit the last Gauloise he possessed in this world. He began:

"Aunt Marguerite, this is very difficult for me. Before I begin, I ask for your forgiveness. When you asked me about my visit to the Manoir on the day before yesterday, I did not tell you all. There was something else. A narrow road led upwards to the crest of a small hill. After leaving the Manoir I took that road. While I rested behind the poplars, a German supply lorry passed me. I followed. . . ."

He told her everything, the name of the Villa, the names of the girls, what he had said to them, how the woman in black silk had ordered him off. He left nothing out. She made neither sign nor comment.

"In a moment of foolishness, I mentioned this Villa to . . . to my headquarters in London in a radio report. The reply came today. Aunt Marguerite, I am ordered by the British Government to enter this Villa, to find out about those who live there and those who visit them. Then I am to be flown to London to tell the story. I do not know to whom or why."

She was no longer Marianne. She was the *tricoteuse* and he the condemned. When she looked up, the guillotine's knife would fall.

"Eh bien." She put down the half-darned sock. Her plump face puckered. "Listen to me. I know about this. I have known since yesterday. The girls of the Villa Mimosa are enclosed and they only see Germans. When you passed, they saw one whom they believed to be a Frenchman. In my view you are a little too tall for the role of Frenchman but let that pass. They saw you, a stranger, one whose bearing is not wholly repugnant to women. So they talked about you, speculated about you."

"How do you know this? Aunt Marguerite, I beg of you——"

"I know because they were overheard."

"You say that these girls are enclosed. Who, in God's name, could have overheard?"

She was silent for a moment, collecting her thoughts. Then she appeared to go off at a tangent.

"We in France are cursed with avarice. Over the centuries, a family collects a little treasure in money or a few hectares of good land. One family is unwilling to let that go to another family, so marriages are arranged between cousins. The treasure remains but the blood becomes thin and this arrangement is not always good for breeding. My sister married her cousin. They have one son. It was the son, my nephew, who overheard the girls of the Villa Mimosa."

"But . . . but what was your nephew doing in this place?"

"He is Gaston the pianist, the hunchback. It was his bow-tie that you wore. In spite of his deformity," Aunt Marguerite said proudly, "he was acknowledged by all to be the best-dressed man in Lille. If one is burdened with a physical handicap, one must triumph in another way. His triumph lies in his elegance." She put down the sock. "It is best that you meet Gaston. He is in Coville at this moment, at the house of my sister." A shadow passed over her face. "He is not required at the Villa until nine o'clock each night but his . . . work may continue till dawn. So he sleeps then, in the attic, and comes to Coville in the hours of daylight. He is not only elegant but a brilliant pianist—and a good son."

This was extraordinary, quite extraordinary. That the labyrinthine family relationships of the Pas de Calais should result in this bizarre contact with the Villa Mimosa was quite absurd—and yet nothing could be more natural. He said, frowning:

"I want to ask you two questions, Aunt Marguerite. If you have known about this . . . this establishment for some time, why did you not tell me? We have no secrets between us, you and I."

She lowered her eyes.

"I am a respectable widow, *mon fils*, and the Villa Mimosa represents a mode of life which every French woman discusses with embarrassment. Your next question—before I put on my hat."

"It is this. When I meet Gaston, it will be necessary to reveal my true identity. Each new person who knows is a new danger, not only to me but to many others. May I rely on his silence?"

"He is my nephew," she said.

*　　*　　*

Gaston was small and bent, so that his head seemed to sit directly on his shoulders. His eyes were bright with intelligence and his long-fingered hands almost woman-like in their fluttering beauty. He listened to Charles without speaking.

"*Enfin,*" he said, "I will tell you what I know. First, there is Madame. I do not know her name but she is stern and honourable. You saw five of the girls, Lucille, Magda, Wanda, Elsa and Monique. Of Monique, I know little. Nobody knows anything of Monique. Wanda the Czech is pretty, deceitful and cruel. She makes jokes about my hump. All of them spoke of you with excitement. There is another whom you did not see. She is Golden Mouse, an Indo-Chinese and a great lady. She is of the honourable house of Li. The German officers who come to the Villa are nearly always the same. Sometimes strange officers come from Paris or Berlin and are accepted. They are a group of close friends and they come because of two things. They know that in the Villa they can talk freely and live the lives of healthy men. Three of them are what the English would call 'gentlemen', the others are of the middle-classes. That you will readily observe for yourself. They are all concerned in some great political enterprise. That is certain." He smiled and broke off. Then he said: "Do you care for music?"

"Very much. I was a member of the Oxford Music Society and I used to play the piano quite a lot."

"And you miss it?"

"Enormously."

"My work, and the place where I do it, may be open to reproach but at least I am doing what I love. I give pleasure both to myself and to others, and in these black days of war that is something."

"I agree."

"Your Government, Monsieur, have ordered you to enter the Villa Mimosa. I go in and out of the military zone at will. I have a little car and a certain Major Hans keeps me well supplied with petrol coupons. I could readily take you in. You could hide in the back. The sentries never examine my car." He smiled. "I flash my light one, one-two and they know it is I. Sometimes they glance at my hump but they always wave me on. Once at the Villa, you could play the piano instead of me—provided Madame agreed—and you could find out what your Government wants to know. What is needed is an excuse, an excuse for your presence."

"And that is something which is not easy to find."

"No. It is very difficult. Monsieur, please do not think me
discourteous if I ask that you allow me to ponder this in silence.
It is . . . not easy."

"Of course."

The room in which Charles sat was hideous. It was obviously
its owner's pride and here was collected all the "best" furniture,
irrespective of harmony.

An Empire clock, silent and motionless for a quarter of a
century, three discordant chairs, two of them spindle-legged, a
satin-wood table with strips of purple silk laid diagonally across,
a stuffed pheasant and a spinning wheel. Charles went on noticing
things. A fly-blown steel engraving of a shipwreck, two polished
brass shell-cases on the chimney piece—

"Monsieur."

The hunchback was contemplating his beautiful hands. He said
absently:

"You are not a Frenchman. Why did you come to France to do
this work? You permit that I ask this question?"

"Certainly. My mother was French, from Béthune. That is
one of the reasons."

"That I see. But you could have stayed with your regiment
and fought at the side of your friends. You chose to come alone
and, if required of you, to die alone. Many of my friends have
died for this same cause. They have given their lives. What have
I given? The skill which is in my fingers—to amuse German
officers and six daughters of joy. I am not proud of myself,
Monsieur Charles."

What was there for Charles to say?

Gaston stood up. The top of his head was no higher than
Charles' chest. He held out his right hand.

"*Au revoir, Monsieur.*"

"*Au revoir, Monsieur Gaston.*" His face showed his disappointment. "Are you going already?"

"Yes. I am going to look for that excuse that we both need. I
will not be long, my friend. A matter of minutes. Please wait
for me."

The pressure of his slim hand was firm. He smiled and walked
lightly out of the hideous room.

Gaston did not leave the house. He went upstairs to his own
bedroom. He sat on his bed and gazed at his hands, moving his
fingers as if he were playing a piano. Then, suddenly, he crossed
the room like a tiger, opened the door, placed his right forefinger

between the hinge and the frame and slammed the door with all his strength.

*   *   *

Charles heard an animal scream of pain. He ran into the hall to see Gaston reeling and stumbling down the stairs. His face was contorted with agony and triumph as he held out a crushed forefinger with blood spurting.

"Voici ton excuse," he shouted, *"voici ton excuse. . . ."*

*   *   *

In the dark of the February night, Charles drove the car with Gaston crouched beside him. His finger had been roughly bandaged by his mother and he occasionally made little hissing noises as the bruised, torn flesh surged with pain. They took a back road unknown to Charles, and at a nudge from Gaston, he flashed his lights one, one-two. The striped bar lifted at once, and he was in the military zone.

Before him lay the incalculable.

Charles stood facing Madame of the Villa Mimosa. She said:
"You have been recommended to me by Gaston. But I have seen you before. You are the man who passed by this house three days ago."

"Yes, Madame."

"You spoke to *mes filles.*"

"Yes, Madame."

"And now you are prepared to entertain my clients—*et mes filles?*"

"Yes, Madame."

"You are aware that my clients are German officers?"

"Yes, Madame."

"And you, a loyal Frenchman, are prepared to do this?"

"Yes, Madame."

She sat back in her chair, putting her folded hands on the table. She looked into his eyes.

"Who are you?"

"My name is Charles Bertin, watchmaker, of Coville."

"I repeat my question. Who are you?"

Charles opened his wallet, took out his forged identity card and laid it on the table. Madame did not look at it. She looked at him.

"For the last time, who are you?"

There was silence. During the early days of Charles' training in England the art of security had been loosely defined as "not talking unnecessarily". Later on, this precept had hardened into "not talking at all" and the need for silence at all times had been dinned into him again and again under harsh mock-interrogation, only slightly the less frightening because it was simulated. Every single rule demanded that he should adhere categorically to his alias and reveal nothing. In direct contradiction, his instinct urged him to throw security to the winds and make this sphinx-like woman his confidante. It was training versus instinct—and the battle fierce but brief. Instinct won. He said deliberately:

"I am a British officer.

"*Tiens!*" At last she leaned forward. There was a faint creak. Could it be the sound of the whale-bone stays he had seen hanging on the line? No. Such a thought was the wildest fantasy. Madame had been born fully dressed.

"You realize, Monsieur, that in telling me this you have made your life forfeit to me?"

"I do."

"Then why do you tell me?"

"I am here in France and in the Villa Mimosa to serve my Government. Without your help, I cannot do so. Therefore I must tell you the truth."

"Your sole and only purpose in coming here, to this house, is to serve your Government?"

"Yes, Madame."

She sat back.

"Your body is straight and strong, Monsieur. You are not a hunchback like Gaston. Under this roof are six girls whose lives are far divorced from those of nuns. From dawn till dusk, their hours pass slowly. Do you, as a British officer, give me your word of honour that you will not profit from a unique situation?"

"I give you my word of honour, Madame."

"And I accept it. I turn now to practical things. I have arranged to send Gaston home. He has given what to him is more than his life. As a serious musician, he is finished. The bone is splintered and he will play the piano again—but with a limp in his fingers. You will occupy his room in the attic. There is a lock on the door and a key. Strange to relate, there is fierce jealousy amongst my *pensionnaires* and I counsel you to keep your door locked. Their code is not so rigid as yours," she said drily. "The German officers

start to come about nine. I will explain you away and your task
is to play what they request. Your back is to the room and you
face the wall. Stay like that. They will soon forget that you are
not Gaston and then is the time to keep your ears open."

"Madame, these German officers have a purpose. What is it?"

"Their purpose," she said, "is to bring peace to a world in
agony. If it were not so, do you suppose that I—I of all people—
would nightly supervise the sacrifice of six human souls? If so,
you mistake me." She stood up. She said formally, speaking to
her employee: "What is your name?"

"Charles is my name, Madame."

"Come with me please, Charles. I will show you to your room
and then present you to my girls."

Charles bowed.

"I am at Madame's service."

5: SEXTETTE IN "A" MAJOR

THE attic bedroom in the Villa Mimosa was very tiny and cold.
The most important thing about it was that it had a window
wide enough for Charles to squeeze through and that the long
drop into the back yard was just possible for an active man. And
the door had a stout lock.

Charles followed Madame downstairs. At the door of the Salon,
he stopped and drew breath. He suddenly remembered how, years
ago as a new boy at Crécy, he had been made to stand on the prep-
room table and give a solo rendering to the assembled House of
"*John Brown's body lies a-mouldering in the grave*". That
experience, terrifying at the time, was trivial compared with
this. . . .

Madame opened the door. Charles saw the narrow room
running the length of the house and the glimmering candles. He
saw the girls of the Villa Mimosa look around without evident
interest and he saw their expressions change. He swallowed. The
palms of his hands felt sticky and there was a fluttering in the
backs of his knees.

"*Mes filles*," said Madame, "please give me your attention."
It was an unnecessary request, for all six girls were gazing open-
mouthed at Charles. "You will be grieved to learn that our pianist
Gaston has suffered a slight accident to his right hand. Until
Gaston can resume his duties, Charles here has consented to play
the piano and to help to entertain our visitors. I have only one

thing to add. The attic is strictly out of bounds both by night and by day." She turned to Charles. "There is the piano in the corner. As you have not played for some time, you may well want to practise. I do not expect our guests for some ten minutes or more. Thank you."

The door closed behind her. Charles walked to the piano and opened it and sat down on the stool. Every note of music he had ever known had fled and he stared helplessly at the key-board, his back to the room. He heard quick footsteps on the parquet floor and the rustle of feminine clothing. Slim fingers ruffled his dark hair and a laughing voice said:

"Welcome to the Villa Mimosa. I am Lucille. You remember?"

"Yes, Mademoiselle. I remember."

He half-turned on his stool. Four girls were clustered around him and a fifth was approaching from the far end of the room. Only one girl sat motionless in shadow. Lucille said:

"Back to your places. I saw him first. Is it not true that I saw you first, my compatriot, my angel?"

There was an indignant cry.

"You are selfish. You want him to yourself," said Magda. "We all saw him together. I am Magda. You remember me?"

"Of course, Mademoiselle."

"And I Wanda. You smiled at me."

"And I Elsa. To me you waved."

"I am Monique."

Charles said desperately:

"I have not played the piano for a long time and my fingers have become unaccustomed. Also, I have forgotten every tune I ever knew. Will one of you not make a suggestion—quickly, before the German officers come?"

Lucille broke in. "We are French, you and I. Play a song of France."

A song of France? The only one Charles could think of was the Marseillaise and that was hardly a suitable choice for the occupied Pas de Calais in 1944. Wait! Something else was coming back to him. If only he could remember how it began. He ran his fingers along the key-board and confidence came flooding. Swiftly he picked out the melody and he heard Lucille's voice, careless as a bird, take up the song.

> *"Auprès de ma blonde . . .*
> *Qu'il fait bon, fait bon, fait bon,*

Auprès de ma blonde ...
Qu'il fait bon dormir!"

That was better. Much better. He looked at Magda, smiling.
"And now you. You choose a song."

"I am Hungarian. Play me a song of my country."

Hungary—Budapest. *Tzigáne-Zene*, gipsy music. Or Liszt?
Better Liszt. He played two movements of the Hungarian
Rhapsody while Magda swayed her shoulders and Wanda scowled.
The girl—it was Golden Mouse—who had been sitting alone rose
up and glided across the floor and silently joined the company.

"Enough of that Magyar drivel," said Wanda. "Play something
Czecho-slovakian, something of value."

Charles rubbed his chin. Dvorák. One of the *Humoresques*. But
this was the girl whom Gaston had described as cruel, the girl
who laughed at his hump. Here was a chance to ridicule her. He
began slowly to play *Knees up, Mother Brown*, gathering pace,
ending with a series of crashing chords.

"I have known it all my life," cried Wanda. "It is magnificent
but I have forgotten its name."

"It is called *Wonderful Windows of Prague*," said Charles with
a cough.

"Of course. Now I remember. Of course. *Wonderful Windows
of Prague*. I heard it first at the knee of my grandfather."

"I am from Strasbourg in Alsace," said Elsa with excitement.
"What can you find for me?"

"That is a little difficult. Strasbourg. Geese. *Pâté de foie gras*,
the finest in the world. Mademoiselle, years ago I composed a
small piece to amuse myself. I now give it a name and dedicate
it to you. This is *The Goose-feather March*."

He played his own composition. It was light and airy as a
goose-feather. He decided to keep the name permanently in
memory of a fantastic night. Elsa was delighted. She said proudly:

"For you all, he plays the work of others. For me he creates a
song."

Charles stood up. He said to Golden Mouse: "I have not had
the pleasure of seeing you before, Mademoiselle. My name is
Charles."

"And I am Golden Mouse. Is it possible that you could play
a song of Indo-China?"

She was modest and of rare, fugitive beauty. It would be
impossible to tell her anything other than the truth.

"Alas, what you ask is beyond me." He racked his brains. "Wait, Mademoiselle. I have an idea but I doubt if it will please you."

"What pleases you, Monsieur, will give pleasure to me."

He played the overture to *Chu Chin Chow*. Golden Mouse pretended to be delighted. Charles looked around carefully. He had played five different things, but in the Villa Mimosa there were six girls. One of them had not asked for a song. But which one? Ah yes. There she was. Rather smaller than any of the others, auburn-haired and little, with the legs of a dancer. It was . . . yes, of course, Monique.

"Mademoiselle, it is your turn. From what country?"

Monique shifted her sandalled feet. She shrugged.

"Play anything you like. I have no special request."

Her French accent was appalling, but her tone was not uncivil. She did not wish to reveal her country and this was her way of saying so.

"But I have played for your friends and I don't want to leave you out. Let us agree to keep your secret. Simply hum a melody to me and I will do my best to follow. Please, Mademoiselle."

Monique hesitated. It seemed to Charles as if she were struggling within herself. Suddenly she flushed under her rouge. She wove her way through the group and leaned over Charles' shoulder. Though her voice was flat and tuneless, the melody was unmistakable. She sang it with a sort of defiance.

It was *Greensleeves*.

The door of the Salon opened. Madame said frigidly:

"To your places, ladies. Our visitors have already started to arrive. I must remind you that this is your drawing-room—and not the back room of a *bistro*. Charles, I want a word with you."

"Certainly, Madame."

The girls scattered as he crossed the parquet floor. On the landing, Madame said quietly:

"The leader of the German group is here. His name is Ramberg, Major Hans Ramberg. Ah, I see that you are as surprised as he was. When I told him that I had engaged a substitute for Gaston, he was very acutely worried and demanded to know who you were. Those who come here are more frightened of their own people than they are of the French resistance, and a stranger could always be a Gestapo man. I was able to set his fears at rest. As soon as I told him that you were Charles Bertin, a watchmaker from Coville, he was greatly relieved. It appears now that you and

Major Hans already know each other—and that you have been spoken to by Field-Marshal Rommel. It is an unusual distinction for a British officer who is not in captivity! For the rest, I said that you were a friend of Gaston's and that you were both reliable and silent. Naturally he wishes to question you. Now come."

Madame opened the door. A fair-haired German officer was standing in her room. She said with formality:

"I have the honour to present Charles, my new pianist. Charles, this is Major Hans. I understand that you have already made each other's acquaintance."

Quietly she closed the door.

* * *

"Cigarette, Monsieur Bertin?"

"Thank you very much, *mon Commandant*. I did not have time on the last occasion we met adequately to thank you for the sausages. But let me do so now."

"It was nothing. And do please sit down, my dear fellow. We are no longer in Panzer Korps Headquarters but in the Villa Mimosa." He flicked a flame to his lighter and lit Charles' cigarette. He sat back and crossed his knees. "Well," he said, "this is very surprising."

"I am surprised myself, *mon Commandant*. Were it not for Gaston's injury——"

"Ah yes, that injury. Gaston crushed it in a door, I gather. Most unfortunate. It remains to be seen if it could not be a blessing in disguise. He is too serious a musician for a place like this." He paused and went on with a frown: "I am beginning to think that you are somewhat of an enigma, Monsieur Bertin. Field-Marshal Rommel rates you highly as a soldier. I know you to be a first-class watchmaker. Madame obviously regards you as a good pianist. I wonder," he said drily, "what your next role will be."

"I am equally curious, *mon Commandant*."

Hans Ramberg leaned forward. His metallic blue eyes were intent and very shrewd.

"By what may or may not have been an unfortunate accident, you have become one of our company. It is certainly unfortunate for you because, for better or worse, you are now involved. The fact is that henceforth you are our hostage. Nobody, man or woman, can light-heartedly enter the Villa Mimosa—and leave it again. If our friends of the *Sicherheitsdienst* were ever to learn of its existence, my brother-officers and I might well stand before a firing squad. One could hope for little tolerance of a house such as this from our celibate Fuehrer. As for Madame and our six charming hostesses, they would rapidly find themselves in a cattle-truck *en route* for Ravensbrueck."

He saw a tiny look of curiosity on Charles' face.

"You don't know about Ravensbrueck? It is a K-Z, one of Himmler's masterpieces, a concentration camp for women. Its true purpose is to intimidate men by degrading those whom they love and long to cherish. The French call it *l'enfer des femmes*. Can you envisage Lucille or Magda or Golden Mouse with their heads shaved, their beautiful and desirable curves reduced to hungry skin, their clothes a mere covering of striped rags? Not a pretty picture, is it?"

"It is horrible, Major Hans."

"I thought you would find it so. The butchers in black have neither pity nor understanding for human frailty and that would be the least punishment one might expect for frequenting this . . . er . . . *ostensible* oasis of love and laughter in the parched Sahara of war." He had slightly emphasized the word "ostensible". He sat back and gazed at the ceiling, inviting a question. Charles asked it.

"You say 'ostensible', Major Hans. Can the Villa Mimosa have any other purpose?"

Perhaps the question had been asked too innocently. Over Hans Ramberg's face flitted that engaging schoolboy grin.

"You are strangely ingenuous, my friend. Come, come. As a good soldier, watchmaker and pianist, you cannot believe that we, who are realists, would risk such punishment in return for brief oblivion in the arms of women—even women like Lucille, Elsa, Wanda, Monique, Magda—and the incomparable Golden Mouse."

He looked at Charles quizzically and spoke after a long pause:

"Madame has described you as being reliable and silent. I hope for all our sakes that she is right. Even if she isn't, it doesn't matter, because you are one of us now and would share our fate. I am tempted to bare my soul to you. It is a well-known German failing, this baring of souls, and is as irresistible to us as cream to a Viennese or garlic to a French cook. I say I am tempted—but I am going to resist that temptation." He smiled wryly. "Once I *did* bare my soul to an English friend—and regretted it."

"Anatole France remarked that Englishmen have two left arms," said Charles sagely.

"He was right. It happened like this. Before the war I was at Oxford—which is the seat of a very great and ancient university. As a German, I was perpetually dismayed by the reserve of the English. I suffered under it for two long years. Then, in an attempt to break down this reserve, I did two things. I took up rowing and I played the mandolin. . . ."

Charles was overwhelmed by a sudden, blinding revelation. He did not betray it by the flicker of an eyelash.

". . . These were my weapons, my muscles and my mandolin, and I used them both very successfully. My fellow undergraduates became my close friends at last and my rooms a cage of singing birds. Then came disaster. One night after my college boat had successfully bumped another college boat, I got drunk. I believed utterly in Hitler then and, in my cups, I was moved to speak of the glorious rebirth of Germany and of strength through joy. Lyrically, I described sunburned Aryans striding up mountainsides, and concentration camps as benevolent institutions designed to lead men and women to a fuller, richer life. I bared my soul. I was Schiller, Goethe and Heine. I was a Valkyrie in full gallop —on a hobby-horse."

Charles could see it all, the brash German undergraduate talking and talking into a void of disapproval.

"When I had finished—with a quotation from Frederick the Great—my companion looked at me as if he had a hair lodged between his teeth. He told me that if I could make myself vomit, I would feel better in the morning. He meant it kindly but I knew that I had committed bad taste, the cardinal sin in the English calendar. I do not propose to commit bad taste again."

His face twisted. An overwhelming urge was upon him to bare his soul once more. There is nobody more eager to reveal all than the reformed rake and that was exactly what Hans knew himself to be. And the man who sat opposite him was no loutish Englishman but a Frenchman and a true European who would not only understand but agree.

He went on, speaking with bitterness:

"Let me only tell you this. My brother-officers and I know at last that we, the whole German nation, have been tricked, bamboozled and shamed. Goethe said that one day Fate would strike the German people because '*they submit to any mad scoundrel who appeals to their lowest instincts, who confirms them in their*

*vices and teaches them to conceive nationalism as isolation and
brutality'*. We *have* submitted to a mad scoundrel. We have turned
Europe into an *abattoir* and we have forgotten God. My friends
and I, here in the Villa Mimosa, in Paris, even in Berlin itself, are
determined to——"

He stopped. The flush faded from his cheeks and his clenched
fists unloosened. He gave a little, shamefaced laugh.

"You see? I was unable to resist the temptation of baring my
soul. Forgive me, Monsieur. All I was going to say was that my
friends and I are determined to bring the war to an end as quickly
as possible. And now it is time for you to go and play the piano."

Charles stood up. He said:

"Thank you, Major Hans."

*   *   *

Charles walked into the Salon and crossed the floor to the piano.
Although he had seemed to look neither to the right nor the left,
he had in fact noted that three or four German officers had arrived
and had already chosen their companions. He sat down on his
stool, acutely aware that he was being stared at. What should he
play? Something easy and long, something that came readily to
his memory and to his fingers. Grieg. *Anitra's Dance in the Hall
of the Mountain King*. That went on and on. He suppled his
fingers and began. At last, he could think.

Ever since Hans Ramberg had brought him the General's watch
a fortnight ago, a formless something had been persistently
scratching on the window-pane of his mind, seeking to enter. Now,
with amazement, he knew what it was. By speaking of Oxford,
Hans had brought it sharply and suddenly into focus.

It had happened long before the war, on a summer evening
during Trinity term. With another man, he had gone to the
Trout at Godstow. He saw the whole scene again, a group of
undergraduates with tankards in their hands clustered round a
fair man who sat on the stone wall by the river, strumming on a
mandolin and singing. Charles heard again the *plinka plinka
plonk* of the strings, and the hush and splash of the waterfall. He
had asked his friend who the troubadour was and he remembered
the answer: "Man called Ramberg. Rhodes Scholar. Quite a nice
chap—for a German."

It occurred to Charles that the man Ramberg was quite a nice
chap—for any nationality.

It was quite fantastic to realize that this man and he were now

unacknowledged allies. It had the quality of a scene from a melodrama. He did an imagined décor. The curtain rises; two
Bachelor of Arts (Oxon) are discovered under the amorous, con-
spiratorial roof of the Villa Mimosa, a *bordel* in France; one of
them is wearing a cheap, French, ready-made suit and the other
is dressed in the uniform and the swastika of the creature they
both long to destroy; *Entré des poules!* What a story to tell Verity
one day! Well . . . possibly. On second thoughts, one could hardly
expect Verity to regard his presence among the ladies of the
Villa with either enthusiasm or humour.

He heard heavy footsteps behind him. A strange voice said
gruffly:

"You. You have been playing that damned piece over and over
again. Don't you know anything else? This is not a funeral, you
know."

"I regret infinitely, *mon Colonel.*"

"Well, play something more lively." Colonel Fritz, who had
left Magda's side, waved a vague hand. "Something cheerful."

Charles hesitated. Then an idea came. His fingers rippled out
the opening bars of *Lili Marlene.*

The effect on Colonel Fritz was immediate. He slapped the top
of the piano violently.

"Not that *verfluchte* tune! I was in the desert with the Ninety-
first Light Panzer Division and every time I hear it, I see the
Tommies chasing us in their skirts with their God-damned bag-
pipes squealing. Play something civilized, something French.
Play *J'attendrai.*"

"Ah."

Charles drew a deep breath. He stood up slowly. Unconsciously
he flexed his muscles like a wrestler. He said deliberately:

"I regret, *mon Colonel,* that you ask for a song which I prefer
not to play."

Fritz's face flushed.

"You prefer not to play it. What the devil are you talking
about?"

The chattering and the clinking of glasses stopped abruptly.
A chair went over with a crash as Captain Paul jumped angrily
to his feet. Eternal bodyguard, he strode to his Colonel's side. His
mouth was a hard line and his blue eyes were icy.

"How dare you speak to a German officer in that fashion. Carry
out my Colonel's request immediately."

Now there could be no retreat. He had done the Baker Street

unpardonable by drawing attention to himself. Charles bowed slightly, warily.

"With the greatest respect, I must refuse."

"You refuse! Did I hear you say *refuse*?"

"That was the word I used, *mon Capitaine*."

The Salon of the Villa was now like a petrified drawing-room scene in a waxworks. *"Twentieth-Century French Drawing-Room During German Occupation, Circa 1944. PLEASE DO NOT TOUCH*. Only the candle-flames were living. Thus it remained for a full, tense minute. Then, suddenly, with a movement by Hans Ramberg, all the waxen figures began to breathe and to become articulate.

Hans strolled leisurely towards the group of three at the piano. He put his hand on Captain Paul's shoulder and said soothingly:

"Gentlemen, we are here to enjoy ourselves, not to bicker. Our good pianist may have a personal reason for not wishing to play a certain song. Am I correct, Charles?"

"You are correct, *mon Commandant*."

"There are a thousand songs in the world—and the girls are becoming impatient. Sit down, Charles, and play something else."

"One moment, Hans." Captain Paul brushed the friendly hand off his shoulder. "This fellow has been insolent to my Colonel. If he has a good and adequate reason for refusing to play *J'attendrai*, I would like to hear that reason. If not, I insist."

Charles looked at Hans and at Captain Paul. Hans gave an almost imperceptible nod of encouragement. Charles began apologetically:

"If you demand my reason, I give it with reluctance. Last autumn, in Coville, a German soldier was killed in a back street. I do not know the circumstances of his death. All I know is that his body was found. In retaliation for this, Himmler sent in one of his Special Commandos. Ten innocent men were taken from their homes and made to dig their own big grave. Then they were lined up in the Grande Place de Coville to be publicly executed. By order of Himmler, they were shot to the refrain of the song you asked me to play." He paused. "That, gentlemen, is my reason."

Colonel Fritz had been sitting with Magda. To her fury, Wanda the Czech was still without an escort. This was her chance. She undulated her way to the piano and gave Fritz a flashing smile.

"Eh bien," she said gaily, "Colonel Fritz was in no way concerned in what has been described. The war goes on outside the

walls of the Villa Mimosa, not within. You have asked for a song. *Mon ami*, I am delighted to sing it for you."

She half-closed her eyes and began to sway, singing huskily.

> *"J'attendrai'* . . .
> *Le jour et la nuit*
> *J'attendrai toujours,*
> *Ton retour*
> *J'attendrai* . . .
> *Comme l'oiseau*——"

The door at the far end of the Salon opened. Nemesis stood framed there, Nemesis in black silk. Madame's voice was like a whiplash.

"Wanda, stop that disgusting exhibition and go to your room at once. At once I say——"

* * *

Midnight in the Villa Mimosa and a candle guttering. Charles took his hands off the keyboard, leaned back and closed his eyes. He knew that his memory and his fingers were utterly exhausted and he only longed for rest. There was a strange silence in the Salon and he turned round. The long room was deserted at last, thank God, and he must have been playing to himself. No. Not quite to himself. One girl sat motionless and alone in a dim corner. He smiled at her, successfully stifling a yawn. She rose and came to him, bringing a chair. It was Monique. She said in her flat voice:

"You must be very tired."

"I am." He hesitated. "I'm afraid I don't know the rules of the Villa. Do you think that the time has come when the hired pianist could go to bed?"

"Yes. I am the only one left and no one else will come tonight." She shrugged. "For me, as time goes on, it is more and more frequently like this. Not that I care. I am . . . a month or two older than the other girls and, like you, I am tired. It has been a long war and there can be no escape for any of us until it ends." She sighed. "But I don't want to talk about myself. You have played the piano all the time and had nothing to eat or drink. Lucille is with Captain Paul and they have left half a bottle of champagne on the table. When he comes down he is going to drive straight to La Roche-Guyon so we——"

"To where?" said Charles softly.

"To La Roche-Guyon. You know. Rommel's Army Group 'B' Headquarters."

"You seem to be very well informed about military matters."

"Oh yes," she said absently. "We all are. Those who come here talk quite freely about such things among themselves. They even discuss the plot."

" 'The plot.' What plot?"

"I thought you would have known. The plot to kill Hitler."

She said the words so casually, as if she were discussing the menu for tomorrow's luncheon. Charles simulated a yawn and tried to keep the eagerness out of his voice.

"I've heard something about it, of course. But tell me more."

"Well, they're going to kill Hitler and the fat one called Goering and the thin one in black who's in charge of the police and wears pince-nez. I forget his name."

"Himmler?"

"That's right. Himmler. And they're going to kill Goebbels as well and take over all the radio stations."

"Do you know when they're going to do this?"

"No. But I do know the names of some of the people concerned —apart from those who come here. You see, Hans and the others forget about us when they talk. Then"—she smiled with painted weariness—"a moment always comes when they remember us. But the big thing is that we can finish the champagne. I'll wash two glasses in the kitchen. Wait."

She went to the table where Lucille and Captain Paul had been sitting and brought the half-empty bottle and put it on the piano. Charles watched her walk to the door holding the two glasses, automatically mincing a little on her dancer's legs.

He stood up and whistled. He had learned enough, quite enough, for tonight. To ask any more might—the English phrase came to his mind—scare the bird off the nest. He tip-toed about the Salon. He saw lipstick-smeared cigarette ends in the ash-trays and one dropped handkerchief. In his excitement, he was sorely tempted to finish one of those half-smoked cigarettes, but refrained. A door banged upstairs and he started. Heavy military footsteps clattered down the stairs, passed the door of the Salon and went on down. From the back of the Villa he heard the whirr of a car's self-starter and then the engine's beat. Captain Paul was about to set out on the long cold drive—he smiled—to their mutual friend Field-Marshal Rommel. *Bon voyage, mon Capitaine!*

Monique came back. She put the clean glass on the piano beside the champagne and gave him a thick sandwich on a plate.

"I stole it from the larder," she said. "It's a good one, with real butter and cheese."

"You are very kind, Mademoiselle. I'll eat it in bed." He began to pour out the champagne.

Monique said quickly: "You take it all. I don't want any."

"I insist on you having some. We must drink a toast."

"Then only a drop, *une larme,* a teardrop. That's enough. You fill your glass."

The champagne, flat but potent, filled Charles' glass to the brim. He raised it.

"Your health, Mademoiselle."

"And yours, Monsieur."

"Wait. We should also drink the health of Captain Paul, our unwitting host."

Monique said with a sneer:

"And that of Lucille who wheedled it out of him. She is a clever one, that Lucille."

Charles drained his glass. He had not eaten for several hours and his mind and muscles had been tense. In this moment of excitement, the wine's reaction was swift. The Salon seemed to swing in a slow half-circle and the flames of the candles duplicated themselves. He sat down on the stool and hiccupped. Better eat something—at once. He bit off a large mouthful of sandwich and ate it slowly. Monique watched him with solicitous, experienced eyes. She spoke as if she were his nurse:

"Better now?"

"Yes. Much better. Sorry about that."

"Eat some more sandwich. It'll do you good."

"Yes, I . . . I think I will."

As he finished the sandwich, the Salon steadied and the candle-flames sorted themselves out. His recent exhaustion had completely gone and he felt full of energy and a sort of gay recklessness. There was an inch and a half of champagne left in the bottle. He divided it carefully between himself and Monique.

"One more toast, Mademoiselle. To the Villa Mimosa!"

"Damn the Villa Mimosa. To solitary beds."

Monique emptied her glass and put it on the piano with a clatter. She said, her painted mouth working:

"Will you do something for me?"

"Of course, Mademoiselle. You have done a lot for me. What is it?"

"Play me that song again, the one you played before."

Charles had played a hundred songs over the long hours, fulfilling one request after another. He shook his head in perplexity.

"I'm sorry but I can't remember which one. Sing me a few bars of it."

She sang *Greensleeves*.

He picked it up at once and her voice stopped. He played it with great tenderness, stressing the lilting melody in the treble keys. Monique sat without a move or a sound. He took his hands off the keyboard and turned on his stool. Monique's eyes were bright with tears unshed. Suddenly what had been hidden was revealed to him. He said, almost in a whisper :

"You're English, aren't you?"

"Yes," she said flatly, "I'm English. May God forgive me."

Monique burst into a storm of weeping.

*   *   *

Long before the cocks had begun to crow, Charles woke up to a slight sound in the attic of the Villa Mimosa. He stared into the darkness, one hand on the butt of the revolver under his pillow, the other on the switch of his pocket torch. Deliberately he pressed the switch and a thin pencil of light bisected the dark and wavered and settled on the handle of his locked door. He saw the handle turn slowly and in vain. He flicked the light off.

There was a faint creak as the stairs took the weight of naked, disappointed feet.

Lucille? Elsa? Wanda? Magda? It was not Golden Mouse and it was certainly not Monique, his compatriot and his friend.

He smiled in the darkness. He would never know.

6: THE RECRUIT

CHARLES woke up an hour before dawn and dressed, shivering. Holding his shoes in his hand, he crept downstairs, tip-toeing along a corridor redolent of half a dozen competing scents. He distinguished *Soir de Paris* and *Shocking* but the others he didn't know. Every door was shut. The salon was as he had left it, a welter of empty bottles and glasses and cigarette ends. He wrinkled his nose at the stale smell and tried the door of Madame's private room. It was open. He sat down at her desk and, after a moment's thought, wrote on a slip of paper:

Madame:

I have taken the liberty of going to Coville to change my clothes. I will report back for duty this evening. I am, Madame,

Yours respectfully,

Charles (pianist).

The hall door of the Villa Mimosa was bolted and the house as silent as the tomb. The bolts were oiled and slid back easily and it was with a sense of vast relief that Charles stepped into the fresh air.

The stars were paling and the ghost of a full February moon hung low on the horizon. He put on his shoes, walking lightly on the frozen ruts, making for the fields. It was reasonably safe to assume that the watchfulness of the sentries would be relaxed at this hour of half-darkness, and he decided to take a chance rather than plunge again into that icy stream. The very thought of it chilled his marrow. He chose the minor control post through which he and Gaston had driven last night and was delighted to see that it was unmanned. But only just! Hardly had he slipped through before he heard the sound of a lorry bringing up the dawn-to-midnight guard.

Once on the safe side of the line, he crouched under a hedge for a petrifying half-hour, waiting until people would be about the streets of Coville. Many a man had found himself on his way to a forced labour camp in the Reich by venturing abroad too early, for Sauckel's minions were ever on the look-out for the able-bodied. It was past eight o'clock when he walked inconspicuously into the town. More than anything else in the world, Charles longed for a hot bath.

He reached the Rue de Voltaire unchallenged. Aunt Marguerite was long up and dressed. Her greeting to him was strangely distant. She made him a bowl of steaming acorn coffee and for breakfast gave him the last of Hans Ramberg's *largesse*, a pair of Frankfurter sausages. He washed and shaved in the kitchen and changed his shirt. He was puzzled by Aunt Marguerite's unaccustomed silence and sought her out in the parlour.

"Well," he said cheerfully, "I am completely refreshed—thanks to you. Now let me tell you about last night."

Her face was like granite.

"I do not wish to hear about last night. The subject is distasteful to me. I am aware that by going there, to that place, you were carrying out the orders of your Government. Me, I am prepared to kill for my country—or to be killed. I am not prepared to be shamed and I hope you will spare me a description of an establishment which robs womanhood of dignity. My nephew Gaston has regained his honour—but at the cost of his finger. It was quite cheap at the price." Her face softened. "And now, *mon fils,* what are your plans?"

"I am meeting Georges at eleven this morning. He will transmit to London that my mission has been completed. Then"—he shrugged—"I have one or two visits to make, and after that I wait."

"Until you are summoned to England?"

"Yes. I shall miss you, Aunt Marguerite."

"And I you."

Charles went to his room and collected his few possessions together. Aunt Marguerite's uncompromising attitude towards the Villa Mimosa was, he saw now, a perfectly natural one. It was that of any decent Frenchwoman brought up within the code of a strict Catholic morality and, as such, was deserving of the greatest respect. On the other hand, some link between the Villa and London had to be established. To ask Aunt Marguerite to be that link would be an affront to this dumpy, ugly woman whom he loved. So it would have to be somebody else. But who? The answer, the obvious answer, came after five minutes thought.

It was Gaston.

* * *

Charles sat again in that hideous room waiting for Gaston to appear. It was odd to think that barely twelve hours had passed since he had talked to Gaston last night and that so much had been crowded into that brief space. He yawned. He supposed that the ladies of the Villa Mimosa would still be asleep. Lucky ladies. Or were they? Were they not already the victims of the mad scoundrel Hitler as surely as if they had been hounded into Ravensbrueck?

Gaston came down. He was wearing a flowered dressing-gown and, though his face was pale, his eyes were bright. He held out his right hand with its bandaged finger. He said, smiling:

"If you would only shake it gently, Monsieur. . . ."

"Is it better?"

"Much. It was X-rayed and dressed in the hospital late last night and this morning I can move it a little. In two, three days, I will be able to play the piano again. I say 'play' but I mean that I should at least make an agreeable noise. That is as much as I can hope for. The German officers are not too critical and my music is only a background. My life as a pianist is over and for that I rejoice. Others have given so much—and I so little." He smiled. "And how was your evening among the ladies of the Villa Mimosa? After all, you are not a hunchback like me."

"Many things happened, Monsieur Gaston." He told Gaston everything up to the moment when he had found himself alone with Monique. The revelation of her nationality was her own secret and he would never betray it. He said at last:

"Now I come to a serious problem, in which I hope—and believe—you can help me."

Gaston held up his bandaged finger.

"I am already committed to you, Monsieur. Please tell me what you require of me."

"It is this: during the next forty-eight hours it is probable that I shall return to England. Tonight may be"—he smiled—"my last professional appearance at the Villa. I can't say yet. But when I go, I take it that you will return."

"Yes. That is my intention." He gave a satanic grin. "It has become my living and, as the Americans say, 'the show must go on'."

"Great events are imminent. All those within the Villa Mimosa are enclosed. You are the only person who can move freely. I want you to become my link between the Villa Mimosa and London."

Gaston raised his eyebrows incredulously.

"Do you mean to tell me, Monsieur, that the Allied Governments would make use of the services of an unknown French hunchback?"

"They would be proud to call on a brave man, Monsieur Gaston."

Gaston stared at the floor, his face a maze of wrinkles. When he looked up his face was clear and youthful.

"What do you want me to do?"

"I want you to keep in touch with a friend of mine who has his own means of communicating with London. His name is Georges. That is all, just Georges. This is his telephone number." Charles gave it. "No. Do not write it down. Write nothing down—ever. Remember it. The first time you speak to Georges, say: *'My name*

is Gaston. *Could you possibly recommend a reliable piano-tuner?'*
Georges will reply: *'Though most of them have been called up, I
do know one who used to live in Lille.'* By this exchange you will
identify each other. Unless you get that exact reply, put down the
telephone at once and try again later. Once you have met and
seen each other and know each other's voice, there will be no
need for further passwords. Tell Georges all that takes place in
the Villa Mimosa and find out the answers to any questions he
may ask you. All clear?"

"Yes, Monsieur. When shall I do this?"

"As soon as I have gone. Now tell me, what is Georges' telephone number?"

Gaston repeated it accurately.

"And what will you say?"

"I will say: *'My name is Gaston. Could you possibly recommend a reliable piano-tuner?'* "

"And what is the reply?"

"The reply will be: *'Though most of them have been called up,
I do know one who used to live in Lille.'* "

"Correct in every way." Charles stood up. "Now I am going to
meet Georges and tell him about our new recruit. I have absolute
confidence in you. *Au revoir,* Gaston."

The hunchback swallowed.

"Au revoir, Charles."

*   *   *

When Charles walked into Notre Dame de Coville on the stroke
of eleven o'clock, a Nuptial Mass was nearing its end. The bride-
groom, who wore full evening dress, was kneeling at the altar
rails and Charles saw that his left leg was missing and that a
rubber-tipped peg protruded from the end of his trousers. He
was lucky to be one-legged. Because of that, he could at least
marry his bride. Otherwise, as an able-bodied man, he would be
working in the Reich. The Mass was being sung and yet another
sign of the times was the absence of bass voices in the choir. The
bride, seen from behind, was a plump body in white, draped in
veiling and wearing white satin shoes. Silently he wished the
couple long life, health and happiness. Little did they know that
two British agents were attending the ceremony.

Georges was kneeling in an attitude of devotion under the
statue of Saint Thérèse of Lisieux. Charles knelt beside him and
was slightly shocked to realize that his neighbour was indeed say-

ing his prayers. It was an unsuspected facet of Georges' character and Charles gladly followed an excellent example. In this time of strain and anxiety he took comfort in confiding in God and, after five minutes, rose from his knees with a new surge of buoyancy. Georges crossed himself and whispered:

"Morning, Charles. What's the form?"

"Couldn't be better. 'Mission completed.' "

"That's all you want me to say?"

"Yes. That's all. When can you transmit?"

"London is standing by for my call-sign at ten minutes past every hour. I think they've all gone dotty in Baker Street." He said enviously: "You certainly are a fast worker."

" 'The difficult,' " quoted Charles smugly, " 'we do at once. The impossible takes a little longer. . . .' "

The two men knelt again for the Benediction. The wedding party followed by friends and relations filed soberly out of the church and the candles were extinguished. Except for one old lady endlessly telling her rosary in a dim corner, Charles and Georges were alone. Georges frowned.

"If I transmit at ten past twelve this morning, the B.B.C. message could come in tonight after the nine o'clock news. Where will you be then?"

"At the Villa Mimosa. I'm going back." Charles smiled. "As my friend Gaston says: 'The show must go on.' I can listen in there. One of the girls, a sad little creature called Monique, tells me that Madame, who runs the place, tunes in practically every night to the *messages personnels* on the B.B.C."

"That's a bit of luck. Who's Gaston?"

"I was coming to him. Big things, very big things, are going on in the Villa Mimosa and it's essential that we keep in touch. So I've recruited Gaston, who knows the form and who can come into Coville every day. I've given him your telephone number and he'll contact you. He will say: *'My name is Gaston. Could you possibly recommend a reliable piano-tuner?'* and your reply is: *'Though most of them have been called up, I do know one who used to live in Lille.'* Got it?"

"Yes, I've got it. What's he like to look at when I meet him?"

Charles hesitated. He said:

"He's small and full of guts. And the forefinger of his right hand is damaged."

"Anything else?"

"Yes. He's a hunchback."

"You might have told me that first."

"When you get to know Gaston, you'll find out that's the least important thing about him. By the way, the official reason for my disappearance will be that Sauckel's thugs have nabbed me at last. Easy."

"Yes. No trouble there. And now, if you don't mind, I'm going to say one more prayer."

"Me too. Goodbye, Georges."

"Goodbye, Charles."

A few minutes later, the two men left the church separately.

Georges rode his bicycle out of Coville by the south-east road. It took him twenty minutes to reach the farm where he lived and worked. He went up to his room and dragged a cheap fibre suit-case from under the bed. Built into it was his transmitting set. He opened the cob-webbed window and looped his aerial over a rusted gutter support. Then he put on his headphones and looked at his watch. Two minutes to go before ten past the hour. He drummed lightly with his finger-tips. He had been walking with death at his elbow for too long and his longing for England and his wife and son was becoming a physical pain. No good thinking about it, no damn good at all.

At exactly ten past, he gave his call-sign on the Morse tapper. It was acknowledged at once. He tapped out his brief message in clear:

'From charles stop message begins stop mission completed stop message ends.'

Swiftly he gathered in his aerial and packed the set away. The cows were coming in for the midday milking. He went down-stairs and across the muck-yard into the long, draughty shed. He dressed in a filthy overall and picked up a bucket and stool. He pushed his head into the hollow of a cow's flank and felt for her bursting teats.

He wished to God he could go to England with Charles.

7: THE SNIPE'S EGG

GEORGES' message was received loud and clear in the house near Sevenoaks. Because of its anonymity and urgency, it was tele-phoned to Baker Street at once and not taken by despatch rider. Squadron Officer "A" smiled slightly and bore it to her Command-ing Officer.

"Charles has come up. 'Mission completed.' "

"What! Already? Are you sure?"

"That's what he says. And if Charles says so, it is so."

"The quicker we get him here, the better. Can you lay it on for tonight? Full moon yesterday. Pas de Calais should be like daylight."

"Yes. I've got the Chiefs of Staff behind me—and the Air Ministry's prepared to give maximum cover."

Her Commanding Officer looked a little worried. He said doubtfully:

"This thing has been yours from the start and I only hope it's going to be worth it. If it isn't, your blood be on your own head."

She smiled. "So be it."

She picked up a green telephone.

"Air Ministry, please."

*　　　　*　　　　*

Squadron-Leader "Croppy" Nesbitt, D.S.O., R.A.F., was about to broach his first pint of bitter of the day in the mess at Temps-ford when the Operations Officer came in. Croppy tried without success to hide behind his tankard. The Operations Officer said apologetically:

"Job for you, Croppy. Tonight—or rather early tomorrow morning. A high-powered Joe to be picked up. Sorry—but it's an urgent one."

British agents working behind the enemy lines were always known as "Joes". Croppy had already whisked a number of them out of France. He put down his tankard with a sigh.

"You might have waited another three minutes. Some day—I hope—I'll be able to buy a pint and drink it. What sort of Joe, male or female?"

"No idea. But I gather you're getting all the trimmings. Briefing at Tangmere—in the Cottage, as usual—at three this afternoon. You'd better have a quick lunch and fly the Lysander over." He smiled and added generously: "I'll drink your pint for you."

"Thank you so very much," said Croppy. "In the next war, remind me to join the Navy, will you?"

Croppy Nesbitt flew the jet-black Lysander with the ladder on its side to Tangmere, left the aircraft at "Dispersal" and made his way to the Cottage. The Briefing Officer was waiting for him.

"Hullo, Croppy. Thought they'd pick on you. The willing

horse is an ass. The job is to pick up a Joe on the field Orange Blossom in the Pas de Calais and bring him home. Pick-up is for 0315 hours tomorrow morning when there'll be bright moonlight. Two Defiants will be over Orange Blossom at 0312 and will shadow you to the French coast. Once clear of the flak, they'll form up to port and starboard and escort you all the way home. But that's not all. It's the whole bloody Lord Mayor's Show— with trimmings. A diversionary squadron of Halifaxes—nine of 'em—will come in over Dunkirk just before three and start dropping a mixed load of bombs and leaflets in the Cassel, Poperinghe and Bailleul area. They should keep the Boche night-fighters busy and give you a clear run."

Croppy sat down and whistled.

"Nine bombers, two fighters and a Lysander—all for one Joe. Who is he, for God's sake? We've already got Hess. Has Goering ratted on the Fuehrer at last?"

"No idea who he is, but Baker Street seem to want him pretty badly."

"O.K. Let me see the photographs."

The Briefing Officer gave him a sheaf of photographs. Croppy sat down and began to study them. He went over them meticulously, inch by inch, until every tiny detail of the topography was deep-etched in his mind. He pointed to a microscopic building under the lee of a beech wood.

"What's this place?"

"House called the Manoir. Believed to be Panzer Korps Head-quarters. The bomber boys have left it alone up to now, but you may be sure it's on the list."

"Huh." His eyes picked out a narrow road that trailed away into nothing. He bent over the photograph and took a magnifying glass. He said: "There's another building here. Any idea what it is?"

"Looks like some sort of villa. Used to be a home-from-home in the country. But it's obviously deserted. The little *midinette* has gone home for the duration."

"Good. And here's the field, Orange Blossom. What's the surface like?"

"Flat stubble. Should be as hard as a rock." The Briefing Officer smiled. "Bring me back a brace of partridges."

"Surely. I'll take my twelve bore and a retriever with me. Anything else you'd like?"

"Yes. A bottle of Chanel Number Five."

Croppy went over the map again. Then he shut his eyes and leaned back, projecting the detailed scene on to the photographic plate of his memory. He re-checked with the actual pictures. A helpful canal ran directly towards Coville, and in moonlight the little stream bounding the military area would shine like silver. He could take a fix on Coville church spire. On a slip of paper he worked out an exact timing, translating it into terms of petrol. A normal fuel load would be ample. So far so good. He telephoned to Met and asked for a weather forecast on the Pas de Calais, say a six-hour period as from midnight. While he waited, he was mentally planning where to cross the French coast, where he could best dodge the flak. He was a very good pilot, eliminating risks in advance, ready, if necessary, to take them in a split second. The Met forecast came in. Over the Pas de Calais there would be what amounted to a full moon, one-eighth overcast, visibility about eight miles.

The decision was his and his alone. He nodded.

"Should be a piece of cake. Right. I'll take it."

"Good. I'll get on to the Air Ministry, who'll get busy."

He knew that Croppy always insisted on some hours of sleep before setting out on an operation. "I suppose you'll go to bed. Pleasant dreams to you. What time do you want a call?"

"Five to one with a cup of tea. Two poached eggs on toast for breakfast, please, and put two flasks of coffee in the Lizzie."

"O.K. Goodnight, Croppy."

"Goodnight."

It was strange to say "goodnight" in the middle of the afternoon. Croppy drew the curtains of his bedroom in the Cottage and undressed and got into pyjamas. Five minutes later he was sound asleep.

By an odd coincidence, Charles went to sleep in the Rue de Voltaire, Coville, at about the same moment. Aunt Marguerite had promised to call him at eight so that he could report to the Villa Mimosa at nine and take up again his duties as temporary pianist.

*   *   *

Just before nine o'clock, the girls of the Villa Mimosa began to assemble in the Salon. Lucille was the first to arrive. She looked eagerly towards the piano and muttered, *"Zut!"* She had hoped to steal a march on her sisters and have Charles alone to herself for at least a moment or two before they should join her. But, alas,

Charles wasn't there. A wicked smile crossed her face. She went to the piano, opened the lid and began to play the first tune that came into her head. There was an immediate patter of feet on the stairs and a jostling at the door as Wanda just managed to get in ahead of Magda—with Elsa a close third. Wanda said with disgust:

"Oh, it's *you*."

"And who did you think it might be? Madame? I'm sorry to disappoint you, *chère amie*." She laughed. "Have you any special request? Shall I play you *Wonderful Windows of Prague*?"

"You are the daughter of——"

Lucille swung round on the stool.

"*Ta gueule*—or I'll beat you. Hold your mouth, I say."

"And I will beat you, too," cried Magda with enthusiasm. "And pull your hair out by the roots. Lucille, where is he?"

"I don't know. Elsa, do you know?"

"No. But he said he would be here to play tonight."

Golden Mouse came into the Salon. She did not join the group but sat alone, her long-nailed fingers woven in her lap, gazing modestly at the floor. Lucille asked sharply:

"Monique. Where is Monique?"

"That one," said Wanda contemptuously. "She has not appeared all day. She has been sitting in her room snivelling. Perhaps she is in love with our pianist. A fine chance she has, at her age. . . ."

The door opened. Monique entered slowly and walked to her accustomed place. She was heavily made up, with violet eye-shadow. Each separate eyelash was a black twig of mascara and her rouge defined and feverish. Her mouth was smeared with lipstick in defiance of nature's contours and her walk was that of a woman approaching the scaffold.

Lucille was the first to speak.

"*Eh bien*," she said. "This is the Villa Mimosa—not the *Place Pigalle*. This is a respectable house, I would have you know. We are ladies. We are not——"

"What did I tell you?" said Wanda with triumph. "She has done it to mask her tears. Are we to permit such a one to sit amongst us, shaming us?"

There were steps on the stairs and the girls looked round expectantly. It was Stefan the Viennese and with him was a strange, dark, good-looking officer whom none of them had seen before. Stefan waved an all-embracing hand.

"Good evening to you, children. This is a friend of mine, a very important man. He comes from Fuehrer Headquarters, in East Prussia, from the Wolf's Lair. His name is Colonel Karl. Karl, these are our dear friends, the ladies of the Villa Mimosa." He looked swiftly from one to the other, choosing. Lucille smiled boldly and he beckoned to her. Monique sat in shadow. It was a long time since he had paid any attention to her and she used to be an amusing little thing.

"You too, Monique."

She stood up listlessly. As she came into full candlelight, Stefan regretted his choice. Under a mask of make-up her face was drawn and haggard, and the smile that she gave him was as false as a set of teeth in a junk-shop window. Never mind. One of the merits of the Villa Mimosa was that one could always change horses in mid-stream!

Lucille looked demurely at the newcomer.

"A bottle of champagne, *mon Colonel?*"

"No," said Stefan boisterously, "two bottles, one for each of us. This poor fellow returns to Fuehrer Headquarters tomorrow and I want his night in the Pas de Calais to be memorable. And now tell me, my friend, what goes on in your East Prussian lunatic asylum?"

Colonel Karl gave a startled glance from one girl to the other. He could hardly believe his ears. The phrase "East Prussian lunatic asylum", used loudly and light-heartedly by Stefan, was enough to qualify the speaker for the *Genickschuss*, the single shot in the back of the neck as practised by the S.S. murder squads. Unversed in the wiles of conspiracy—as was the whole military hierarchy to which he belonged—Colonel Karl was horrified. In a continent where every telephone line could be tapped, where hidden microphones could pick up every scrap of conversation, where children were bribed and cajoled into betraying their parents, the spirit of revolt should wax unseen and unheard. And here was Stefan relaxed and laughing, saying fearful things out loud in the presence of witnesses. . . . He said in shocked tones:

"My dear fellow——"

"Oh, it's quite all right." Stefan slid an arm round Lucille's willing waist. "Our little sweethearts of the Villa Mimosa know all our secrets. Lucille here has even offered to hang the Fuehrer on one of her silk stockings—if only she could get near enough to him."

"Nobody can get near him. Everywhere he goes, he is surrounded by fawning sycophants. They say that the Devil looks after his own. He certainly looks after our beloved Fuehrer. The other day he decided that he alone must approve the cut of a new military greatcoat. It was to be worn by Major von dem Busche and this seemed like a heaven-sent chance. Under this new style greatcoat, Major von dem Busche secreted three hand-grenades and then reported for inspection. He was prepared suddenly to clasp the Fuehrer in his arms and blow himself and Adolf to Kingdom come."

"And what happened?"

"Nothing. Satan whispered in Adolf's ear and the inspection was cancelled at the last moment. And General Tresckow, von Bock's Chief of Staff, has had his pistol cocked for weeks, waiting. Keitel or Jodl or one of the others is always between him and Tresckow's target."

"Pray God, the time will come. I may tell you, Karl, that the orders we get are more and more maniacal. He moves Divisions that don't exist in Panzers that don't exist driven by fuel that doesn't exist. Even General von Wolfram, who is loyal to his oath, is beginning to despair."

Lucille yawned deliberately, ostentatiously. Stefan smiled.

"Be patient, my little one. Your time will come. Give us another five minutes. It is rare that we get a visitor from the Unholy of Unholies. How about the new secret weapon, Karl?"

"The V.1? The bombardment of London is scheduled to open at the end of May. It is expected to do one or both of two things: to reduce London to ashes, and to bring Winston Churchill to his knees. If it fails to do that, it will compel the Allies to invade the Pas de Calais, where most of the launching ramps are—and where your XVth Army is waiting." He shrugged. "Being divinely inspired, all things are clear to the Fuehrer."

"It will take more than a few flying bombs on London to change Allied strategy. I don't believe for a moment that they will land here, launching ramps or no launching ramps."

"Try telling the Fuehrer that. You know, of course, that Himmler is now commanding an S.S. Army in the field, and making one mistake after another. A Division is to move in here in March."

"General Wolf *will* be delighted. And Ribbentrop, what's he up to?"

"*Von* Ribbentrop if you please. Still telling the Fuehrer how decadent the British are. He bases his knowledge of England on the Oxford Union."

"One last question—before we surrender to our real conquerers, the delicious ladies of the Villa. What news of Goering?"

"None. He is entirely out of favour and spends his days painting his toe-nails pink and wearing a toga. Nero of the Third Reich, he throws himself to the lions." Colonel Karl stood up laughing. "I now declare this military conference to be over. If only we had some music, we could dance."

Lucille jumped to her feet.

"I can't think where our pianist is. I'll go and ask Madame."

*   *   *

Charles had already arrived at the Villa Mimosa. During the early afternoon, before going to bed, he had collected three strong electric torches—in case he should have urgent need of them before the dawn. He had used Hans Ramberg's pass into the evacuated zone, possibly—he told himself with excitement —for the last time.

He was admitted by Marie the housemaid and walked upstairs. Outside the door of Madame's room, he paused. Madame reminded him sharply of a certain Miss Twye who had once been his governess and who seemed to spend most of her time telling him to wash his hands and face. He glanced at his hands now. They were reasonably clean. He knocked.

"*Entrez.*"

She was sitting timelessly at her desk. She raised her pencilled eyebrows.

"Good evening, Charles. So you have returned?"

"Yes, Madame."

"I had your note. I find it necessary to recall to your mind that you are my employee and that you may not leave this house again without my permission."

"Very well, Madame." He hesitated. "Madame, I have a favour to ask of you."

"What is it?"

"I . . . I am told that you have a wireless set on which it is possible to listen to broadcasts from the B.B.C. in London."

"Who told you this?"

He looked at her steadily.

"Madame, I am unwilling to betray a confidence."

"Your loyalty does you credit. I will not press the question because I know the answer. It was Monique. You talked to her alone last night when the others had gone to bed. It is natural that she should tell you. You and Monique have . . . certain things in common. I will deal with her later. What service do you ask of me?"

He glanced at his watch. It was eight minutes past nine.

"Madame, every night a series of code messages are broadcast at a quarter past nine, from London. To the Germans, they are meaningless. To the few who understand them, they are deeply significant. It is possible that a message may come through in a few minutes which concerns me—and it is vitally important that I should hear it."

"And suppose I refuse?"

"I have not even considered such a possibility."

"You flatter me, Charles—and yourself. Be kind enough to lock the door."

Charles turned the key. Madame went to a table behind her and lifted the domed lid off what purported to be a sewing machine. She sat down and slowly turned a dial. The Germans were jamming that night and the first sound Charles heard was like the wailing of an amorous tom-cat; Madame moved the dial a fraction and the wailing stopped. A voice like that of a Pont Street dowager said clearly: "And that is the end of the news."

Now for it. Charles listened intently, scarcely daring to breathe. "Bom-bom-bom-BOM. *Ici Londres. Voici quelques messages personnels.*" The French voice paused and then spoke very deliberately and slowly: "*The nightingale will sing this evening.*" To hell with the nightingale. What Charles wanted was news of a snipe. . . . "*The fleas have jumped on Paul.*" Let the bloody fleas jump on whom they liked. . . . "*The tricoteuses are impatient.*" They were ready, were they, the knitting women who cackled as the heads rolled bloodily into the basket. . . . *The snipe will lay an egg at a quarter past three tomorrow morning.*"

Thank God! Everything had worked. Pick-up at three-fifteen from the field Orange Blossom. In less than six hours from now he would be on his way to England. He said to Madame, his eyes bright and his fingers trembling:

"That's all I want to hear. I've had my message."

She switched off the wireless calmly, put the domed sewing-machine lid back over the set, unlocked the door and returned to her desk.

"And now what?"

He said to her, laughing:

"A few minutes ago you forbade me to leave the house without permission. I now humbly ask that permission."

"When do you want to go?"

"At a quarter past three tomorrow morning. An aircraft of the R.A.F. is coming from England to a field near here. It will pick me up and take me home."

She gazed at him unblinking.

"You will have played the piano for two nights only. There is the question of your wages——"

"Madame, I am honoured to have been of service. If, however, you insist——"

"I do insist."

"Very well. If I might have a bottle of champagne—*Reserviert Für Die Wehrmacht*—to bring home to the girl I am going to marry...."

"I will see to it, Charles." She stood up. "I confess that you are a most beguiling fellow. This girl of yours is lucky. Our visitors have been without music all this time. Go and earn your bottle of champagne."

"Madame, there is one more thing."

"I am no longer capable of surprise. What is it?"

"May I have a scrap of paper? Thank you." He drew a large letter L. "As the aircraft comes in, the pilot will look for three lights, one here at the top of the L, one at the angle and one at the end of the bottom stroke. He will land into the wind, guided by the three lights, and taxi back for take-off again into the wind. Is that clear to you?"

"Perfectly." Her face was wholly without expression.

Charles went on eagerly: "I have brought three torches from Coville. I can only hold one of them."

"And who, do you suppose, will hold the others? Is it your suggestion that I shall place myself in a freezing field at a quarter past three in the morning for the purpose of signalling to a British aircraft?"

"I know it is a great deal to ask, Madame."

"The English have a genius for understatement. Have you decided who is to complete the trio?"

"Yes."

"Who pray?"

"Monique."

There was a long silence. The door of the Salon opened and

Charles heard a burst of laughter and the clinking of glasses. Fingers tapped lightly, deferentially, on Madame's door.

"*Entrez!*"

It was Lucille. She gave Charles a lightning glance and said: "Forgive me, Madame. The German officers are demanding music, as they wish to dance."

"I am sorry that there has been a delay. Charles, please go to your work at once and play what the German officers request."

"Certainly, Madame."

"Thank you. And, oh, Lucille."

"Yes, Madame."

"Ask Monique to come and see me immediately."

"Certainly, Madame. She is sitting with Colonel Stefan at the moment, but I am sure he will be prepared to yield her up. . . ."

*   *   *

That night there were wings on Charles' fingers and the tunes came tumbling out. He played a selection from *Die Fledermaus,* impishly slipping in *It's a long way to Tipperary,* and went on to *The Merry Widow*—into which he slyly introduced the Coldstream regimental march. The new officer—Colonel Karl Somebody, who came from the Wolf's Lair—Hitler's Headquarters— was delighted, and interrupted his ardent pursuit of Lucille to put a slightly tipsy arm around Charles' shoulders and to insist that he, too, should have a glass of champagne. When Charles stood up to clink glasses, the Colonel immediately sat down on the stool and banged out a chorus in which everybody joined. Charles found himself standing beside Wanda, who, as if accidentally, pressed hard against him. He said to her under cover of the loud singing:

"I don't see Monique. Is she having a night off?"

"No. She spent the day blubbering in her room and then had the impudence to come down painted like a street girl. None of us wished to be associated with one like that, we who pride ourselves on our *chic*."

"So Monique is in disgrace?"

"Yes. Madame sent for her, you may be sure, and told her to wash her face and to stay out of sight. She will not appear this evening. She is no loss."

The Colonel twirled round on his stool.

"Everybody link arms!"

Golden Mouse slid a timid arm through one of Charles' while

Wanda clutched the other. As the chorus of *Wien und der Wein* crashed out, the whole company began to sway and to sing. The spirit was one of reckless intoxication, made the more exhilarating by the sense of danger that pervaded every nook and cranny of the Villa. Hans Ramberg was the apostle of even wilder abandon. He shouted for a Russian song and did a barbaric Cossack dance in the middle of the Salon, squatting and kicking and whooping. When he finally collapsed full length, Magda and Stefan launched into a Hungarian Csárdás, swinging and stamping, knocking a table over so that the spilled champagne fizzed and bubbled on the floor while the girls clapped their hands, beating time to the measure of the dance. Time had sped and it was with a shock that Charles saw that more than three hours had passed since he entered the Salon. It was ten to one—and in less than a hundred and eighty minutes, God willing, he would be airborne and droning through the night sky. He searched in his mind for an appropriate song and found it.

Adieu, mein kleiner Garde—Offizier. . . .

8: JOY AFFIRMATIVE

AT the same time that Charles was making his musical farewell to those still left in the Salon of the Villa Mimosa, an R.A.F. orderly woke up Squadron-Leader Croppy Nesbitt in the Cottage at Tangmere.

"Five minutes to one, sir, and a nice drop of moonlight outside. I've made you a nice cup of tea, sir, and there's a nice drop of rum in it to keep the cold out."

"Good man."

Croppy had slept well and dreamlessly. He sat up in bed and drank his tea. There certainly was a nice drop of rum in it. He handed the empty cup to the orderly and asked for breakfast in ten minutes.

"Certainly, sir. With a nice couple of poached eggs on toast, like you said, and a nice cup of coffee."

"You think of everything."

As was his invariable practice before setting out on these clandestine operations, he stripped naked and examined each garment before he put it on, to make absolutely certain that there was nothing which, in case of disaster, could give anything away to the enemy. No theatre-ticket counterfoils, telephone numbers, addressed envelopes, cheque-books, stamps, cigarettes or matches. Every pocket was empty and the only thing he carried was his identity disc—with the notable exception of a loaded ·32 Walther automatic which fitted snugly into the top of his right flying boot. Before breakfast, he went out of the Cottage and looked at the sky. The moon was riding high and he could feel the February cold inside his nostrils. Smelled all right. He telephoned to Met and asked for a final forecast on the Pas de Calais, from two a.m. until five. While he waited, he rechecked his course. Met came through almost at once. Bright moonlight, one-eighth overcast, visibility ten miles. Looked like a piece of cake. Sorry. Looked like a nice piece of cake.

His escorting officer came in while he had breakfast. Croppy explained his flight plan.

"I propose to cross the Channel at zero feet and the French coast here, at Joanne-sur-Mer. May be some light flak. When I've picked up the Joe, I'll come out over Pointe Caroline, so if the Defiants miss me over Orange Blossom, they'll know where to find me on the way out."

"The Defiants won't miss you. They'll be sitting on your tail while you're over France and then form up on either side to bring you in. What with them and the Halifaxes, should be quite a party."

" 'Party's' the word." He wiped a tiny smear of egg off the side of his mouth with his napkin and stood up. "Who's the Joe?"

"Search me. But whoever he is, Baker Street wants you to bring him back alive."

"We aim to please," said Croppy sententiously. He telephoned to Dispersal and spoke to the Flight-Engineer. How was the Lizzie? "Sweet as a nut, sir. Radio checked."

"Good. I'm coming over straightaway."

With his escorting officer, he drove to Dispersal. The black Lysander cast a shadow in the moonlight. Croppy checked the inter-com helmet and the passenger's parachute and made sure that a flask of coffee was by each seat. He always took coffee, but never drank it. He glanced at his watch. 2 a.m. dead. He climbed into the cockpit, adjusted his parachute straps and buckled on his Sutton harness. He switched on the engine. The propeller swung jerkily like the leg of a marionette and then spun sweetly. While the engine warmed, his eyes were looking expertly at the dials and his hands checking the controls. Everything was O.K. He jerked up one thumb to the Flight-Engineer and waved a gloved hand to the escorting officers. Brakes off. The Lysander moved slowly forward and wheeled and bumped towards the end of the runway. To the Escorting Officer, it looked very small and fragile and lonely.

Croppy opened the throttle and the Lysander bounded forward. Fair stood the wind for France.

*　　*　　*

At 0246 hours, just as a little light flak from the Ack-Ack batteries of Joanne-sur-Mer was hosing up harmlessly aft of the Lysander's tail, Charles tapped on the door of Madame's room in the Villa Mimosa.

"Entrez!"

Madame was at her desk. Over her black silk, she wore a tightly buttoned overcoat, and her head was wrapped in a woollen scarf. Monique was sitting beside her, her fingers nervously twisting. Her face was entirely devoid of make-up and she looked drawn and middle-aged. Madame began curtly:

"I sent Monique to her room some hours ago and she has been resting. I have told her nothing of what you require of her. She may or may not be willing to help you. The one thing I can assure you of is her silence."

"Good." He looked directly at Monique and spoke in English. She started at the sound of that familiar tongue and seemed to shrink back into her chair.

"Listen to me, Monique," he said. "I have decided to take you into my confidence and to ask your urgent help. I am a British officer. I am as British as you are yourself and that is why I come to you. In less than half an hour from now, an aircraft of the R.A.F. will land on a field close to here and take me to England. I have been working in France for our country, yours and mine, and the time has come for me to return."

He stopped and looked at her with concern. Her mouth was opening and shutting and she seemed to have difficulty in breathing. She was like a woman who hears with horror the footfall of a ghost. When she could speak, her voice was little more than a whisper.

"You're . . . you're English? Reely English?"

"Yes, Monique. I'm English."

She flung her two hands over her face. She wailed.

"Oh God, what must you think of me?"

Madame spoke firmly but not unkindly.

"Now, Monique, you must pull yourself together. This gentleman has taken you into his confidence and for that you should feel flattered. He could have picked any one of my *pensionnaires,* but his choice has fallen on you. Dry your eyes, child, and remember that. He has singled you out and asked for your help. Are you prepared to give it?"

"I'll do anything. Anything. Only tell me what you want and I'll do anything."

"Good girl," said Charles. "Now I want you to pay attention. I have here three torches. Madame will hold one, I'll hold one and you'll hold one. We'll go very quietly to this field together and I'll show you where to stand. The aircraft will be looking for our lights; without them he won't land. When he sees them, he'll open and close his engine twice as a signal and you'll flick your torch off—on—off—on. Then he'll land into the wind, taxi round our little flarepath and I'll jump in. Once I'm aboard, he'll take off at once and go lickety-split for home. That's all. Think you can do it?"

Monique got to her feet. Still sniffing she groped in her memory to find the polite, the refined phrase that a young lady should use when talking to a gentleman. It came pat to her lips.

"I'll be ever so pleased to oblige. . . . And now, if you'll please pardon me, I'll just get my coat. It'll be chilly out."

While they waited for Monique, Madame drew on her gloves.

"May I ask you a question, Charles?"

"Of course."

"What is your rank in the British Army?"

"Major."

"Thank you. As you are no longer in my employ, I shall now address you by your rank and not by your Christian name. Oh, of course. Your wages."

She handed him a beautifully wrapped-up parcel.

"I have put in three bottles, Major. It is Veuve Clicquot, the widow, and I hope you will drink it in memory of me. One bottle is for your *fiancée,* one for you and one for your pilot. Please present it to him with my anonymous compliments."

"You are very kind."

"Not at all. You have been a very good pianist and my *pensionnaires* will miss you. Theirs is a dreary, repetitive existence and you brought a breath of fresh air into this . . . this curtained world. I have been wondering, Major, how to explain away your

sudden disappearance and the answer, of course, is simple. I will
officially assume that you have been press-ganged for forced labour
in Germany. Able-bodied men vanish every day all over France
and nobody—least of all Army officers—asks questions. The
Sicherheitsdienst or the S.S. do Sauckel's work of recruitment and
it is wise to steer clear of them. All that is easy. There is another
thing which is not so easy." She paused. "By the way, are you
worried about time?"

"No. We must leave this house by three. The field is ten minutes
away, which will give us five minutes in hand. In affairs of this
sort, one arrives exactly on time. What is your next problem?"

"Monique."

"How so?"

"Your coming and the revelation that you are her compatriot
has made her feel deeply ashamed of her position. You will know
that she springs of an English class whose ideal is 'to keep themselves to themselves'. She realizes now that she has betrayed that
class. 'Class' could be even more important to her than country.
Perhaps in her heart of hearts she has always known it, and bottled
up her pride. I don't know. But what I do know is that she will
never enter the Salon of the Villa Mimosa again. To ask her to do
so would be the most inhuman cruelty." She raised her eyebrows.
"I suppose," she said tentatively, "that you couldn't . . . er. . . ."

Charles frowned for a moment. Then he shook his head.

"Sorry, Madame. I couldn't. Not possibly. Sorry." He looked at
his watch. "It's three minutes to three. Ah, here's Monique."

She had put on a little rouge and some lipstick in honour of
the occasion. She wore a faded overcoat with a fur collar and a
pink artificial silk scarf.

They left the Villa Mimosa by the kitchen. The night was clear
and cold and quiet, and then they began to hear the boom and
engine surge of bombers coming in high over the Channel. The
sound increased to thunder that seemed to reverberate off the
flat frozen land as a squadron of Halifaxes flew in battle formation across the stars. With a snarl, the German night fighters
streaked up from coastal airfields.

Monique was a pace or two behind Charles. She said timidly:

"Funny, isn't it, sir? They don't usually come over at this time."

"Yes. It is odd. But you mustn't call me 'sir'. My name is
'Charles'."

"Oh, I couldn't call you that, sir, not any more."

"Why not, Monique?"

"Well, you're sort of different now. When I called you 'Charles' before, I didn't know who you were, see. If I'd known, I wouldn't 'a had the sauce."

"Rubbish. You go on calling me 'Charles'."

"There's one more thing I want to say to you, before you go, sir. It's this. Don't tell anyone in England that you saw a British girl doing . . . well, the sort of thing I have been doing. If my Mum and Dad knew, they'd die. So would Gran. They all think I'm dead."

"I won't tell, Monique."

The stealthy trio had reached the edge of the stubble. It was long, hard and level in the moonlight and, miraculously, still without obstructions. Charles licked his finger and held it up. What very little wind there was came from the east-north-east. Fine. He took Madame's arm.

"I want you to stand here and, the moment you hear the sound of a single aircraft, shine your torch slightly upwards. He'll be coming in pretty low and looking for you. I'll be fifty paces away on your right, so copy what I do. All right?"

"Certainly, Major. You may rely on me."

"I do." Suddenly, impulsively, he bent forward and kissed her forehead. Even in the half-light, he could see that she was blushing like a girl. He said, laughing:

"Goodbye, Madame."

"Goodbye, Charles. And God speed."

He hardly heard her benediction. He said to Monique: "I'm going to walk a hundred and fifty paces, down here along the upright of the imaginary L. Can you see me?"

"Yes, sir. Quite clear."

"Then follow."

"It'll be a pleasure, I'm sure."

Four full minutes to go before the aircraft was due. And now two more aircraft had turned up. They looked and sounded like Defiants and they kept swooping and diving, kicking up a God-awful shindy over Orange Blossom; why the hell couldn't they go somewhere else, having a high old time up there, I suppose, well push off for the Lord's sake and have a high old time somewhere else. . . .

"A hundred and fifty. Here we are, Monique—and you know what to do."

"Yes, sir. I know all right."

"I must run back now and take up my position. The pilot

should come in at any moment. I can't begin to thank you for what you're doing. The whole thing depends on you."

"I'm ever so glad. Reely I am."

He held out his hand. "Well, goodbye, Monique."

"Sir, you . . . you wouldn't kiss me like you did Madame? It . . . it 'ud make a big difference to me if you would."

"Of course I will. Gladly."

He kissed her lightly on the forehead. Then he ran across the rutted stubble and crouched down fifty paces from Madame. It sounded as if distant battle had been joined between the German night-fighters and the Halifaxes—and those bloody Defiants were still overhead, blast them. Anyone would think they'd specially picked on the bloody field.

*　　*　　*

0259 hours.

Croppy Nesbitt, once well clear of the coastal Ack-Ack, put the Lysander's nose down to hop the hedges of the Pas de Calais. He flew with his map on his knee, checking his position. The shadow of his wings flowed across the cold fields as he looked for landmarks. Ah! There it was, the silver glint of the canal. He flew along the right of it, throttling back, glancing continuously over his left shoulder. *Tout va bien*—in fact, *tout* went so very *bien* that he began to sing.

> "*The moon hath raised her lamp above*
> *To light the way to thee, my love,*
> *To l—i—g—h—t the way to theee, my love. . . .*"

Coville should be pretty close now but there should be a winding stream first, the stream that separated the town from the military zone. Good. There it was, to starboard. He took up his song:

> "*Her rays upon the waters play*
> *To tell me eyes more bright than they*
> *Are watching through the night. . . .*"

Coville church in sight. Croppy wheeled and reset his course on a heading of 298 degrees for Orange Blossom. He crooned:

> "*I come, I come, my heart's delight,*
> *I c—o—m—e, I c—o—m—e, my heart's deee-light. . . .*"

0314 hours.

There they were, by God, three torches in an inverted L, pricking the half dark. Croppy opened and closed his engine twice and the torches winked their welcoming signal.

Down, down went the Lysander's nose and lifted up again as he cleared a hedge. The wheels touched down on the frozen stubble. Now brakes on gently and the wings rocked as the Lysander taxied between the two torches, wheeled in a semi-circle and came back to the first light, her nose to the wind, the propeller easily spinning. A man came belting across the field and scrambled up the Lysander's ladder, laid a parcel tenderly on the floor and slammed the open door. He put on his inter-com helmet and said breathlessly:

"All aboard."

"Right. Off we go. Buckle on your parachute harness."

"O.K."

The propeller became a roaring prism as the Lysander surged forward and disdainfully lifted its heron's legs over the boundary of Orange Blossom.

* * *

"Monique."

"Yes, Madame?"

"Dry your eyes, child, and be proud of yourself. You have taken part in a great adventure."

"Yes, Madame. I know. But him being English, like me. . . . I wished I could have 'a died."

"Now, Monique, as we go home"—Monique winced at the word "home"—"I want to talk to you very seriously. You must never breathe a word to a living soul about what has happened. Everybody will think that Charles has disappeared into a German labour camp. Well, let them think it. May I have your promise that you will never reveal the truth?"

"I'd rather have my tongue dragged out by the roots."

"I believe you. Now, there's something else. I have decided to change your room. From tonight onwards, you will sleep in the attic."

"Sleep in the attic." That was upstairs under the roof. There was no heating up there as far as she knew, while her own room was at least warm. Funny of Madame to put her up there, nearest the bombs, as the other girls said. Maybe she'd done something wrong, like being saucy to one of the German officers or something.

Suddenly she stopped dead. The real significance of what Madame had said burst on her in a blinding flash of light. She said, stammering:

"D-d-does that m-mean that f-from now on, I-I-I won't ever have to-t-to. . . ."

"Yes, Monique. It means exactly that."

. . . Sunday School in Brixton . . . a white frock with a blue sash . . . the sound of the buses outside . . . the lumpy hassock hurting her little girl's knees when she knelt down . . . the confession, the absolution, the single drawn-out note on the harmonium. . . . *Oh Lord open thou our lips. . . . And our mouth shall shew forth thy praise.* . . . The old bellows working like a cart-horse and the old geezer pumping away with his elastic-sided boots. . . . Monique struggled to remember. The words came sweetly.

"Oh come, let us sing unto the Lord;
Let us heartily rejoice in the strength of our salvation. . . ."

*   *   *

A solicitous voice spoke in Charles' head-phones:

"Hullo there aft. You quite comfortable?"

"Yes, perfectly. I could sing the Hallelujah chorus right now." Croppy chuckled.

"Don't. By my stop watch, you got aboard in twenty-three seconds. Pretty good, that. Have a quick look behind you and tell me what you see."

Charles peered into the racing moonlight. The Lysander was flying at about fifty feet and all he could see was the bare country-side. Then he saw that the two aircraft—Defiants, he thought—that had been kicking up such a din over Orange Blossom had swooped down to fly on a parallel course. They were keeping station a hundred or so feet above. Charles spoke into the mouth-piece:

"Hullo. Looks as if we're being followed by two Defiants."

"We are. They are your own personal bodyguards. And over to the east the sky is cluttered up with Halifaxes playing hide-and-seek with the Jerry night-fighters—all for your benefit. V.I.P.— that's you. Your name Winston by any chance?"

"No."

"Roosevelt? Stalin? Montgomery? Eisenhower? Vera Lynn?"

"No. Not even Beaverbrook. My name's Charles."

"Mine's Croppy. Now this is the form. I'm going to keep low, right down here, and cross the French coast at the Pointe Caroline. The Defiants will scram and disperse so that any flak the Jerries throw up will be all over the shop. Once over the Channel, I'm going up to twelve thousand and the Defiants will come alongside again. And so to Tangmere. Estimated Time of Arrival about ten to five. It's a piece of cake."

"Talking about a piece of cake," said Charles. "I've got something to go with it. A special present for you."

"What's that?"

"Bottle of champagne. Veuve Clicquot. With the compliments of"—he smiled—"a girl friend of mine."

"Good for her. The last Joe I picked up gave me half a dozen eggs and a bloody great slab of Brie. Now mind your eye. Here comes the flak."

He switched off the inter-com and banked hard to port. The wing swung down as a fiery fountain spurted aft and to starboard. Twisting and turning, the Lysander climbed steeply and, far below, Charles could see the bright geometry of searchlights, brushing the sky, searching. He saw the land break and the calm, moonlit levels of the sea. Up, up, up went the Lysander—and then, with a triumphant surge, the Defiants were alongside, their turrets swinging, their four Browning ·303 machine-guns spitting. It could have lasted ten seconds or ten minutes—and then Croppy spoke cheerfully on the inter-com:

"Hullo there, Charles. See that?"

"Yes. What was it?"

"Focke-Wulf 109 came up to have a squint at us. When he saw the Defiants, he sugared off and pretended we weren't there. Bright boy! He wants to get home all in one piece to the Frankfurter and the little woman. How are you feeling?"

"Couldn't be better."

"I'm going to talk to Tangmere in a minute. For tonight, Tangmere's code name is 'Figleaf' and we're 'Tadpole'. Ought really to be 'Caterpillar'."

"Why?"

"Think what caterpillars do to figleaves, old boy. Here we go."

There was a click and then Croppy's voice spoke in clear:

"Hullo, Figleaf, hullo, Figleaf. Tadpole calling. Over."

The reply came instantly:

"Hullo, Tadpole, hullo, Tadpole. Figleaf answering. Any joy? Over."

"Hullo, Figleaf. Tadpole answering. Joy affirmative. Get some ice ready and two—repeat two—glasses. Be with you in fifteen minutes. Out."

The Lysander slid down the steeps of the sky. The sea cast

itself lazily against England and dissolved in a fringe of foam. The fields on either side of the runway were English fields. As the aircraft slowed, the mist that had come unbidden to Charles's eyes cleared. The Lysander stopped and when the sound of its engine ceased, there was an overwhelming silence, a silence in which every little sound was magnified. Charles stamped with his cheap French shoes on the tarmac, rejoicing to feel his own land beneath his feet. Croppy swept off his flying helmet and grinned at him.

"Well, there we are. Absolute piece of cake. And now what about that something to go with it?"

"Certainly. I've got it here. And thank you most awfully."

"Pleased—*and* proud," said Croppy. "Service before self, that's our motto."

They walked side by side to a waiting car. A W.A.A.F. officer was standing by the radiator. She waved to Charles and put out her hand. It was, of course, Squadron Officer A. She had seen him off six months ago and here she was to meet him on his return.

"Welcome home, Charles." She laughed. "I'd better tell you at once that I amended Croppy's wireless. I said that *three* glasses would be required, not two. Now tell me, did you have a good trip?"

"Magnificent. Everything worked according to plan, as they say. If I'd known you were coming to meet me, I would have brought you a spray of mimosa."

"Bring me one next time. And now while you and Croppy open that bottle, I've got some telephoning to do. I'll join you in the mess in five minutes."

Charles and Croppy went into the mess. The ice-bucket was full and there were three glasses on a tray. The cork came out of the bottle with a loud report and a whoosh of champagne hit the ceiling and dripped down on to the back of Charles' neck. He wiped it with a dirty rag of handkerchief.

"That's lucky," said Croppy. "Damn lucky."

9: ENTR'ACTE

It was well after five o'clock before Charles set out from Tangmere for London. The staff car was driven by a F.A.N.Y., a nubile young woman in a military greatcoat who introduced herself as "April". *"Oh to be in England,"* she said, *"now that April's here."* Charles and Squadron Officer A sat in the back. The moon, whose light had served him so well, was waning now and the English countryside was dark and bitterly cold. He found it extraordinarily difficult to accept the fact that the fields were English fields and that he was home. He kept on being worried because Squadron Officer A talked to him in English carelessly and out loud, as if it didn't matter. The car slowed down to pass through a village. Over a shop he saw the name: *A. Hobden, Saddler & Harnessmaker*, and, a few yards farther on: *J. Winter, Confectioner & Tobacconist*, and then a swinging sign over a shut pub: *The Rose and Crown*. But the shops of Coville that he knew so well seemed to come between: *H. Dufort, Charcuterie, Albert Nicolas, Pompes Funèbres* and *Café Jeanne d'Arc, Grande Dégustation*. He needed something more than a few English names over a few English shops to convince him—and it came.

Halted at a hooded traffic light, he lowered the window. A pungent, familiar, all-pervading smell laced the morning air and he could just make out a scrawled notice in a shop window: FRYING TONIGHT. BRING YOUR OWN PAPER.

In a split second of time he was whisked back over four years to the sweat, ache, obscenity, laughter and hunger of Caterham and the bite of his recruits' heels in the asphalt, eff-ite, eff-ite, eff-ite . . . get a hold of it . . . eff-ite, eff-ite—squa-a-a-ad halt. Squa-a-ad, dis-miss . . . and then the glorious, greasy, amber, sickle moons of potato and the vinegar-sprinkled mounds of rock-salmon. . . . No other country in the world wafted that smell. No other country would dare. The Villa Mimosa receded into the realms of fantasy and the girls were ghosts. Charles was home.

"I've got you a room at Brown's Hotel," said Squadron Officer A, "and your luggage will be arriving at eight this morning." She smiled. "I chose Brown's because there are two entrances, one in Dover Street and one in Albemarle Street, and I thought you'd like that. People like you get used to alternative escape routes. Your first appointment is at three this afternoon with the Chiefs of Staff. They are . . . well . . . very much interested in the Villa Mimosa. They'll ask you a lot of questions. My own view is that we're on to something really big—even bigger than any of us imagine."

"Will you be there?"

"I shall be, as it were, in attendance."

"What about this morning?"

"There's nothing scheduled for this morning." Again she

smiled. "But I have reason to suppose that you'll find plenty to do. Most people, when they come back from the field, spend hours wallowing in a hot bath. By the way, how did you get into the Villa?"

"Played the piano."

She chuckled.

"E.N.S.A. behind the enemy lines! You have unsuspected talents, Charles."

They had reached the outskirts of London and dawn was busy about the eastern horizon. Charles fell silent, well content to blink and to yawn and to rejoice in the sight of familiar landmarks. Sloane Square . . . Sloane Street . . . Hyde Park Corner . . . Piccadilly. It was as if he had never been away.

The porter at Brown's looked without surprise at the tall, unshaven figure in dirty trousers, a fisherman's jersey and a crumpled beret. In the visitors' book, Charles began to write "Charles Bertin" and then crossed it out and substituted boldly "Major Charles Addison, H.M. Forces". There was such a lot to remember. The porter took him up to his bedroom with, thank God, a bathroom attached, and shut the door.

Charles looked at his watch. Ten to eight. He put the two remaining bottles of Veuve Clicquot on the dressing-table and drew his ·38 Colt revolver, spilling out the cartridges, ranging them like extracted teeth in front of the bottles. Then he sat on the bed, picked up the telephone receiver and asked for Verity Gale's number in Sussex. The call took four minutes to come through. While he waited, he found that his fingers were trembling and that he kept humming odd snatches of songs. The second the bell whirred, he grabbed the receiver. A strange woman's voice answered and said querulously:

"Hullo."

"Is that Newick 218?"

"Yes."

"May I speak to Miss Gale, please?"

"Sorry. You can't speak to Miss Verity. She's away for the day."

His heart sank like a lump of lead.

"Away? But . . . but, I must speak to her. This is Charles Addison. Do you know where she's gone?"

"No, I don't. Miss Verity left early this morning before I was up and I don't know where she's gone, I'm sure. What name did you say it was, sir?"

"Major Addison. Miss Verity is my fiancée and . . . and I've just come home from abroad. Er . . . who are you, please?"

"I'm the new housekeeper, sir. Would you like to leave a message?"

"Yes, please. Would you ask Miss Verity to telephone me at Brown's Hotel, London—she knows the number—the very moment she comes back. She can ring up any time, night or day, and if I'm out they'll take a message. And please tell Miss Verity that——"

An impersonal voice broke in:

"Toll calls are restricted to three minutes. I am disconnecting you now."

Charles sat down on his bed. He was conscious of numbing disappointment. During the recent days and nights he had not allowed himself to think of Verity because something, anything, might have gone wrong. Only in the last five minutes, since he had been alone, had he surrendered and let her in completely with eagerness and joy. And now this had happened—after all those long months of separation when their only link had been their prayers. He stared at the flowered carpet, not seeing it. Why had she to choose this day of all days to be away? If only——

Fingers beat a familiar tattoo on his bedroom door. He listened incredulously. He said aloud, "Oh dear God." He shot across the room and flung the door wide open. Outside stood Verity Gale. Behind her towered an immense Guardsman, holding two packed suitcases. The Guardsman put the two suitcases down and saluted. As a figure seen through gauze, Charles recognized his friend and servant, Guardsman Pegg. He said huskily, "Hullo, Pegg. Would you mind waiting outside for a moment?" Verity stepped into the room. She was infinitely more beautiful than he had ever imagined. She gazed at him, dirty, unshaven as he was, and her face was transfigured. She slipped into his strong and most welcoming arms.

A notice in the bathroom strictly adjoined guests to limit themselves to five inches of bathwater. After five months of life in provincial France, Charles thought it reasonable to allow himself a bonus of an inch a month. He lay in the greatest luxury in ten inches of bathwater and talked to Verity and Guardsman Pegg through the slightly opened door. An electric iron and an ironing board had been produced by the hall-porter and while Verity pressed the creases out of his uniform trousers, Pegg was getting a shine on "them boots and buttons".

". . . I was sound asleep and was wakened by the sound of the telephone ringing and ringing in the study. I thought it must be a wrong number because nobody in their senses would ring up at that time of the morning but I went downstairs in my dressing-gown. It was Squadron Officer somebody or other and she asked me if I was Verity Gale and I said, 'Yes! I was,' and then she said that Major Addison had returned unexpectedly from overseas and would be arriving in Brown's Hotel shortly before eight. Then she hung up."

Charles swirled the bathwater over his torso.

"So what did you do?"

"Dressed like a flash, rode my bicycle to the station and caught the milk train to Victoria. I was lucky enough to get a taxi and here I am. I didn't have time to do a thing to myself and I look terrible."

"Pegg."

"Sir?"

"Does Miss Gale look terrible?"

"Nossir. Smashing, sir."

"My own view exactly. Who told *you* to turn up?"

"Sarnt-in-waiting woke me up at half past five, sir, with orders to report to the Piquet Officer at seven. Piquet Officer said he'd had a buzz on the blower from a lady officer and that I was to report to you, sir, having picked up your luggage previous." He coughed. "You been abroad, sir?"

"Yes, Pegg. How did you guess?"

"It's them clothes, sir." He shook his head. "I wouldn't want the Adjutant to see you, not in them, sir."

"God forbid that he should," said Charles fervently. "How are you getting on?"

"Ready in five minutes, sir."

"Verity, how are the trousers?"

"Done. By the way, don't imagine that this sort of thing is going to continue, your lying in a bath while I do the work."

"We'll see about that later, my love. Pegg, chuck me in my trousers and shirt, will you?"

"Coming up, sir."

Five minutes later, Charles came into his bedroom. The shabby French watchmaker had vanished down the waste-pipe. In his place was a tall, smiling man, lean-faced, dark-haired and blue-eyed. He seemed to have increased both in physical stature, bearing and authority and Verity's knees weakened for love of him. Six months of absence was a long time.

His job done, Guardsman Pegg departed until eight a.m. the following morning. When he had gone, Verity walked over to the dressing-table and looked at the two bottles of champagne. She picked one of them up and read aloud slowly: *"Reserviert Fuer Die Wehrmacht."*

"What does it mean?"

" 'Reserved for the German Army.' It's for you. A present from a friend of mine."

"Oh." She put the bottle down and took instead a handful of cartridges. "I needn't ask you what these are. They're things you kill people with." She swung round and faced him. "You've been in France, haven't you?"

"Yes, Verity." There could be no point in keeping up a pretence any more. "I've been in France."

"Then . . . then those letters marked 'G.H.Q.' were all bogus."

"No. The letters were not bogus. The only bogus thing about them was the address."

She came to him and looked at him with that candid gaze that he knew and loved so well.

"I knew you were doing something pretty desperate," she said, "so you didn't fool me at all. I suppose I can't ask you where you were in France or what you were doing?"

"I can't tell you where I was, but I can tell you what I was doing." He grinned at her. "Mine was a sedentary occupation, mending watches for German officers. When I wasn't doing that, I was keeping my hand in at the piano." Could it be possible that only a few hours ago he had been in the company of Madame and Monique and Golden Mouse . . . and Magda and . . . what were the names of the other girls?—Wanda and two more, oh yes, Lucille was one. Elsa had already vanished into mists of unreality. "I'll tell you all about it one day, when the war's over. At least," he added carefully, "I'll tell you as much as I consider suitable for the ears of a delicately nurtured girl."

"I've only one more question to ask you." She swallowed. "Will you be going back?"

He considered it and answered her truthfully.

"Certainly not to . . . er . . . where I was before. I should think that's out of the question. I'm supposed to be working in a forced labour camp in Germany at this moment so I dare not turn up there again. In fact I don't think I'll go back to France at all. My work there is done." He shook his head and frowned. "I loathe

having secrets from you—but I must." He took her in his arms
and touched her eyelids very gently with his finger-tips. He said
with a sigh: "I can hardly believe you're real. Everything else is
so shadowy."

"I promise you I'm real. How long have we got?"

"The whole morning's ours."

"And then?"

"At three this afternoon I go to a meeting. I don't know how
long it will last but I think it may be some time. How long can
you stay, darling Verity?"

"I'll return to Sussex when you go to your meeting. I've got to.
I'm coping with a sick father, three acres of vegetables and sixteen
Hereford bullocks. Look, this is Friday. Couldn't you come down
for the weekend?"

"There's nothing I'd like better in the world."

"Or me. Telephone me tonight, the minute your meeting's over,
and then come winging down."

"I will."

There was a tap on the door. Charles said, "Blast!" and opened
it. A floor waiter handed him a copy of *The Times* and said
gloomily that the dried egg was running out in the dining-room
so if they wanted breakfast. . . .

*   *   *

It was a strange London through which Charles and Verity
wandered. German aircraft had been over in the early hours of
the morning dropping both high explosive and incendiaries, and
long-suffering Cockneys, who had put up with far worse, referred
to it tolerantly as "the Baby-Blitz". There was a rash of strange
uniforms about the streets of the West End—Americans and
Free French and Norwegians and Poles and God knows what.
Even the sentries outside Buckingham Palace were in battledress
with steel helmets, and tapped with their rifle butts in salute
as Charles passed. He acknowledged this recognition a little
awkwardly, restraining an automatic impulse to sweep off an
imaginary beret and bow. As he crossed the road to make for
Birdcage Walk and his bank in Whitehall, he had the misfortune
to come face to face with his Regimental Lieutenant-Colonel. The
immaculate figure stopped.

"Good morning, Charles."

"Good morning, sir." Charles found no consolation whatsoever
in the fact that if they had met three hours ago, he would certainly

not have been recognized. Introductions were made. Colonel
Jimmy said genially:

"How do you do! So you're the young woman I was to have
met six months ago—before Charles started polishing the seat of
his pants in the War Office. Come and have some luncheon with
me, both of you. Or has Charles got to scuttle back to his pen-
pushing?"

"We'd love to," said Verity with deceptive swiftness, "but, alas,
Charles simply must keep on driving that quill, mustn't you,
darling? So may we some other time?"

"Of course. Delighted. Any time." He looked with a shrewd,
hawk-like eye at Charles. "You've lost weight—and you're
improperly dressed."

"Improperly dressed. How so, sir?"

A bony finger was extended to tap Charles' tunic.

"Persons who have been dropped into enemy territory should
wear parachute wings half an inch exactly above the left breast
pocket. See to it, Charles, see to it. I'm delighted to have met
you, Miss Gale." He chuckled. "Come and visit me when you're
next in London. Goodbye."

"I will. Goodbye, Colonel."

Charles and Verity had reached Storey's Gate before he spoke.
He said, half laughing, wholly affectionately:

"Cunning old devil."

The cashier at his bank welcomed Charles cordially and pointed
out that he had an accumulation of five months' pay. It was one
of the benefits of service in the field which Charles had forgotten.
As he left the bank, he said, "I can't remember what things cost
here," and Verity said soothingly, "The maximum price for
luncheon is five bob no matter where we go."

They chose Boulestin. The *Maître d'hôtel,* an old friend,
found a grouse in the larder and a bottle of Nuits St. Georges in the
cellar and the time passed all too quickly. Charles took Verity to
Victoria and found her a corner seat. She said, "I'm so happy I
could weep—and you'll come down tonight when your meeting's
over?"

"I will."

The train went out. Charles straightened his shoulders. Now
—back to the war.

*   *   *

Always arrive five minutes early for parade. Charles turned up diffidently at Great George Street well before three o'clock to find Squadron Officer A waiting. Security precautions at street level were thorough and the photograph on his identity card, as well as his signature, was checked before he was given a temporary pass. With Squadron Officer A, he was escorted down four flights of stairs, passing further check points manned by armed Royal Marine sentries. Through a bomb-proof door, he entered a bustling, troglodyte labyrinth of passages, bright with strip lighting, air-conditioned and curiously antiseptic. Over his head were huge iron girders bearing the weight of several thousand tons of concrete. From this place, this man-made cave deep under the streets of London, stretched the invisible filaments that linked the battered city to every theatre in the world in which soldiers, sailors and airmen fought. To those who worked—and frequently slept—in this sound-proof tomb, knowledge of the weather and of the activities of the Luftwaffe came second hand. At this moment, a notice board—whose message was continuously changed—informed the cave dwellers that the weather was "FINE" and the skies "ALL CLEAR". Long might they both remain so!

Charles followed Squadron Officer A through a door marked *Officers' Waiting Room*. He said to her:

"Thank you so very much for telephoning Verity—and Pegg. They both turned up at eight." He smiled. "You are the most thoughtful person."

She waved an airy hand.

"It's all part of the Baker Street Service. We aim to please."

"It's quite extraordinary. It's only a week ago today since I wheeled my bicycle past the Villa Mimosa and . . . er . . . said, '*Bonjour*,' to the girls. And now, here I am—in the heart of things." He glanced around the bare brick walls. "If only there were a few out-of-date copies of *Horse and Hound*, this would be rather like a visit to the dentist. How long will it last?"

"Some time, I should think. Why?"

"I promised Verity I'd come down to Sussex as soon as it's over."

"I very much doubt if you'll make it."

A senior Royal Marine officer came into the waiting room and shook hands. He said cheerfully:

"Right, Addison. We're ready for you."

As Charles stepped through yet another steel door, a strong

smell of cigar-smoke tangled in his nostrils. He was in the heart of things.

*   *   *

Charles did not go to Sussex that night. It was well after midnight before his meeting broke up. He walked with Squadron Officer A as far as Hyde Park Corner when, to his amusement, he saw daubed on a wall the exhortation "SECOND FRONT NOW!" A taxi, hurrying in the direction of Chelsea, consented to stop and to take Squadron Officer A, and Charles walked along Piccadilly alone. At the corner of Clarges Street, he was accosted by a young Englishwoman who flashed a pocket torch first at his face and then at her own before saying cheerfully, "*Bonsoir, chéri.*" At Berkeley Street corner, a young Frenchwoman went through the same routine and said coaxingly, "*Good evening, darling.*"

Arrived at Brown's Hotel, he telephoned to Verity at once. She was awaiting his call and he explained that his meeting had gone on and on. He would come down by the first available train in the morning and stay until Sunday evening or until the crack of dawn on Monday morning when he had another meeting—elsewhere. Verity was very disappointed but choked it back as best she could and they went on to speak of themselves and their future and of the great love that they bore for each other, using up every second of their three allotted minutes.

The friendly night-porter made him a cup of coffee and a spam sandwich, which he took up to his room. The black-out curtains were already in place and he sat on his bed. He was exhausted and exhilarated. Exhausted by tension, long concentration and lack of sleep; exhilarated by having been present at the forging of a plan that was at once daring, fantastic and separate—and yet woven into the grand strategy of the war.

In the early hours, long before the dawn, the Luftwaffe struck at London. He prayed fervently to God that no bomb would kill or disable him now for he had been chosen as the instrument by which great things might be accomplished.

10: DANCE OF THE FIREFLIES

MAJOR-GENERAL JOHN SOUTHERDEN, Director of Subversive Activities, The War Office, had an enviable nickname. The initials of his appointment, D.S.A., were interpreted by his staff as standing for "Director of Sex-Appeal". There were three other reasons for this. In picking his female associates, he reversed the normal order of things, choosing first for beauty and second for brains—with security limping along in the rear. His wife Araminta had been the Deb of the Year (1923 vintage), his personal assistant Angela a Digby Morton model and his F.A.N.Y. driver April a one time film-starlet. He explained airily that the perpetual society of one or other of these three graces provided a most beneficial stimulus to his work.

The General was forty-six, a Horse Gunner with a maritime taste for pink gin. He had a puce face, a bristly moustache and his body was thin and hard as nails. Even his voice had an abrupt, parade-ground quality and any casting director would have given him the part of a bone-headed British officer at sight. This appearance of his was wholly deceptive. Serving under Wavell in the lean, desert days had taught him the arts of bluff and duplicity and when, to his disgust, he was posted to the War Office, he continued to practise these arts on those whom he regarded as his enemies in equal parts, the German nation and His Britannic Majesty's Treasury.

On arrival in Whitehall, he had spent his first weeks in assessing the strength of the enemy on the home ground. These were his conclusions. Inside the War Office sat two entirely different breeds of men, the civilian staff, who were permanent, and the military staff, who were mere birds of passage, civilians outnumbering soldiers by about two to one. The civilians—who held the tightly-knotted purse strings of the Treasury—were commanded by a Director of Finance, Z Branch (D.F.(Z)), a herring-gutted gentleman known to the General as "Barebones Scrooge" or merely "Scrooge".

The wicked world beyond Whitehall came to Scrooge secondhand. Files piled up in his In-tray relating to every theatre in which troops were serving—places which Scrooge had never seen and never would see. These files contained new ideas, new proposals, new plans, plans that would have made his hair curl if he had had any hair left. A dedicated man, it was his duty to examine, to comment upon, to question and if possible to reject every military proposal which in any way involved the expenditure of money or material. Only thus could Economies be Effected and Financial Rectitude Observed. As General Southerden observed acidly: "Old Scrooge can always be relied upon to find a problem to every solution."

The Director of Sex-Appeal had breezed into the darkened wordy arena of the War Office some eighteen months ago. He had soon found his way around the labyrinthine corridors and taken Scrooge's measure. The thing to do was always to add a few expensive items to every proposal, items which could light-heartedly be offered up as sacrifices to the Gods of Finance. Hitherto this scheme had worked reasonably well. Hitherto. . . .

On Monday 21st February, 1944, a TOP SECRET file entitled OPERATION FIREFLY was put on General Southerden's desk. It concerned an establishment in the Pas de Calais called the Villa Mimosa and its contents were calculated to reduce old Scrooge to a cinder.

*   *   *

Charles Addison reported to the Director of Subversive Activities in the War Office at ten a.m. exactly. He had come up from Sussex by the milk-train and spent the last two hours in Brown's Hotel completing notes he had made during the weekend. The General's P.A., Angela, had already procured a War Office pass for him and he added it in his wallet to that already issued by Hans Ramberg. It was a pleasant thought that he was now officially free to enter either the War Office in London or the militarized zone in the Pas de Calais.

When Angela ushered him into General Southerden's office, the D.S.A. said cheerfully:

"Good morning to you, Addison."

He waved a hand towards the shattered window. "The Luftwaffe had the damned impudence to drop a bomb in White-hall early this morning and the only window left intact in the War Office belongs to the C.I.G.S. Even the Germans quail before Brookie's disapproving stare. Means that my P.A., Angela, has to work in her overcoat. Now then, you and I are going to be closely associated so I shall call you 'Charles'. You've been away for the weekend?"

"Yes, sir. In Sussex. Herding bullocks with my young woman."

"I'm so glad. Good practice for herding humans. Have a cigarette, sit down and glance at this file before I send it on its rounds. I may tell you," he added grimly, "that Operation Firefly will be a Sunday-school picnic compared with the battle I'm going to have with old Barebones Scrooge."

" 'Barebones Scrooge', sir?"

"Yes. The Treasury watch-dog. Lives in a kennel on the second floor and chews the meat off all my most succulent bones. He'll break his porcelain dentures on this one."

Charles read the file slowly and carefully. Even the cold and precise terms in which it was set down could not rob Operation Firefly of its drama or of its high adventure. It was conceived on an impudent scale and soldiers of three nations would die in its performance. It would be brief, fierce and bloody and its reward would be fourfold. It would seem fully to confirm Hitler's belief that the Pas de Calais and nowhere else had been chosen as the lodgment in the forthcoming Allied invasion of Europe and would therefore silence the tongues of the doubters in the German High Command; it would test the strength of the enemy coastal defences and serve to destroy radar stations, naval guns, air-strips and launching ramps; in Moscow, it would give some satisfaction to the demanding, distrustful Stalin; lastly, it would provide admirable cover for yet another operation contained within it, a daring and stealthy foray to which Charles had already given the appropriate code name "Operation Sabine".

He closed the file and handed it back to General Southerden. With the air of a sultan, the General rang a bell and the sylph-like Angela appeared.

"Angela, I want you to walk this file round the relevant branches right away and tell them to get cracking with their comments. It's TOP PRIORITY so don't let anyone sit on it. I must have it back by nine o'clock tomorrow morning. And tell the exchange to divert my telephone calls to Colonel Crispin for the next half hour.

"Certainly, General."

As the door closed, the D.S.A. cocked a remarkably shrewd eye at Charles.

"Well, what do you think of it?"

"Given ordinary luck, it should work, sir. My main problem is going to be transport."

"Yes, I've been pondering that. But I gather you've got a radio contact in Coville."

"I have indeed, sir. Man named Gaston. Between us we ought to be able to fix something."

"How many chaps do you want?"

"As few as possible. Eight in all, with one reserve."

The General mentally pulled the pin out of an imaginary hand grenade, counted four and rolled it over the desk towards Charles.

"In other words, four Americans, three British—plus you— and one reserve."

The grenade exploded silently. Charles sat back and said incredulously:

"Americans, sir? Did I hear you say 'Americans'?"

"You did. A—M—E—R—I—C—A—N—S. Operation Firefly is an Anglo-American undertaking and your Expedition Sabine is a part of Firefly. Therefore the team, your team, will be evenly divided—with the one reserve British. Dammit man," he went on warmly, "if the Americans were kept out of this, it would be worse than the Boston Tea-party. There'd be hell to pay. It would shake the Grand Alliance to its foundations. You know yourself how the Americans go for dames. Well, this is a natural. Dames, danger and Purple Hearts—what a prospect! My God, how I envy you. To think that, while you're on this beano, I'll be sitting here in the War Office on my fanny, arguing the toss with old Scrooge, makes me sick." He paused. "And, by the way, we've got to keep the French out. If de Gaulle got wind of it, he'd gallop his high horse round to the P.M., sing a verse or two of the Marseillaise and then loose off a broadside about violation of the Sovereignty of France and all that. So not a word to Dorset Square —until it's over." He glanced at his watch. "I'm taking you to a meeting at Combined Ops at eleven and sending you up to Oxford this afternoon to spend a day with the Inter-Services Topographical boys. My F.A.N.Y. April will take you—and you will sit in the back of the car, not the front. Any questions?"

"Yes, sir. When will Firefly be launched?"

"This is February the 21st. It should take about ten days to mount. Say March the 2nd or 3rd, weather permitting. Anything else?"

"Not at the moment, sir. Other things will crop up."

"Good. We've got a quarter of an hour in hand." He sat back and gave Charles a rollicking look. "Now tell me about the dames themselves."

"The dames, sir?"

"Yes. The Villa Mimosa popsies."

"Ah yes. Of course." So close had Charles been only a few hours ago to his beloved Verity that he found it difficult to clothe the shadowy women of the Villa Mimosa with faces and with flesh. He thought of them as a group. They were Madame's *pensionnaires*. To make them individual and separate, he had first to remember their setting, the long Salon with the high ceiling and the flames of the candles and the piano with his back to the wall. Slowly they emerged from their half-world and lived

and breathed, each with her own features and fingers and voice
and clinging, competing scent. There was a map of France on
the General's wall and, looking at the Pas de Calais absent-
mindedly, he saw them again, in their perfumed prison. He
frowned.

"Well, sir, there are six of them—and there's Madame. Madame
could be any age between forty-six and seventy and——"

"We'll take Madame as read," said General Southerden, "and
get on with the popsies."

"Thinking of them from this distance, they seem, oddly enough,
to fall into pairs. There's Elsa and Lucille. Elsa is from Alsace,
pretty in a rather heavy-featured way and shows signs of being in
love with one of the German officers. She's plump and not very
intelligent. For her the Villa Mimosa is the line of least resistance
and she's really a housewife *manquée* who would be much happier
cooking dumplings in her own kitchen. I link her with Lucille
because they're so utterly different. Lucille is a Parisian, tall, slim,
blonde, chic and cynical and a natural bed-hopper. She has what
Voltaire described as '*le diable au corps*' and the Villa Mimosa
—or its equivalent in Berlin, Madrid, Vienna or Clarges Street—
is her habitat."

"I knew a girl like that in Athens once," said General Southerden reminiscently, "but let that pass. What about the
others?"

"My next pair are Wanda and Magda. Wanda is a Czech and
Magda Hungarian. They loathe each other, not only racially but
personally, and would gladly scratch each other's eyes out. Wanda
is thin, fair and pretty, Magda dark, slumberous and tigerish.
Wanda has a very ugly streak of sadism in her and pokes fun at a
friend of mine who happens to be a hunchback."

"What a bitch."

"Yes, she is rather. Now we come to Golden Mouse and
Monique."

The General rubbed his hands.

"I can't wait to hear about Golden Mouse."

"The trouble is, sir, that I know practically nothing about her.
I don't think anybody does. She is Indo-Chinese and her mother
is"—he smiled—"of the honourable House of Li. I don't know
how or when or why she came to the Villa. I think of her as
being very beautiful and quiet and . . . and remote. She is, as it
were, *in* the Villa Mimosa but not *of* it—in spite of the fact that
she plays the normal role of a *pensionnaire*. She wears a long,

concealing coat and her eyes are downcast. Her hair is jet-black and she has the sun in her skin. I'm afraid that's all I know about Golden Mouse."

"Highly provocative it is, too, if I may say so. I can hardly tear myself away from the subject. What's the last one's name—Monica or something?"

"No, sir, not Monica. Monique."

"Same thing."

"Yes," said Charles with surprise, "I suppose it is. I hadn't thought of that. Monique—or Monica—is a little older than the others and must once have looked like an engaging tabby kitten. I believe she was a dancer—and anyway, she takes no further part in the activities of the Villa."

"Nationality?"

Charles gazed directly at the General. He did not hear the traffic of Whitehall. He heard instead a thin pleading voice speaking in the silence of a frozen French field of stubble . . . *"Don't tell anyone in England that you saw a British girl doing . . . well, the sort of thing I have been doing. If my Mum and Dad knew, they'd die. So would Gran. They all think I'm dead"* . . . and to that he, Charles, had replied: *"I won't tell, Monique."* So be it. He said curtly:

"Sorry, sir, I've no idea."

The meeting in Combined Operations Headquarters lasted until half past one, when Charles had a brief, preoccupied sandwich lunch in the Silver Cross. General Southerden's ex-film starlet driver April was waiting to motor him to Oxford and, disobeying orders, he sat beside her in the front seat. During the last ten days, he reflected, the war appeared to have thrown him perpetually into the society of nubile women.

He called first of all at his old college and was lucky enough to be given a room and an invitation to dine at High Table. His next visit was to the School of Geography, when he was able to contribute still further to the considerable topographical data on the Pas de Calais. April was still waiting when he came out and he realized with guilt that he had forgotten all about her. "Yes," she said in answer to a question, "there *is* somewhere I can get a bed. One of those ghastly female transit camps, all Brasso and khaki bloomers. But they don't know I'm in Oxford . . . or anything."

"Lucky old them," said Charles cheerfully, "they've got a treat in store. Come to the Randolph and have a drink on your way to the bloomers and the Brasso."

He took her to the Randolph and, because he was an old friend of the house, managed to get her some sherry. Then he excused himself to telephone Verity. The call took a long time to come through, the line was very bad and he could hardly hear. When he came back, April was deep in conversation with a Captain in the United States Marines. Charles left them to it and made his way through the polyglot streets of Oxford to his college. His room was bare and comfortless, and dinner, at a sadly diminished High Table, seemed a pallid ghost of pre-war days. Only the conversation, dry and donnish, was unchanged and tactfully he eked out his single glass of port—it was the Taylor '12—which he took with the Dean. Before going to bed, he wrote a long letter to Verity.

He told her of his great love for her and of how, suddenly and for no reason at all, he would be aware of a sharp sense of loss because she wasn't by his side. It seemed that he would be in Oxford for at least another twenty-four hours and that his future appeared to consist of endless conferences. This was strictly true, so his only lie was one of omission. He went on to write: *"A Don told me at dinner that during the Blitz some London evacuees were housed here in college and that they strung clotheslines across the quad and hung out their washing. Everybody was outraged and went around the place muttering the word 'blasphemy'."*

Charles put down his pen. In writing these words to Verity, the vision in his mind had not been one of plebeian nappies in an Oxford quad. It had been the sharply remembered sight of a clothesline that ran from a back, first-floor window to the branch of a tree. On it six sets of women's panties and several pairs of silk stockings cavorted in the breeze and at the far end dangled Madame's whalebone stays. It was this frippery that had brought him to Oxford. It was this frippery that would bring him back to France.

*   *   *

While Charles pored over maps and discussed shingle and tide-fall in Oxford, significant movements were going on elsewhere.

Summoned by the glow of Firefly, officers and men were discreetly drawn from Special Service Forces training all over Britain. They left their units without elaborate farewells and made their way to a certain south coast port. A depot ship—H.M.S. *Claddah Burn*—slipped into the harbour unheralded and under cover of darkness, soldiers out-numbering the sailors on board. These Commandos, who had arrived in twos and threes by train or truck, were unobtrusively ferried out to join their comrades.

The men who gathered were of many regiments and corps. They were Guardsmen, Highlanders, Riflemen, men of the county regiments, lantern-jawed neutrals from the mountains and bogs of Eire, all of them indissolubly linked by the fact that they were Commandos. Amongst them were an anthropologist, a school-master, an interior decorator, a financier, a road sweeper and a Regius Professor of Byzantine Greek. There was, of course, a bank clerk. There always was. Every man of them was physically hard after months of rock-climbing, speed-marching and swim-ming. They were experts in the use of their own and of the enemy's weapons; they handled explosives with swift and familiar skill; some of them had met the enemy before and were avid to meet him again.

Security was rigid. Commando flashes were taken off sleeves so that these men, on their rare visits ashore, seemed merely a few of the many soldiers training in the area. There was strict postal censorship. No telephone calls were allowed. No thirsty Commando might enter a pub for a pint and a game of darts and—above all—NO GIRLS.

Not a single soul, officer or man, aboard H.M.S. *Claddah Burn* believed that Operation Firefly was anything other than yet another bloody silly exercise thought up in the bloody War Office by some bloody brass-hat who had too bloody little to do. And then an event occurred which made the bored Commandos scratch their heads and think again.

American Rangers, volunteers to a man, filtered into the town and were taken aboard, armed to the teeth.

That night Lance-Corporal "Quiff" Perkins (who had tattoed on his hairy forearm the assertion "I LOVE GLAD" and who was soon to die) remarked to his pal Rifleman Ron Harper (who loved many unacknowledged Glads and who was soon to be carried home with a shattered pelvis):

"There's something up, Ron. Definitely. Stands to reason. The bloody War Office 'ud never sugar the Yanks about like they do us. They wouldn't bloody dare. Stands to reason."

The two men were leaning on the taffrail. Ron spat thought-fully into the tranquil sea.

"Too bloody true, Quiff! There's something up all right. Definitely."

                    *   *   *

On Tuesday evening, Charles returned from Oxford to London, the exchange of topographical data completed. His temporary driver April, who seemed mysteriously to have acquired a faint American accent overnight, picked him up at the School of Geography and they set off in the February dusk.

Charles had much to ponder and plan and they motored in silence until they reached the Lambert Arms. There he ordered a drink for April and himself, left her in the bar and, on an impulse, telephoned to Baker Street. The guarded news from Squadron Officer A was such that he hurried back to the bar, swallowed his drink in a gulp and said, "Sorry—but we've got to press on. Fast as we can do it."

"You're always in a hurry. Where to? The War Office?"

"No, Baker Street. Know your way?"

"Sure."

She had slim fingers and she drove beautifully. As they swept past Northolt, they could hear the roar of fighter engines warming up for instant take-off. It was an ominous sound and, to distract April's attention from it, he asked her a question:

"By the way, I forgot to ask you. How was the female transit camp last night? All Brasso and khaki bloomers?"

April changed skilfully into top gear. She answered briefly:

"Search me."

Arrived at Baker Street, Charles went immediately to Squadron Officer A's room. She handed him a decoded radio message.

"That came in three hours ago. Doesn't look too good."

Charles sat down and read the message with mounting anxiety.

> *"For charles from gaston most urgent stop message begins stop madame deeply suspicious of colonel otto plausible new-comer to villa stop otto claims to be close friend of colonel johnny but cannot check as johnny vanished stop fear gestapo net closing in stop message ends."*

He put down the message and stared at Squadron Officer A with narrowed eyes.

"You say it doesn't look too good. It looks damn bad to me.

Colonel Johnny turned up at the Villa one night last week, tight
—and in a staff car with a driver. You may bet your boots that
the driver talked. I would—if I was kept *outside* the Villa
Mimosa for three hours on a February night. Now the Gestapo
have pinched Johnny and planted one of their own boys. It's
miraculous that it hasn't happened before now. They've all been
sitting on a land-mine for months now and it's started ticking.
The only question is—when will it go up?"

Squadron Officer A selected a cigarette from her case and lit
it with deliberate slowness. She appeared to meditate. She said
at last:

"In my opinion, not yet. The German mind is both methodical
and thorough. Bismarck said once: 'We Germans fear God:
nothing else in the world.' It isn't true, Charles. The Germans are
frightened of the bizarre. They are frightened of it because the
bizarre is a thing you can neither kill, eat, plan against nor set to
music. The Villa Mimosa is the epitome of the bizarre. Therefore
they will take a little time to face up to it. Once they grasp the
fact that Madame and her six girls have been insolently trailing
their petticoats within a stone's throw of Panzer Corps Headquarters, they will be very angry indeed. When they find out—as
they will because they are very thorough—that deadly conspiracy
has been added to the laughter and the love-making, they will be
even angrier. Then, and then only, will they start applying
method. They won't want merely to catch one or two traitor-
Lotharios—but the lot. So they'll hold their hand." She paused.
"Pray God my judgement is right."

"How long do you give it?"

"How long do you want?"

"Ten days—as from yesterday."

She shook her head.

"It's too long. A week at most."

"I think you're right." He took a sheet of paper and wrote:

"For gaston from charles stop message begins stop tell
madame vital to keep suspect colonel otto in play as long as
humanly possible stop if necessary she should promise collabora-
tion in future stop special for georges things hotting up nicely
here stop stand by at two hourly intervals for further instructions stop merde stop message ends."

"Can you get that coded and transmitted to Georges?"

"Yes. He'll get it within the hour."

"And now may I talk to General Southerden?"

"Yes. Use the green telephone. It's a secret line."

Charles was put through to the Director of Subversive Activities at once. He began:

"Charles Addison here, sir. I wonder——"

"What have you done with my driver April?"

"She's here, sir. We got in from Oxford half an hour ago."

"High time too. My wife Araminta is in the Cotswolds, Angela has retired to bed with 'flu and you and April spend the day gallivanting round Oxford. I'm beginning to feel like a blasted monk. The quicker we get Operations Firefly and Sabine under way, the better."

"I quite agree, sir. I want to talk to you about that very thing."

"Come to the War Office right away. I've got your American opposite number with me and we can all three dine together. And bring April with you."

"I will, sir. See you in about twenty minutes."

Charles' opposite number turned out to be a thin drawling Major from Minnesota. His name was Thayer B. Cavendish. General Southerden introduced them briefly.

"I'll leave you two together for a bit, and meet you later for dinner. Where shall we dine, Charles?"

"Why not come to Brown's, sir? I'm living there."

"What's the cellar like?"

"First class, sir."

"Right. Brown's it is. Say nine o'clock. That'll give you time to get acquainted—and me time to pour a glass of sherry into April. In the meantime you may talk freely to Cavendish. The lid's off."

"Good, sir."

When the General had gone, Major Cavendish frowned and shook his head.

"Funny that. He didn't strike me as the sort of guy who'd worry overmuch about cellars."

"He means the wine cellar."

"Oh, gosh." He gave a slow smile. "I certainly beg his pardon."

The two men took wary stock of each other. Strangers now, they were to become firm and trusted friends in action. Infinitely more foreign than the French, whom he knew and loved and whose tongue Charles spoke, the Americans came from strange places with strange names—names like Manhattan and Martha's Vineyard and Brandywine and Colorado and Chevy Chase. They were lusty, potent men who drank prodigiously and ripped up the quiet, narrow English roads with their half-tracks and heavy trucks, speaking a language of their own, distributing gum and silk stockings and Chesterfields. But it was a far cry from Minnesota to the Villa Mimosa. . . .

Charles said with the ghost of a sigh:

"Well . . . I gather we're in this together."

"That's right."

"How much do you know about it?"

Major Cavendish smiled.

"Enough to make me want not to pass it up. No, sir, not for all the gold in Fort Knox."

"Splendid. Now let me supplement what the General has told you. I'll start at the beginning. Just over a week ago, on Saint Valentine's Day, I happened to pass by what looked like a deserted Villa. . . ."

He told the whole story. Aunt Marguerite and Gaston and Georges came into it and Madame and the girls, five of them; Hans Ramberg and his fellow conspirators; the piano and the candle-light; the Lysander skidding in on the frozen stubble—and then the plan within a plan. Major Cavendish listened without a word. When he had finished, Charles said apologetically:

"It may sound a bit crazy but I believe it'll work. Anything you're not clear about?"

"Yes. Two things. How did this guy Gaston get you into the Villa?"

"Put his right forefinger in a door and slammed it on himself."

Major Cavendish winced and lit a cigarette. He said thoughtfully:

"I guess I'd deem it an honour to shake that right hand of Gaston's."

"Very likely you will. What's the other thing?"

"When the General told me about it, he said there were six dames. Now you say five."

"Yes. The sixth . . . er . . . dame is a girl called Monique. She doesn't . . . take any part in the Villa's activities."

"Sort of assistant to Madame?"

"Sort of," said Charles. He stood up. "Now what I suggest is that you and I go to Great George Street—we've got an hour in hand—and visit the Map Room. I'm having a model made of

the Villa itself and that should be ready tomorrow. I want you
to know the place inside out so that you can find your way round
it blindfold. Have you picked your team yet?"

"Yes. A Lootenant, a Top-Sergeant and an enlisted man. What
about you?"

"General Southerden's picking my chaps for me. I haven't been
in England for six months and I'm a little out of touch. Well,
what do you feel about it all?"

Major Cavendish smiled his slow smile.

"I'll be happy to serve under your command—Major."

"My name's Charles. What's yours?"

"Thayer."

"O.K., Thayer. Tally-ho for the Map Room."

Major Thayer B. Cavendish left Brown's Hotel just before
midnight. By then, a tentative date had been fixed for the
launching of Operations Firefly and Sabine. Every extra day's
delay was dangerous now. The R.A.F. had been out flying
innumerable sorties over the whole coastline of the Pas de Calais
at zero feet and the mosaics of the imminent battle area were
very nearly complete. The Commandos and Rangers, after a
suspicious start, were slowly integrating, as photographs of wives,
girl-friends and children were shyly or boastfully exchanged.
Cooped up in H.M.S. *Claddah Burn,* they needed one full-scale
exercise before putting to sea on the real job. This exercise was
scheduled to take place on Thursday night. That left two full
days and one night before their D-Day in miniature. On Saturday
there would be no moon and the Channel would be dark. High
tide at the Pas de Calais at twelve thirty-five p.m.

On Saturday, February 27th, 1944, the expedition would sail.

By gross misuse of his rank, General Southerden wheedled two
whiskies and soda out of the night porter. He sat back and said
genially:

"Now we come to your team, Charles. I've got your three chaps
and one reserve. Your second-in-command is a Subaltern, Brian
Manning of the Greenjackets. Got an M.C. in North Africa. Keen
as a young fox-hound. Then Sergeant Fergus Forbes, some sort
of Highlander and a pious, steady type. Go anywhere, do anything
as long as he can sing a hymn while he's doing it. Your last man
—to keep you happy, Charles—is a Guardsman. Terence O'Flynn
from the Micks. When he isn't fighting, he's doing time—and

vice-versa. Same composition as the Americans. By the way, what do you think of Thayer B. Cavendish?"

Charles considered his reply. He said slowly:

"I think he's absolutely first-class. He's quiet, intelligent and reliable. More than that, sir, he sees this thing as it is—not as a dirty joke. I'm well content."

"I am too." The General stifled a yawn and stood up. "Well, goodnight, Charles. If you hear a bomb coming at you tonight, duck, for God's sake."

"I'll be under the bed like a flash. Goodnight, General."

*   *   *

Wednesday, 24th February, 1944.

Charles and Thayer drove in the morning to the Duke of York's Headquarters in Chelsea. There, behind locked doors, was what looked like a three-feet-high doll's house—on the roof of which the constructor had humorously stuck a Tricolor. Charles was considering the front elevation carefully when General Southerden was admitted. He greeted them boisterously.

"Morning, Charles, morning, Thayer—if I may make so bold. Can't keep on calling you 'Major' like a damned *maître d'hôtel.*" He chuckled. "Now give me your opinion of this pretty thing. Sorry about no clothesline. Other than that, is it accurate, Charles?"

Charles peered at the back of the model. There was a kitchen door—which was important. He said frowning:

"I think it's fairly accurate, sir. I only saw the place once by daylight."

"Ah, but you haven't seen all. Watch." With finger and thumb, he gently lifted the hinged roof. There revealed was a tiny attic bedroom, no bigger than a large match-box. "That, of course, should have a plaque in it saying 'Charles Addison slept here'. Now we come to the . . . er . . . *chambres d'amour.*" He lifted the attic floor. A microscopic staircase led downwards into a corridor set with six minute doors. "Wonderful, isn't it? But the big thing I want to know from you, Charles, is"—his voice sank into a blood-curdling whisper—"WHO SLEEPS WHERE?"

"I . . . I . . . I'm afraid I haven't the slightest idea. The only time I ever tip-toed along it was one very early morning and then all the doors were shut."

"You don't even know which one Golden Mouse sleeps in?" said the General wistfully. "You really don't?"

"I really don't, sir."

"Pity, Charles. Pity." With a sigh, he replaced the attic floor and then the roof. "And now I want you both to come along with me to Combined Ops for a talk with the Navy."

"The Navy" was a young Lieutenant named Tim Something-or-other who commanded a motor gun-boat. He had the face of a schoolgirl and a slight stutter. When the full nature of Operation Sabine was explained to him as well as the part he would have to play, he blushed bright pink and his stutter became even more pronounced. Maps and charts were produced and exact details worked out. As one who rightly considered himself somewhat of a Don Juan, Tim had one or two ideas of his own.

As dusk fell, Charles went back to Brown's Hotel, packed his bags and paid his bill. His next appointment was on the following morning at a south coast port within reasonably easy reach of Newick. If necessary, he could bicycle over from Verity's house. After all, he was well used to bicycling—and you never could tell if and when he'd see Verity again.

*   *   *

Dinner was over.

Charles and Verity sat facing each other at either end of a long, shining refectory table. The room was illuminated both by a log-fire and by candle-light. Two Georgian candle-sticks caught and held the flicker and glow of the logs in their silver stems and between them was a bottle that had recently contained champagne. Across its label was stamped in red RESERVIERT FUER DIE WEHRMACHT.

There had been a long silence between them, a silence that held in it a strange and unfamiliar element of tension. At last Verity rose, put down her napkin and walked to the fire. Charles joined her at once, standing beside her and putting an arm around her shoulders. She remained motionless and without response. Then, without a word, she slipped out of the clasp of his arm and sat down in a deep armchair, pointing to another chair on the far side of the fire. He sat down and said to her, speaking with tenderness:

"Something's troubling you, my darling. What is it?"

"The awful thing is that I don't know."

She gazed into the depths of the fire. There was the ghost of a frown on her forehead and, looking at her, Charles was again conscious of a sense of incredulity that this most lovely and sought-after girl should have placed herself and her future in his keeping. She was wearing a clinging red blouse of Indian silk, through which ran threads of gold, and a wide skirt of black velvet. On the third finger of her small left hand glimmered the ring he had given her, an eighteenth-century sapphire with a filigree pattern of pearls. A day or two ago, General Southerden had barked at him: "Engaged, are you? What's she like?" and he had tried to describe Verity. "Well, sir, she's dark with dark eyes and very small, slim hands and feet. In fact, she's sort of slim all over."

"Slim all over!" Those were poor words he had used to describe her most exciting body. She was graceful in the extreme, walking or standing or sitting, and her clear skin seemed almost to radiate its springing health. She looked away from the fire and directly at him with a steady, candid glance. Only the fingers of her right hand slowly and absent-mindedly twisted the ring.

"That's not quite true, Charles. I do know. It's this. Before you went away to France, you and I were terribly close, so close that very often it was quite unnecessary to speak. You remember?"

Of course he remembered. It had happened a hundred times and this wordless oneness of thought had seemed to him to be the most natural thing in the world.

"While you were away, I missed you dreadfully. No single night passed without my praying for you and for your safety. In spite of your letters from 'G.H.Q.' "—she smiled—"I knew that you were constantly in danger and I pestered the Almighty. I pestered him selfishly because in this bloody war countless thousands of people need prayers, and the whole weight of mine was for you."

"I prayed for you, too, Verity."

"I was aware of it—all the time. When I knew that you were home and safe, I was overjoyed. That's a small word to use. I came dashing up and we met in Brown's. But your Guardsman Pegg was there and when we *were* alone at last, the waiter knocked on the door and . . . and talked to us about dried egg. I could have killed him. Is this all very shameless of me, Charles?"

"No. It's not shameless."

"Then you came down for the weekend. My goodness, I was looking forward to seeing you. You didn't come on Friday evening—not till Saturday. The moment you arrived I knew in my bones that something had happened. Something had come between us—and whatever it was, it was a lot more important than . . . than dried egg—or me. You were, and you are, pre-occupied with"—she shrugged—"I don't know what. Oh, I don't mean that you were off-hand or discourteous, because you could never be either of those things. But I keep looking for Charles, the Charles I knew so well, and I don't find him. You, the man on the other side of the fire, are thinking of and living in a secret world of your own and I'm outside it." She paused and swallowed. "You . . . you didn't meet any girls in France or . . . or any special girl? Because if you did, you'd tell me, wouldn't you?" She gave a great sigh. "There you are, Now I've said it."

Charles was silent for a long time, contemplating his finger-nails. He said at last:

"You spoke a moment ago about 'this bloody war'. Well, that's all there is to it. For better or for worse, I'm a soldier, and through no wish of my own, I became involved in what pompous people call 'a certain phase' of this bloody war. I'd be much happier with the battalion but I'm in this thing now and I can't back out. I loathe being secretive with you because it implies that I don't trust you. I *do* trust you—absolutely. But these secrets are not mine to share. They concern others and the lives of others. You ask me if I met girls in France. Of course I did." He coughed. "Six at least. But compared with you, my darling, they simply don't exist. I am a single-minded person and you are my sole and only love."

"Promise?"

"Of course I promise."

She gave him an oblique look, as old as the glance of Eve. Slowly she raised her arms to clasp either side of the chair's back.

"It's been lonely without you," she said slowly. She half-closed her eyes. "You're quite sure that, compared with those French girls, you don't find me a sort of . . . of yokel?"

He gave no answer. He stood up and crossed and stood behind her chair. She lowered her raised arms, clasping her slender fingers behind her neck, pressing her shoulders back into the chair. Her small breasts lifted and her eyelids closed. She half whispered:

"You're *quite* sure, Charles?"

"Sure about what?"

"That I'm not a yokel?"

"I'm quite sure."

There was a tap and the door of the dining-room opened. The

voice of the housekeeper, cold with disapproval, warm with satisfaction, spoke:

"Excuse me, I'm sure, for disturbing you, Miss Verity, but
there's a telephone call from London for the Major." She paused
to give her sentence its full import. "It's from a lady."

"Thank you, Mrs. Masters. The Major will come at once."
Verity straightened her hair and her blouse. She said, smiling
to hide her chagrin, "Do you remember the waiter with the dried
egg at Brown's?"

Charles walked quickly into Mr. Gale's study and picked up
the receiver. He said curtly:

"Charles Addison."

"Hullo, Charles. Sorry to interrupt. It's me." "Me" was
Squadron Officer A. "I've just had a message from Gaston. It's
so important that you'd better know about it at once."

"On an open line?"

"Yes even on an open line. I'm in a call-box. This is how it
reads: *'Colonel otto definitely identified as black sheep stop
villa situation critical stop can provide transport stop hurry
repeat hurry or we really will be in the merde this time.'* Have
you got it?"

"Yes, I've got it. I'll telephone you back in ten minutes with
the reply. What's your number?"

"No. Don't do that. I'll ring you again in ten minutes from
another call-box."

"Right. Goodbye."

He went back to the dining-room. Verity was standing before
the fire. He was instantly aware of her change of mood. She had
become separate.

"I'm terribly sorry. It's the bloody war again. May I have a
sheet of paper and a pencil?"

"Certainly."

She gave him a sheet from the desk. He sat down at the table
and began to draft his reply, frowning, crossing out words. Verity
lit one of her rare cigarettes in silence, looking at him with a
strangely remote gaze. At last Charles was satisfied. He had
written:

*"For gaston from charles stop message begins stop tell
madame to confide in otto that senior conspirator general
expected villa sunday night stop this should postpone any
action stop imperative you keep villa as going concern till*

then stop special to georges things have almost reached boiling point here message ends."

He put down his pencil and listened. The dining-room door was half open and he heard the ringing of the telephone from Mr. Gale's study. He said quickly:

"It's for me."

"Oh."

He dictated the message to Squadron Officer A. She said with her unassailable calm: "I think we'll find that Otto will swallow that bait. I'll get it coded and away at once. Goodnight, Charles."

"Goodnight."

He went back to the dining-room. Verity had not moved from her place before the fire. She asked with studied lack of interest:

"Same lady again—or another one?"

"Same lady."

"Not one of the ones you met in France?"

"No. Not one of those."

"Well, that's a relief. Charles, there's something I was going to ask you, or rather discuss with you, but I'm a little diffident about it now."

"Please ask it."

"It's this. I haven't had a holiday from here for nearly a year. As you know, my father's much better and I had arranged with Mrs. Kingsley, who used to be a nurse, to come for a week and sleep in. And old Tom Foster from Piltdown, who was herdsman to Lord Bindley, can always cope with the farm if I go away. On Monday I wrote to my aunt Joanna and asked if I could come up and stop with her for a few days. She's got a house overlooking Richmond Green. Her reply came this morning. She wants me to come up for a week as from Monday." She paused. "The point is, would you like me to come—or will you be too busy being rung up by strange females?"

Monday. By Monday Operation Sabine would be over and he, Charles, would either be dead, in a German prison camp—or home. He said warmly:

"I'd love you to come. There's only one thing. You know the Baby-Blitz is on."

"So they tell me," she said with indifference. "But it's you and your work I'm thinking about and wouldn't want to be a nuisance or a bore to you."

"You could never be either. Please come, darling Verity."

"Very well, I will."

Gone utterly was the yielding, impulsive person he had known only a few moments ago. He realized with sadness that to recapture her now was beyond his power. It was one of those things.

"What time have you got to leave tomorrow morning?"

"I've been thinking about that. The place I've got to go to is just sixteen miles away so if I get away from here at about eight——"

The vanished girl came back swiftly, as suddenly as a flash of light. Verity took a step forward, her dark eyes luminous, and put her head on Charles' forearm. She was like an excited school-girl.

"Listen," she said. "I'll drive you to wherever it is. I've got at least three gallons of petrol left out of the ration. That means we won't have to say goodbye after breakfast."

It was hard, desperately hard for him to say "no". But he couldn't possibly let Verity come to where he was going, to that harbour of stealthy ships where Firefly was taking lethal shape. He put his two hands on her shoulders.

"There's nothing I'd like better but——"

She stepped back. Her face clouded. She said:

"But my kind offer is declined with thanks. Sorry, Charles. I didn't want to embarrass you." She swallowed. "I suppose your damn secrets will be over one day. In the meantime, it's not much fun being outside. How will you get to your . . . your mysterious rendezvous?"

"There's an R.A.S.C. supply depot a mile or so from here. They're bound to have some sort of transport going my way."

"And if they haven't?"

"Then I'll ask the C.O. to take me in his staff car."

"You must be a very important person, Charles. You make me feel more like a yokel than ever. Ah well, back to the byre. It's time to water the bullocks."

She went into the hall and put on an old sheepskin coat and a pair of wellington boots. He said to her:

"May I come too?"

"Of course. If it will amuse you."

They went out together, separate from each other, in the darkness of the February night.

•　　•　　•

Thursday, 25th February, 1944.

Two Hunt class destroyers, H.M.S. *Galway Blazer* and *Coollattin,* sailed into the harbour during the morning and moored alongside, in full view of the town. With them were four motor launches. There was no attempt at concealment but the presence of these six ships *did* divert attention from the motor gun-boat that tucked herself discreetly away behind the hull of H.M.S. *Claddah Burn,* the depot ship. A carpenter went aboard the M.G.B. and vanished below, and there was the muffled sound of hammering from the mess deck. In the opinion of the puzzled Coxswain, the Skipper had gone flipping nuts.

The lesson of Saint Nazaire had not been forgotten. A rumour was deliberately started that the two destroyers and their attendant motor launches were part of a new formation to be called the 34th Anti-Submarine Striking Force, destined for service in Far Eastern waters. To confirm this rumour, tropical kit was openly issued to all the ships' companies in the hope that some know-all would talk. A know-all *did* talk—and one of his indignant audience put pen to paper in a letter to the First Lord of the Admiralty.

Sir:

I feel it to be no less than my duty to inform you of a grave breach of security in this town. Today, the crews of two destroyers and four motor launches were publicly issued with tropical clothing in preparation for service overseas. The destination of this force and its future role is an open secret and is discussed freely in Licensed Houses. It is your duty, Sir, to bring to book those who, by culpable carelessness IF NOT WORSE, are endangering the lives of our gallant sailors.

I am, Sir,

Yours etc.

"SILENT—AND PROUD OF IT."

Everything was working out very satisfactorily.

The wind got up in the evening and by eleven o'clock it was blowing hard from the north-east. Laden, grumbling and swearing, the Commandos and Rangers left the comparative comfort of H.M.S. *Claddah Burn* and clambered into the spartan guts of two Infantry landing craft that had arrived to join the miniature fleet. They put to sea—and soon Commandos and Rangers and sailors alike were lurching to the rails. A mock attack was carried out on a lonely beach and the windy darkness spattered with the staccato of blank ammunition. Soaked to the waist, the soldiers re-embarked in the L.C.I.s and only prayed for *Claddah Burn* and the peaceful anchorage of the harbour.

But the voyage had done its work. In shared endeavour, sickness, cold and misery, the British and the Americans had become a completely integrated force. The Commandos had learned new and strange oaths and the Rangers had added a touch of Billingsgate to their already salty language.

Lance Corporal Quiff ("I love Glad") Perkins wrung the seawater out of his saturated socks, emptied his boots and offered a limp cigarette to his new pal "Butch" Treite of the U.S. Rangers.

"I thought I'd die 'laffin'," he said, "when that officer son-of-a-bitch went into the drink. Oh boy, oh boy."

"It certainly was bloody funny," said Butch. "Definitely."

11: DEATH OF A COLONEL

Friday, 26th February, 1944.
COLONEL RUPPRECHT, nicknamed "Johnny", had been a close friend of Rommel. That was long ago, centuries ago. The Field-Marshal—who was himself suspect—could be of no help at all to Johnny in his present predicament.

He sat shivering in what had been a servant's bedroom in 84 Avenue Foch, Paris. It was a commodious and elegant house and the Gestapo, whose Headquarters it was, treated the lower floors of the building with respect. They had less respect for the servants' bedrooms and for those whom they housed there.

It had happened on Sunday last. Five days ago. Five endless days and five endless nights.

Colonel Johnny had been to a conference at La Roche-Guyon with his friend Field-Marshal Rommel. The meeting had broken up early and, blithely unaware that his car was being followed, he had driven into Paris and, as usual, stopped off for a champagne cocktail in the Crillon Bar. There he had been joined by a genial stranger, an officer of Colonel Johnny's own rank, who insisted on paying for a second champagne cocktail. He had introduced himself formally with a bow as "Otto", and suggested another drink at the Ritz Bar where, he said, his wife was awaiting him. Colonel Johnny was in no hurry. Paris and the bars of Paris were a great deal more to his taste than the austere *bistros* of Coville.

"We can go in my car," said the genial Colonel Otto, "and my driver can take you back here in half an hour to pick up your own car."

"Splendid," said Colonel Johnny. "*Allons-y.*"

Gaily they went out together into the Place de la Concorde and Colonel Johnny was a little surprised to find himself sitting between two hard-faced men in black raincoats. He was even more surprised to feel a Lueger pistol pressing against his ribs—and was sick with fear by the time the car stopped outside a tall, elegant and closely guarded building in the Avenue Foch.

His own driver who had taken him in a drunken moment to the Villa Mimosa had talked. The ubiquitous Gestapo had listened. It had been as simple at that. *Kinderspiel.* Child's play.

His tunic had been stripped of its badges of rank, stripped of all that Colonel Johnny had earned since the war began. Then, locked in what had been a servant's bedroom, they had begun to ask questions about the Villa Mimosa. Who was Madame? What were the girls' names? What were the names of the debauched officers who frequented this . . . this filthy *bordel,* this flagrant insult to the dedicated, celibate Fuehrer? What subjects did these libertines discuss among themselves—and with which women?

He told them that he knew nothing of Madame—nor did he remember the names of the girls. He said that the officers who went there were strangers to him. He could not remember any particular subject of discussion.

To stimulate his memory, they laid him face downwards on a sofa and beat him on the nape of the neck with a rubber truncheon until he was senseless. They threw a bucket of water over him to revive him and took up the truncheon again. He told them then the names of the girls. He mumbled that that was as much as he knew. They rolled him over and beat him on the genitals, one blow for the Villa Mimosa, one for Madame, one for Lucille, one for Elsa, one for Magda, one for Wanda, one for Monique and two for Golden Mouse because her blood was impure.

All that had happened on Sunday. Since then they had left Colonel Johnny alone, to yelp and to crawl about the floor like a dog with paralysed hind-quarters after a motor accident.

The key rattled in the lock of the servant's bedroom and Colonel Otto, flanked by the two men in black raincoats, came in. He said quietly:

"Good morning, Herr Rupprecht. You notice that I call you

'Herr' and not 'Colonel'. I do this because you are no longer an officer in the Armed Forces of the Reich. Now I want to talk to you again about the Villa Mimosa."

"I have told you all I know."

"Ah, yes. So you have. You told me the names of the pretty creatures who administer to officers living under extreme tension. What could be more harmless or more natural than that these gallant, harassed fellows should seek brief oblivion from their responsibilities in the arms of women? Is not that what you implied?"

"It is."

"But what you did *not* tell me is that the Villa Mimosa has yet another function. You did not tell me that you, Hans Ramberg and all the other criminals are traitors and swine. Did you forget?"

"I . . . I don't know what you mean."

"I think you do. Since our last meeting on Sunday, I have been to the Villa myself and made the acquaintance of Madame and the girls. As a friend and confidant of yours, I was made welcome. The girls all spoke of you with laughter and affection. Colonel Johnny—appears to have been a very popular person. I basked in your reflected glory. So much did I ingratiate myself that I even dared to follow in your footsteps and invite one of the girls to a *tête-à-tête* in her bedroom." He sighed. "When in Rome. . . . It is rare indeed that one's duty leads one along such primrose paths."

"Whose body did you soil?"

A little of the geniality went out of Colonel Otto's face. He was like a small boy who had been rightly slapped.

"You are a civilian. For insulting a German officer, I could have you beaten again—but I want you to be able to stand up. That is essential, that you should be capable of standing up. I chose my girl at once. It was not difficult. In my profession, we are trained to select the foolish and the loquacious. My light-of-love and I went upstairs and, after a suitable romantic interval, she talked. My God, how she talked! I now know that a group of criminals are conspiring to murder the Fuehrer and to betray Germany. You, Herr Rupprecht, 'Johnny', are one of them. I require the names, ranks and regiments of *all* the others."

Far below Colonel Johnny could hear the muffled sound of traffic. People were coming and going on the pavements of Paris. He closed his eyes. Sweet Saviour, only give me strength to be silent. . . .

"Pick him up."

The two men in raincoats dragged Colonel Johnny to his feet. So bruised were his agonized genitals that he was unable to walk. But he could stand and look Colonel Otto in the face. Thank God he could stand.

"Well?"

Dumbly Colonel Johnny shook his head.

"Put his coat around his shoulders and bring him down."

"*Jawohl, Herr Oberst.*"

Each movement was a separate, realized pain. The wooden stairs were narrow and precipitous and the descent to the ground floor took a long time. Two cars were waiting outside. One was Colonel Otto's own staff car and the other a troop carrier containing some half-dozen soldiers. Colonel Johnny was pushed into the back seat of the staff car between his two silent escorts. Colonel Otto said, smiling through the half-open window:

"In case you are curious about our destination, I will tell you at once. We are going to the Pas de Calais, the setting of your little love-nest."

The staff car swept up the avenue, the troop carrier following. Colonel Johnny saw a passer-by look the other way and furtively cross himself.

Houses gave way to factories; factories to fields. As the surface of the roads became less good, the speed of the staff car increased and the jolting worsened. Hour after unendurable hour went by, each minute filled with pain. Sometimes the troop carrier was close behind, sometimes it fell back a kilometre or more, but it was always there. Colonel Johnny had begun to slide into blessed oblivion when the staff car slowed down and stopped. The troop carrier screeched to a halt and the soldiers let down the tail-board, and lifted something out. It was a coffin.

"*Heraus, heraus.* We have now entered the Pas de Calais, a most suitable place for our little ceremony. Bring him into the wood."

There was a clearing in the wood and a convenient screen of saplings between it and the road. Colonel Johnny, supported under the arms by the two men in raincoats, was taken, his feet dragging, to the far end of the clearing. The toe of his shoe struck a spent cartridge-case and he knew, with nausea, that the clearing had been used for this purpose before.

"You are capable of standing?"

"Yes."

"Then stand against the stump."

How many men, close to God, had stood here before him? The words of Colonel Otto spoke softly, ingratiatingly:

"The names of your fellow conspirators. *All* the names, please. In return for those names, I can promise you your life. Those who assist us in our enquiries do not find us ungrateful. It is even possible that your officer status could be restored—after, of course, a period of probation."

The soldiers were forming a single line, fingering their weapons. Colonel Johnny managed to say one word.

"*Nein.*"

"For the last time?"

He shook his head.

"As you wish." Colonel Otto swung on his heel and gave a curt order to the firing party.

"*Legt an.*"

The men raised their automatic rifles. They were suppressing their giggles with difficulty. A bird alighted on the coffin, relieved itself and flew off chirruping into the depths of the wood. Sweet Jesu, receive my soul——

"It is customary for ex-officers to shout '*Heil Hitler!*' before they die."

"Long live Germany!"

"*Feuer!*"

The crack of the automatic rifles burst like a redhot explosion in Colonel Johnny's brain. He sagged and fell and lay twitching. And then, wonder upon wonder, he heard with living ears echoes reverberating in the cold stillness. He heard the chirruping of the bird in the wood and he heard roars of laughter, rich, ribald, back-slapping guffaws of laughter. In pain and shame, he dragged himself to his feet. The men of the firing squad were doubled up with mirth, pointing and shaking their heads helplessly.

Colonel Otto, his jovial face creased with a grin, strode over.

"Forgive me, my dear friend. That was only a joke, a little joke at your expense. The cartridges were blank. *Es war lustig!* If only you could have seen yourself! No doubt you have emulated the bird who perched on your coffin! *Ach. Du lieber Gott.*" His grin broadened. "Now, the names of the officers, please."

Colonel Johnny drew himself to his full height. He sucked in his cheeks, gathering together all the spittle in his mouth. Miraculously, he was no longer in physical pain. Fear had conquered pain and now fury conquered fear. He spat in Colonel Otto's face.

The firing squad, no longer laughing, looked at each other furtively and in horror. Murderers to a man, they were aghast at this . . . this blasphemy. The grin remained on the muscles of Colonel Otto's mouth but his eyes hardened into the dead blue of slate. With his left hand, he took out a handkerchief and began to wipe his cheek. Still wiping, he took his Lueger in his right hand and shot Colonel Johnny in the stomach, counting out loud, *ein—zwei—drei—vier—fuenf—sechs——*

He went back to his car. The Corporal in charge of the firing party turned Colonel Johnny over with his foot and shot him again between his glazing eyes. They put his body into the coffin, lifted the coffin into the troop carrier and drove away. They were still silent and shocked by the dreadful insult they had seen.

The bird, frightened by the firing, took refuge, chirruping on the topmost branch of a distant tree.

Arrived in Coville, Colonel Otto went straight to Gestapo Headquarters and gave his orders.

He had decided not to raid the Villa Mimosa until tomorrow, Saturday night. The "weekend habit" had spread from England into Germany and tomorrow he could count on a full attendance. He wanted all, not just one or two. As to the raid itself, he would require, say, a dozen men to surround the house. There were two entrances, one at the front and one at the back. A Gestapo man would be stationed at either door. The prisoners would be conveyed from the Villa in a Black Maria, a *panier à salade*, a salad basket. The French had thought up this light-hearted name for a sinister vehicle. A searchlight would be mounted on the roof of the Black Maria and he, a keen photographer, hoped to get a shot or two of the girls' exodus. Reichfuehrer Himmler, who collected such *objets d'art*, would be most amused. Access to the Villa would present no difficulty. He was himself *persona grata* not only with the girls but also with Madame and he would be admitted readily. Any questions?

Resistance? Colonel Otto smiled.

Visitors to the Villa Mimosa hung up their weapons in the hall—and in any case, men shed their courage with their trousers. There would be no resistance. Any other questions?

Accommodation overnight?

The cells of Coville prison should be made ready temporarily

to house approximately twenty new occupants, seven or eight
of them women and the rest men. On Sunday morning, they
would be transported to Paris, to the Avenue Foch, for interrogation. Anything else?

Should the Villa be discreetly guarded during the next twenty-
four hours?

Quite unnecessary. Nobody within its walls had the slightest
suspicion and the presence of a guard, no matter how discreet,
could give the game away.

"As well as that, I must remind you, gentlemen, that the Villa
Mimosa is within the evacuated area and even if they wanted to
run away, there is nowhere for them to go. That is all. *Heil
Hitler!*"

"*Heil Hitler!*"

Colonel Otto dined alone. He had another reason, a purely
personal one, for postponing the raid until tomorrow and for
making sure that the Villa was unguarded. That afternoon, he
had killed a human being. The shedding of blood always had a
queerly aphrodisiac effect on him and he wanted a woman.
Tonight he proposed to visit the Villa Mimosa in a private
capacity.

*   *   *

Even as he rang the bell, Colonel Otto heard the tinkling of
a piano. Gaston, the little hunchback with the maimed hand,
was maltreating Mozart. For that alone he would get an extra
ten years. Old Marie the housemaid—another candidate for the
salad basket—admitted him and, as a token, he hung up his
Lueger in the hall, giving the holster an affectionate pat. He
was never unarmed and carried a small, loaded automatic in his
hip pocket. As he mounted the stairs, he saw the figure of Madame
in her black silk—soon to be changed for the striped pyjamas
of Ravensbrueck. She inclined her head to his bow.

"I wonder if I might have a word with you, Colonel?"

"Certainly, Madame."

He followed her into the room on the landing. She sat down
at her desk. French women of her class—which was unmistakable
—always made him feel as if he had six fingers on each hand.
Still, she would look rather different when the *coiffeuses* of
Ravensbrueck had been over that iron grey hair with the clippers.
The very thought of it was socially reassuring.

"I will be frank with you, Colonel. In a house such as this, we have to be very careful. If the *Sicherheitsdienst*"—Colonel Otto put on a shocked look—"if the *Sicherheitsdienst* were to learn of our existence, we would be in very serious trouble. When you visited us on Monday last, we treated you with a certain reserve—in spite of the fact that you are a friend of Colonel Johnny's. We had hoped that Colonel Johnny would have visited us himself during the week to tell us something about you. But he didn't come." She raised one plucked eye-brow. "Have you any news of Colonel Johnny?"

This was rich. Really rich. He smiled.

"Let me answer several questions at once. Firstly, you are perfectly right to be suspicious of strangers. I applaud your caution. Secondly, it is not surprising that none of your clients recognize me. I am a member of the *Abwehr*, the secret service, and between the *Abwehr* and your *Sicherheitsdienst* there is both hatred and distrust. As for Colonel Johnny, I saw him this very morning in Paris. We had a drink together in the Crillon. He was his usual gay self and sent you all his love. He has been posted, as from this afternoon." Here Colonel Otto paused while his sense of humour came into full play. "Johnny has been posted to a liaison job with the Luftwaffe"—he waved an expressive hand—"you know, up in the clouds."

So Colonel Johnny was dead and this creature had killed him. The Villa Mimosa was in deadly, imminent peril. Madame said easily:

"So that's the explanation. I hope Colonel Johnny will be happy in his new appointment. We are all very fond of him." She leaned forward. "Now that I know you to be a member of the *Abwehr*, I am tempted to take you into my confidence."

"I should be honoured to respect any confidence you give me, Madame."

"It is this. On Sunday night, that is the day after tomorrow, we are to receive a special visitor, one who has never been here before. He is a General and I gather that he is coming from Hitler's Headquarters for some sort of a political discussion with my clients. Even Major Hans, who is no respecter of persons, holds him in great awe. I am arranging a modest celebration and I hope that you will be able to come. I invite you because you have satisfactorily explained yourself and I regard you as being one of us, one of our little *coterie*."

Colonel Otto had been trained to conceal the excitement that welled up inside him. He wrinkled his brow.

"A General from Fuehrer Headquarters. Do you happen to know his name?"

"No more than I know yours. To me you are simply 'Colonel Otto'. There are few rules in this house. The strictest of them forbids the use of anything other than Christian names—and I do not know his."

"It is of no importance. I am sure I will be able to arrange to be here. . . . On Sunday night you say. At what time is the General expected?"

"At nine, half-past nine. The usual time."

Such a plump partridge as a General from Fuehrer Headquarters was well worth waiting for. The raid on the Villa Mimosa would be postponed until, say, midnight on Sunday. The better the day, the better the deed! Colonel Otto absent-mindedly fingered the left breast pocket of his tunic. Reichsfuehrer Himmler would surely consider this worthy of a decoration. Certainly an Iron Cross; possibly even with Swords.

He stood up. He had served his country well today. Now he was going to serve himself.

"With your permission, Madame, I would like to join my brother officers in the Salon."

She inclined her head.

"Of course. They and my *pensionnaires* will be delighted to see you."

Colonel Otto entered the Salon with a certain swagger. Lordly Caliph of a harem transplanted (no doubt by carpet) from Baghdad to the Pas de Calais, he was now ready to look the women over. He was a little dashed to see that three minor officials of the Court, so to speak, had preceded him. They were Hans Ramberg, Gerhard and Stefan.

Lucille, the slim blonde Parisian, was perched on Hans' knee, playfully twirling his hair into two devil's horns. Elsa, the plump Alsatian, sat beside Gerhard looking at him with the eyes of a lovesick spaniel, while Magda danced a languorous foxtrot with Stefan. The hunchback was playing whatever tune it was very badly.

A pretty sight to see—with the siege of Leningrad lifted and the Bolshevik hordes sweeping to the very frontiers of Hitler's

Germany! With the Anzio beach-head widening every hour; with Berlin, Stuttgart, Leipzig, Regensburg and half a dozen other cities crouching under a nightly hail of bombs; with an eager Allied army poised and ready to spring across the God-damned English Channel. Like Boccaccio's youths and maidens, this riff-raff had fled to the hillsides to listen to the sound of lutes, to tell and to practise dirty stories while plague ravished their city below. A pretty sight—but one that would not last much longer. Colonel Otto checked his mounting disgust. But was he not here for a similar purpose? Was he not Satan reproving sin?

His choice of woman, alas, was restricted to one of two, Wanda or Golden Mouse; Golden Mouse or Wanda. But which? He had already possessed Wanda, the talkative one. The other one, the silent one, was of mixed blood and in every respect beneath the contempt of a member of the master-race. Therefore he desired her.

Avoiding Wanda's bright and possessive eye, Colonel Otto addressed himself to Golden Mouse. She received his advances modestly and without expression. She allowed him to buy her a bottle of champagne. She suffered him to stroke her knee. Then she gave him a sideways glance.

"Is it permitted to ask a question?"

"Of course."

"May one ask about Colonel Johnny? I ask because you are his friend."

Colonel Johnny again! Drunken, roystering and treacherous, the swine must have had an attraction for women. If only his female admirers could have seen him in the Avenue Foch crawling like a paralysed dog on the floor, they would soon have changed their minds. He put on a doleful expression.

"I doubt very much if Colonel Johnny will come again. He has been posted to . . . er . . . flying duties. First Madame asked me about him—and now you. Really, I am becoming quite jealous." He laughed. "What had Colonel Johnny got that I haven't got?"

Verdammt. That was a slip of the tongue. In speaking of Colonel Johnny he had used the past tense. Had Golden Mouse noticed? He gave her a furtive glance. Her fingers were still demurely linked in her lap and she had given no sign. But in case she had heard, he went on quickly to smother his mistake with words:

"We are not doing justice to the champagne. There is still half a bottle left. Could we not drink it—upstairs?"

Gaston ran his fingers lightly up the keys of the piano. There was quietness in the Salon broken only by Hans Ramberg's whispered love-making. From under downcast lids, Golden Mouse saw the hand that stroked her knee. The thought of being touched by that hand filled her with horror, for she sensed now that there was blood on its skin. She spoke in a soft murmur.

"I am going to ask you to be patient, *mon Colonel*. Perhaps tomorrow night. . . ."

"But why not tonight? Why not now?"

"There is a reason."

What right had this Asiatic, this non-Aryan woman of the Villa, to talk to him of 'a reason'? Was she not here for a purpose? Did she not realize that he, a German officer, was doing her great honour? He began angrily:

"But you are only a——" He stopped, biting back the word.

"I am aware of my status. But I am also a woman, *mon Colonel*," she said in uncomplaining reproof.

He took his hand from her knee. She rejoiced to be free from the touch of an unclean thing. Unconsciously Colonel Otto assumed a more familiar role—that of interrogator.

"You speak of a reason. What is this reason?"

"I beg of you not to ask me. It will cause me embarrassment to answer you. All I ask for is . . . rewarding patience."

"I insist."

"Very well. I am your servant. Sometimes a woman wishes to give more than her body. But the fulfilment of such a wish is only achieved by patience." She fluttered her black eye-lashes. "I hope that you understand my words."

He did. He understood them very clearly and he was flattered by them. He sat back and filled their two champagne glasses.

"I drink to—tomorrow night."

"And I too. *A demain!*"

"*A demain.*"

Later, much later, Wanda said to him with a thread of jealousy:

"I thought when you first came that you were interested in that Chinese girl."

It had, of course, been true. The remote and elusive image of Golden Mouse was with him now. Two hours ago, she had

merely been one of the girls of the Villa Mimosa on whom his
glance had happened to alight. He had chosen her with a mingled
sense of desire and guilt, desire because he wanted a woman,
guilt because she was of contemptible breed and therefore un-
worthy. But her proximity had excited him strangely and her
withdrawal had angered him. When he knew its flattering cause,
desire for her amber body had become overwhelming and now
no power on earth could keep him away from the Villa Mimosa
tomorrow night.

Wanda began to undress. Thin and white-skinned, she was
only a stop-gap, an immediate answer to the physical need roused
in him by the killing of Colonel Johnny. She was a poor, pale
thing of no account.

With his tunic half-off, he suddenly paused and listened. From
the Salon below, he could hear the measured sound of the piano.
He scowled. He wiped the imagined spit off his face. That damned
hunchback had certainly chosen a macabre composition with
which to serenade him.

Gaston was playing a funeral march, the entry of the gods
into Valhalla.

12: VERITY

Saturday, 27th February, 1944

CHARLES ADDISON had been awake for more than an hour before
the waiter at Brown's called him with a cup of tea. He had not
slept at all well and felt unrefreshed and exhausted. "All through
the night in vain, with candle in hand, he had hunted the ugly
beast." Operation Sabine was no longer a daring adventure.
Rather like a visit to the dentist, it was a thing to be endured,
and he would be damn glad when it was over. It was odd to think
that by this time tomorrow it *would* be over—for better or for
worse. Thank God for that. The hours of waiting had become
intolerable.

Guardsman Pegg arrived at five past eight and turned on
Charles' bath, filling it to the regulation five inches exactly.
When he heard the water gushing in, Charles wondered gloomily
when he would next have a bath. In prisoner-of-war camps you
got a shower once a week—if you were lucky. In the grave,
nobody wanted any sort of bath at all. As Charles shaved, Pegg
set to work on his buttons, belt and shoes until Charles told

him not to bother. Pegg enquired with stern disapproval:

"You're not thinking of wearing battledress, are you, sir? Not in London, sir."

Charles put down his razor and laughed out loud. History had unwittingly come to his aid and he had little doubt that, nigh on three hundred years ago, some bewhiskered Coldstreamer had equally well disapproved of his officer's turn-out on Tower Hill. Everything was going to be all right. Operation Sabine was like the rising of a tide, buoyant and surging. Charles cocked his head around the bathroom door.

"I wouldn't dare, Pegg—not with you about the place."

"That's good, sir. Mind you, sir, some gentlemen in Line regiments *do* wear battledress in London. But not us. Not unless we got to. You going away for the weekend, sir?"

"Not quite. Only for tonight. I'll be back tomorrow morning." He said it confidently, believing it to be true. "So if you can turn up at nine instead of eight, because it's Sunday——"

"I will, sir. And I'll take these things back to Wellington and run the iron over them. Must have you looking your best of a Sunday. I've laid out your battledress. Will that be all, sir?"

"Yes, Pegg. That will be all. And thank you very much."

"It's a pleasure, sir. See you tomorrow morning, sir."

"You will."

After breakfast Charles insisted on paying his hotel bill up to date. Yes, he wanted to keep his room but he didn't expect to be back until some time in the early morning. Might he have a cup of tea and the *Sunday Times* at nine? Ordering these normal things reinforced the confidence that Pegg had unconsciously given him. The day was cold and clear with a pale blue sky and he decided to walk to Baker Street rather than take a taxi. He was restless and full of energy and in need of physical movement.

As always, Squadron Officer A was there. She gave him the decoded radio messages that had come in overnight and he read them, trying to put himself into the mind of the sender. It looked as if everything had been organized perfectly. All he had to do now was to allow for the unpredictable.

"Well," she said, "how do you feel about it?"

"I think it's going to work." He looked like a worried man. "It'd better! Guardsman Pegg is busy pressing my trousers for Church Parade, so to speak, and I can't possibly let him down."

"No, you can't—not possibly. By the way, we're moving a new wireless operator up from the south as a replacement for Georges. Georges has had a long time in the field and the last few days must have been a terrific strain."

"I agree. And what about Gaston?"

"I've been thinking about him too. Once Operation Sabine is over, there's going to be a pretty big blood-bath in the area and we don't want Gaston to fall into it. As the Villa's pianist, he's one of the first people the S.S. will go for. And there's that housemaid—what's her name?—Marie. You'd better bring her as well." She half-smiled. "It's one way of coping with the servant shortage. Import your own—from France."

"You think of everybody, don't you? Don't you ever think about yourself?"

"Amongst other . . . er . . . duties, I'm the Welfare Officer and Marie comes under welfare."

"When do I see you next?"

"Tomorrow morning—sometime. I'll be there to meet you."

"You always are." He stood up. "Well, *au revoir*, my old friend."

"Merde," said Squadron Officer A.

Charles took a taxi from Baker Street to the War Office. General Southerden's P.A., Angela, was typing the last page of the TOP SECRET file concerning Operation Firefly for submission to the Director of Finance (Z).

"Good morning, Major Addison," she said. "You're expected but the General's busy. I'll tell him you're here." She picked up the telephone and announced his arrival.

Charles heard every word of the General's staccato reply: "Good. But don't let him come in here for God's sake. And in five minutes you can bring me in some brown paper and string."

"Very well, sir. How much string?"

"Balls."

"I beg your pardon, sir."

"Sorry. I mean yards."

She put down the receiver and shook her head tolerantly.

"Operation Firefly's gone to his head—not to mention Sabine. Came in early this morning skipping like a lamb and promptly sent me out to buy him a sheet of white cardboard, a bottle of black ink and a mapping pen. I don't know what he's up to but, by goodness, he's having fun. Would you like *The Times*?"

"Thank you very much."

Charles read *The Times*. He read it for the second time, absent-mindedly, thinking about Sabine. Angela finished her typing and checked it, controlling her giggles. She found some brown paper and string in the filing cabinet and knocked on the General's door.

"Come in and tell Charles he can come in in two minutes."

When Charles entered, General Southerden was tying the last knot of a flat parcel. He gave a cheerful wave.

"Good morning to you. Got that 'eve of the point-to-point' feeling? Cold in the saddle and the jump as big as Bechers?"

"Bechers is a cut-and-thrust compared with this."

"I know. It's hell hanging about. The great thing is to keep busy. Stops you thinking. The weather's on our side up to now and tonight should be pitch dark. I've called a conference in H.M.S. *Claddah Burn* at three this afternoon, so I thought you and I could drive down together and have a quiet glass and a bite of luncheon on the way. Angela, got that file ready?"

"Here it is, sir. All checked."

General Southerden signed it with a chuckle and flourish.

"That'll wreck old Scrooge's weekend for him. My only regret is that I won't be amongst those present when he sees it. Right, Charles. Off we go."

*   *   *

April drove them down to the south coast, stopping on the way at the Roebuck. General Southerden was in splendid form, reminiscing about his life in the Army. He had parachuted into Italian Eritrea, ridden a bicycle into the harbour in Hong Kong, been tight in Damascus. Charles found himself forgetting about Operation Sabine, on one occasion for as long as twenty minutes at a stretch.

A tender took them out to H.M.S. *Claddah Burn* and, at three o'clock, all officers were summoned to the ward-room. The curtains were drawn. What the Commandos and Rangers saw, they saw by torch-light. It was a beautifully made model of a section of the Pas de Calais coast, with steep cliffs rising on the left flank to slope into a valley of sand-dunes and rise again on the right. The torches cast long shadows, the sort of shadows that would be cast by searchlights—or by the illumination of flares. General Southerden gave the officers five minutes to study the model before he spoke:

"Please pay attention. What you see before you, gentlemen, is the scene of Operation Firefly. I'm going to tell you about it quite informally, so don't hesitate to ask questions as we go along. Right?

"Operation Firefly is a raid on the Pas de Calais coast. It takes place tonight and you will be ashore in all for something under three hours. You will sail in the two Infantry landing craft which you already know and in which you were recently so violently sick. Tonight, you'll all be happy to hear, the sea looks like being as calm as a duckpond. You will be escorted halfway across the Channel by two Hunt-class destroyers, H.M.S. *Galway Blazer* and *Coollattin,* who will then come home leaving you in the tender care of your motor launches. The less shipping there is in the Channel the better, as we don't want enemy radar to pick you up and track you in. Talking of enemy radar, 'window' will be used extensively."

"Pardon me, General, sir, but what the heck's 'window'?"

"Metallic strips dropped by R.A.F. and U.S. bombers tuned in to German wavelengths. These strips look like God knows what on enemy radar screens. Simple, effective and highly confusing. The bombers can't give you close cover because the night promises to be as black as original sin, but they *are* going to bomb airfields and other installations on either flank. Distraction stuff. Any other questions up to now?"

"No, sir."

"Good. Having arrived—we hope unobserved—an hour and a half before high tide, which is at 0135 hours G.M.T., you will scale the cliffs in two separate groups, British on the left, Americans on the right. A United States officer with a radio set will be attached to the Commandos and a British subaltern will land with the Rangers. The call-sign will be 'Popsie'. Very appropriate, if I may say so. Once on the cliff's crest, you will proceed to kick up hell's delight. The more din you make, the more I like it. We want the Germans to think that this raid is bigger than it is and you will be assisted by 'noises off'. Your specific targets, to be shown to you in a moment in detail, are two naval guns, one on each cliff, and a radar station"—he pointed—"here. For this purpose, limpet mines and hand-grenades should do the trick and, as well as that, you'll have Bren guns and Stens." He paused. "Now I come to the most important part of Firefly. I must have a clear corridor, so to speak, between the two forces. I want the Germans pushed and held back on either flank so that anyone coming down that corridor can make a break for the sea."

"Pardon me, General, but is anyone likely to come down that corridor?"

"I most profoundly hope so. Have you ever seen the State opening of Parliament with troops lining the route? Well, you're the troops—and the golden coach drawn by the Windsor Greys is a one-horse show compared with what's coming. I can't tell you what—or who—it is because it's TOP SECRET. But I assure you, gentlemen, that whatever or whoever he, she or it is or are, they are eminently desirable." He coughed. "I use the word 'desirable' in its fullest sense. Do I make myself clear?"

"Not quite, General, sir. I guess——"

"Having done your stuff," said General Southerden swiftly, "you will re-embark in your luxury yachts and sail for home. In on the flood, out on the ebb. One last word. Please do not be deluded by any wishful thinking you may have seen in the papers." His voice hardened. "This is no picnic on a French beach. The Germans are tough, resolute and brave fighters who will give blow for blow. Remember that and hit first. That's all there is to it."

He frowned and, after a moment, went on with solemnity: "Some days ago, I organized a hand-picked mixed force of British Commandos and American Rangers to undertake Firefly. Today that force is no longer mixed. It has become a force of Allies. 'A fellow sickness makes us wondrous kind.' That is all. Keep your feet dry, gentlemen, and good luck to you."

As they chugged in the tender across the darkening harbour, Charles said with admiration:

"That was a damn good speech, sir. The only thing that surprises me is that you haven't smuggled yourself aboard one of the landing craft. How did you manage to resist?"

"Strength of mind, Charles; pure strength of mind." They arrived at the quay and General Southerden climbed into the car. He waved carelessly to Charles.

"Well, bring 'em back alive. Goodbye."

Dusk fell.

As the flood tide mounted and was moved by the pulse of the sea, motor gun-boat 331 shifted perpetually, squeezing her weeping fenders against the black side of *Claddah Burn*. The buzz had been around the messdeck that whatever was brewing was going to come to the boil tonight, and speculation was gloomy.

The issue of tropical kit could only mean one thing: they were going to the flipping Arctic.

As the tender drew away from the depot ship, Lieutenant Tim Something-or-other, R.N. (nobody ever remembered his full name because it was long, Irish and hyphenated), rang for his steward, presented his compliments to the Coxswain and requested that he come to the wardroom. So fair and boyish did this young Captain look that on one occasion (after a three-day running fight in the Narrows) he had been denied entrance to an "A" film and the memory rankled. The Coxswain and he had served together since 1942 with mutual respect.

"Good afternoon, sir."

"Hullo, Coxswain. What I say from now on is confidential. We're going out on a job tonight and Number One is ashore at the Base, hanging around for sailing orders. In the meantime, as they say, 'Be Prepared'."

"Aye aye, sir."

"The job is to pick up some V.I.P.s from the Pas de Calais and deliver them here, the initials 'V.I.P.' standing, in this case, for 'Very Important Poules'. You will have noticed certain modifications and additions to the messdeck—curtains, lampshades and a dressing-table—and you may have wondered what it's all in aid of."

"I certainly did, sir. And I'm not the only one."

"Well, now you know, Coxswain. The Royal Navy," he went on warmly, "has a long tradition of hospitality and I have further decided to augment ship's stores in these V.I.P.s' honour—without charge either to Their Lordships or to the British taxpayer. Got a signal pad?"

"Aye aye, sir."

"I want you to go into the town now, before the shops shut, and buy the following items," said Lieutenant Tim dreamily. "Six lipsticks—and one can't be fussy about colours in wartime; six boxes of face powder and six powder puffs—swan's-down if possible; six combs, one pot of rouge and one pot of that black stuff women put on their eyelashes."

"Mascara, sir?"

"That's the word, Coxswain," he said admiringly. "Anything else that occurs to you?"

"Box of face tissues, sir."

"Of course. Add it on. What it is to be a family man!"

"As a matter of fact, sir, I'm a bachelor."

"Then you are deserving of my warmest congratulations."

The Coxswain made his way aft to his friend the Chief Engine Room Artificer.

"Want anything in the town, Chiefie? I'm just going ashore to buy some lipsticks and powder-puffs for the Skipper."

"Well, well, well." Chiefie shook his head. "You *do* surprise me. I always thought the Skipper was one of *us*. Never occurred to me that he was one of *them*. . . ."

*   *   *

Five and a half hours still to run; three hundred and thirty minutes; a frightening infinity of crawling time. Charles decided to do two things. He would go to church and then see Verity.

He had some difficulty in finding a church that was open, but he discovered one at last in a back street. It was an unwelcoming church that gave one a feeling of intrusion. As he knelt in its cold emptiness, he remembered meeting Georges in Coville, under the statue of Saint Thérèse of Lisieux. It seemed a very long time ago —and yet it was only a matter of a few days. And now Georges was coming home—please God. As he had walked into this forbidding place, he had been diffident and uncertain what to ask for. Now of course he knew. Please God they were all coming home. That was his prayer.

So secret would be his destination after leaving Verity that he dare not employ a civilian car driver. The R.A.S.C. came unofficially to his rescue, driving him the sixteen miles to Verity's house and undertaking to wait and take him on elsewhere.

Verity was overjoyed to see him, thinking that he had come for the week-end. The herdsman had been out with a gun, there was wood-pigeon pie for dinner and it wouldn't take two minutes to make his room ready. The shadow that had been between them had vanished completely.

He put his two hands on her pliant shoulders. Slowly he shook his head.

"I'm terribly sorry but I can't stay. I've only got just over an hour."

"But . . . but this is Saturday night. Where have you got to go—and why are you in battledress?"

"To the bloody war."

"Oh."

She took a pace backwards, withdrawing her living warmth from the touch of his hands, separating herself from him.

"More secrets, Charles?"

"Yes," he said wearily, "more secrets. I hope and believe this is the last."

His tension communicated itself to her. She knew with certainty that he was going into danger and that he might never come back. She wanted desperately to ask questions so that she could enter this man's life even more deeply and share his danger if only in spirit.

"But if . . . if you're going to the bloody war, how can you be in London next week when I come up?"

"I'll be there."

So whatever it was was brief. That was at least something. She traced a pattern on the carpet with the toe of her shoe. She said, looking away from him:

"Are you expecting any telephone calls during the next hour from mysterious females?"

"No. Definitely not. Nobody knows I'm here." He opened his arms. "You've gone away. Come back, to me, Verity."

She could hear her housekeeper stirring in the kitchen. At any moment she would be coming in to lay the table. She said in a low voice:

"I want to. If you knew how much I wanted to, you'd be more than slightly shocked." She looked at him with a candid gaze. "Let's go out."

They left the house together hand in hand, crossing the darkness of the yard, cracking the iced puddles with the weight of their steps so that the puddles splintered and turned into frozen flowers. In the long, low-roofed shed, the shutters were bolted against the night and the bullocks stood in a long line, chewing and sometimes rattling a head-stall chain, the candle-light flickering on their straight, fat, flat backs. She was in love and frightened for her man and as shameless as Eve before the serpent came and she led the way up a ladder and into the hayloft to be alone with her lover who might die tonight. Below they could hear the rattle of the chains and smell the bullocks breathing. Mixed up with it was the smell of dung and hay and clover and roots and the burnt reek of guttering candles . . . and oh, dear God, there were candles in the Villa Mimosa, too, but the smell that went with them came out of cut-glass bottles and, anyway, the Villa Mimosa was remote from Verity by a million miles and she was his love and his only desire.

*   *   *

Because the driver was there and because of many things, she said goodbye to him formally, as if he were a person who had happened to come in for a glass of sherry.

"You won't forget to telephone me tomorrow, will you, so that we can arrange where and when to meet on Monday?"

"No, indeed. I won't forget. Goodbye, Verity."

"Goodbye, Charles."

She stood in the cold porch of her house watching the red tail-light become smaller, until it flicked out of sight. She went on standing there, listening to the sound of the car's engine until it was lost in the thunder of the silence that encompassed her. She shut the door, trying to shut out the terror of the night with it, and went upstairs. In her room she gazed for a long time at herself in the looking-glass. She was consumed with a new and immense curiosity, looking at every feature of her face, wondering. Then, suddenly, she knelt by her bed and began to cry and to pray.

* * *

At eight o'clock that night, the Commandos and Rangers paraded in full battle order on the deck of *Claddah Burn*. They wore a strange mixture of uniforms, khaki blouses over dark blue Naval jerseys and, the mark of the Commando, heavy rubber-soled boots. To the delight of the Rangers, three men from Highland regiments had insisted on their right to wear the kilt and preserved a dignified silence in response to American wolf-whistles and calls of "Hi-ya, Fanny". Live ammunition and hand grenades were distributed and, the parade dismissed, the men split into their small battle-groups and were taken to the landing craft. The boom opened. A channel had been re-swept through the minefield outside the harbour and through this the landing craft nosed gingerly to make for their rendezvous with the faster destroyers and motor launches. By a quarter to ten, the tiny armada was at sea, guns cleared and tested, dipping for France.

Operation Firefly was under way.

13: TREASURY RULING

THE Director of Finance (Z Branch) had spent the whole of his adult life in the War Office. Aged fifty-one, he took sardonic pleasure in his nickname. To be known as "Barebones Scrooge" indicated that he had served the Treasury faithfully and well. It was, he thought, a foreshadowing of that O.B.E. which would set a modest crown on his career.

In peace as in war, Humphrey Hogarth (for that was his unlikely baptismal name) had tolerantly watched the arrival and departure of countless military gentlemen. They marched ebulliently into Whitehall, rolled up their sleeves and blundered into wordy battle. Experience had taught him all the tricks of the bluff but naïve soldiery and he immediately recognized and isolated all those items which had been put in in order to be taken out. The war he waged on behalf of his mentors was one of attrition and the end was sure. He lived in Weybridge, Surrey, and in appearance was an exact replica of a clean-shaven Mr. Pooter.

During the morning of February the 27th, his confidential clerk put a TOP SECRET file from the Director of Subversive Activities into his In-tray. Scrooge disliked working on Saturdays but as this file was marked IMMEDIATE, he decided to consider it that evening in the comparative quiet of Weybridge. Strictly speaking, it was against the rules to take TOP SECRET files out of the War Office, but as the Treasury made the rules, Scrooge felt that he might allow himself a little latitude.

To his extreme annoyance he had to stand with a lot of private soldiers in the corridor of the train all the way to Weybridge. He did so while mentally drafting a complaint to the railway company. His afternoon's work in the garden was unrewarding. Dinner consisted of soup, whale steak, a tough and detestable mammal, and there was an electricity power-cut. It was, therefore, with a surgeon's zest that Scrooge picked up a fountain-pen turned scalpel and prepared to castrate the TOP SECRET file.

By a pleasant coincidence in time, Scrooge began reading at the very moment when H.M.S. *Galway Blazer* and *Coollattin* cleared the boom and tested their guns.

TOP SECRET AND IMMEDIATE
To: Director of Finance (Z)
From: Director of Subversive Activities
Para 1. *Enclosed with this file, you will find an outline plan Operation Firefly within which is contained a second plan Operation Sabine. Both Firefly and Sabine have been agreed in principle by the Chiefs of Staff.*
Para 2. *Also enclosed with this file are our more detailed pro-*

*posals for that part of the Operation Sabine for which the
War Office will be responsible.*

At this point, Scrooge idly began to read the two enclosures to
put himself, as it were, "in the picture". By the time he had
finished, he was fighting for breath. When, with the aid of two
digestion tablets, he had recovered his physical composure, he
read on:

Para 3. *You will observe that Operation Sabine presents certain
unusual features for which, as far as I am aware, there
is no exact precedent. With your longer experience of
Treasury rulings, you may however be able to guide on
our ad hoc solutions to these problems. They have been
arrived at after discussions with the military branches
concerned. A summary of these views is given below.*

"*Unusual Features . . .*" oh my sainted aunt! "*No exact precedent. . . .*" That at least was a matter for congratulation.

Para. 4. CLOTHING AND NECESSARIES. *The Director of Clothing
and Equipment appears to have decided views about
clothing for these ladies. He considers that their upper
and outer garments should be provided by a money allowance. This allowance must be sufficient to cover what we
have in view. He would deprecate what he calls "a
Windmill Standard" of outer clothing being forced upon
these ladies by any inadequacy of the allowance and
insists that some system af close inspection be instituted
to ensure that the provision (in cash and in kind taken
together) meets with minimum requirements. He doubts
whether the type of underclothing and night wear provided for the Women's Services would necessarily be
acceptable to these ladies. He is, however, very willing to
co-operate in any measures which may finally be decided
and expresses his personal interest. He is willing to
inspect. Certain extra-regulation expenditure will, no
doubt, be necessary to cover the cost of cosmetics, etc.,
which, he considers, are normally part of these ladies'
equipment and without which they would be less amen-
able to interrogation.*

"Windmill Standard" of outer clothing? Cosmetics? Did the

Director of Subversive Activities seriously think that he, Scrooge, would jeopardize his future O.B.E. by approaching the Treasury for a request for face-powder? Grimly, he turned to the next page.

Para. 5. DISCIPLINE AND RELATIVE RANK. *The Adjutant General's branches find grave difficulty in conceding Officer status to these ladies and we are thus open to any alternative suggestion which you think proper.*

*We had inclined to the view (*NOT *repeat* NOT *acceptable to Director of Women's Service) that "Madame" should enjoy the relative rank of Senior Commander (with pay and allowances appropriate to that rank) on account of her heavy responsibilities in controlling or attempting to control her little team—the members of which, we thought, should similarly have the relative rank of Subaltern.*

This, this was a personal affront. Scrooge's own unmarried sister Adelaide was a Senior Commander. She had been promoted to that rank after five selfless years devoted to the Provost Branch of the Women's Services. Was Adelaide to call "Madame" her Sister-in-Arms? Was Madame to be entitled to slap Adelaide's back? Only over Scrooge's dead body! Gritting his teeth, he read on:

The Adjutant General's branches, however, have pointed out that the application to these ladies of Section 40 of the Army Act (Neglect or Conduct to the Prejudice of Good Order and Military Discipline) and Section 16 of the same Act (Disgraceful Conduct) might well prove difficult to apply. A footnote to Section 40 provides that "neglect must be wilful or culpable and not merely the result of forgetfulness, error of judgement or inadvertence". This footnote would provide a let-out for the ladies and thus render court-martial proceeding nugatory. In all the circumstances, therefore, we would be prepared to agree that our fair visitors should be regarded as "Sutlers or Camp Followers" under Section 23 and 182 of the Army Act.

"Fair visitors" indeed! In the past, Scrooge had had to come down heavily on the incurable romanticism of the soldiery and it would give him the keenest pleasure to do so again. The whale steak lay in his stomach like a lump of lead and he thought that a turn in his freshly-turned back garden might be beneficial. He put on his overcoat and went out through the kitchen. The night was very dark and silent—until he heard the slow whooping of air-raid sirens from the darkened, distant city. A few days ago, the Germans had had the effrontery to blow in his War Office windows. They had been replaced before those of anyone else—which was something. High overhead, he heard the tiger-humming of the Nazi squadrons and then the barking of Ack-Ack batteries. He hurried indoors. He could not bear to hear, actually to hear, all that money exploding in the sky.

Para. 6. ACCOMMODATION, RATIONS, FUEL and LIGHT and USE of W.D. TRANSPORT. *Director Accommodation (Women's Services) and Director Victuals and Vehicles have collaborated on these vexed questions.*

The alternatives appear to be (a) money allowances to provide these services or (b) the establishment (for security reasons) of some simulated Villa Mimosa, made ready for these ladies at the public expense.

Either alternative is open to the gravest objection. Politically (a) money allowances offers advantages. In the case of (b) it is difficult to contemplate the position of the Secretary of State in Secret Session, defending, at the Despatch Box, the setting up of even a simulated establistment of this kind. Women Members of Parliament, it is felt, would react violently. You will no doubt therefore advise us as to the likelihood of securing Treasury approval for an adequate money allowance. As regards the use of W.D. Transport, the branch concerned suggests, without much enthusiasm, that some provision could be made enabling the ladies to ride in the front seats of certain specified W.D. Vehicles—provided always that the journey were associated with interrogation of an official nature. In this connection. . . .

Scrooge looked up from the file with annoyance. The last stick of bombs had fallen uncomfortably close. Really, he wished that the Germans had been briefed before setting out that Surrey was merely a dormitory area. He finished the file sitting in a little home-made air-raid shelter under the stairs.

> . . . *In this connection, they do not favour the indis-*
> *criminate use of W.D. transport for this—or still less for*
> *recreational purposes—even on repayment.*

May I hope to receive your comments and, I hope, your agree-
ment as the two operations in question, Firefly and Sabine, are
due to occur at a very early date?

John Southerden, Major-General,
Director of Subversive Activities.

27th February, 1944.

Scrooge took a sheet of paper and began gleefully to draft his
reply. So arctic would it be that Scrooge begged leave to doubt
whether either operation would ever take place.

*   *   *

It was some time later when Scrooge emerged from under the
stairs to the sustained soprano of the All Clear. He had put the
air-raid to good use and his official reply to General Southerden
was complete. It was, he considered, a masterpiece in repression.
So utterly astringent was it that he felt that he deserved a little
celebration. As he drank the last of the Ovaltine, he read what he
had written, mentally rubbing his hands.

To: Director of Subversive Operations.
From: Director of Finance (Z).

I am concerned as to items in Paras. 4, 5 and 6—in fact I
am concerned with every single suggestion emanating from the
Military branches.

Firstly, I must remind you that money voted by Parliament for
one purpose may, on no account, be expended on another. This
principle stems from the time when the profligate King Charles II
expended on his mistresses money which the faithful Commons
had voted for his Army. We must therefore avoid, and be seen to
avoid, any similar indiscretion. I refer to the expenditure of
public money upon what is virtually a maison tolérée *(lit:*
tolerated house) when the object in view is merely the acquisition
of information by a process of interrogation. Here are my com-
ments on your detailed suggestions.

CLOTHING AND NECESSARIES. Your para. 4.

I am at a loss to understand the reference to a "Windmill
Standard" of outer clothing. Am I to assume that female labour

in windmills in the old days was poorly clad like the sansculottes *of the French Revolution?*

On the whole, I come down in favour (if "favour" is not too strong a word) of a money allowance. I am reluctantly prepared to go to the Treasury for this. If you will submit what is fitting and if I can agree, I will put it up. Before doing so, pray read my next comment.

DISCIPLINE, RELATIVE RANK, ACCOMMODATION, RATIONS, FUEL and LIGHT and USE OF W.D. TRANSPORT. Your paras. 5 & 6.
I group your paragraphs together.

I confess that I am aghast at your proposals and those of the military branches concerned. I can almost—I repeat "almost" —bring myself to regret that there are no establishments in this country analogous to the Villa Mimosa to which these ladies could be attached for rations and accommodation. The nearest analogy is perhaps a convent—which would also go far towards solving all questions of discipline, relative rank, fuel and light and use of W.D. transport. Those who frequent the cloisters do not disdain the use of the humble bicycle. You may therefore wish to consult the Chaplain-General as to the practicability of finding a suitable cloister—which could prove a very satisfactory saving of public funds.
Until this avenue has been explored and the reactions of the Chaplain-General tested, I feel unable to approach the Treasury with your alternatives.

Humphrey Hogarth,
Director of Finance (Z).

28th February, 1944.

Something attempted, something done, had earned a night's repose. Scrooge went to bed.

14: PARACHUTIST EXTRAORDINARY

AT the guarded entrance to Tangmere airfield, Charles dismissed the car and was taken by R.A.F. transport to a single-storey building on the far fringe of the perimeter. There he was awaited by the Briefing Officer, a professionally cheerful gentleman who affected to regard Operation Sabine as a light-hearted undergraduate rag in which, alas, he was not going to be allowed to take part. With some acerbity, Charles turned down a suggestion that he should blacken his face. He consented to turn out his pockets, yielding up, with the greatest reluctance, a letter from Verity. It would be posted back to him tonight and await him at Brown's Hotel on Monday morning.

"Your team has arrived and so, by the way, has this parcel from the War Office."

Charles opened the bulky parcel. It seemed to contain six articles of women's clothing and there was a note inside which read:

> *Dear Charles:*
>
> *As it is reasonable to assume that* les girls *may be* en déshabillé *at the late hour of your arrival, I am sending you six gowns, serge, unlined, Women's Services, for the use of, so that the pretty creatures may be well wrapped up for the journey.* A bientôt!
>
>

Yours ever,
John Southerden.

"I like that," said the conducting officer. "I like it very much. I only wish I could be there to see you arrive, hung with hand-grenades, a Sten gun in one hand and a dressing-gown in the other. Your team looks as tough as they make 'em."

Eight men, their faces blackened, were standing in the shadow of the building. As Charles approached, they formed into line and Major Thayer B. Cavendish stepped forward.

"Hullo there, Major. All set and rarin' to go. Meet the boys." He led Charles along the line.

"Lieutenant Brian Manning, British Army."

"How do you do, Manning."

"Lootenant Clark H. Vance, United States Army."

"How do you do, Lootenant." Or should he have said "Mr"? Or just "Vance"? He didn't know.

"Sergeant Fergus Forbes, British Army."

"Evening, Sarn't."

"Top-Sergeant Josef Kowalski, United States Army."

"Good evening to you."

"Guardsman Terence O'Flynn, British Army."

"Good evening, O'Flynn."

"Good evening, sor. I'll thank you, sor, for leave to speak, sor?"

"Yes, O'Flynn?"

"It's not the British Army I'm in, sor. It's the Irish Guards."

"*Quis separabit?*" Charles smiled. "But I confess that I see very clearly what you mean."

"Private (First class) Izzy Cohen, United States Army."

"Good evening, Cohen."

"And this is the one reserve. Lance-Bombardier Smith, British Army."

"Good evening, Bombardier. It doesn't look as if you'll be coming with us. We've got a full house. But stand by."

"Very good, sir."

Charles stepped back a few paces and then faced the team.

"Right. Stand Easy. First of all, I take it that you've all done parachute jumps before." He paused. There was a murmur of assent. "Good. Now, the next thing I must tell you is that we only take volunteers for the sort of job we're doing and, having heard what it is, any one of you is free to back out. All clear? I'll tell you in outline what we're going to do and then go into details and show you a model.

"We're going to be dropped at eight hundred feet on to a field called Orange Blossom in the Pas de Calais. A fire is being lit on the dropping zone to guide us in. Having landed, we make our way to a house called the Villa Mimosa in which there is a Madame, a housemaid and six young women. There will also be some . . . er . . . visiting German officers, who, oddly enough, are on our side. On the other hand, if they resist, you will use force. Our job is to kidnap Madame, the housemaid and the girls—and as many German officers as we can scoop up—rush them to the coast where a motor gun-boat will be waiting and bring them to England for interrogation. The Navy, the R.A.F. and a mixed Anglo-American raiding force are combining to give us cover and a clear passage. The whole operation—which is appropriately called 'Sabine'—is regarded as being of the highest importance by the Chiefs of Staff. Any questions on that?"

A figure sprang to attention, took one pace forward and saluted.

"Forbes, sir."

"Yes, Sarn't Forbes?"

"Please, sirr, would it be in orrder to have a word with ye on your ain?"

"Certainly, Forbes. The rest of you dismiss and I'll join you in a moment inside the hut. Thayer, you take over and show them the model. Now, Forbes, what's your trouble?"

"Wi' great respect, sirr, I would like tae ask ye what sorrt o' a hoos this is?"

Charles frowned. It was a question he did not expect and he was embarrassed by it. He answered with hesitation:

"I thought I'd made that pretty clear. Its very name, Villa Mimosa, is surely indication enough."

"In other worrds, sirr, it's a hoos o' ill fame?"

"Yes," said Charles flatly. "That's one way of describing it."

"And the girrls who dwell therein," went on Sergeant Forbes sternly, "are therefore scarlet wimmen."

"I hadn't thought of them in those terms myself, Forbes, but, speaking biblically, I suppose they are."

Sergeant Forbes drew himself up. In his gaunt face, his eyes burned with all the fervour of one who had sprung from the loins of Covenanting forebears.

"Wi' great respect, sirr, I must tell ye that it's not possible for me to volunteer for this operation."

"Not possible! But——" Charles checked himself. "Of course, Forbes. I said that this was a volunteer job and so it is. We take the reserve in your place. I accept your decision without question."

"Sirr, I'd like to explain."

"You don't have to. I said it's a volunteer job."

"I'd prefer to, sirr. It's a question of principle. I'm a married man, sirr, wi' twa bairns. The day I joined the Army, I made a promise tae ma wife that I'd always keep masel' to masel' in this particular respect. Ye'll pardon me, sirr, but I would'na take kindly to consortin' wi' hoors."

They were standing facing each other in the gloom. Charles struck a match and peered above the left breast pocket of Sergeant Forbes' tunic and at the single medal ribbon that was stitched there.

"I notice," he said pleasantly, "that you've been awarded the Military Medal—and they don't give those away with the rations. I don't know what you got it for, but whatever it was, you've done a braver thing tonight. I'm proud to have met you, Forbes."

"I appreciate your attitude to ma sentiments, sirr."

"Now as to practical things. As you know all about Operation Sabine, I'm afraid you'll have to spend the night here on the air-field. Nothing personal about that. Just elementary security. And ask er . . . the reserve—what's his name?—to come and see me."

"Lance-Bombardier Smith's the name, sirr. Guid luck on the trip and guidnight, sirr."

"Goodnight, Forbes."

The door of the hut opened and shut, opened again. A figure in battledress and jumping boots came out and saluted.

"Lance-Bombardier Smith reporting, sir. You sent for me."

"Yes. One of the British team has fallen out—for wholly creditable reasons—and I want you to take his place. How do you feel about it?"

"Absolutely delighted, sir."

"You do, do you?"

There was something familiar about that voice and that phrase. A thought, an incredible thought, crossed Charles' mind and he dismissed it as absurd. But was it so absurd? Was it not absolutely and consistently in character? Again he struck a match and stared into Bombardier Smith's face. Though it was made up like a nigger minstrel, its grin was unmistakable. Charles only dropped the match when it burned his fingers. He drew a deep breath. He said:

"General Southerden, may I ask you what the hell you're doing dressed up as a Lance-Bombardier and looking like a coon?"

"Ah, hullo, Charles. I had hoped that you wouldn't penetrate my little disguise until we were airborne. I'm coming with you on Operation Sabine. I confess to you that Golden Mouse draws me to her side like a magnet."

"So you fixed Sergeant Forbes."

"I did no such thing. Forbes is the unfixable type. All I did was to exercise a little psychological skill in choosing him. I know these Covenanting Highlanders. Brave as lions, proud as Lucifer and pious as Sunday-school teachers. But let the word 'hoor' come into their heads and they're away like a redshank."

"Thank you. You've made everything crystal clear. There's only one question that remains to be answered. I consider it to be of importance. Who's commanding this team, you or I?"

"You are, Charles."

"I'm glad to hear it," said Charles grimly, "very glad indeed. To begin with, you'd better begin by addressing me as 'sir' and not 'Charles'. You're to be the first to drop—you have parachuted before, I suppose? Of course you have, you took care to tell me on the way down—and I hope you'll be the first aboard the motor gun-boat. If, in the meantime, I catch you making a pass at Golden Mouse or anyone else—and Madame, in my opinion, is more suited to your years—I'll have you court-martialled. Is that perfectly clear?"

"Yes, sir."

"Then fall in," said Charles, "shut up and keep out of Major Cavendish's sight."

He strode into the hut. The men were clustered around the model of the Villa Mimosa. He began crisply:

"May I have your attention for a moment, please? I've decided to take the reserve, Lance-Bombardier Smith, on this trip. Sorry, Sarn't Forbes, but you'll have to stand down. The Director of Subversive Activities at the War Office, *with his usual considera- tion for others,* has sent us six dressing-gowns in which to wrap up the ladies of the Villa Mimosa. Lance-Bombardier Smith is detailed both to carry and distribute these garments. The rest of us will have Sten guns and hand-grenades. Right. Major Cavendish, will you carry on with the detailed plan?"

*   *   *

It was a quarter past ten and Operation Firefly drove steadily through the darkness. The midships column consisted of the two packed landing craft, with their escort of motor launches keeping station to port and starboard. *Galway Blazer* and *Coollattin* drew circles of sea-water around them and there was little sound other than the whispering of the wind, the yielding wash of the bow-waves and the steady throbbing of the motor launches. At first there had been conversation in the landing craft and the occasional tinny whimper of a mouth organ playing *The Road to the Isles* or *Stardust*. Soon these human sounds ceased. Men were content with their own thoughts. The admission "I Love Glad" tattooed on still living skin was poignant and true, and many a man said his quiet prayers.

A light blinked.

"Galway Blazer and Coollattin to Firefly stop we are leaving you now and will pick you up on the way home stop good luck to you and singe that mans moustache."

*   *   *

Eleven o'clock dead. Time to go.

Squadron-Leader "Croppy" Nesbitt led the way with Charles, the team following, across the tarmac to the Dakota that waited at the end of the runway.

"Shouldn't take us more than forty minutes to get there," he said. "I've been before and I know the way. You're the Joe I picked up a fortnight ago from the same field. I recognized you at once. Can't you keep away from the place? Got a popsie down there?"

"Six of 'em."

"No wonder you're going back! Have you settled your order of jumping?"

"Yes. This man Bombardier Smith is the sort of honorary Wardrobe Mistress and he's going first. I'm going last. The whole stick shouldn't take more than a few seconds. Who's your despatcher?"

"Ex P.T. Instructor, a quick worker who gets on with the job. I've had the door taken off so that you can get out all the faster. It may be a bit noisy and cold but I'm afraid you'll have to put up with that. Well, here we are. Bring me back another bottle of champagne if you can."

The Ex P.T. Instructor looked like a benevolent all-in wrestler. He hooked up the eight parachutes to the static line, talking all the time. "You lucky people dropping down to a real egg omelette, a glass of red wine and a nice, warm French four-poster bed to follow, I wouldn't wonder, pardon me, sir, you're number four, that's right, there's one gentleman I know came down smackeroo on a running pheasant and he didn't go short of his supper that night, no fear, now are you all happy and comfortable, that's the ticket, first you'll hear a buzz and see a red light and as soon as that red light turns to green, well, I don't want you to leave me, gentlemen, but I think you ought to go as the old song has it, you're last out, are you, sir, last but not least as they say. . . ."

The Dakota's engines woke, the slip-stream flattening the grass. Charles looked along the men's faces. They were grim and unsmiling and only Izzy Cohen's jaws moved rhythmically. The engines swelled into a crescendo and the Dakota, her wings straining and quivering, bounded along the runway and lifted and surged into the night sky.

The timing of Firefly had worked out to the minute. It was six minutes past eleven when the motor launches' chugging died away and the landing craft came in on the tide, still miraculously unobserved. The ramps went down silently. Commandos and Rangers waded ashore and split to keep clear of the sandy bay, certain to be mined. Spikes were thrust into crevices in what looked like solid rock and ropes looped around them. Men began to climb, gripping and heaving and sweating and slipping. R.A.F. and American fighter-bombers, their engines snarling and their

cannon firing, swooped in on either flank, drowning the noise of
falling shingle and that of Sten gun barrels clinking against rock.
Only a few yards more to the barbed wire on the cliff's crust. . . .
Lance-Corporal Quiff (I love Glad) Perkins spat on his hands. At
that second a voice above challenged harshly.

"Halt! Wer da?"

Silently Perkins drew the pin out of a hand-grenade. The
spring flew back. A strong torch blazed in his face, blinding
him as he flung—and a Schmeisser opened up on him at point-
blank range. He was dead and falling down the cliff before the
grenade exploded.

Firefly was alight.

The Dakota slewed and swung in the darkness as Croppy
peered down and ahead. At last he saw what he was looking
for, a tiny flickering point of light, that flared and faded as the
wind stirred it. A buzz sounded in the freezing cabin and his
voice spoke on the intercom:

"I've picked up our beacon now and we'll be over the dropping
zone in two minutes. I'll circle it once and then come down to
eight hundred. Get ready to go, please."

Eight men moved cumbrously to the open door, where the
despatcher waited. They formed a single line, pressing tightly
against each other's back, hearts hammering, muscles taut, mouths
dry. Charles found himself yawning and hating the very guts
of the despatcher, who kept on talking when all he wanted to
do was to pray——

"You lucky people, how I envy you, arms close to your sides
now and spring to attention like you was on parade, it's easy"—
his voice rose to a sudden shout—"out, out, out, out, come on
lad, out, out, OUT."

The slipstream tossed Charles like a leaf in a thunderstorm
and then he was falling, falling, falling right into the heart of
the bloody fire, but he wasn't falling at all, thank God, he was
floating and swinging, he was the daring young man on the
flying trapeze whose movements were graceful all girls he did
please and nobody could ever steal his love away. . . .

15: RAPE OF THE SABINES

ALL day long and in the hours before waking, the amber, elusive image of Golden Mouse had haunted Colonel Otto. He despised her and he wanted her. She was with him as a wraith when he made his arrangements for tomorrow night's coup. These arrangements were harsh and practical things. Golden Mouse belonged suddenly and bewilderingly to the spirit. In the watches of the night, a startling and most disturbing idea had come to him. As a Nordic, he acknowledged it to himself with shame but his need of her transcended racial purity. It was that he should recruit Golden Mouse into his own organization and employ her as his personal assistant. Other officers of his service had "secretaries". Why not he? By becoming his servant and colleague, she would purge all past sins, and even a woman of mixed blood would be acceptable to his masters provided she were given the status of agent. He gazed into the imagined future with mounting excitement. He would install her in an apartment in Saint Germain. Dressed in her concealing gown with its innumerable buttons, she would move about and between his Louis XIVth furniture, receiving his guests with decorum, always obedient, always faithful. And there would be his journeys. . . .

At the thought of his journeys, Colonel Otto's eyes gleamed. Golden Mouse would be available to accompany him on his stealthy expeditions to Holland, to Italy, to Vienna, to the south of France—where the scent of living, growing mimosa would overwhelm the memory of the name of the house in which he saw her first. Last night, she had shyly asked for his patience—with the hint of more subtle submissions to come. He would continue to exercise that patience tonight—in the knowledge that those entrancing submissions would be made far from the brief and sordid beds of a Pas de Calais *bordel*.

The day passed slowly for Colonel Otto, as it did for others.

On that Saturday morning, Rommel had called a full conference at La Roch-Guyon and it was after dark before the staff officers arrived back to the Pas de Calais. After a long, official and dispiriting afternoon of work, the thought of the Villa Mimosa was uppermost in their minds, and one by one they were lured by its siren song. No Lorelei ever sang so sweetly.

Hans Ramberg was the first to arrive, just as the clock was striking ten. He saw Madame outside the door of her room on the landing.

"Good evening, Major," she said. "I am glad to see you. I had hoped that you would come tonight because I am giving a little private celebration."

"It couldn't be more welcome. We are all coming, Gerhard, Stefan, Fritz, Paul, all of us. If only Colonel Johnny were here, it would complete the party. I hear from Colonel Otto that Johnny has been posted to the Luftwaffe. He detests flying, poor devil." He sighed. "There was a conference at La Roch-Guyon that went on and on. The Field-Marshal is pretty gloomy about the Atlantic Wall, I can tell you, and what we need tonight is exactly what you provide—wine, women and song." He frowned. "Talking of women, I haven't seen Monique for some days. I trust she hasn't left you? But of course she hasn't. There's nowhere for her to go."

"How right you are! We are all prisoners. No, Monique hasn't left. But recently she has been helping me and I have kept her out of the Salon."

He said, with a droll look: "Come, come. You're not going to tell me that she has retired—or, even worse, reformed. I thought that the Moniques of this world never retired."

"You have little knowledge of human nature, Major. Monique *has* retired—for good. But I hear your friends arriving and I must not detain you. There is no need to order or to pay for champagne tonight. Everything is free—with the compliments of the Villa Mimosa."

"May I know what we are celebrating?"

She smiled.

"I hope to make an announcement a little later. In the meantime, *amusez-vous bien!*"

"*Merci, Madame.*"

When Colonel Otto rang the bell and was admitted by Marie, he could hear from the hall the sounds of laughter, dancing and singing upstairs. The criminals and their paramours were obviously enjoying themselves—for the last time, he reflected grimly. Tomorrow the whole collection of degenerates and traitors would be under lock and key—with one notable exception. He added his Lueger to the little armoury of weapons already hanging on hooks—as their owners would dangle on hooks in the near future! With this agreeable thought in mind he climbed the stairs, only pausing to make sure that his hip-pocket automatic was in its accustomed place. To be in uniform and unarmed gave him a sense of near-nudity.

Madame's celebration was being a huge success. The officers and girls were clustered around the piano, all of them swaying and singing, all of them with glasses in their hands. He was vastly relieved to see that Golden Mouse was amongst them. He would have found it hard to forgive and forget if she had not been in the Salon.

At his entry, Wanda slipped out of Paul's encircling arm and tripped across the floor to greet him. She kissed him with abandon, leaving the mark of her lipstick on his mouth. Her breath smelled of wine and her hair of cigarette smoke and she looked like a Bacchante. She poured him out a huge goblet of champagne and clinked glasses, clearly constituting herself his special girl. He drained his goblet and Wanda at once refilled it. Really her devotion to him was quite touching and could be put to good purpose. Having made sure that Golden Mouse had noted his arrival in the Salon, he proposed to withdraw—with Wanda. Colonel Otto considered himself an adept at the art of playing off one woman against another and his disappearance with Wanda was calculated to evoke in Golden Mouse that most potent of all stimuli—a touch of jealousy. As for Wanda herself, he proposed to save himself any possible embarrassment in the future by disposing of her in the traditional Gestapo manner. Tomorrow night, she would be shot "while attempting to escape".

Now there was no hurry, no hurry at all. The night was young, the wine was flowing and the hunchback at the piano excelled himself. Laughing, Colonel Otto suffered himself to be half-dragged towards the group and he, their potential murderer, was one with them, singing in chorus: *"Trink, trink, Brüderlein, trink. . . ."*

Colonel Otto was not the only armed man in the Salon.

*   *   *

Fifteen minutes to midnight—and the din from the Salon below was getting louder and louder.

Monique stood precariously on a heap of cushions piled on a chair that she had lifted on to the bed in the attic of the house that had once been the *mise-en-scène* of her sad livelihood. She had managed to push the attic's skylight open and by hanging with her finger-tips on the ledge—it didn't do a girl's nails any good—she could just peer out into the darkness towards the direction of the flat field where she had gone in her one moment of triumph to help Charles the British officer get away from her country's enemies.

England *was* her country. Funny how she hadn't thought of England as being her country for years and years, not really until Charles had played that tune on the piano. And she hadn't thought of anyone being her enemy either. Foreigners weren't anything special. They were just men who were nice or nasty, generous or stingy and she'd met both sorts. In her adult years, there was hardly any manifestation of the tiger, the ape and the donkey who dwelled within the skins of men that she hadn't met. And it wasn't a foreigner who had let her down in the first place. It was an Englishman, a true-blue Briton with a bow-tie and a little ginger moustache and a way with the ladies; a proper Charley he had been, if ever there was one. In thinking of England, she thought of mean streets and garish dance-halls and the awful disapproval of that awful old lady, Gran, who was always telling her that she'd come to no good and that being in a troup of entertainers wasn't respectable. Well, Gran was right. She *had* come to no good.

The night was ever so dark. She could hear the noise of gunfire from the coast. Men again! Always either fighting or making passes. Oh, it was lovely to be up here in the attic and not down in the Salon with the others. And then suddenly she heard a special sound in the night sky. It was a separate and individual sound, the sound she was listening for, and she heard it to the exclusion of the far-away shooting and shouting and the thumping in the Salon below. A single aircraft was up there and it wasn't flying very high. With all her strength, she pulled herself up and stared into the blackness. For a moment she could see nothing. She shut her eyes and counted ten. When she opened them, she almost cried aloud. The tiny flicker of a distant fire had started and was getting bigger and flaring as petrol was poured and the noise of the aircraft was getting louder as it came lower and lower. . . .

Monique let go of the sill and clambered down. She was shaking all over as she opened the door and began to descend the steep stairs to the first floor and the corridor of shut doors where she once used to sleep. She passed her old room with averted eyes and reached the stairs leading down to the Salon.

Someone was coming up—no, it was two people, a man and a woman. She pressed back against the wall to let them pass, not looking at them but at the floor.

A man's voice, strange to Monique and sharp with suspicion, inquired:

"Hullo. Who's this?"

Wanda answered contemptuously:

"She used to be one of us, but now she has taken the veil. Her name is Monique and she helps Marie with the sweeping and cleaning. Come, Otto."

"Are there any others whom I haven't seen?"

"No. Only this one. And you, Monique, what are you doing out of your attic?"

"I am going to see Madame."

"See that you keep your nose out of the Salon. It is no place for a novice tonight."

The two moved on along the corridor and Monique crept downstairs. Madame was at her desk.

"Yes, Monique?"

"The fire is alight, Madame."

"And the aircraft?"

"It flew low over the fire. Now it has gone."

"Good." Madame's face was impassive. "Return to the attic and wait. We shall see Charles again—very soon."

"Yes, Madame."

As she tip-toed back to the attic, she heard Wanda and the man she had called "Otto" laughing in her room.

*　　*　　*

"No bones broken?"

"No. I guess we're all O.K."

"Thank God for that! Keep close behind me."

When he was still a hundred yards away from the Villa Mimosa, Charles Addison heard the muffled stamping and the laughter and the singing. He stopped and his team gathered silently around him. He spoke in a whisper.

"Well, this is it. Thayer, I want you, Manning and Kowalski to guard the back door. If anyone tries to make a break for it— shoot only as a last resort. Any man, I mean. If it's a woman, just scoop her up. I'm going in by the front door with you, Vance, and you, O'Flynn, and you Lance-Bombardier—what's your name?—Smith. Got your dressing-gowns ready?"

"Yes, sir."

"What's that other parcel you're carrying, that flat thing?"

"Just a little idea of my own, Charles."

"Don't call me 'Charles', or you'll find yourself in the glass-house for insolence. What's that parcel?"

"Sorry, sir. It's a sort of . . . well, a sort of notice. It's quite inoffensive, I assure you, sir."

"That's a change. Georges, where's your transport?"

"Backed up against the far side of the Villa." He chuckled. "It's the Black Maria."

"How the hell did you get hold of it?"

"Nothing easier. It always fills up in a garage run by one of my boys. This evening my chap slugged the driver and I pinched his clothes. They don't fit very well but they'll serve."

"They suit you very well, if I may say so. Cohen, you stand by the Black Maria and shovel the boys and girls inside as they come out. Any questions?"

"I'll thank you, sor, for leave to speak, sor?"

"Yes, O'Flynn."

"Sor, I wouldn't want to be ridin' inside a yoke the like of a Black Maria." He crossed himself furtively in the darkness. "Me Da, sor, was a divil in the drink and thim yokes is terrible bad luck, sor."

"I quite understand, O'Flynn. My compliments to your father. Sorry I even suggested it. On the way to the coast, you and Cohen sit in front with the driver. Right. Now we all know what to do, so let's get on with it."

Silently the group split up. Charles walked up the familiar path to the Villa Mimosa and rang the bell.

The door opened, releasing a surge of noise. Charles stepped swiftly into the hall. Old Marie peered at him and gasped. He said to her:

"You remember me, Marie? Charles the pianist. You are to go with this gentleman here. You will come to no harm. Vance, take her outside and hand her over to Cohen." He collected the row of weapons off their hooks. "Chuck these in the front of the Black Maria and come back."

"O.K., Major."

The smell of the Villa was instantly familiar to Charles' nostrils. It was a mixture of stale scent and candle-grease. The three men stood listening to the thumping upstairs and to the beating of their own hearts. Vance came back. He said in a whisper:

"She's fainted. Izzy's taking care of her."

"Fine. Now follow me upstairs, all of you, and don't make a sound."

The door of the Salon was closed. Charles stood for a moment on the landing as Guardsman O'Flynn shifted his Sten gun from the crook of his right arm to his left. Then he rapped on Madame's door.

"*Entrez.*"

Madame rose from her chair, a stately figure in black silk.

"Good evening, Charles." A tiny frown passed over her waxen face with its plucked eyebrows. "Forgive me. I should have addressed you as 'Major'. I am enchanted to see you. What are your orders?"

She asked the question calmly, but Charles could see the slight trembling of her fingers on the desk.

"Good evening, Madame. I give you no orders. I ask for your help. How many people are here and who are they?"

"Four of my *pensionnaires* are in the Salon. Monique is in the attic and"—her thin lips curled in disgust—"Wanda has taken Colonel Otto to her room. As for the officers, they are Major Hans, Gerhard, Stefan, Fritz and Paul."

"Which is Wanda's room?"

"Gaston knows. He has asked me to request that he be allowed to . . . to deal with the two alone. He is armed and prepared."

"So be it. You have authority and the girls will obey you. Will you please come with us into the Salon? I want you to order them, the girls, to line up along the left wall. My friends and I will look after the men." He smiled. "Are you prepared to do this?"

"Certainly, Major."

She crossed the landing and quietly opened the door of the Salon.

Looking over Madame's shoulder, Charles saw a fantastic sight. Holding each other by the waist, a chain of men and girls wove in and out of the furniture, stamping and yelling the words of the Horst Wessel song pounded out by Gaston on the piano. One officer—it was Gerhard—was standing on a chair. He had combed his black forelock down over his forehead and his upper lip was smudged with the travesty of a moustache in grotesque imitation of Hitler. At his shout of "*Halt! Sieg Heil!*" the music stopped and everybody flung up a right arm and screamed "*Heil Hitler!*"

Then the music started again and the human daisy-chain straightened to goose-step round the room.

"Paul, you take the right, O'Flynn the left. Smith come behind me."

Charles stepped into the Salon of the Villa Mimosa.

For a moment nobody saw him. Then Lucille, who was leading the chain, looked in his direction. Her mouth opened. She glanced to right and left to see two men in foreign uniforms, their faces blackened, Sten guns at the ready.

She wriggled herself out of the fingers clasping her waist and stood stock-still. A delighted smile spread over her face.

"Quiet, children! Quiet—and regard who has come back to us! It is Charles himself, our beloved pianist." She advanced a step and put her head on one side. "*Bonsoir, chic type.* You remember me? Lucille."

The goose-stepping chain broke asunder. Gaston shut the piano lid with a slam and darted across the Salon to Charles' side, drawing a revolver. He swung round on his heel to face the bewildered room. Madame's voice was calm and authoritative in the deep-breathing hush.

"*Mes filles,* the Villa Mimosa is finished. Our last party is over. *Les jeux sont faits.* I order you to stand in a line along the left wall. You too, Lucille. At once."

As the four girls disentangled themselves, Charles spoke curtly:

"Officers to the right. Please do not compel us to use force. Thank you. We have all met before, gentlemen. You and I, Major Hans, are specially old friends. Now listen to me. The Villa Mimosa is surrounded by British and American parachutists and escape is impossible. It is in your own interests not to resist. Your activities are known to the Gestapo and if you were to remain in France for even a few more hours, you would meet a Nazi hangman. Your friend Colonel Johnny has been executed already. I give you my word of honour that this is true. Arrangements have been made to take you to England immediately by sea. There you will be treated as prisoners of war. O'Flynn."

"Sor."

"Watch that man in the chair."

"Me eye's upon him, sor."

Gerhard, caricature of Hitler, had bent his knees. Now, with a grunt, he flung himself bodily at Charles. O'Flynn took a swift pace to the right and his mighty fist flashed upwards. There was a sickening sound like a butcher splitting a shin-bone and

Gerhard staggered back wiping the blood off his mouth. Elsa, who loved him, ran to him and put her arms around him, sobbing and gulping. Hans Ramberg, his face ashen, was staring at Charles incredulously and in the slanting eyes of Golden Mouse there was a great brightness as she saw her long journey's end.

"One more thing before we start on our way. A distinguished General from the British War Office has thought fit to equip the ladies with garments for the sea-voyage. Lance-Bombardier Smith."

"Sir."

"Distribute your offerings."

"Sir."

As General Southerden advanced into the Salon, Lucille threw back her champagne-coloured mop of hair and laughed out loud.

"Figure to yourselves, children. *Enfin,* we go to England. We go to visit Winston Churchill and—Sherlock Holmes. *Quel joie, enfants!* In England are not only the English but also Americans, thousands upon thousands of Americans, all of them with dollars and silk stockings, all of them lusty millionaires. In England nobody will cut off our hair because of revenge. Rejoice, children!" She turned her gaze on the shocked and white-faced German officers. "As for you, *Messieurs,* at last I can say what has always been in my heart. *A bas les Boches!* Charles, consider me at the disposal of the Allies." She looked at the dressing-gown offered her by General Southerden. "And you, *mon petit,* what is this? A dish-cloth? Do you seriously expect a woman of France to arrive in England to visit Winston Churchill wearing a dish-cloth? You are out of your mind, *mon petit caporal.* Present it to Marie in the kitchen."

"Gaston."

"Yes, Charles."

"There are two more upstairs.. You know where they are."

Gaston grinned, flashing his teeth.

"I know only too well. My little sweetheart Wanda and her Gestapo lover are together."

"Take one of my men and bring them down."

"No, Charles, I go alone. This is my personal affair and my pleasure." He raised his revolver. "I have this and the *cochon* upstairs has nothing. I do not think Wanda will laugh at my hump tonight. . . ."

*　　*　　*

Colonel Otto heard the music and the thumping stop, heard
the slam of the piano lid. He said sharply to Wanda:

"Why are they suddenly silent?"

She sat up in bed, clasping her knees.

"I don't know—nor do I care. Come to me, Otto."

"But listen."

"There is nothing to listen to. Come to bed. Or do you want
to go downstairs and dance with your Chinese girl? I saw your
eyes when you looked at her."

"You talk like a fool."

"Me! You call me a fool when it is you who are standing half-
dressed in the cold, listening to nothing. Come to bed, I say."

Colonel Otto crossed the bedroom in his bare feet and half
opened the door and listened. From below, he could hear a man
talking in French. It was as if this man had commanded silence
and was addressing the others. His voice was unknown to Otto.
Then there was a jumbled sound and staggering footsteps immediately followed by a woman's pitiful sobbing. Colonel Otto's eyes
narrowed. He crossed the room to a chair. From the hip-pocket
of his trousers he pulled his automatic and clicked off the safety-
catch. He said to Wanda:

"Come to the door and listen."

Grumbling, she got out of bed, put on a flowered dressing-gown
and thrust her painted toe-nails into sandals.

"Is my bed not warm enough for you—that you must stand
listening at a door. I thought you were a great Colonel. Instead,
I find that you are a great coward. And that pistol of yours!"
Her lips curled. "This is a house of women—*mon colonel.*"

"Be quiet and listen. Who is that talking?"

"Who indeed? How should I know?" She cocked her head on
one side. She frowned and a little impish grin settled on the
corner of her mouth. She shrugged. "It could be the voice of
Charles. Our dear friend Charles."

"Who is Charles?"

"One who used to play the piano here. We all thought he had
been sent to Germany." She twined her arms around his neck.
"Do I no longer please you that you——?"

He gripped her wrist, freeing himself from her embrace.

"Leave me alone, damn you. Something is happening down
there and you wish to keep me here. If it is a trick and if you
have any part in it, I promise you that it will go hardly for you.
I am going down to the Salon."

"You are going down—like that! You wish to hold me up to shame me in a respectable house. You are not a man. You are a pig." She darted out of the door screaming "Madame, Madame——"

At the top of the stairs the hunchback, Gaston, was standing with a revolver in his hand and a grin on his face.

Wanda stopped half way between the two men and pressed herself against the wall, whimpering.

Colonel Otto fired first. In the narrow corridor, the bang was deafening. Gaston lurched against the banisters, coughed and spat out a mouthful of blood. He steadied himself and, with his maimed finger, pressed the trigger of his revolver again and again. Colonel Otto's shooting became wild. There were still two unspent cartridges in his automatic when he sagged and folded over at the hips and collapsed on the floor like a punctured rubber doll.

Nobody ever knew whose bullet killed Wanda.

* * *

In her English south coast port, the motor gun-boat started up engines a few minutes before midnight. Exact timing was essential to the success of Operation Sabine and the Captain cast off on the stroke of twelve o'clock. The vessel made her leisured way out of harbour. Once out of the swept Channel through the minefield, she cleared her guns, did a short, testing speed-burst and settled down on a steady course, churning up a glimmer of phosphorescence in her wake.

On the bridge the young Captain talked to the Coxswain, explaining his plan.

"I'm going to stop and cut engines about two cables offshore. Then we'll lower the dory and Number One will take her in quietly with Wilmot and Earley while we loaf around and wait for Number One's signal. I expect about twenty passengers in all, boys and girls mixed, so it'll mean two trips in the dory. All officers, British, American and German, will travel in the wardroom with Madame. Other ranks and popsies in the mess deck. Looks pretty cosy down there, don't you think?"

"Very snug indeed, sir." He chuckled. "What I like best is the notice over the heads: '*Toilette des Dames.*' Pardon the liberty, sir, but you are a one!"

"Yes," said the Captain modestly. "Came to me all of a flash, that did. '*Toujours la politesse.*' And talking of flashes, Coxswain, Operation Firefly appears to be getting under way."

The M.G.B. had been doing a steady twenty knots and had passed mid-Channel. Now the muffled light of the Pas de Calais was in view. Star shells were flinging cascades of light into the sky over the far cliffs. Already the sounds of the land battle rolled across the salt, the sniggering of machine guns and the grunt and crump of three-inch mortars. Overhead, Royal Air Force and American fighter-bombers appeared to be having it all their own way, hammering and blasting and scorching a path between Commandos and Rangers.

The Captain addressed himself to the wheelhouse.

"How are we doing, Number One?"

The First Lieutenant made a rapid calculation from the spread chart.

"Just over five miles offshore, sir."

"Let me know when we're one mile off."

"Aye aye, sir."

The Captain rang down SLOW AHEAD to the engine room and the wind blew less strongly in their faces. Comparative quietness settled over the motor gun-boat. A gull, frightened by the firing on shore, took off from her nest in the cliffs and flew over the vessel, protesting. Captain Tim glanced up at the pleasant, peaceful sound. Enemy gull? Gull of the French Resistance? *Mouette maquisarde?* Or just gull complaining at the violence of men? A stickler for the ancient courtesies, the Captain had managed to get together a small posy of early primroses and snow-drops and these he proposed to present to Madame as soon as she stepped aboard one of H.M. ships—with the compliments of Their Lordships. This whole adventure was very much after his own heart and as his craft thrust her bows into the light swell, he murmured to himself:

> "... *English posies*
> *Kent and Surrey may;*
> *Violets from the undercliff*
> *Drenched in Channel spray....*"

But he should be remembering his duties as a host rather than quoting verse.

"Coxswain."

"Sir?"

"You got some of that black stuff women put on their eye-lashes?"

"I did, sir. And when I asked for it, the girl in the shop gave me ever such a look."

"In fact she misjudged you, Coxswain."

"She certainly did, sir." He added bitterly: "Me—of all people!"

Number One's voice spoke from the wheelhouse.

"Captain, sir."

"Yes, Number One."

"One mile off, sir."

"Thank you. Coxswain, stand by to lower the dory as soon as we stop."

"Aye aye, sir."

From the shore, the sounds of firing had become fitful and then, suddenly, there was a mighty explosion on the right flank followed by a wild outburst. The Captain rang down STOP to the engine room and the M.G.B. eased and rocked a little as the waves slapped her sides. The dory splashed into the water and Number One and two ratings jumped into her and chugged off into the dark.

"Now I'm going to circle very slowly. Signalman, keep your eyes peeled for a blue flash from the shore."

"Aye aye, sir."

He rang down SLOW AHEAD and the M.G.B. took up her stealthy patrol.

* * *

On shore, surprise had been complete.

The Germans were confused and uncertain as to the scale of the attack and threw up star shells to alert the area and to summon reinforcements. With great restraint, the Rangers held their fire until they reached the pillboxes that defended the naval gun on their flank. Then and only then did they open up with all they had. What had looked like a single attack became two separate battles and the Germans yielded ground yard by yard as they waited for the Panzers that were already clanking up from the south to surround and seal off the widening perimeter.

A Black Maria with a blinking searchlight on its roof swept imperiously past one of these clanking columns and was brought to a standstill by the leading Panzer slewed sideways across the narrow road. The driver of the Black Maria jumped down from the cab shouting, "Gestapo!" and waving furiously at the Panzer crew. From inside they could hear the pounding of fists and the yelling of men's and women's voices and they made haste to clear the way. Battle or no battle, that was a vehicle that no man would dare halt or delay. The driver climbed back and manoeuvred his huge prison van past. As it crunched in the icy ditch, the window of the cab was slid open and a genial voice said in what sounded like English, "And a very happy New Year to yiz all." A hand came out and lobbed something that rolled under the Panzer's hull.

The Black Maria was several yards away and gathering speed before the grenade exploded.

*   *   *

The First Lieutenant saw an enormous vehicle that looked like a furniture van sink axle-deep in the wet sand and stop. He stepped forward and inquired politely:

"Major Addison's party?"

"Yes. Sorry we're five minutes late. Got held up on the way."

"That's all right, sir." Georges had unlocked the door of the Black Maria and the First Lieutenant watched with amazement as a string of men and women assembled in the gloom. "How many are you in all, sir?"

"Twenty-one."

"That means two trips in the dory and I'm afraid you'll have to wade out. It's only a few yards and it's not very deep."

"Right. German officers first, with you, Manning, Kowalski, Cohen and O'Flynn. Now, gentlemen, one after another please and, I repeat, don't make us use force."

The M.G.B., a blue light flashing from her bridge, nosed in shore as the prisoners and their guards waded into the sea and climbed aboard the dory. As it vanished, Charles gave his orders.

"We don't want the girls to get their feet wet so we'll take them out to the dory piggy-back. Thayer, you carry Golden Mouse. Vance, I'm allotting Lucille to you and then I want you to come back for Magda. Georges, you can take Elsa and I'll take Monique. All clear?"

"Er . . . what about me?" said General Southerden plaintively. "Don't I get anybody?"

"You certainly do. You get Marie first and then come back for Madame. Lucky old you. Think you can manage it?"

"I'm not sure. With great respect, Madame's a bit of a heavy-weight. I think I'd be safer with Golden Mouse, honestly I do."

"Ah—but would Golden Mouse be safe with you? I doubt it. You have your orders, Bombardier."

"I look forward more than I can say," said General Southerden with feeling, "to meeting you in the War Office on Monday morning—sir."

"And I you—Bombardier." He turned to the girls. *"Ecoutez, Mesdemoiselles. . . ."*

The dory came back. With a giggle and a cry of *"Allez-oop"* Lucille mounted on Vance's back and he walked into the sea. He put her into the dory, passing Thayer with Golden Mouse as he came back for Magda. Georges and a sobbing, frightened Elsa splashed waist-deep in the ebb as General Southerden approached Marie with distaste.

Monique was standing alone. Charles said to her in English: "Come on, Monique. Up you jump."

"Sir . . . you haven't told anyone about me, have you?"

"No. Not a soul."

"Because I'd . . . I'd rather die—like . . . like Gaston."

"Nobody will ever know. I promise you." He bent his broad back. "Come on, Monique. We've got to hurry."

She climbed on his back and put her thin arms around his neck. He waded into the sea. Only one person was left—Madame —and a breathless General Southerden was already on his way back for her. He saluted her with formality and said in what he hoped was perfect French:

"Voulez-vous monter sur mon dos, si'il vous plaît?"

He turned round and bent double. Madame shrugged and lifted her skirt. She was about to accept General Southerden's invitation when a strong searchlight blazed on the cliff-top and cast a dazzling, spreading beam on the dark waters of the bay. The unexplained light from the M.G.B.'s bridge had been spotted and the Germans were looking for what could be the invasion fleet. Charles shouted from the dory:

"Hurry up for God's sake."

"Coming, sir."

With Madame on his back, General Southerden staggered into the curling surf. The searchlight fell short of the M.G.B. and danced on and steadied and settled on the dory. Almost immediately, a hose of machine-gun fire ripped into the shallow water. General Southerden lurched forward, pitching Madame head-

first into the sea. The dory swung and Charles leapt in, grabbing
Madame and half-lifting, half-shoving her over the gunnel. He
seized General Southerden under the arms and hoisted him on
board. He spat out a mouthful of sea-water and said anxiously:

"You're not hit are you, sir?"

"No. Put my foot in a blasted hole and ricked my ankle. Let's
get to hell out of here."

The dory drifted out to sea as two power-worked double
Oerlikons on the M.G.B. got the searchlight's range and blew it
and its crew into what they hoped was eternity.

The girls of the Villa Mimosa clambered up the short rope
ladder and stood in a bewildered group on the M.G.B.'s deck.

"All aboard?" said Captain Tim. "Good, We'll abandon the
dory." He rang down SLOW AHEAD and the bow-wave lifted.

"Steady as you go, Coxswain. Ladies down the forward hatch,
please, and officers in the wardroom. Ah, this must be Madame.
Excusez-moi but it looks as though you'd swum out to the dory.
Cookie will get you some blankets and cocoa. In the meantime,
please accept this . . . er . . . little bouquet—with the compliments of the Royal Navy."

"*Merci, mon Commandant.* You are too amiable. No, I did not
swim out to the little boat. I was *jetée*—thrown into the sea by
this . . . this gentleman."

"Tut, tut. How very careless." The Captain glanced at General
Southerden, whose lips were twisting with pain. He said sharply:
"Are you all right, Corporal?"

"Pretty well all right, Ricked my bloody ankle that's all."

"Don't use words like that to me. You've got no damn right to
talk like an officer."

"Sorry, sir."

"You'd better lie down in my cabin and someone will come
and look at it once we're under way. By the way, haven't I seen
you somewhere before?"

"No, sir," said General Southerden. "Quite categorically—no,
sir."

"You seem very sure about it."

"I am, sir."

It was Madame who at once volunteered to render first aid.
Swathed in a blanket—she had refused absolutely to divest herself of any single, saturated garment in the proximity of men—
she unlaced General Southerden's boot, took off his sock and

tightly bandaged the ankle. Cocoa and "medicinal brandy" were produced and, as Madame withdrew, Charles said with solicitude:

"How do you feel, sir?"

"Splendid, Charles. Madame is a remarkable woman. Beautiful hands, and fingers like thistle-down. Is there anything left in that bottle?"

"I don't think you ought to have any more, sir. Can't have one of my team coming ashore both lame *and* tight."

"Rubbish, Charles. Pour me out a glass at once. Thank you." He raised himself gingerly on one elbow. "Look here, I've been thinking about this. We've got to keep my part in this dark. We've simply got to. If Monty ever found out that I'd been dropped on the Villa Mimosa and ricked my ankle while carrying a middle-aged lady piggy-back into the sea—well, I don't suppose he'd exactly throw his beret into the air and cheer. It isn't the sort of thing that would appeal to his somewhat astringent sense of humour. He'd feel that 'The Lord, Mighty in Battle' wouldn't approve. As well as that, I'm meant to be chairborne."

"How will you say you did it?"

"Tripped over a pew while taking up the collection at Matins. That ought to get me promotion." The strains of *Alexander's Ragtime Band* played on a gramophone sounded faintly from the messdeck. "Sounds as if there's quite a party going on below," he said wistfully. "Do you think I could get my boot on again?"

"Certainly not. You stay here and rest that ankle of yours. I'll nip down and see what's going on."

"Give my love to Golden Mouse. Ask her to come and sit by the patient's bedside and tell her not to bother about bringing a bunch of grapes."

"I'll do no such thing. One more word out of you and I'll send in Marie the housemaid."

Charles went through the wheelhouse and down to the messdeck. The M.G.B. was cracking along at 1,800 revs now, with her nose well up and her stern well down, kicking up a peacock's tail of soap-suds, smacking the steepish swell, roaring like a lion. The First Lieutenant looked up from his chart, grinned at him and jerked up one thumb. The record of *Alexander's Ragtime Band* had screeched to an end and was replaced by *The Teddy-Bears' Picnic*. It was to the thumping of this that Charles entered the narrow room.

The music came from an ancient gramophone with an enormous horn. A plaque on the sound-box said that it and the records had been DONATED BY THE LADIES OF MID-BEDS who could hardly have foreseen that the instrument would ever be put to this use. Lucille, who had discarded her serge dressing-gown, was dancing a fox-trot up and down the sloping floor with Guardsman O'Flynn, and Magda was doing her best to teach Izzy Cohen the *Csárdás*. Monique and Golden Mouse sat silently side by side while Elsa repaired the ravages to her tear-stained face and swollen eyelids by liberal applications of mascara. It was quite extraordinary to realize that the M.G.B. was at sea, at war and at action stations and that Operation Sabine was nearing its end.

Charles crossed the floor and sat down beside Monique. She asked at once:

"How's your friend, sir? The one that hurt his foot."

"He'll be all right, Monique. He was lucky. It's only a ricked ankle. He'll have to hobble around for a day or two. That's all."

"I'm ever so sorry."

"It's not serious. But tell me, how do you feel yourself?"

"A bit frightened actually, sir."

"Frightened of what, Monique? The dangerous bit's over."

"Not for me it isn't. Not by a long way. You don't know Gran."

"No, that's true. But we'll fix Gran—somehow. Don't worry. The secret's ours." He spoke across her to Golden Mouse: *"Et vous, Mademoiselle?"*

"Thank you, *Monsieur*. Me, I am extremely content. Because I have been wicked for a long time, I have not considered myself worthy to approach the Deity with my prayers. But He, whoever He may be, has heard the words I left unsaid and it is by His Hand that I am here. I bow in submission and in gratitude."

"It is by His Hand that we are all here, Golden Mouse."

She looked at him with bright, slanting eyes. Then her lashes dropped.

"You are right, *Monsieur*. I am justly reproved for thinking only of myself. Forgive me."

He smiled at her and stood up and used her own humble phrase. "I am your servant."

As Charles recrossed the floor, Lucille wriggled from Guardsman O'Flynn's reluctant arms and put her pretty, laughing face to his.

"Eh bien, beau musician! Are you not going to dance with me, Lucille, who saw you first?" She pirouetted and waved her fingers to the scratched overture of *The Gondoliers*. "Come."

Charles shook his head.

"Sorry, Lucille. Some other time. I've got to go and talk to the German officers."

" 'The German officers'," she said scornfully. "You mean our prisoners. Tell them from me, a Frenchwoman, *à bas les Boches*!"

"I never knew Frenchwomen were so tough."

He went back through the wheelhouse and up to the bridge where Major Cavendish was drinking cocoa as he peered into the racing dark. Charles touched him on the shoulder.

"Can you come into the wardroom for a minute or two?"

"Sure, Charles."

The German officers were sitting in a dejected group, staring at the floor. At Charles' entry, they stood up. Charles spoke in French:

"Which of you is the senior German officer?"

After a moment's hesitation, Colonel Fritz stepped forward.

"I am."

"Then it is to you I speak. There is no need for me to introduce myself again. You all knew me as the pianist of the Villa Mimosa, as 'Charles'. My name is Addison and I am a British officer. This is Major Cavendish, of the United States Army. After arrival in England you will be questioned as prisoners of war. That is the normal procedure. But I suggest to you, Colonel, that the situation between us is far from normal. You were not taken on the field of battle—but . . . elsewhere. I beg of you therefore to listen to what I have to say and to believe in my sincerity." He paused. All eyes were upon him. He went on slowly:

"I am in a unique position to know that we, all of us, no matter what uniform me wear, are dedicated to the same cause. Our common purpose is peace and the lifting of an intolerable and obscene burden off the shoulders of men. It is in your power to help us to achieve this. I hope with all my heart that you will not withhold this help. That is all. And now, sir, have I your permission to speak personally to Major Ramberg?"

Colonel Fritz said stiffly:

"That is as Major Ramberg wishes."

Charles looked directly at Hans Ramberg. He said in English: "Well?"

Hans Ramberg hesitated. Then he too spoke in English, groping for half-forgotten words:

"Please to say what you wish in the presence of my brother-officers. We . . . we are one."

"Very well. It is this. When you believed me to be a French

watchmaker, you treated me with courtesy and indeed generosity."
He smiled. "The sausages you gave me that day in the Manoir
were a God-send to a hungry man. In the Villa Mimosa, you
honoured me with your confidence. These things will not be
forgotten. Nor can I forget the moment when I saw you first. I
too was up at Oxford, but not at your college. You were playing
a mandolin on the terrace of the Trout at Godstow one summer
night long before the war. Please remember those days and help
us to restore them."

With Thayer he went up on deck. The M.G.B. had slackened
speed as she neared the minefield and the harbour, and it was
possible to talk in the gusty dark.

Thayer said reflectively:

"Everything's happened so darned fast. I sorta feel as if we
hadn't left England yet and yet here we are almost home and
dry. There's only one thing that I'm real sorry about."

"You're thinking of Gaston."

"I certainly am. I'd looked forward to shaking that little guy's
hand."

"That 'little guy' as you call him was no ordinary man—and
when I say that I'm not thinking of his hump. I'm thinking of
him, and in the little time I knew him I got to know him very
well. In his heart, Gaston was a soldier condemned by his shape
to play a piano. Well, he achieved more than he'd ever hoped
for. He died in action. God rest his brave soul."

A distant light blinked from the shore and was answered by
the signalman on the M.G.B.'s bridge. The Captain rang down
SLOW AHEAD and the bow-wave diminished. Charles found himself
yawning. Operation Sabine was over. He had no sense of elation
or triumph as the M.G.B. steadied in the sheltered waters of the
harbour. He only wanted to go to bed and sleep and sleep. He
saw the vast hull of the depot ship and he heard ropes thudding
on the M.G.B.'s deck as the crew, their vigil at an end, stood
down from the guns.

"CUT ENGINES."

The grumble and bubbling stopped and the sound of English
voices was clear in the quiet night. From the galley of the depot
ship came the smell of fish and chips.

16: OPERATION FATTED CALF

Action was followed by reaction, climax by anti-climax. After the Lord Mayor's Show—the dung-cart.

Charles woke up in Brown's Hotel at the entry of Guardsman Pegg. During the very few hours he had been in bed, he had slept badly, confused and wrestling with half-waking dreams in which he was either falling through the sky or swimming endlessly in a drowning sea. He sat up in bed, his dark hair tousled, his eyes bright and staring.

"Good morning, sir, and a very nice morning it is, too. You look as if you'd been having a bit of a night out, if I may say so. Cup of black coffee 'ud do you the world of good. That or a brandy and port mixed, same as the Adjutant has. You seen the news, sir?"

"No. What's happened?"

"Big raid on the French coast. Us and the Yanks. I've brought you up the paper."

Charles skimmed the meagre report. A mixed force of British and U.S. troops, with air and naval support, had landed on the Pas de Calais coast late last night and, having successfully achieved all their objects, had withdrawn in the early hours of the morning. During the course of the raid, two big naval guns had been destroyed, a Radar station had been attacked and much valuable equipment brought home. Heavy casualties had been inflicted on the enemy. British and American losses were slight. A list of those killed, wounded or missing would be issued later.

Charles put down the paper. He could hear Pegg moving about the bathroom and the noise of water gushing. *"Killed, wounded or missing."* He said the words aloud with dawning horror. Somehow it had never occurred to him that men might die because he had once wheeled a bicycle past the Villa Mimosa. He was sick at heart. How many would never hear the sound of gushing water again—or any other sound? In God's name, how many wives had been widowed to clear a path for the human rag-tag and bobtail snatched out of a French *bordel*?

Pegg's head came round the bathroom door. He inquired with some suspicion:

"Pardon me, sir, you weren't by any chance on last night's lark, were you, sir?"

Charles shook his head slowly.

"No, Pegg. I wasn't on that lark, I . . . I was on another lark."

"Ah well, as I said before, sir, you'll be twice the man on a cup of black coffee—or the other thing, with a raw egg beaten up in it. Your bath's ready, sir, so if there's nothing else. . . ."

"No. Nothing else. Thank you so much for doing my uniform. See you tomorrow morning."

"You will, sir."

When Pegg had gone, he telephoned to Verity. Her voice answered at once and he knew that she had been agog for his call. Yes, he was back from wherever he'd been and was in Brown's Hotel, safe in bed. No, he hadn't been on that raid, at least not exactly. How had she slept? Oh, oh, oh. That wasn't too good. When was she coming up?

"First thing tomorrow morning. Will you be terribly busy being mysterious during the week?"

"I have got several people to interview and I shall have to be 'on call', so to speak. Big things are afoot in London. It's the same old thing, 'the bloody war'. But at least it isn't being fought on the battlefield this time. I am counting the hours till you come."

He put down the receiver. Now that Operation Sabine was over, there could be no possible reason for being secretive with Verity any more. If he was going to share his life with her—and that was his most ardent intention—he proposed to take her completely into his confidence and tell her the whole truth about the Villa Mimosa. Once he had done that, he would return to the battalion and start being a soldier again. That was what he had joined the army for. He hadn't joined it to play a piano in a bawdy house or to shovel five women in dressing-gowns into a stolen Black Maria.

He was in his bath when General Southerden arrived, an immaculate figure in uniform. Could it be true that this was the self-same black-faced Lance-Bombardier who, a few hours ago, had pitched Madame head-first into the sea? So resplendent did the General look that Charles had to remind himself that a salute would be inappropriate when all he had on was a towel around the torso.

"Good morning, Charles," said the General genially. "I thought I'd set your mind at rest by telling you at once that I've decided to overlook the numerous incivilities you offered me last night."

He waved a tolerant hand. "Heat of the moment, that sort of thing. Forget it."

"You are very kind, sir. Very kind indeed." He coughed. "And how is Lance-Bombardier Smith's ankle this morning?"

"You will be grieved to hear that the poor fellow died last night and was cremated immediately. R.I.P. Very sad. *Dulce et decorum*, etcetera."

"In return for accepting Lance-Bombardier Smith's demise, sir, I have a favour to ask of you."

"Ask it. And get dressed like a good chap. Thayer will be here in ten minutes."

"Well, it's this. You know I'm going to marry a girl called Verity Gale. Up to now, I've kept her out of all this. She doesn't know a damn thing about the Villa Mimosa and it's high time she did. She's getting restive and I quite agree with her. I'd get restive if she went around the place being mysterious. Verity is coming up to London tomorrow morning and I propose to tell her the whole story right from the beginning. I'd like your permission to do so. Frankly, even if you don't give it to me, I'll tell Verity all the same."

"You are an ass, Charles. If I had the good fortune to be engaged to Verity Gale, I would have told her long ago. Always tell women secrets unless you happen to be emotionally involved in the secret. You're not. Therefore tell her all—with my love." He paused. "As a matter of fact, we might be able to use Verity."

"Use Verity! What the hell do you mean, sir?"

"Just an idea that crossed my mind. And don't be so damned indignant. This is war—not a Lonely Hearts Bureau. She lives in Sussex, doesn't she? Of course she does. In Newick. Anything else?"

"Yes there is. Once we've sorted this thing out, I'd like to rejoin the battalion."

"We'll see about that later. By hook or by crook, we've got to make this pay off and it's not going to be easy." He stood up and walked across the room, limping a little. "And we haven't much time. Now that Firefly is in the papers, you can bet your boots that de Gaulle's boys will be round at Baker Street first thing tomorrow morning declaiming in classical hexameters and demanding this and that. Thank the Lord they don't know about Sabine yet. When they *do* find out, the garlic really will be in the soup. And now let's go down and see Thayer."

General Southerden described the situation and gave his orders.

The security authorities had taken over and split the party. Madame, Monique and Marie were staying at Squadron Officer A's flat. The other four girls had been tucked away in a house in Shepherd's Bush under the baleful eye of Senior Commander Hogarth of the Women's Services Provost, God help them. Hans Ramberg and his brother-officers were in separate cells in a special wing of the prison off Wood Lane.

"I want you, Charles, to interrogate Madame, Monique and Hans Ramberg. That leaves Lucille, Elsa, Magda and the other officers to you, Thayer. Having found out as much as you can, change over and begin again. What we want to find out, in order of importance, are the answers to the following questions. Who is concerned in the anti-Hitler conspiracy, what has been done and what is going to be done? Everything should be subordinated to that. The next thing is D-Day. If indeed the Nazi High Command believes that we've picked on the Pas de Calais, what more can we do to confirm that erroneous forecast? The R.A.F. urgently want the exact locations of those launching ramps, and we want to know their purpose. We believe that the Germans are going to bombard London with pilot-less aircraft but we want to be sure. Other things are strength and location of troops, morale, defence works, God knows what. Everything's useful." He paused and frowned. "It's a hell of a lot to expect from the Villa Mimosa but if you're patient and put up with the irrelevant, you should get something. My own strictly unofficial view is that the security boys are all wrong in locking them up. The girls won't talk in an atmosphere of cold baths and carbolic and I don't blame them. Neither will the men." His eyes gleamed. "If only we could have an old-fashioned party. . . ." He sighed. "Ah well, any questions before you get cracking?"

"Yes, General. I guess you haven't mentioned Golden Mouse."

"I propose to interrogate Golden Mouse myself. Anything else?"

"When do we meet again?"

"Here—at six o'clock. Don't forget that it could be in your power to alter the whole course of the war." He smiled. "Makes the talkative Field-Marshals look faintly comic."

"It certainly does," said Thayer. " 'How I won the War—in Bed by Lance-Corporal Lucille.' Well, I'm off to the jail-house."

*　　*　　*

Thayer B. Cavendish stopped his car outside the vast nail-studded door of the prison and was admitted at once. He was escorted to the Governor's office. He gave the Governor a Chesterfield cigarette and lit one himself.

"Well, sir, how are the boys this morning?"

The Governor smiled.

" 'The boys,' as you call them, are still a little dazed. We bedded them down in separate cells but, of course, they had time to talk before being admitted here. They've all had good breakfasts—and a cigarette ration."

"Have I your permission to supplement that ration?"

"Strictly speaking, no. On the other hand, if you think it would help with your interrogation, I'm prepared to turn a blind eye."

"You'd be surprised," said Thayer, "what guys and dames will do for a pack of Chesterfields. O.K. Let's go."

They walked along a high, echoing gallery, netted below with wire mesh to prevent suicides. At a locked cell door, the Governor stopped.

"Number One's in here—and the others in the cells alongside. I'll give you a pass-key which you must return to me before leaving the prison. Good luck to you."

Thayer unlocked the cell door and stepped inside. A grey-faced German officer rose to his feet and faced him.

"How do you do?" said Thayer. "I guess you and I became acquainted last night and I've just come along to ask you a few questions. Cigarette?"

"Are you also proposing to give my brother-officers cigarettes?"

"Sure, sure."

"Then I will accept with pleasure. I am the senior German officer and you will understand that I am unwilling to be privileged. As to your questions, I will answer them in advance and at once. Under the terms of the Geneva Convention, I am permitted to give you my number, my rank and my name. That is all."

"I guess I've never been to Geneva, Colonel," said Thayer meaningly.

"Nor I. Nevertheless, it exists—both as a city and as a source of international standards. My number is 305344, my name Stefan and my rank that of Colonel."

"Very glad to know you, Colonel. Now getting around to this crazy guy Hitler. . . ."

*   *   *

INTERIM INTERROGATION REPORT
ON THE CASE OF
"Madame"

Conducted by Major Charles Addison, Coldstream Guards.

"I prefer not to give my name. I am known as 'Madame'. I am unmarried, a Catholic and a Frenchwoman who loves France. I lived in the country in a large house with my parents. Early in 1943, a senior German officer was billeted on us. I had been brought up to hate, fear and distrust all Germans. When I was a child, I knew the word *'Boche'* before I knew the word 'German' and I therefore prepared to hate this man. Because my parents were old and proud and unwilling to sit at table with a *Boche,* it happened that he and I usually had supper together. I found after a little while that I could not hate him. He was a person of infinite courtesy and our conversation, stilted at first, warmed as we found out that we cared for the same things. He was devout, as I was, and we spoke more and more freely of Christendom and the old traditions of Europe. Ours was a friendship of the mind. In April of that year, the Gestapo came and took this man and hanged him. I knew then that he was not only a great idealist but also that he had been concerned with practical things. He had dared to plot against Hitler. I banished the word *'Boche'* from my vocabulary for ever.

"As a woman, I could not carry on his work. But I determined to provide a roof under which men who felt and thought as he did could meet in secrecy and safety. It was the smallest service I could do in his memory and for my Country. When my parents died from *la grippe,* I was free. I shut up the big house and went to the Pas de Calais where I was unknown and where there were many soldiers—amongst them Hans Ramberg whose name I had heard as a close friend of my hanged Colonel.

"You will know that Hitler had transformed a continent of families into a land mass peopled by the hungry and the homeless. I gave shelter to those in need of it. My girls will tell you their own devious and unhappy stories and how they came to my door. I knew nothing of the physical side of life nor did I realize how utterly Hitler had debauched the moral standards of centuries. How could I, a middle-aged, socially segregated Catholic spinster foretell that the presence of women would transform my house into . . . into what it became? When it was borne upon me that the officers who came had not one purpose but two, I

was shocked beyond measure. I had become engulfed in the full
tide of this ugliness without knowing. To permit it to continue
would cut me off from my Faith. I told myself with horror that I
should close the Villa Mimosa and run away. Three considera-
tions halted immediate flight. Neither my family nor I have ever
had any admiration for those who take to their heels; if I were
to leave, my girls would be subjected to even grosser indignities
at the hands of grosser men; I loved France. Those were my
reasons. After a night of mental torment, I begged God's indul-
gence, bought myself a uniform of black silk—and stayed.

"I owe my life and the lives of my girls to Major Addison and
his comrades. From all of these gentlemen, English and American,
I have received more courtesy than I deserve."

Major A: "What do you know of the anti-Hitler plot?"

Madame: "I only know that it exists. You will remember that
I remained *outside* the Salon. My girls, who lived the full,
shameful life of the Villa, can tell you much more than I. Those
with whom they were intimate were not reticent. The officer with
most knowledge of this plot is Major Hans Ramberg. I have a
personal request to make."

Major A: "What is this personal request?"

Madame: "More than anything in the world, it is my wish to
see a priest. Am I permitted to do this?"

Major A: "Of course. It will be arranged this afternoon."

INTERIM INTERROGATION REPORT

ON THE CASE OF

"Monique"

Conducted by Major Charles Addison, Coldstream Guards.

"My real name is Monica but I used to call myself 'Monique'
to sound foreign. I am English. I went abroad in 1938 with two
other girls in a dancing troupe. Our name was *'The Tantalising
Trio'* and we did all right. Just before the war started we were
in Naples and our manager got the wind up and did a bunk with
the other two girls, leaving me stranded. I became very friendly
with an Italian gentleman and he looked after me until 1943
when he was put in prison for being on the Black Market and I
was stranded again. A Swiss gentleman in the confectionery took
me to Paris but after a bit he did a bunk, too. I got a job washing
up but that didn't last and I went to Coville with an Austrian
gentleman in the perfumery. This Austrian gentleman had to go

back to Austria and I really was in the cart with Coville full of German soldiers. I was told by a nun that I could always get something to eat and a roof to sleep under in a place called the Villa Mimosa so I went there and Madame took me in.

"German officers used to meet there and Madame had no idea what was going on at first. When she did find out, she was in ever such a state, crying and saying her prayers, but it was too late then and none of us could get away. I didn't like doing what I was doing but I must say that the German officers treated us all right and never took undue liberties, as you might say. It's funny. If anyone had ever had the sauce to tell me that I'd end up doing what I was doing, I'd have laughed them to scorn. But after a bit it doesn't seem to matter any more and it's not really *you,* anyway. As long as Dad and Mum and Gran didn't know, it was all right, except when I remembered I was English; so I had to stop myself thinking about England and Dad and Mum and Gran or I couldn't have gone on. Since the night the aeroplane came I haven't worked in the Salon or upstairs. I've just lived in the attic on my own."

Major A: "Tell me, Monique, what do you know about the anti-Hitler plot?"

Monique: "Well, I know that a lot of high-ups are in it. The German officers used to talk about it in the Salon among themselves but when they took us upstairs they only told us about their wives and showed us photos of their kiddies."

Major A: "Can you think of any specific 'high-ups' who are concerned in this plot? Can you tell me any names?"

Monique: "Yes, sir. There's one who's an Admiral and he's got a name like 'Canary'."

Major A: "Is it possible that you mean Admiral Canaris?"

Monique: "Yes. That's the gentleman's name. He's up to the neck in it."

Major A: "You are sure of this? It is very important."

Monique: "Dead certain. There's another called General Beck. He's in it. Field-Marshal Rommel isn't in it yet but they are trying to get him in, and if they succeed it's all up with Hitler and the others, so they say."

Major A: "Can you think of any other names?"

Monique: "Not really. I only heard bits and pieces. The one who knows it all is Major Hans. And, sir, I'd like to go home but I'm frightened."

Major A: "Have you ever heard of the 'Official Secrets Act', Monique?"

Monique: "Not really, sir."

Major A: "You will. Thank you very much indeed for your invaluable help. I would like you to rest until after luncheon and then you and I are going for a drive together."

Monique: "I'll do anything you say, sir."

INTERIM INTERROGATION REPORT
ON THE CASE OF
Major Hans Ramberg

Conducted by Major Charles Addison, Coldstream Guards.

"My name is Hans Ramberg, my number 643520 and I am a Major. Under the terms of the Geneva Convention, that is all that I am permitted to tell you."

Mayor A: "That is all you are prepared to say?"

Major R: "That is all."

*   *   *

Before luncheon Charles Addison made two telephone calls. The first was to Westminster Cathedral, where he inquired at what hour it would be convenient for a French-speaking priest to hear what might well prove to be a protracted confession. Five o'clock? He would arrive punctually with the penitent. His next call was to the Duty Officer at the War Office. Immediately after luncheon he would be bringing in a lady who wished to sign a document in duplicate, acknowledging that she was subject to the provisions of the Official Secrets Act. These things done, he poured himself out a stiff drink. It went down his throat like a torchlight procession.

At two o'clock he called again at Squadron Officer A's flat. Monique was waiting for him and he drove her at once to the War Office where she obediently signed the Official Secrets form. Charles took a copy and put it in his pocket. Monique appeared to be wholly without curiosity as to the purpose of this. He talked to her, sitting on a park bench overlooking the Serpentine.

"This morning, you told me that you wanted to go home but that you were frightened. Who are you frightened of?"

"Dad and Mum and Gran. But Gran most."

"Listen very carefully to me, Monique. I can tell you now that soldiers, British and American, died on the beaches of the

Pas de Calais last night in order to bring you here in safety. I dare say they were frightened too—but they got on with the job. I want you to face up to Dad and Mum and Gran this afternoon."

Her face blanched.

"I couldn't. Honestly I couldn't. They'd ask . . . questions."

"That's what I'm going to protect you against. Did you fully understand the document you signed in the War Office this afternoon?"

"No, sir. Not reely-reely. I signed it because you said I should."

"Then let me explain. That document means that you've undertaken never to divulge an official secret to anybody—and the word 'anybody' includes Dad, Mum *and* Gran."

"But I don't know any official secrets, sir. Reely-reely I don't."

Charles turned and looked directly at Monique.

"Your life and everything concerned with it since you left England are an official secret. Now do you understand?"

The car stopped at the corner of the Brixton street where Monique used to live. Charles said cheerfully:

"I'll go in first and break the ice. You follow in exactly fifteen minutes."

"Sir, I'd rather not. I'm scared. I'd much sooner stay dead. Honestly I would."

"Rubbish, you're alive and you're not scared. This is operation Fatted Calf."

"You don't know Gran."

"I hope to rectify that omission in the next two minutes. Promise me that you won't run away."

"All right," she said despairingly. "I promise."

He walked a few yards along the street. Number 35 was a small stucco house with a patch of sooty front garden in which a china gnome fished eternally in a dried-up pool. The windows of the front room were elaborately draped with lace curtains and the whole squat house exuded an atmosphere of shabby but determined respectability. Charles was daunted at the task that lay before him. Thank the Lord he wasn't in Monique's high-heeled shoes! He rang the bell.

After a long wait the door was opened by an elderly, grey-haired man in shirt-sleeves and braces. His collar was open and he had the querulous look of one who resents being woken up from a

Sunday afternoon nap. There was no need whatsoever for Charles to ask who he was. The resemblance between father and daughter was unmistakable. Charles saluted.

"Good afternoon, sir. My name is Charles Addison and I would very much like to have five minutes conversation with you." He smiled. "Forgive me for disturbing you on a Sunday afternoon. I wouldn't do so if it were not important."

"Are you sure it's me you want?"

"Perfectly certain."

Monique's father stared at this army officer in puzzled curiosity. Then he opened the door wide.

"Come in," he said, "and I'll ask you to wait for a minute in the hall while I tidy the front room and get my coat on. We . . . we weren't expecting company."

"Please don't bother."

"If I didn't tidy the place, the wife 'ud never let me hear the end of it." His forehead puckered. "You'll pardon me, but is it bad news?"

"No. It's very good news."

"Well, that's a change. I'll tell the wife. The kettle's just on the boil so maybe you'd care for a cup of tea."

"I would indeed."

"May I have the name again?"

"Addison. Charles Addison."

Charles stood in the narrow hall. He heard the sounds of furniture being moved and cushions being slapped. From the kitchen came the rattle of cups. Monique's father came back. He had fastened his collar and put on a coat.

"Now if you'll come into the front room, the wife'll give you a cup of tea."

"How very kind of you. I'd like to meet your wife very much—and also your mother if she's here."

"Gran? How do you know about Gran? As a matter of fact Gran's been bed-ridden this last three years and she's stone deaf since the Blitz. This is the wife. This gentleman says he's got good news, dear."

Charles shook hands with a faded, frightened woman whose face was twitching like a rabbit. She mumbled that she was pleased to meet him and that she hoped he'd pardon the parlour. She poured out three cups of strong tea, slopping the tea into the saucer. Then she sat down on the extreme edge of the sofa and waited in fluttering anxiety. Well, here goes——

"I said I had very good news for you. I have. It is about your daughter Monique."

There was silence. It was broken by a long, shuddering gasp. Monique's mother, her face blotchy white, reached out a shaking hand toward her husband. He got to his feet. His voice was harsh.

"I knew you'd made a mistake. We got no daughter Monique. We did have a girl once, Monica, but we don't want to know nothing about her. Far as we're concerned, she's dead. Dead and buried. That's all I got to say. I'll trouble you to finish your cup of tea and leave Mother and me alone."

"You are doing your daughter a great injustice, sir."

"You'll permit me to be the judge of that. And now I'll trouble you——"

Monique's mother seemed to gather all her strength together. She cried wildly:

"Don't you harken to him, sir. If he doesn't want to hear about our Monica, I do. Where is she? For God's sake, sir, where is my little girl?"

"Your daughter is waiting in a car a few yards away from this house. In five minutes time, she will ring your bell."

"She'd better not have the sauce to——"

"How can you demean yourself, talking that way—and you a sidesman!" Monique's mother was no longer a rabbit. She was a tigress. "Calling yourself a Christian and taking up the plate."

Charles had an ally. He said evenly:

"Before Monica rings that bell, I am going to tell you something—whether you, sir, want to listen to me or not. I am talking now to Monica's mother. Would you, madam, recognize your daughter's handwriting?"

"Course I would."

"Then be kind enough to glance at this form signed by your daughter an hour or two ago. It relates to the Official Secrets Act. Do you know that writing?"

"Yes I do. That's Monica's."

"Please pass it to your husband. Do you, sir, also agree that that is your daughter's signature?"

"Yes. But I don't see——"

"You will in a minute. Monica—we knew her under the code name of 'Monique'—has been working in secret and in constant danger of her life for the British Government. A few hours ago, she and her colleagues were snatched from their post of duty in occupied France and brought home to England. If she had stayed any longer, she would indeed be 'dead and buried'—at the hands of the Gestapo. Her safe arrival in this country has cost British and American lives. That is some indication of how highly we rate her work. She will tell you nothing of it—ever. Nor will I."

He put down his cup with a clatter and rose to his feet.

"When that bell rings, am I going to answer it and take Monica away—or are you going to answer it and take your daughter into your arms? The decision is yours."

Monique's father was staring at the floor. Charles looked with exaggerated interest at a petrified flight of china ducks on the flowered wall-paper. Mallard—or were they teal? The Sunday afternoon silence of Brixton deepened in an oppression that was almost tangible. Charles heard the muffled sound of a car's door slamming; he heard the garden gate open and the hesitant tap-tap of frightened footsteps on the tiled path; he saw Monica's mother's hands go to her mouth. Then, after an unendurable thirty seconds of indecision, the bell rang shrilly, stridently in the hall.

Monica's father stood up. He said gruffly:

"All right, Mother. I'll go."

Charles waited in the car. Monica had been in there for nearly half an hour. Operation Fatted Calf must have worked. Time for him to go or he'd be late for Madame and her priest.

He had slipped the car into gear when he heard footsteps that were no longer frightened but buoyant. Monica's thin, tabby-kitten face was tear-stained, but her eyes were bright. Charles switched off the engine.

"Well?"

"It's all right. It's all right. Mum's putting a hot-water bottle into my bed. And I've seen Gran."

"And how was Gran?"

"It's funny. She's deaf and she doesn't seem to realize I've been away at all." Monica sniffed. "All she said was I wasn't to forget to wash my hands and face before supper. And I've been scared stiff of her for years. It's funny."

"Things have a habit of working out like that—thank God."

Monique hesitated.

"Dad says that you're welcome to a glass of port wine . . . if you'd like to come in again."

Charles repressed a shudder. "Please thank your father very

much and say I'd love to—some other time. I've got to hurry back now and pick up Madame. And you'll turn up at Brown's Hotel, Albemarle Street, at eight o'clock tonight, having thought out the answers to those questions I put to you."

"I'll be there, sir." She shook her auburn hair. "You're always doing things for people, for me and Madame and the others. I wish I could do something for you." She traced a pattern on the pavement with the toe of her sandal. "You got a young lady, sir?"

"Yes, Monica. I've got a young lady."

"A steady?"

"Steady as a rock."

"I'm glad." She swallowed. "Ever so glad. She's lucky."

Charles started the engine.

"*Au revoir,* Monica."

"*Au roovoire, Mussyour,*" she said in her execrable French. Monica ran home.

17: "GERMANY CALLING"

THE good people of Coville were coming out of Mass on that same Sunday morning when two seemingly unrelated facts were brought to the attention of the *Sicherheitsdienst.* Neither the Black Maria, the *panier à salade,* nor its driver could be found. Furthermore, Colonel Otto, who had called a conference at eleven o'clock to issue detailed orders for tonight's raid on the Villa Mimosa, had not arrived. An orderly was sent to his rooms and returned with the disquieting news that the Colonel's bed had not been slept in. Half an hour of discussion and speculation ensued before it was decided that the two Gestapo men in belted raincoats should take a car and drive discreetly past the Villa Mimosa just in case the Colonel might have paid the establishment a private visit—in the course of his duty.

The two men set out. Their names were Kurt and Gustav. They talked in monosyllables about the impudent raid launched last night by the Anglo-Saxons and the Americans. The enemy had been repulsed—with a bloody nose. But German casualties had been heavy and a comb-out of the dolts who had failed to give the alarm until the Allies were ashore had already been ordered by Fuehrer Headquarters. Himmler's Special Commandos were closing in to conduct the inquiry and to mete out summary punishment.

There was a pale blue sky with wind-ripped tatters of cloud. In spite of the cold, the snowdrops would not be long delayed.

Outside Panzer Korps Headquarters, there was much activity. The car swept past the wrought-iron gates and climbed the long, poplar-lined hill at the back. Both Gestapo men noted that a large flat field of stubble had been left unspiked against parachutists. In its middle was heaped the black remnants of a fire. To have left this field thus was a serious neglect of duty on the part of General von Wolfram and would be reported to higher authority. The car breasted the hill and began the run down. They saw a mouldy hay-cock with a farm cart resting on its shafts beside it. Beyond, where the road became a track, stood the Villa Mimosa.

Kurt was driving. He said in a low voice:

"I'll go past it slowly and then reverse as if I had lost my way. You keep your eyes skinned."

"Agreed."

The car bumped over the track and drew level with the gate of the Villa. Gustav said sharply:

"Halt."

The car stopped. The door of the Villa Mimosa was wide open and swinging on its hinges. The two men looked at the building from blind window to blind window. Kurt said:

"I'm going to take a look inside. Come."

They got out of the car and drew their pistols and cocked them. Then Kurt strode up the garden path and stopped at the door. He shouted loudly into the hall.

"Gestapo. Is anyone there?"

The only sounds were the creaking of the door in the wind's eddies and the drip, drip of a water tap in the kitchen. An officer's greatcoat hung on a peg. Kurt looked at the tab sewn on the inside pocket. The coat had been made by a Berlin tailor in 1942 for "Major Hans Ramberg". He grunted. "So, staff officer to General von Wolfram. His name is on our list. Now I go upstairs. Stay here and be on your guard. I am far from satisfied."

With his finger on the trigger of his pistol, Kurt crept upstairs. He kicked open a door on the right. It was a small room with a desk, two chairs and a domed sewing machine. Another door faced him on the landing. Again he raised his boot and the door swung open. He saw dimly a long narrow room with a high ceiling. He stepped inside and pulled back a plush curtain. A chair was overturned on the floor. Empty champagne bottles and dirty glasses stood on the tables ranged along the wall and there was a strong smell of guttered candles and of recent feminine occupation. Kurt walked the length of the room and struck a single, absent-minded note on the piano. The silence swallowed the sound at once. He shut the piano lid and returned to the landing. He saw a flight of stairs leading upwards and his eyes narrowed. Perhaps the explanation of this silent and deserted house was to be found up there. He called softly:

"Gustav!"

"*Jawohl.*"

"There is nothing on this floor. Now I try farther up."

He began to climb the stairs, very slowly as if testing the strength of each step. The feminine smell that pervaded the Villa became even more pronounced and it was threaded now by another smell that was strangely familiar to his nostrils. He had smelt it before many times but he couldn't think what it was. He reached the landing. It was dark but a tiny chink of light filtered through a thickly curtained window on the left. He jerked the curtain to one side, letting in a shaft of pale sunshine. That was better. Much better. He half turned—and reeled back against the wall in horror.

Beside him, not a yard away, a dead hunchback was propped grotesquely against the banisters. His eyes and his mouth were wide open and there was a revolver at his feet. Though death was his trade, Kurt shuddered at that baleful, sightless, triumphant stare. He muttered, *"Ach, Du lieber Gott,"* and forced himself to look away. What he saw in the corridor gave him a sense of nightmare. He shut his eyes and opened them again. Nothing had changed. A half-naked woman was crouched there in tousled death, her bare white breast spattered with black blood. Beyond her, Colonel Otto in vest and pants reached out as if to claw her with his dead hand.

Kurt heard a guffaw of laughter from below. Laughter—in the presence of this waxen carnage! He was pale to the lips as he walked downstairs. Gustav was holding up a white square of cardboard and giggling. He said:

"I have been going to Berlitz School and I speak very well English. This I find. It was by the vind down-blown. I make for you translation."

UNDER NEW MANAGEMENT

CHANGE OF ADDRESS

THIS BUSINESS HAS BEEN TRANSFERRED
(BODILY)

To LONDON!

We regret any inconvenience to regular patrons and assure
all clients of prompt and personal attention. Enquiries and
appointments may be made by telephone to:

HUMPHREY HOGARTH
(Director of Finance (Z))
The War Office
Whitehall S.W.1.

BOOK NOW AND AVOID DISAPPOINTMENT.

God Save the King!   The Stars and Stripes
for Ever!   Vive la France!

*   *   *

A voice came out of Germany and snarled in English homes.
It was as rich as rancid pork fat and it had within it all the
malice and suggestiveness of an anonymous letter.

"Germany calling; Germany calling; Germany calling. This is
station Hambursch, Bremen and D X B on the thirty-one metre
band. Here is the news in English.

"Last night the war-monger Churchill, prodded into activity by
International Jewry, launched an unsuccessful Anglo-American
raid against the Atlantic wall. If, as one can only suppose, the
operation was designed to test the strength of the German
defences, its result will give its author much to scratch his head
about. The raid may be compared with Churchill's sinking of
the *Athenia* in so far that it cost many British and American
lives and achieved—precisely nothing.

"I now address the mothers, the widows and the children of
those who died—and particularly the Americans. It has been said
that Britain will fight to the last Yankee and at last you know
this to be true. At the behest of the arch-schemer Roosevelt, your
men crossed the Atlantic to take part in a European war in which
they are in no way involved. Today, they seek no more glory, no
more Purple Hearts. They lie in a French cemetery, many
thousand miles away from their homes. Their bodies were

brought here from the coast by the German Army, by those whom you have been bamboozled into regarding as your enemies. They were buried today with military honours—a little sketchy perhaps because the war goes on. But the intention was to do them honour. The Fuehrer respects those who die in battle. Not all of your men could be identified. Lueger and Schmeisser bullets, incendiary shells fired over open sights, mines, bombs and even barbed wire have rendered some of your men unidentifiable. During the next days, more will be picked out of the tides. Ladies and Gentlemen of America—it is a pitiful and wasteful recital. I take no pleasure in telling it."

The speaker lied. He and his master Dr. Goebbels were cock-a-hoop with delight. Operation Firefly was a heaven-sent introduction to American wave-lengths.

"And now to England—to some mean house in a mean street in an English town. I speak to one person. All I know of her is that her name is 'Glad'. Tattoo marks on human skin are usually too discreet to give a name and address, and the words 'I love Glad' tell the undertaker little. Your Lance-Corporal is dead, Glad, and you had better look for a new boy-friend. Why not choose one from amongst the tens of thousands of Americans, white and coloured, who are occupying your ancient land?

"Thank you for your attention. There will be further news in English from Station Hambursh, Bremen and D X B on the thirty-one metre band at nine-fifteen p.m. G.M.T."

There was no need to wait until nine-fifteen.

Hamburg, Bremen and Station D X B were back on the air again within half an hour. News of the raid on the Villa Mimosa had been flashed to Dr. Goebbels.

The speaker begged leave to amplify his earlier news bulletin in which he had stated that the Anglo-American raid launched against the French coast last night had achieved nothing. This was incorrect.

Bereaved parents, wives and sweethearts would rejoice to learn that their loved ones had not died in vain. They had died in order that hordes of women who already infested the West End of London should be augmented by five foreign prostitutes.

It could now be revealed that a tiny clique of criminally stupid traitors holding military rank had frequented a certain house in the Pas de Calais to consort with loose women and to plot against the Fuehrer. An Anglo-American force of parachutists, using the abortive raid as cover, had seen fit to kidnap these women and their paramours, leaving behind a would-be humorous notice giving their destination as London. France was well rid of these creatures and Germany of these officers whose families had been taken into protective custody.

An unarmed Colonel of the German Security Service, visiting the house on duty, had been brutally murdered in cold blood as had been a hitherto unidentified woman and a French hunchback. Large-scale arrests were imminent. General Wolf von Wolfram, Commander of a Panzer Division in the area, had been stripped of all his decorations by order of the Fuehrer. Later, the General had accidentally shot himself while cleaning a revolver.

In General de Gaulle's London Headquarters, the broadcast account of the raid on the Villa Mimosa caused a storm of anger and indignation. To the traditional phrase *"perfide Albion"* could now be added *"perfide Amérique"*. The Commander-in-Chief sent for his Liaison Officer, a high-nosed Colonel of Cavalry who had served in Indo-China and in Beirut before making his way to England. This high-nosed Colonel was icily instructed to present himself tomorrow morning at Baker Street and demand the immediate handing over of the kidnapped ladies to the Forces of Free France.

18: MIMOSA IN MINIATURE

CHARLES and Thayer met again at Brown's a few minutes before six. Both men were exhausted and bitterly resentful of the Sabbatarian licensing laws that closed the bar inexorably until seven o'clock. Charles began.

"Well," he said, "I've talked to Madame, Monique and Hans Ramberg, in that order. Madame was very forthcoming and told me as much as she knew. Frankly, it doesn't help us much. She was a sort of Cerebus——"

"Sort of what?"

"Cerebus. Multi-headed dog that guarded the entrance to Hades."

"Hades being the Salon?"

"Exactly. With hell one floor farther up. Monique produced what she called 'bits and pieces'. They are pretty startling and we'll have to cross-check. Canaris is implicated and so is Beck— with my old friend Field-Marshal Rommel as a likely starter. I

imagine that there'll be more to come from her when she's had
time to settle down and think. Hans Ramberg was my big disappointment. He wouldn't utter a bloody word. I let him sweat.
After lunch, I restored Monique to the bosom of some . . . er
. . . English connections of hers and Madame to the bosom of
her Church. Hans is our problem-child. How did you get on?"

"I've had a heck of a day," said Thayer. "I interviewed Stefan,
Fritz, Paul and Gerhard. I guess they took their cue from Hans.
Number, name and rank—that's the lot."

"So they wouldn't talk, either?"

"Not a damned word. There's nothing I didn't try, from
Chesterfields to Bourbon, but those guys made a Littleneck Clam
seem positively loquacious. Once we'd been over the Geneva
Convention routine, Gerhard *did* open up. Wanted to know
how and where his girl-friend Elsa was. I told him she was O.K.
and being cared for and I thought to myself, 'Now we really
can go places.' So we did. Back to Geneva. And to think we
practically snatched those boys off the scaffold. . . ."

Charles could see it all. These were regular officers who followed
the military rules both by instinct and tradition. On board the
M.G.B. they had been together and all that had been required
to establish the Geneva pattern was one word from that strange,
incalculable man, Hans Ramberg. The word had obviously been
given and a policy of non-co-operation would be rigidly observed
unless and until some influence could be brought to bear on the
man who dangled the puppets. If Hans could be induced to
break silence, they were home and dry. But, for God's sake, how?

"Having drawn blank in your London Sing-Sing," said Thayer,
"I went to see the girls. I used to fancy myself with dames."

In Shepherd's Bush, Thayer had been confronted by Senior
Commander Adelaide Hogarth. It was an ordeal to which no man
should be subjected. Adelaide had a light cavalry moustache and
an eye like a rusty gimlet. She considered it her duty to attend all
interrogations in the role of chaperon, and in her daunting
presence nothing of political or military value had emerged.
Magda had sulked. Elsa had blubbered—and even the vivacious
Lucille had been cowed by the awful disapproval of Adelaide's
eye. Sadly and thirstily, Thayer had left.

"The fact is, Charles, we gotta spring those dames out of that
dump."

"I agree," said Charles absently. "If only we could repeat
Sabine and parachute into Shepherd's Bush. . . . But if we did

that, we'd be arrested for causing a breach of the peace."

Charles lit a cigarette. Thayer was quite right. As long as the girls of the Villa Mimosa remained in Shepherd's Bush under the antiseptic discipline of Senior Commander Hogarth, they would never talk. They had been prisoners in the Villa. In London, their prison was much more rigorous and was without benefit of the anaesthetics of human companionship, music and wine. Within the limits of propriety—for this was England—these three things should be restored to them. He remembered General Southerden's phrase: "If only we could have an old-fashioned party. . . ." But to ask Senior Commander Hogarth to yield up her charges for a party, old-fashioned or otherwise, would be like inviting a hungry tigress to share out the horse-flesh.

Suddenly Charles heard a well-known voice in the hall of the hotel, a crisp, confident voice giving orders.

"A private room please . . . oh yes, at once . . . and some candles, say a dozen to start with. Nonsense. Surely Brown's Hotel can produce a few candles. And a piano. Yes, I said a piano. P—i—a—n—o. I don't care a damn whether it needs tuning or not. And present my compliments to the wine-butler and ask him to come and see me right away. Tell him to bring a list of the champagnes. Champagne, candles and a piano and . . . er . . . you might care to make a note. The bill is to be sent to Humphrey Hogarth, Director of Finance (Z), The War Office, S.W.1."

Speechless, Charles and Thayer went into the hall. General Southerden waved a cheerful hand. Around him stood a smiling, excited group of girls.

"*Bonsoir*, Charles! You remember me—Lucille?"

"And me—Magda?"

"For me, Elsa, you composed the *Goose-feather March*."

"I am your servant."

Charles shook his head incredulously at General Southerden. "How the blazes did you do it, sir?"

"The security boys wouldn't play. Pack of frustrated old nursery governesses looking down their noses and bleating. So I took the bull by the horns—or rather the lion by the mane. Went to Number Ten and knocked up the Old Man. He was in bed drinking brandy out of a rose-bowl. Saw my point at once." General Southerden triumphantly displayed a half-sheet of paper.

It was headed: ACTION THIS NIGHT.

* * *

The hour was approaching nine o'clock when an irate resident
of Brown's Hotel stormed downstairs and begged leave to inform
the night-porter:

(a) that he and his wife had been regular visitors to Brown's
Hotel for over forty years

(b) that he and his wife were prepared to eat smoked snoek
and to put up with the worst that Hitler had to offer in
the way of aerial bombardment

(c) that he and his wife were NOT prepared to put up with a
respectable hotel being turned into a blasted *palais de
dance* and

(d) that unless that damned piano shut up, he and his wife
would leave Brown's Hotel first thing tomorrow morning,
BAG and BAGGAGE.

Charles shut the piano lid and looked around the curtained
room, dim with smoke. It smelt, felt and looked like the Salon
of the Villa Mimosa in miniature. It was fantastic to realize that
London bobbies pounded their beats on the pavements outside
and that a darkened Buckingham Palace stood a few hundred
yards across the Green Park. General Southerden, wholly at his
ease, was deep in conversation with Golden Mouse. Thayer was
showing both patience and tenacity in his approach to the
bovine Elsa. As a subject for interrogation in detail, Elsa was
unrewarding. She seemed wholly insensitive, both mentally and
physically, to what had gone on in the Villa Mimosa other than
that which concerned her beloved Gerhard, and was genuinely
unaware that the house had any purpose except its ostensible
one. But she had heard names and, being a German speaker, had
remembered them. Canaris was one of those names—and Major-
General Hans Oster, his chief *Abwehr* Assistant. If only she could
see and have a talk to Gerhard, she was sure she could remember
some more. With a peasant's cunning, she stated her price.

Magda had leaned over the piano while Charles played. She
had no pity for Wanda but grieved for the hunchback Gaston.
It was bad luck on him—a true gentleman—to have to die in his
tormentor's company. But the good God would set that right.
The plot to kill Hitler? Oh, a great number of people, high
and low, were concerned. One of them was Field-Marshal von
Witzleben and yet another the Military Governor of France
itself, Stuelpnagel. These Germans were all the same. They
explored their souls and talked, but did nothing. If it had been

Budapest, Hitler would long ago be dead. The man whom Hitler had most cause to fear was a Colonel, a man with one arm and only one and a half eyes. His name was von Stauffenberg. All the plotters knew that he, von Stauffenberg, was the bravest of them. They relied on him to do the deed. She did not know when or how.

"Give me a drink, a cigarette and play me a Hungarian song."

He had given her a glass of champagne, a cigarette and played *There's only one minute in life*.

Now he rose from the piano stool and walked across the room and sat down on the sofa. He was immediately joined by Lucille. She fluttered her eyelashes and gave him a reproachful look.

"*Eh bien*, so you have decided to talk to me at last."

"When I was a little boy," said Charles gallantly, "I was always told to save up the cake till the end."

"Please consider me entirely at your disposal either as an answerer of questions or"—she twinkled—"as a piece of cake. You have just played a song for Magda. The words of this song are 'There is only one minute in life'. This is true. Because there is only one minute in life, I do not wish to waste a second of it. I was interested in you, Charles, from the first moment I saw you. I knew in my bones that you were a man, a real man, and not one who takes a woman lightly. I knew that you could never be a *client* of the Villa Mimosa or of any such house, and because of that I desired very much to have a love affair with you. To be possessed by you would restore much that I have lost." She glanced meaningly at the ceiling. "Do you live in this hotel?"

"Yes."

"Which floor?"

"The fourth."

She slid a warm hand into his, entwining his fingers. Her voice was low and challenging.

"Then it appears to me that we are wasting our time. Will you not take me to your room on the fourth floor and there put to me all these important questions?" Her clasp tightened. "The answers would come to me more readily in the dark."

"This is not the Villa Mimosa, Lucille."

"Nor I, at this moment, a woman of the Villa Mimosa." The liquid blue of her eyes hardened into ice. "You may be a good pianist and a brave parachutist, but you are also a big fool. I did not say that I desired to have an affair with you. I said 'a love affair!'" She looked sideways at his face and saw the answer in his set features. She blinked, shrugged and laughed. "Please do

not flatter yourself. There have already been a thousand men.
There will be a thousand more. For once, it would have been a
joy. Consider what I said as a *ballon d'essai*, something I sent up
to see which way the wind is blowing. Alas, it does not blow in
my direction—yet. Perhaps if I am good and tell you all you want
to know, you may change your mind. Now, ask your questions."

"The first and most important one is——"

He stopped. Fingers were beating a private tattoo on the door
and Charles gasped. He scrambled to his feet as the door opened
and Verity Gale walked into the room. She said with composure:

"I'm sorry I'm late, General. The Germans dropped some high
explosive in the road and we had to go a long way round. Hullo,
Charles. Won't you please introduce me to your friends?"

Outside, the feather-mop searchlights were dusting the clouds
and the rescue squads searched broken masonry for the living
and the dead. German bombers had come and gone, leaving
many of their dark escort on Kentish fields. Within Brown's
Hotel, the candles had guttered, the bottles were empty and the
piano was silent.

In that darkness, desired by and denied to Lucille, Charles
talked in whispers to Verity.

"When you came into the room, it was as if somebody had
turned the light on. Suddenly the girls looked old and tawdry
and you, in their midst, like a posy of spring flowers. But tell me
everything. Why and how did you come?"

"It was all very surprising. I was mucking out in dungarees
and Wellington boots when that slim, limping, elegant General
of yours turned up out of the blue. I was looking quite frightful
but he didn't seem to mind."

"What time was this?"

"Oh, about twelve—why?"

"He must have driven down the moment he left Thayer and
me. He didn't say a word about where he was going, the wily
old devil. What happened then?"

"I gave him a glass of sherry and rushed up to change. When I
came down he swore me to secrecy and then told me the lot."

"The lot?"

"Everything. All about your Aunt Marguerite and you being
a watchmaker and meeting Rommel—that must have been *quite*
a moment—and seeing the girls of the Villa Mimosa and then
you playing the piano inside and being picked up by the R.A.F.

and brought home. Do you remember the night you came to dine and some woman kept telephoning?"

"I remember it very clearly."

"You nearly lost me that night, Charles."

His arm tightened around her pliant shoulders.

"But you came back."

"Oh yes, I came back. I came back because I knew that whatever you were going to do was dangerous and that *you* might not come back. But you're here, thank God, and now we're in it together." She paused. Charles could hear the measured sound of her breathing. "General Southerden asked for my help. He seemed to think that a completely fresh mind was now essential. You know how he talks about horses. Well, he said that you and Thayer were bogged up to the hocks in the Villa Mimosa and that to put me, an untried filly, at the jumps was a long shot but it might come off. Nobody has ever called me an untried filly before, but I suppose he meant it kindly. So here I am."

"Tell me what you think of the girls."

"I was fascinated. In my ignorance, I've always thought of women like that as a class. But they're not 'a class'. They're real people. There's only one of them that falls into the 'class' category."

"You're thinking of Lucille?"

"Yes. She loathed me at sight and I didn't exactly take to her. Did she make a pass at you before I arrived?"

"I suppose," said Charles, " that it could be called a pass."

"I thought so. No wonder she looked stilettos at me. I liked Golden Mouse enormously. The Honourable House of Li may well be proud of her. Magda was charming and a fervent patriot. She talked to me about Hungary with tears in her eyes. Even Elsa was anxious to please and desperately respectful. Monica kept on telling me what a gentleman you were—which was a little embarrassing—and how lucky I was. As if I didn't know. . . . She is your absolute slave. I think I'm a little jealous of Monica. And now tell me about the most important one of all, the one I haven't met, Hans Ramberg."

Charles stared into the darkness. What could he tell Verity about this strange man? What did he really know of the man whose true being lurked inside the schizophrenic skin of a German officer who was not only "correct" himself but had imposed an equal rigidity on his fellow captives? He said:

"Hans is the hub and the heart of the whole thing. We've been

given a number of names by the girls—some of them pretty
surprising names—but without Hans we can't link them up
together. We've got the pieces but we haven't got the picture.
Now let me think what I know of him. He was Staff Officer to a
Panzer Korps General, now deceased. He's a friendly, generous
man and philanderer. Oddly enough, I saw him first long before
the war."

"Where?"

"At the Trout at Godstow. He was a Rhodes Scholar and I
happened on him one night when he was playing a mandolin by
the waterfall."

There was a long silence. Verity said:

"I think you'd better go now, my darling. This is Brown's
Hotel—not the Villa Mimosa—and we've got our lives before
us." She took a deep breath. "Do you know that feeling one gets
in the very early morning, when it's grey, just before the sun
comes up?"

"I know it very well."

"I've got that feeling now. Sleep well, my darling."

The searchlights were switched off and the birds shaking the
frost out of their feathers before Verity closed her eyes.

Within the house at Shepherd's Bush, Senior Commander
Hogarth scowled at the clock, tapped with her military shoe on
the floor and poured herself out another whisky and soda. Ten
past two and still no sign of her prisoners. She disapproved whole-
heartedly of General Southerden's "candle-light and kindness"
plan. Brain-washing—preferably with carbolic soap—would have
been *her* method of interrogation. The girls ought to have been
in bed long ago—as indeed three of them were, but not under
Senior Commander Hogarth's forbidding roof.

The front door bell rang. At last! She put on her cap and
flung General Southerden a muscular, quivering salute. To her
surprise, he was alone.

"Good evening," he said. "I'm afraid I've got some rather disturbing news for you."

"Disturbing, sir?"

"Yes, dammit. The girls have done a bunk."

"Done a bunk, sir? But how?"

He answered wearily. "Brown's Hotel has two entrances, one
in Albemarle Street and one in Dover Street. While we were . . .
er . . . saying 'goodnight' in the lobby, Lucille, Magda and Elsa

nipped out into Albemarle Street and were last seen making towards Piccadilly, hotly pursued by two American G.I.s and a Polish Air Force Sergeant. They vanished into the Blackout." He shrugged. "What's bred in the bone. . . ."

"And the Chinese one, sir?"

"Ah, Golden Mouse. While we were chasing Lucille, Magda and Elsa, Golden Mouse strolled into Dover Street, caught a taxi and told the driver to go to Free French Headquarters. By now"—he sighed—"she will without doubt be in the society of her beloved Colonel. I confess to you that I—envy that man."

Senior Commander Hogarth's ample bosom swelled. She said icily:

"In spite of your rank, sir, I must remind you that you are subject to the Provisions of the Army Act. Section 40 of that Act specifically mentions 'Neglect' and with the greatest respect, I suggest——"

"How I envy that man," said General Southerden with feeling. "Goodnight and bad luck, old girl. . . ."

19: THE WATERFALL

BREAKFAST at Brown's. At half past nine April reported with a staff car, and Charles and Verity drove to the War Office. Charles' interview with General Southerden was brief and he came out folding a piece of paper that ordered the temporary release of Major Hans Ramberg, German prisoner-of-war. Armed with this "open sesame", he arrived at the prison a few minutes after ten.

Hans Ramberg stood up as Charles entered his cell.

"Good morning to you," said Charles. "You've had breakfast? Good. I hope you'll be pleased to hear that I'm taking you out for the day. No point in sitting around here moping. Come on."

Verity was standing by the car. Charles introduced Hans at once.

"This is my friend Hans Ramberg, Staff Officer to the late General von Wolfram. My fiancée, Verity Gale."

"How do you do. Charles has told me a lot about you and how kind you were to him in France." She shook hands. "I've been looking forward to meeting you."

"I am honoured to meet Miss Gale." He shook his head in bewilderment. "But I do not understand——"

"You will. The lady driving the car answers to April. I'm afraid I don't know her other name. Verity, will you sit between us in the back? You know your way, April?"

"I should—by now."

The car swept along Western Avenue and past Gerrards Cross. A convoy of Army lorries with mounted searchlights rumbled towards London, and Hans watched them, a frown on his forehead. He was groping in his mind for the meaning of a half-forgotten English phrase and it came to him suddenly as the car entered Beaconsfield.

"Is it permitted to ask a question?"

"Of course."

"When you were presenting me to Miss . . . Miss Gale, you said I was Staff Officer to the *late* General von Wolfram. This word 'late'—does it not wish to say that a person is dead?"

"Yes. I'm afraid it does. We heard on the German wireless that your General had shot himself 'accidentally, while cleaning a revolver'. You know as well as I do what that means."

Hans' face, already pale and set, took on a grey tinge. He said, stumbling over the words:

"Yes. I understand. It means that the Gestapo have come for him. He would never do such a thing *freiwillig*, by his own wish. But he was a good man, loyal to his oath and to the Fuehrer. He was not one of us. To kill him or to compel him to kill himself is murder. He was a man without guilt."

"It is in your power to avenge the murder of this guiltless man."

The car crawled through High Wycombe, teeming with soldiers in training for the assault on Hitler's Europe, and began to climb the frosted slopes of the Chilterns. The March sun, red as a blood orange, pierced the morning mist that lay flat and still. Hans stared straight ahead, his mouth a thin line. At the hill's crest, he half-turned his head. His blue eyes were full of grief.

"For this murder of General Wolf, it is I who am to blame. For the death of Gaston and of Wanda, I am also to blame. In the Villa Mimosa were girls and laughter. Now this house is become a . . . a mortuary."

"Unless you help us, all Europe may become a mortuary."

"Now I am confused and very sad. Please permit me to think."

"That is what Verity and I want you to do. To think." He paused. "You see, the whole thing now depends on you and on you alone."

"That I do not understand. I am only *one* of your captives. My

brother officers and I are soldiers and as such must remain silent.
The girls of the Villa are not bound by tradition. They are already
your Allies. The first words of Lucille, who had been the willing
lover of us all, were '*à bas les Boches*'." He went on with bitterness: "Perhaps she hated us all the time. Who can tell with a
woman?"

"Who indeed?" said Charles dryly. He cleared his throat. "For
reasons with which I will not weary you, neither Lucille, Magda
nor Elsa are . . . er . . . available for interrogation at the
moment. Golden Mouse has reverted to her original loyalty and
I wish her nothing but joy. My respect for her and for the
honourable house of Li is profound. Madame has entered into
a period of contemplation and of penitence. Wanda is dead.
There only remains Monique—and you."

"Then men have died for nothing. The Villa Mimosa is a
ruin and all your endeavour is wasted."

"I most profoundly hope not. It is up to you."

The car descended the hill and sped in brittle sunshine along
the straight. Beyond the Lambert Arms there was a sign-post
re-erected since the threat of invasion had vanished. It read
OXFORD 16 MILES.

The car stopped outside the Trout at Godstow. Charles and
Verity got out but Hans sat bolt upright in the back.

"Come along," said Charles. "Sorry I haven't got a mandolin."

"But . . . but it would be incorrect for me to enter this place
now. It could lead to difficulties. I am wearing the uniform of
the German Army."

"Oh that," said Charles carelessly. "That doesn't matter in
the least. What do you suppose—that the landlord will empty a
pint of mild and bitter over you? England is teeming with free
troops, free Danes, free Norwegians, free Poles, free French—
and they all wear comic uniforms. You'll be mistaken for one
of the free. Pity it's not true."

"I used to visit this place when I was an undergraduate. I
could be recognized."

"If you were, he or she would probably buy you a drink.
Hostilities cease by the waterfall." He held the door of the car
open. Hans got out. They walked together along the terrace. At the
entrance to the tap-room, Hans hesitated. He said awkwardly:

"I would like to stay here, outside, by this river for a little
while. I know I am your . . . your prisoner but if you allow me

to stay here by myself, I could feel that I was free. We Germans are adept at deceiving ourselves."

Charles glanced at Verity. She gave an almost imperceptible nod.

"I will give you my *Ehrenwort,* my word of honour, that I will not seek to escape."

"Quite unnecessary. Come in when you're ready."

Charles and Verity went into the tap-room. Two old men were talking in rumbling, complaining voices about the rising price of sheep-dip, and a young R.A.F. officer and his bride sat entranced in their own private, fleeting world. Charles ordered two drinks and they sat together in the corner. He said to Verity in a worried voice:

"I said that I'd be guided by you, my darling. But nothing has happened."

"More has happened than either of us know. Please go on being guided by me. Ask him nothing. Don't put a single question to him. Let it simply be what you said, 'a day out'."

"But Verity——"

She laid her hand on his.

"I know how desperately important it is. I know it could be the difference between peace coming and the war going on and I still beg of you with all my heart to ask him nothing. Every single instinct I have tells me I'm right."

Ten minutes passed and then a quarter of an hour. The door of the tap-room opened and Hans crossed the floor. He gave a little bow to Verity.

"I am most grateful to you for this moment of freedom. I have listened to the waterfall and its music was even more beautiful than the songs played by our good pianist Charles in the Villa Mimosa." He smiled. "My mind has been washed by the water of this river. And now, please, I would like to go back to the prison."

*   *   *

In his cell, Hans Ramberg took a sheet of lined paper and looked at it for a long time. Then he wrote:

To Major Charles Addison:
My dear friend,
   I hope you will forgive me, your prisoner, for addressing you in this way. It is a familiarity which will not be repeated.
   I bare my soul to you for the last time.

Germany has lost the war. My friends and I have known this for a long time. Our leaders, the Nazis, also know this but they continue to fight because the Allies offer Germany no hope and no terms. We are told night and day by Goebbels that the words "unconditional surrender" mean unconditional and everlasting slavery for all, and because of that Germany must fight on until the last man is destroyed. My friends and I were determined to kill Hitler so that we could say to the Allies that we ourselves, Germans, had rid Germany of our evil leaders. We could sue for peace with a little honour.

I can be silent no longer. Chivalry has unloosed my tongue. I ask myself, as a Staff Officer, what I would wish to know if our situations were reversed. The men of whom I now write are honourable Germans. When the Allies have won victory, I pray God that this will be remembered. . . .

Hans took a fresh page. He wrote on steadily, pausing only to search for a word. Twilight settled about the corners of his cell so that it was hard to see. It was time to put up the blackout frames and he did so. A moment later, the prison lights were switched on and he went back to his wooden table and picked up his pen.

A warder brought him in a meagre supper of bread, margarine and cocoa. He said in a friendly voice:

"Writing a letter to the missus, sir?"

"No. Not to my wife. I . . . I am a bachelor."

"Some people have all the luck! Well, lights out in forty minutes so you'd better get on with it fast."

"Yes. I will do that. Get on with it fast."

Hans Ramberg reached his last paragraph. He wrote:

I have written fully and for one purpose only. It is so that the war, already lost to us, may be more quickly at an end. I do not consider that I have betrayed my country. I hope that my words may save something of the true doomed Germany I love. General von Wolfram will surely have need of a staff officer in Valhalla and I propose to place myself at his side. To you and to Miss Gale, I send my gratitude. I will pray for your happiness.

Long live Germany!

Your affectionate friend,

Hans Ramberg (B.A. Oxon).

The lights went out all over the prison. Hans folded the twelve sheets of paper in the darkness. He knelt by his bed. Many many months ago, he had prepared for such a moment as this—in case the Gestapo caught up with him. He did not wish to belabour the Almighty with overlong supplications and his prayers were brief. He stood up, feeling inside his mouth with the tip of his tongue until he touched a tiny glass capsule lodged in a hollow tooth. Deliberately, he worked it loose. He was without fear and only consumed by an immense curiosity. From far away in South London, he heard the thin wailing of an air-raid siren. The sound was taken up by other sirens until it seemed that the whole, darkened city was whooping and carolling. How very odd that his compatriots should come at this moment!

He bit hard on the capsule, crunching the glass. How very odd——

SUBSMASH!

J. E. Macdonnell

"Subsmash!" is published by
Constable & Co. Ltd.

The Author

J. E. Macdonnell is an Australian from Queensland. In 1934 he joined the Royal Australian Navy as an Ordinary Seaman, Second Class. He served in pretty nearly every vessel in the R.A.N., and after twelve years gained a commission. 1945 saw publication in Melbourne of his first book, *Fleet Destroyer*. Other successes he has written are *Valiant Occasions, Gimme the Boats* and *Wings off the Sea*. He joined the staff of the *Sydney Bulletin* in 1948.

Subsmash! is the latest of his "Jim Brady" novels, which have firmly established Mr. Macdonnell as an outstanding writer about the sea.

CHAPTER ONE

Australia, 1959.

A red sun lowering into a flushed ocean stared upon a solitary, moving submarine. The vessel was crawling across an immense circle of sea, towards an edge bitten in the west by the stone headlands of Sydney Harbour. As the colour faded from all but one quickened track of water, the sombre craft was held more closely within the tightened wheel of the horizon.

The vessel's foredeck casing was not level, but swelled into a black hammer-head of a nose; yet her stem where it met the water was very fine, so that she ran along with two thin spurts of liquid curving upward. These twin bow-waves ran aft to meet the saddle-tanks which bulged her belly, and slipped over them in little catspaws of white foam.

"Starb'd twenty."

The voice from the bridge was quiet but assured. Lieutenant-Commander Eric Ransome, D.S.O., Royal Navy, tilted his body a little to counter the list as the rudder went over, his eyes on the opening between North and South Head. He was small and squat, with a strong thick look about his shoulders. Fourteen years ago, towards the end of the Second World War, he had been injured by a rifle-shot from a merchant ship he had ordered to heave-to. The bullet had gone in through his left cheek, just below the bone under his eye, and out through the flesh under his left jowl. It had been a nasty wound, but it had healed neatly except at the point of entrance, where it had a strong tendency to pucker, drawing his eyelid down on his cheek and giving him the look of a bulldog.

"Ease to ten," said Ransome.

This cryptic order was repeated, and the helmsman below in the control-room allowed his steering wheel to spin back through his fingers. When the brass pointer on the helm indicator fingered ten he steadied his wheel, reported "Ten degrees of starb'd wheel on, sir," and waited for the next expected command :

"Midships."

Now the helmsman took off all his wheel—the rudder was

fore and aft, neutral. As he spun the spokes he looked at the
ship's head, as indicated by a thin black line on his gyro compass.
So that when he heard his captain say "Steady!" the helmsman
could answer at once:

"Two-seven-eight, sir."

"Steer two-seven-four," Ransome ordered.

So H.M. Submarine *Diana* received, some weeks after she had
left Singapore, the final command which would place her torpedo-
loaded bow neatly in the watery gap between the Heads of
Sydney Harbour.

She slid her long, low, ugly length through the gap and shaped
up to her berth just as the first street-lights began to pierce the
dying day in the city ahead of her. British naval craft seldom use
harbour pilots. *Diana* had men on her bow and others on her
stern; a small party waited for her lines on the pier of Garden
Island dockyard. She would lie there a day or two before shifting
back up-harbour to a more permanent berth at Balmoral Naval
Depot.

She edged warily towards the pier, which stalked on long legs
into the water to meet her. From her bows two lines went through
the air, whistling, and struck at the pier viciously, like the fangs
of a snake. Three minutes later she was bound head and stern,
her bulging tanks snuggled in against large wooden catamarans
which kept them from damaging contact with her moorings.

Ahead of her, grey and lean and quiet, lay a large modern Fleet
destroyer: the mongoose and the snake were lying together.

Diana's wardroom, into which four of her officers had come
for a pre-dinner snort, was small, compactly fitted-out, and cosy.
There was a table with a brown baize cloth, padded benches
around it bolted to the steel deck, a bookcase, a locked pistol-
cupboard, and two coloured photographs. The walls—bulkheads
and ship's side—were a clean white.

In one of the photographs a pretty girl with an empty face
reclined in a pose of eternal suggestion; her sister in the second
photograph suggested less, but displayed more. At the table a
man with a nose and chin like a lobster's claw sipped his gin
and water and gazed up at the shadowed curves and smooth
white legs. His nutcracker face was thoughtful. He was the
navigator, his name was Thornton, but for as long as he could
remember he had answered to nothing but "Pilot".

"I think I might step ashore," Pilot decided. "Heard a thing
or two about the talent in Sydney."

"You might as well," a morose companion agreed. "God knows when we'll get the chance once that bloke starts his fun and games."

Pilot glanced at the speaker, a long, cadaverous man with a swooping nose, a narrow jaw, and untidy grey eyebrows over closely-set greenish eyes. His features had something of the same sharp outline as Pilot's, but there the similarity ended. Pilot's mouth and eyes denoted humour and friendliness; the thin nose and thin mouth of the other man, Lieutenant Deevers, showed him to be pessimistic, disagreeable, perhaps even shifty.

"What bloke?" Pilot asked. "Brady?"

"Our little lord and master from now on," Deevers assented unpleasantly. "Captain Brady, R.A.N." He gave a slight, sour emphasis to the letter "A". "Boss of the destroyer-flotilla—newly-appointed, anxious to shine."

"Hm," said Pilot, returning his attention to the photographs.

"One thing about our colonial hosts," Deevers continued as he poured himself a fresh drink, "they're workers. They know little about submarines—got none of their own. Believe me, with this Brady fellow in charge, we'll be working our guts out licking 'em into some sort of shape." He lifted his glass, and ended with a teeth-showing lift of his lip:

"And Brady's come up from the lower-deck."

"That has its advantages." A cool, deep voice spoke from the doorway.

Four heads swung towards the man standing there. He was lean, wide-shouldered and tall. The faces of Deevers and Pilot were like poor preliminary sketches for his dark, eager and aquiline profile—and he was one of those men whom one always thinks of in profile, as of the clean-cut edge of some weapon. He looked back at them from eyes of quite startling brilliance—the brilliancy of steel, as though they had been polished by the wind.

From beside the newcomer's shoulder, with its four gold rings on the white shirt, Lieutenant-Commander Ransome looked at his officers with thunder in his face.

"Captain Brady," he introduced his visitor tightly.

They were on their feet now, and the glasses were on the table. Ransome made them known to the destroyer captain, who nodded at each name, a brief recognition which was not enlarged in any way when Ransome came to the torpedo officer, Deevers. Brady had a cigarette in his hand. He held a lighter to it, smiling

at them over its little golden spear-point of flame. Pilot held out
the room's one chair and he sat down, lowering himself through
a leisurely breath of smoke.

"Yes," he said pleasantly, "a crawl up through the hawse-pipe
into the wardroom has its points." He turned his head quickly
and looked straight at Deevers. "You don't agree?"

Deevers swallowed. His pale green eyes widened a trifle; his
mouth formed a nominal smile.

"Why yes, sir. Yes, of course." For an instant pride made him
hesitate, then he added:

"Please understand, sir, I meant no disparagement in what I
said. It's—it's just that your rise to command of a flotilla from
the lower-deck is—well, sir, it's a bit unusual."

Brady's cool gaze told him that his words had camouflaged
his real feelings about as effectively as a sheet of glass. He dropped
his eyes to the table. For a moment Brady stroked the ash-tray
with the tip of his cigarette.

"I didn't come aboard to talk shop," he said, addressing them
generally in the same pleasant tone, "but now the subject's been
brought up. . . . Yes, I'm afraid you will be working pretty
intensively at first. As Lieutenant Deevers mentioned, I'm quite
new to the flotilla. I think you may blame that fact for your
having been brought all the way down from Singapore—we
wanted a large, modern boat to work with."

He drew his trimmed cigarette-end to a fresh glow, holding
their attention away from the discomfited Deevers. He wanted to
make it plain to them that the British submarine, just arrived on
this Commonwealth station, would not be judged by its torpedo
officer.

"However," he went on, "that's tomorrow. We've got all night
before my ship, *Scourge*—she's lying just ahead of you—starts
chasing you over the briny. Which brings me to the real purpose
of my visit." His smile took in Ransome, whose weather-dark
face had relaxed a little. "You must be feeling a trifle cramped
in here; in fact, you must be heartily sick of it. That thing of
mine's not a destroyer—she's a young cruiser, as you may have
noticed. We can seat you all at dinner tonight."

The little table was ringed with smiles, which Brady felt were
not merely dutiful. Pilot answered for them.

"I believe the beer is seven per cent alcohol in Sydney, sir?"

"Something like that, yes," Brady grinned. "You'd better stick
to gin." He rose so lithely from his chair that he surprised them.

"When you're ready," he told them, and with a look at Ransome stepped out through the door.

It was twilight above deck. The British commander waited until they were at the submarine's little gangway, reaching from her casing to the pier.

"I'm damned sorry about that, sir," he began.

"Forget it," Brady told him crisply. "The day juniors pack up slamming seniors in the Navy will be the day. It was his bad luck we dropped in on him like that."

"Nevertheless, sir. . . ."

"If you're worrying about the lower-deck comment," Brady spoke on top of him, "I'm not. Not now, old chap."

He smiled down into the bulldog face level with his shoulder, and understanding was between them like electricity bridging a gap. Brady knew that his last words, cheerfully spoken, had been accepted as an admission that his mess-deck beginnings had once been cause for heartburn. But not now—and Ransome treated the phrase as if it had been a plea, and said no more. The two men stood in silence for a moment, while Brady smoked his cigarette and Ransome regarded the lights already reflected in the harbour water.

"By the way," Brady said suddenly, "I've been asked to a do ashore tonight, after dinner. Reserve officer—knew him during the war. He's an obstetrical surgeon now—making piles of dough. How about coming along? I won't know anybody else there. It's a sort of housewarming, as far as I can make out. He's moved into a new place down at Whale Beach—it'd be a pleasant run in the car. Eh?"

"Why, yes," said Ransome, surprised, "of course I'd like to come. Be a bit late though, won't it?"

"Doesn't matter with this bloke," Brady grinned, "or this party. We'll push off as soon as we can, all the same." He stepped on to the gangway, tossing his cigarette-end into the water. "You'll be along soon?"

"Very soon," responded Ransome.

"Right, then," Brady nodded, and the sudden note of the bosun's pipe sounded through the dusk as he crossed to the pier.

Captain Brady walked back to his destroyer slowly, hardly noticing the gleam of open water beyond the submarine, or the rigging of ships in for refit, black against the darkening sky. The remark he had overheard from Lieutenant Deevers had sharpened a sting of awareness in his mind. So they still thought about his lowly beginnings: he had thought those forgotten, but here was a British officer down from Singapore, and he knew.

The bow of his own ship cut out the scene across the dockyard; he could see the pennant number painted on her side. The name *Scourge* came under his hand as he strode up the sloping gangway. He said crisply to the officer waiting to receive him:

"They're all coming, Number One. And they look thirsty. I'll be in my cabin. Let me know when Lieutenant-Commander Ransome arrives."

"Aye, aye, sir," the first-lieutenant answered. He was a big, paunchy man with square shoulders and a square face which smiled quickly but never as though the smile came from deep inside. He seemed to hesitate, then he said:

"Will you and Lieutenant-Commander Ransome be staying in your cabin, sir?"

"No," Brady replied at once. Then he understood what was behind his second-in-command's question. "We'll join you after dinner," he added more slowly, and waited for Cowan's smile to die. As first-lieutenant, Cowan was president of the wardroom mess, and theoretically the captain entered it only on invitation. Brady had been in command of his new ship less than a week, yet already he sensed that Cowan preferred his absence from the wardroom.

But the shallow smile remained on the large square face.

"Of course, sir. We'll be delighted to have you."

Brady nodded, and turned forward towards his cabin. There was no outward change in his demeanour as he walked along the steel deck, any more than the shape of a radio set changes when it is switched on. But already the circuits of training and experience had awakened to receptive life, telling him with dispassionate certainty that Cowan felt some animosity, vague yet perceptible, towards him. It was only a feeling, there had been no actual surliness or questioning of orders—and of course there never would be, in a Service as tightly disciplined as this one. But it was there, and that "delighted to have you" was part of it.

With any other officer Brady would have dismissed the matter from mind, believing that so long as such a man did his job efficiently, he was at perfect liberty to hate his captain's guts. But Cowan was his second-in-command: if Cowan disliked him, the whole ship's progress towards Brady's ideal could be slowed down. Cowan might have his paintwork spotless, his gun-drill might be perfect, he might have the crew exercised thoroughly in seamanship. But it took more than material proficiency to make a fighting craft: you had to have *esprit de corps,* every man's pride in his vessel, complete confidence in the officers' teamwork. . . . Brady's look was troubled when he reached his own quarters.

He stepped into the little pantry and made some final arrangements with his steward about the meal for his guest. "I'll have some bottles and glasses on a tray, Benson," he called back as he passed through to his cabin. He did not like a *tête-à-tête* to be spoiled by a man standing around serving drinks. He saw that Benson had already laid a table in expectation of Ransome's arrival, and indeed it was not long before the first-lieutenant knocked at the door. The British commander had come aboard and was with him.

"Take a pew," Brady invited, slapping the wide arm of a chintz-covered easy chair. "We'll have a drink before we feed. You'll join us, Number One?"

"Thank you, sir," Cowan answered civilly, "but *Diana's* team is on board. I think I should get down there."

Brady nodded. That was fair enough. "We'll be with you later," he said, and Cowan departed.

Ransome asked for gin, and Brady handed it down from the tray. He poured beer for himself. He offered a carved wooden cigarette-box, but Ransome shook his head and pulled out a pipe. The bowl was blackened, scraped thin, and had a half-inch crack running down the left side. The mouth of the stem had been nearly bitten through. Ransome stuffed the bowl full from an old pouch, clamped the stem between his white teeth, and lit up from Brady's match. The scarred side of his face closed into a prodigious wink. His work on the pipe made a sound like a rotary-pump and produced rapid wreaths of smoke.

"And you submarine blokes worry about chlorine gas," Brady marvelled.

The two commanders had relaxed into the companionable mood that followed from their conversation at *Diana's* gangway. As they talked now, however, Ransome was studying the officer before him. Until the inquiries he had made in Singapore after learning of his new assignment to Australia, he had not heard of Captain James Brady, R.A.N. But he knew well enough the calibre of a man who could haul himself up from ordinary seaman to the rank of captain, even with the accelerated promotion of a world war to help him on.

It must have taken the most single-minded application, Ransome reasoned: a relentless discipline of work and study beneath the watchful eyes of waiting senior officers. And years of that would surely make a man a martinet, determined both by natural bent and toughness of experience to exact the utmost from his subordinates. Now he himself was one of those subordinates, detailed to work with and under this self-made commander. Yet so far he had not found Brady overbearing, and he had noticed few signs of strain in his manner. Ransome drew on his pipe and wondered what the future might reveal.

Brady had an inkling of his visitor's thoughts; he was used to other officers studying him like that while they tried to disguise their interest. To them he was a queer bird, an unusual specimen, something quite apart from their own regulated channels of advancement. Once he had enjoyed their carefully casual questions, but now the game of suiting his replies to the questioners did not amuse him. Public attention and his years of achievement had left him with an attitude of which he was less conscious: the habit of feeling that he was expected to be equal or superior to his brother captains in the discharge of every duty. He really wanted to be friendly with Ransome; but this was partly because he wanted to learn what Ransome had to teach.

Brady was certainly practised in the finding, tracking and destroying of submarines. But methods of detection and Asdic control had developed enormously since the Second World War. He felt that it was not good enough for him to become proficient in methods of attack, learned in the anti-submarine school at Watson; he wanted to know the methods of evasion, to share in imagination the thoughts and even the emotional reactions of the experts underwater. Ransome must be a bright boy, one of the brightest, to get command of the Royal Navy's newest and largest submarine. Brady believed that frankness with this specialist would serve him best. He pulled at his beer and waited for his chance.

Ransome had been speaking of the war. "It dies hard, you know," he concluded, face puckered round his pipe, "and yet it's more than fourteen years ago. The only officer in my wardroom who's seen war service is Number One. I suppose you find the same?"

"Much the same," Brady agreed. "My Number One—and the gunner, of course. I shipped with him, way back, when I was a petty officer on B-gun. But I've got a pretty taut hand in my Asdic instructor. Remember *Swordsman*—five U-boats in one day in the Atlantic? Well, Slocum was her HSD then—or Underwater Control Rating, first-class, as they call 'em now. You'd better keep your tail tucked in when we're tracking you tomorrow."

Ransome smiled, then tapped his teeth with his pipe. "*Swordsman*," he said thoughtfully. "Wasn't her Old Man a chap named Brookes?"

"Brookes it was. Did you know him? He was captain of my first destroyer, the old *Scourge*." Brady was delighted that the Englishman had heard of the man who had taught him most. "He retired about three years ago," he went on. "Buried himself on Green Island, up in the Reef. As for the *Scourge*, she was scrapped after the war, but this ship we're on was named after her...."

"And there are several younger Brookes on Green Island," Ransome completed his thought. They smiled at each other, a trifle glumly. "No, I never met Brookes," Ransome continued, "but if your Asdic man—Slocum, is it?—was with him long, he's bound to be good, five U-boats or no. Looks as if our exercise in the morning is going to be interesting."

They both laughed; then Brady felt that his opportunity had come.

"I've got a pretty keen bunch of captains in this flotilla," he said soberly. "All of them with Atlantic experience. I've got Slocum, too, but . . ." he hesitated, "well, a man has to keep on the ball with those fellows. Even apart from that, it doesn't do my crew any harm at all to gain first contact."

He saw the interest on Ransome's face tighten into disbelief, then into something hard like granite. God, Brady thought, he thinks I want him to give his position away to me tomorrow! His sense of shock was followed by anger, but he went on in a friendly and casual tone:

"There's only one way to do that, as I see it, and that is to learn how the other half lives, sort of thing. I'd be glad if you could arrange for me to transfer to *Diana* out there tomorrow. I'd like two hours with you if possible."

"Your Number One should jump at the chance of playing skipper," Ransome said. He knew that Brady had been aware of his misunderstanding, and he kept his voice even.

"I think it would be a good thing if I came over to you after manoeuvres and the main exercise," Brady clinched the matter.

"That would be best, sir," nodded Ransome.

Inwardly, Brady began to smile. The older man, now very much the junior officer, had not been entirely to blame for leaping to the wrong conclusion. Brady reflected that he could have made his meaning more plain or his approach more direct. Perhaps, after all, he had not chosen the best moment: he had crowded the fish and then been clumsy with his strike. As these thoughts passed through Brady's mind, Ransome looked up from knocking out his pipe. Sub-hunter and submariner regarded each other steadily, then their eyes lit with a gleam of mutual comprehension and amusement.

Brady rose to his feet. "Let's have a bite before we look in at the wardroom," he suggested, and pressed a buzzer on the bulkhead. "Must get a move on, if we want to be at Whale Beach tonight." He nodded at Benson in the doorway, and the steward withdrew to fetch the first course.

"Do we change out of uniform," Ransome asked as he seated himself at the table, "or go as we are?"

Brady, pacing the carpet, pulled at his nose. The gesture gave him a boyish look. "As we are, I think," he answered. "I haven't met Farley, this Reserve bloke, since the war, but I doubt if he's altered. The beggar would be in uniform himself if he could. You know the type—a Reserve who's more pusser-built than regular Navy."

"A lot of 'em were like that," Ransome agreed. "Damned good thing in a way—I had a lot of respect for Reserves in the war. Came from one job, learned another."

Brady nodded, and sat down as Benson reappeared with the soup. "Tastes fine," Ransome said after a moment in response to Brady's look, and they fell to with one accord.

The senior wardroom in *Scourge* was forward, under the bridge. As Captain Brady pulled aside a brown curtain and ushered Ransome in, the talk of the assembled officers died away and those who were seated scuffled to their feet. Cowan, waiting near the doorway, came forward at once with his shallow smile, while Brady waved his hand deprecatingly to the men behind as if to say: "Now look, chaps, I don't want you to stand up when I come in; please sit down."

None of them did so; they were expectant and not quite at ease with the two commanders among them. When Cowan, as president of the mess, had welcomed the visitor, Brady took Ransome along the loose line representing *Scourge*, introducing his gunnery-control officer, his surgeon and engineer and radar officer, the lieutenants in charge of Asdic and torpedoes, until he came to Mr. Seymour, his gunner. Ransome was surprised by the gunner's quick and youthful handshake.

"I imagine," he said genially, "you've got some pretty nifty gadgets on board, Guns?"

"That's for sure, sir," Seymour grinned. "I could open up and let you have a look at some of 'em if you like."

"Seymour," Brady said, "is only half joking. Come and sit down before you're trapped for a gunnery course." He urged Ransome towards the two large chairs left suggestively empty. Seymour's expression as Brady turned away had a hint of affection in it, and Ransome guessed that the two men were close in trust and respect—old shipmates, both gunnery, and both from the lower-deck.

He settled into the chair beside Brady's and looked about the room, nodding at those of his own officers who caught his eye. "I see what you mean," he said.

"Eh?"

"You said something earlier about a young cruiser."

Brady chuckled. "Gimme the boats, eh? I imagine there's very little derision in that old cry now. This mess"—he took a glass for Ransome from the steward's tray held down to him—"would be as big as a couple of messdecks on the old boats. Which brings me to my favourite heretical contention—that comfort in no way detracts from efficiency." Brady took a drink for himself, and the steward, smart in starched white, withdrew from earshot. "I know, because I shifted from a small mess holding about eight seamen petty-officers to a cabin holding me. The sybaritic life didn't make me less efficient—or at least, I had no kicks from the Old Man." He grinned.

"I wouldn't know," Ransome joked, and Brady's mind went back to the butter-box of a wardroom on the submarine.

"But you wouldn't transfer back to general service?"

The nuggety submariner shook his head. "Sometimes," he admitted mildly, "I do wonder why not."

Brady saw Cowan coming towards them, a glass of beer in one hand, the other dragging a chair behind him. He subdued his slight annoyance: he would have preferred the first-lieutenant to await an invitation, but Cowan was the president of this mess, after all. He said pleasantly as the big officer placed his chair before them:

"I'm afraid we're talking shop, Number One."

"I'd hoped you were, sir." Cowan's smile stretched a little. "Makes it easier for me to break the rule."

Again Brady felt the twinge of annoyance. Cowan's reply and his smile were almost . . . cocky. Not enough for him to be slammed down; not nearly enough. But there was that about his demeanour which decided Brady that he would, when opportunity arose, slam him down hard.

"What's your problem, Number One?"

Cowan took a gulp of his beer. "Hardly a problem, sir." Brady saw the line of wetness left round his mouth. Cowan removed it with his tongue. "It's just that I'm interested in the future—the technological future of the Navy."

He drank again, and Brady wondered suddenly just how many beers Cowan had already sunk this evening.

"As opposed to the passing parade," Cowan continued flamboyantly, "represented by—well—this destroyer."

With his last words he had shifted his eyes to Ransome. For a long three seconds the submarine commander did not speak, and Brady knew intuitively that Ransome was sharing his own irritation. "I suppose you agree with the ideas of the missile boys?" Ransome said at last.

"Why yes, sir!" After he had spoken Cowan nodded quickly at the submariner, his smile wide, and Brady realized with distaste that he meant to flatter Ransome's perspicacity. "I don't suppose you've been aboard one of the American atom-submarines, sir?"

"No."

"Don't you think, sir," said Cowan, leaning forward in a confidential position, his elbows on his spread knees, "that those three or four atom-subs of the Yanks have made all our stuff obsolete?"

"You're not serious, are you?" Brady came near to grinning at the curtness in Ransome's voice.

"Yes, sir, of course." But Cowan sounded a little uncertain. He recognized that tone, Brady judged. "Their endurance, their underwater speed. . . ." He went on more quickly, gathering assurance with his words: "The great weakness of submarines has been their inability to stay submerged for very long. We only had to sit on top of one of 'em for long enough and he had to surface. You know that, sir. But with these American boats —what hope have we got? Weeks, they stay down. And now they're fitted with missiles. . . ." He chuckled and relegated the world's navies to the scrapyard with a sideways gesture of his hand.

"I really think you believe in your conclusions," Ransome pondered, and Brady sat back, waiting.

"I don't think there's any question about the capabilities of the new boats," remarked Cowan with a touch of smugness.

"No question at all," Ransome nodded. "The atom-powered boats are fast, both on top and underneath, some are fitted with guided missiles, and they can cruise pretty well indefinitely."

"Well, sir. . . ."

"The only reason I'm not worried about our employment for years to come," Ransome told him, his voice clipped, "is that at the moment there are no more than four atom-powered submarines in existence. As opposed to that, the Russians have some four hundred conventional types, and we own one or two ourselves. . . ."

"But their missiles, sir—they can stand off and blow hell out of a target miles inland. Their fire-power. . . ." The smile had slipped from Cowan's large face.

"Their fire-power is considerable," Ransome conceded, slightly nettled by the interruption. "But there are still only four of them. The nine seas cover a hefty slice of operational water. And while an enemy mounts four hundred conventional submarines, you must be able to meet his threat with destroyers—killer ships. That is what you are serving in now. A killer ship."

"Yes, sir. But you must progress," Cowan muttered.

"Of course! I'm conservative, but only to a degree. In my own boat I've got equipment I would have given my eye-teeth for during the war. So have you—vastly improved Asdic, the 'Squid' and 'Limbo' to clobber us with depth-charges, all those things. And that's the stuff you'd use, not those four atom-subs. . . ." He stopped, and grinned at Brady. "I'm sorry. Perhaps it was Nelson who made that rule against talking shop; anyhow, it's a damn good one." He applied himself to his glass.

"Not at all," said Brady with a grin he tried to keep from looking satisfied. "You were pulled into it. Eh, Number One?"

"Yes, sir," dutifully.

"Maybe the automatic ship will come," Ransome resumed more kindly, "atom-propelled and all the rest of it. But even then that ship will have to sail either in or on the sea. So don't get starry-eyed. Seamanship"—he drained his glass and, leaning forward to place it on the low table before him, looked up into Cowan's face—"seamanship is, has been, and always will be the prime concern of a fighting Fleet."

"Exactly," Brady concluded, and stood up. "We're shoving off now, Number One. The lieutenant-commander has been short on his shore-leave a long time. Everyone seems to be happy. . . ." His eye wandered among the mingled officers, passed across a steward bearing a tray of salted nuts and sausages on sticks, came to rest lightly on the first-lieutenant's paunch. "I know you'll see to it that they get what they want: plenty of smokes, plenty of food, and—ah—sufficient to drink."

"Yes, sir," said Cowan.

CHAPTER TWO

CAPTAIN BRADY'S car, a six-months-old Jaguar, gleamed richly in the pool of light at the foot of his destroyer's gangway. During the day it stood in the shade of a tall pile of steel-plating farther up the pier, but it had been brought down to the *Scourge* ready for use. As Ransome settled into his red leather seat, he expressed his admiration.

"Your father own a kangaroo farm? Or is he in diamonds?"

"Not quite," Brady smiled. "I'm not married."

"And this brute's got the lot, eh?"

"That's about it."

Brady fitted the ignition key into its slot, and the harsh power of the starter-motor died into the whispering hum of the engine. The big black car moved off, with Brady navigating carefully among the reels of electric cable and tangled anchors and other bric-à-brac of a naval dockyard. At the wide main gate a policeman saluted, and then the road stretched deserted up past a sandstone cliff on one side and some dark warehouses on the other. Brady pressed his foot down and the two-hundred horsepower under the bonnet responded with a surge that forced Ransome back against his seat. Before he could speak there was a slight hesitation and then the car was in top gear, gliding smoothly and almost without sound up towards the city.

"I dunno," Ransome said with a grin, "I've got a wife and three kids. . . ."

"I'd swap this for any one of 'em," Brady replied, and the sudden fervour in his voice made Ransome pause before he commented dryly:

"They're not hard to come by, you know."

Brady nodded. "So I hear." He had to swing hard right at the top of the hill. "St. Mary's Cathedral," he pointed out, and the subject appeared to be closed.

As the car moved down behind Sydney Hospital and into Macquarie Street, Ransome looked about him with the interest of a sailor in a port he was seeing for the first time. But one cannot see much of a city from a car window at night, and though Brady occasionally drew his attention to some notable feature, Ransome soon resigned himself to the hypnotic effect of lights flickering across his eyes, closed them, and dozed. Brady had by now fallen silent. He was in fact again worrying about his second-in-command.

That Cowan was a bit batty about atom-powered ships and guided missiles was not a cause for anxiety; he would be dangerously insensitive if these things did not impress him. But his attitude to Brady—that half-hidden insolence, founded perhaps on resentment or a sense of inferiority—could be very infectious among the ship's crew, and as an epidemic would be difficult to check. A sailor caught out in a misdemeanour growled about his punishment but ruefully appreciated the cleverness of the top brass in catching him; it was entirely different if he could justify himself by whining: "Why pick on me, when the Number One couldn't care less?"

The Jaguar halted, then took off smoothly from the harbour bridge toll-gates towards the bridge itself. Brady thought: there's always some blasted thing to worry about! You reach the top, you get command of a whole flotilla, you should feel like a million—and you feel these pricks digging in and keeping the old stomach rolling.

What had Ransome said? "Your Number One should jump at the chance of playing skipper." Perhaps that was the answer, if it was a feeling of inferiority that prompted Cowan's behaviour. Well, tomorrow might show that Cowan could be cured; the taste of responsibility worked wonders with some men. Brady felt a little cheered. He glanced at the speedometer, glowing from the polished maple dashboard, he felt the car's smooth power under his foot, he remembered what he had been able to pay for it, and the hard planes of his face creased into a grin. What the hell had he really to gripe about? His long struggle had brought him to an enviable position which peace would consolidate, or war improve. He knew his job, every wrinkle of it.

He was sure of himself. With boyish elation he said to Ransome:
"I think this might turn out all right tonight."

The submarine skipper turned from his drowsy contemplation
of the light-sparkling harbour below them. "I expect it might,"
he replied. "Where are we?"

"North Sydney. This area—farther up, of course, Newport,
Avalon, Whale Beach—is about the best. One beach after another; trees, too. I'd like to settle here one day. I'm from the
bush, you know—Queensland. Up here you've got everything—
bush, and the sea as well. Just about perfect."

"A little expensive?"

"Damned expensive. But it would be worth it. I've been thinking quite a bit about it lately." He swung the car into Miller
Street; a tree-thick park slid darkly by; intimacy came into
Brady's voice. "Kids, down on the beach every weekend. Somewhere to come home to in port. You know how it is. I'm thirty-
six. About time I organized something."

"More than time. It's none of my business, of course, but I'm
surprised you've held out so long."

"Maybe it's because I've gone flat out for promotion. No time
or thought for much else. But now I think of Brookes, up on
Green Island. He had no children." Brady paused, then repeated:
"I'm thirty-six. It worries me." He added no more, and Ransome
made no further comment. Both men sat in quiet companionship
during the rest of the thirty-mile drive.

They left the city behind, and the Jaguar's headlights burned
a white swathe through the trees of French's Forest. The road
was smooth and well-marked, and almost deserted. The stitches
of the yellow line passed under the long bonnet in swift and
rhythmic sequence. Ransome noticed at one moment that the
Jaguar was doing eighty-five. Soon after that it slowed steadily,
and a mile or so north of Avalon turned off the main road. Brady
drove carefully between a scrub-hung hill rising on the right,
and a dark slope dropping away out of sight on the left. Several
hundred feet below, the Pacific beat in a lazy and never-ceasing
surge against the cliffs.

The headlights washed over the polished bodies of half a
dozen cars ahead, parked where the road ended. Beyond and
above them, at the top of a wide concrete drive buttressed from
the cliff by a sandstone wall, loomed a huge glass-fronted house,
pouring out yellow light and the sounds of many people enjoying themselves.

"This must be it," said Brady, switching off the engine. "If you sink a few, don't wander round the garden. Farley told me that the sea's two hundred feet down, and there's nothing between you and it but a low wall. All set?"

They climbed out and walked up the drive. A few yards short of the wide steps leading to the front door, Ransome halted. He stared out across the light-glinting water below them, at the sombre black of the cliffs across the bay, north to where the incandescent sword of Barrenjoey Lighthouse swept in its disciplined circle. Then he turned and looked at the long frontage of the white mansion.

"Some place," he murmured, thinking of his small flat in Portsmouth, the frequent discussions on school fees and children's clothes, and his wife's liking for little adventures like this one he was enjoying.

"Not a blade of grass or a tree in the lot, I bet," Brady demurred. "But," he nodded, grinning, "expensive."

As they mounted the steps, Ransome could see across a terrace through big windows into the living-room. Even in that short glance his view encompassed a TV set and radiogram, what looked like a film-projection unit, a cocktail bar, and several huge vases of brilliant flowers.

"H'm," he said, "friend Farley was wise to leave the Service."

The front door stood open, but Brady pressed the bell. There was no answer except for a din of conversation from the packed living-room. Fishing in his pocket, Brady stepped into the hall. "This'll bring him out," he said, producing a small silver object which he put to his mouth. He took a breath, and the next instant the sound of a bosun's pipe shrilled through to the guests.

A large man seemed to explode from the living-room doorway. Ransome got an overpowering impression of size and joviality, of welcome radiating from the grin on a red face. The man came down on them like a battleship, his right hand thrust out before him like a ram.

"My God, Brady, that brought back memories!" he boomed, gripping the destroyerman's hand with one of his own and his shoulder with the other. His glance ran down the visitor's uniform, and his grin widened.

"I thought it might," Brady played along. He got his hand back and turned. "This is Lieutenant-Commander Ransome. He's got _Diana_. She's a submarine, just in, and I knew you wouldn't mind. . . ."

"I know she's a submarine, Brady! A fraction under two thousand tons, surface speed eighteen knots, six tubes for'ard, two aft. How are you, Commander? Delighted you came." He pistoned Ransome's hand. "Come on in, come on in. You fellows must be dehydrated. Come on then, and meet some people."

Beaming, Farley introduced them round. The next few moments were a hurried kaleidoscope of faces and smiles and hands and colourful dresses, backed by the height and beauty of the vases of flowers.

"I'll fix you fellows up with something," Farley confided in a subdued boom, "but don't go away, Brady. I've got something to show you, my boy. Something. . . ." He emphasized his point with a wagging forefinger as he backed off through the crowd.

"Phew," said Ransome as they found themselves to be a little island among the talk and movement.

"Don't believe all you see," Brady told him, smiling. "He's nuts on the Navy, yes, but that's the limit of his peculiarities. I hear he's one of the very top boys in his operating theatre." He looked around him. "He must be," he ended.

Ransome did not speak. He was staring down the long room, and automatically Brady shifted his glance to follow. Then something which Brady would describe later as like a fist in the stomach, opened his mouth and narrowed his eyes.

He saw at first only that the girl was lovely. He took an immediate and general impression of her charm of face, her honey-coloured hair, her slender figure sheathed in some white stuff which was both clinging and cool, and her intent look directed upon himself.

"I say," Ransome murmured beside him. Now the girl knew that Brady was looking back at her, but she did not avert her gaze. Her expression changed and became quizzical—it was an admission of having been caught. Brady wet his lips and then he smiled. He could think of nothing better to do. The girl said something to a woman beside her, and then she came towards them.

Brady noticed during the girl's approach that her bare arms and shoulders were a tanned brown against the white of her dress, and that her shoulders were square, as straight as his own had ever been on a parade ground. Then she was close to him.

"Captain Brady, isn't it?"

He saw that her eyes were hazel, and slanted slightly at the corners. He smiled into them with frank pleasure.

"Yes. This is Lieutenant-Commander Ransome."

She smiled at Ransome and held out a brown hand. "How do you do, Commander? I'm so. . . ."

"Well, well, well!" Farley's voice boomed behind them. "I see you've got yourselves acquainted. No doubt about you sailors, eh? The prettiest girl in the room. Yes. Here you are, you two. Down the hatch with that." They took the drinks. "Now I'll show you something, Brady! It'll make you green . . . no, we'll have to belay that awhile, people at the door. Now don't get lost, shipmate. I'll be back at the double. Look after 'em, Beth."

Brady took a pull at his Scotch and the girl said:

"Come on, let's get it over with."

She touched his arm and the two officers followed her out of the room into a corridor which Brady guessed must run back towards the cliff behind the house. At the end of this passage there was a door, and set in the door, a round window.

"That looks almost like a porthole," said Ransome.

"For Pete's sake don't let him hear you say that," the girl admonished. "It *is* a porthole."

"I see," murmured Ransome, and glanced at Brady. The girl's fingers were on the door-knob when Brady asked:

"And whom do we have the honour of addressing?"

"You mean what's my name?"

"Fair enough," he grinned. "Who the devil are you?"

"I'm Beth Farley—the daughter of the house."

"Farley . . . ? But he's never mentioned a girl to me."

"I'm not surprised. When you were with him during the war I was in pigtails and about ten." She turned the knob, and paused. "You mustn't misjudge him, you know. It's really your fault, both of you. Normally he's quite sane. It's only when he gets mixed up with salty types like you that all this nonsense springs out." Her smile belied the words. "Look in there," she said, pushing the door open. "Maybe that will explain why I prefer the medical side of him."

They stepped into the room.

The first thing that Brady saw—partly because it had pride of position, mounted against the end wall—was a huge old wooden steering-wheel. Its spokes had been recently varnished and the brass boss in the centre shone brightly, reflecting, with the metal-tipped spokes, the light from a small electric lamp appropriately placed overhead. On either side, navigation lights gave out their red and green glow, and near them two standards were bolted to the floor: a wheelhouse telegraph and a revolution indicator, as spick and span and sparkling as ever they had been aboard ship. The side walls were punctured freely with the scuttle rings of portholes, each one giving a view of a painted seascape behind. At the end of the room opposite the steering-wheel, a short length of destroyer's cable was strung between two stanchions. In one corner stood a large, old-fashioned telescope.

Those were the main decorations—the rest of the space was cluttered with a dockyard assembly of naval junk, from a boat's oar to a topmast weather-vane.

"Farley's Folly," said Beth. Brady turned and saw her watching him, her expression half amused and half pleading.

"He's certainly got it well set up," said Brady promptly. "Though I've seen old sailors' dens more cluttered than this. Eh, Ransome?"

Ransome nodded. The girl asked:

"Then this sort of thing—it's more or less normal?"

Brady knew he must not overdo it. "I wouldn't say that. But you find lots of men who've come ashore on the beach who like to remember the old days. I know a three-badged seaman whose front fence is made of old destroyer cable, painted white. Quite effective, too."

She looked at him keenly, and he wasn't sure whether he had quieted her suspicions. Then she said, quietly:

"That's very nice of you. Now we'd better get back into circulation. I expect you'd like another drink?" She switched off the lights, and Brady remembered, with a pang of affection for Farley, that she had not needed to switch them on.

They returned to the main room, where Beth led them to a long table weighted with bottles and glasses.

"What's wrong with the cocktail bar?" Brady asked as she handed him a decanter of Scotch.

"Nothing, except that it's fully occupied." She took up three glasses and he filled them, one by one, glancing at her face as she looked down in absorption. He liked the vivid effect of her lips against the smooth brown of her skin. Suddenly, more than anything, he wanted to ensure that he would meet her again, and soon.

Ransome had no sooner received his whisky than two women bore down on him, exclaiming something about "submarines" above the hubbub; in a moment he was towed away helplessly, glass in hand. Brady turned back to Beth and grinned.

"That's fine. Perfect organization."

"Oh?" She sipped her drink, her right elbow cupped in her left hand, and looked up at him.

"I haven't much time," he said, and remembered her frankness outside the museum door. "Look, I'd like to see you again. Soon. Are you tied up with anybody? Could you come surfing with me?"

She said at once: "I'd like that very much."

"Tomorrow afternoon, after four? We're going to sea in the morning."

She shook her head slowly. "No, I couldn't manage that. I have a lecture at three, and couldn't possibly be back here by four. It would have to be Saturday." She smiled suddenly, and he saw her teeth white as sugar in the brown of her face. "That would be much better. You could have the whole day away from your ship, here. You wouldn't have to talk shop more than half the time."

"Fine." Smiling back at her, he was quite conscious of the quality of the feeling in him. He had met and liked many pretty girls before, but this emotion was more acute—the essence. "You go to lectures?"

"M'm? Oh. At the Uni. I'm doing medicine. Final year, in fact."

"Obstetrics?"

"Heavens, no! I've seen enough of Dad up at all hours. No, just general practice—if I make the grade, of course."

"You will. But you won't make it a full-time career? Don't you want to get married?"

"Naturally."

He drained his glass and reached for the decanter. A peculiar sensation moved in him. Still leaning forward, he looked up at her sideways.

"You should marry a bloke like me. While he's at sea you could press on in your own world."

The words, their expression, his smile, were innocuous. Yet for a moment, as they looked at each other, they seemed to be surrounded by silence in that large, loud room.

"So there you are," boomed Farley breezily. "I see Ransome's hooked already. Now, Brady, you come with me."

"He's seen it, Dad. I took both of them in."

"Oh." Farley looked disappointed. Then he brightened.

"What'd you think of it, eh? Remember, my boy—when you build your house, lay aside a room for old memories."

"I will," Brady lied. "You've certainly got it fitted out pusser's-like. Where on earth did you scrounge that wheel?"

Farley took his arm.

"There's an old ship-chandler's in Erskine Street, right down near the docks. One of the last of his kind. He refits yachts and things. And he's got a big yard behind the shop—I'll take you down one day. But you'll need a few quid with you. The stuff he's got lying about there! You won't be able to leave the place. I pick around in it all day." He chuckled, a deep sound. "I almost missed a Caesarean section I was listed for, couldn't make up my mind between an engine-room telegraph and a revolution counter. I finished up taking both of 'em."

"So I saw," Brady murmured.

"You have to be careful, Brady. It gets you, you know. You'll be worse than me—you've had about twenty years in. I got to the theatre fifteen minutes late that day—first time that's happened."

"Everything was all right?"

"Oh, yes, both doing well."

"He's really quite brilliant in the theatre," said Beth. Brady was not sure, but he thought he detected a defensive note in her words.

"I'm sure he is. I'd like to see him at work."

"Would you?"

He looked at her, and a great longing compounded of all his years of struggle and loneliness surged in him. It was the first time he had ever felt like this, and the force of it took him by surprise. She asked again: "Would you?"

"Of course I would. I saw an appendicitis operation once, in a destroyer. I'll never forget that as long as I live."

"All right, then." She looked at her father.

"Now look here, Beth. . . ." He turned to Brady. "I work in an operating theatre, old man—not a picture theatre. In any case, it's out of the question—obstetrics, women, you understand?"

"Of course."

"Don't be so stuffy, Dad. It can easily be arranged. Not obstetrical, naturally. There is other surgery."

Farley pulled at his nose. "I don't know." He looked at his daughter with a suggestion of exasperation. "Some time, perhaps.'

Brady felt embarrassed. "Look, really it doesn't. . . ."

"I'll fix it," she told him calmly. "Now, Dad, there's poor Mrs. Townsend in the corner on her own."

"Oh, all right, all right. Help yourself there, Brady. I'll be back." He shouldered his bulk through the press.

"I'd like another drink, please."

"Of course." He got it for her.

"Thank you for being so nice about his museum. He's only a big kid, you know."

"Don't worry about it. I haven't seen a room like that before, but a lot of Reserve chaps are like that. I suppose their time in the Navy was such a hell of a departure from their usual lives that it's made a lasting impression. I think it's a good thing, actually. I won't pretend it doesn't please me to see an ex-naval type still keen."

She nodded, looking up into his face. Quite suddenly, she asked: "How old are you, Captain?"

"My name is Jim," he smiled. "I'm thirty-six, and I've had only seventeen years in the Service."

"I see. Dad mentioned. . . . You're not married?"

He knew a score of facetious answers to that question. Now, he said simply: "No. I suppose I've been too busy to do anything about it."

They turned together to put their glasses on the table, and his arm brushed against hers. She said quietly:

"Come early on Saturday. About ten?"

All the banter and by-play he was used to employing with women seemed to have dried up within him.

"I'll be here at ten," he said.

Since his commission—and before—Captain Brady had been at some choice parties, in most of the ports of the Nine Seas. But none of them had passed so swiftly as this one. It seemed he had no sooner arrived than guests were offering their platitudinous excuses and hunting for coats. He looked at his watch—it was almost two o'clock. He wanted to be the last to leave, and they were, Farley pressing another couple of drinks on them before Ransome at last said he would really have to be getting back.

Farley heaved his bulk to his feet. He held out his hand with the thick fingers outspread.

"It was damned nice having you two. You must come again. I mean that!"

The two officers murmured politely, and they all walked to the door. Farley stood on the threshold, gazing out over the sea towards Barrenjoey Lighthouse. The sky was star-powdered, cloudless and calm. In the silence his voice boomed:

"I saw you two together damn near all night. Why don't you marry the girl?"

Brady's answer was instant and unprepared.

"I'd like that very much," he said.

What he remembered afterwards was that nobody, at first, laughed. Only Beth was looking at him, her brown face and red-lipped mouth serious. Then Ransome chuckled.

"That's what I like about the modern age—romance! Come on then, Skipper—there's a long day tomorrow."

Brady nodded. "Good night," he said to Farley, and smiled at the girl. Then he turned quickly and followed Ransome down the steps and the sloping concrete to the car.

They had reached the safety of the main road and were picking up speed when Ransome fitted his pipe-stem between his teeth and asked: "When are you seeing her again?"

"Saturday." Brady changed the subject. "How'd you find the old boy?"

"He'd love you as a son-in-law."

"Whoa there! You're damn near as bad as my mother. Every girl in Toowoomba would give her all to marry me—Mum thinks."

Ransome struck a match and grinned into his little cave of light. "Farley looks as if he could provide a hefty dowry," he said slyly.

"Don't imagine I'd turn it down," Brady played along. "These insistent self-made blokes are all wet. A rich father-in-law makes for a very happy marriage." Then he yawned. "God, I'm tired." He pressed harder with his foot and the car responded with a smooth surge.

Neither officer spoke much after that. Ransome was relatively wakeful. As they swept between the tall gum-trees of the forest he smoked his pipe with leisurely enjoyment, and he was thinking: this fellow seems a very pleasant chap indeed; hard, certainly, but then he would need to be that; and quite sure of himself. He slumped more comfortably into his seat, and mused: lovely girl . . . how nice to be at the wedding . . . it could happen . . . often happened like this . . . for instance, Moira and himself. They had met, met again, often, and he had married her in six weeks. Wartime, of course. But if it was there, it was there, and Brady was old enough to know it when it hit him—he would

have had experience enough, with looks like that. The girl was
sensible, too. Old Farley would be delighted. A naval wedding,
all hands in uniform. Here, it would be whites. Especially
effective, the white drills, the contrasting gold of ranks, the glittering swords outside the church. . . .

Brady drove on, the powerful headlights cutting shadows
beyond fences as he turned, swathing the road when it ran
straight. He remembered her face, the tanned honey of her skin
and the lips red against it. He thought of her, of her body,
and instinctively he forced that thought aside. As he did so, he
recognized the nature of the suppression; he realized that he had
never been so restrained before in his thoughts about a woman;
and he knew why he felt as he did about this one.

CHAPTER THREE

At precisely seven o'clock in the morning, Captain Brady's
steward opened the door of his master's cabin. He stepped in
over the coaming, balancing the cup of tea in his left hand as he
had often done in a gale of wind. He stopped at the bunk:

"Are you awake, sir?"

The brown face lying sideways on the pillow made no response.
Benson looked down on it dispassionately, seeing the strong chin
and the straight mouth, the nose large and hooked. But he was
not concerned with his captain's looks, only with his consciousness. He had come with Brady from his last ship, and had stood
like this before him on more mornings than he could remember.
He repeated the absurd, traditional query:

"Are you awake, sir?"

You did not lay your hand on an officer when waking him,
short of the threat of an approaching torpedo. This time Brady's
face wrinkled as he came up from deep sleep. He opened his
eyes and said at once:

"What's the weather?"

Benson answered as promptly—question and answer were
almost a ritual.

"Fine and clear, sir. Breakfast in fifteen minutes, sir?"

Brady nodded and swung his legs out of the bunk. He took
the tea and his mouth was grateful for its hot, clean taste.

"The oldest gear I've got, today, Benson. I'll be in the
submarine."

"Oldest gear, aye aye, sir. Double-fried, sir?"

"M'm. No," Brady corrected quickly, impelled by his night-before stomach. "Scrambled."

"Scrambled, aye aye, sir. Is that all, sir?"

At his lord's nod, Benson withdrew. Brady finished his tea standing, then walked into his small bathroom. In the pantry, Benson heard him whistling under the shower and his own tanned face lightened. He trapped a bit ashore last night, was his irreverent judgment. Whoever she was, she had his blessing. Looked like being a good day.

Meteorologically speaking, there were all the indications that Benson was right. As Brady climbed the steep iron ladder to the bridge he felt the eastern sun biting nicely into his back, and he could see the wide expanse of the harbour glittering and shimmering, right up to the wooded foreshores. The wind was very light. They should have an easy start.

"*Diana* getting under way, sir," the signal yeoman reported briefly.

Brady nodded. From his height he could look down upon the whole length of the submarine: her bulbous nose, her bulging belly-tanks and her after-part tapering to the thin tail. He picked out Ransome's squat figure on her bridge, then distinguished Deevers and saw him bend to speak into a voice-pipe. A second or two later a slow churning began under *Diana's* stern, and smoothly she moved away from the pier. The hammering of her diesels sounded as far as *Scourge's* bridge in the morning air. Another minute and she was well clear, her low stern swinging round towards Pinchgut Island and her bow aiming for the open sea past Bradley's Head.

"Good morning, sir. Ready in all respects for sea. All hands on board, singled up fore and aft."

"Good morning, Number One," Brady answered. Cowan's face was smooth and shining from the morning's shave. His eyes were puffed. "A good night?"

Cowan grinned. "Just so long as it's not rough at sea, sir. Yes, it was a good ding. Those poor beggars lapped it up. Pity you couldn't have stayed on, sir."

Brady acknowledged this false sentiment with an equally conventional nod of regret. "What time did they leave?"

"Oh, they were all tucked in bed by two o'clock, sir."

Brady was not sure that he liked Cowan's ready understanding that he wanted the submarine to dive with its officers safely sober. Then he smiled inwardly at his prejudice—if Cowan was quick on the uptake, wasn't that all to the good? He said pleasantly, "I'll be transferring to *Diana* some time this morning, on completion of squadron exercises. I'll want you to carry out a few runs on her, Number One."

Cowan looked surprised; then he replied carefully: "Aye aye, sir. If I may, I'd like to take over for a bit during the squadron manoeuvres."

"Of course. By the way, I'll be returning the squadron to base before I join *Diana*."

Cowan caught on to that quickly, too, and Brady noticed his relief. Driving a destroyer alone on an empty sea was a different proposition to being in command of the squadron leader with three other ships in company. Cowan smiled, and for the first time since he had met him Brady realized that the expression was sincere.

"Thank you very much, sir. I'll look forward to it."

Brady nodded. He had paid his Number One a nice compliment, and was pleased with the result. He looked at his watch, and then at *Diana's* low shape turning to round Bradley's Head. It was time to cast-off.

"All right, let's get out there."

He stepped up to the raised grating round the binnacle, took his binoculars from where they hung by their black strap, and slung them round his neck. His movements were as good as the spoken word. Cowan advanced to the edge of the fore windbreak and raised his hand, palm upwards, to the cable officer on the fo'c'sle. The lieutenant raised his own hand in acknowledgment, gave an order, and the head-rope was thrown off the pier bollards and hauled in. A similar gesture towards the quarterdeck produced the same quick result. *Scourge* was held now by a wire spring, which ran from under her bridge aft to the pier.

Brady gave his orders carefully, nursing the destroyer's fifty-thousand horse-power. He had handled her only twice before, and was thankful that on this almost windless morning he could treat her gently. Her sharp bow eased forward slowly, and then in against the pier-fenders, under obedience to the starb'd screw and the rudder-face; while her stern swung out towards clear water.

"In spring."

Cowan raised his hand again, and the cable officer did the rest. As Brady looked aft to check his position, he saw a pair of tall masts moving very slowly behind the ferry-pier at the end of Garden Island. They belonged to two of his other ships, which had already left their buoys and were under way, ready for their leader.

Everything was as it should be. He turned back to the binnacle and he thought in that instant of Beth, and of Saturday. A feeling of intense well-being rose in him. He had found the girl he wanted. He was in command of a powerful new ship, and of a well-drilled squadron of destroyers with a special function to fulfil. He was due for a pleasant day of exercises he could handle, with no danger to be expected from any quarter. Life could hardly be sweeter than it was. He bent to the wheelhouse voice-pipe and gave the order which would drag *Scourge* away from the pier.

Clear in the fairway, he put one screw ahead, the other astern, and swung his rudder over. The destroyer turned with hardly any forward motion until her knife of a bow was aimed a little to the right of Bradley's Head.

"Midships. Half ahead together. Two-double-oh revolutions. Steer oh-eight-five."

Scourge shuddered a little and then moved towards the sea. Astern of her the other ships of the squadron took station. Ferries and sailing-craft passed them, the ferry-boats listing slightly as their passengers clustered to the rails. The line of long grey ships made a clean and powerful picture, the guns advancing from the turrets, the disciplined seamen on the upper-decks omitting to answer the calls from the waving sightseers—a fine scene on the sun-sparkling water.

Ashore, unseen, unknown to the appreciative onlookers in boats and round the harbour, the Subsmash organization was prepared for action.

The officer known as SM4, commanding the submarine squadron based on Balmoral, checked his communications system (which took in the naval transmitting-station near Canberra), and made sure that his specially trained team of deep-sea divers was on call at Rushcutters—it might be needed should *Diana* fail to surface after submersion. Shipping had already been warned of activity in the area, designated Nan Alfa (NA) on charts, east of Barrenjoey Lighthouse. The R.A.A.F.'s Neptunes were available for search-operations from the Richmond air-base, as was a helicopter to transport SM4, divers and a specially trained medical officer to the scene of any emergency. There was a com-

munication track kept open for high-priority signals to and from
Nan Alfa, and the "Coast-flash" system for long-distance telephoning ensured that extra divers could be obtained without delay.

None of the members of the organization supposed that he
would be vitally employed this morning; theirs were routine
duties, undertaken without apprehension. But all were standing
by as *Diana* poked her bulbous black nose out between the headlands and passed from sight of the grey hunters behind.

She had plenty of time, for they would play among themselves
for an hour before they began searching for her with their sonic
fingers. When the destroyers emerged into the open Pacific, Brady
saw the low silhouette of *Diana* coursing northward. But he led
the squadron straight out towards the weld of blue sea and bluer
sky, until the masterful, weathered cliffs had sunk to a dark blur
edging the horizon astern. He looked all about him, a normal
precautionary check, noting the distant smoke of two merchant-
men hull-down to the south, and a bigger ship shaping up for
the Heads, and then he began his squadron manoeuvres.

For half an hour the four ships twisted and turned at high
speed, breaking formation, regaining it, simulating bombardment,
avoiding bombs and torpedoes; and once only did the squadron
commander hoist a ship's pendants to his yard-arm—the traditional "bottle" for a manoeuvre clumsily executed. At length,
satisfied, Brady formed-up in line astern from the leader; it was
time for Cowan to assume command.

The first-lieutenant stepped up beside him on the grating, and
Brady said quietly, "Alter course ninety degrees in succession."

Cowan repeated the order to the signal yeoman, who understood at once what was happening. The brightly coloured flags
hauled up the foremast, whipping in the wind of *Scourge's* passage.
They hung there a moment, were repeated on all the ships down
the line, and then they hauled down. Executive!

Cowan gave his orders and *Scourge* came round in a fast, tight
turn. At the spot where she had turned, and still keeping their
mathematical distance astern of her, the rest of the squadron
came round in her wake.

For twenty minutes Cowan discharged his responsibility surely
and efficiently. Then Brady said, "All right, Number One, that
will do nicely," and shifted two steps to the right. The movement
returned command to him. Cowan stepped down and walked
to the fore windbreak. The waiting signalman heard Brady
order:

"Request permission to carry out SMX (submarine-attack exercise)."

The signal went off to H.M.A.S. Watson, the Asdic training school near South Head, and would be repeated to everyone interested—Belconnon, the wireless station near Canberra, SM4 in his office at Balmoral base, headquarters at Potts Point.

Brady took his squadron southward, and while the ships were turning he sent a signal to *Diana*, low-lying to the distant north, telling her he was about to begin their joint exercise. A subtle change came over his bridge-team of officers and men. This was the most important part of their work; interest supplemented their alertness. Manoeuvres were important, but commonplace; now the destroyermen were to fulfil their prime function. Limbo, the big three-barrelled mortar on the quarter-deck, would be loaded with drill projectiles, but the finding and tracking and the final firing-run would be the real thing. Nor would any man relax until the submarine had come up again after she had dived. Nobody mentioned it, the thought was kept well in the background of consciousness, but they all knew that *Diana*, once down, would be surrounded by an enemy more real and implacably destructive than a whole squadron of destroyers.

By the time *Scourge* had led her consorts right round, so that they faced north again, *Diana* had vanished. They would find her, of course, for the exercise area was not large, and one purpose of the exercise was to drill the Asdic control teams in attacking runs; but it might not be easy.

"Sweep from Red eight-oh to Green eight-oh," Brady ordered.

Assuming that he was screening a convoy, with submarines suspected of operating ahead of the line of advance, Brady stationed his ships in arrowhead formation, with *Scourge* in the van. Petty Officer Slocum's experience regardless, luck would be needed for the squadron leader to make first contact. Asdic range was limited, and *Diana* could be making at a fast clip towards either edge of his screen.

When they were almost up to Barrenjoey Lighthouse, with the tall tower standing like a bleached bone on the lip of its cliff, Brady lifted his binoculars. Almost at once the big concrete house on the hill overlooking Whale Beach showed in his magnifying lenses. He could see Farley's white painted flagpole clearly enough, but there appeared to be no movement on the terrace. Farley would be in Macquarie Street now, or in the operating theatre. Beth would be sitting in a lecture-room, or peering through a lens at some bug or other. A student . . . it made her seem schoolgirlish; yet if she had been ten years old when he and Farley had worked together, she would be rising twenty-six at the end of her studies. Ten years difference between them. You were as old as you felt. Reassuring, sometimes, those ready cliches —for certainly he felt young on this bright morning. Two days to Saturday.

"Echo bearing Red six-oh. Range one-five-double-oh yards."

The Asdic control officer's voice crackled through the bridge loudspeaker. Brady lowered his glasses quickly and turned towards the wheelhouse voice-pipe. From the edge of his eye he saw the yeoman busy at the halyards, bending on the red pendant which would tell the rest of the squadron, "Contact!"

"Bearing zero-one-five. One-five-double-oh yards. Echo pitch slight high."

Cowan said: "He's coming towards."

The 'speaker continued reporting flatly: "Extent of target five degrees. Classified submarine."

That was what they were waiting for. Brady assumed the attack. The red flag hauled up to the yard-arm. Brady ordered:

"Action Limbo!"

Cowan jiggled the microphone of the armament-broadcast out of its socket and repeated the command.

"Port one-five. Steer oh-one-five. One-five-oh revolutions." Then to the Asdic Control Room, the A.C.R., where Slocum was seated before his instrument: "Set speed one-five knots. Depth one-double-oh feet."

These quotients were set on the range-recorder, a gleaming black box cluttered with levers and a moving tape of iodized paper. On the top right-hand corner was fitted a short metal arm, and at the bottom of its arc waited electrical contacts. This was the firing-arm. It had not yet begun to move.

The bridge 'speaker cleared its throat again: "Echo bearing oh-two-oh. Drawing right. Echo pitch moderate high."

The target was coming faster towards them.

The Asdic officer's voice, unemotional, efficient, reported: "Estimated submarine course one-six-oh. Drawing right. Speed four knots. Ready to attack."

"Steer by Asdic," Brady commanded, "attacking with Limbo."

That was the permissive order to the A.C.R. and the weapon's crew to carry out an attack. The quartermaster at the wheel was now steering by an Asdic repeater, not his compass, and was kept

directly on to the target's course with electronic exactitude.
Down aft, the big mortar was also following Asdic, and automatically allowing deflection for the target's speed and course.

Scourge moved in closer to five hundred yards, her Asdic pulses,
transmitted down through an oscillating piece of quartz, tapping
at the steel hull of the submarine. On the range-recorder the
firing-bar now moved smoothly in its arc, closer and closer to the
firing contact. The resonant ping of the Asdic set on the bridge
was almost simultaneous with the returning peep. The firing-bar
touched, the electrical circuit was made.

"Fired by recorder!"

The Asdic officer's voice was drowned by a succession of three
coughing booms. Three dummy projectiles flew forward over the
bridge, described a graceful parabola and then dropped into the
sea three hundred yards ahead.

"Instant echoes," reported A.C.R. "Carrying out stern sweep."

With his extended sonic fingers, Slocum began to sweep an
arc to either side of the destroyer's stern. Then: "Echo bearing
Red one-seven-oh. Classified submarine."

They had passed directly over *Diana*; she was now clear behind
them.

Brady turned from the binnacle. It had been a text-book run,
but *Diana* had taken little avoiding action. He kept his voice
expressionless as he addressed the navigator:

"All right, open the range. Give me a longer run this time."

CHAPTER FOUR

Two hours later, Brady considered that they had had enough.
The target had been found each time, and each time they judged
that they had battered her open with their omnisciently-placed
"charges". He was perfectly aware that Ransome down there had
been making it easy for them, but that was the intention. Next
time, with the squadron practised under their new leader in
concerted attack, he might turn on a trick or two.

"Make to the squadron," Brady ordered: "Disregard my movements, return to base."

The yeoman stepped to his signal-light.

Brady had been granted permission to stay out of harbour
after completion of the squadron exercises. Now, with his three

charges heeling over on the turn back towards the distant Heads, he was ready for his extra-curricular training.

He laid his binoculars on the chart-table and nodded to Cowan.

"All right, Number One, take over. We'll exercise the sea-boat at the same time."

Diana, signalled to the surface by grenades, was waiting off the starb'd beam, the slight seas rolling up and over her saddle-tanks. Her long black body gleamed wetly in the sunlight. Within ten minutes Brady had been deposited on her port bilges, under the bridge, and the sea-boat had pulled off towards *Scourge.* The crew rowed automatically, staring with interest at the quarry they had been hunting all morning.

Lieutenant Deevers had been posted to help Brady aboard. The torpedo officer's thin, sharp face could not be disguised, but his voice was pleasant enough as he invited the visitor to ascend by the footholds cut into the vertical side of *Diana's* bridge. A moment later Brady had swung himself lithely over the top and was standing in the presence of Lieutenant-Commander Ransome, who saluted him and smiled.

"Good morning, sir."

Brady returned the courtesy. "Nice day for it," he grinned as they strolled forward a little, leaving Deevers and the lookout behind them. The black steel was drying quickly in the hot sun. "What's the drill now? I'm in your hands."

"Ah . . . it's mainly Christian names aboard at sea, sir."

"Right, Eric. Are these the only hands you have on the bridge?"

"In patrol routine, yes. We might have to get down in a hurry. By the way. . . ."

"Yes?"

"If we surface later on, and you want to come up top, would you mind telling the officer of the watch from the control-room? I'm pretty strict on what bods are allowed on the bridge, and it will put the officer down there in a stew if he has to stop you."

"Of course," Brady agreed at once, and Ransome seemed relieved.

"I'll make a diving signal, then we can get under and start the run. Excuse me."

He stepped aside to a voice-pipe, and Brady looked about him. *Diana's* bridge structure rose high from the upper-deck, clear of everything except the heaviest seas. Directly below him the fore-deck casing ran to the bow. It was liberally punctured with holes, both for lightness and to get rid of water swiftly when surfacing.

That was what was usually hit by shells, Brady reflected—the real pressure-hull was below the casing: here and there he could see its steely curve.

He looked down over the port side and saw the valves, fitted into the tanks every few feet.

"Stay there, sir," Ransome said to him, and gave an order in which Brady caught the word "vent". Watching, he saw a valve suddenly jerk up from its seating and heard the thud of its opening. A small spurt of spray spat upwards. Ransome said beside him: "The bottoms of those tanks are free-flooding— they're open to the sea. Compressed air keeps the water down. When we vent a tank, the valve opens as you saw it then, and of course air is released and water comes in. We go down."

"Your tanks are open at the bottom? One imagines that a submarine is always buttoned up tight. Tight as hell."

Ransome smiled. "One cruiser captain we had aboard was amazed—and a little worried, I suspect—that we don't close all water-tight doors when we're dived."

"I understand his feelings," the destroyerman commented dryly.

"Yes, but it's too inconvenient. We have men shifting fore and aft all the time. But a submarine is perfectly safe—until you forget that it can be dangerous."

"M'mm. At least this looks familiar territory." Brady glanced around him. There was not a fraction of the instruments his own bridge mounted, but what there were seemed recognizable enough. The main difference was in the thickness of the two periscope standards, one behind the other, which lifted their rectangular faces about fifteen feet above the deck. "One's an auxiliary?" he asked.

"Yes and no. This chap here is the search periscope. We get on to a target with it. The other one is the attack instrument— its lens is not much bigger than my thumbnail. Being so much smaller, of course, it leaves a much slighter wake."

"I see. In any sort of a chop that thing would be well-nigh invisible to even a good lookout."

"We hope so, yes. Well, if you'd like to go below . . . I imagine your Number One's wondering what the hell's keeping us."

Brady glanced across at *Scourge*, whose every feature was distinct in the strong sunlight. He saw that the sea-boat had been hoisted, and that a dozen curious faces were staring at them from upper-deck and bridge. He stepped towards the hatch.

"Straight down, sir," said Deevers politely. "The ladder leads into the control-room." Evidently he wished to ignore Brady's last visit to *Diana*, with its unfortunate consequences for himself.

"Thank you," Brady answered crisply, and eased his feet on to the ladder. The hatches through which it descended were just large enough to admit his shoulders. As he climbed down inside the steel shaft, with his shirt billowing in the strong current of air, he smelt that peculiar odour—a compound of diesel oil, heat, sweat and bilge-water—which always reminded him of the time in the Mediterranean when he had boarded his first submarine.

He dropped the last few feet into the control-room, where the first thing he saw was the figure of the navigator, dressed in black football shorts and a black T-shirt, bent like a question-mark over the little chart-table. He recognized Pilot's nutcracker face. Then a voice said beside him: "Good morning, sir, I'm Dan Ullyet, engineer officer. I am to show you around."

Brady turned, vaguely remembering that he had seen his guide at *Scourge's* wardroom splash yesterday evening. Ullyet looked absurdly young, and he was almost perfectly handsome. Brown clear skin, black hair, straight nose and mouth, and a pair of brown eyes that seemed eager to be helpful.

"Good morning, Chief," Brady returned easily. "I'm here to look and listen and learn. At the moment all I want is a place where I'll be out of the way."

"Yes, sir. This corner near the blowing-panel will do nicely."

Brady was eased into a spare foot of deck beside a big panel bristling with shiny steel levers. A senior-looking rating, with a sweat-rag flung over one burned shoulder, a small, quiet man whom he was later to meet as the outside engine-room artificer, waited in front of this impressive array.

Brady turned to ask Ullyet a question and a klaxon blared harshly through the boat. Again.

"Always twice," Ullyet explained, "in case the first time's accidental."

It seemed to the destroyerman not more than a couple of seconds after the diving-signal had sounded that the look-out came dropping down the ladder and into the control-room. Things began to happen, fast.

There was so much for him to see, on this his first trip underwater, that only prime impressions fixed themselves in his mind. Ransome dropping in, then Deevers, reaching back up and shoving levers——

"One clip on, both clips on, pin inserted!"

Sharp, yet calm, almost casual. There were now two hatches shut between them and the waiting water beginning to swill up and over the dried bridge. Meanwhile the man beside Brady had played a virtuoso performance at the blowing-panel, causing a succession of thuds as the vents opened outside on top of the tanks.

"Main vent hand-levers to open!"

A pause, while checking lights flashed, then:

"All main vents checked open!"

The sea was now free to enter through the bottom of the ballast tanks; the air would be rushing out through the vents on top, causing the white spurts which the destroyer captain had seen dozens of times when his enemy had dived to get clear.

Brady's alert stare was attracted by movement to the left of the ladder and main periscope tube. He saw two hydroplane operators sitting there on a long bench before huge depth-gauges and two curved instruments which looked like, and were in effect, spirit-levels. Inclinometers. The after-operator spun his big wheel and Brady saw the pointer come to rest on fifteen degrees of dive. He knew then that the submarine was being helped down, not only by the destruction of buoyancy in her tanks, but by the hydroplanes aft acting as a rudder in the vertical plane and driving her under.

He was surprised that there was so little tilt in the control-room; the submarine seemed to be simply sinking, rather than diving down at a sharp angle. Something else struck him as strange—the silence. When he had dropped into the room his ears had registered the hammering thud of the big diesels.

"We're on electric power?" he turned his head to Ullyet.

"That's right, sir. In the engine-room they've stopped both diesels and shut the exhaust muffler valves on the pressure hull. Otherwise we could get salt water in the cylinders, and that could bend the con. rods, water being incompressible. As soon as the clutches were taken out we went ahead on the main electric motors." Ullyet rubbed his nose with one finger. "Oh lots of things happened, sir. The electricians have shut down battery ventilation, started the clearing fans, switched on the hydrogen eliminators. Lots of routine things like that."

"I see," Brady lied. "Er—I noticed we went down quite smoothly, no tilt at all. This wasn't a crash-dive, then?"

"Crash-dive, sir? There ain't no such animal, except in novels. Whenever we dive, no matter what the circs, we get down in a hurry." The engineer pointed to the depth-gauge. "You see?"

Brady was astonished to see the long black pointer at sixty feet, and still revolving. He was sure that only a few seconds had passed since the last hatch had been clipped into position.

"That's nothing, sir," Ullyet continued. "I think the skipper is going to flood. . . ."

"Vent 'Q' inboard!" Ransome's voice rapped.

"Watch this," Ullyet warned, and then his voice was drowned in a screaming rush of compressed air. A brief white mist formed. At once Brady felt the pressure on his ears. The blast whined to silence, and a rating called: " 'Q' vented inboard!"

Ullyet touched Brady's arm and pointed. The depth-gauge indicator seemed to be turning like a spoke in a bicycle-wheel.

"We flooded 'Q'," the engineer explained "Emergency tank. It holds ten tons of water and fills in six seconds."

Brady nodded, impressed. He thought: every destroyer captain should spend at least a week a year in a submarine.

"Hundred and fifty feet," ordered Ransome.

The destroyerman followed fairly clearly what happened next. Ransome's first-lieutenant was standing in front of a rectangular box, which lighted up when he turned a knob to outline the words: "No. 1 tank pumping." Shortly afterwards the light went out, and Brady assumed that somewhere someone had finished pumping that particular tank. At the same time the two hydroplane operators, one on the fore planes and the other on the after ones, twirled their big wheels, checking *Diana's* headlong drop and levelling her off. He could see the bubbles in their inclinometers coming gradually back to zero.

Nobody was taking any notice of Brady. He looked about him, the first chance he had had of a quiet study of this novel room. Glancing up, he saw that it would be difficult to poke his hand through the pipes, wheels, gauges, pump-panels and ventilation lines to touch the deck-head. The sides of the control-room were the same—there was hardly a square-inch of space not taken up by instruments.

There were close on a dozen men present, but there was no sound but the distant whine of the electric motors. Each man sat or stood before his instruments, quiet, intent—the periscope watch-keeper near his lever which would raise and lower the thick brass tube, the Asdic operator in his little compartment a few feet to Brady's right, and the helmsman before his strip gyro-compass, a group-up-group-down switch to the motors and the big revolution-per-minute dial. Brady saw a coloured space-comic poking out of the hip-pocket of his overalls.

"Hundred and fifty feet, sir," said a broad Scots voice.

Ransome nodded and turned aft. Seamen gave his broad-shouldered figure passage as he came over to Brady, his scarred cheek crumpling with his smile. "We'll stooge round here a bit until *Scourge* gets into position for her run. Then I'll come up to eighty feet and see what your Number One can do." He looked at his watch. "Nice time for a pre-lunch snort."

For an instant the usually ready response to that suggestion failed the Australian; then he remembered the Royal Navy rum issue—afloat, aground, in harbour, even probably in the face of the enemy. It seemed there were many things he had yet to learn about service in British submersibles.

"Thank you, Eric, I am dry. Must be the excitement."

They walked the few paces forward to the wardroom, and Ransome hauled out a chair for Brady at the head of the table, where he had sat yesterday afternoon. The submariner bent to a wooden locker which formed an extension to one of the padded benches, like a seat, and came up with a bottle of Scotch. As he sat down, Ullyet sauntered in, whistling soundlessly to himself, and squeezed into a place along the bench opposite his commander. Ransome placed his elbows on the table, guarding the upright bottle, and looked towards the door. There came a sound of humming from outside and Pilot showed in the door-way. He said "Good morning" respectfully to the visiting captain and slid up beside Ullyet. Ransome rubbed his nose and then rested his chin on his fingers. In another moment the first-lieutenant, a red-cheeked, fair-headed young man, wandered into the mess. Brady had been introduced to him on *Scourge* the night before, and remembered that his name was Wetherell. He too squeezed in beside Pilot.

His chin still on his interlaced fingers, Ransome looked at them. Then he placed his fingers before his nose and tapped them gently together into a steeple above the whisky.

"You will appreciate, sir," he said to Brady with unsmiling irony, "just what this gathering means. It means that the ship under my command is an engineering marvel—that there is no need for any supervision whatever in that department. My charts and tide-tables and all navigational appurtenances are in tip-top shape—that department, too, is perfect and requires no work done in it. And so it follows—I suppose—that the gentleman responsible for the overall supervision of those duties also finds himself without employment."

His glance flicked to his first-lieutenant. The three officers watched him with polite attention. Ransome said, with emphasis:

"Damned vultures! I haven't even got the cork out yet and they're on to it!"

"You're wasting an awful lot of time, sir," advised Ullyet respectfully. "All the ice will be melted."

"Ice?" Ransome looked at the engineer. "Captain Brady is not one of your shoreside floozies," he said. "Your wit is misplaced, as usual. Even a surface fish knows. . . . Ice in a submarine!"

"Ice in a submarine, sir," Ullyet persisted gently. No one else spoke. They waited.

"All right, all right," Ransome growled, "what've you been up to?"

"As you will agree, sir," said Ullyet politely, his cultivated voice contrasting with his grease-spotted shorts and round-necked singlet, "engineers are a race apart. As has been proved several times aboard this bucket, sir, they are magicians. *Voilà!*"

He leaned sideways and jerked a none-too-clean towel from what it had been hiding on the end of the table. There, frosted on the outside, waited a jug crammed with ice-cubes and surrounded by glasses.

Ransome stared at Ullyet, whose handsome young face was registering benign pleasure at his surprise. "You're a magician all right—when you want to be. But *I* make out your fitness reports, not Captain Brady. I shall expect to see that jug filled at this time every day from now on—or else."

"The ice is melting, sir," the first-lieutenant prodded gently.

"Then pour the ruddy drinks!"

Number One took up the bottle.

Brady leaned back and watched them appreciatively. He had never seen a mess quite like this before. The three junior officers were completely at ease with their commander; they chaffed his chaff, and yet the respect was there. He especially liked the fact that Ransome did not alter his attitude with them because he had an officer senior to himself in the mess. This was Ransome's command and here he was lord.

"There you are, sir," Number One said with a quick smile, and handed him his drink. They lifted their glasses to a low chorus of "Cheers", and as Brady drank his eye caught a lacquered plaque screwed to the end bulkhead in front of him, between the two lounging ladies. It was a simple rectangle of painted wood, and on it in faded gold letters was printed *Diana's* creed:

I EXPECT EVERYTHING WILL BE ALL RIGHT

They were in the mess for ten minutes, and Brady answered questions on destroyers and asked a few of his own. He noticed that, earlier skylarking regardless, none of the officers had a second drink. Then a knock sounded at the door.

"Yes?" demanded Ransome.

"Officer of the watch, sir—hydrophone effect bearing one hundred and seventy, range three miles, destroyer sir," the messenger reported.

"Right!" Ransome stood up. "Would you come to the control-room, Captain? *Scourge* is panting on the hunt."

Brady nodded. As he stepped out into the passage he saw Wetherell quietly stowing the whisky bottle back in its locker. A commander can afford to go easy, he reflected, if all hands do the decent. He remembered that Deevers had been absent from the wardroom, but discarded the thought that it had been a deliberate arrangement. Not with this team. Even in his short time on board he knew that Ransome had a happy ship.

"There's a spare set of headphones outside the Asdic cabinet," Ransome told him in the control-room, and pointed. Brady walked aft a few steps and poked his head into a steel box about three feet square, where an operator sat before the black and white dial of his instrument. He held a stop-watch in his hand, and Brady guessed he was checking the revolutions of the screws of the ship he could hear on his hydrophones.

"You're still in contact?" he asked.

"Yes, sir, we got her loud an' clear." The seaman reached past him and unhooked the spare phones from the bulkhead. Brady slipped them on and heard a rushing beat of sound, minute but distinct. It was curious to know that he was listening to the thrashing of his own ship's screws from three miles away and a hundred and fifty feet down out of sight.

"Them propellers are in good shape, sir," the Asdic man told him, "no whistlin' or screechin' noises like if they had bits chipped out of them."

"They ought to be," Brady nodded, "they're brand new."

He noted the bearing on the dial, and that it was not changing.

Cowan was coming straight for them, though he could not yet have detected them. It will be good if he contacts us, Brady reflected—good for Cowan and good for the crew's impression of his competence. Then he had another thought—out there, even with her modern Asdic, *Scourge* had no idea of where her target was. The target on the other hand was listening to her plainly and easily, at much more than her hydrophonic range.

"Eighty feet," Ransome ordered.

Wetherell was now at his instrument. The planesmen twirled their wheels. The inclinometer bubbles moved away from zero as *Diana's* nose slanted upwards.

"Burn oxygen candle for'ard and aft and run CO_2 unit on air," instructed Ransome.

Back in his position now by the blowing-panel, Brady looked at Ullyet.

"Just normal routine, sir. Freshen up the boat a bit."

"H.E. increasing, two-five-oh revolutions."

That was twenty-five knots. *Scourge* was picking up her feet. Had she gained contact? Brady looked round at the faces. The report had caused no untoward interest. The planesmen worked their wheels, the helmsman had cocked one side of his backside off his seat, easing the weight; Number One leaned on his order instrument and Ransome was relaxing with one hand on an overhead ventilating line.

If the destroyer was in contact, Brady could imagine the alertness on her bridge and down in the Asdic Control Room. But here, in the control-room of the quarry, the only feeling he could identify was resigned boredom. He got the impression that they knew they could turn or increase speed or drop a hundred feet and slip easily away from the searching sonic fingers. Defensively, he thought: All right, then, but if we had two destroyers up there. . . .

A clear, resonant tok, tok, tok sound rang against the submarine's hull.

"What's that?" he said sharply.

"That's your Asdic pulse, sir. They're on to us."

"Starb'd fifteen," ordered Ransome.

"Starb'd fifteen, sir, Fifteen degrees of starb'd wheel on, sir."

Brady felt no heel. He guessed that the totally encompassing water outside was holding *Diana* steady as she swung. She was turning all right, fairly fast, as he could see from the black lubber's line on the compass. And still the gentle, malignant sound of *Scourge's* Asdic pulse tapped against her hull. That would be Slocum, holding his target in an embracing fan of sensitivity, feeling the course-alteration, following. . . .

"Midships," Ransome said, "steer oh-two-oh." He walked across to Brady. "I'll stooge along on this course for a bit. Then another slight alteration back again—not too much, just enough to give 'em some practice."

Though the submariner had stated the purpose of the exercise quite correctly, Brady was nettled by the suggestion that things would be made easy for *Scourge*. We're not that bad, he thought. Slocum had this plumber's pipe all right—he had it and he'd hold it.

"Eric, I want you to do something for me," he said casually. "Shake him off. Go through your tricks."

"All of them?" Ransome grinned.

"All of them," Brady said quietly.

And between them, as before, suddenly there was understanding. They smiled at each other, with Ullyet watching, but Ransome's step was quick as he returned to the periscope standard.

"Group up! Two-four-oh revolutions! Starb'd twenty-five. One-twenty feet!"

Wheels spun, and this time Brady felt *Diana* heel as she turned on the angled face of her rudder. He felt something else—a tightening of alertness in the control-room. Trained to keep every facet of a changing tactical situation in his mind, he applied himself to this one. He knew the relative positions of hunter and hunted, and he knew that with her rudder over the submarine was heading round towards the destroyer, fast. Her turning-circle being so much smaller than that of the bigger, heavier, surface ship, she could change course inside *Scourge's* track and the destroyer could cut across the arc so travelled. Unless they were very watchful up there. . . .

The helmsman was sitting square on his seat now; the planesmen leaned forward a little, their eyes never leaving the depth-gauges. Pilot had come upright from his bored stance against the chart-table and Ullyet had quietly moved off somewhere from the control-room. Brady grinned to himself.

He heard Ransome give the straightening-up order, and a voice report, "Hundred and twenty feet, sir." Keeping the relative positions in his mind, he had forgotten the gentle sound of *Scourge's* contact with them. The helmsman reported himself on-course and in the silence following his voice Brady listened. There it was—insistent, omniscient: "tok, tok, tok."

The submarine ran on for a few minutes. Once Ransome walked to the Asdic cabinet and put the phones on. He came back to the periscope tube and ordered her down another thirty feet. He waited. When the resonant pulsing against the hull continued unbroken he went and stood directly behind the first-lieutenant, his legs braced apart. Then he gave his orders.

For fifteen minutes *Diana* twisted and dropped, speeded-up and slowed-down, snaked sideways and vertically through the lightless depths to throw off her pursuer. Once she crept through the water at barely steerage way, a tiny motor turning her screw, and with every moving thing in her apart from that motor shut down. Once Ransome said, "We'll cavitate," and in response to his decision the big twin screws abruptly thrashed and bit at the water, hurling back behind them a maelstrom of tossing, bubbling water, "knuckles" which could confuse the echoes sent back to an Asdic set's receiver.

He went down deep, very deep, and *Diana* hung there motionless, at negative buoyancy, just holding her own. The weight of one man walking for'ard would have sent her nose down. It was while she waited there, almost at her maximum designed depth, the whole boat absolutely quiet, transmitting no sound whatever to be picked up by sensitive hydrophones, that Brady received his most telling impression of that novel day.

Ransome had stepped forward a pace, closer to Number One, and Brady could see the shiny brass periscope tube. There was not much light in the control-room—most of it being directed straight on to instruments—and so he was not sure at first what it was he saw. He kept his stare on the periscope tube, and then he saw it again. Down the tube's side, coursing erratically through the lubricating grease which covered it, ran a tiny trickle of water.

No much, hardly anything at all. He could easily have missed this alien entry. Yet that water was forcing its way through the heavy water-tight gland surrounding the periscope. To the destroyerman, his mind already worked upon by the alertness of the control-room's crew, that quiet trickle seemed to shout a warning—"I'm outside, waiting, thousands of tons, waiting. . . ."

At two hundred and fifty feet the pressure of sea-water is one hundred and twenty-five pounds per square inch. *Diana's* hull was supporting a weight of thirty-eight thousand tons. She was holding back this colossal pressure by means of her circular I-section frames, fitted every eighteen inches—a circle being the best engineering construction for withstanding such a crushing force.

She was supporting something else. A feather-weight impulse, yet heavy with implied triumph. "*Tok, tok, tok*" came *Scourge's* sonic tapping.

"All right," Ransome growled, "take her up out of this." He turned his head to look at Brady. "You've got a good boy up top. Had enough?"

"Let's get up," Brady grinned, "that blasted tapping is getting on my nerves!"

He meant it. His mind, quickened by the unusual circumstances, envisaged clearly the demoralizing effect that sound would have on a crew if they knew it would be followed by the sledgehammer concussion of depth-charges.

Diana was angling smoothly towards the surface; the tilt was noticeable. Ransome stopped her at sixty feet. *Scourge* was still in contact, still playing with them, and there was a strict ritual to be observed before the submarine dared to rise to within anywhere near the draught-level of the destroyer's knifing stem.

Brady heard a sound. He stared up at the deckhead. The noise was as if a sheet of canvas was being ripped a few inches at a time: a regular, rhythmic noise, the sound of the destroyer's screws tearing through the water.

In a few seconds the whole control-room was filled with the evidence and echo of the onrushing destroyer—it was a huge reverberating cavern. The uproar reached an almost unbearable pitch, scourging the long, hollow metal ear which was the submarine. The power of fifty-thousand straining horses was transmitted through grinding gears and spinning shafts of two huge clover-leaves of phosphor-bronze; these sent all that strength and menace beating down through troubled tons of water to lash the frail sounding-chamber floating below.

With a scream of straining gears the destroyer's engine-room was directly over them—and then she was past, the roar of her passage fading quickly into a distant, rhythmic thrum, thrum, thrum of whirling screws.

A sharp clang rapped against the pressure hull. Brady knew what that was plainly enough. He'd ordered the hand-grenade heaved overboard dozens of times—"Try that one for size!"

"What do you reckon?" he grinned at Ransome.

"They could have given us a severe shaking with a depth-charge," Ransome smiled back. "I'm going to surface now."

"Good."

Brady watched the procedure with interest, but he was ting-ling with memory of the destroyer's win. He felt that his elation was a bit childish, and tried to justify it by thinking factually: Ransome *had* tried everything in the book, and Slocum had held him. Cowan too had handled the destroyer well. Of course, Ransome had been confined to the exercise area, and there may have been times when he could have fired a torpedo down *Scourge's* throat. Even so, it had been a good effort, and he would tell them so when he got back.

Through his hydrophones Ransome checked precisely where the destroyer was. She had lost contact herself, and Brady was forced to recognize again the submarine's superiority in detection. Then Ransome ordered a smoke-candle fired. This marker, pouring out smoke when it reached the surface, was projected from an under-water gun by compressed air. The destroyer would sight it at once, and clear out of the vicinity.

With the marker reported fired, Ransome kept his craft on a prearranged course for a set period of time. Then he fired a second candle. The two plumes of smoke would indicate his position exactly. He waited a minute or so, keeping the boat on its set course, then he ordered:

"Thirty feet."

It took only a few seconds. The needle quivered on the mark, then steadied. Ransome spread his short legs round the periscope well in the deck, his arms reaching out on either side of his body. He snapped his fingers.

The periscope watchkeeper moved his lever. Wires ran over pulleys and a faint whirr filled the room. The periscope, housed deep down in its well, rose smoothly. Ransome bent down, his hands reaching for the handle-bars, and came up with the instrument so that his eyes were at the twin lenses before the glass face-piece broke surface.

Standing to one side of him, Brady saw Ransome's left eye suddenly glow with blue light. It was the sunlight, shafting down through the lenses into his face from thirty feet above. The destroyerman became conscious that he wanted to see that sunlight very much. Then Ransome began to move. His arms hanging over the handle-bars like a great bat, he trained the lens round, trailing his feet in a peculiar motion round the edge of the periscope well. He completed the circle and stepped back. He raised his finger to Brady.

At first Brady could see nothing clearly. The lens was being washed over like a car's windscreen in very heavy rain. Then the wave dropped clear and the outside view leaped into focus: blue sea flashed with white, blue sky and white clouds, brown cliffs and yellow beaches backing the sea, and a long grey ship half a mile away on the beam. He felt Ransome's hand on one of the handle-bars, twisting. Abruptly the destroyer jumped closer, so that he could see every detail of her structure, and heads watching them from the bridge. Either the lookouts were very much on the ball or *Scourge's* radar had picked up this water-surface eye.

"Magnification four times," Ransome muttered, and took his hand away. Brady twisted the lenses back to normal. He knew he was waited for, but the experience was too novel for him to forego it so soon. He trained the periscope round to the right, but the sea seemed to be empty. Then he sighted something that looked like an old man with his head back on a stiff neck. There was something sinister about that fixed stare. He realized he was looking at the attack periscope.

He stepped back from the lenses, and Ransome commanded: "Stand-by to surface!"

Wetherell carried on at once: "Open all main vents. Open lower lid." After a pause, punctuated by a resonant clang, his orders came in a quick staccato sequence: "Ready to surface, sir. Slow ahead together. Blow one main ballast, blow six, two, four. . . ."

The E.R.A. beside Brady played his blowing-panel with hands like striking snakes. Shining levers slammed into place and air at four thousand pounds per square inch burst into the ballast tanks and blew the water out. There was no nonsense about that air. In a few seconds *Diana* had exchanged her neutral weight for positive buoyancy. She lifted out of the water in a flurry of foam and Ransome ordered: "Open up!"

The signalman's ready feet disappeared up the vertical ladder with monkey-like speed; there was a pause and then the brother clang of the upper-hatch's opening. A dazzling beam of sunlight fell down into the control-room. A shower of salt-water sparkled down the light-shaft, and Ransome ran up the ladder with the same agility as his predecessor.

On the bridge, voice-pipe covers were unfastened and the water drained into buckets. Those pipes had been shut before the submarine dived, but the covers had been under great pressure.

Orders came down the pipes and soon the quiet of the control-room was filled with the thud of the diesels. A strong draught flowed past Brady as the big engines gulped in the fresh air, clearing the fuggy atmosphere. A voice-pipe buzzed again and the visitor heard Ransome's voice:

"Captain Brady on the bridge."

Without smiling he heard Number One's interpretation:

"From the captain, sir, would you care to go up on the bridge now?"

"Thank you, Number One."

Up in the fresh air, Brady by habit stared right round the horizon, taking in *Scourge* as his eyes swung. Satisfied that all ships within his range of visibility had been accounted for, he turned back to Ransome. "Champagne," he grinned, expanding his chest.

Ransome nodded, smiling, then glanced across at *Scourge*, where he could see a group clustered about the sea-boat.

"Will you stay to lunch? Or do you want to get back home?"

"What's on?" Brady asked. Now that he could see his ship he itched to be with her again.

"What's for lunch, Pearson?" Ransome asked the signalman.

"Train-smash and bangers, sir. It's ready now."

"Stewed tomatoes and sausages," interpreted Ransome.

"Grim, but descriptive. No thanks, Eric, I'd better get back. Sea-boat?"

Ransome nodded and looked at the signalman. The call for the seat-boat flashed across the glittering sea. Brady said, under the clatter of the lamp:

"I really enjoyed that. There should be more of it. Time permitting, I'd like to send all my captains out with you, one per day. All right?"

"Certainly. It's the obvious drill, yet so few destroyer types do it." Ransome pulled at his nose a moment. "I wonder if you'd be interested in seeing the other side? At Balmoral they've got a couple of good films on escape drill. I think you'd find the principles of escape routine interesting. You could see a couple of bods dressed in immersion suits and so forth."

"I'd like that," Brady nodded. He heard the rattle of the sea-boat's oars. "I'll give you a ring this evening, and we'll arrange the captains' visits as well. But I won't be at Balmoral on Saturday!"

"You won't need escape routine for Saturday—I hope."
Ransome gave him a warm, quick smile.

"Oars! Hook on for'ard!" bellowed a voice beneath them.

"My God!" Ransome ejaculated, realizing that he had omitted
to provide a boat-party for his senior officer's transport. He swung
round to stare over the side and saw the signalman grab hold of
the bowman's boathook.

"Two hands and a bosun's pipe on the bridge at the double!"
he snapped into a voice-pipe.

Brady walked to the after-end of the bridge, on the side opposite to the sea-boat. He had taken three steps when two seamen
jumped through the hatch on to the bridge and then dived down
on to the upper-deck casing. There was a smart first-lieutenant's
hand in that, he thought—those two must have been waiting in
the conning-tower.

With seamanship and tradition satisfied, Ransome looked at
Brady and saluted.

"Your boat's alongside, sir."

"Thank you, Eric," the captain replied, as if he had no knowledge of these high-speed manoeuvres. "Return to base now,
please. Don't bother coming down. And thanks for the ride."

"Aye aye, sir." The informality of the last half-hour had been
banished. Ransome saluted again as his guest climbed over the
bridge rail and handled himself down to the casing. As Brady
stepped into his boat Ransome ordered "Pipe". The shrill
cadence pierced out over the water.

"Bear off for'ard," rapped the coxswain, and the boat pulled
away smartly.

Brady waved to Ransome above him and settled down in the
stern-sheets. He looked back at the submarine. He could see the
valves plainly on the bulge of her saddle-tanks, the long row of
them, shut tight now, holding the pressured air in and the water
out. The boat pulled past the bow, sharp where its stem cut the
water, but bulbous a few feet farther back, where he could pick
out the mouths of the torpedo tubes. He had seen much in his
time aboard her, but not a fraction of what there was to look at.
He knew that they had six torpedoes loaded into her bow-tubes.
A hell of a wallop, he thought—each warhead equal in rupturing
effect to a cruiser's full broadside.

"*Diana* getting under way, sir," the coxswain reported.

Brady nodded acknowledgment. A swirl had started under the
snake's tail, growing into a continuous tossing. It reminded him

that he had done no more than poke his head into the engine-room. There was so much he had missed. Another time, perhaps.

Diana had turned, and now her water-lapping tail was towards them. Her silhouette was very slender above water-line, the bulging side-tanks almost under. If she lowered herself a few feet more there would be hardly a vulnerable part of her open to entry from a destroyer's shells. Depth-charges, or the Limbo's mortar ammunition was the only answer: explode about her when she had dived, using the deep water's incompressibility to enclose her in an iron-hard, crushing fist. . . .

Brady smiled to himself. The violent days had gone. Now it was rockets to the moon, gravity-defying satellites: peaceful days like this one, back alongside the pier every afternoon in time for libertymen. No danger, just routine. Tons of time. Time to work on a future.

The oarsmen were pulling smoothly, elbows into sides, eyes in the boat, feeling those other eyes watching their every stroke from beside the tiller—this trip could help or harm the coxswain when he came up before his captain for a recommend for petty officer. But the captain was thinking neither of the crew's efficiency nor the coxswain's prospects. He was thinking of Beth.

She might like him, but marriage could be miles beyond the limit of her intentions; she might want to settle herself in practice first; she might lose her interest once she got to know him better; there might be, there would certainly be, other men of whom he knew nothing. . . .

"Oars!" the coxswain's voice rode over his thoughts. He stood up and was on the platform at its foot before he realized that Cowan had gone to the trouble of rigging the heavy gangway for him; a Jacob's ladder would have done as well. Had this brief hour of command altered Cowan so much? It certainly could have done—command, complete responsibility, projected a man into a larger world.

The pipes twittered and Captain Brady stepped on to his own quarterdeck.

CHAPTER FIVE

HER day's work done, her crew just that much more experienced and proficient, destroyer *Scourge* was snuggled back against her pier at Garden Island.

With most of them dressing for leave, the petty officers' mess was crowded, so Ben Slocum had slipped down to the bathroom to put his white shirt and black tie on.

He finished knotting the black silk and noted the mirror's sad and worried comment on his face. He rubbed his hand down his shaven cheek, up and down, slowly, his eyes looking at the tiled deck. But the mirror faithfully reflected what it saw—a brown pug-nosed face, the skin weathered to the shiny toughness of old leather, the eyes quiet and set well in under the eyebrows: and a pair of ears, the sharpest, most sensitive set of ears in the Fleet, organs which could distinguish fish chirping and porpoises whistling through the Asdic oscillator, ears which were not large but small, perfectly formed, and tucked in close to his head . . . worth more to *Scourge's* captain than all her Asdic sets and Limbo mortar put together.

Still looking at the deck, standing before the mirror, Slocum pressed his lips together in an odd facial equivalent of a sigh. He reached back to his hip-pocket and produced a comb. He was parting his brown hair when a step sounded in the passage out-side and Petty Officer McCook came into the bathroom.

Slocum saw him in the mirror. McCook was his go-ashore oppo, a fairly small man like himself, but perky, with a dark face and black hair and a smile which was a natural for a tooth-paste advertisement. Aboard and on duty, he was captain of B-turret's twin guns; off-duty, now, he was simply thirsty.

"Strike me up a gum-tree!" he invited. "I been looking every-where for you. Come on then, come on, you'll do. Let's get stuck into it."

"Okay, Stan, I'm just about set. Where'll we go—First and Last?"

"It's the first pub, ain't it?" McCook patted down his own thick mat in the mirror, and said casually, "I hear the Old Man sent for you. Everything all right?"

"Crowd of bloody old women in this hooker. Yes, she's apples. He just talked for a bit about the Asdic exercise."

"So now we're townies with the skipper, eh? What'd he have to say? Nice things?"

Slocum shrugged into his uniform coat. Captain Brady had been more than nice. He had talked in the friendliest way about old James Brookes, telling his visitor that he too had served in destroyers with him. Then he had looked at Slocum and told him that the submarine had done everything it could to escape

Scourge's Asdic pulse, and that Slocum had done an extremely competent job of holding her. And that he, Captain Brady, was proud of his ship's performance.

Slocum had come out of the sea-cabin with a lifting pride in his own heart. He knew that Brady was not given to fulsome praise, and he felt that his real compliment lay not so much in what he had said, as in the fact that he had said it. The captain had known that his praise would not go to Slocum's head—and it was this implication of the interview that had made the Asdic man feel on top of the world.

Then when the other thing had crept back into his conscious-ness, destroying his pleasure in his captain's approbation, he had felt almost savage. The force of his feeling had surprised him—he was normally an equable man.

"Well?" McCook asked, "what'd he say?"

"Oh, he was pretty nice about it. Just said we'd done a good job of holding that sub. down there. That's all."

" 'We' held her, eh? Yeah. . . . You should be feeling jacked-up and rarin' to go then."

"Sure, sure. What are we waiting for?"

They drank fairly steadily in the "First and Last", that hostelry nearest the sailors' landing-place, Man-o'-War Steps. They were both seasoned topers, and throughout the years of their friend-ship they had drunk most of the world's liquors, in most of its ports. They were both new to their present ship, *Scourge* having been not long in commission, and before that McCook had not seen Slocum for close on two years, which time he had spent in an aircraft-carrier. Yet closing that gap were fifteen years of friendship, and the dark little gunnery-man could see as plainly as the frosted glass in front of him that his old shipmate was not at all "jacked-up and rarin' to go", as he should have been after a personal wrap-up from his skipper. Slocum, McCook knew, was worried. He felt vaguely irritated—this restraint on his friend's part was spoiling what should develop into a first-class run ashore.

Slocum put his glass down on the bar and moved it in a small circle, spreading the wetness round.

"Stan," he said, his eyes on the glass, "how about coming out home for tea? I'm spliced now, you know," he added quickly.

"I heard about it," McCook nodded. "But not from you," he went on belligerently. "You might play that bloody Asdic set like a piano but you wouldn't know what comes out of the end of a fountain-pen. Two letters in two years!" He lowered the level in his glass and placed it gently on the counter.

"I'd like to come out home, Ben," he said. "It sure wouldn't hurt a man's guts to fill it with home-cooked scran once in a while. But I tell you what—I reckon you oughta ring the missus first. No offence, mate, but I been home with blokes before. 'Sure it's all right! Listen, cobs, I bring someone home, one of me mates, see, and the missus loves to see 'em. She'll be apples.' Oh yeah . . . ! What happens? We lob home and she's either screamin' at him before we open the gate or else she freezes cold enough to make ice-cream shiver. I'll be in it, Ben, love to, but I reckon you oughta give her a tinkle first. You on the phone? She likes a beer herself?"

"Sure she does," said Slocum. "Maybe you're right. I'll whip out and ring her now. Set 'em up again."

Slocum went out into the street and McCook set them up again. He waited, then started sipping at his beer. He had finished it and had ordered a replacement before his friend came in through the glass-topped door.

"Where the hell you been?" McCook growled. "Up to the ruddy G.P.O.?"

"Not that far," Slocum said quietly, "I had to wait a bit at the phone."

"Well?"

"I couldn't raise her. I should have known—she'll be out shopping."

"At half past five?"

"Eh?" Slocum hedged: "She often shops a bit late—misses the crowd, y'know!"

"Sure," McCook said neutrally. He was not at all sure, but he thought he had an idea of the cause of his friend's worry. He had known him a long while, and at any other time Slocum would have grinned and joked about his wife probably being half-sozzled down in the pub. Now he invented excuses. The situation was not original: it was just a hell of a shame that it had happened to a bloke like old Ben. If it really had happened, of course. . . .

"Come out anyway," Slocum was saying, "I want you to meet Marge."

"I'll do that," McCook said suddenly, and at once hoped he had not sounded too definite. He wanted to meet this Marge. "Let's shove off then," he grunted, and drained his glass.

Slocum lived in a semi-detached cottage in Bondi: one of those tiled, hunched-together abominations that crowd in a red rash of roofs down to the long crescent of golden sand.

They could not get a taxi. There were plenty of cabs, but at this Quay end of town there were plenty of customers waiting to jump into them.

"A man oughta be in gob's uniform." McCook growled. "Let's get a bus."

The trip through the peak-hour traffic was jerky and slow. McCook became morose. His run ashore had begun well, drinking in the old place with his old cobber, their thirsts whetted by a successful day at sea with the new skipper. Everything should have been jake. It wasn't. He had had enough beer to make him want more, but not enough to dull the discomfort of the crowded, jerking double-decker bus. All this was time wasted—in the old days, pre-marriage, they would have rolled out of the pub at six-thirty, fed in town, and have been ready and thirsty when the pubs opened again at seven-thirty. Now he was crowded into a packed bus; he couldn't even smoke.

Even bus trips, like slow convoys, come to an end. They jumped down and McCook noted with a thirsty eye that the stop was ten feet away from the "Astra Hotel". They walked down the hill, concrete and bitumen on one side, the beach on the other where the long rollers of the Pacific ended their run on the sand. The sun was setting but plenty of light lingered in the vast bowl of the sky; it was still warm and heads dotted the surf like black currants in a pudding. McCook ran his finger round inside his collar.

"Man oughta be in there," he grunted.

"A good time for sharks, now," his friend answered. "We go down here."

His voice was quick, nervous. McCook began to wonder if he'd done the right thing in getting mixed up in this. He could have found plenty of drinking oppos in the "Fortune of Fights" or the "Macquarie". They turned into a side-road called Francis Street and McCook felt a brief touch of shame—Ben had obviously wanted him to come out here tonight; maybe the poor devil wanted someone to share his worry with. It helped a hell of a lot if you could talk about things. Slocum stopped at a wooden gate in front of a red-brick cottage. In a sudden surge of fellowship, McCook slapped him on the shoulder and grinned, "After you, cobber."

The front door up on the small veranda was closed. In this

heat, in McCook's home-town of Dubbo, in central New South Wales, that meant only one thing. But here in this packed pen they called a suburb you never knew; you kept it shut or you had a dozen bods a minute peering in.

Slocum, apparently, knew the reason for the shut door. He did not knock, but took out his key. He swung back the door and called in a half-hearted tone:

"You there, Marge? I've brought a cobber home."

He was answered by the mewing of a hungry cat.

"Come on in, Stan, and get your feet under the table. I'll feed that bloody cat and then we'll see what's in the fridge. I keep half a dozen on tap for bludgers like you."

McCook grinned dutifully and stepped into the hallway. Slocum's jocular tone wouldn't deceive even the cat, he thought. He followed the Asdic operator out into the little kitchen, and noted automatically that it was clean, tidied-up. He watched Slocum swing back the refrigerator door, and there was something in the way he did that, a certain quickness of movement, that prepared McCook for what his friend said.

"Well I'm damned! That grog was there this morning. Hell . . . I know—one of them blasted neighbours has been in and borrowed half a dozen."

McCook was as certain as of anything in his life that he knew where that beer had gone. He felt an uneasy embarrassment. The truth was hackneyed enough—if a sailor picked a stinker he was in for real trouble; the circumstances of his livelihood accentuated the chances a woman had of doing the dirty. But even though he knew a score of sailors in domestic strife ashore, McCook had never come into close personal contact with such a situation. And this time it was his best pal.

"Forget the grog," he advised, "they'll be open in a few minutes. I tell you what—I could go a cup of plu."

"Sure. Just a sec and I'll fix the cat."

"Gimme the cat's meat and I'll do that. You put the kettle on."

"Okay."

Slocum opened the fridge door again, and came out with a half-eaten leg of lamb. He placed the meat on the sink and McCook whistled.

"Strike me, this plurry cat's a prize Persian or somethin'?"

"No, she's a bitzer—bits of everything," Slocum smiled. His face looked tired. "But we seem to be fresh out of cat's meat."

McCook fed the cat out in the pocket yard at the back of the house, heard someone next door pull the chain, thought of his home in Dubbo with a paddock on either side, and came back into the kitchen. Slocum had the tea made and they sat down at a little table.

"I s'pose you're hungry, Stan?"

"Hell no, I had a big tea on board," McCook replied. He smacked his lips. "Ah, that's good. Nothing like a cup of the old plu." He looked round the tiny room. "You're set-up all right here, mate."

"Yes, it's big enough for the two of us."

"No kids yet, eh?"

"Just as bloody well!" The words were out quickly, without thought.

"Yeah," McCook murmured.

They sipped their tea, and the silence grew. Both men knew it could not go on like this—the woman who should have been there, whose absence in that kitchen seemed like a shout, would have to be talked of directly. Slocum put his cup down in the saucer and pushed it to one side.

"She won't be home, Stan," he said. He was looking at the table and his face was miserable.

"Do you know where she is? Is it—often like this, cobs?"

Slocum nodded, looking briefly into his friend's face.

"I dunno where she is. Only guess. But she was out late last night and I thought it'd be okay tonight. I thought maybe we'd all go up to the local afterwards—give her a bit of life. It gets lonely for a girl home here all day—you know how it is."

McCook nodded. Sure, he knew how it was. Poor little bitch. Nothing to do all day—except get a job to help out, maybe, or produce a couple of kids. That'd keep her occupied, keep her mind off whatever it was on. What was her trouble? Grog, or the old wily what's-'is-name? He was about to put the question, tactfully, when he realized that though the subject had been broached, old Ben hadn't taken him that much into his confidence. He changed his mind and said:

"How do you feel about her, Ben? Like when you was married?"

"Worse," Slocum answered at once. "I'd do anything for her, Stan, and she knows it. Maybe that's the trouble—you read about these things. But I can't help it. I can't help the way I feel, can I? That's why I married her. It ain't wrong for a man to want to do things. I bring her little things, all the time I'm doing that." He rubbed his forehead with the tips of his fingers. "She don't seem to care. Sometimes she hardly looks at what I bring her. Y'know —hankies, a bottle of scent. . . ."

The words tumbled out. McCook got up and put both cups on the draining-board. He turned round and lit a cigarette, leaning against the sink, looking down at his friend. You poor old bastard, he thought—always like that, always good for a soft touch, all the mess knows it. And now you're tangled with this tramp. . . .

He shook off his thoughts. "I feel like a beer. Let's get up there."

"All right." Slocum got up at once. "Come on, then."

At the front door of the "Astra", Slocum said quietly, "Lounge, Stan?"

"Jeez no, Ben! I don't like drinking in those places. And you have to tip the bludgers in there."

"I want to go in the lounge, Stan," Slocum repeated. He walked up the steps and into the foyer. Then McCook understood. He walked in a pace behind him.

Even though he had wanted to meet Marge, and realized now that the most likely place to look was in the lounge, McCook felt embarrassed as they came up to the big glass doors leading into the table-filled room. This could be mighty uncomfortable— especially if she were with someone. He consoled himself with the reflection that she wouldn't be so damned stupid as to muck around so close to home. You didn't foul up your own backyard.

There were only three couples in the lounge. Slocum walked across the room and sat down at a table in line with the door. That's very bright, McCook thought as he pulled out a chair— she could see him and beat a quick retreat. But maybe Ben wouldn't mind not finding her out tonight; maybe he still had belief in her moral innocence, and wanted it to stay that way. He said:

"You ever done this before, Ben? Come lookin' for her?"

Slocum shook his head. "I just want you to meet her."

"Yeah, sure. Two beers please," McCook said to the waiter.

The gunnery-man's smile was noticeably absent that night. It was the most unpleasant hour he had ever spent. They drank three beers, and before long McCook found his own eyes flicking to the door every time there was movement there. Slocum's eyes hardly left it. Tension grew between them. McCook knew now that if she walked in there would be trouble. It was no time to discuss his friend's domestic life; you don't launch into a serious discussion about the hell your life is when the main architect of your distress might intervene at any moment.

At half past eight Slocum looked at his watch and then picked up his glass and emptied it.

"We'll go down to the 'Bondi', Stan," he decided.

"Look, Ben." McCook leaned forward with his elbows on the table. "Let's give it away, huh? It's nice in here, we're settled in okay. Let's press on regardless, cobber. She won't turn up tonight."

Slocum looked at him. McCook was shocked. Slocum's eyes were bleak, and his face was cut with lines of weariness.

"I want to shift down to the 'Bondi', Stan. I want you to come."

McCook stabbed his cigarette out in the ash-tray and picked up his cap.

They spoke little on the short journey to the bottom of the hill. Slocum walked quickly, and McCook's eyes were drawn round the bend of the bay to where the strings of promenade lights repeated themselves in the dark smooth surface of the sea, the yellow reflections drawn-out and wriggling as the deep sea breathed and moved. They passed a cinema, garish with light, the silent cars drawn up outside, waiting. A few yards farther on and they had turned into the lounge of the "Bondi Hotel", its colonnaded verandas staring out at the ocean.

Inside the doors Slocum halted, so abruptly that McCook bumped into his back. He followed Slocum's gaze across the room.

The lounge was full, but this was the loudest table. Braced for trouble, McCook took in the five people there with swift, intense comprehension. There were three men and two women. He forgot the men. One girl was sitting back quietly, not laughing, her face serious. From his position McCook could see her right hand, rubbing slowly and suggestively along the thigh of the man next to her. Nympho, he judged at once—you often found it with a nice face like that. He forgot her and his stare locked on to the second girl.

As he had expected, she was blonde and brassy, pretty as paint. She had a cigarette in one hand and a glass of whisky floated in the other. Her reddened mouth was open wide in a loud laugh and she was leaning forward to look up into the face of the man across the table. That man had his back to them; but McCook saw her eyes sight Slocum. She drew back from the table and the laugh eased from her flushed face. Then her features set in an expression of apprehension and recognition.

Bloody lovely, McCook thought grimly. Slocum stepped forward.

Veteran of many bar-room brawls, in much more dangerous places than this, McCook rapidly studied the space around the table, and then the men. It was not easy to judge them, sitting down, but they seemed of average size, and fairly drunk. The main danger, he decided, lay with the man opposite the blonde. They stopped beside him.

The noise of the room beat about them in almost solid waves of sound. But McCook heard the blonde say:

"Hullo, Ben."

She leaned back, the glass in her hand, and she was smiling again, her heavily made-up face putting boldness before anxiety. The three men looked up at them. The other girl had taken her hand from her companion's thigh and was staring at the table.

"Hullo, Elsie," Slocum said. His voice was strained. He turned his head and said to the quiet girl:

"Marge."

McCook jerked his head to stare at her. Through his astonishment and disgust, remembering her rubbing hand, he saw that she was quite attractive, in a serious way. Her features were fine and her brown hair, gleaming in the lights, was worn low on the nape of her neck. She said to her hands in her lap: "I thought you'd be at sea tonight. What do you want?"

The three men looking up at Slocum were amused. The one opposite the blonde was craned round in his chair. McCook saw the smile widening on his course dark face. A surge of anger twisted in the gunner's guts. For God's sake, Ben, don't stand there . . . !

"I didn't say I'd be out all night," Slocum said.

"So you're here. What do you want?"

"I want you to come home. I have a friend here with me. This is Stan McCook."

The girl did not look up. She took her glass and drank slowly. She put her glass carefully back on the table.

"So?"

The blonde laughed, a half-drunken cackle. The man whose thigh had been receiving attention leaned back so that he could see Slocum behind his wife's head. He smiled, fatly.

"You don't want to break up a nice little party, sailor. Pull up a chair and have a drink. Come on now, they're on me. Had a good day at Rosehill. What'll it be? Beer?"

Almost sick with repressed rage McCook looked at him. He saw a fair, plump face, still young, grinning over a silk shirt and a flashy tie. A shrewd young face, watchful behind the smile.

"Come home now, Marge," repeated Slocum.

"You heard what the man said. You want a drink or you don't."

Standing beside his friend, a little behind him, McCook saw a little knot of muscle run along Slocum's jaw. This is it, he thought. Ben'll go for the bludger with the dough, I'll take this slob in front of me as he gets up. A nice downward chop. The other bloke. . . .

Slocum touched his arm.

"Come on, Stan."

"What?"

"Come on!" Slocum repeated, low and vehement. He walked away from the table. McCook took a step to follow him, then halted. He turned his head back, glaring at the girl. She took no notice of him. His stare grabbed at each of the men in turn. No one moved. McCook muttered something obscene and walked slowly towards the door.

Slocum was waiting on the footpath. He was smoking in quick puffs and he said at once, without explanation:

"I'll wait for them."

"Them?"

"Yes. I've got to know, Stan."

I could tell you without waiting for them, chum. Remember that Gloria dame who used to wait for the mat'loes at Man-o'-War Steps? Couldn't get enough of it? All same here, chum, except this bitch is quieter. That makes her deeper.

"But she's on to you now. She knows you'll be waiting."

"No, Stan, she'll think I've gone home. It won't worry her."

"D'you want me to stick around?"

"That's up to you, Stan. I'd like you around."

"Sure. I'm . . . bloody sorry, Ben."

"Yeah."

"Look, we better beat it from here. I feel like a drink. They'll be in there a while yet."

"Sure."

Slocum's voice was tired and flat. He moved off towards the public bar. McCook ordered two middies. He waited till they came, then he asked: "That bloke she was with—the well-fed slob. You know him?"

"Sure. That's Walshe. Everybody round here knows him. He's the local S.P. bookie."

"Nice type. Flash bastard. Tons of dough the way he talks."

"He's got it. He gets taken by the cops about every three weeks —just for show. Never goes up himself—one of his stooges takes the can for him. Mugs!" Slocum finished bitterly.

"He might get taken tonight—all by his lonesome," McCook growled.

They had two more beers, without talking much. There was nothing to tell now, it was all plain enough. And McCook found it hard to talk—Slocum stared at the bar, his face set in a mask of pain.

"We'd better get out there," the gunner suggested, "if you want to catch 'em. I'll get a couple of bottles."

Slocum straightened up without speaking and they walked out. The night was still warm, and young. McCook went into the near-by bottle department and then they crossed the wide concrete road. Beyond it were trees and lawns reaching down the slope to the promenade. Beyond that lay the quiet, clean sea.

They sat under a tree, shaded from the street-lights. McCook opened a bottle and handed it across. Slocum took a swallow and then placed the bottle on the grass. His eyes were on the door to the lounge thirty yards across the street.

"If they turn to the left they'll be going to Walshe's flat. It's just along there a bit, past that fairground."

"Waterfront, eh? Nothing but the best," his friend grunted.

They sat there, silent. It occurred to neither of them to worry about Walshe's fighting ability. Used to looking after themselves —it was a natural result of long naval experience in every kind of dive—they had already noted that their quarry was out of condition. And with what he contemplated he would hardly have company around.

Slocum turned to pick up his bottle, taking his eyes from the hotel. McCook said, quietly: "It looks like the flat."

Slocum's head jerked back. Five people had come out of the main door. They stood on the footpath, and McCook could see plainly that Marge had both her arms round Walshe's waist and was looking up into his face, which was turned down, almost touching hers.

Two men and the blonde wandered off towards the cinema. Walshe waved his free arm to them, and McCook saw him look carefully but casually up and down the street. He did not even glance towards the dark trees. Then he said something to the girl and they began walking to the left towards a glare of light which burst from the fairground.

McCook made to rise and Slocum held him back.

"I know where they're going. We've got plenty of time."

They waited fifteen minutes, finishing their beer. Then Slocum got up, his bottle in one hand. He looked down at it, and McCook read his thoughts like a printed page: a beer bottle, smashed against a tree, the neck held in your hand, made a murderous weapon, sharper than a razor. With a twist of disgust on his mouth Slocum threw the bottle to the grass. "Let's go," he muttered.

They walked quickly now, keeping to the tree-shaded side of the street. Past the fairground, then on to a point opposite a large block of flats, with shops on the ground floor. Slocum led the way across the road and straight into a hallway, lit dimly by one lamp. A rectangular cluster of locked letter-boxes was fitted into the wall on the left. They found the name easily:

J. WALSHE: FLAT FOUR

"First floor," Slocum muttered, and McCook nodded, remembering the shops around them. He followed his friend up the staircase to a large square landing, where Slocum stopped at a door with a modernistic "Four" painted on its bland face.

They stood there a moment, silent and tensed. A faint light was diffused through the open fanlight above their heads. There was no sound, not in the whole building. Then a girl's voice, sharp with ecstasy, came through the fanlight. . . .

Slocum turned the handle and flung the door open.

Even in that moment McCook reflected that Walshe must have been drunk with eagerness not to have locked the door; then he was across a small lighted hall and through an archway, running to where Slocum was bending over a bed in the dark, heaving with both hands.

The girl was against the wall, where her instinct for flight and a demented heave of Slocum's hand had flung her. She crouched forward, her body pale in the dimness of the bedroom, her white shoulders meeting the light coming through the open archway from the hall. Her face, staring in shock, was shaded by her uncoiled hair.

McCook's brain was too excited, with part of it listening for interfering steps from outside, for him to appreciate clearly the violence of the next few minutes. But the scene was impressed so vividly on his subconscious that afterwards he could recall it with absolute clarity—Walshe lifting himself from the bed and punching his balled fist straight into Slocum's face; the seaman shaking his head and closing in, his arms curved out like a grab; the bemused bookmaker, lifted half off the bed and then hurled down to the floor with a shock that jarred his breath from his lungs in a great gasp; Slocum dropping beside the winded seducer and hammering with hard blows at his face; Slocum snarling when McCook reached him and dragged him backwards and away.

"All right, Ben, all right! D'you want to kill the bastard?" McCook panted. He was heaving as he spoke, striving to overcome the crazed strength in his friend's arms and shoulders. He felt resistance slacken suddenly. Slocum pushed himself to his feet. He stood there, looking down at the bloodied face on the floor, and now his hands shook and his mouth quivered with reaction. He did not look towards the woman against the wall.

A hoarse voice, punctuated with panting breaths, spoke from the floor.

"I'll sool . . . the boys . . . on to you for this."

McCook bent over him. "We've got a few boys on board!" he snarled. "We'll take you first and then we'll bust up your business every Saturday. And if the cops want to know why, I'll tell 'em. See if you can buy your way out of that rap!"

He straightened up, and Walshe turned his face away from them, pulling himself up painfully by the bed.

"Come on, mate," McCook said in a controlled voice, and took Slocum by the arm. Slocum turned towards the hall, his head hanging. McCook glanced at the woman. Like Diana at the pool, he thought viciously, her attitude surfacing a memory of a painting he had seen. She was staring at Walshe.

Slocum wished with an almost overpowering urge to look at her, to go to her. He had no anger left in him now. Shame saved him. With his head still down he walked out through the archway. McCook shut the front door of the flat quietly behind them.

The girl heard the door click shut and she ran quickly to the bed. Walshe was dragging himself up on to it. He felt her hands on his shoulder. He turned his head and mouthed:

"Get to hell out of here! Beat it! D'you hear me? *Beat it!*"

CHAPTER SIX

NEXT morning at precisely seven o'clock Benson opened his master's cabin door and stepped in. He repeated his question, and when Brady opened his eyes, greeted him, "Good morning, sir."

"M'mm. What's the weather?"

"Fine and clear, sir. Paper forecasts a wet week-end tomorrow, sir."

"What!"

"Don't worry, sir—that means there won't be a cloud in the sky."

"I hope you're right, Benson. All right, then."

"Aye aye, sir." The steward withdrew to his pantry. Brady lay a moment quickly reviewing his day ahead. This morning he was to see the escape routine at the Balmoral submarine base where *Diana* was now berthed. He had arranged it with Ransome last night after she had moved. SM4, the officer commanding the submarine flotilla, would certainly ask him to stay for lunch, and Ransome would join in, because *Diana's* team fed in the base's wardroom ashore during their berthing period there.

He turned his head and idly watched the play of light-gleams on the white-painted ceiling, reflected from the shifting water outside the porthole. This morning the eagerness with which he usually looked forward to a new experience was missing. It would be a completely Navy day—things naval, talk naval; he would be surrounded by it, limited, confined to the same old Service rut.

He consciously digested this new feeling. He had heard older messmates complain of it, but he had never been affected himself before. His Service life had been too full and busy, gaining promotion, gaining facility in the new spheres to which he had been admitted by award of each gold ring. Then he grinned slowly as he realized that Ransome, SM4, Cowan, the familiar preoccupations of his seventeen years at sea, naturally seemed uninspiring beside his new interest in Beth.

Benson saw the look on his captain's face and halted in the doorway. Then he coughed and entered.

"Five minutes past seven, sir," he advised reproachfully.

Brady sat up, smiling, and swung his legs out of the bunk. "Benson."

"Sir?"

"What would you do if I failed to sit down at your blasted breakfast-table right on the dot of seven-thirty? Eh? What the devil would you do?"

Benson rubbed his nose. "Well, sir, there's a dozen things I might do. I might go lookin' for you, I might take it back to the galley, or I might—I might think it was the best thing that ever happened in this ruddy outfit, sir! Ah—breakfast usual time, sir?"

"Usual time," Brady scowled, and got to his feet. He looked at Benson's face and read in its abrupt tightening the steward's thoughts—"They're all the same, these bludgers: lead you on and then smack you down." He replaced his scowl with a twisted grin.

"Best clothes today, Benson. I'm visiting the Royal Navy."

"Best clothes, aye aye, sir."

With the breakfast-table cleared, Brady lit his first cigarette of the day and sent for the first-lieutenant. Cowan came almost at once. He knocked and stepped in. Brady looked up and gestured to a chair. Cowan's attitude was respectful; the cynicism had gone, Brady realized, and was replaced by sincerity. Brother, he thought briefly, that shot of command worked wonders.

"Good morning, Number One. You're the boy again today. I'm shoving off to Balmoral—Ransome tells me their escape drill is worth seeing."

"Yes, sir, I imagine it would be. I wouldn't mind sitting in myself."

"I was reading through the B.R. on the local Subsmash routine last night. I had no idea there was such a hell of a lot for us to do."

"Yes, sir? I'm afraid I haven't studied it."

"I suppose not many of us have," Brady agreed. "No one ever expects to have to put it into operation, eh?"

"I dare say that's it, sir."

"Yes. Ransome tells me submarines haven't much to worry about these days. Nevertheless, I want to see the escape drill. If anything did happen on our exercise, we'd be the bunnies, you know. Senior Search Officer, I think I would be called. But that's not what I wanted you for."

He ashed his cigarette with quick little flicks of his forefinger.

"I learned a lot down there, Number One. I want you to go down in her on Monday. In fact, I'm sending all the squadron captains down in rotation. Ferris from *Lockyer* can go on Monday afternoon, I think, and you in the morning. All right?"

"I think it's a very good idea, sir."

"Yes. All right, Number One." Brady stood up. He picked up a blue-covered book from the table. "I'd like you to read through the Subsmash routine. It's quite interesting—in a seamanship way."

He handed the book to Cowan, smiling. The officer took it, then glanced up into Brady's eyes.

"Ah—that missile business the other night, sir. I—well—we've got some pretty nifty gadgets ourselves. It's not until you have to use them that you fully realize it. . . ."

"I thought you might," Brady nodded. His faced showed nothing of the pleasure he felt. It must have taken something for Cowan to admit what he had.

"Yes, sir." Cowan took up his cap. "When do you expect to be back?"

"After lunch, I should think. If I'm delayed, I'll let you know. Usual leave."

Cowan smiled at him and left.

Brady looked at his cigarette. It was only half finished. He sat down on the settee and leaned back. Nice and open, that last grin of Cowan's. Yet the change was not so revolutionary: he remembered an officer who had been universally judged the biggest pig in the Navy—until he finally got his own command. It did that to you, made you think and gave you understanding. . . . First-lieutenants and others were required by regulation to be given periods in command, but the reason was not solely to make them professionally competent in handling their ships. There was another reason—that it helped them to appreciate the captain's problems.

Brady got up and put his cap on, then walked to the pantry door. With practised facility Benson dropped his cigarette into a saucer on the sink in front of him and turned so that his back hid the evidence.

"Sir?"

"I'll be out of the ship for lunch, Benson," Brady told him, seeing without expression on his face a curl of smoke rising from over the steward's shoulder. "Back for dinner."

"Certainly sir!"

"And put that thing in your mouth instead of burning my crockery."

"Ah—aye aye, sir."

Brady left the cabin. Benson turned back to his sink. He took up the cigarette, shaking his head slowly.

"You cunning old bludger," he muttered irreverently, and took a draw. "But you'll do me."

The first-lieutenant, officer of the day and quarterdeck staff were waiting for the captain. "Pipe," ordered the officer of the day as Brady set foot on the gangway. When he had got into his car and driven off, the destroyer settled back into her daily routine.

"That man there!" Cowan said suddenly. The young officer of the day stared, and then dutifully snapped:

"Able Seaman Lawson! At the double!"

The seaman addressed swung round in quick trepidation, then came doubling aft, putting his cap on straight as he came. He halted in front of Cowan, saluting.

"Sir?"

"You know the regulations regarding wearing caps on straight? You're an Asdic rating, aren't you?"

"Yes, sir."

"Sydney native?"

"Yes, sir." The eyes, respectful, pleaded.

"Very well, then. I catch you again with your cap flat aback like that, you know what it means?"

"Yes, sir."

"Send Petty Officer Slocum to me."

"Aye aye, sir!"

Lawson turned smartly and doubled for'ard, thankful to get out of the way. He knew what Slocum was in for, but that was too bad—his leave was safe for tonight.

Cowan paced aft along the quarterdeck, debating what he would say to Slocum, the petty officer in charge of Asdic ratings. It did not occur to him to wonder that two days previously he would merely have told the officer of the day to have that man's cap put on straight, instead of handling the incident himself, and taking it as far as Slocum. He turned back, and by the time he had reached the officer of the day Slocum had come along the upper-deck.

"You know why I sent for you, Petty Officer Slocum?"

"Yes, sir."

The Asdic operator's voice and bearing were listless. Cowan's voice sharpened a little.

"Things like that are minor offences, Petty Officer Slocum, but you know they can develop into general slackness. This is a new ship. If she starts off slack, she'll stay that way. You'll tighten up in your department. I don't want a repetition of this jack-me-hearty business. All right?"

"Yes, sir."

Cowan hesitated. It was difficult to charge a senior rating with sounding uninterested.

"Pass the word round in the petty officers' mess: all regulations regarding dress will be strictly enforced, especially in harbour. Carry on."

"Aye aye, sir." Slocum saluted and turned away for'ard.

"Looks a bit washed-out, One," the officer of the day commented. "Probably on the turps last night."

"I expect so," Cowan said curtly. "Keep an eye lifting for breaches of dress. And you'll spend your whole watch on deck. All right?"

"Yes, of course," the officer of the day nodded. Cowan walked off, and the lieutenant looked after him curiously.

Captain Brady would not have been much concerned about Lawson's defection, or even about Slocum's washed-out appearance. But he would have been pleased by his first-lieutenant's unusual interest in the ship's discipline.

As it was, Brady was content enough, driving over the great spread of Sydney Bridge, with city-bound traffic coming towards him, but his own outward lane almost free from cars. His tyres hummed on the smooth bitumen, the vast bowl of the summer sky arched lightly over the blue and white harbour, and glancing to the right as he crossed the long bridge, he could see grey ships against the green of Garden Island. He had had a good day yesterday, he was looking forward to an interesting morning, and tomorrow he would be with Beth.

He sent his car up the slope of Pacific Highway and along a traffic-crowded Miller Street. He had passed the Independent Theatre when a van coming out on his right caused him to brake hard, annoyed with his own remissness. A head poked towards the window and a strident voice called:

"All right, mate, you ain't at sea now!"

He moved on again, more watchfully. He didn't cut much ice

here in Miller Street. He'd been used to closed-shop privileges for a long time. When he came outside one day it would be like this—he would have to start right from the bottom, with no weight to throw around.

What the hell was he worrying about? He had years to go yet. But then the longer he left it the harder it would be to get a berth outside. Efficiency in tracking submarines wasn't much chop in George Street. And Beth might want him out sooner; might want her husband around all the time.

There it was: the end-all of these novel thoughts about civil life and retirement from the Service. Beth. He was a hell of a long way ahead of himself! She mightn't give a tinker's damn if he served in the Navy or served in Kamchatka. He'd know that tomorrow. He'd know all right, for sure.

He turned in carefully through the gate at Balmoral Naval Depot, and the sentry came across quickly, saluting.

"SM4," Brady said.

"Yes, sir. Captain Brady, sir? He's expecting you. Second turn down there on the left, sir."

Step back from the car, rigid salute again. Brady drove on, back in the arms of recognition and security and respect.

He stopped the car in front of a large brick building which faced a grassy slope, dotted with trees, descending to the harbour. Down there the black superstructure of *Diana* could be seen, diminished by distance, on the far side of a pier. Leaving the car he walked up some stairs to the first floor, and turned left where a sign directed him to the office of Commander Blain.

He had not previously met the C.O. of the Fourth Submarine Flotilla. As he stepped into the Commander's room from the outer office, a man whose straight, slight figure showed him to be about forty, but with grey hair and an old face, got up from a desk and came to meet him.

"Good morning, sir. Blain."

"Hello, Commander, it's kind of you to have me over. Is Ransome up yet?"

Blain looked at him, briefly and cautiously, from under stiff grey eyebrows.

"I mean up out of bed yet," Brady amplified. "Submariners. . . ."

Blain smiled, relaxing. "Strangely enough, he's been up for an hour or so." He was easier now; their ranks were close enough, and Blain was in a responsible post. Normally, on a home station, he could have had more ships under him than Brady had. "He's been in and out of here looking for you, so I think we'd better look for him. Where's my pipe?"

Blain turned to his desk and picked up an old pipe, already filled, from an ash-tray which had once been a four-inch cartridge. Waving his match out, he said round the pipe-stem: "Ransome tells me *Scourge* put up a jolly good show out there. He couldn't shake her."

"Thank you," Brady smiled. He was about to add something deprecatory, then changed his mind: the ship had in fact done well. Blain began ushering him towards the door.

"You're the first destroyer driver we've had over here. I'd like to see it more often."

"You will," Brady promised. He preceded the commander through the ante-room and along the passage. At the top of the stairs he turned his head. Blain's limp was so noticeable that Brady's eyes automatically dropped to his right leg. He knew the submariner had seen his look, and he said pleasantly, "Sciatica, so early?"

"No," grunted Blain, "a little present from a Jap bayonet." He waved his hand towards a near-by window. "You have a really lovely harbour here. I'd heard about it, of course, but strangely enough it came up to expectations."

"You haven't been on the station long?" Brady asked, falling in with Blain's apparent wishes as they started down the stairs.

"Only a month or so. That gives me almost two years to go here."

"And then . . . ?"

"Then I'm resigning and staying here. So far as I'm concerned, this place is near enough to paradise. The children love it—they're as brown as Tamils already."

They were walking slowly down, Blain holding on to the banister rail. Brady glanced sideways into his face. The submariner was not smiling; his expression was serious. Brady filled in the story: a Jap bayonet, obviously from a prison guard—you didn't meet enemy bayonets in a submarine—and that would account for the grey hair; a hard war for this man, to whom the pleasantness of life in sunlit Australia would appeal strongly. "I'm glad to hear it," Brady said, and meant it. He had definite ideas on migration. The country needed Britishers like Blain.

They crossed the footpath outside and Brady opened the near-side door of the Jaguar. The C.O. smiled his thanks and slid himself carefully into the seat. The car twisted down a steep road to the harbour-level, and Brady ran it along to some wharf buildings which backed on to the slope. The two officers alighted.

"Look at it," said Blain, nodding outward. "And I've been in Rio's harbour."

Pleased by the Englishman's appreciation, Brady glanced across the water, which sparkled warmly over the deeper colours of green shading into blue beyond *Diana's* pier. Farther off, three or four tongues of land came lapping down: peninsulas clothed thickly in bush green, relieved in flashes of white by the trunks of tall gums and occasionally by the red roof of a house half-hidden in the forest. In the distance the dominant face of North Head stood straight up from the sea, a necklace of white foam at its base: the guardian of all this warm beauty.

"I sometimes wonder what Captain Cook thought of it all," Brady smiled. "It must have made his day."

"I'm sure it did. It's the best cure for a liver I know. Ah—here's Ransome."

The squat figure rolled up, his eye almost closed under the effect of scar and grin.

"Good morning, Eric," Brady greeted him genially. "Got all your tricks laid out?"

"You, sir," Ransome replied, nodding, "are privileged. The escape coxswain himself has agreed to the morning's instruction. And will instruct personally."

"I see," said Brady, looking suitably impressed. "Then we mustn't keep him waiting."

They moved off abreast, and Ransome said:

"Actually, I know the beggars are tickled pink that Captain D himself is interested enough to drop in."

"You'll get on," Brady told him, matching his grin.

"There's a film as well," Ransome said. "It shows chaps under instruction escaping from the bottom of a big water-tank in the U.K. Using free ascent—that's replaced the old Davis escape gear now."

They were almost up to a two-storey brick building. Brady's gunnery-trained eye picked out the coxswain at once. He was a tall man, dressed cleanly in white drill shorts and shirt, white stockings and shoes, and he stood beside the door, at ease, waiting, his shoulders back and his arms stretched straight behind him. He could have been a gunner's mate on the parade ground. Brady had seen enough to appreciate the casual but instant discipline prevailing on board a submarine; judging by this fellow it would seem that submariners, for all their easy routine, could be sticklers for drill in other circumstances also.

Ransome stopped at the door and the coxswain snapped to attention. His eyes stared straight ahead at the brick wall opposite.

"This is Chief Petty Officer Ponsonby, sir," Ransome said formally. "Captain Brady, Coxswain."

Ponsonby's hand rose and remained at the salute a moment, quivering. Brady found himself, with an inward grin, saluting back just as smartly.

"Morning, sir." The voice was clipped.

"Good morning, 'Swain," Brady answered easily. "At ease, please."

Ponsonby relaxed into something slightly less rigid than an upright iron bar. "All ready, sir," he informed Ransome. "I suggest the film first, sir, then I'll get a couple of hands into immersion suits in the swimming baths. M'mm."

In his interest in what had been laid out for him, Brady missed that first "m'mm". He was to notice later than it ended every speech, and sometimes each sentence, the coxswain uttered. It sounded as though Ponsonby was communing with himself on the correctness of what he had just said, and had found it good.

"Right," Ransome said. "Would you come in here, sir?"

Brady stepped in through the door, the coxswain standing smartly aside to let him pass. The destroyerman concealed his delighted appreciation. Ponsonby, a lower-deck rating, had by his example wiped out the easy camaraderie of the senior officers and had stiffened them into formality—Brady's own salute, Ransome's pukka request to enter. . . .

Brady found himself in a small room cluttered with marine impedimenta—racks of escape suits, rubber breathing tubes, goggles, bottles of compressed gases, ropes, weights and a pile of face-masks. Three petty officers were in there, all coxswains, and at Ponsonby's rapped "Gangway!" they straightened up in hastily-hidden surprise. Brady nodded pleasantly to them, and passed on through another door. The next room was almost as full as the first, and had the same smell—the peculiar tang associated with rubber, wet rope, all salted from use—but it was larger and held a film-projector.

The three officers seated themselves, the door was shut from the outside, and a screen was rolled down over it by an able seaman, who then posted himself at the projector after telling

Ponsonby as he passed: "All set, 'Swain." And Ponsonby took up his stance directly in front of his gold-braided audience.

"The film you are about to see," he informed them, "shows the escape drill as taught at H.M. training establishment in Gosport."

He kept his eyes mainly on the Australian, and Brady was not sure if he had been singled out because of his seniority or because of his ignorance.

"Here you will see demonstrated the new method of free ascent," Ponsonby continued. "It has been found to be the safest, quickest method of getting from a sunken submarine to the surface, depending of course on the depth of water. M'mm. You will notice that the men under instruction in the film are cautioned that they must breathe out slowly and continuously on their way to the surface. This is most important. At a depth of, say, two hundred feet, the air in a man's lungs is at considerable pressure. If he leaves the submarine and rises to the surface, holding his breath until he gets to the top, it is possible that his lungs will burst with the pressure inside them. M'mm. We will now see the film."

He walked to the door and snicked off the light. The projector began whirring at once.

Brady was so interested that he forgot to smoke. He had seen many British training films during the war, and this one possessed the same clarity of exposition. He watched the trainee submariners enter an air-lock at the base of a huge water-tank which reminded him of a wheat silo on his native Darling Downs. The men wore breathing masks. The chamber they occupied was then filled with water, and an instructor opened a steel door into the main body of the cylindrical tank. Each man in turn discarded his mask and left the air-lock.

The camera followed him up through the column of water. He rose quickly by his own buoyancy, breathing out a slow stream of bubbles as he ascended. On the surface a brace of instructors waited to escort him, blowing and gasping, to a ladder outside the tower.

A spoken commentary pointed out that the air pressure in a man's lungs when he entered the base of the tower was fifty pounds per square inch. When he surfaced, the surrounding atmospheric pressure was about fifteen pounds: a difference which, if he had not breathed out on the way up, could easily have ruptured his lungs.

The film flickered off, the light went on under Ponsonby's ready hand, and the officers looked at one another.

"Nothing to it, eh?" Ransome smiled. "Who wouldn't be a submariner?"

"It looks all right in a tank," Brady commented. He was thinking of the darkness and pressure and fear in a water-filled submarine two hundred feet down under the sea. He said:

"I've read a lot about all the inventions designed to assist rescue from a sunken boat. Now they find that the natural way is the best after all."

"It was ever thus," Ransome answered, "providing you're not down too deep," he qualified.

"And then?"

"Then we use a special immersion suit. Coxswain?"

"Two suits and two instructors are waiting, sir. If you'd like to come out to the pool, sir. . . . M'mm."

The outer room was empty as they passed through. Brady found two of its earlier occupants standing beside a long swimming pool in an adjacent building. The water looked green and inviting. Beside each man on the spring-board lay a yellow pack about one foot square.

"This," pontificated Ponsonby, taking up a pack, "is an immersion suit. It is made of rubberized cotton, and painted yellow for easy sighting by rescue boats or aircraft.

"You will note that the suit is sewn in such a fashion that it has plenty of gas pockets. It is inflated when in the water by releasing the valve on a bottle of CO_2. It is sealed round the neck and wrists by rubber bands. It carries with it goggles, light, bright yellow gloves and an inflation tube by which the floating man can blow up his suit if it should tend to deflate through rough seas. M'mm.

"There is another important feature. Urine. The man floats on his back. He might be in the water some time. If he urinates the liquid will gather in a pool round the small of his back, round his kidneys. This gathering of liquid, especially in cold weather, can lower a man's resistance. The acid also attacks his skin chemically. So an absorbent pad like a large napkin is supplied. At least one man omitted to put it on before he clad himself in the immersion suit, and he died. M'mm. We will now demonstrate the suit."

Nappies and life-saving immersion suits for men emerging from a submarine two hundred feet down. . . . No one smiled

—the instructor's method of delivery forbade the slightest levity. He nodded to one of his henchmen and the petty officer pulled off his shoes and took up his pack.

"That is the only requirement—apart from the absorbent pad," they were told. "Off shoes before donning the equipment."

Brady was surprised to see the size of what spilled out from the small yellow pack. The petty officer slipped into the suit with practised facility, the bulky padded material making him look more like a space-traveller than a submariner. He got the nod from Ponsonby and jumped into the pool.

He lay on his back and pulled a valve and there was a hiss of gas and the suit billowed to fullness about him. He blew a whistle, switched on his light, let gas out of the suit, re-inflated it with his own breath, and floated there, quite at ease. Then he paddled with his gloved hands and manoeuvred himself to the side of the pool.

When he had discarded the suit Brady noticed that the only wetness about him was his own perspiration. Now I know what to look for, he thought, remembering the outsize yellow figure floating on the green water. He put the grim impression aside— sailors are a superstitious lot—and said: "Thank you, Cox'n. Most interesting. I don't suppose you've had to use this gear yourself? In actuality?"

"No, sir. If all hands do their jobs down there, there's not much danger of having to use this stuff. M'mm."

"Now," put in Ransome, looking at his watch, "it's time to inspect *Diana's* wardroom. I warned them I expected ice at all times from now on." He smiled at Brady. "Thank you, 'Swain. An excellent demonstration, all very clear. You'll have a nip, Arthur?" he finished, turning to Blain.

The C.O. intimated that he would have a nip. Ponsonby saw them out, as formal as ever, and it was not until they were walking down the pier that they relaxed. They crossed the narrow gangway to *Diana's* foredeck, and Ransome led the way to the forehatch, which gaped open in a surprisingly large rectangle.

"We load torpedoes down through here," Ransome explained, and led the way down the ladder. "This is the torpedo-stowage compartment. The actual tube-space is through that hatch there. You can see the tubes."

Brady looked with interest—he had not come this far for'ard yesterday. He saw the banks of white-painted torpedo tubes, six of them, three on either side mounted on top of each other like giant gun-barrels. Almost two feet in diameter, each long tube was cluttered with a lacework of pressure-pipes.

"Up here," Ransome reached up and touched what looked like a thin water-pipe running the length of the compartment, "our B.B.S."

Brady saw that the pipe was fitted at regular intervals with what looked like nozzles—the apparatus resembled a fire-spraying system in an office ashore. He shook his head.

"I'm stumped—B.B.S.?"

"Built-in Breathing System. Remember the face-masks in Ponsonby's room? Each one has a hose; it plugs into one of those nozzles. Up top under the casing are three cylinders of oxygen and nitrogen, at four thousand pounds pressure. If this compartment floods—it's one of the escape compartments, by the way—each man can plug in to the breathing system through those demand valves and take what oxygen he wants while he's waiting to escape."

"Like a suckling baby?"

"Exactly. We also have breathing-tubes without the masks—more convenient sometimes."

"But four thousand pounds per square inch—you must have a decent-sized reducing valve?"

"It is a hefty one, yes. Reduces it right down to comfortable breathing pressure. They can also inflate their life-jackets with it."

"I see." Brady looked round the compartment, noting the shining spare torpedoes racked-in against the boat's side, and he was impressed by the casualness with which Ransome discussed the horrible possibility of flooding. He himself once, many years before, had ordered a magazine in a cruiser flooded; he wished not to even think about that, and would certainly never willingly discuss it. Different ships, different cap-tallies, he thought, and tried not to imagine what this dark, cluttered space would be like, full of water two hundred feet down. . . . But the macabre possibility had been much in the mind of the submarine's designer. On *Scourge* they had a few lifeboats and carley rafts if she went—here, high-pressure cylinders, oxygen and nitrogen, built-in breathing system, demand valves, face-masks, escape hatch. . . .

He deliberately lowered his eyes from the sinister-looking air-pipe and then he saw that the compartment was lined also with bunks, mere canvas stretched over iron frames, and lashed back against the boat's side. He saw something else, and the sight provided a welcome note of comic relief. Each bunk was painted crudely with its owner's insignia: Buggy's Pit, R.I.P., Taffy's Tent, Mac's Sack, Head's Heaven. . . .

"Eighteen men bunk in here," Ransome offered.

Brady nodded. Submariners must be a devoted tribe, he reflected —even now, with the big hatch thrown back, the place was a hot gloomy cavern, redolent with the stink of oil and grease, bilge-water and sweat. At night, underwater, eighteen men asleep, it would approximate to his idea of a basement back-room in hell.

"Someone mentioned," Blain said dryly, "a gin *avec* ice."

"I detect a note of disbelief on the last word," Ransome grinned, and led the way through the door, "but I've got a bright engineer boy—or I'd better have," he ended grimly.

Brady followed him through, lifting his feet to clear the coaming and bending his head to miss the top of the hatchway. He noticed that the door was very thick, and its clips strong, eight heavy handles of polished steel. Swung over, those clips would take up on eight sloping wedges on the door, jamming the rubber of the door-edge against its facing in a water-tight seal.

They followed Ransome down a narrow passage to the ward-room, where he halted in the doorway. Five faces looked up at him expectantly, five resigned faces waiting over a cluster of glasses on the table. His gaze flicked to the table-end, and, satisfied, swung round to Brady.

"It worries me, sir," he said soberly.

"How they knew?"

"Yes. I made no mention of your coming on board today. Yet here they are—gathered for the debauch."

"Good morning, sir," Wetherell greeted formally, "would you care for an iced drink, sir?"

"I certainly would!" put in Blain, "even though I don't believe it."

"There are submarines—and submarines, sir," said Dan Ullyet. "Or rather, engineers—and engineers."

"There's no damned modesty—not in this mess," Ransome growled rudely, and squeezed himself along the padded seat. "Come on then, let's see this marvel."

The engineer raised the towel, and the drinks were served quickly and passed round. Everyone drank gin and water, and though Brady detested the mixture—to him it tasted like eau-de-Cologne—he swallowed two glassfuls without grimacing. He put his glass down and watched Ullyet fill it again.

"How are you fellows finding it ashore?" he asked. "Enough invitations?"

"Some get more than others, sir," replied Wetherell. "We haven't been in very long, but the torpedo officer already has his legs under the table. In some beach suburb, I believe."

Brady glanced at Deevers, and saw the self-satisfied smirk under his swooping nose. The engineer read Brady's look accurately. He said, generally:

"Obviously it's not his face. Our Torps has hidden charms."

"Seldom hidden," Number One offered.

"Ever tried to hide a lower-boom?" inquired Pilot.

"Jealously," Deevers said, and grinned widely at Brady, "they're all jealous."

Brady smiled slightly, trying to hide his distaste for the torpedo officer's expression; he felt that there was more than friendly raillery in the others' comments, also. He emptied his glass, and was relieved when Ransome suggested:

"The other half, sir? No? Then we'd better get ashore and up there if we want to feed."

Brady climbed the ladder into the clean hot sunlight and walked down the gangplank to the pier. He waited for the others, and he was thinking: there's always one, it's never perfect; not even in a mess like that one. Deevers had some queer attraction for women, and he was the type who would come back aboard and talk about what he had done, and who with. He couldn't be shut up—he would confuse good taste with envy, and be provoked by disapproval to even more intimate revelations.

"I don't suppose we can all pile into the Jaguar?" Ransome suggested.

"I think so. Feet off the woodwork, though."

Brady opened the rear door of the shining black beauty, and felt an absurd pleasure when Ullyet whistled in appreciation. They jammed in, and the Jaguar whined powerfully up the hill to the main buildings of the depot.

In the long wardroom, its big windows looking down on the harbour, Brady had finished his salad when the steward approached.

"Excuse me, sir, you're wanted on the phone."

"Oh?" Brady rose at once, his thoughts going instantly to his ship.

"In the corner there, sir."

He walked quickly to the phone and took up the receiver. "Yes? Brady."

"Good Lord! Do you always speak like that on board? Remind me never to join the Navy!"

"Why, Beth!" His pleasure went into his voice over the wire.

"That's better. But now I know your other side, remember?"

"Did you have any trouble getting me?"

"Not at all. Your first-lieutenant—also with a voice like a damned rasp until he knew he wasn't talking to a poor able seaman—told me where you were. Now, how do you stand down there? Finished lunch yet?"

"Yes—only sweets to come."

"Good. I've arranged it for this afternoon. Two-thirty."

"Have you now! Arranged what?"

"The operation, of course." She ended the silence with: "Well? I thought you said you'd like to see one."

"Yes, I would—of course. What is it? Not too gory, I hope?"

"You can always leave the theatre, you know. It's an upper lobectomy—dissection of tubercular tissue from the lung."

"That's funny," he said, and a vague excitement began to stir in him. "We've been talking about lungs all the morning here. Air pressure in same, things like that."

"Oh? Then you're well up on the subject."

"Nasty," he drawled, grinning at the wall.

"I must shove now, James. The operation is at Royal North Shore Hospital, thoracic section. It's at the back, behind the main entrance. Ask for Dr. Thomsett—he's one of our top lung boys. I've told him about you. It's all right with him, as long as you keep your hands in your pockets, sort of thing. By the way, don't broadcast it around—it *is* a bit unusual to let a layman in."

"I understand—and thanks. Till tomorrow, then?"

"Tomorrow?" There was a faintly-surprised query in her voice. For an instant he felt the most acute disappointment. Then she said:

"Tomorrow—yes, of course. Looking forward to it. Good-bye now—two-thirty, remember."

"Good-bye, Beth."

He heard the phone click and put up his receiver. He walked slowly back to the table. Surely she hadn't forgotten their appointment for tomorrow? There had hardly been a moment when he hadn't been thinking of it, even two hundred feet down under the Pacific. Perhaps he was banking too much. . . . But then surely that "Looking forward to it" had been genuine enough?

"All well?" Ransome asked, smiling up at him.

"Yes," Brady nodded. He made to pull his chair out and then changed his mind. He would let Cowan know that he wouldn't be back this afternoon, and then go to the hospital. "I'm afraid I must shove off now. Look—I think I'll have Beth and her father down for dinner on board on Sunday night. Join us?"

"Thanks, yes."

"About six, then. Good-bye," he said to Blain, "thanks for this morning."

"Pleasure, sir."

Brady looked into the grey-haired face and he hoped that Blain had not heard his invitation to Ransome. For a moment he hesitated—but no, his cabin space was limited, and he wanted Sunday night to be cosy.

"Happy surfing," Ransome murmured maliciously, and turned back to his sweet.

"You'll keep," Brady grinned, and made for his cap.

CHAPTER SEVEN

BALMORAL was on the North Shore, and Brady did not have to cross the harbour bridge to get to the hospital. Even so, he found the traffic heavy, and he throttled the big car back with impatience.

He had plenty of time, but he was excited at the prospect of seeing a major operation, of looking at a bared lung, perhaps even a beating heart. Influenced by this emotion, he felt as he had sometimes done before in his life, that he would like to have been a surgeon. He remembered the fascination which had gripped him when he had seen a naval surgeon perform a run-of-the-mill appendicectomy in the old destroyer *Scourge*, when he had been Petty Officer Brady. Now he was to witness something really worthwhile. Not what, but who you know, he grinned to himself as he swung the car into a narrow street which would bring him to the back of the hospital buildings.

A pity Beth would not be there, to take his hand and introduce him to this alien territory. He was in uniform, too, which would make him even more conspicuous. But then she had organized everything—Thomsett was the man to meet, he must go straight to the top boy. Things should be smooth from there on in.

He parked the Jaguar among cars with doctors' insignias prominent on the number-plates, and stepped into a high, cool hall. A nurse came towards him and he smiled and asked, crisply:

"Where is the thoracic section, please?"

"Up the stairs, sir," she answered at once. "The theatre doors are at the end of the passage."

"Thank you."

Probably she thought he was a naval surgeon. That's it, boy —the confident approach, as if you owned the place. (His self-satisfaction was to be pricked later on, when he recognized that nurse in the operating theatre and realized that she had been told to look out for him.) From the top of the first flight he saw some swing doors, and walked towards them. The doors opened and a thin, bony woman backed out, a mask rumpled down under her chin and a try of instruments in her hands. She turned and saw him.

"Good afternoon. Captain Brady?"

"Yes, Nurse," he answered, relieved.

"I am Sister Affleck."

"Oh—I beg your pardon."

"Mister Thomsett is not here yet. But he shouldn't be long. In the surgeons' room there you'll find a cap, mask and gown. Also canvas shoes for your feet. They go over your own shoes. Excuse me now, please."

She strode into another room, from which came the hiss of steam. He rubbed his nose, grinning a little. He had worried about his reception. . . . He had been received, recognized, corrected, briefed and detailed-off in six brisk sentences. Maybe he wasn't so much out of his own disciplined element after all.

Inside the surgeons' room he searched for a moment along clothes-hooks before he sighted the articles he wanted laid out neatly on a small table at the end of a row of hand-basins. Over-shoes, gown and mask. He was wondering how the mask tied on when Sister Affleck came in, talking to two young men students.

"Scrub up," she ordered, "at least ten minutes with that brush, mind you. Then into the theatre—a nurse will show you how it's set up."

"Yes, Sister," the taller young man replied dutifully.

Before Brady could appeal for help with the mask, she had brushed past him and through a single swing door into the theatre. He turned to the two students, who now had their backs to him as they bent over their basins. The tall one took up a large slab of common soap, turned on the hot water with his elbow and started scrubbing.

"Bloody old battleaxe," he grunted. "Sex-starved, of course." The lather rose thickly on his hairy forearms.

"Why don't you do something about it?" chided the other, a short, plump fellow.

The tall one grinned, and scrubbed faster. "I do it for love, not for punishment."

"I have always maintained," said a deep voice from Brady's right, "that medical students are arrogant, uncouth and obscene. Your observations on the most competent theatre sister in the hospital confirm my diagnosis. Eh?"

They swung round guiltily towards the man behind them. Brady turned also, and saw that the new arrival had a rugger forward's body and a craggy face under a short, steep forehead.

His grey eyes beneath bushy black brows examined each student in turn.

"Sorry, sir," the tall one broke the silence. "We—er—didn't hear you come in."

"Evidently," said the big man dryly. He nodded to the basins. They turned back gratefully and resumed scrubbing. The deep-set eyes swung towards Brady, and one of them closed in a wink.

"Captain Brady?"

"Yes. Mr. Thomsett, I believe?"

"That's right. Nice to have you with us."

The tall student looked back over his shoulder—apparently he had assumed Brady in his gown to be one of the theatre assistants.

"I see you've managed all right?" Thomsett looked his guest up and down.

"Not quite. This mask. . . ."

"I see. Here we are. One string over the ears, the other under your chin. That's it. I think you will agree with me, Captain, when I say that instruction is never wasted—there is always someone around who needs to learn."

Brady smiled. The tall student coughed. Thomsett began scrubbing his own hands.

"This is a teaching hospital, hence the presence of these two sexually sensitive young gentlemen. You are familiar with the operation?" he inquired of the scrubbers, his deep voice echoing from the white tiles before them.

"Well, sir. . . ." began the tall student.

"Quite." Thomsett rotated his wrists and forearms under a

jet of water, and took up the soap again. "Upper lobectomy. I suspect that the left upper lobe will need resecting. We shall remove one rib, and you will see the heart, beating. In the pericardium, of course. A sight, I may say, not many of us have seen."

Brady listened, intent.

"You will also see something of an interesting branch of anaesthetics. Oxygen and anaesthetic gases will be induced through a tracheal tube—the normal mask is unsuitable for this particular job." They all stared at him. "Obviously, with the lung exposed, the patient must not breathe. So the anaesthetist will use a rubber bladder—poor fellow has to squeeze it by hand —and through this she will get her oxygen and anaesthetics direct. Directly into the lungs. Understand?"

The students nodded, their faces serious. Thomsett gave his hands a final rinse and stepped back from the basin. With their hands held in front of them, trailing drips of water, the students followed him straight into the operating theatre, pushing the swing door as he did, with his shoulder. Brady went in behind them.

He got a first general impression of white severity, of gleaming instruments, and of the penetrating smell of anaesthetics. Then he distinguished half a dozen gowned figures moving purposefully and silently about the room, and a woman lying quiet on the operating-table with the big lamp, almost three feet across, suspended above her. He was easing towards a corner, being careful not to touch anything, when a cheerful voice called to him from the far side of the table.

"There you are, James. Wend your way over here."

He felt acute pleasure and relief: Beth was here, and that explained her hesitation when he had said on the telephone that he'd see her tomorrow. She had assumed that he knew she would be present this afternoon. He judged from the easiness of her greeting that she was much senior to the other two students, or else that she was close to Thomsett socially, probably through her father.

He walked across and smiled into the slightly-smiling eyes looking at him over her mask. She was wearing rubber gloves, and so he did not go too near.

"I didn't realize you'd be here."

The corners of her eyes crinkled. "I wouldn't let you stumble into this on your own. But it will cost you a drink—nice little pub down the road."

"I might do that."

Suddenly he didn't want to banter with her, not in this room, and he was glad when she said, "I want you to meet some of the people here. Don't touch anything, please."

He followed her carefully round the theatre, and a man with gloved hands met them with his eyes.

"This is Dr. Trantor, the senior assistant. Captain Jim Brady, Bruce."

"How are you, Captain?" Trantor nodded. He had a pleasant voice, but there was little else Brady could judge about him behind the mask and under the cap. He seemed to be about his own age, medium height, a strong, full figure, but undistinguished beneath the loose anonymity of the white gown.

"A bit out of my depth," Brady grinned.

"The novelty will wear off—after the fourth hour. Excuse me now?"

He walked over to where Thomsett was studying an X-ray negative pinned to the wall. Brady saw ribs, and two darker oblongs which he presumed were lungs.

"What's he do?" he asked in a low voice.

"Assists Thomsett. Helps keep the incision open, ties bleeding points, things like that. But you'll see it all. Down here."

He followed her again to the end of the table, feeling respect for her in her strange environment. "Colin?"

A short fat man came upright from fiddling with a valve on the anaesthetic machine. Brady's impression was of a pair of soft brown eyes.

"Yes, Beth."

"This is Jim Brady. . . . Colin Hagar."

"Oh yes, your sailor friend. How are you, Jim?" the anaesthetist said easily.

"Fine . . . so far." Brady liked the other's friendly familiarity and the knowledge that Beth had been speaking about him. That one word "friend" seemed somehow to establish a certain relationship between him and Beth. He was about to say something further to Hagar, thinking at the same time what a nice bunch they seemed to be, when Thomsett's voice brought his head round.

"When you are ready, gentlemen."

"Stay here with Colin," Beth advised him, "you'll see everything." She stepped up to the table. Brady waited beside the anaesthetic machine, his eyes and mind intent. He began to feel

a little restricted behind his porous mask, and for the first time
really believed that he might faint. He pushed the thought down,
and looked at the patient.

A woman of about forty-five, she lay on her back, injected with
pentothal, her eyes closed. Her face was a foot away from his
stomach, right at the head of the table. Two nurses tried to lever
her on to her right side. They strained, and automatically Brady
made to help. He quelled that impulse before his foot had moved.
This is something, boy, you keep well out of. . . .

"Solid bod, isn't she, Sister?" Thomsett grunted. He called to
an orderly working on a gas cylinder. "All right, Tom, bear a
hand here."

They turned the woman on to her side, and the nurses buttressed her there with two straps passed across her body.

"Jim."

The anaesthetist gestured with his head. Brady stepped over
beside him. Hagar had a thick instrument down the patient's
throat. At its end a light shone.

"Take a look."

Brady bent over and peered down.

"Vocal cords. See 'em?"

Brady nodded. He could see the cords plainly. They looked
like two short pieces of white elastic, side by side. They were
vibrating slightly, an effect of the muscle-relaxant. In them, he
thought with wonder, were the range of tone of a Caruso's voice,
or the shades and inflexions of his own. Hagar touched his
shoulder and he stepped aside.

Then Hagar inserted a long rubber tube. Brady saw it was
the continuation of two corrugated tubes which ran from the
machine. Hagar turned a small wheel, and immediately began
squeezing and releasing a rubber bladder. Still watching the
patient, he asked:

"Are you here because you're connected with submarines? I've
done a spot of lecturing on lungs, air pressures and things for
them from time to time."

The remark was so apposite to his whereabouts of only a few
hours before that Brady almost said yes. Then he hesitated—
why was he here? The interest, of course. Yet there was something
else and she was standing facing Thomsett, beside Trantor. Yes,
that was his main reason, not consciously thought about till now.
He wanted to see Beth in her world, to learn something about it,
as she would of his.

"No, not really. Though I did learn a little about lungs this morning—went through the escape-drill."

"The coots are mad," Hagar said without malice. "I went down in a submarine a month ago. Once was enough. You'll learn something about lungs here today. See this?" He held up the bladder. "I'm breathing for her now. Here."

Brady had to take the rubber bag—it was thrust at him. Gently he squeezed.

"Don't be frightened of it. Needs quite a bit of force."

Obediently he squeezed harder. Beth's eyes flicked up to him. Hagar moved over to a table against the wall and busied himself with a phial and a hypodermic syringe. Brady became uneasy: he knew nothing of what he was doing, or of the operation of the machine. Then the tall student spoke beside him.

"Let's have a shot at that, will you, sir?"

Brady handed over the bladder with relief. Hagar came back, followed by a nurse who strung a sterile cloth across the patient's neck on two steel stanchions, leaving her face visible on the pillow. Hagar nodded his head at the cloth.

"That's there because the wound will be fairly high up on her side, just under the shoulder. Pretty close to me. And I'm not sterile. Okay?"

"Have got," Brady acknowledged. The anaesthetist resumed control of the bladder, caught Thomsett's eye, and nodded. At once the student left the machine and stood beside Beth, facing the surgeon. Brady turned to face him also, looking over the sterile cloth barrier.

The big surgeon, his head not far from the lamp which focused a brilliant circle of white shadowless light on the Dettol-treated skin, held out his hand. Gently and carefully Sister Affleck laid a scalpel in his palm. The surgeon placed his left hand on the woman's side, his spread fingers tightening the skin. With the knife poised, while Brady scarcely breathed, he looked up at his students.

"I have often read," he said dryly, "of a knife being slapped into a surgeon's hands. That's maybe. As for me, this thing is damned sharp. I treat it accordingly."

Then he bent his head and the knife slid smoothly and firmly across the brown-tinted flesh. In that instant there flashed into Beth's mind the memory of the first time she had cut human skin, in the dissecting-room. The skin then had been incredibly tough. Now, under these fingers, it opened like a white furrow behind the plough of the knife.

Unconscious of Brady standing at the head of the table, conscious of nothing but the lengthening wound, beginning to gape now, Beth watched, her eyes above the mask narrowed in the intensity of her interest. She was not looking at a woman's body. The woman had vanished. She merely saw skin, and bubbly yellow fat; and she used her anatomical knowledge to visualize what was beneath the area Thomsett had cut, strove to see, beforehand, what the knife would reveal.

Blood seeped into the wound—rich, red blood, vitally alive, vividly coloured against the white tissue. Sister Affleck, on Thomsett's left, handed him a pair of forceps. He took them in his left hand, and with a deft snick fastened their toothed jaws over a bleeding vessel. He glanced up across the table.

"That's something you young fellows want to learn. And practise. Using forceps and scissors with your left hand."

They nodded.

"Try it some time. Try closing a pair of forceps with your left hand."

He put out his own left hand and Sister Affleck laid the instrument in it. Thomsett held the forceps up. Slowly, while they watched, his thumb and forefinger came together, until the jaws slipped with a grating snick into place. Looks easy enough, Brady judged. Thomsett handed the forceps, jaws first, to the tall student.

He slipped his fingers clumsily into the holes of the handles; he shut the jaws, and they would not clip together.

"Not so easy, eh?" Thomsett grunted. "Beth?"

The girl took her eyes reluctantly from the wound. There she could see the outline of a rib, sheathed in its protective periosteum. She was impatient for Thomsett to confirm what she knew she should see when the rib was cut and removed. She took the forceps from the student, fitted them quickly to her fingers and with one movement snicked the teeth together.

Expressionless, the surgeon's black-browed eyes looked at her from above the white mask.

"Been practising, eh?" he grunted.

Brady's eyes as he stared at her, however, were loaded with expression. He knew little of anatomy and less of surgery, but character-study with him was a different pair of forceps altogether. He had judged accurately the intentness with which she had watched the preliminary incisions, and he knew that the quickness of her movements with the forceps was a measure of her impatience for the surgeon to continue.

You're a devoted girl, he thought—devoted to your profession, eager for competence in it. I could walk out of here now and my time wouldn't have been wasted.

He liked what he was thinking about her, and he knew why he liked it. They were alike, completely of one mind, she with her surgery, he with his gunnery and seamanship. The same driving force, the same devoted application, was in both of them. He looked at her, he looked at Thomsett, and then down at the gaping wound, and he knew that this strange experience he was undergoing held a deep significance for him.

Trantor, the assistant, spoke to Sister Affleck. She laid in his hand a short instrument, more like a chisel than a knife. Carefully, for he had to use considerable pressure, Trantor ran the blade along the rib, scraping off the protective sheath. Presently the rib lay bare, creamy white, clear of the lips of the wound, in which broad retractors held the tissue widely apart.

Wholly fascinated, Brady saw Thomsett take the big silvered pliers Sister Affleck had ready. The surgeon glanced sideways at the anaesthetist, watching over the sterile cloth strung between the two stanchions.

"Let that lung down a bit, will you?" he ordered.

Still watching, Hagar stopped squeezing the bag. So intent was Brady, he hardly breathed himself. He saw the full, rounded sponge of the lung—like bluish marble it looked, and pitted here and there with black specks—begin to shrivel; its dimensions grew smaller, as a sponge does when the water is pressed out.

Now, with the surface relaxed, and not distended with gas, he could see the minute and multitudinous sacs honeycombing its surface. The lung sank down, and the rib was clear above it. Thomsett placed the open jaws of the rib shears around one end of the rib. He squeezed, hard. There was a distinct snick in the enclosed quiet of the theatre. Again, at the other end. Trantor lifted the six inches of rib bone and dropped it into a kidney bowl. Thomsett nodded to the anaesthetist.

Almost immediately the lung swelled, until it was fully distended—apparently as hard as marble, though it was, as Thomsett felt it, actually soft and spongy.

Brady craned his head round the edge of the sterile cloth. But he could see nothing beneath the lung, only, behind its apex, the clean, glistening cavity of the pink chest wall. Thomsett turned from the table. He held his hands clear from his sides and walked across the theatre. He stood a moment before the lighted X-ray plate, while they watched him. Then he came back, and took up the upper lobe of the lung, three of his fingers down inside the cleanly-defined cleft which separated both lobes. He looked up at Beth. His voice was clipped.

"Woman from the country—lungs would be pink. Miner's lungs—black." His finger pointed. "These black specks there—see 'em? Bunnerong powerhouse. Rib retractor, Sister."

He returned to the X-ray plate, and Trantor took the vice-like instrument. He fitted its two vertical blades inside a rib on either side of the wound. He juggled it, making sure it was secure. Then he turned the ratchet. Gradually the two ribs were forced apart. Trantor twisted, harder.

God, thought Brady, they'll crack! Trantor twisted. The wound was now six inches wide. Brady glanced sharply at Thomsett. The surgeon was staring at the X-ray plate. Trantor twisted. Only the habit of rigid discipline kept Brady from calling out a warning. He was no surgeon, but any fool could see no woman's ribs would stand that mechanical pressure. Maybe this was Trantor's first thoracic operation, maybe he was one of those butchers you read about who didn't care anyway.

Thomsett turned back. He felt the intensity of Brady's stare. His eyes blinked a little, in puzzlement. He looked down at the wound. Brady breathed out in relief. Then Thomsett swung round, walked a few steps, and casually rinsed his slippery gloves in sterile water.

Trantor, broad and bulky, was quite visibly exerting considerable force on the screw. At the moment that Brady had made up his mind to warn him, to tell him no bone could stand that levered pressure—after all, he was an adult naval captain, he knew something of pressures, he wasn't a tongue-tied medical student—at that moment, Thomsett came back. Trantor stopped turning.

"A little more, I think," Thomsett answered his look.

Trantor twisted. Thomsett nodded. He reached over and felt the retractor. It was solidly anchored. The wound was now so wide that Brady could see the whole of the upper lobe, and a good deal of the lower.

"Strong, aren't they—ribs?" the surgeon grunted.

"Yes," Brady spoke for the first time, and meant it.

For the next fifteen minutes there was no sound but the shuffling of Thomsett's canvas-covered shoes on the floor as he shifted position, and the occasional gruff asking for a special kind of forceps.

Knife—scissors; carefully, slowly, they cut, dissected—tissue, branches of the pulmonary artery, arteries of the lung's apex. And all the time the surgeon's big fingers, deft, tender almost, cleared the section of the lung which was to be cut away.

Once Brady, standing behind the sterile cloth between its two stanchions, gazed down at the patient's face. Her head on one side, she was—or seemed to be—sleeping peacefully. Her hand, with the nails neatly manicured, rested beside her cheek on the pillow.

Hagar pressed one finger-nail. It showed white a moment, then red as the blood flowed back.

"Condition good," Hagar murmured.

Her face was calm, as though normally asleep. Then Brady lifted his head, so that he could see over the sterile cloth. The contrast, coming abruptly, shocked him. Below the cloth her body was almost literally cut in half.

Smiling a little grimly to himself at his imagination, he looked round the theatre. A young nurse stood over against one wall, her hands clasped before her. It was her job to pick up any fallen instruments, or tissue, and to keep Thomsett's wash-bowl cleanly filled. Calmly, visible above the mask, her youthful hazel eyes gazed upon this red-edged violation before her. The anaesthetist spoke.

"She's waking up, Sister. Pethidine."

Brady stepped back swiftly, clear of the anaesthetic machine. His brain was alert, eager to witness and commit to memory the procedure which must be adopted instantly if the most frightful thing he could think of were not to happen.

He shot a glance at the operating group. Thomsett and Trantor were intent at their task; Beth was leaning forward, her brown forehead furrowed in concentration. Surely they must have heard? Now the anaesthetics sister came across the room, a phial in her hand. Brady's senses willed her to run!

She walked up to Hagar, and past him. Then she lifted a hypodermic syringe from a table, filled it calmly, and handed it over to the anaesthetist. With equal calmness, he injected its contents into the blood-transfusion tube. Then he handed the syringe back, and continued with his interminable squeeze, squeeze, squeeze.

Brady swallowed. He stepped forward.

"You said she was waking up?"

Hagar nodded. "Yep. I'm keeping her pretty light, you know. The trend these days." He saw the puzzled frown above Brady's mask. "Oh, I see. Yes, I see. . . . No, nothing like that. Hell no. Even if she did come right out, she wouldn't feel anything for a bit. Quite a bit. But it was nothing as bad as that. Hell, man, what do you think I am? A bloody student?"

"Captain," said Thomsett.

"Yes?"

Brady walked carefully round the machine to the middle of the table. Held by the surgeon's fingers within the wound was a piece of tissue as large as his palm. It was black, the delicate fibre squashed by handling. As Brady watched, the surgeon excised. He held the tissue up.

"That's it. Teeming with baccili. Rotten with it."

He dropped it into the bowl Sister Affleck held out.

"It goes to pathology now." He laid his scalpel down, turned away, and rinsed his hands. Then he came to the table again. "Can you see there, Captain?" He dug his right hand deep into the wound, and as Brady watched, lifted the remainder of the lung aside.

"Pretty well one inch thick—as much pressure in there as in a garden hose."

Brady, Beth and the two students craning forward saw the aorta, the main blood vessel from the heart. It was thick, and full, and almost the size of a garden hose—red, and pulsing. Thomsett pulled the lung back farther.

And now they looked at the heart. Brady's first fascination was replaced by surprise. In his imagination the human heart was firm, solid, like the hearts you bought in a butcher's shop. Here, beneath its protective sheath, it palpitated loosely—it looked almost flabby. In, out, as large as his hand, pulsing, contracting; with the aorta swelling in sympathy, the muscular pump sent the cleansing, rejuvenating swirl of red blood round the body. Thomsett removed his hand.

"All right, Sister."

The needle and suture were already in her hand. She passed them over.

It was not easy to pierce the tough tissue, even with the sharp needle held in forceps. As Thomsett worked slowly and thoroughly through each layer, cauterizing and tying vessels as he went, Beth itched to try at least one layer of stitches. She knew that sometimes the surgeon allowed his assistant to finish off the operation, after making sure that there was nothing left open which could later bleed. But her hopes here remained unfulfilled.

Once, her heart jumped. Thomsett had ordered quietly:

"Count the sponges."

Sister Affleck nodded to a nurse. Quickly the nurse ran her eye over the stained cloths hanging on a wire against the wall. She turned to pick up a sponge near the instrument tray on the operating table.

"Nurse!"

The voice, sharp with authority, cut through the room. The nurse stared at Sister Affleck.

"Count those sponges! Count them with your fingers. Then count them again!"

"Yes, Sister."

Slowly, this time. Then the nurse picked up the sponge on the table. She had begun to walk to the wire when the sponge was taken from her hand. Sister Affleck shook the blooded square of cloth out vigorously.

"You *must* shake them out. Shake them individually. Like this. Do you understand that?"

Vehement nods of the sister's head punctuated her machine-gun speech.

"Yes, Sister."

"Right. Now count the sponges—properly."

Brady listened with relish. His meticulously trained character revelled in this thoroughness. It was then that Thomsett, who had been waiting for the sponge-count, gestured at Beth with the forceps and needle. Her hand was out, about to take the forceps, when the surgeon spoke:

"Remember that, young lady. We could damn near build a new hospital with the money paid out in damage suits through sponges left in."

Beth nodded and, flushing, withdrew her hand. Thomsett dropped his eyes to the wound. Brady knew he had noticed the eager gesture.

"Sponges correct, sir," reported Sister Affleck.

"Thank you," said the surgeon, and took up a drainage tube.

In the lounge of the small hotel near the hospital Brady paid the waiter and took up his glass.

"Here's to our patient," he smiled. "Long may she breathe."

Beth smiled back briefly, and drank.

"You really enjoyed that, didn't you?" Brady asked quietly.

Beth had been staring at the table, her brown face serious. She looked up at him, and a smile pouted her lower lip.

"Yes, Jim. Yes, I did. He's got a wonderful pair of hands."

Brady crossed his legs. He was smiling inwardly at her seriousness, and he felt the need of some relief from the drama of what he had been through.

"M'mm. At his age, though, it's just mechanical. Refined butchery."

"Oh, what rot! Do you imagine it came to him naturally? Think of the years of practice. Years!"

"All right, all right." Brady smiled openly. "Have you a smoke?"

She opened her purse and handed a packet across.

"I'm convinced more and more," she said quietly, "that dissection is the answer. Hours and hours of dissection. It's absolutely essential if you're to be anatomically expert. And if you're not anatomically expert you haven't a hope."

Sipping his drink, Brady was delighted that she was talking to him in this way, not talking down to him, but discussing what they had seen professionally.

"I got a different impression."

"What? How on earth could you? You *must* know your anatomy."

"All right. For surgery, yes. No argument. But I thought the important bloke was the anaesthetist. Remember the way he handled that lung? And the way he brought her out—the sticking plaster was hardly over the wound when she coughed and came round. That boy really knows his stuff." He grinned suddenly. "Good money too, I should say."

She smiled back at him.

"It's a pity you didn't feel this way five years back—then we could have teamed together."

He lit her cigarette, and she looked at him over the match flame. "You liked it in there?"

"It was fascinating," he said slowly. "Thomsett had her life in his hands—to coin a phrase," he smiled deprecatingly. "I've never seen anything so completely fascinating in my life. Every detail. . . . I'm sure I could describe that operation five years from now, cut by cut."

"I suppose it must have been a novel experience."

Her voice was light, but she was looking at him with curious interest. She sipped her drink, laid the glass down, then said

quietly: "I feel the same. I've been dissecting or watching operations for close on three years now, and the same fascination is
still there."

"It always will be with you, Beth. I watched you. . . . We're
a bit alike, you know." He spoke cautiously, searching for the
right words. "Application to the job covers it, I think. Even now,
like you, I still get a hell of a kick if I see something new, or
interesting, in the Navy. Like the escape drill this morning." He
circled his glass on the table, looking down at it. "Maybe it's
because we haven't grown up properly yet. Not . . . blasé, y'know?"

"Jim?" Her voice was so low that it brought his head up, his
forehead crinkled as he stared at her. She had her elbows on the
table, her fingers twisted into a steeple under her chin, and her
eyes were gazing at him steadily. He saw the smooth brown of
her skin, the red curve of her mouth, and he thought: God, you're
lovely! She said: "I like you very much, Jim!"

"I want you to, Beth. You know that, don't you?" She nodded,
smiling a little. "I've hardly stopped thinking of you since the
party. I've never met a girl like you before. I haven't felt like
this about anyone before."

He saw her eyes shining, and emotion tightened his throat;
then someone laughed suddenly in the corner of the room. A girl's
voice came, knowing, half-giggling: "What are you trying to get
me tight for?" A man's voice mumbled, warningly. The mood
was broken. Brady lifted his glass and recklessly swallowed the
whisky. He looked round for the waiter and Beth exclaimed:

"Heavens, Jim, the time! I must be off!"

"What?" He swung back and stared at her, seeing her stuffing
the cigarettes back in her purse. "Oh hell no! I thought we'd
have dinner somewhere."

"Sorry, dear," and his disappointment made him miss the
affectionate epithet, "but I have to be in town in half an hour.
It's quite important, really. You go through town, don't you?"

"I go through town," he said sulkily.

She hesitated, thinking how lovely it would be with him tonight,
after this. . . . But they would be waiting for her in town. There
was tomorrow.

"I must go now, Jim."

He stared at her, and for one moment she thought he was going
to question her, to ask who she was meeting, to spoil it all.

"Right!" he said. "Remind me to get some smokes down
below."

CHAPTER EIGHT

AT a few minutes to seven that night Lieutenant Charles Deevers was alone in the officers' sleeping quarters of H.M. Submarine *Diana*. He was engaged in knotting his civilian tie carefully under his white collar, and he was thinking.

Lieutenant Deevers was not a popular member of the submarine's mess, and he knew it. He also knew why—he believed that it was because of the envy of his less-favoured shipmates. It did not worry him in the slightest. Things had always been so, and he was quite used to it. There was only one man in his life for whose judgment he had the least concern, and that man was the commanding officer of the ship he happened to be serving in. So long as he carried out his professional duties efficiently, there was no question of his shore leave being curtailed—and shore leave was an obsession with Deevers; leave, and what it brought him.

His messmates had got to know him very quickly. They had learned that the most oblique reference to a woman was grabbed by him as an excuse to enlarge on his pet subject. What no one did know was that Lieutenant Deevers, R.N., kept in a locked drawer a thick file of the most revolting pornographic photographs, some of them bought in Japan, the rest in Cairo. The photographs were well-fingered and dog-eared.

There was something else that his messmates had not fully appreciated about Deevers—that in a strictly limited sense he was a cunning thinker, a man to whom the sighting and the chase were almost as deliciously rewarding at the final pulling down of the quarry. Deevers was thinking now.

He would not go back to Coogee tonight, even though he had promised to do so. The girl he had met in the beach-front hotel was pretty enough, and she had that sort of figure—sun-browned, lithe, freshly-clean—characteristic of Australian beach girls. There were plenty of them, apparently, and Deevers felt that he had landed in a happy hunting-ground. The one at Coogee had been easy, but she was inexperienced. The night had been almost completely wasted—he had gained neither physical nor mental satisfaction. So it would be another hotel tonight.

He slipped on his coat, a light Assam cloth bought in Hong Kong, and grinned at his narrow reflection in the mirror. Then he bent down to his drawer beneath the ship-side bunk and from under a couple of shirts took a slim plastic capsule. He checked the contents and dropped the container into his shirt pocket. Prepared, he took up his brown hat and stepped out into the passage.

He caught a bus, not because he could not afford a taxi, but because he had half an hour to fill in before the hotels reopened. The bus conductress was neither pretty nor otherwise desirable, but she was female.

"I say," he smiled up at her, "would it be too much trouble for you to put me off at the 'Bondi Hotel'?"

Deevers hadn't the sort of face which was posted out from Hollywood, stamp-signed for eager fans, but he was quite aware of the value of his cultivated voice and manner, and his careful habits of dress. His awareness was vindicated now when the conductress smiled suddenly and brightly.

"No trouble at all, sir. You just leave it to me."

"Thank you so much. It's very good of you."

He leaned back in his seat, his face sober, and self-satisfaction flowed warmly through him.

He had timed it nicely to the hotel. He wanted to be in the lounge early, so that his loneliness would be quickly apparent. He had long since established the value of his pose as a lonely naval officer, gentlemanly and well-bred of course, to whom it would be a social sin not to extend the welcoming hand of a drinking circle: a cultivated man who would be a graceful asset to any company bent on pleasure.

He walked in through the wide front doors and saw at once that somebody else shared his wish for an early arrival. She was quite pretty, she had well-kept hair shining down on to the nape of her neck, and she was at a table alone. Feeling in his pockets for cigarettes, keeping his eyes down so that the direction of his advance would seem to be casual, he came to the table next to hers.

He pulled out a chair near her and with a companionable sigh lowered himself into it. The girl glanced at him and resumed tapping her fingers against the side of her glass. He put a cigarette between his lips, hesitated while he looked at the table, then turned in his chair to face her.

"Forgive me for asking," he smiled, "but I seem to have left my matches on board. I see you're smoking—would you mind . . . ?"

That one had worked before, too. Now, quite naturally and casually, he had told her he was a seafaring man; obviously, with his accent, an officer. If she liked, it gave her an easy opening for conversation, provided her with a pat question.

Then he knew that he would have no need here of subterfuge.

She looked at him, and a little thrill ran up his spine and dried his throat. He had seen that look before—only once in all his experience, in Athens, and he would remember the night that followed for the rest of his life.

She handed him the matches on her table. Feeling her steady, responsive stare flushing both his memory and his desire, he drew out a chair opposite hers and sidled on to it. "What are you drinking?" he asked.

From the way she answered "Whisky", he knew that his judgment had not failed. She was the type, as the other had been. He said casually to the approaching waiter, "Two whiskies, please," then lit his cigarette—inwardly cursing, while he objectively enjoyed, the slight trembling of the match-flame.

He saw her looking at his hands, he saw her lips open and the pink tip of her tongue appear. God, how lucky can you be! That he was the first in here tonight. She was ready for anyone. They were like that, her sort; they couldn't hide it, were incapable of controlling what was urging them on. Like the Armenian girl in Averoff Street in Athens. . . .

"Thank you." He nodded at the waiter. "That's all right—keep the change."

"Thank you, sir!"

He took up his glass and raised it in a smiling gesture, looking into her eyes, then allowing his gaze to move gently down her face until he was staring at her mouth. He sipped his drink and lowered the glass.

"Now," he began, and he had never felt more pleasantly sure of himself in his life, "I hope we are going to exchange confidences. I mean in the matter of names."

She sipped her own drink, and he thought with devoted application to the job in hand of what a couple more whiskies would do. "My name's Slocum," she told him composedly, and sipped again.

"It must have been your father's," Deevers said with smiling conviction. "Tell me—what else do the family call you to distinguish you from him?"

She hesitated, reading his intentions in his eyes as if to make doubly sure what they were (and that was the moment, he recognized, when another woman would have drawn back), and then surrendering to her general impression of his sun-burned virility.

"Marge—Marjorie," she said at last, and he realized with some satisfaction that the correction was due to his gentlemanly voice and appearance.

"Marjorie Slocum. M'mm. Rolls nicely off the tongue." He leaned back and surveyed her with admiration. "I'm known as Charles Deevers—naval officer."

"My husband's in the Navy," she murmured, looking into her glass, testing him.

"I see," he replied evenly, and his mind was alertly examining the possibilities. So far he had nothing to worry about. "Where is he now? You're waiting for him?"

"Like hell I am."

"Trouble? I'm sorry to hear that."

"Don't be. We separated, some time ago. The usual thing— another woman."

She looked at him, and he was not for a moment fooled. I know why he's on the outer, my darling—he's a clod, an ignorant peasant, no good for you. But wait. . . .

"You're English. You must be from the submarine."

"That's so," he said easily. "And your husband?"

"I don't want to talk about my husband."

"Good girl, neither do I. I say, that stuff'll get cold. Have a fresh one."

Afterwards, back on board, he derived immense pleasure from dwelling on how he had delayed their leaving for her home; remembering how the whisky had worked on her; how by exerting the promise of his manner he had raised her to excitement, then let her down by seeming to lose interest: until in the end he had broken through all her superficial pretences and her dignity, so that it was she who invited him to the house. . . .

By nine o'clock he was ready himself, he was feeling the strain. You can hold off a good thing too long. He got up and she rose with him, taking his arm as they walked between the tables. Her fingers played with his muscles, kneading them slowly and suggestively, and feeling rose in him in a blind red surge.

They stepped out into the warm starlight of the summer night, and with pressure on his arm she turned him towards the garish brightness of the cinema. As they walked away from the main doors of the hotel into the shadows, they missed seeing two men in petty officers' uniform step into the entrance to the public bar, farther along towards the fairground behind them.

"Down here," she said a few minutes later, and led him into a side-street running back from the foot of the hill. Its darkness was relieved only slightly by spaced street-lamps. Her pace quickened a little; he dragged his own.

"Look, darling, we have to be sensible about this. What about your husband?"

"He has left me. He won't be home—he sleeps on board his ship. There is no one in the house."

He reflected that even if the husband did show up, he could always claim dignified and annoyed ignorance of the situation, and leave at once. Embarrassing, maybe even unpleasant, but not dangerous. Oh yes, he could manage it well enough.

She stopped at a gate and they both slipped in quickly, up a short concrete path and on to a tiny veranda. A moment later he was in a dark hallway, and she was snicking the lock of the front door into place.

He allowed her to pull him by the hand a few paces down the hall and into the living-room. He felt her lean sideways. When the shaded table-lamp flicked on he looked at once at the windows —the blinds were drawn right down. She turned, pressing her body against his so that he felt the firm weight of her breasts through his thin coat, and looked up at him with her mouth a little loose. Half closing her eyes she whispered: "Wait a moment."

She squeezed his hand sharply, then turned and walked hastily from the room.

He was sitting in a chintz-covered armchair, smoking nervously, when he heard her come in. He swung round, to see her in a white silk robe with a silver dragon crawling round it and bursting into fire-spitting life on her shoulders—a garish thing, probably brought back from Singapore by her husband. Under it she was evidently wearing nothing.

"You're . . . beautiful."

She smiled, and sat down on the arm of his chair. The lower half of the robe slipped aside, and the smooth swell of her thigh was close to his hand. He lifted his hand; she quivered slightly; then he deliberately leaned away to stub out his cigarette in an ash-tray near by.

Her own hands moved in a helpless gesture, and she stood up quickly, waiting in front of him. Still he sat in the chair, not now to arouse her further, but to drink into his memory the way she looked. The robe's whiteness provided a striking contrast to her sunbrowned skin and shining brown hair; it made her torso even more intriguing than the tight dress in which he had first seen it. It also made her seem little more than a girl.

Deevers felt the nervy roiling in his stomach rise into his throat; yet for a moment he met her pleading gaze without an answering sensuality, until his eyes were drawn down to where the white robe had fallen open from her throat. At once she made an almost imperceptibly supple movement, and the robe slipped off her shoulders and down to her elbows, held there like a stole.

He would always remember the feat of self-control by which he kept on looking at her without moving. Then she put her hands on his shoulders and leaned forward to mould her mouth against his. This time he could not keep quite still.

She felt his touch and drew back her head; she was breathing deeply, and in her face was gratitude, purpose and longing.

"Yes," she said, "yes."

McCook nodded at the look of inquiry in the barmaid's face as her hands reached out to their empty glasses.

"Not a bad drop," he commented, and licked his lips. "The beer, I mean."

Slocum smiled briefly, and turned his head to stare restlessly round the room.

"For the love of Mike, cobs!" his friend expostulated, "turn it up, will yer? She ain't worth worrying about, I tell yer. You been like a walking corpse ever since it happened. What's the use, mate? Why should you sweat blood over a tramp like that? She's rotten—rotten as hell. Far as you're concerned, she's dead! Now for Gawd's sake forget it and get this inter yer guts."

He spoke brutally, and he knew it. He felt brutal. He stared at Slocum's strained face and he thought what he had thought the other night: why did this have to happen to you, old feller? How many blokes did he know who lusted their way from port to port—yet old Ben here never in his life had a bit out of watch; and he comes home to this bitch. He could control himself, and maybe that was it—Ben was just too plain decent and normal —too much married, for the likes of her.

"Sorry, cobs," he grunted, and rubbed his fingers across his mouth. "Tell me to pull me great head in."

"No, Stan, you're right. That's how I've got to think of her— dead and rotten. But I can't."

"I know. Here, sink this—the chloroform'll do you good."

He lifted his own glass and over its edge idly surveyed the other side of the projecting, oblong bar. There was a man standing there on his own, and he caught McCook's eye and nodded, smiling slightly. McCook nodded back automatically before he recognized him—a leading seaman he had served with in the carrier.

He lowered his glass and a sudden jolt tipped it sideways, so that some beer splashed on his hand. An unpleasant voice growled beside him:

"Move down, sailor boy—you want the whole flamin' bar?"

As he jolted sideways, off balance, he took in the scene: the big bar was not a quarter filled; there were yards of empty space on either side of him—the shove had been deliberate. In a flash, guessing who had sent the man, he released his hold on the glass and stepped back into the clear. There were three men, but he kept his eye on the one who had shoved him—a hard, coarse face, the eyes wary and cold. McCook felt Slocum behind his left shoulder. His stomach was a tight knot of tension, but his voice was level.

"So Walshe didn't have the guts to come himself. He sent his apes."

"Walshe? I don't know no Walshe. But no slob in a pansy uniform calls me ape and gets away with it."

The blow was sharp and vicious, aimed below the level of the bar at McCook's stomach. But the seaman's tautened senses had allowed for it—his right hand flashed down and beat the blow aside. The thug's fist, slowing, smashed into the front of the bar. He gave a coughing grunt of pain.

"I'll have your guts for that!"

"You might. Any time. There's some there, mate—not like the dingo louse who sent you."

"Now's the time, bastard! Out the back—and don't think you can run outa this." These weren't the sort to fight in a public bar, where they would be stopped almost as soon as they began.

McCook turned and picked up his glass. He emptied it deliberately. Slocum said: "My cobber's got nothing to do with this. She's my wife."

The three men looked at him. McCook put the glass down and said quietly, "Come on, Ben."

They walked round the end of the bar, towards a door on the far side of the room. It led out into a courtyard, flanked by

garages and a men's lavatory. Slocum pushed open the door.
"There's three of them, Stan."

McCook shook his head. "They'd only wait till the pub closed.
We're in, Ben. Keep beside me, keep your back to the garage
wall. We'll take 'em all right—they're dingoes, not used to any
opposition. Remember that."

They walked across the half-lit concrete yard and heard the
door open behind them. Feet thudded on the concrete and
McCook hissed, "The wall, Ben, and use yer feet!"

Afterwards the two of them tried in vain to put into coherent
sequence what happened. McCook remembered the first thug
coming at him with hands up and face snarling; he remembered
striking first and feeling his fist sink into a liquor-soft belly,
and thinking that they might take these toughs after all. Then
his conscious thoughts were submerged and confused beneath
flailing blows, while his fighting brain retained an instinctive
and long-experienced appreciation of the tactics of his opponents.
Two men were at him, with Slocum grappling the third in fierce
but undisciplined effort. He hadn't the fighting skill of his friend;
he lacked McCook's harder nature.

Silhouetted against the rectangle of light streaming from the
lavatory door opposite him, McCook saw the first thug's foot go
back, then flash forward. The foot was aimed at his groin, and
if it had got there it would have crippled him. Instantly, automatically, as he had been trained to do in unarmed combat during
the war, he raised his own foot, the sole of his shoe at right
angles to his shin, his whole leg rigid.

The thug's shin-bone, sweeping forward, jarred with sickening
force against the bottom of McCook's shoe. He cried out with the
pain and stumbled forward. McCook's right hand, the fingers
extended, close together in a rigid vertical wall, chopped down
at the side of the exposed neck. It was a killing blow, and it
could have dropped the thug in a crumpled heap. But the second
man punched at McCook's face, and his driving arm deflected
the chop, so that the seaman's hand jarred against the side of the
first man's face, against solid bone.

He grunted with the force of it, but bore in against McCook,
grabbing him round the waist. McCook knew what was coming.
He tried to twist his body to one side, clear. His head jerked back
under the second man's fist and the next moment a knee jabbed
viciously upwards and an abrupt shock of pain exploded in his
groin.

He knew he was being punched in the face, but he felt nothing above the nauseating agony between his legs. He heard a grunting gasp from below and beside him:

"Stan . . . Stan!"

He was on his own. Through the pain that shocked and sickened him there surfaced the red mist of a murderous rage. His eyes squinted almost closed, he felt down with his hands, found the face of the thug who had kicked him. He knew what he was doing, and he needed only one hand to do it. He got the heel of his open hand beneath the man's nose; to make sure of his leverage he pressed his hand hard in against mouth and teeth. Then with all his strength he shoved upwards. There was a muffled shout of pain, and McCook knew that one thug was out of the fight.

He swung his head groggily, his eyes almost closed with exhaustion. He saw the third man rising from Slocum's sprawled figure on the concrete, his head craned back, glaring at McCook with panting hate and intention. Then something came between him and the light from the lavatory door. McCook heard a hard, tight voice snarl "Mongrels!" and saw the speaker's foot take the rising man square between his shoulders. The thug hurled forward and his face smacked nakedly against the concrete.

In these few seconds McCook had been instinctively trying to fend off the punches of his remaining attacker. He heard the thuds of other blows, delivered powerfully with fresh strength, and felt the thug sag against him. He pushed him aside, and the man stumbled along the garage wall, then broke into a weaving run for the street at the end of the courtyard.

"Let him go!" their saviour grunted, "Here, hold up now."

McCook squinted painfully at him. He recognized the leading seaman he had nodded to in the bar.

"Nice work, Rodgers," he mumbled.

"Grab your cobber," Rodgers urged. "The barmaid phoned for the cops just after you came out. Come on, give us a hand."

His face numb, and the pain in his groin easing into a dull steady ache, McCook bent down and between them they hauled Slocum to his feet. They staggered towards the gate opening on to the street, and passed something grovelling on its knees, one hand to its face. Through the hand came a low muffled groaning.

"Tell Walshe," McCook gasped, his voice punctuated with his panting breath, "we'll be out tomorrow to wreck his joint."

"Skip that," Rodgers said urgently, "come on!"

They reached the narrow back-street and turned left. Fifty yards up they came to a garage, with a dark lane leading down beside it.

"This'll do," Rodgers grunted, and steered both of them into the lane. They lurched down it almost to its dead-end, then they lowered Slocum on to a patch of long coarse grass.

"All right, Ben?"

"I'm alive. Where are we? What happened?"

He levered himself up on one elbow and McCook pushed him back. As he wiped at Slocum's face he told him.

"You were down, I was on the way. Rodgers here jumped in at the right time. Your bloke is out to it back there, and my bastard's gonna have a hell of a sore snout for a long time. The third one got away. Barmaid phoned for the cops. They'll find two of Walshe's boys there."

"Leave off, Stan—that hurts. Where's this?"

"Dead-end lane up from the pub a bit."

"Yeah, I know." Slocum sat up, feeling his face. "How are you, Rodgers? I remember you in the bar. Thanks for the help."

"Forget it. What are you fellers going to do now?"

"Back to the ship," McCook answered definitely, "I've had a gutful for one night."

"We're going to my place," Slocum put in weakly.

"Like hell we are!"

"Listen, cobs, it's my house. And it's just up the road. We'll go home and wash up."

"Ben," McCook said quietly, "we can't go to your place."

"She won't be home," Slocum said bitterly.

"She might be. You want her to see you like this? She'll know who done it. She'll think those bastards towled us up. She'll like that."

"I wanna go to my place. It's my place."

"You can come to my joint," Rodgers said, "there's only Mum there."

"We'd frighten six months' growth out of her" McCook grinned painfully. "Thanks, pal, but we'll get back to the Island."

"I'm goin' to my place."

McCook stared at Slocum trying to get up.

"You can't stand up, you bloody galah," he said, affection mingling with pity in his voice. "All right, then, let's go. But we get a taxi."

When they reached the back-street they looked to their right. A small crowd of men was gathered about the yard gate of the

hotel! The three seamen turned the opposite way, and emerged
into a brightly-lit street which ran down towards the promenade.

"They'll need an ambulance back there," McCook said viciously,
and then he whistled shrilly. A taxi swerved into the kerb. Slocum
was leaning heavily against him. He opened the rear door and
bundled him in. Then he turned and shook Rodgers's hand.

"Thanks again, cobs."

"Any time," Rodgers grinned.

McCook nodded good-bye and got in and shut the door. He
gave the driver the number of Slocum's house in Francis Street,
then looked at his friend. The Asdic instructor was sprawled on
the seat, his eyes closed, his breathing heavy.

"Poor beggar," McCook thought. "When you're down you cop
the lot." Then he thought of the reason for all this, and his mouth
tightened into a hard thin line. The cause of it all—and she'd
copped nothing; nothing except what she wanted to cop.

The cab swung right into the street above the promenade and
moved smoothly towards the hill. The slope of trees and the
dark sea were on their left.

She'll love this, McCook thought, and his lip twisted—she'll
pretend she doesn't want us there, and all the time she'll be
gloating, remembering how we mucked up her little party with
Walshe. Maybe she'll even get a kick out of Walshe going to the
trouble to do them over—think maybe that he did it partly for
her. Oh, she'll love it!

Slocum's street near the bottom of the hill was coming up.
McCook saw the corner and bitterness swirled sourly within him.
He glanced at Slocum. The petty officer was lying where he had
bundled him in, exhausted, his eyes closed. As the taxi-driver
began to turn McCook made his move.

"Belay Francis Street, mate," he said softly, leaning forward,
"make it Garden Island."

"It's your dough," the driver answered amiably, and swung
his wheel back. The taxi moved on up the hill.

He stretched his body slowly and gently, feeling the girl's tousled
head on his arm, nestled in against his shoulder. She was so still
that he thought she was asleep.

"Darling," she whispered into his hot shoulder, in answer to
his movement. How lazy, lazy like a satisfied cat, were a girl's first
words following successful love-making; throaty, exhausted of
identifiable accent, bare of particular emotion.

He twisted himself a little so that he could look at her. He coughed, a low inarticulate clearing of his throat, a deep masculine sound that he knew would mean more than words. But then there was nothing he wanted to say.

"Sweetheart," she murmured, and he felt the movement of her eyelids in against his shoulder, "you're terrific."

He shuddered without movement, deep in his mind. The Armenian girl had not been vulgar, like that—she had allowed her exhaustion to shout silently to him. But then what could he expect of a pick-up in Bondi, a sailor's wife?

"M'mmm?" he answered, his voice a rising inflexion, and kissed her gently. Not on her lips, but near the corner of her mouth; partly because he had no need now for her mouth, but mainly to show her that though they had passed through a period of the most uninhibited intimacy, now, even after that, she still had his gratitude, his most tender respect.

He had never known it to fail.

"Oh, Charles," she whispered, and rubbed her hand across his bare chest. Her fingers came up and gently caressed the taut line of his throat—his head lay back without a pillow. Never fails, he thought—they always want to feel, afterwards, that the man still likes them; relieved to know that respect and affection is still there.

Now, also, he could think—his eyes on the dim ceiling, lit diffusedly by the blind-filtered street-light outside, seeing the cracks in the white plaster, and considering how soon could he get away, get back safely on board, where he could relax completely in his own bunk, reviewing the night with lascivious satisfaction.

He eased his leg. The girl, mistaking the movement, raised herself, her lips coming down to meet his. He let her kiss him, then he drew his face gently aside.

"Darling. . . ." His voice held a note of tender reproach.

It was not only that he could not help her now; he did not want his experience spoiled. He smiled and brushed the hair back from her damp forehead, gently forcing her head back on to his arm. Her eyes looked up at him, and he found himself vaguely disgusted by what he saw in them. Quick now—there's an answer to this one.

"Your husband," he said, his voice low and intimate, "tell me about your husband."

Her hand drew back from his chest.

"Him . . . ?"

There was annoyance, as well as distaste, in the word.

"Yes. You see, I must know something about him."

He smiled at her, and there was promise in his gesture. She breathed in and twisted a little, so that she lay on her back.

"He's in a destroyer. Something to do with the Asdic. He instructs in it. I think he's the senior man in . . . whatever he does."

"Is the name of his ship *Scourge*?"

"Yes." Her eyes looked sideways at him, curiosity replacing the look of a moment before. "Wait a minute he's exercised with your submarine, hasn't he?"

He nodded at her, then looked up at the ceiling to hide his silent laughter. A pity he couldn't tell the mess! The man had hunted them with electronic weapons—and now he, Deevers, had hunted and dragged down his wife, with the oldest, most potent weapon in all creation. *Scourge's* chief Underwater Control Rating: why, there was a development of the joke there; if they failed to come up, it would be *Scourge's* U.C.R. who would find them, bring help and rescue, so that *Diana's* torpedo officer could come ashore and. . . .

Steady there . . . the one thought you never allowed to reach conscious deliberation; push it back, keep it back—the darkness, the black pouring water, choking. . . . He twisted involuntarily, failing to crush what had surfaced in his mind. Blast her husband! This had never happened before, at a time like this.

"Darling," she whispered, and her hand came back, searching. He twisted forcibly away from her, swinging his legs out and down on to the floor, and he remembered only just in time to calm her, to keep unspoiled their experience.

"I'm sorry, sweetheart, but I must go back. I don't want to go —you know that! But if he comes—we don't want tomorrow night upset, do we?"

She watched him, silent, as he dressed. "Tomorrow night?"

"Try and keep me away!" He cupped her cheek in one hand and kissed her with just enough pressure on the lips, feeling her respond. Before the kiss could harden, he came upright. Exactly right! He smiled at her from the door, whispered, "Tomorrow, darling," and went out.

He caught a taxi without difficulty, and as it rolled up past the "Astra Hotel" he leaned back in his seat, smiling round his cigarette.

The other, forbidden thought was well subdued now. He was

reliving the night, from the moment she had first looked at him, and he had known. It was a pleasant review, and it was not until an hour later, in his bunk, that the other thought, the black water, returned unbidden to his mind. Then he wondered briefly, without actual fright, if his obsession with women could have something to do with keeping that thought crushed down.

CHAPTER NINE

SATURDAY began with a perfect morning. The sun lifted out of the sea, looked down upon the stone city and the embayed harbour with its saving fringe of trees, and found them good. Its strong light drew gold from the beaches, deep blue from the harbour, and faced the gums and jacarandas and cassia bushes with gleaming green.

That was the impression Brady received when he looked out of his cabin scuttle—colour in the harbour, the sombre grey of the great bridge leaping in delicate steely tracery from point to point across the water, and over all the vivid blue well of the deep sky.

Already, at half past seven, the morning was warm; it would be a perfect day for the beach. Weather, beach, cool green seawater the whole day and night before them—all the ingredients were there, and yet as Captain Brady swung his legs down from his bunk, he was not altogether happy.

Saturday morning was the time of captain's rounds, when the professional competence of every first-lieutenant in the Navy was tested. On Saturday morning *Scourge* was scrubbed and swept and polished and burnished, and it was Brady's duty to inspect the results. From the domestic point of view, it was the climax of the week's work. Today there was only one snag—captain's rounds began at eleven o'clock; but if Brady were to be at Beth's house at ten, as he had promised, he would need to leave the ship not later than nine-fifteen.

He got up, stretched, walked into the bathroom, washed his face and slowly took his electric razor from its case. He had heard in other ships, many times in his experience, the pipe: "There will be no captain's rounds this morning." But this was his ship, she was new, and he had done Saturday rounds not more than three or four times. Begin with a tight discipline, then, later, you can afford to relax it—that had always been the way he worked.

He began to shave, his face on one side, a frowning furrow above his nose between his eyebrows. All right, he thought, a little pugnaciously—I have responsibilities, and by God I've discharged them! But a man's responsibility doesn't begin and end with the Navy—what about his own private life, his hopes of marriage, and children? This morning up at Whale Beach could be the most important one of his life—this morning his responsibility was to himself, not to messdecks and store-rooms which would be spotless anyway.

His decision made, he finished shaving and twisted the cord round his fingers before replacing the shaver in its leather case. In the pantry, Benson heard a not very tuneful humming from the bathroom, before the sound was drowned under the hiss of the shower.

The steward lit a cigarette, smiling as he waved the match out. So we're on to something tasty ashore today, are we? Maybe we could use three eggs this morning; maybe we could use some lead in the old pencil? Good luck to you, sport—and I hope she keeps you ashore the whole ruddy week-end.

"Benson," Captain Brady said as he pushed his emptied plate back and drew his coffee-cup in front of him, "why the three eggs this morning?"

"Well, sir, you can get mighty peckish in the surf, specially on a day like this when you stay in a long time."

"So I'm going surfing? You've been reading my letters?"

"No, sir," Benson answered easily, "I saw you holding up your swimming togs. I agree, sir—you could do with a new pair. Maybe if I was to slip ashore this morning. . . ."

"You can slip ashore for the week-end, Benson—without worrying about my shopping."

"Thank you, sir. More coffee, sir?"

"Yes, please. By the way, I'll want you back for dinner tomorrow night. I shall probably have three guests, a lady amongst them. I'll confirm the number in plenty of time."

"Yes, sir. Anything special for dinner, sir?"

"I'll leave that to you. I'll need Scotch."

"Yes, sir. I'll put on something nice and delicate."

"Not too delicate—there's only one lady. Now ask the first-lieutenant to speak to me."

"Aye, aye, sir."

Brady had not finished his second cup of coffee when Cowan knocked at the open door.

"Morning, Number One, come in, please. Coffee?"

"Thank you, sir."

Brady pushed his cigarette-box across while the ready Benson laid a fresh cup and saucer before the lieutenant. The steward poured and Cowan drank.

"Now, Number One," Brady said, his voice easy, his attitude casual, and his eyes watching the lieutenant's face, "I'm leaving the ship at nine-fifteen—I want you to do rounds."

"Yes, sir." Cowan put down his cup.

"Give her a good run through. And include the gunner's store this time—I hear his yeoman has worked hard there this week; we don't want to waste his effort."

"Gunner's store, aye aye, sir," Cowan answered automatically, and wondered how this aloof being had heard about the activity in the gunner's store.

Brady nodded, and Cowan rose, taking up his cap.

"I'll be off all day, possibly tonight."

"Yes, sir—have a nice week-end."

Cowan had turned at the door; Brady's awareness tautened, but the lieutenant's smile was genuine; Brady smiled back.

"Thank you, Number One," he said amiably, "I'm having dinner guests on board tomorrow night. You might like to come up for a nip later on in the piece."

"If I'm on board I'd like to, sir."

He went out, and Brady wondered again at the influence Cowan's period in command had had on his outlook. Then he shoved back his chair. "Benson," he called, "Harris tweed coat, flannels, white shirt, suède shoes, cravat."

"Play togs on the way up, sir," Benson answered cheerfully—for there had been that in Brady's voice which allowed latitude. "Them trunks'll do for today, sir, but I still think I ought to look out for a new pair ashore."

"All right, for heaven's sake! But if I'm not off this craft by nine-fifteen you'll have something to look out for!"

"Yessir," Benson grinned, "the best flannels, I presume, sir?"

Brady took the big car smoothly across the bridge and up the hill of Pacific Highway, an overnight bag on the seat beside him, and he could not remember any time in his life when he had felt so completely happy. He was on his way to see her, he was free for the week-end, and he had no doubt at all that Farley would insist on his staying overnight.

When he swung into the French's Forest Road and the massed music of summer cicadas beat in through his open window, the sound reminded him nostalgically of his own Queensland bush, where he had hunted wallabies as a boy with an old pea-rifle. Inevitably he thought of his present position, and his object on this glorious summer morning. He had come a long way—a hell of a long way! And thinking back over his career from the time when he had joined the Navy as an ordinary seaman, he felt doubts slide insidiously into his mind to warn him—things were too good, too smooth; his happiness was too complete.

He passed a big American car with a surge of speed and as he brought the Jaguar back over the yellow line he wriggled himself into a more comfortable position. Too happy be damned, he told himself—other men had become captains, other men met and loved and married the women of their choice: why shouldn't he? Beth was waiting for him at Whale Beach, thinking of his coming as she dressed herself to meet him: the ship was all right, the squadron was all right, it was peacetime, there was no toil and fear and danger any more. He would accept these things, enjoy them, win her for himself. . . .

At the end of his journey he eased the car up the steep concrete driveway and parked it on a level apron fronting a double garage. As he opened his door he saw the overnight bag. Grinning a little, he decided to leave it there—he could have been too optimistic. He slammed the door and started towards the steps, enjoying the superb view across the bay to where Barrenjoey Lighthouse reared from its rocky lip.

When he turned his head he saw Beth standing on the top step. "Hullo, Jimmy," she called down to him. "Dead on time—as expected."

He smiled, finding the diminutive delightful. She was wearing shorts of white linen, complementary to her white thong sandals, an eye-catching contrast to the smooth brown of her slender legs. No coquetry—she waited for him with her legs apart, like a boy. He walked up the steps, still looking at her—she had a green blouse tucked into the shorts, simple and boyish and cool-looking, nice against the honey of her hair. He came up to her, his expression a little wondering at the picture she made, and saw how her hair, brushed, caught the morning sun and gleamed as she moved her head.

"Hello, Beth—what a lovely morning."

In his thoughts she already belonged to him. She saw him with his coat slung over his shoulder, tailored flannels, brown hawk face, smiling at her like a boy, and she thought how many women he must have had, before coming to her who wanted him most, and for life.

"I have my costume on under this. This sun's too good to waste."

"No argument. Give me three minutes." He turned on the step. On impulse, she walked down with him, smiling up at him. When he opened the car door she reached in and brought out his bag. She felt its weight and put it back on the seat, and snicked the catch open. Then she looked back at him over her shoulder.

"How did you know?"

"Come again?"

"I rang the ship this morning but you'd left. I was going to ask if you could stay overnight."

"Serves you right for sticking your pretty nose in where it has no business," he teased. "I *was* staying the night—with a tit-bit in Newport. Now I suppose I'm trapped here."

"You are, darling." She handed him the bag. "Your tit-bit can find someone else to eat her."

He took the bag. He wasn't sure about that "darling"—it could have been the easy camaraderie of her medical set. They started up the steps and she slipped her arm through his with complete naturalness. Her darling, he knew, meant darling.

A big heavy curtain was drawn across the plate-glass windows of the living-room against the sun's level entry. Beside the curtain Farley watched them come up the steps. He saw the muscled manliness of the seaman and the boyish loveliness of his daughter; but his real feeling, deep and a little sad, was in his thought: if you could see them, Edna.

Yet his voice was cheerfully booming when he stepped from the front door and greeted Brady:

"Hullo, James, me boy. Nice to see you're decently dressed."

"Sorry about the clothes," Brady grinned, "but I'll soon fix it. Come on, harum-scarum—where do I berth?"

Holding his hand, she led him into the cool dimness of the hall. "Here we are—next to my room."

He followed her in. The room was cosy: a wall-to-wall carpet, built-in furniture, twin beds, a full book-case and a small radio set on the reading-lamp stand.

"Thank you," he said, setting his bag on one bed, "now beat it."

"Why?" she said pertly, but moving to the door. "I'm almost a doctor, you know."

"But I'm not a patient—yet."

"I'll bet you've got knobbly knees," she mocked him, and slammed the door a second before his bunched cravat hit it.

He changed quickly into shorts over his trunks, a light beach shirt which he left open outside his shorts, and a pair of sandals. "Hey!" he called, "I didn't bring a towel."

"Can do," she answered him from outside the door, and opened it, stepping into the room. "May I come in?"

"Doesn't that door rate a lock and key?" he growled.

She came up to him, close to him, smiling.

"Would you want to use it—against me?"

Her head was tilted back a little to look at him; he saw the smile ease from her face, and her eyes drop from his, slowly. He put his hands on her arms, feeling them smoothly firm, and her eyes came up again. For a moment they stood like that, barely breathing, their eyes locked together. He dropped his hands.

"Come on," he said roughly, "where's that towel?"

At the front door, the towels slung over her shoulder, she asked: "You've got your car keys?"

"Yes, but I thought we just walked down to the beach?"

"We'll go to Avalon. There's a pastry shop there makes the nicest bread rolls. We could bring some back for lunch."

They waved to Farley doing something with a hibiscus tree at the end of the garden, and ran down the steps to the garage, talking, laughing, about nothing. In both their minds was the significant memory of that moment in the bedroom.

It took only a few minutes to get to Avalon. He stopped the car in the grassy park and they walked quickly to the edge of the slope leading down to the beach. As though by signal, they stopped. They were close to the southern edge of the beach, and slowly Brady took in the scene.

The colour shouted to him—the green grass of the slope, the long crescent of golden sand reaching right round to its binding hook of rough grey rock, a mile to the north; while meeting the beach, ending their thousand-mile run, the big combers of the Pacific lifted and crashed down in a symphony of green and flashing white—each wave powerful yet lazy, running in for the shore in a long smooth green hump, a liquid ridge whose upper edge sharpened until it frayed into spray, then curled over, farther, and broke and tumbled and crashed into abrupt white, flinging up its final defiant spouts before spreading out fast into a great apron of froth which slowed and steadied and then withdrew, sliding back beneath the next shining breaker.

The blue sky, puffed with white clouds, arched gently over the varied and vivid colours of beach umbrellas mushrooming along the sand; the heat of the sun, nearing its zenith, beat against the sand and grass, water and trees, and bathed the brown bodies stretched out above the sea's threshold. Permeating everything was the never-ceasing murmur of falling waves.

"I want to live up here," Brady said suddenly. "I don't care what it costs—this is it."

Her fingers played along his bare forearm.

"There are some nice little timber houses, darling—not more than four thousand pounds."

"A house here, with what you've got in beach and forest, would be worth ten thousand anywhere else, if you get what I mean."

"I'm with you. And Dad would like you so close." She glanced up at him slyly.

"That's what's called in Navy parlance passing the can," he accused her, grinning. "Come on—let's go down."

They ran down on to the sand, kicking off their sandals, and Brady delighted in the warmth of it sliding between his toes. He rigged the big beach umbrella Beth had brought, while she slipped off her blouse and shorts. On his knees, forcing the umbrella spike deep into the sand, he turned and looked up at her. Then he sat back and stared at her with bold and open admiration.

"Tell me," he said, "how come you're still pure and single?"

"That's easy, darling." She dropped on her knees beside him. "I waited for you."

She flipped out a towel and lay back on it, her head in the shade of the umbrella, the rest of her golden-brown body out in the sun's caress. "Let's warm up before we swim," she said, and breathed in deeply. Exercising considerable restraint he kept his eyes on her face, leaning a little over her, resting on one elbow.

"Take your things off," she said, "then come back here."

He nodded, feeling his throat dry, and slipped off his shirt and shorts. As his arms moved, shedding the shirt, she watched the rippling of his muscles in his back and shoulders, her anatomical eye noting the breadth of his shoulders and the slenderness of his waist, and she knew how he had won the boxing titles her father had told her about.

He threw his clothes up under the umbrella and turned to her again. He saw her arm move and felt her fingers on his back, stroking idly, and then pressing gently, pressing him down. He resisted that pressure as he would have done a fifty-ton ram. The kiss was light, not hard, nor passionate. She stroked his hair back from his forehead.

"Why didn't you kiss me in the bedroom?"

"You know why." He looked at her soberly. "It's going to be hard, Beth."

"I know, darling. But the time depends on you." She smiled slightly, but her eyes were serious.

"You will marry me?"

He felt her breasts move under his arm as she breathed in. Her smile reached her eyes. He eased himself back and lay down, his head on his hand, beside her. So this is how it happens? As simple as that.

"Your work," he said matter-of-factly, "your medical business?"

"Blow my medical business! My mind might be a bit woolly for a few days, but I'll make it. One or two doctors are married, you know—even some students."

Why am I talking like this? he wondered, feeling the dryness in his throat and the excitement in his stomach. Yet he said: "Your father will be surprised."

"Blow him too!"

He raised himself on his elbow again and saw that she was smiling delightedly, almost laughing. He wondered at that, also —not knowing that she was seeing the adult soberness of his expression belied by the youthful shallowness of his breathing, his tongue wetting his lips.

"Come here," she said softly.

On the way down to her Brady forgot his formality of speech, even the dryness in his throat. He reached her, and he remembered only the sweet wonder of her lips taking his, responding with abrupt passion, for a moment straining. . . . Then his head was on her shoulder and she was gently brushing his forehead with her finger-tips.

"Home is the sailor," she murmured, and pressed her cheek against his temple. He lay there, feeling her with him, feeling the gentle strokes of her fingers, and his tension was soothed away, leaving the inner warmth of a deep and encompassing gladness.

They jumped into the surf, swam and played there; dried

themselves in the sun, ran down to the sea again; enjoying the cold touch of the deeper water and its pale green translucency, so clean and fresh.

Under the umbrella, the sun burning into their legs, she prised off her bathing cap and fluffed her hair out. Then she sat down beside him, lowering herself with one hand on his shoulder. How long will it be like this, he wondered; how long before I forget that even when she touched my shoulder I got a thrill from it?

He lit her cigarette and he put aside his self-analysis; wondering was for the future; now he was in the present, filled with the precious delight of shared emotion. He gave himself to it, conscious of her smooth left arm over his drawn-up knee.

"Look, darling," she said.

Out beyond the line of breakers, beyond the clustering black heads of surfers waiting for a wave to bring them in, a youth was lying flat on his long polished board, his hands on either side paddling furiously, his head craned round, watching the smooth green ridge swell behind him into the wave form.

Gazing appreciatively, Brady remembered that the water in a wave is not in forward motion—it is only the form that moves, like a rolling-pin being rolled along under a stationary tablecloth.

The stern of the surf-board began to rise on the watery slope descending towards it; with a swift muscular movement of arms and legs the rider sprang to his feet, one foot in front of the other, his arms balancing his body. He had timed the wave perfectly. Upright on the narrow board he stood, his bronzed body wet and gleaming in the hot sunlight, his eyes on the distant beach, a splendid picture of youth and vigour.

Brady estimated his forward speed at something like twenty knots. The huge wave was toppling into white foam at its crest, but still the rider held his place, the stern of his board hidden by foam, the bow sloping to meet the foot of the wave, twin bow-waves spurting on either side—polished wood, white bow-waves, deep green of the comber, golden-bronze body, foam dazzling white on the ridge's crest, and beyond them the vivid turquoise of the deep sea.

Brady's thoughts changed from those of an idle sunbather to the mathematical judgments of the sea-captain. There would be hundreds of tons of water-weight in that half-mile-long wave, and the origin of its swell was in the persistent frictional force of a high wind somewhere out near New Zealand. The wave was toppling so prettily because its roots, deep down and moving over

the upward-sloping bottom of sand, were being retarded in speed
through friction—friction the origin, and the end. The top of
the wave, unretarded, was moving faster than its feet, and so was
falling forward, like a man tripping over a stone and lurching
forward in slow motion.

Nature had created that wave. A thousand miles to the eastward
the sun had heated a balloon of air; the balloon had risen, its
place taken by colder, heavier air; the convection circle had
begun, growing gradually faster, more violent in its movement.
The lowermost periphery of the vast revolving air-sea had brushed
continuously against resistant water—creating first ripples, then
wavelets, then deep watery ridges twenty or thirty feet high.
Somewhere out there the wind had died, the roaring combers
had subsided, but the swell, the form of the upheaval had run
inexorably on. Now the primeval powers of wind and water were
being used by a youth of twenty to gain two minutes' pleasure.

"He's probably thinking it's time for lunch," Brady murmured,
almost to himself.

"What's that, darling?"

He grinned at her shamefacedly.

"Nothing, really. Just pondering a bit heavily on the origin of
things. I'm often like that—but it's not dangerous."

"That wave?"

He looked at her quickly in surprise.

"You're a seaman, you were staring at a wave—it wasn't hard.
Tell me." She turned on her stomach, lying stretched out on the
towel, looking up at him. "Tell me about it."

Her expression was sober, interested. Speaking slowly, gathering his thoughts into words, he told her what he had been
thinking. "And all he was concerned with, probably, was his
lunch or if his girl-friend was watching him," he finished, with
the self-conscious grin she was coming to like so much. "In their
way, certainly to him, just as important as my wanderings."

She dribbled a handful of sand into a little cone and said
quietly, "I'm glad, Jim." And, at his inquiring look, "I'm like
that—always digging down into origins and reasons. D'you know
I sometimes wonder how . . . well, how a knife cuts. You know
what I mean? That sort of restless probing almost got me into
trouble once. We were watching an adrenalectomy—dissecting
an adrenal gland from a man's kidney. It's by no means a
common operation, and the surgeon was top man in his field.
The tricky part was over, and I asked him what actually caused

anaesthetic to paralyse a patient. He looked at me as if I were
nuts. Later on I asked the anaesthetist, even though the surgeon
was listening. He didn't like it, and later I guessed why. He
didn't know."

"But," Brady smiled, "surely it just . . . well, drugs the brain?"

"Of course it does. A wave swells up out of nowhere, a lad
jumps on it and rides it in, rain falls, nitrous oxide drugs the
brain. But how?"

"Sorry," Brady said, "go on."

"It seems that when an anaesthetic is administered, everywhere
else the oxygenated blood is doing its normal work—supplying
fuel for the body's functions. But in the brain there is complete
disregard of the nerves' warnings, when the scalpel cuts. The brain
cells, because of the anaesthetic agent carried in the blood, are
incapable of utilizing their full requirements of oxygen. And
that renders them insensible to messages from the cut nerves."

Beth brushed the sand from her hands.

"Yet even that hypothesis is not definitely proved," she went
on, "and anyhow it only begs the question. So we still don't
know exactly how an anaesthetic drugs the brain." She smiled up
at him. "But imagine the looks if I went round the med. school
asking what an anaesthetic does!"

"Maybe we're a couple of James Watts's poring over a kettle,"
Brady grinned, yet he was pleased at her revealing the likeness
between them.

"Just as well he did."

"Do you know we've talked hardly at all about our marriage
—the wedding, kids, things like that you're supposed to natter
about for weeks? Instead—waves and anaesthetics."

"We've plenty of time."

"Maybe. But I tell you this—whatever time may bring, this
marriage of ours is going to be nothing if not damned practical!
Beth," he added inconsequentially, "I've never been so bloody
happy in my life!"

"What a lover!" she smiled, but he saw her eyes were dancing.
"You've got me, that's why." She touched his bare forearm with
her fingers. "But let's be practical for a bit—we *are* going to live
somewhere up here?"

"Nowhere else."

"Lovely. Y'know, the War Service Homes people will advance
a salty old veteran like you almost three thousand pounds towards
a house."

"I know, yes. Speaking of money, I might be able to manage without 'em—I've been single a long time. Also, while we're on this interesting subject—how long before you'll start earning anything?"

"Ages yet; I'm not even through. Then a couple of years at Sydney Hospital, resident, then I have to build up a practice."

He smiled at her serious face.

"I wasn't fair dinkum, you know."

"But I am. You don't have to worry, Jimmy. Mother had money of her own—when she went, she left most of it to me."

He wanted to say something flippant, the subject of money having got a little out of hand; but she was looking at him too seriously. He said, quietly:

"I'd like to know about your mother."

She had been talking for almost an hour, with Brady learning of the youthful woman who had shared Farley's early work and disappointments, feeling he would like to have known her, when Beth reached for her clothes and pulled out her wristwatch.

"My sainted aunt!" she breathed, "he'll be ropeable. Do you know it's twenty to two?"

She made to rise and his hand went out. He said, leaning forward:

"I wish she could have known about us."

"So do I, darling—I like to think she does." Then she smiled, brightly. "On your feet, lover boy, or poppa-in-law will cut us off without a penny."

CHAPTER TEN

"WHAT the blazes have you two been up to?" Farley boomed from the top of the steps. "You should know better!" He glared accusingly at Brady, "If this happened aboard *your* ship . . . !"

"But we're not on his ship, yet," Beth said lightly, and kissed him on the cheek. "We've brought you some of those bread rolls. Now give the poor man a drink while I shower."

"So now we shower!" Farley growled, watching her skip through the door. "Isn't the blasted Pacific Ocean enough?" He glowered, then grinned at Brady. "Nice bit of goods, eh? What do you think?"

"If you come inside out of this blasted sun and give me a drink I'll tell you, Bruce," Brady laughed. Then he reflected:

Bruce. Perfectly natural. He was in his mid-thirties, and Farley
was to be his father-in-law. There need be no quivering pleading
for a daughter's hand here, or questions about the state to which
she had been accustomed.

"Beer?" Farley asked, going behind the bar; and, at Brady's
nod, "Not that I need an appetizer. Two o'clock! Don't you
feed in the middle of the day?"

"Had other things on my mind," Brady grinned.

"Really? Let's take a pew."

They sat down in the big living-room, Brady placing himself
so that he could see through the plate-glass windows over the
cliff to the sea, beating in white froth at the base of the farther
promontory.

"What other things?" asked Farley abruptly.

Brady took a deep pull of beer and lit a cigarette from a wooden
box. "I'm going to marry her, Bruce," he said quietly, and waited
for the boom of surprise.

"Are you now?" said Farley mildly.

"For God's sake man! Is that all?"

"What the hell am I supposed to say? She's pretty, right age,
nice bank-balance, nice legs—so a cove comes along, not what
I'd have picked myself, of course, and wants to marry the girl,
and I'm supposed to do hand-springs! When's the day?"

"The day . . . ? We—well, we haven't decided yet."

"What the hell did you talk about all morning, then?
Destroyers?"

"No, waves."

"Waves?"

Brady was pleased to see the bland face turn puzzled.

"What a lover!" Farley grunted. "I always thought this
damned electronic Navy had gone wishy-washy. Now, my boy,
we must have a little talk."

"I'm not a blasted boy!"

"No? That makes it all the easier then. Man to man, eh?
Now—can you keep my daughter in the state to which she's been
accustomed?"

Brady leaned back in his chair and roared with laughter.

"Pipe down, you clot! She'll hear you." Farley looked over
his shoulder.

"So daughter rules the roost, eh?" Brady chuckled. He pressed
his advantage. "Of course I can keep her as she's been used to—
ever since I got tangled up with this man-hungry offspring of

yours she's been telling me what a top-flight surgeon you are.
I'm sure we can keep her happy, between us. Let's see now. You
must be pulling down close on three hundred a week. . . ."

Beth came in, saying, "Well, what's the subject? Us? You've
relayed the glad tidings?" She seated herself on the arm of
Brady's chair, her hand ruffling his hair. "What do you think,
Dad? I've done all right, eh?"

"That's arguable. He's got a face only a mother would love,
but—*fait accompli*, I suppose."

Father and daughter looked at each other, and there was something in his large happy face that drew her from Brady's chair
to his. She leant down impulsively and he leaned forward, his
arms closing round her. Brady looked out of the window.

"Well, that's over," said Farley, and pushed her away. His
voice was suspiciously throaty. "Get back to your inamorata."

"With pleasure, darling."

"Hey, what about lunch!" Farley exploded. "*My* stomach's
not churning with fancy feelings."

"If you must be prosaic," Beth smiled, and holding out her
hands pulled Brady up. "Come on, then, I'll fix something."

"Thank you so much," her father growled, and grunted himself up on to his feet.

It was an informal and animated luncheon, taken on the
kitchen table. Beth's talk and eyes were radiant, and even Farley
allowed glimpses of his secret happiness to escape from under his
normal heavy phlegm. Brady was sipping his coffee when he
realized that Farley had not once mentioned the Navy or his
hobby of collecting things maritime. Of course, he remembered,
he had begun most of that silly business on the night of the party
himself, by blowing the bosun's pipe in the hallway. Perhaps
Farley had merely talked as he thought they wanted him to talk.
He liked collecting bric-à-brac from old ships, certainly, but
maybe his interest went no farther. It seemed so, from his
conversation now.

A feeling of complete contentment warmed Brady, Smiling,
putting in a word, he looked at them—Farley big and heavy and
genial, straddling a wooden chair, a lump of cheese in one hand,
a coffee-cup in the other, looking up at his girl; Beth on the
corner of the table, swinging one bare brown leg, nibbling noisily
at a spear of celery, her face smiling, her eyes dancing, the world
hers, unworriedly accepting her fortune. . . .

Creeping, sliding in, came the doubt. Wasn't it all too perfect? He had never won anything as easily as this. He crushed the thought down so vehemently that he actually shuddered slightly, and shook his head. Beth was looking at him.

"Anything wrong, darling? Cold feet?"

He answered quickly, his voice injecting a sudden sobriety into the happy atmosphere.

"No. I was thinking it's too good to be true." She leaned side-ways a little and he took her hand. "I was also thinking I'd like Ransome to know."

"Only Ransome?"

"Mainly Ransome, yes."

She looked at him critically. "You've known him so short a time, Jim. Yet you like him very much. Why don't you ring him up?"

"Of course," he said brightening. "I should have thought of that."

"Before you do, phone a telegram through to your mother and father. If you make it urgent they may deliver it this afternoon."

"They deliver till nine at night," he grinned boyishly. "I ought to know—at one time, to make money for a push-bike, I used to deliver telegrams in Toowoomba."

"Bully for you."

"What shall I say about our honeymoon in Queensland?"

"We'll see them before that, even if we have to fly and you can wangle only a few days' leave."

"Oh?"

"That's right. Has it occurred to you—no, it wouldn't, of course—that your mother and father might like to see what's got hold of you before the fatal knot is pulled tight?"

"That would be lovely."

"I think so, Jim," she smiled, and pouted a kiss at him.

"If I may interrupt all these gay plannings," Farley put in heavily. "As you mentioned, it's not legal yet, and it won't be without the provision of a best man. I suggest Ransome."

"Damn it all, Daddy, I wanted to say that!"

"Then why didn't you?" he asked, but he said it very gently in face of her frown.

"My gunner's mate," grinned Brady, "would envy the snap in that voice. Anyway, the suggestion's in the ring, and it won't have to be kicked around much. I'm sure old Ransome will be in it, sword and all. He's dining with me on board tomorrow night, and we'll celebrate then. The bride will also be there."

Farley sat forward, clattering his cup in its saucer.

"Not without me she won't!"

"All right, Pop," Brady conceded with a sigh, "but this is the last time you play gooseberry."

"Pop . . . !" Farley spluttered.

"Righto me lad," Beth broke in briskly, "telephone."

After lunch Farley went to his room to lie down. Beth led Brady out on to the front terrace. They lay side by side in long deck-chairs, the sea and cliffs before them. A slight haze blurred the even weld of sea and sky. Beyond the small curve of the beach the measureless expanse of swelling water lay sparkling like a floor of jewels in the afternoon sun, and as empty as the sky.

Only on the surge's fringe, a few yards out from the beach, was there any invasion of the sea's vast privacy.

"Look at 'em." Brady waved his arm lazily at the surfers. "Some of them probably think they're out quite a way, but. . . ." His gesture widened to include the reach of the sea.

"Man's dominion stops at the shore, eh? But you surely don't subscribe to that?"

"I do. We merely scratch the surface—almost literally."

"Our best man digs down a bit deeper, though."

"A maximum of about three hundred feet." He turned his head and smiled at her. "Out in the Pacific they've got soundings of close on seven miles."

"Jim?"

"Yup?"

"Tell me things—you know, mother and father, brothers and sisters, all that. We've got all afternoon."

"Surely you have people here week-ends?"

"Usually, yes. But this week-end I reserved."

"Scheming little minx. All right, what d'you want to know?"

"I expect if you started at the beginning it might be helpful. What sort of kid were *you*?"

He stretched his long body luxuriously, placing his hands behind his head, his eyes squinted almost shut against the hot sunlight beyond the terrace eaves. His body was relaxed, but his mind was stimulated to acute awareness by the tremendously significant events of that day.

He lit a cigarette and began to talk, and imagination, taking up the thread of thought, shot its swift shuttle back across the long hard years, weaving a picture so real and vivid that Beth, listening with the eagerness of devoted interest, could almost feel she had lived through them with him. Once, when he told her of his struggles at the Grammar School, when he had been called a guttersnipe by a rich and snobbish lout, she reached over and laid her hand on his fore-arm. He continued talking, but he felt the gesture, and its implication.

She listened with her mind and she was looking at his face and the muscled body bared under the open beach shirt, and she was thinking that there must have been other girls, many of them, who would like to have caught him. But she mustn't think of that.

He glanced at his watch and sat up in surprise. "It's almost four o'clock. You poor little devil—why didn't you stop me?"

"Why should I? It was important entertainment."

Her face serious, she stared out over the blue carpet of the sea, now flowering with little white flashes under the suasion of the on-shore afternoon breeze. She meant what she had said. Brady's story had given her more understanding of his character —she knew now what it had meant to him to conquer his sense of inferiority, to attain his confident self-assurance. This know-ledge made her speak of a subject which had been in her mind since they had talked of Thomsett's chest operation.

"Jim?"

Now come the detailed questions, he thought. Actually he was a little tired of his own story—he had compressed years of experience into an hour's telling.

"Yes, darling?" he smiled, and was conscious of his tolerance.

"You've served the Navy a long time. Would they let you go?"

"You mean resign?"

His head came up to stare at her. He felt a jolt of interest— this was not what he had expected; this was something he himself had vaguely thought about only a few days ago.

"Yes—resign."

He let his head fall back on the cushion; his burned face was calm, but his mind was running swiftly; he remembered the morning he had awoken with a novel distaste of the time-worn formality the day offered him; the way he'd begun to imagine settling into his own home, near a beach somewhere, when previously the only home he had desired had been his ship; he thought of children, coming home to them, running with them to

the beach. . . . Now if he had children they could quite easily be a
year older before he saw them again, a year of changes irretrievably
missed. He *had* served the Navy a long time. . . .

"I suppose I could resign," he said reflectively, and she felt the
feather of a hopeful thrill at his tone of voice. "I signed a bond
to serve for five years after I was commissioned—that's been
redeemed long ago, of course. Yes, I imagine there's nothing to
prevent my swallowing the anchor—as they say we say. Except
that I've just been given command of the squadron."

She tried not to sound too eager, to keep her voice flatly
practical.

"Wouldn't this be the time to give up that command? I mean,
before your captains got used to you? It seems to me you could be
replaced more easily now than if you were halfway through the
appointment."

"Hey, now. . . ." he began, grinning at her, and heard Farley's
heavy step behind them.

"Ah—I enjoyed that," Farley boomed, and stretched his arms
sideways and back. He looked down at them. "Young love—I don't
think. But then you're both middle-aged." He yawned, and
dragged over a cane chair. "Well, what are you talking about?
Waves again?"

"Yes," Beth answered him, "and how to get away from them, in
one easy lesson."

"Eh?" Farley sounded mystified enough, but he looked quickly
at Beth and leaned forward. You've caught on pretty smartly,
Brady thought—you two have talked about this before. Which,
he had to admit, was perfectly natural.

"She wants me to chuck the Service," he said flatly.

"I see. And will you?"

"Now hold on a minute!" He sat right up and looked at each
of them on either side of him in turn, his glance shrewd. "You
two are in cahoots on this."

"That's right," Beth said, her voice was flat as his had been.
"I want you with me all the time—selfish female, aren't I?—
and Dad thinks you're wasting your time and talent in the Navy."
She swung her bare legs over the side of the deck-chair and sat
facing him. You're lovely when you're serious, he thought
irrelevantly.

"Look, darling," she went on, "in a Navy our size your chances
of getting higher than captain are pretty slim. Right?" He nodded;
he wasn't the only commander who had pondered along those

lines. "Now I see it this way. Now, you're still young; but if you stay in the Service, you'll certainly draw good pay for another ten or fifteen years, and at the end of that time you'll be too old to come outside and start afresh."

He nodded again. When he looked into her face, he saw the anxiety beneath its seriousness.

"Jim, darling," she said quietly, "sooner or later you *have* to come outside. You've done more than your bit—right through the war, and after it. Why waste time? Why spoil your chances of starting in a new profession?" She repeated: "Sooner or later you must come outside."

He looked out over the sea, and they respected his silence. He was not thinking of the element he had sailed on for almost twenty years; he loved the Service, he still could be exhilarated by the lines and the speed of a warship, but there was no salt water in his veins. He was a bush-boy, and he loved the Navy for what it was—interesting, highly efficient, adventurous—not because it had its being on water; he could grow to love any other profession which offered the same incalculables.

He put a cigarette slowly into his mouth. His strong nose jutted above his hands, cupped against the breeze. He exhaled a deep breath of smoke.

"You're right, of course. I've known it for a long time. Earlier—before my four rings—we used to talk about it in the mess. Several chaps I know wanted to have a stab at life outside—the usual reasons, wives, kids, home life; and, as you said, we all knew that we'd have to take a shot at it some time. Lieutenant-Commanders have to retire at forty-five. But there was always one thing that stopped us doing anything about it—and it still applies to me no matter what reasons you advance for my coming outside."

"I know, Jim—you have no job to come out to."

He nodded. "There it is—nice and compact and wrapped-up. And unbeatable."

"Not at all, darling."

"What?—we live on your money?" His voice was brutal. He recognized his tone and regretted it instantly.

"Yes," she said calmly, and he stared at her in astonishment. "For a time that is, if necessary. You are not one of those fictional heroes who idiotically refuses any help his wife could give him. You are not the sort of man who has to prove his ability to make his own way, on his own. You would use my money to help you get started."

There was no query in her statements. He tapped at the end of his cigarette.

"Yes, I would use your money," he said slowly. "After we'd bought a house, I'd have to." He glanced up from the ash-tray and his grin seemed to her young and almost cheeky. "Now that's decided, what exactly does Captain Brady, gunnery officer and seaman, do in Civvy Street?"

Her answer came instantly and definitely: "Medicine."

"I see," he answered, and it was their turn to be astonished. Recovering from his calm acceptance of the possibility, she pressed her advantage.

"You told me you would like to be a surgeon. You talked intelligently of the operation you saw. You're a mature man, you're used to concentrated application. Your age? There's a man of forty-six in my term now."

Odd that she should mention a man of forty-six taking on a new profession, because he had already remembered a rear-admiral who had come outside and begun a law course at the University. He was now a barrister, a judge's associate.

Brady heard Farley's chair creak, but he did not hear the big man step quietly inside. Staring at the sea, his eyes receiving only the impression of colour, no definition of movement or feature, he was reflecting that if Admiral Morrison could do it. . . . And there was the precedent—no one could laugh at his going back to school, sitting at lectures with youngsters of twenty. Morrison had sat with them, argued probably, discussed legal points seriously with students young enough to be his sons. Only now did he fully understand what a determined, yet flexible mind the admiral must have. And Morrison had been married for years —he had lacked Captain Brady's incentive to begin, and learn, and practise all over again.

"It will be hard," Brady said slowly.

"It will be damned hard," Farley grunted, and leaned over him to place the whisky decanter on the cane table. "I don't know about you, Jim, but your decision's put me in need of a drink."

"Makes two of us."

"And baby makes three," Beth said, putting her arms around him from behind. "Darling," she murmured into his ear.

Two whiskies later Brady chuckled suddenly.

"Y'know, this has made a hell of a difference to me."

"No doubt," Farley said dryly.

"I mean, an hour ago I was worried because things were too good to be true—I've always doubted things when they go too well. But now I've been pitchforked into six years of blasted study I'm on an even keel again. The Fates are laughing their heads off at me—that'll keep 'em occupied nicely."

"There's something else to this arrangement," Beth smiled, "and I thought of this one all by myself. I imagine it will take some time for you to get out; so you might as well move in with us and come home to Momma each night for a square meal."

"Hell, I couldn't do that—but I will," Brady grinned at her.

"Good. There's plenty of room."

"Paying guest, of course," Farley growled.

"Like hell—look what I'm taking off your hands."

"There's something in that," Farley admitted. "Another one?"

Brady made to drain his glass, and halted it half-way to his lips. His mind was clear now, and he wanted it that way for a while longer.

"No thanks"—he shook his head. "Look—I think I might take a stroll down to the beach."

"All right, Jim," Beth said, and he was glad she did not get up with him.

They watched him walk down the steps, and out of sight beyond the garage.

"He's got a lot to think about," Farley said thoughtfully. "But it should make you happy."

"Dad," she said after a moment, and clasped her hands round her knees, "now I'm worried."

"A little late for that, my pet."

"I don't mean that. I mean—it seems too good to be true."

He looked at her, her chin on her knees, and he thought: nothing's too good for you, my baby; your mother and me had thirty years of goodness, and thank God we accepted it and enjoyed it gratefully.

"You'll have your ups and down, but I expect everything will be all right."

"That's funny." She looked at him quickly. "Those exact words —Jim told me they're painted on a plaque in the submarine's wardroom. Dad?"

"M'mm?"

"I think I'll ask John and Betty up this evening; the Priors too."

"I didn't think you'd hold off the whole week-end." Farley chuckled. "But I'm taking it easy—dinner on board tomorrow night."

The dinner on board was a complete success; it could hardly have failed to be so.

Brady had driven Beth on to the pier in his car, Farley following in his own. *Scourge* was sailing early in the morning, and there was no point in returning to Whale Beach. His mind was settled: he would resign at once.

He had thought long and carefully, walking down to the beach, sitting on a sand-hillock in the westering sun. There had been rear-admirals in the Australian Navy promoted from the lower-deck, but none, as far as he knew, from the seaman, executive, branch. It was quite unusual that he had risen as high as he had, and there was little hope that he would get much farther. Beth's reminder, that sooner or later he must get out, did most to influence his decision.

His mind was made up as he drove on to the pier, but when he saw his ship, lying long and grey and quiet, an odd restlessness came to him. He got out of the car and looked at *Scourge*. What now of his keenness to work the squadron up, of his pleasure in Cowan's growing interest and appreciation, of his captains' visits to the submarine? His inspection of *Diana*, his intent listening to the escape coxswain, his careful reading of the Subsmash routine, his chief activities of the past week, in fact—all were pointless now, wasted.

Soon he would no longer be commanding officer of this beautiful new brute of a ship; he would not even be in the Navy. He heard the click as Beth, wondering at his delay, opened the car door. All right, he thought almost savagely: it was my decision, no one twisted my arm, so let's pack up self-pity. He stepped quickly round the front of the car and opened the door, scenting Beth's perfume as she moved.

"Sorry, darling, just mooning a bit."

"I understand." She took his arm. "Can we have a lovely night? I'm looking forward to it so much."

He almost said: "Okay, okay, I know I'm like a kid with its toy taken away." He smiled and gestured to the gangway. "You'll enjoy it, even if only for the novelty. There's Ransome—grinning like the original Cheshire."

The submariner's short thick body rolled towards them, his

tough face smiling so that the scar almost closed his eye. "Well, well, what wonderful news!"

"I'm a faster worker," said Beth, holding out her gloved hand. Farley's car pulled up behind them.

"Eric," Brady said, "while we're on the subject, and still sober— I'd like you to be best man."

"Of course. Just tell me the date, and rig of the day. Ah—here's someone who's going to enjoy his naval time."

They turned to greet Farley, distinguished-looking in dinner clothes, and Beth was glad because Ransome's instant acceptance of the invitation showed that he reciprocated Brady's feelings for him. She reflected that Jim must know many more like Ransome— but there was plenty of time to meet them.

In the cabin they relaxed with sherries before them. Benson, watching from his pantry, grinned to himself. "What a slasher! a little hum-twicer! No wonder the old boy's got ants in his pants. He might even marry her. Be a mug if he didn't."

"Benson!"

The steward jumped. Hurriedly he laid his cigarette in an ash-tray hidden behind a kettle, and stepped into the cabin. "Sir?"

"Benson, this is Miss Farley. Steward Benson."

"Pleased to meet you, Miss Farley."

"Hello," Beth smiled, and Brady was pleased that she hadn't used his surname.

"Benson's looked after me like a mother for the last five years."

"And made a good job of it," Beth conceded. "But soon your work will be lightened."

"Will it, miss?"

"Yes, Benson," Brady said easily, "we're going to be married."

"Oh, I am pleased to hear that, sir! May I offer my congratulations, sir? And you, miss?"

She looked up at him: what tales *you* could tell, she thought. He seemed genuinely pleased, and she smiled. "Thank you very much. You might give me some tips on cooking."

"Oh, I don't do no cooking, Miss Farley—the galley looks after that. I just make morning tea and such, as the captain's personal steward. In fact, to tell you the truth, I don't like cooking."

"But you like your grog."

Benson's head jerked round at the booming voice. He looked into a large quizzical face which reminded him of . . . ?

"Flinders Naval Depot, just before the war ended," said Farley. "Remember a certain week-end up the Line, and a certain face that had fallen flat outside the police office? M'mm"—he looked up at Benson with his head on one side—"not a bad job on that eye and mouth, even if I say it myself. Eh, Benson?"

"Yes, sir," the steward gulped, "you did a very good job, sir. I remember you now. You was a surgeon-lieutenant then, sir, yes sir, I remember you very well now and I. . . ."

"So, Benson," a stern voice spoke on top of his, "and all the time I assumed that those scars were won fighting valiantly, against the common enemy. Instead, you were paralytic drunk."

"Well, sir, I seem to remember me and me cobber had a jug or two, but it was that blasted—I beg your pardon, miss—that footpath in front of the police office."

"Never mind, steward," Beth smiled, nodding understandingly at him, "your past lapse has served a good purpose. I know now that drinking is severely frowned on in the Service. That would apply of course even more strictly to senior officers. I will remember that."

Benson grinned at Brady, who growled at him: "I'll see you in the morning."

"Never fear, Benson," Ransome chuckled. "You know where to bring your complaint of unfair treatment."

"It's a conspiracy," Brady charged; he was delighted that Beth had so patently clicked with Benson—and through him, with the ship. "Do something with that cigarette in there or you'll burn the place out."

"Yes, sir."

"Having finished your smoke, you might be good enough to serve dinner?"

"Dinner, sir? Certainly, sir." Long experience had taught Benson the exact line to toe, and he knew he had reached it now. He left the cabin, hiding his grin. A smart chick, that one: going home to her every night would make a nice, sweet, easy commission both for Brady and for himself left on board. . . . He served the meal with disciplined precision, as if to impress on Beth the efficiency with which Brady had been cared for in the past.

The guests talked little shop: Service matters crept in only once, when Brady said: "Big day tomorrow, Eric, with Cowan and Captain Ferris as your pupils. I'd like you out there nice and early. Sorry, but we'll waste half the morning otherwise."

"I thought of that," Ransome nodded, "and *Diana's* leave is up at midnight tonight. I'll start early enough. Should be an interesting day."

Brady agreed absently; he had already forgotten all about submarine exercises, for he was looking at Beth and she at him.

CHAPTER ELEVEN

NEXT morning, a little before daylight, submarine *Diana* went to sea.

Flakes of foam slid past her black sides; the water struck against and broke on her sharp bow with flashing blows, clear white against the dark sea. The land glided back into obscurity, and when the sun rose, flaming crimson on the level of the water, the submarine's wake, long and straight, stretched itself out through a day of immense solitude. To the south the topmasts of a ship running for Melbourne rose slender and upright above the sharp edge of the horizon, lingered, and vanished like an illusion.

A dawn squall, coming up from ahead, dissolved into the short deluge of a hissing shower. It left the ship glistening from radar-mast to belly-tanks, and with shining casings. She ran on easily into the whitecaps, and the navigator's pencil-line of her course on the chart had as its visual counterpart the broad gleaming path of the rising sun. Moving along with her, heard subconsciously by Ransome as he stood on the bridge, was the sustained and monotonous swishing of the waves, coming at her, meeting her cutting stem, hissing down her metal sides, fading astern, flanking the long white ribbon of her wake; the sound of the restless sea mingling with the muted hammer of the diesels, the short creaking plaint of some fitting as she rolled; or, now and then, a loud sigh of wind.

Ashore, far behind her below the curve of the ocean's cheek, the Subsmash organization had not yet been fully alerted. It was too early, and in any case *Diana* would not dive for some time; now, she was an ordinary ship, well-found and seaworthy, under capable command, coursing to the eastward on the surface, buoyant, powerful, safe.

Lieutenant Deevers, officer of the watch, wished Ransome would go below: then he could indulge himself in his thoughts of yesterday evening. Now he had to make a pretence of alertness, sweeping the horizon regularly with his binoculars, even though the sparkling sea was guiltless of any presence other than their own.

He had got back to *Diana* just before midnight, yet he could feel his tiredness safely enough; the man's shallow mind revelled in the feeling: he thought of it and enjoyed it like a medal-winner studying the beribboned evidence of his triumph.

A voice-pipe buzzer pitched sharply across the quiet bridge. He levered himself upright and answered it, listened, then turned to Ransome.

"First-lieutenant on the bridge, sir?"

"Yes, please," Ransome nodded, and pushed his cap up a little from his forehead and rubbed his eyes. Nice party last night—almost too nice. His head was clear of whisky, but he could do with some sleep. That was why he was on the bridge now, filling his lungs with fresh air before confining himself for a day in *Diana's* funny innards. Brady was right to give up the sea—he'd served more than long enough to entitle himself to the comforts of existence a bricklayer took for granted.

Take me now, he pondered—seven o'clock, and already on the job for more than two hours; and upwards of fifteen thousand miles away from Moira and the children. Alone in her bed she was waking to loneliness, to facing the day without his companionship: who to talk to at night, to discuss the children with, the little intimate and significant things? Today, and tomorrow, and a hundred tomorrows.

Brady was right. It was no place for a married man. For a man like Deevers . . . what a foul fellow he is, the lipstick not even washed off properly—perhaps deliberately. But he can't be got rid of down here; Singapore perhaps.

"Morning, sir."

"No need to be so damned bright about it," Ransome growled. He looked at Wetherell's face. "You should have brought your sun-glasses up," he added pointedly.

"Like the eagle, I can look into the sun," grinned the first-lieutenant, then shuddered. "A week at sea would do us all good," he muttered.

"If it will help I'll restrict your leave in Sydney," Ransome offered.

"It's not as bad as all that," Number One said hastily. Then his professional instincts over-rode the by-play and he stared about him.

To him, just up from the stale and oily interior of the submarine, the boat had a shower-wet freshness; the long clear stretch of the foredeck glistened; slanting sunlight splashed on the brasswork and darted over the glass compass-face in lines of gold;

and the drops of rain-water here and there on the bridge rail
were as limpid and sparkling as drops of dew. Here outside the
boat was quiet, the only sounds those of hissing water and sighing
wind. The sun, rising lonely and splendid in the pale sky, saw a
solitary vessel moving purposefully on the glittering sea.

"We'll have two visitors today," Ransome remarked, his arms
out straight before him, his hands on the bridge rail.

"Yes, sir?"

"Captain Brady's first-lieutenant this morning, and the captain
of *Lockyer* after lunch." He glanced briefly at his deputy. "You
know we're firing torpedoes this morning?"

"Yes, sir. I've come up to relieve Torps. I presume that *Scourge*
is recovery ship?"

"Yes. All right, Torps." Ransome spoke over his shoulder.

Deevers came forward a couple of paces. "I'm all right, thank
you, sir—both firing torpedoes are checked."

Ransome's words had been an order for Deevers to go below;
not an expression of interest in his welfare. "You checked them?
You must have been up early."

"No. sir, the T.I. has everything in hand."

"Has he now! I prefer my torpedo officer to be on hand,"
Ransome said coldly.

Deevers recognized the tone, and the most prudent response.
"Of course, sir," he answered crisply, and reported to Number
One: "Course due east, speed ten knots, we're on the chart, no
ships in sight."

"Have got," Wetherell nodded, and took Deevers's binoculars.
The torpedo officer went down the vertical ladder without a
further glance at the sunny morning.

Ransome looked idly round the bridge, noting that the look-
out was staring aft over the wake, out of earshot. He wanted to
talk to his deputy about having Deevers relieved on return to
Singapore. He dismissed the idea as soon as it was born—the
officer complement on *Diana* was too small, the first-lieutenant
was of necessity too close to them for his captain to discuss an
officer's removal. If Deevers went, it would have to be solely on
Ransome's unaided decision.

He glanced at his watch.

"Alter to the north in ten minutes' time," he ordered. "The
squadron should be coming out now."

The squadron, with *Scourge* in the van, was at that moment

approaching the starb'd turn which would take the four ships out between the Heads.

"Coming on the bearing, sir," reported the navigator.

"Starb'd twenty," Brady ordered.

He heard the navigator repeat the words, the dispassionate repetition of the coxswain below in the wheelhouse, and was surprised by a flood of nostalgia—how many times more would he give an order like that, hear it acknowledged with that calm efficiency?

His seaman's eye was watching *Scourge* swing, feeling her lean, scanning the open sea she would soon be traversing, noting the position of the ferry, now on his port bow, but his momentary regret had him thinking of the resignation he had written out after his guests had left last night. He had kept it brief, only mentioning his decision to do medicine; the senior officers who read it would appreciate that he had given his action considerable thought, but there was no point in going into details. The envelope, with his hopes of the future, and of Beth, would by now be caught up in the routine of the G.P.O.—unrecallable, headed inevitably for Navy Office in Melbourne.

The die was cast. Even if he should rescind his decision, he would be remembered, when promotions were being listed, as the captain who had once resigned his commission; an officer who, no matter what his degree of experience or competence, could not be considered for higher posting—he had done it once, he might resign again, he was mentally out of line for bigger things.

"Ease to ten."

That reasoning apart, he knew he would never go back on his decision. Valuing flexibility in small matters, he saw the worth of firmness in bigger ones. And there was Beth. . . .

She'd love this though, he realized suddenly—before he left, he might take her out one day, bring old Farley too, in his Reserve uniform.

"Midships." Pause. "Steady—steer oh-nine-oh."

He must tell her that while thinking of her, quite clearly and consciously, he had not for one moment been remiss in his seamanship. Could the human brain be divided into quite separate compartments, like twin engines, each section operating efficiently and independently? One thinking of the woman he loved, the other conning a three-thousand-ton Fleet destroyer through Sydney Heads?

Already he was thinking medically. . . . The thought amused him, so that when Lieutenant Cowan stepped up beside him and spoke, the lieutenant was confronted with a genial grin. Reacting normally, he smiled back.

"Torpedo-firing orders unchanged, sir? First run at ten o'clock?"

"That's right. She'll fire two torpedoes, two runs—the first for your benefit, the other for Captain Ferris."

"I'm looking forward to it, sir."

"I imagine you are; I'd like to have seen a fish fired myself."

"Well then, would you like to go down this morning?"

Instantly, Brady was tempted—the arrangements could be made easily; he would very much like to see what went on in that torpedo-tube compartment during an actual firing. And then a voice mocked: what the hell for? What's it to you how a torpedo fires from a submarine? You'd be better off rubbing-up on your chemistry symbols!

"No thanks, Number One." He shook his head. "This is your picnic. Pilot! Take her out ten miles, then alter to the north."

"That crew pulls damned well," Wetherell muttered, his glasses up.

"A ship is known by her boats, Number One," Ransome quoted pontifically, also watching the sea-boat approaching *Diana's* black side.

"And Brady's a pretty taut hand, eh?"

"Captain Brady is a highly efficient seaman, if that's what you mean."

Number One glanced at the near-by look-out, then muttered:

"Sorry, sir."

"That's all right," Ransome grunted. "In fact"—his voice lightened—"I have to brush up on routine myself—I've got to be damned efficient in a few days' time."

"Sir?"

"Captain Brady has asked me to be his best man."

"Well I never!" Wetherell pronounced slowly.

"You doubt his choice?"

"Not at all," the lieutenant grinned. "I was thinking of the captain getting spliced. Though that's silly. Like when you see a friend's child after a year or so and you remark with wonder how he's grown. Men get married, kids grow up. . . . You've met the lady?"

"She's a lulu," Commander Ransome said expressively. "You, by the way, and against my wishes, are invited to the do."

"Nice—very nice. We'll have to dub in for a present."

"Oars!" came a sharp voice below them. A few moments later Cowan climbed up over the bridge and Ransome smiled a greeting.

"Morning, Cowan. You know Bob Wetherell, my Number One?"

"Been under the table with him, sir—or almost. Morning, Bob."

"Yes, I remember, first night in port," Ransome nodded. "Right! Clear the bridge! I want to slam a tin-fish into our friend over there."

"We've still got Slocum," Cowan grinned as he headed for the hatch.

Ransome pushed his lips out in amiable deprecation. "We'll see about that," he promised. "Now try to make that ladder without breaking your neck."

Brady watched the boat pulling back, then his eyes returned to the submarine; he felt a stir of excitement as he remembered that this would be as close to the real thing as killer-ship and hunter could get. Ransome would fire his torpedo directly at them, but it would be fitted with a practice head and it would be set to pass beneath *Scourge's* hull. Apart from those necessary precautions, the hunt would be parallel to reality. He knew that this morning Ransome would give nothing away, and he felt that he wanted to "kill" the submarine quickly and surely—a sort of going out with glory. . . .

"Bosun's mate," he ordered. "Petty Officer Slocum on the bridge."

Brady was watching *Diana's* sinking bridge pushing a small cliff of water before it, when Slocum appeared.

"You sent for me, sir?"

"Yes, Slocum," Brady said genially, his eyes still on the diving submarine. "I especially want to make a quick contact this morning."

"Yes, sir."

Brady turned quickly at the listless tone: Slocum was normally as keen as salt in his special field. Now he was staring at the deck, his face carved into lines of worry.

"What's wrong, Slocum?" Brady asked quietly.

"Nothing, sir." The answer was expected, as was its lack of

spirit. Brady looked up at the navigator beside the binnacle.

"Sea cabin, Pilot," he called crisply, and, to Slocum, "come with me."

Brady went down the ladder, thinking fast. The squadron had been disposed for the exercise; he had at least fifteen minutes before he need commence hunting; *Diana's* periscope standard was disappearing beneath a feather of wake—all was well there. Now there was only Slocum. Obviously there was something wrong, and whatever the reason, it was of prime importance that Slocum should be on his toes at this time, with a submarine just dived. It was highly unlikely, of course, but Slocum's skill might be required if anything went wrong.

He walked along the passage to his cabin, and held open the door.

"Come in and sit down."

"Yes, sir."

Slocum sat down on the edge of an armchair and Benson appeared from the pantry, his eyes on Brady. The captain shook his head and Benson understood at once. He left the cabin, closing the door, and walked out on to the upper-deck, as Brady knew he would. Brady looked at Slocum.

Brady knew men, and this man particularly well—knew him to be of oaken loyalty and as dependable as anchor-chain. He decided on his approach even as he leaned forward in his chair, holding Slocum's eyes with his own.

"You're in strife, old chap," he said soberly. "Let's have it."

Slocum lowered his gaze to his cap. He turned it nervously in his hands on his lap.

"It's personal, sir."

"I know that." Brady could pronounce with confidence there —any trouble on board would sooner or later have reached his ears. "You are an important man on this ship, Slocum, and especially so right now. You understand that normally I'd mind my own business, unless you came to me first—but with a submarine dived out there, and my senior Asdic rating worried sick about something, well, that brings me into the picture—officially. You see that?"

His voice and his look were kindly—naturally so, for he liked Slocum and respected his ability. In his years of command he had been confronted by most types of domestic conflict among his men, and often his detached advice had borne happy fruit; he hoped it might do so now.

"I see that, sir."

"Come on, then—money, or is it your wife?"

Slocum's mouth tightened. His cap lay still. Brady waited, knowing that Slocum could tell him, in effect, to mind his own business; he certainly could not be forced to speak on a domestic problem which concerned only himself. And it seemed he was not going to speak now.

"All right," Brady said, and leaned back. "I only wanted to help you. That's all."

"Yes, sir."

Slocum got up and walked to the door. Brady swung his chair round to face his desk, ostensibly to study a file of papers, actually to hide his disappointment and to give Slocum time to get out before he himself returned to the bridge. Then he heard feet on the carpet, and looked over his shoulder. Slocum stood beside him and spoke without preliminary.

"My wife's a tramp," he said steadily, in a low voice.

"Sit down," Brady gestured, and turned his chair to face him. "You're sure, of course?"

"Me and McCook caught her at Bondi."

Brady saw the pain in his face. You poor devil, he thought—it's usually the nice blokes. He waited, letting his commiseration flow out to the other man. Slocum stared into his eyes a second, then his gaze shifted slowly to the right and fixed on the sky through the open porthole. He began to talk.

Brady listened without interruption to the sordid story. Description was sparse, but the gaps could be filled in easily enough. Slocum paused, and rubbed his fingers in a tired movement across his forehead. When he went on, his voice was edged with anger.

"She was at it again on Friday night. The coxswain saw her, in the pub lounge. He told me and McCook." He stared up at Brady, a stabbing sort of look. "It was a naval officer this time. An R.N. type."

Now Brady knew the reason for that edge of anger—one of Slocum's own kind had moved in against him, not a bludging bookmaker, but a naval man—and an officer.

"Royal Navy?" Brady spoke for the first time. "But how did the coxswain know? Officers go ashore in plain clothes."

"The 'swain knew all right—he saw him once when he went aboard *Diana* on business. He was officer of the day. We dunno who he is or what he does, but he's in that submarine all right —he's in her now!"

God, Brady thought, what a shocking situation! He rubbed his chin with nervous movements, then took up a cigarette and offered the box to Slocum. Deevers, of course! He was as sure of that as he had been of anything in his life. Just as sure as he was that sooner or later Slocum would identify Deevers—and when he did, and took action, the resultant proceedings, if they got into the papers, would rock the Service. Rating's wife seduced by naval officer! The Sunday papers would jump at it.

He watched Slocum lighting a cigarette with shaking fingers and appreciated again the cause of his anger—he could take on a bookmaker, he could fight thugs, but against an officer his hands were tied; except that he could break Deevers through legal methods. The woman was worthless, and Slocum knew that —there was no advice or help to be given there. But a Service scandal was a different matter! Slocum had to be stopped. Brady's mind went straight to the stopping-point.

"The coxswain could be wrong," he said quietly.

"He could be, but he's not."

The voice was hard. Brady leaned sideways, looking down at the deck, his chin supported on his thumb. He glanced up at Slocum.

"I'm damned sorry about this, Slocum. I know words won't help, but I want you to know I appreciate your feelings. I only hope getting it off your chest has helped a bit." He paused. "What are you going to do?"

Slocum drew twice on his cigarette.

"I'm not sure yet, sir." Brady felt a flicker of hope. "We handled Walshe and his mugs all right, but there's only one way to get at this other mongrel."

Brady tried again.

"I'd think long and hard before trying anything like that. The girl's not worth it—why get yourself into more trouble?"

Slocum's answer was quick and almost vicious.

"I'm not in no trouble, sir! But he'll be when I find him!"

Brady cursed his stupidity—he had hit on the one thing which would inflame Slocum's anger: the suggestion that a lower-deckman was heading for trouble if he stacked up against a superior officer.

"I didn't mean you were in trouble that way," he said quickly. "I referred only to what's happened with your wife. But there are some things I must say. First, you must be absolutely sure that the coxswain's identification is water-tight—and remember he saw this officer only once, and briefly, before he recognized him

in a crowded lounge. I hate to think what a clever lawyer could
do with that. And I want you to think of what a court case will
mean—at the moment a handful of us know your story; you can
imagine what the papers will do with it. Think hard about that.

"Also, this business concerns me, professionally. I understand
your feelings, but I have a squadron of destroyers out here, and
our purpose is to hunt and find that submarine. You are my senior
Asdic rating. I want you on the ball. Is that clear?"

His voice was still kindly, but crisp.

"You don't have to worry about that, sir."

"I'm pleased to hear it. Now I must get back to the bridge. If
you wish, we'll talk further about it later on."

Slocum stood up, and for the first time he smiled, a rueful
twist of his lips.

"I won't worry you no more, sir. It was decent of you to listen.
We been together a long time, and . . . well, it helps for you
to know." He turned quickly and left the room.

Brady looked at the door, then at his watch. He had not more
than five minutes before the exercise was due to begin. The
coxswain was the man for him to see, but he would have to
move very carefully—if Slocum found out, the idea that his own
captain was trying to cover the torpedo officer would simply
strengthen his resolution.

Brady thought hard, smoking in quick nervous puffs. He'd
have to use the ship's normal routine, the expected routine. He
got up and pressed the buzzer beside the bridge voice-pipe. The
navigator answered at once.

"Get the Asdic team closed-up. Coxswain on the wheel."

"Aye aye, sir."

Brady turned back to his desk to crush out his cigarette.
Jabbing it in the ash-tray, he caught sight of a blue-covered book
lying on the blotting-pad. He had been glancing through it only
an hour before—the book of reference detailing the Subsmash
organization, how to rescue the crew of a submarine sunk in a
workable depth of water. He grinned tightly. He was dealing with
real troubles and grown men, not the plot of a D-class Hollywood
melodrama. Jamming on his cap, he made for the bridge ladder.

On the bridge in the bright sunlight he lifted his binoculars to
study the nearest destroyer, *Lockyer*, the familiar long grey shape
and the white flash of her bow-wave against the blue sea.

"Coxswain?" he spoke into the wheelhouse voice-pipe. "On
the bridge, please."

He had spoken easily, giving a perfectly natural order. Casually he strolled clear to one side of the bridge, knowing his isolation would be respected. He leaned on the windbreak, thinking of the chief petty officer who would now be turning over the wheel to a helmsman. The coxswain. . . . It was a rank and title of peculiar force in a destroyer. The coxswain was the senior man on the lower-deck, a man whose authority there was almost as forceful as the captain's. He was responsible for discipline, he took the wheel when the ship went into action or approached a coast or harbour, and he stayed there till the business was finished. He was the incorruptible link between captain and men, the confidante of captains, the stanchion of competence and probity. Brady knew as he waited that some time that day the coxswain would have come to him—not with news of the bookmaker and his thugs, but to inform him that a naval officer was known to be mixed up in Slocum's sorry business.

A step sounded behind him and a deep steady voice said:

"Coxswain, sir."

"Morning, 'Swain," Brady answered, and looked at the man standing at attention before him. He saw a tall, rangy figure, neatly dressed, the cap's peak projecting forward over steady eyes and a large straight nose. The coxswain had been at sea longer than himself—his face was seamed like a relief map and his weather-toughened skin was the colour of well-used leather.

Brady turned casually so that he was facing seaward. The coxswain turned with him.

"I've been talking to Slocum."

"Yes, sir. The submarine officer?"

"That's right. You're quite sure?"

"I made sure I was sure, sir. He's in *Diana* all right. Matter of fact, I was going to see you when we got back to base."

Brady nodded.

"It's nasty. It could be a damn' sight worse. I think Slocum might cite him as co-respondent. You know what that could mean?"

"Yes, sir. I. . . ."

"Yes?"

"I dunno why the hell I told him what I saw. I must've been all burned-up myself. It was . . . rotten, seeing that submarine bloke with her."

Brady nodded again.

"I imagine it was. The whole business is rotten. That's why I want it stopped where it is. You understand?"

"I think so, sir."

"If Slocum blows his top over this it'll do no good whatever —he said himself his wife's a tramp. There's no hope there. I hold no brief for the submarine officer, whoever he is. But anything Slocum does won't alter *his* nature, either. He'll go quietly for a month or so, then he'll be up to the same caper with somebody else. There is also a strong possibility that he doesn't know who that woman's husband is."

"Yes, sir."

Brady looked sideways, holding the coxswain's eyes. "No good will come of this," he repeated, and waited three seconds. "You can't identify that officer, coxswain. You thought you recognized him, but now you're sure you're wrong. As soon as we get back in you'll visit *Diana* on some pretext and you'll come back and tell Slocum you made a mistake." Brady's voice was low, conversational—he was not ordering, he was giving information on how a mission should be carried out; he knew his man.

"Aye aye, sir. I hope it works."

"There's no 'hope' about it—if you can't identify the man, there's no case, no case at all."

"Yes, I see, sir."

"Good. I don't like this any more than you do, but it has to be this way. That's all."

"Aye aye, sir," the coxswain said smartly, and saluted.

Brady heard his feet clattering down the ladder, then stepped over to the binnacle.

"All right," he said to the bridge team in general, "let's get started. Signalman? *Diana* dived at eight-forty for four hours for exercise SMX. In position . . . give him that, Pilot. I am about to commence exercise. Usual addresses."

"Aye aye, sir," the yeoman muttered.

Lieutenant Cowan had watched the diving routine in the control-room with fascinated interest. His situation was novel enough, but he was impressed by more than that—he had gradually come round to Brady's way of thinking.

The main influence had been his period in command. For several hours he had been in sole charge of *Scourge,* a unique experience for a man who previously had kept only a four-hour watch on the bridge, knowing that a few feet away in his sea-cabin was a captain who could instantly take all responsibility on his experienced shoulders. But this time there had been no one else—he was the boy, they came to him, and the feel of such power and authority was sweet, as well as educational.

Then there was the realization that Brady had been proved right. Watching the practised movements of these submariners among their maze of instruments, he had quickly come to the conclusion that a sub-hunter who had never dived knew only half the score; he was like a hunter tracking an animal of whose physical capabilities he knew nothing. Cowan realized also that though the missile-men and rocketeers were smart, Ransome and his impeccably trained team were no slouches either.

By the time Lieutenant Deevers, the torpedo officer, came up to him, he had begun to enjoy himself.

"Morning, Torps," Cowan said, with the geniality of the guest. Deevers nodded back, his lip lifting in what was meant to be a smile—he still felt sour about Ransome's tone on the bridge, and now he had this Australian clot to shepherd through the torpedo-tube space.

"Commander thinks you should see the loading of a torpedo."

"I'd like that very much, yes."

"All right, let's get on with it."

Pleasant bird, Cowan reflected wryly, and followed Deevers's thin form down the narrow passage through the crew's quarters. He stepped over a high coaming, noting the thick solidity of the water-tight door, and was in the torpedo-stowage compartment. He could see the twin banks of tubes through the next door, but his eyes were drawn to what was waiting a few feet in front of him.

He stopped beside it. The torpedo, almost two feet in diameter, lay in its cradles behind and in line with the rear door of one of the tubes; on its left an empty space between two more torpedoes showed where it had been stowed.

The weapon was long and shone even through its coating of grease. Cowan's instant impression was of smoothness—the whole shape was beautifully streamlined, from the twin sets of counter-revolving screws to the practice blowing-head, painted bright yellow for easy sighting when its compressed-air tank brought it to the surface after the run. The compartments housing the rudder controls, the diesel engine, the big air-vessel, the practice head, were joined by bolts counter-sunk in horizontal fluted holes—there was nothing to retard the torpedo's forty-knot speed.

Cowan saw torpedoes almost every day of his life aboard

Scourge, but here there was a difference. The destroyer's tinfish were auxiliary weapons, to be used as a last resort against a weighty cruiser or carrier; she had her main-armament guns and her Limbo mortar's depth-charges to carry out her principal function. But these long shiny shapes were *Diana's* king-hitters. *Scourge* would need to race at top speed into the fire of an alerted enemy's heavy guns to deliver her torpedoes: *Diana* could creep unseen to within half a mile of her target and spit out her secret messengers, each capped with half a ton of explosive.

Here was one of those messengers now, and it was ready to be loaded into its tube, to be loosed at *Scourge.* Beside the chart-table in the control-room a polished lever would jerk back; one hundred and forty feet farther for'ard, a punch of air at a pressure of three thousand pounds per square inch would enter the tube. Snug in its steel womb the torpedo, for a fractional instant, would resist; long enough for the propellant air to build up and exert its full force. Under the vehement thrust the shining cylinder would speed forward. A metal lug projecting down from the top of the tube would catch against a small steel hook in the top of the torpedo as it raced past. The powerful engine would start instantly. Before the torpedo had lost its initial impetus it would be running on its own engine, twin propellers keeping it on course, acting in concert with a vertical rudder.

A few yards ahead of *Diana's* bow, water pressure would act on a hydrostatic valve; the two horizontal rudders behind the spinning screws would move, bringing the torpedo back to the correct depth-setting, the depth to make it miss *Scourge's* belly by a few feet. In the control-room they would feel the concussive thrust of the compressed air, and the slight lift as the submarine's bow shed the torpedo's weight. The propelling air would be sucked back into the tube-space—if it had followed the torpedo past the bow-cap it would have risen to the surface in a large revealing bubble.

". . . Petty Officer Trunnion," Deevers was saying. Cowan put aside his imaginings and looked up. "Our torpedo instructor— he'll give you a run around what happens."

"Pleasure, sir."

Cowan saw a small fat man in greasy overalls. He was smiling tentatively, and Cowan got the impression that the smile could willingly extend into a genial grin; he was also impressed by a pair of eyes that looked at him with keen intelligence from between chubby folds of fat.

"Good morning," Cowan smiled back. He was not all averse to Trunnion's instruction, being confident that he would have forgotten more about torpedoes than Deevers, an ordinary executive officer detailed as torpedo officer, had ever known.

"We'd better start with the tubes, sir."

Cowan followed him forward towards the banks of white cylinders, seeing out of the corner of his eye Deevers step back and sit down on the ladder leading up to the torpedo-loading hatch. He climbed on to the steel grating behind the breeches of the tubes, and Trunnion pointed to the heavy rear door of a lower one.

"That's the firing tube this morning, Number Four. We pump the fish out with compressed air—but you'd know that?"

"Yes," Cowan nodded, "we mount ten of 'em. But I'd like to know how you manage the little detail of water—we were down to sixty feet when I came for'ard."

"No black magic about it," Trunnion smiled, and rubbed his fleshy nose, leaving a scar of black grease. "There are two doors —bow-cap at the other end, and the rear door, here. The bow cap's shut now, and the tube is dry. We just open the. . . ."

"How do you know the tube's dry?" Cowan broke in.

"Good point that—the *Thetis* was lost because they thought the tube was dry." He leaned forward and worked back a locking device in the centre of the concave door. A small hole was revealed. Picking up a slender length of metal hanging on a chain Trunnion rammed the hole with it. Nothing came out.

"That's how," he grunted, straightening back. "If the bow-cap had been accidentally left open and the tube was full, you'd get a nice jet from that hole."

Cowan's lips pursed in a soundless whistle. You'd get one hell of a jet of pressured water if that *door* were opened and the tube wasn't dry! A flooding inlet from the sea outside, two feet wide. . . .

"There's another important safety device, inside the tube," Trunnion said. "As you'll know, the fish's engine is started by a hook coming up against a lug in the top of the tube as the fish shoots forward ahead of its compressed air."

"I think I've got it," Cowan said, nodding. "When you load the torpedo you must make sure its starting-hook doesn't come up against the lug?"

"You've got it." Trunnion's voice sounded grim. Cowan glanced at him curiously.

"A big worry of mine," the instructor answered the look. "I've never known it to happen, but it could."

"You mean the engine starting prematurely . . . ?"

"That's what I mean. There are stops in there to prevent the torpedo—while we're loading it—from coming up against the firing-tripper. If the stops weren't fully engaged. . . ."

"Then . . . ?"

"Then the engine would start to run. We'd have what we call a hot run on our hands. Several nasty things could happen then —the air vessel of a torpedo is loaded with air at four thousand pounds pressure. If it got loose. . . ." He glanced sideways at his listener, his face creasing so that his eyes were almost hidden. "Ah well, we wouldn't know much about it anyway."

"Remind me to watch the firing from the control-room," the destroyerman grimaced.

"The commander wants you up here to watch. We're doing a firing-run at *Scourge,* and maybe he thinks the control-room might be a bit crowded with visitors there."

"I expect he does," Cowan answered briefly. Suddenly he felt he didn't want to hear any more about possible accidents; he had a sailor's superstition about tempting Fate.

"What are those nozzle things on that pipe?" he asked, bending to look back into the stowage compartment.

"That's our built-in breathing system," Trunnion told him. "In case of flooding, we plug in with our masks or breathing-tubes. That canvas comes down and forms a trunk to the escape-hatch."

"Well, thanks, Chief. We won't be firing for a bit? I'd like to take another look at the control-room."

"You'll be right, sir—*Scourge* has to find us before we let her have one. See you later."

"Yes." Cowan bent his head and stepped back into the stowage compartment. Deevers levered himself up from the ladder.

"Know all about it?"

"Enough, I think. All right if I watch in the control-room while *Scourge* makes her run?"

Deevers nodded, and Cowan got the feeling he was pleased to be rid of him. "You can find your way back? Straight down the passage."

"Thanks." Cowan passed through the next hatch, and was struck again by the heaviness of the door and its clips.

Ransome was straightening up from the Asdic cabinet when

Cowan walked into the control-room. He smiled at his guest. "I was about to send for you. We've contacted *Scourge* and I think she'll be starting her run in. Here."

He handed Cowan the spare set of phones. The control-room was quiet, and the lieutenant heard clearly in his phones a steady, rhythmic beat.

CHAPTER TWELVE

Scourge's bridge was also quiet. Brady stood against the fore windbreak, his hands on the turned-over copper edge. Here there was little wind, the design of the bridge superstructure deflecting it out and upwards. Behind him Mr. Seymour, officer of the watch, stood at the binnacle, handy to the wheelhouse voice-pipe, swaying easily as the ship corkscrewed in the increasing swell.

On their starb'd beam the three ships of the squadron were disposed in line-abreast—the squadron was steaming northward in a searching sweep almost three miles wide. Every ship was operating her Asdic, the sound-beams overlapping in an embracing fan of sensitivity. If the submarine were hiding in that area ahead of them she would be detected; the successful ship would remain in contact, and the others, directed by the squadron leader and guided by the destroyer in contact, would rush in to the attack, dropping hand-grenades to simulate depth-charges.

Scourge's bridge was quiet and intent, but elsewhere the crew went about their normal duties, for this exercise occupied only the Asdic team. On the quarterdeck three seamen were engaged in the never-ending battle with rust—the sound of their chipping hammers came rhythmically to the bridge, at that distance a pleasant pointer to normal working routine. On B-gun deck directly below Brady two fo'c'slemen were greasing the pins of the guard-rail stanchions, ensuring that if the ship had to go into action the guard-rails could be dropped instantly to clear the line of fire of the big twin guns.

Brady watched them idly, hearing the resonant ping of the Asdic transmission from the loudspeaker on his left, with no answering peep of contact, and he was thinking that neither of those two men busily engaged under his eye had ever lowered those rails in action; he wondered briefly if they thought their precautionary work pointless. The violent days had gone, sliding back into the limbo of merely remembered things; and the weapons of destruction had become so terrifying powerful and embracing that the violent days might have gone for ever. Now they were only playing at war; now, certainly, was the time to leave those games and begin the new reality of a lifetime with Beth. The violent days were surely gone. . . .

"Wind's veering to the south-east, sir," Mr. Seymour, the gunner, offered conversationally. Brady nodded, turning his head a little in acknowledgment. He had already noticed the shift in direction, and the wind's increasing strength, as he had already studied the forecast, which predicted gale-force winds tonight. But they would be snug in harbour well before the big wind struck; and in any case a gale was of little significance to a Fleet destroyer and a submarine—both classes of ships were designed to make their way against bad weather, even to fight while so doing.

But Seymour's casual words did spark a thought in his mind. He glanced out at the sea to starb'd, judging its force as the waves ran level with him. He judged, and the thought died—the boat recovering the torpedo could ride much rougher seas than those.

A sharp "peep" pitched across the bridge. "Contact, sir," Seymour reported unnecessarily; and, a moment later, "classified submarine".

Brady took his place behind the binnacle.

For fifteen minutes *Scourge* hunted her quarry, her sonic fingers in constant echoing contact with *Diana's* steel hull. From his own ship's alterations of course, and from the pencil lines on the plot he could see by looking down through the viewing-screen into the room below, Brady knew what Ransome was up to as clearly as if the submarine had been on the surface. He also knew that Slocum was at his best, enveloping the target, following her wherever she dropped and twisted and fled. He wondered: what is he feeling down there? Is he filled with hate, feeling in the Asdic pulses his own vengeful intentions tapping at the submarine's hull, knowing he had his wife's seducer as securely gripped in his power as he has his vessel?

Brady grinned at himself: Slocum was probably simply absorbed in his job.

He gave an order and *Scourge* went in to the attack.

Three times the squadron made its run-in, and three times the flung grenades belted their triumphant message against the submarine's hull. The destroyers' success was no reflection on Ransome's competence—had he been faced with only one ship, or had he been able to retaliate with torpedoes, the success-story would have been different; but with four anti-submarine vessels on top of him, he had no hope of evasion once contact had been established.

Satisfied with his ships' manoeuvring, Brady hauled them off and made the signal returning them to base. The exercise plan, carefully prepared and to be meticulously followed, now required Ransome to make his actual firing-run at *Scourge*. The destroyer was to steam on a set course to the north, zigzagging normally as she would if proceeding in wartime or screening a convoy. *Diana* would line her up and fire one torpedo. Then she would surface, a sea-boat from *Scourge* recovering the missile in the meantime. After lunch ashore the captain of *Lockyer* would go aboard the submarine, and out at sea again the second torpedo would be fired. At present there was no point in wasting the time and fuel of the three destroyers not employed.

Scourge cruised in a circle for ten minutes, until Slocum reported that he had lost contact with *Diana*. During that time Brady watched his squadron wheel to port, seeing the decks lean as the rudders went over, the bow-waves streaking back against the grey sides like the flashing strokes of a giant white brush. Then they were right round, and he was looking at their stems, low-hung at twenty-five knots, spawning mounds of tossing white on the blue sea. Those were the dominant colours of his years afloat: the white of wave or bow-wave, the blue of deep water; the blue of sky and the white of clouds. It was time for a change, he grinned to himself—the green of leaves and grass.

"Shall I set course, sir?" the navigator asked, and wondered secretly at the genial look on his captain's face—surely he'd seen enough of destroyers!

"Yes, please," Brady turned back to his business. "Start the zigzag." A moment later he felt his own ship heel, and said to Seymour: "Post extra look-outs. I don't want to miss that torpedo."

"They're on their way, sir," the gunner answered, and pointed to the foremast, where a seaman, his binoculars slung round his neck, was climbing carefully up to the crow's nest.

"Right! Warn the sea-boat's crew they'll be needed any time from now on."

"Aye aye, sir."

Scourge cruised northward. Now Barrenjoey Lighthouse was on her port bow—they had been up and down past it all morning

—and Brady braced his legs apart as the waves, coming at her from starb'd, screwed her nose down into the valleys streaked with white.

The wind was rising, he felt; he turned his cheek and was sure of it. If the gale reached them sooner than he expected, he might cancel the second torpedo firing. Twenty-one-inch torpedoes cost many thousands of pounds, and he did not relish the thought of trying to find one in gale-driven seas and perhaps returning to base without it. But the time for decision was not yet. If the seas really got up he would confer with Ransome when he surfaced after this firing; the worst result, after all, would be that he would get ashore earlier and have more time out at Whale Beach.

His mind on Beth, his thoughts moved farther. Navy Office might act quickly on his resignation; in important things like the command of a destroyer squadron they usually did. He could be relieved sooner than he expected. It was a mere two hours to Melbourne by air—his letter would be there now; for all he knew, a posting signal might be racing through the ether already. If it were, this would be the last time he took a ship to sea—he would spend the rest of his Service time in harbour turning over to the relieving captain.

It might be a long time before he experienced this again—the mile-long wave swelling up under *Scourge's* engine-room, the momentary pause until she moved on with the thrust of her screws while the wave passed amidships. Now the destroyer's bow dipped to the trough and her stern lifted; he could plainly feel the brief shaking as the propellers came closer to the surface. Then the stern slid on and a smooth hill of water was left behind, marbled white where the wake ran up and over it. The sight reminded him of the youth on the surfboard, seeming to slide down the green face of his wave. But he was dependent on its forward motion for his own; *Scourge* was a separate entity, superior in speed and strength to any wave. . . .

The sharp buzz from a voice-pipe cut stridently into his thoughts. His head jerked round. The buzz came again, loud and long, imperative with emphasis and urgency.

Seymour was at the open mouth of the pipe in two bounds. For a moment his head hid the pipe, then he swung round and upright, his eyes grabbing at Brady's face. His voice sprang crisp and emphatic across the bridge.

"Heavy underwater explosion, bearing Green eight-five!"

Brady leaped for the binnacle, his brain working at lightning speed. Green eight-five would be the natural bearing for the

submarine to fire from, on their beam; but it was Slocum who
had put the urgency into that report. It could not be any ordinary
or expected sound that had startled Slocum's expert ear: something was wrong with *Diana*. He reached the wheel-house voice-
pipe and his orders clipped out fast and sure.

"Starb'd thirty, full ahead together!" To the bosun's mate, his
youthful eyes round with interest: "Cox'n on the wheel!" To
the signal yeoman, staring at him, waiting: "Recall *Lockyer*!"

The yeoman nodded, two quick jerks of his head, but he did
not turn to his signal lamp.

"Will I send 'Subsmash', sir?"

There it was, out in the open, and Brady calmed his surging
feelings. What did he know of submarines? It might have been
a torpedo exploding well clear, or almost anything but the one
he dreaded.

"Not yet. Get *Lockyer* back, full speed. Pilot! Put us on the
chart—exactly. Guns!" The pause in his speech and the demand
in his eyes brought Seymour to him quickly. "In my cabin . . .
a blue book on the desk, Subsmash organization." Brady spoke
in a low voice. Seymour turned without speaking and jumped
for the ladder.

All this time *Scourge* had been swinging round. A disembodied
voice came up the pipe: "Cox'n on the wheel, sir." Her nose
wiped round the horizon, she was feeling the increased thrust of
her screws, and as she came into the eye of the wind her motion
became progressively more violent.

Now she was forcing directly into wind and wave. Her speed
magnified the effect of the seas. High ridges of water swept down
upon her from the southward—long rolling furrows of dark
green topped with foaming white, which met her thrusting bow
and exploded up over her flares in abrupt cascades of spray.
Most of the water surged down the fo'c'sle deck until it met the
breakwater; balked there, it washed to both sides and streamed
away seaward. The rest of it was picked up by the wind and
flung towards the bridge, where it drove into the faces of Brady
and his officers.

Now at her full speed ahead, the destroyer rose and plunged
and screwed down sideways, crunching water from under her
sharp bows, rolling water from her cambered decks, trucking her
masts of violent sweeps across the clouding sky. The only stable
part of her equipment was that which normally swung with the
slightest breeze—her ensign, stiffened by the tide of air, stood

out rigidly from the main mast. Red, white and blue, it streamed
from the halyard, and only the extreme after-edge of it oscillated
in tiny snapping movements. On the foremast above the bridge,
the radar aerial swung round and round with unimpassioned
efficiency, shafting out its electronic particles at the speed of
light. In all that windswept waste there was nothing unrecog-
nized from which to echo—the particles lost themselves in the
vast immensity of the Pacific.

Wiping his wet face with a sodden handkerchief, ignoring the
need for oilskins—this mad bucking would ease when he slowed
her down—Brady wondered why he had not heard the explosion
himself: water was an excellent conductor, better than air. He
decided that *Diana* must have been a mile away, and only the
concussive shock, not the sound of the explosion, had reached
out to *Scourge's* hull. He was lifting his glasses for the tenth time
to study the area ahead of the bow, when Seymour's voice reached
him above the howl of the wind.

"Bearing right ahead, range half a mile!"

One part of Brady's mind wondered briefly why Seymour, a
gunnery officer trained to identify the object sighted, had failed
to name it this time. He put his glasses to his eyes and then he
knew why. Seymour would not have seen anything like this before.
It was not an eruption, nothing like the wall of water hurled
up by a depth-charge: it was simply a big, quiet bubble, which
swelled but did not break. The bubble subsided, and as they
stared another took its place; smaller this time, smoothing the
sea about it; then came a quick succession of even smaller swell-
ings: surface evidence of catastrophe in the depths below.

"Half ahead together," Brady ordered. There was no doubt
now. To take that time to affect the surface the explosion must
have been a deep one, and powerful. A torpedo would have been
fired at periscope depth, a mere thirty feet; its explosion would
have flung a scarf of white spray into the air. He spoke to Slocum
himself, even though the Asdic ping was innocent of any echoing peep.

"Any contact yet, Slocum?"

"No, sir," Slocum's voice came quickly from the loudspeaker.
"I'm sweeping well on either side of the bearing, but nothing yet."

"You must find her, Slocum, we must have her pin-pointed."

"Yes, sir, but if she's on the bottom it mightn't be easy. I'm doing
all. . . ." His voice was audible to all on the bridge; its sudden
cessation brought their heads round. The echoing peep, blurred

with interference, but still identifiable, pitched across the bridge a second before his voice.

"Contact, sir! Bearing Red oh-five, range one thousand!"

It was something, it was a small triumph: they had found her. Brady moved swiftly back to the binnacle.

"Slow ahead together! Steer oh-eight-oh! Tell the engine-room —stand-by for manoeuvring!"

He came upright from the voice-pipe and his squinted stare caught at the signal-yeoman.

"Send 'Subsmash'," he ordered, his voice harsh.

With the submarine coursing to get into firing position, and Number One on watch at the order-panel, Ransome leaned back against the chart-table. For the next ten minutes or so there was little for him to do. They knew *Scourge's* bearing and range, the beat of the destroyer's screws travelling much farther through the conducting water than the comparatively minor tapping of her Asdic pulse; they were well clear of her, travelling on a converging course which would put them forward of her beam. Through their magnifying hydrophones, they had heard her steaming northwards, offering herself as target to their torpedo.

Ransome's eyes dropped to the chart, and he noted idly that the depth was round about thirty fathoms—an average of two hundred feet. Waiting for word from the tube-compartment for'ard, he let his eye run on, hearing Wetherell behind him give a quiet trimming order. There was no other sound in the control-room except the muted whine of the electric motors—*Diana* was at one hundred feet, quite stable, below the turbulence of the windy surface.

Barrenjoey, Whale Beach, Avalon, Newport, Collaroy, Dee Why—the names met his roving eye; Long Reef, with the mark "Bomboras" beside its spiky outline, warning the seaman of boiling whirlpools where waves crashed over half-submerged rocks; "Water Tower", marking a prominent identification useful for navigation on the plateau above Collaroy. Whale Beach— nothing there of navigational use, only the name of the beach; nothing of a large white house on the cliff, nor its happy connection with a man one hundred feet below the surface and another on a bridge at sea ten miles to the east of it. . . .

A buzzer sounded, short and loud in the enclosed quiet. The seaman who answered the phone listened, then looked at Ransome.

"Ready to load Number Four tube, sir."

Ransome took a precautionary glance round the compartment.
Course two-eighty, in towards the land; speed six knots; target
contacted, well clear; depth one hundred feet. Everything was in
order—his check had been automatic.

"Carry on," he ordered crisply. The seaman spoke into the
phone and Ransome said to Wetherell:

"As soon as they're finished for'ard we'll come up to periscope
depth and take a look." He glanced at his watch; it would not
take long to load the torpedo. "You can get the attack-team
closed-up now."

"Aye aye, sir."

In the torpedo-stowage compartment directly abaft the tubes
Cowan kept clear to one side, leaning his back against a canvas
bunk marked "Mac's Sack". He had heard Deevers report ready,
and now he watched the long torpedo hauled forward towards
the rear door of its tube. The torpedo-men handled it easily—
Diana was quite steady at this depth. Apart from the steady hiss
of air from the ventilating punkahs and the grunts of the men as
they hauled on their tackles there was complete quiet, no sound of
wind or wave to indicate that he wasn't ashore in some machine-
shop instead of being in a submarine below a pressured column
of water.

Down on the steel grating beside the rear door Trunnion
looked up at Deevers. The torpedo officer nodded. Trunnion
unlocked the vent, and probed it with his metal reamer. Dry.
Then the unlocking lever, and finally the big clips. Cowan saw
the heavy circular door swing silently open, and looked into the
dark maw of the tube. Deevers said:

"Control-room? Number Four tube rear door open."

Every detail, every movement, Cowan thought, premeditated
and checked and reported. Deevers said:

"Come on then, let's load the thing. I've got something waiting
ashore tonight even if you haven't." He chuckled. Cowan noticed
that no one laughed. Deevers stared sourly at Trunnion, who
interpreted the look behind a bland face. He gave an order and
the tackles tightened and the long steel shape moved forward.

As only one torpedo was to be fired there were three men apart
from Trunnion in the compartment. The brightly-painted head
was about to enter the tube when its smooth progress was
halted.

"Now what's wrong?" Deevers demanded irritably.

"Nothing much, sir." Trunnion examined the point where

the torpedo rested in the cradle. "Stuck here, sir. All right, men
—take her back a bit to clear her."

"Take it back . . . !" Deevers fumed. "The damned thing
should have been fired by now. Come on, put some weight into
it! D'you think we've got all day? I've reported we were loading.
Pull your fingers out!"

So there we have it, Cowan thought wryly—we've reported
we're loading, and we must prove to the captain we're efficient.
You clot—Ransome wants safety, not speed. His reflections were
interrupted.

"Hop in there behind the tubes," Deevers told him, glancing at
him briefly.

Cowan hesitated. "Do you think there's room?" His voice, in
the novelty of his position, was uncertain.

"I know there's room. This is mainly for your benefit, you
know—it might be a good idea if you saw it."

Swift annoyance flushed in Cowan's face. He was senior in
rank to Deevers, he had been spoken to sneeringly in front of
able seamen, but he was angered chiefly by Deevers's plain nasti-
ness. There was no need for it—they were not trying to break
records for loading. Perhaps it was due to the pointed lack of
appreciation of Deevers's humour a few minutes before.

Cowan held on to his anger.

"Very well," he answered coldly, and easing past the men,
climbed through the hatch on to the grating behind the tubes.
Everyone was conscious of the silence in the compartment.
Because they expect unanimity of purpose amongst their officers,
sailors are embarrassed by even a slight conflict between them.

"All right, all right," Deevers snapped, "what are we waiting
for? Get it moving, Trunnion."

They bent their backs and silently took the weight on the
tackle. They themselves might call Petty Officer Trunnion by
all sorts of names behind his back, but no officer, not even the
captain, called him by his surname. Regulations required, in
fact, that the prefix of a man's rate be given before his name,
whether he were able seaman, leading seaman or petty officer.
And common courtesy required that the senior torpedo rating
in the boat be addressed properly in front of his men.

Deevers had succeeded in getting their backs up. Trunnion
gave his orders and the men heaved sullenly. The nose slid into
the gaping hole; the practice blowing-head vanished from Cowan's
sight, then the big pressured air-vessel, then the engine-room with

its starting-hook. The torpedo stopped again, its tapered tail and twin screws and rudders still outside the tube.

"*Now* what's wrong?" Deevers demanded from where he stood back in the stowage compartment.

"Nothing wrong, sir," Trunnion answered him, and the calm politeness in his voice was an unpunishable insult. "We've run out of tackle, sir, it's two blocks." Cowan could see that the tackle was now vertical—it could only lift, not heave forward.

"Right," Trunnion said to his men, his tone now crisp, "shift tackle to the tail."

Quickly the hook of the lower block was secured to the big steel wedge which fitted over the very end of the propeller shaft and prevented the screws from turning, or being damaged.

"All right, girls," Deevers said from behind them, his voice sarcastic, "we've mucked around enough. I want it in on one heave."

Cowan heard Trunnion whisper "Easy!" in a warning tone; then heard Deevers order raspingly:

"Stand-by! One, two, six—*heave!*"

Disgusted, viciously the men heaved. The rest of the steel shape shot forward into the tube. It may have been their extra strength, it may have been that the engaging stops were faulty. The torpedo slid in, jerking momentarily as it came up against the stops; the tackle was slack and the wedge on the shaft dropped with a steely clang to the deck; the torpedo moved on. The firing lug did its job with unimpassioned efficiency. The diesel engine started with a clattering roar.

"*Jesus!*"

Trunnion's exclamation was lost behind the strident hammering of the engine. The steel tube and the steel compartment magnified its noise ten-fold. For an instant they glared at the spinning screws, their brains numbed by novelty and danger. Then Trunnion, standing in the stowage compartment with Deevers, flung himself forward, his hands scrabbling at the hatch, his eyes on the open rear door of the tube.

"The door! The door!" he shouted, his voice cracking with urgency. Cowan jumped forward, at the same time as the seaman on the other side of the tube. Bent down towards the door, his head met the other's shoulder. His feet slid uncontrollably backwards on the greasy steel grating. As he went down, taking the seaman with him, their bodies sprawling across the open mouth of the tube, he heard above the scream of the heating engine, the sharp persistent buzzing of a telephone. It was the last thing he heard.

Denied cooling water, racing inside the heat-confining walls of the tube, the engine went up first. Heated by the engine and already under four thousand pounds per square inch pressure, the violence in the air-vessel was stirring: the shock of the engine exploding was more than it needed.

Directly behind the tube, in the stowage compartment, Trunnion heard nothing—his ear-drums were blown in before a vast breath of air picked him up like thistle-down and flung him to the after-end of the compartment.

Deevers heard the roar. He was twenty-five feet away, his hands scrabbling frantically at the clips of the water-tight door, his mind activated by one desperate thought. The explosion slammed him against the bulkhead, crushing the breath from his body. He slid down to the deck, gasping, his head turned forward, his eyes fastened on the cataract of green water plunging through the shattered bulkhead behind the tubes.

He saw a man washing towards him, a black shape tossing and tumbling, and he began to slide towards him. His bemused brain dimly realized that the deck was tilting down. He came up against the ladder leading to the torpedo-loading hatch and with desperate strength he gripped the rungs. Water was boiling round his knees when he hauled himself upright. He staggered back towards the after bulkhead door—beyond that was dryness, and air, and safety. His hands were on the clips, tugging, his gasping face was pouring with sweat from the heat of the compressing air, when a voice screamed at him, reaching him above the steady roar of the eager sea.

"No! No! You'll flood the boat!"

His hands still tugging, he twisted round to look at Trunnion, coming for him on hands and knees, only his head above the lashing water. He had one clip off when Trunnion's hands grabbed him round the thighs. The next second he had lost his grip and was sliding and splashing down the inclined deck.

He shook his head, shaking his eyes clear of water, and pushed himself up with his hands on Trunnion's shoulders. The torpedo-man came up after him. They stood in front of each other beside the ladder, gripping its rigidity in this world of tugging water. Trunnion felt a fumbling at his legs. Without taking his eyes from Deevers he bent down and grabbed with one hand. Daniels, a rating who had been with him in the stowage compartment, handled himself up the ladder-rungs, coughing with violent spasms.

". . . open the door!" Deevers was screaming, "our only chance! We can shut it again!"

Trunnion could not hear him but he guessed his meaning.

"No!" he shook his head emphatically. "Open it, it stays open . . . flood the boat!"

Deevers stared back at him. He was panting in quick little jerks through his open mouth; his eyes glared into Trunnion's with demoniacal rebuff of everything he had said. Keeping one hand gripped round the ladder Trunnion reached out and twisted his other fist into Deevers's shirt. Then he stared about him.

There were ways, there was something they could do. He strove to bring sense and intelligent thought out of the chaos of shock and fear in his brain: this had been allowed for, there were escape measures provided. Life-jackets! The B.B.S.! There were the jackets, not ten feet away, stowed in their neat little boxes. They had to get to them. This was no normal flooding. The air would not be simply trapped under pressure in the compartment as the water rose; it would be escaping through what was left of the bows, even now bubbling up to the surface, reducing their chances with every second.

"Life-jackets!" he shouted at Deevers and released his hold. He had taken one step towards the stowage boxes when the boat gave a violent tilt downwards. Only a desperate out-flinging of his hand caught the ladder and prevented him from being thrown down under the black, rising water.

The lights went out.

Trunnion was engulfed in darkness and silence. He could see nothing, hear nothing; he could feel the coldness of the water rising up round his shoulders and the heat of the compressed air on his face. Then he felt something else—the start of a throbbing pain in his belly. Instinctively, panting for breath, he lowered one hand and rubbed it tentatively across his stomach. He pressed, and a jolt of pain shocked through him. .Then he brought his hand up, holding it in front of his face, looking for signs of blood. He stared for three seconds before he realized he could not see, and that the water would have washed any blood away.

He felt the cold grip round his throat; water washed into his panting mouth and he tasted the oily foulness of it. Hysteria rose in him, flooding into his brain, bubbling into his throat. His mouth opened to form a scream. With all his will and manhood he crushed the scream back. He forced himself to think.

In the few seconds since the explosion the boat must have dropped a hundred feet; he knew from the weight on his arms as he clung to the ladder that she was tilted acutely down by the bow. Therefore the for'ard end of the compartment would be full, from deck to deckhead: that should mean that their end, aft, would retain its bubble of air, like a corked bottle, half-full and tilted. The air could not escape through the water—it was being pressed tightly against the deckhead above them.

Shortly they should hit the bottom. On the configuration of the bottom their lives depended. If the bow landed on a rise the water inside would surge backwards and their pocket of air could flow out; if the boat slewed over on its side they would be flung under the oily surface.

His mind twisted away from the ghastly possibilities. Almost with relief he fastened on the pain in his belly. Something was torn in there, he knew it. Something had happened when he had been blown back—it had been caused either by the force of the explosion or by a blow against a projection.

He felt a fist rapping at his ribs. He guessed it was Daniels, and that the seaman was shouting something. He shouted back "I can't hear you! Ears gone!" and then a violent contractive spasm tore at his guts.

Instinctively he doubled over, gasping with the shock of the pain. His face went under the greasy water and he had swallowed several mouthfuls before he could straighten up again. With his eyes squinted closed against the searing of the oil he strained his head back, straining to keep his mouth clear. Dully he realized that the cold ring had risen no farther up his throat. The pressure of water and air in the compartment was equalized.

Then *Diana's* torn-open bow struck the bottom.

The submarine's whole hull was a resonant steel sounding-board. In the control-room they had heard the distant roar and clatter of the dry-running engine. It was Ransome's snapped order which had sent the telephone buzzing its query as Cowan was blown into oblivion.

He had ordered "Shut water-tight doors!" and the heavy hatches were slamming through the boat, the clips thudding home, dividing her into tight little compartments, when the torpedo blew up.

The effect was more violent than of a pattern of depth

charges; the force was that of a direct hit. *Diana* reeled under the club of the explosion and her hull vibrated and rang like an enormous tuning-fork. The control-room was a huge reverberating cavern. A bulb was shaken from the deckhead and exploded with an unheard pop beside Ransome's sliding feet; from above him cork in the paint was jerked loose and showered down in a fine white rain. Then came a noise like real rain—the sound of water washing violently back through the casings.

The ringing ceased, the rain through the casings faded into silence. The deck tilted like a seesaw, and in the sudden quiet a high-pitched, gibbering scream sheared out and slashed horribly at the officers' lacerated nerves.

Ransome had been shouting orders, though he knew that if the two for'ard compartments had flooded, he had no chance of holding her. Clinging with one hand to a ventilating pipe overhead, the first-lieutenant was operating his order-panel, knowing that it would be a miracle if the stokers manning the pumps aft had not been hurled off their feet. When the screaming began, Ransome's head jerked round. His stare took in a man braced against the door of the Asdic cabinet, retching on the deck through abrupt nervous strain, and swung on to find the origin of that horrible sound. He saw the periscope watchkeeper standing with his hands gripped round a pipe and his head back and his mouth strained open, and Ransome knew that if the screaming did not stop, his whole crew might panic.

He released his grip of the chart-table and slid down the sloping deck, bringing up with a jolt against the blowing-panel. His face hard and purposeful, he clawed his way across to the watch-keeper and his big hands went out to the man's throat. One hand grasping the back of his neck, he clamped the fingers of his other hand over the open mouth. Sharply, he knocked the man's head back against the brass edge of a big gauge. His head sagged forward; the screaming stopped.

"I can't hold her, sir," Number One called. His voice was urgent, but steady. Ransome did not answer. He leaned sideways so that he could see the depth-gauge: the needle in front of the hydroplane operators, still in their bolted-down seats, was swing-ing round the bland face of the dial quickly and smoothly. It was coming up to one hundred and fifty feet.

Ransome handled himself back towards the periscope. The coxswain, who had closed-up at the forward hydroplane for the firing-run, extended his hand. Ransome grabbed it and hauled himself up beside Number One. The two officers looked at each other, and between them was the understanding of catastrophe and the need to keep calm, to think. Ransome shifted his eyes to the depth gauge.

"We'll hit the bottom shortly," he said, his voice dry and rasping. He coughed to clear his throat. "Depth here is about two hundred feet."

With the attack-team closed-up the control-room was crowded. At Ransome's words every head turned to the gauge. One hundred and eighty feet. *Diana's* engines had been stopped, then ordered astern to take the forward way off her. Only a few seconds had passed and nobody knew yet whether the intention had succeeded. They could only hope that the boat was dropping down, angled by the bow, and not driving forward and down as well.

"As soon as we hit, get a damage report," Ransome ordered Number One. Wetherell nodded, watching the gauge. Two hundred feet. The needle still swung. They could not afford much more depth and ascend alive.

The black needle moved on, travelling now on the downward slope of the right-hand side of the gauge, towards the boat's maximum designed depth; moving efficiently, dispassionately, offering its message, unmoved by the fear in the faces and minds willing it to stop.

Two hundred and five, seven, eight. . . .

"God!" Number One burst out, "it can't. . . ."

Abruptly he was flung against Ransome. They landed on the deck in a tangle of limbs, feeling other men on top of them, hearing the tearing crunch as *Diana* ploughed over the bottom, feeling her frame shuddering, grinding. . . .

The shaking ceased, the grinding of metal stopped; there were only the grunts and curses of men.

"Up!" Ransome snarled, "get up, damn you!"

They struggled clear and he scrambled to his feet. His legs felt an almost even keel and his eyes saw their depth—two hundred and ten feet, a fraction more. He lurched to the conning-tower ladder, shouldering men aside, and when he got there he turned round to face them, panting, his stare steady, surveying them one by one.

"Anyone hurt?" He kept his voice level. A dull chorus answered him. The coxswain said, a grin in his voice: "Feeling a bit low, sir."

Mentally Ransome thanked him, appreciating the deliberate effort behind the grin. The men looked back at Ransome with anxiety but without panic.

"Right, Number One," Ransome said briskly, "we'll have that damage report."

He knew that he had to maintain normal discipline and routine, had to show his crew that this extraordinary situation was still part of their Service lives, anticipated in their training and provided for by their mechanical facilities. He thought of waiting until he could speak to all of them left alive, *en masse*: but that might be possible only when he had them crowded in the escape-compartment aft, and then their concentration would be required for what they had to do. Many of his seamen were with him now in the control-room, and now was the time to give them a boost—their demeanour would communicate itself to the stokers and others when the time came for escape.

"Listen to me, men," he began, and realized that if ever he had given an unnecessary injunction, he had just then. He understood also that he had to keep his talk technical—there must be no suggestion that they might lose their heads.

"We can assume that there was a dry run in Number Four tube, and that the air-vessel went up. By the way we came down, the fore-ends and the torpedo-stowage compartment are flooded. Now, we have. . . ."

"Sir?"

Ransome looked at Number One, as did every other face.

"Engine-room and after-ends report no damage, sir, no casualties."

Ransome nodded acknowledgment. Behind his sober expression hope was leaping—the after escape-compartment was clear and dry and safe. It would be horribly unpleasant, but they could get out. He turned back to the men, and the coxswain, understanding, admired his calm acceptance of this vital news; Ransome might have been receiving a report on the bread supply.

"We have," he resumed, "a very strong submarine. You heard the report from aft. The escape-compartment is clear. We have plenty of air, and the CO_2 machine to purify it, as well as oxygen cylinders. We're at two hundred feet, not much more than the escape tower you've all been through at Gosport."

He talked on, and it took all his willpower to stand there before them, when his professional instinct was urging him to get on with the score of things waiting for his attention. But he knew he had to attend to the human element first. Out of the corner of his eye he could see Number One listening on the phone, and knew he was talking to someone in the accommodation space, the compartment directly beyond the water-tight door of the control-room.

"We have destroyer *Scourge* up top, with a highly experienced captain in command. They will have heard the explosion, and will now be on their way to us. We have every chance of making it up top. But there's no hurry—it was starting to blow when we dived, and there's no point in getting up there before the destroyers are on the scene ready to haul us aboard."

He had finished—there was nothing technical left to say, and he would not appeal to their steadiness; they must believe he took that for granted. He was relieved when Wetherell said, his voice controlled but urgent:

"Sir? Word from the accommodation space. The stowage-compartment bulkhead's holding—but it's leaking through communication and voice-pipe trunking."

An electric awareness was in the room. The leaking bulkhead was not important; where it was pierced by electrical leads and voice-pipe glands, it was expected to leak; and even if it went, Number Three bulkhead, the one protecting the control-room, was undamaged and would hold. There were seamen and artificers and stoker petty officers in the accommodation space—their messes took up almost all of it; but they could be got through into the control-room in a few seconds. What everyone was thinking was that under the removable corticene squares of the deck in there lay great banks of batteries, more than three hundred of them, all filled with acid, eager to combine with salt water and produce choking chlorine gas.

"Coxswain! In there with buckets! Four men!"

"Yes, sir!" Tall and hard, the counterpart of *Scourge's* senior rating, the coxswain stabbed his finger and four seamen followed him to the bulkhead door. Everything they wanted would be in the crew space—buckets in the messes, and a plenitude of mopping-up rags. . . .

His eyes on the water-tight door, Ransome ordered Wetherell to release a marker buoy.

"Marker buoy—aye aye, sir."

Though he knew the next compartment was not flooded, the coxswain knocked off the clips gingerly. He left two on, and waited a moment. Ransome also watched. No water trickled through. With a definite gesture the coxswain cleared the door and heaved its weight back.

They smelled it at once—faint, but unmistakable; the acrid odour of chlorine. One of the four men started to cough.

"Come on, smack it about!" Ransome snapped. "That will only tickle your tonsils."

The coxswain jumped through and the others followed. They found an engine-room artificer and two seamen already at work mopping up the wet deck. Without orders the four men dived into the near-by messes for buckets and cloths. The coxswain stood back a little, smelling the gas, trying not to cough, and with expert eyes appraised the farther bulkhead. It was not bulging, but in half a dozen places water was seeping through the glands of leads and voice-pipes. At one point on the starb'd side a thin jet curved out and splashed on to the deck.

"Get a bucket under there," he ordered, pointing.

But it was the tightly closed water-tight door which fascinated him. He wished there was room in the narrow space for him to work—standing inactively there, his eyes and his mind were drawn back to that door. The men mopping below him were talking, but he hardly heard them.

"Old Nobby Clarke was in there, poor bastard. I hope he got it sudden."

Hundreds of tons of water pressing against that door. . . . Not only the weight in the two compartments, but the tremendous pressure of a column of water over two hundred feet high.

"What happened? How come a dry run? Gawd, I hope the Old Man gets us outa here soon."

The bow must be blown right open. . . . It would be quiet in there now, dark as a tomb. It was a tomb. They'd be washing about in the currents. How many? Only one fish to be fired. Not more than five of them.

"Torpedo officer . . . old Trunnion, too. Four kids—Jesus . . . !"

Must take a muster soon as I get back. Wonder the Old Man didn't order it right away. He's got enough on his mind. Got to help him. That bloke screaming. . . . Can't have that when we flood. God, if someone starts to panic then! The Old Man's handling it right. Got to help him. Got to keep them calm, keep calm myself.

Stop thinking about that door. Deevers . . . never liked him; liverish bastard, always ready to shift the subject to the old what's-'is-name. Dirty. Not clean dirt, dirty dirt. The floosies'll be waiting a long time now. Easy—he's in there, what's left of him. Pack it up—you're supposed to help the Old Man, not fly into a flap. Keep your mind on it.

"Keep it up," he said to the mopping party, "I'm going back to the commander. Baxter—in the corner there. Watch it, now. We got to keep this down till the time comes to get out. I'll be back."

He hurried aft to the control-room and found the engineer-officer talking to Ransome. The captain glanced at him.

"We can hold it all right, sir."

"The bulkhead, the door?"

"Holding, sir. No bulges. Door's tight as a drum."

"I'll take a look, sir," said Ullyet.

"Do that, Chief—the batteries too. Then get busy on clearing the escape compartment aft."

"Got 'em working on that now, sir." He stepped through the bulkhead and they heard his cough down the passage as the gas caught his throat.

"The boat's tight everywhere else," Ransome said to the coxswain, knowing the others could hear. "Get the men sitting down wherever possible. Impress on them that the less they exert themselves the less oxygen they use."

"Aye aye, sir. Ah—we'll make it all right, sir."

"Yes, I'm sure we will."

In the flooded stowage compartment it was quiet—absolutely so. At this depth, on the bottom, there were no currents. The oil-scummed water lay in the submarine's bow without movement. Its power was latent—quietly, steadily, the enormous force of its weight pressed against the bulkhead, searching for entry, finding it around the glands, squirting in thin jets out into the crew-space beyond; a persistent relentless pressure, waiting to exploit the slightest weakness in the steel wall holding it back.

A black, lightless tomb in which nothing stirred: foul with the pungent odour of oil floated up from hidden places, and the hot smell of air heated by great pressure. A place to sap the manhood and the will of the two figures clinging half-way up the steel ladder to the torpedo-loading hatch. . . .

Able Seaman Daniels was under the water, drowned by weakness and terror. Lieutenant Deevers was highest on the ladder, his head almost against the hatch; Petty Officer Trunnion, his chubby face twisted into folds of pain, stood one rung below him,

on the ladder's other side. Even with his head held back the
water was against his chin, just below his mouth. To ease the
strain, when he could no longer stand the cramp in his neck
muscles, he would dip his head forward, and then he had to keep
his mouth tightly shut.

Their lives were dependent on the pocket of air forced up by
the water into the horseshoe-shaped recess of the hatch; the shock
of the grounding had swirled the water back and so deprived
them of most of their precious air supply.

They did not talk; there was nothing to say. Deevers knew
Trunnion had no hearing, and the torpedoman's bemused mind
was activated by a dull hatred of the officer for his attempt to
open the water-tight door and endanger the boat. Trunnion was
not motivated by noble ideas of self-sacrifice for the sake of
others. He would have taken almost any means of escape from
his present frightful position. But dully in his mind, weakened
by fear and the agonizing pain in his guts, was the knowledge
that the officer should not have done what he had. His feeling
was as simple as that. You were in strife; the rest of the boat
was tight: you did not open the water-tight door of a flooding
compartment. And so he hated Lieutenant Deevers.

The thinking of Deevers was less simple but more narrow.
There was a pocket of air available, and it would last only half as
long for two men as for one. The destroyer would get a diver
down as soon as possible, and a diver, strong and fresh, could open
the torpedo-hatch from outside. A man, if he were careful, could
avoid being blown out with the air-bubble; he could wait till
the water filled the whole compartment and then he could climb
out and begin his free ascent to light and air.

One man. There was enough air in that pocket to keep one man
alive until the diver should come, tapping his message.

Salvation for both men lay a few feet away: the oxygen from
the undamaged bottles in the casing outside was waiting in the
B.B.S. pipes, and it would keep them alive indefinitely. But the
face-masks, without which they could not plug into the demand-
valves, were under the black water. Deevers was too fearful to
leave the present safety of the airlock; Trunnion was too weak.

Those had been Deevers's thoughts after the bow had struck
and they had climbed up the ladder, when his brain had been
working normally, insofar as fear allowed normality. Long
minutes had passed since then. The air pocket had now been
fouled with CO_2 from the breathing of the two men. The symp-

toms of CO_2 poisoning are laboured breathing, heart palpitation, sweating and flushing of the face. Both Deevers and Trunnion had these symptoms. CO_2 cyanosis also causes the brain to function abnormally, and the result may be that the mind is not aware that it is issuing most irregular instructions to the body.

That was why Lieutenant Deevers suddenly took his right hand from the ladder, felt for Trunnion's face, and pushed it under the water.

Trunnion was caught unready. His head went back and the water poured into his open mouth, oily and choking. But he retained his grip on the sides of the ladder. With an effort that wrenched his injured belly he pulled himself forward, lifting his head clear of the surface. He let go with one hand and raised it, clawing unscientifically through the rungs at Deevers. His hand was struck aside.

"You . . . rotten . . . bastard!" he mouthed, his words interrupted by gasps of pain.

He felt a disturbance in the water as Deevers swung his body sideways and drew back his foot. He knew with frantic certainty what Deevers was aiming for, and bent his own body away in a desperate bow. But his feet and hands were still on the ladder, and he could not withdraw nearly far enough. The next moment Deevers's foot took him with cruel force in his stomach.

The shocking pain of the blow drove Trunnion's mind over the edge of consciousness. His fingers on the ladder opened. Deevers kicked again. It was wasted effort. There was a soft surge of sound in the quiet compartment, a few lappings of water against the deckhead, then the silence returned, broken only by the panting of the survivor.

CHAPTER THIRTEEN

EMERGENCY   UNCLASSIFIED
FROM: Captain (D), *Scourge*.   TO : AIG 1051.
SUBSMASH "DIANA" DIVED POSITION 110 DEGREES BARRENJOEY
HEAD 4 MILES AT 1045. NAVY ORDER 800 REFERS. SUBMARINE
CONTACTED. HEAVY UNDERWATER EXPLOSION. "LOCKYER" IN
COMPANY. MEDICAL OFFICER IN "SCOURGE". ENDS.

On the special track for priority signals, kept open while a submarine was at sea, *Scourge's* message flashed to the naval

wireless station outside Canberra; it was immediately teleprinted
to Naval Base Headquarters at Potts Point, overlooking Garden
Island and the great dry-dock. From there the Subsmash organization went into action swiftly and smoothly.

Commander Blain was told that a helicopter was standing by
to take him out to the searching ships. The port diving-party at
Rushcutters Bay was warned, and the big decompression chamber
there was made ready, for two hundred feet is a long way to
come up in free ascent. The admiral's signal caught the two home-
coming destroyers of Brady's squadron as they were shaping up
for the Heads, and ordered them to return to the area of the
sinking, to sight and rescue survivors.

Brady on his bridge was not concerned with these shoreside
bustlings, but with conning his ship up to the marker-buoy
which the signal yeoman had sighted ahead, a little on the port
bow. Its rounded red and yellow was plainly visible now, the
buoy tilted to the left under the pressure of wind and waves.

Scourge was riding more easily with reduced speed. Brady had
the Subsmash book of reference on the chart-table beside him,
but he had not opened it. His mind, sharply retentive at any
time, had been stimulated by the disaster to his friend's boat, and
he remembered vividly most of what he had read. He knew where
Diana lay, and his task was cut by half. From now on it was
chiefly a matter of seamanship. Thank God he had had the foresight to learn what would be happening now in the submarine,
and how they would escape. Ransome and his men should reap a
rich benefit from the two days' instruction they had given him.

Above his head, at the end of the upper yard-arm, a large red
flag whipped in the wind; it indicated, as required by the blue
book on the chart-table, that *Scourge* was the ship of the Senior
Officer, Search Force.

"Slow ahead together," Brady ordered. He took her down clear
of the buoy, knowing that Ransome would hear her screws even
if his hydrophone were out of commission. He had to be quick,
but he must also be careful; and he knew that Ransome would
not begin the escape until he was sure that the destroyer was
ready to receive his men. This, with any sort of luck, Brady
could tell him by S.S.T.—underwater supersonic telegraphy. But
first he had to have a picture of how *Diana* was lying—he must
not drop a ton of anchor on her, or foul her with heavy cables.
He gave a wheel order to bring the ship round east of the buoy,
and then spoke to Slocum.

Down in the Asdic Control Room, Slocum was operating his set with the most concentrated attention. The distant explosion of *Diana's* torpedo had sounded to him something like a fire-cracker set off in a long drain-pipe. The echoes, dulled by distance, had swelled into his ears, then faded, swelled and faded again. He had not been in Asdic contact with the submarine and so did not know her range, but he knew she was outside his own maximum field of detection; he deduced that the volume of sound reaching him indicated a heavy explosion. He had reported this urgently and automatically—no thought of his wife's lover had entered his mind. Now he was in contact again. With virtuoso fingers he moved his operating wheel, playing the sonic beam slowly along *Diana's* grounded hull. He could answer Brady's question with confidence.

"Submarine lying three-one-five degrees, sir."

"Good work, Slocum," said Brady crisply. *Diana* was lying almost north-west—that coincided with her intercepting course. "All right, Pilot."

Waiting, the navigator ordered the echo-sounder to be switched on. This instrument, sited in the chart-house outside Brady's cabin, worked on much the same principle as the Asdic set, shafting out sounds which echoed from the bottom. Brady took *Scourge* out, then brought her back directly over the submarine, course north-west. The tiny shafts pulsed down—returning from the bottom, the stern, over the casing, up over the bridge, down again on the fore-casing, the bow, and back again from the ocean-bed—pulsations which tapped gently at *Diana's* contours and produced a pattern on the iodized paper of the instrument above. Satisfied, Brady ordered: "Make to *Lockyer*—'Submarine lying three-one-five degrees, two hundred and ten feet. Remain astern, stand by to pick up survivors.' Then make S.S.T. contact with *Diana*. Ask the position."

This was a crucial signal. He had no idea of the present situation inside the submarine. Someone must have been alive to release the marker-buoy, but that was fifteen minutes ago. By now the boat could be swirling with chlorine gas; she could be flooded throughout, the escape-hatches jammed. If he got no reply to his underwater signal he could do no more; if *Diana's* crew was dead, she would be merely a problem for the salvage specialists.

He put these grim thoughts away from him and conned the ship slowly round the buoy. Until he knew which escape-hatch *Diana's* men would use, he could not anchor his vessel. The

natural position to anchor was astern of her, so that the southerly
wind would drift him down upon her as he veered his cable.
But then if they escaped through the after hatch, the one near
the stern, they would rise and strike against *Scourge's* bottom.
The alternative was to anchor south-east of *Diana's* stern,
manoeuvre his ship well to port and then let go a second anchor;
after that he could veer, and drift back until his bow was above
her bow, and his cables were laid clear on either side of her.
Scourge would then be straddling her with the long legs of
anchor-chain, but would herself be out of the way of rising
survivors. If anyone was alive for'ard, *Scourge* would have to
send a diver down; the bow was not the best place to operate
from, but Brady would have the advantage of being able to
drop a man right on to the submarine's fore-casing.

He saw the yeoman hauling up the message carrier on its thin
cord and stepped across to meet him. He read the first sentence
printed on the signal form and a surge of thankfulness and hope
thrilled through him. Some of them still lived.

"Flooded to accom. space. Five inc. Cowan presumed dead.
Will escape aft. Ransome."

The brief message told Brady more than enough. It must have
been a torpedo explosion to flood for'ard; poor Cowan would
have been up there, watching. But regret for the loss of his
Number One must not be allowed to hinder his thinking and
action now. Ransome would have most of his men in the control-
room, waiting, and Ullyet would be busy preparing the steering
compartment for the time when they would open the escape-
hatch in its deckhead. His own S.S.T. message would have brought
lifting hope into those fouling spaces. They still had an unpleasant
experience ahead of them, but that would be a merry-go-round
compared with the alternative. . . .

"Helicopter approaching from starb'd, sir," the yeoman called.
Brady spared it a glance—the queer-shaped craft was over the
distant Heads—then forgot it in what he had to do.

"Port twenty," he ordered, "half ahead together. Make to
Lockyer—'Clear my line of advance'."

It was neat manoeuvring, performed by a man grown master
in his profession. Brady had let go his starb'd anchor, and had
veered out and then altered position to port, ready to let go his
second tonnage of anchoring iron, when the wireless office sent
up a special weather report. The navigator took it and came over
to the binnacle.

"Wind expected to increase to gale force by two o'clock, sir. South-east."

"Nice of it," Brady grunted, and dropped his upheld arm. The port anchor dropped with a hammering clatter of racing cable. "We won't be able to lower boats. Organize half a dozen—a dozen if you can—of the strongest swimmers in the ship. Plenty of heaving lines, grass as well. Scrambling-nets, life-buoys—you know all that."

"Yes, sir."

Unspoken between them was the realization that these preparations were the first-lieutenant's job; the navigator, next in seniority, was now Cowan's relief.

"Guns?"

"Sir?" Seymour looked up from beside the grating.

"Who's the best diver in the ship?"

"Petty Officer McCook, sir. He's standing-by. Diving-pump's rigged, and the underwater torch and Cox gun are ready. Air-lines connected to the compressor."

"Good work, Guns. We'll work from the fo'c'sle."

"Good thing you had that gear shipped on board, sir."

Brady looked down at his old shipmate's cynical grin, then stared out over the fo'c'sle, where the cable officer was veering on both cable-holders. His request had raised sceptical brows ashore on the Island. It was all very well, he had argued, for the Subsmash book of reference to talk about underwater cutting torches, and Cox guns for shooting hollow bullets into a sunken hull so that an air-pipe could be screwed into the bullet; but what destroyer carried all that specialized gear, and how long would it take the diving-boat from Rushcutters to get out and put a diver down?

"You're taking this Subsmash business a bit seriously?" the dockyard officer had smiled.

"It might be serious—flooded at a couple of hundred feet," Brady had answered curtly.

"All right, all right," the official had grinned, "you can have your damned gear. But I want it back as soon as you've finished playing round out there. Understood?"

"Understood and will do," Brady had smiled, knowing that he had gained for himself a reputation for touchy fussiness. . . .

"You'll want him down on the fore-casing?" Seymour asked.

"Yes. Send him up here for instructions."

"Aye aye, sir."

A stammering roar reached his ears, faded in the wind, came

again. He looked up, then reached for the radio-telephone. "*Scourge* to helicopter. What have you got?" Brady's memory of the Subsmash organization did not run to who came out in helicopters—though he had hopes.

"SM4," the pilot answered, "Commander Blain."

Thank God for that, Brady thought. He said: "Lower your passenger on to the fo'c'sle. Then remain and search for survivors. Report your fuel state periodically."

He clipped the phone back. Things were happening now, converging on the wave-washed area of sea above the crippled submarine. The cable-party would look after Blain on the fo'c'sle; the chief bosun's mate was providing heaving-lines and light grass ropes to be swum, if necessary, out to *Diana's* surfaced men; *Lockyer* was back in position, actually now over his anchors, and the other ships of the squadron were only two miles away, bucking through the seas at high speed. The admiral's signal had been repeated to *Scourge*, and Brady hoped he would not dispatch more ships. He knew his squadron, and did not want to have to impress his wishes on captains who were strange to him.

His eye was on the figure dangling from a thin wire, descending from the helicopter towards the fo'c'sle, but his thoughts were on the relative positions of destroyer and submarine. He spoke into the engine-room voice-pipe: "Captain speaking—engineer officer."

The man in charge of *Scourge's* fifty thousand horse-power was a lieutenant-commander, a grizzled pipe-smoking black-ganger who had learned his lathes in the Merchant Navy, joined the R.A.N. for the war, liked it, and transferred to the regular Navy. He was as reliable as his own new turbines.

"Engineer officer, sir," the voice came thinly up the pipe.

"Hullo, Chief. I'm veering on both cables and am now over the submarine's bow. I'll hold her there. There's a gale forecast for this afternoon. I'm putting a diver down on to her bow, and I might need the engines to keep me in position. I don't think both anchors will drag, but they might."

"Have got, sir. We'll be standing by."

"Right, Chief."

"How are they down there, sir?"

"Only for this wind I'd say they're home and dry. It could be a bit tricky getting 'em on board. All but five are alive."

Blain was on the fo'c'sle now, his grey hair blowing.

"That's all, Chief."

Brady shut the voice-pipe cover and straightened up. The force of the wind, even with the ship stopped, made him screw up his eyes. He felt drops of water on his face and looked at the dipping bow. The air was whipping the crests of the waves into smoke, but it was not strong enough to lift the spray over the bridge. Then he raised his head to the heavens and a few more drops of rain hit him. It had been a blue and white morning when they had put to sea, but now the dominant colour was grey—grey seas under grey squadrons of clouds, scudding up from the south-east on the vast breath of the wind.

Rain would obscure visibility, the sighting of survivors. He must post look-outs all along the ship, as high up as he could; the yellow of life-jackets would not contrast as vividly with dull grey as with sunny blue.

He heard a tread on the bridge ladder and turned. Blain came limping towards him. "Morning, sir. Bad business."

Brady nodded. The submariner's grey face looked harsh in its seriousness. "What's the position? S.S.T. worked?"

Blain did not ask, "Have you tried S.S.T.?" Brady knew he could work with this officer. "Yes," he replied, and went on quickly: "Torpedo explosion in the bow—I presume. She's flooded to the accommodation space. Five men only were for'ard. Ransome will send the rest up as soon as we are prepared. *Lockyer's* ready astern. I've two anchors down, and my bow is directly above hers."

"You'll send a diver down?"

"Of course—though I don't know if he'll do any good. What do you think?"

"Yes," Blain nodded definitely. "If the air-vessel went up, the nearest men would've had it. Anybody in the stowage compartment—I'm not sure. Air and water do funny things. There might be an air pocket they could keep their heads in. And they've got the B.B.S." He nodded again. "Yes, we must send a diver down."

"Here he is," Brady said. "All right, McCook."

McCook came over dressed in overalls, ready for the dive.

"This is SM4, Commander Blain. The two for'ard compartments are flooded, but we think a man or two might be in an air pocket." Memory stirred. "Possibly on the ladder under the fore-hatch," he said, looking at Blain. The submariner nodded. "Tap with a spanner—even if they don't know Morse they'll hit back."

"Yes, sir. Then you'll lower the torch and Cox gun down?"

"No, they'll go down with you. A minute might make the difference. Get oxygen down through the hatch, then cut your escape hole in the ship's side. Even if you could open the hatch, anybody inside would be blown out with the escaping air."

Blain listened to Brady's crisp instructions with approval—this destroyerman had learned a lot! But there was something of greater significance. "You can't begin cutting yet. The gear's on its way out now."

"We've got it on board," Brady told him. "One set, anyhow. I organized it from the dockyard several days ago."

"I see," Blain said slowly, and his lips twisted in a taut little smile. "We'll get those boys out," he finished abruptly.

To a civilian or to a surface sailor, the air in *Diana's* crowded control-room would have seemed foul; to the submariners the heat, the smell of diesel oil and bilges and sweat were normal. There was another smell—the odour of fear. Men can control facial expressions, their voices, their actions under stress. But no man, with fear churning in his guts, can control the exudation of acid from his glands. Ransome knew that all in the control-room were considering one unpleasant prospect. He could not hope to divert their thoughts, but he might allay their fear. Now was the time to speak to them about the escape.

"Pay attention, please," he said calmly, and pushed himself up from the chart-table. The mopping-up party had been withdrawn from the accommodation space above the batteries, and the water-tight door was now tightly shut. Casually the coxswain moved round until he was standing opposite the captain—making two distinct points of support for discipline and calmness.

"You know the senior officer of the search group has made contact with us. There will have been one hell of a panic ashore —I think you can imagine that!" One or two smiles rewarded him, and the coxswain grinned.

"We'll be spread all over the papers tonight, sir."

"I should think we'll make the afternoon editions," Ransome nodded. "By now the whole destroyer squadron will be waiting for us to show up. I am waiting for word from Captain Brady to begin the escape. And that is what I want to talk to you about. There won't be time once we begin flooding."

He badly wanted to smoke. For a moment he thought of allowing one smoke all round. It might convince them of his belief in their chances—that they would be free so soon that there was no need to conserve oxygen. But suppose something went wrong, here or up top? Bolstered hopes wouldn't be worth as much then as relatively untainted air. He took his hand from his pocket.

"You need have no worry about striking any part of a search ship as you go up—Captain Brady will have disposed the squadron about us in a wide circle. Once you surface you will be sighted at once—there will be scores of look-outs ready. If you have to wait before being picked up, there's nothing to worry about there either—your gas-containers on the life-jackets will be checked before you leave, and you can float for hours, if need be. Try and keep one arm raised, and remember you have a whistle. But I'm sure all that won't be necessary—there'll be eyes like hawks on you.

"Now—the jumping wire. You know, of course, that it runs directly over the escape-hatch. Before you leave the hatch, push yourself to one side and you'll clear it with no trouble. Then release the valve to inflate your life-jacket as you go up. Don't forget—clear the wire before you inflate your jacket. We've all been up through the water-tower at Gosport, but none of us has had to escape from a sunken submarine before; this won't seem so very different, once you have by-passed the wire.

"You will find it somewhat different from Gosport when we start to flood the escape compartment. There will be little light, if any, though we'll have underwater torches. Then, as the water rises round us, the air will become hotter—quite hot, simply because the air will be compressed. You've all pumped up a push-bike tyre at some time; you'll recall how the cylinder of the pump got warm; same principle here. The water will rise and it will be oily on top, black. Keep it out of your mouth and eyes if you can—your goggles may help. But it will rise only to a certain level, until the pressures of water and air equal each other. Then it will stop, and that will leave a free space of a few feet below the deckhead. We shall be getting fresh air from the B.B.S., of course. You will go out through the hatch as you've been taught —each man moving along, passing from one demand-valve to the next, until he reaches the canvas trunk. Then a quick duck underneath, a kick sideways as you leave the hatch—the wire!— and before you know it you'll be in good clean water, heading for the top."

Ransome paused, then added: "Cox'n, you'll ascend first."

"Yes, sir," the coxswain answered at once, understanding that the first man up must not be a senior officer, yet had to be someone able to explain concisely and fully to Captain Brady the position down below. Ransome made his intention explicit, for the benefit of those who might not have understood:

"As soon as you're up I want you to give Captain Brady the complete picture—especially the number of men still to come. When I reach the surface you will know we're all out."

"Yes, sir." The coxswain, and the men, accepted that, too. The captain had many privileges: being the last to leave the ship was one of them. . . .

"Now," Ransome resumed, and looked at them keenly—they were holding on well, and he had to stress this last point without causing them extra anxiety—"the old business of breathing out all the way up. Let's face it—we're in an unusual situation. Damned unusual. Under these circumstances you might forget what you were taught in the escape drill. But there'll be no instructors to grab you here. *You must remember to breathe out, slowly, continuously.* I will try to remind each one of you just before you get into the trunk. If I don't, or can't, I want somebody to call 'Breathe out'. Is that clear? There's a squadron of ships waiting on top for us; the escape compartment will be in perfect working order, including the B.B.S.; we have plenty of life-jackets; there is every reason for us all to get out of this with nothing worse than a nasty memory—provided we all breathe out on the way up. Before you know where you are you'll be gulping in good old Aussie freshers. Now—any questions?"

They shifted and looked at him, at each other. One or two coughed nervously. The voice that spoke was high-pitched, youthful, and only an apparent effort kept it from quavering.

"Sir—how long will it be before we start to escape?"

Out of the mouths of babes . . . thought Ransome. There wasn't a man among them, from coxswain to commander, who wasn't thinking of that question, and only one was young or frightened enough to put it into words. He looked at the speaker, who returned his attention with widened eyes. Able Seaman Menotti had been born in Soho, and his Italian parentage was evident in his black hair and olive skin. His chief distinction was that he was the youngest person on board; a loading number in the gun-crew, Ransome remembered. Why, he thought—you're not much older than my boy. His instincts urged him to speak kindly to the youngster: but he knew that that might precipitate breakdown. Of all the men in that room, this one had to be treated formally.

"It won't be long, Able Seaman Menotti. The senior officer up there will be placing his ships to receive us. As soon as he does, we'll get the word on S.S.T."

Menotti lowered his eyes, and Ransome could see that his breathing was shallow and quick. He wished that he could send a man up with him—but once out under that two-hundred-foot column of water, every man would be on his own.

"All right, then," he ended briskly, "let's sit down and move as little as possible. All we have to do now is to wait."

Behind Number Four bulkhead, aft of the control-room, Ullyet and his stoker-mechanics were vitally busy. For the last half-hour they had been preparing this and the next compartment for flooding. The big twin diesels were still and silent now, as were the electric motors. Beyond the fifth bulkhead, *Diana's* deck rose at an angle to meet the stern, and there was not room for an average man to stand upright. In there were the stokers' mess and two torpedoes and the great hydraulic pistons which worked the rudder and the after hydroplanes; and it was from the hatchway there that the crew would have to escape.

First, his young, good-looking face running with sweat and smeared with grease, Ullyet had shut off all sources of oil. The black water would pick up quite enough from the machinery anyhow. Then he had made his men lash down all loose gear, and heave out the spare batteries. Next, the strong twill trunking stowed round the escape-hatch had been unfolded downward, and the lines attached to the bottom edge of it had been threaded through small ringbolts in the deck, hauled tight and secured. The trunking now looked like an artificial hollow tree, except that it was suspended in mid-air, only its roots—the lines—touching the ground. Wriggling between these roots, the men would have to ascend inside the tree to reach the hatch. Meanwhile the life-jackets had been got out from their stowage-boxes, and the gas-containers checked for faulty valves and strength of flow. Breathing equipment for each man had been unpacked from a locker and laid out with the jackets. Face-masks had not been provided in the after compartments; instead there were short hoses, each with a mouthpiece which could be spat out when necessary. The other end of each tube could be plugged into the demand-valves on the B.B.S. pipes. Ullyet had tested this system and found it working normally. He had checked his supply of underwater, pressure-tight torches, and had made sure that all

the tools he might need were handy, before the flooding began.
Now he called to the chief stoker.

"All right, Chief—we'll crack the flooding-valve."

The chief stoker made his way forward in the cramped space.
He was a very fat man and his main characteristic—apart from
professional skill—was a runaway tongue which, allied to a
restraining hand, pinned an unfortunate victim to boredom as
if to a dead wall. But now his tongue was stilled. He reached over
to the glass-fronted panel above the flooding-valve and took out
the big wheel-spanner. He hooked the steel claw of the spanner
round the rim of the valve, and before he pulled he looked
round at Ullyet.

Ullyet understood that look perfectly. In here they were dry,
they had air. Outside, the vast weight of the sea lay upon *Diana*
with almost crushing force. Now they were to open a tiny crack,
deliberately creating a breach for that enormous pressure. Yet
just because every square inch of the escape-hatch was supporting
a weight of one hundred and twenty-five pounds, it could not be
opened until the water had been allowed in, and the pressure
equalized. If the water were denied entry by a sticking valve, or a
damaged inlet, they would rot inside the submarine. The flooding-
pipe was five inches in diameter—and it had to work.

"Crack it," Ullyet ordered, and stepped aside.

The chief stoker brought the heel of his open hand against the
spanner. Nothing happened. He tapped again. He was too gentle.

"You'll need more than that."

"Yes, sir." This time he hit the spanner quite hard. The wheel
turned a fraction. Again. A hiss which was almost a high-pitched,
minute scream sounded in the compartment, and a thin flash
of silver leaped across the room: a tiny jet of water so extraordinarily forceful that it had nearly the power of a bullet.

"All right," said Ullyet, and the chief stoker hastily shut the
valve. "Remind me to keep all hands away from that valve
when we crack it again." He took a sound-powered phone from
its clips and spoke to Ransome.

"Ready for flooding, sir."

"Good," Ransome's voice came back thinly over the wire.
"We've just got the go-ahead on S.S.T. We're coming in now."

On *Scourge's* windswept fo'c'sle, McCook was being dressed
for the dive. Brady watched from the bridge, curbing his impatience, for this was an operation one hurried at one's peril.

McCook was sitting on a cable-holder, and a relief diver was attending him. He had already donned a thick woollen jersey and socks; the tough canvas suit had been pulled on and adjusted; huge, eighteen-pound lead-soled clogs had been laced to his feet with half-inch ropes. A shoulder-pad had been fitted to receive the helmet, and now the big dome was being lowered over his head. It settled on the heavy brass corselet which was attached to the suit, and the attendant braced himself and pulled hard: the helmet engaged its threads and locked into place. McCook looked out through a glass face-piece, not yet screwed tight.

A tap on the head and he lumbered to his feet. Around his waist the relief diver secured with lanyards the breast-rope, a strongly plaited life-line, and the rubber air-pipe laced with steel wire. A long sharp knife in a sheath of brass was put into his left hand, to make sure that he knew its position. Meanwhile, McCook tested the telephone inside his helmet.

All gunners are trained diving-officers. Mr. Seymour was in charge on the fo'c'sle. He gestured, and the sailors on the pump turned the two big wheels. The air hissed through the distributing channels in the helmet, and the clank of the pump cylinders was a soft thud-thud in McCook's ears. Awkward in his boots, he moved across to the ladder slung from the ship's side, and carefully backed out on to the rungs. He could feel the plunge and lift of the ship as the waves rolled at her below him. One slip with those clogs and the open helmet. . . .

Two forty-pound weights were slung on to his back and chest. He was nearly ready now, and Seymour peered into the helmet to give his final instructions.

"Shot-rope is on your right: it will lead you straight to the hatch. Soon as you're down, try to make contact with anybody inside. Then the oxygen, then the hole in the side. We'll lower the Cox gun, oxygen-container and torch beside you. All right?"

"Yes."

"Number One was for'ard when she went. He might still be okay."

McCook nodded understanding behind the glass. Cowan was in all their thoughts—they knew and liked him. With a gesture suggesting tenderness, Seymour reached out his hands and screwed the face-piece as tight as it would go. Then he smiled and saluted McCook with a tap on the helmet. McCook began to descend.

The cold grey water crept up his thighs, back and chest; it swirled over his face-piece and he was under, testing the air-valve by the side of his head.

It did not take him long to drop down the shot-rope, a strong line secured to a heavy iron weight which now rested on the submarine's fore-casing. He came gently to rest there, and stumped round slowly like a dream walker as he identified his position. A line bearing a cluster of metal fruit—the oxygen-bottle, the cutting-torch and the gun—swayed down into his field of vision, and he took it and towed it about with him as he walked. The bridge loomed blackly on his right, he turned left and stared curiously at the bow. One side of it was curled back like a carelessly opened jam tin, the edges jagged like fingers of torn steel. But he had no time to study the damage. At the fore-hatch, the large opening through which *Diana* had loaded her torpedoes, he put down his knife and pulled a spanner from his belt. Kneeling, he tapped hard. The sound came sharply through his copper helmet.

No sound came back. The heavy, silent sea enfolded him. He tapped again. It was not enough that men should still be living in that flooded compartment—there had to be a wakeful intelligence to benefit from what the diver could do. McCook tapped a third time.

Lieutenant Deevers was barely alive; his own exhalations had been gradually poisoning him. But he had set all his hopes on a diver reaching *Diana*, and his dozing mind slowly woke to the significance of the sounds which rang out abruptly a few inches above his head. Blindly he groped for a spanner, any steel tool with which to send ringing back the evidence that he still lived. He found nothing. Below him, all around him, were a hundred tools: but they were down on the deck and he was high on the ladder, his head now and again actually touching the hatch. He had neither the strength nor the courage to desert his pocket of air, vitiated as it was.

The tapping came again. Frantically he bunched his fist and pounded against the deckhead. But his fist had only an inch or two to travel, and its sideways swing was confined by the horseshoe shape of the hatch. He could hardly hear the sound of it hitting the steel.

The tapping came again. His eyes closed, his mouth open and moaning, Deevers rubbed his fist across his chest in the extremity of his horror and need. He felt something hard under his knuckles.

Fingers fumbling, he drew from his shirt pocket his metal cigarette-case.

With desperate strength he struck upwards, and the case almost slipped from his fingers. He clasped his hand tightly round it, and beat again, a frantic tattoo. Two taps answered him. He had been heard! Rallying his swimming senses, he tapped out slowly in Morse: a . . . i . . . r.

Two understanding knocks. A pause, then McCook told him to keep clear of the Cox gun bullet. But Deevers, exhausted by his effort and panting in the foul air, had slumped against the ladder, its second rung under his armpit and all his attention devoted to keeping his head pressed up against the hatch and his mouth above the water.

McCook wasted no more time in communication. Assuming that his warning had been understood, he began untying the heavy underwater gun from its line. As he did so, he spoke into his telephone. "On deck there!"

"Yes?" Seymour's voice was not wholly filtered of excitement by the long thin wire.

"I've made contact. One of 'em's alive, anyhow. I'm firing the Cox bullet into the fore-hatch."

"Good work, Mac! Where is he? Under the hatch?"

"Yes."

"For God's sake be careful with that bullet! Can't you warn him to bend down, keep clear?"

"I have, but he doesn't answer. I can't waste time."

"All right, get the oxygen into him. Then start on the hole."

"Okay. Here goes with the gun."

The Cox gun had a broad cylinder for barrel, which ended in a pistol grip. It fired a large hollow projectile whose hardened point could penetrate the toughest steel, and whose other end was threaded to take the nozzle of an oxygen-pipe. Through the comparatively thin steel of *Diana's* skin the bullet would project upwards of an inch.

McCook bent down slowly, feeling the increased pressure in his ears, and thinking: I hope it's Cowan, and I hope to God he's got his head clear. He thought of tapping again, but remembered that the poor devil in there would be gasping for breath. The need now was oxygen, and quickly—a minute's delay could be fatal.

He pressed the muzzle of the gun against the hatch and pulled the trigger.

Deevers did not hear the puncturing thud of the bullet, even though his forehead was resting on the conductive steel of the hatch-coaming. He had lost consciousness. Only after several minutes did he become aware of the sibilant hiss as the oxygen entered his prison. He opened his eyes as though to see what was causing that thin, steady sound, and felt a cold jet playing over his right cheek, drying the sweat. Then he knew. He put one hand up, and his fingers touched the sharp point of the bullet—two inches from the crown of his head. The significance of its closeness escaped him. He knew only that he was breathing easily, gloriously fresh oxygen which swirled its particles in his bloodstream and revitalized his brain and his body. The tapping began again.

This time he listened eagerly, understanding the slow Morse perfectly. How many of you are alive? McCook asked him. Only me, he answered. Was he capable of free ascent? Yes! Deevers tapped back exultantly—he was feeling exhilarated by the oxygen. Then the diver told him he would cut a small hole in the side of the submarine. Were there any ballast tanks in the path of the torch? No—if McCook cut well up just under the casing there was only the pressure hull.

McCook had no trouble in reaching the point where he had to cut. Standing on the sandy bottom, a weird figure in the undulating world of water, he got to work. The white-hot flame of the cutting-torch penetrated quite easily where the great grip of the sea had failed.

CHAPTER FOURTEEN

"I DON'T like it," Blain said to Brady on the destroyer's bridge. "That sea's rising fast. I wish they'd start coming up."

"There's a lot to do down there, especially in the escape compartment."

"I know, but Ransome should be ready by now." Thinking of the survivor for'ard, Blain added: "I wonder who he is?"

Brady was wondering, too. Seymour had kept the bridge informed of McCook's progress, but no identification of the trapped man had come up. It wasn't important enough to worry the diver about.

He looked at his watch. Almost two o'clock. He stared at the navigator, who was taking bearings on the coast, ensuring that the ship was not dragging her anchors. Brady was about to ask if the swimming party was ready, but checked himself: the question merely stemmed from his desire to do something, not from a genuine need for information. He could see the half-dozen men ready on the fo'c'sle, and the lines coiled on the deck.

He looked skyward, towards the spinning anemometer. He knew that the wind force was thirty-five knots, and increasing; soon it would be blowing a full gale. *Scourge* was meeting the waves rhythmically enough, rising and plunging, but he could detect a jerkiness in her movement; the cables were grinding in the hawse-pipes, and now and then she was brought up against their frictional weight laid out along the sea bottom. It was that weight, more than the biting of the anchors' flukes, which was holding her. If the wind force overcame the cables' restraint, he would have to use his engines. The thought did not please him. He expected *Diana's* men to come up ahead of his bow; but he had no knowledge of the possible deep currents here, ocean sets which might sweep them awry and bring them up under his chopping screws.

Everything was ready now: the ships were in position, the surgeon waiting, the helicopter prepared to fly men with bends to the decompression chamber—there was nothing more to do but wait for Ransome's move. And to think, perhaps. As neatly as the top of an egg did this climax of his career fit the events of the past few days—his finding of Beth, his hopes of the future, the deaths in *Diana's* bow, all working to crystallize his desire to get outside to a normal life with wife and children. Then he remembered: Cowan had offered to let him take his place in the submarine, and it might have been he who had been for'ard watching the torpedo firing. At this time! With a girl he had waited years to meet now about to marry him, their lives together already begun. . . . "I hope it's Cowan," he muttered aloud.

"What's that?" asked Blain sharply, his edginess showing.

"I was thinking it must be unpleasant down there—starting to flood," Brady half-lied.

"It'll be damned unpleasant," Blain growled, and together they stared ahead at the empty, white-whipped water.

The coxswain pushed young Menotti before him and raised one hand so that Ransome could see him above the press of bodies in the escape compartment.

"All hands in, sir," he reported.

"Shut the door," ordered Ransome.

The coxswain hauled on the heavy water-tight door and with

all his strength slammed the clips home, forcing them tightly up the slanting wedges. "Door shut, sir, all clips on tight."

Now they were all in the after-end of the submarine. For two-thirds of her length for'ard *Diana* was empty, deserted. A hundred and forty feet away from them McCook was cutting into the tough steel of the pressure hull, but they did not know that. Nor did they care, nor think about those five men in the torpedo-stowage compartment. They were dead, they had vanished from conscious memory. The survivors were concerned only with the ordeal ahead of them, and with controlling the emotion which could prevent them from winning through. The air in the crowded compartment already seemed unbearably hot, and it was fouling quickly with their burnt-up breath. They were surrounded by machinery, the deckhead was inches above them, and the space available seemed even less because the emergency lighting was so dim. Few men without underwater experience could have survived these conditions; but so far panic had not overcome the crew of *Diana*.

At Ransome's order they supplied themselves with life-jackets, took off their shoes and with great difficulty wriggled into the yellow suits, helping one another to adjust the urine pads. At once they felt the extra heat, and most of them were glad to plug into the demand-valves of the breathing system. Watching, Ransome was relieved that no man had tried to do that before his order—they were still disciplined. He looked at them, the sweat stinging his eyes, then at Ullyet. The engineer passed him a waterproof torch, and said quietly: "Ready, sir."

"Very well. Coxswain, take off three clips, slacken the fourth."

"Aye aye, sir."

His face composed, the coxswain squeezed through the crowd, ducked into the shaft of trunking, and stood up beneath the escape-hatch. He spun off the three clips, then eased the last one by a few threads. That hatch would be under considerable pressure from below when Ullyet flooded, sufficient to make the turning of its clips very difficult. He reappeared and made a sign to the commander with one yellow-gloved hand.

"Crack the valve," Ransome ordered.

Beside the big valve, Ullyet gestured sideways with the wheel-spanner. "That man—keep back clear."

The crowd eddied as the seaman pressed sideways. Satisfied, Ullyet bent and secured his spanner. Silent, the mouthpieces of their breathing-tubes swelling their lips, they watched him. He knocked the spanner, and the hissing noise began at once. He twisted farther and the thin jet grew into a tumbling cascade, splayed out like water pouring over the lip of a bedroom jug. The men felt a cold pressure round their ankles. A few more turns and the five-inch valve was wide open; there was a hard pouring sound, as from a fire-hydrant a foot from the deck.

Within a few minutes the flow was broken into bubbles and gurgling, and then the inlet was under the surface, the sea's entry being shown by the water-level, silently rising. Up it came, smoothly and quickly: up round their knees, over the thick pistons of the steering machinery, over the stokers' mess-table, the CO_2 machine; brimming round the kit lockers, filling and then hiding a small basin against the bulkhead, drowning the familiar things they had lived with for so long—the relentless rise submerging any hope of regaining the dry sections of the submarine, committing them to escape or death.

Water is incompressible; under its inexorable force the air in the compartment was squeezed, compacted against the deck-head. The temperature rose as rapidly as the sea: now the men were cold below the solar plexus, intolerably hot above. There was a continuous roaring noise in their ears. The air became hotter still: cheeks burned, scalps prickled, eyes felt bruised as if before a furnace-blast. Most of the men put on their goggles: clear sight would be impossible now, anyway. Suddenly Ransome felt his ears pop. A sharp ache started in his head.

I should have warned them of this, he thought. He looked round at their faces—there was not much else of their bodies visible. In the mouths compressed about the breathing-tubes he saw fear: but a controlled fear. I should have told them of the ears and headache . . . if they break now! Then suddenly he had a revulsion of feeling against himself. These men would not break. They were frightened, yes—but so was he, scared stiff. And not for the first time in a submarine. These were his men, he had sailed with them a long time, and a longer time still with men of their breed. They would not break.

The emergency lighting failed.

"Switch on torches," Ransome ordered. His voice was a cackle with the pressure against his larynx. He flicked the button of his rubber-sheathed torch. The light shone on a ghastly scene.

The water, black, scummed with oil, was almost to his chin; he knew it would not rise much higher. All about him men strained their heads back to escape the foulness, cracking their heads against deckhead projections. Their goggle-lenses gleamed large and glassy, like the eyes of huge insects. A swirl in one corner drew his attention. A small man could not keep his head above the water. He was struggling to find some raised base for his feet. He found it, and almost at once slipped off balance. His head went under with open mouth; his insect eyes, staring in terror, could not close. Ransome spat out his mouthpiece and instantly gasped in the hot and foetid air. Before he could shout, the small man's mate grabbed him, holding him up, hugging him to his chest. The man's goggles, oily now, had in fact saved him from pain; he rubbed at them gratefully and ineffectually with a yellow fist.

Ransome turned towards the hatch, shining his torch into his own face. "Hatch vent!" he cackled at the coxswain.

In the reflected light of the crew's torches he saw the coxswain wave his hand. The next moment he had disappeared.

The coxswain came up inside the twill trunking. He knew what he had to do—next to the opening of the valve, it was the most crucial part of the escape. In the hatch there was a small vent. It could not have been opened earlier, but now the pressure inside the submarine was almost equal to the pressure outside. When he opened that vent the air trapped within the trunking would escape; the water would rise to take its place, thus completing a liquid column from the deck of the compartment to the surface of the sea. Because the base of the trunking was below the compartment's water-level, only the air inside the twill shaft would be lost, and the water in the compartment would remain where it was now, level with their chins.

It took him only a moment to open the vent. The air hissed out; he felt it tugging at his body. Then he screwed off the last clip of the escape-hatch. The big circle of steel, with equal pressure above and below it, opened as easily as if *Diana* had been on the surface. The way was clear.

He ducked back into the compartment and his head came out of the water, streaming. He waved his gloved hand at Ransome. The commander nodded, and the coxswain heard his croak: "Breathe out!" He took a deep lungful from his demand-valve, spat out the mouthpiece, bent beneath the trunking and a second or two later was rising smoothly towards the surface.

The escape continued regularly, and after the first half-dozen men had gone Ransome did not bother to see that they plugged into the next demand-valve as they moved along the breathing-pipe towards the trunking. Soon fifteen of them had gone up, and a calm confidence replaced the apprehension in Ransome's mind. Everything was working well—but then, why shouldn't it? This compartment had been designed for precisely what they were doing now. If every man followed his training there was no reason why all of them should not reach the surface unharmed.

The sixteenth man was Leading Stoker-Mechanic Osborne, a lean, lank individual with bulbous eyes and a protuberant Adam's apple. Osborne had spent almost all of his time below decks, and had been in engine-rooms since he was seventeen. He could not remember the last time he had been on the bridge, and his contact with *Diana's* upper casing had been confined to the few steps he took along it on the infrequent occasions when he went ashore. He was a conscientious man, and while he waited his turn at the trunking his commander's exhortation ran through his head: "Breathe out on the way up!" There was one man at least, Osborne knew with grim determination, who would not be caught by the natural inclination to hold his breath.

He felt Ransome's touch on his shoulder and looked for a moment into the sweat-running, tough, calm face. Ransome had not put on goggles because they hindered vision. The commander pointed to his mouth—talking had become almost impossible— and Osborne knew well enough what he meant. He nodded, then lowered himself under the foul water and wriggled up inside the trunking.

He remembered that from stem to stern *Diana* carried a long, strong jumping-wire of tough, serrated steel. It reached up over her periscope standards and bridge, over her direction finding coil and four-inch gun, over everything in fact that might obstruct her passage under an anti-submarine net. It also reached directly over her after escape-hatch. Owing to his rather secluded life below decks, Osborne had only a vague idea of the height of the wire above the hatch, and hence of the movement needed to avoid its tight-strung menace.

"Breathe out," he muttered to himself; and with that single thought filling his mind he bent his legs, released the inflation-valve of his life-jacket, and projected himself like a missile towards the circular opening above him.

He got through, but because of the partial inflation of his jacket he was travelling lighter and a bit faster than his predecessors, was already fuller in figure, and had far less control of his movements. His kick sideways at the hatch-coaming was inadequate. He met the jumping-wire with his left temple and

cheek. Its steely roughness scraped down his face, twitching off
his goggles, rasped his bared neck and jolted against his shoulder.
Pain and shock tumbled as a kaleidoscope of fire through his
brain and for an instant almost dissolved into blackness. His
instinct for life fought to keep him conscious. Fortunately, his
jacket was not punctured to admit water and drown him. He was
swept on upwards, and the pain in his face and neck did not
distract him from the determination to empty his lungs as he
had been taught.

Osborne broke surface with his shoulders right out of the water,
and fell back, supported by his life-jacket. The left side of his
face was flayed and weeping, his collarbone felt as if it were
broken, but he was alive. He was feeling the salt whip of the
wind on his injured cheek, but he was breathing clean and
abundant air and he could see the rescue ships all around him
shouldering, like himself, a world of changing colour and light.

Down in the foetid hell of the escape compartment Ransome
was craving for the men to move faster, to reduce the numbers
so that he too could go. The contrast between icy water round
his body and superheated air round his head was sapping his
energy and self-discipline. Mechanically he touched his Number
One on the head and saw Wetherell dive beneath the water. It
would be better if he himself had something to do, some new
responsibility to engage his weakening will. It was no good
telling himself that he had to set an example: that was a matter
of mental stability, increasingly disturbed now by the thought
that he could do nothing against physical enervation; if he lost
his mouthpiece, if the B.B.S. failed, he would last no longer than
ten seconds; firmness of mind, even when rooted in bodily habit,
could not withstand material change. . . . With a great effort he
remembered that every detail of his present circumstances had
been foreseen, understood and countered by human minds, which
had utilized these very changes in the plan of escape; he had only
to contribute the mental effort which could not have been
calculated: his own will.

Recovering, he blinked about him in the eerie glow of the
remaining torches, saw the engineer, and tapped him on the
head. The goggled face, distorted by the mouthpiece, flashed with
black scars of grease, stared back at him; then unbelievably, the
goggles moved from side to side in refusal. Anger out of all propor-
tion to Ullyet's disobedience surged through Ransome. He wanted
no nobility here! He wanted these men out, as fast as they could

leave, so that at last he too could duck down and leap up to life.

"Get . . . out!" he croaked furiously.

"I'm waiting with you. You might need an engineer."

Through the pressure on his ears Ransome barely distinguished the words. Abruptly, the anger left him. He was not influenced by Ullyet's loyalty and courage, but simply by weakness: he could not sustain any definite feeling for long. His head turned and he saw Able Seaman Menotti waiting beside the trunking.

Menotti was not a tall youth, and his head was craned right back. Ransome could see the strained muscles of his neck running down like cords into invisibility beneath the black water. His round lenses were staring straight at a female nude figure, a picture pasted on the deckhead above a stoker's submerged bunk. The nude smiled back at him intimately. . . .

Ransome touched him and saw the startled face turn blindly to his own, invisible behind his torch beam. Here was something he could do, something he must do: he turned the torch and shone it on his own features, so that his eyes could carry assurance to the frightened boy. He nodded encouragement.

"Breathe out! Don't forget—breathe out and you'll be all right. Up you go."

Menotti stooped, came upright inside the trunking, and could see nothing at all. The escape compartment had been dimly lit by the torches, but in his memory it seemed dazzlingly bright compared to the deep tomb he was in now. There he had been with his shipmates, he could see their faces, he knew the commander was there to help him. Now he was on his own, two hundred feet down in the lightless sea.

The fear which he had restrained before his mates swamped him in a flood of hysteria. Wildly he kicked at the deck, shooting himself up through the hatch, missing the jumping-wire by a miracle. Madly he worked his hands up and down, clawing himself higher with all the strength of his crazed-animal will. Over his mouth his lips were clenched in a tight unreasoning resolve to keep to himself his stock of precious air.

When Menotti had left the escape-hatch his lungs had been filled with air at a pressure of close on a hundred and forty pounds. When his head and shoulders shot above the surface, leaping into the atmospheric pressure of fifteen pounds, his lungs could no longer contain their expansive breath.

The gale had come slewing across the sea and had struck them.

The rest of the squadron, under their own power, were riding it more easily than *Scourge,* her nose tied to her cables. But the rescue work was proceeding satisfactorily. *Diana's* men were surfacing not far ahead of the destroyer's bow, and Brady's swimmers got to them quickly, securing the lines round their waists, giving the signal to haul in. Ransome's coxswain had reported the position to Brady, and was now in the sick-bay under the surgeon's eye. Considering the depth, they had all come up in good shape—only Osborne had needed medical attention.

On the bridge Brady stood behind the binnacle, his hands grasping it and steadying him against the destroyer's wild plunging. For half an hour now his eyes had hardly left the sea ahead. He was watching one of the swimmers bending on his line to a man conspicuous in a yellow life-jacket, when the yeoman called:

"There's another one! Just behind the other. . . . *Jesus!*"

Brady's glasses came up quickly. In the powerful lenses he saw the first man spluttering as the life-line went round him; obviously he was all right. He lifted his sight to the man who had just appeared, and horror thrilled through him. He knew—even as his shocked memory fought to recall where he had seen something like this before, and remembered the operating-table of the thoracic section and the pinkness of the lung between the edges of the rib-retractor. For a moment he stared at the lolling head, the black hair plastered over its face, the obscene protuberance . . . then a wave slopped over the focused figure and he lowered his glasses. He was sure that the man was dead, and he felt something retching in his own throat.

"Why?" he shouted to Blain above the howl of the wind, and feeling relief in the action, "why didn't he breathe out?"

Blain dropped his glasses until they hung on their leather strap. His face was a grim grey mask. "It's natural to want to hold your breath. It's a wonder more haven't come up like that."

Brady looked at the fo'c'sle. The hands on the pump were having trouble keeping their footing as *Scourge* lifted and lunged and then, snubbed by the cables, buried her snout in the troughs. He called Seymour to the cable-party telephone. "How is McCook doing, Guns?"

"He's nearly finished, sir. It can't be too pleasant down there. I can't pay out too much line or it might snag. He's probably being jerked about a bit."

"I know. Tell him to try and speed it up. I don't know how much longer I can stay at anchor."

There was a pause, then Seymour said with a mixture of diffidence and concern: "The man's alive in the submarine, sir."

"I know he's alive. So is McCook—now."

"I see. Yes, sir, I'll tell him."

More than fifty men had gone up through the circular hatch, and now it was almost comfortable to stand in the escape compartment—on the assumption that everything is relative. Continually Ransome thought: it's too good to be true, we can't be getting out so smoothly; and just as persistently his common sense told him the compartment was designed precisely for its present purpose.

Only two to go, including Ullyet. He felt ineffably weary. His mind turned to the supply of nitrogen and oxygen: a lot of men had been draining the B.B.S. reserve—could there be enough left? Involuntarily he drew in deeply and felt the cold draught flow reassuringly down his throat. He must not think like that. The second man ducked under the trunking to make his bid, and he was alone with Ullyet. He would have liked to talk with him; he wondered if the engineer was as weak as he was himself. He lifted his yellow-gloved hand above the water and shone the torch on it. Ullyet removed his goggles and gripped the extended hand; for a moment their eyes locked. Then the engineer filled his lungs, spat out his mouthpiece, and in the next second was gone. Ransome was alone.

For perhaps thirty more seconds he remained in the compartment, his eyes following the torch-beam as he shone it slowly round. An observer might have thought that he was taking a last reluctant farewell of his command, of a vessel he would be lucky if ever he saw it again. But the real reason for his delay was his weakness. His body was so numb with cold that he could barely feel the deck; he was breathing comfortably through the demand-valve—why exchange this safety for the forceful sea outside, the malignant, waiting sea? Why make the effort?

The deck moved beneath his feet.

He stumbled, and his outflung hand caught at the breathing-pipe. Hanging there, his eyes smarting and squinted, his sluggish brain trying to understand that movement, he had concluded that he had merely staggered from his own faintness when, undeniably, the deck shifted again, a definite lurch. At the same time he heard clearly a grinding, scraping sound outside on the casing. Fear shocked him into coherent reasoning. The submarine was moving on the sea-bed. Already her hull was tilted a little.

If she rolled . . . if she rolled the bottom of the trunking would lift above the water-level: the compressed air would jet out of the hatch: he would go with it, flung out with the force of a bullet.

He did not stop to question why she had moved, whether it was because of a deep current, or an inequality of the bottom on which she was lying. Impelled by the threat he pulled and paddled himself hurriedly to the trunking, clutched the rough twill with one hand and grabbed Ullyet's swinging breathing-tube with the other. Breath after breath he drew the rich mixture into his lungs. Then he dropped his torch, jerked the mouthpiece free, and went down under the foul liquid.

Breathe out . . . jumping-wire. . . . He slid upwards through the hatch, brushing it with his shoulder, and kicked sideways with his left foot against the coaming. The kick cleared him of the wire, and when he had risen thirty feet he inflated his jacket. Up, up—smoothly as in a lift, feeling his hair plastered down over his face; the water pressed into his ears and rushed down past the surface of his skin, giving a sensation of calm, terrific speed. And all the time, through a small aperture in his compressed lips, he breathed out a thin jet of bubbles.

He felt himself rising faster, and he opened his eyes and tried to distinguish the light of the surface. But he could discern no change above or around him: on all sides a luminous liquid cave spread illimitably away, its shimmering vistas leading nowhere.

He wondered briefly if he were breathing out slowly enough— or, dreadful thought, too slowly. He must relieve his lungs of their pressure, yet must not rid his body of all its air, for he had no idea of how much higher he had to go. You were not taught a rate of expiration in the training-tank, nor how to judge your rate of ascent: you were told only to breathe out, breathe out. . . .

He shot clear of the water, right up to stomach-height, and fell back in a small welter of foam: out of the calm silence of the deep sea he was born into a howling world of grey wind and driven spray, of waves rearing and rushing upon him as if to roll him under and down whence he came. . . . A voice bellowed, "Take it easy, cobber!" and strong arms were about him and he felt other hands fumbling round his waist.

"Last one . . . !" he gasped, drinking the air, spitting salt water, shaking his head to clear his eyes of the lashing spray. He was not afraid now. The sea was violent, but he had sailed through fiercer gales than this one. And he could feel that savage rope tugging round his guts. *"Scourge!"* he shouted to his rescuers, of whom he could distinguish only brown faces and mats of streaming hair, "take me to *Scourge*!"

"Aye aye, sir," came the answer, and Ransome knew then that they had recognized him as the commander, the last to come up. He closed his eyes, feeling the waves battering over him, feeling the rope dragging, and the strong hands on his shoulders.

"Thank God!" Brady said, and shook Ransome's hand in both of his own. Smiling, coughing, then breathing in short jerks, Ransome was seated on the grating. His wet yellow suit had just been stripped from him and lay near the binnacle. Its waterproofing at neck and wrists had been fairly effective, but the two sailors detailed to help him to the sick-bay had provided him with an oilskin against the flying spray.

"Jim," he responded, and then lowered his head into a towel. Brady put his hand on his shoulder.

"I'll get you below to the sick-bay."

"Not yet." Ransome's scarred face reappeared. "How many?"

"According to your cox'n, all of them from the after-ends except one. His name's Menotti. He didn't breathe out."

"Oh." Ransome's hands began to shake—delayed shock and exhaustion. "I told him . . . Jim, you've got a diver down?"

"Yes. There's a man alive for'ard. We're cutting him out."

"But she's moving! She started to move as I left!"

"McCook said he thought. . . ." Brady looked keenly into Ransome's face; his lips were beginning to quiver over the chattering teeth. "You're sure? I thought he'd imagined it."

"Perhaps it's the swell—I only wonder she hasn't shifted before this. And that you haven't dragged."

"We have. I'm holding her with the engines."

"So that's the grinding noise I heard—cables."

"What's that?" Brady bent his head—even behind the windbreak the gale was a howl of sound. He must not detain Ransome, but this was terribly important. "Cables?"

"Yes. She could roll on top of him."

Brady stared out at the smoking sea for a moment. There were forty hundredweight of anchors which could claw at *Diana's* hull, and tons of cable whose rasping friction alone could turn her over on her bilges, crushing McCook. There was also a trapped man alive down there, a man filled with hope, a man he would leave to suffocating death if he hauled the diver up. That man might be Cowan.

He knew that McCook was nearly through, and that Seymour would have reported any further shifting of the submarine. His glance came back to Ransome.

"We'll wait," he said.

Deevers had not noticed the vessel's movement; he had noticed nothing but the spearpoint of flame he could see under the water below him, as the torch cut his exit through the steel. He did not feel the cold; he was filled with a drunken exhilaration and now and again he broke into a song, sometimes verbal, sometimes hummed. His bloodstream was saturated with oxygen.

This would have no bad effect on him. Pure oxygen might have sent him into convulsions, but this was mixed with CO_2 from his own lungs. The only danger was that it might make him careless, when he was still two hundred feet from safety. He was truly drunk, as surely as if he had been swilling whisky. Like many drunks, he was cunning. They had tried to keep him here, they had pulled him back from the door, when beyond it had lain safety. They hated him, and they wanted him to stay here and drown like a rat. He chuckled! Now who was drowned! Now who lay under the water, and now who was breathing wonderful air, watching the circle to freedom and life grow rounder under the melting touch of that torch!

What a tale to tell! What an experience to worm his way in with! It would be laid on after this. Marjorie. Her own husband would have found him, made his rescue possible with his Asdic set. Oh, that was rich. A pity he had to keep it to himself. But he would tell her—yes, she would appreciate that. She would appreciate him, too, when he came to her as a hero, a man who had kept his head where all others had failed. He would tell her how he had succeeded, how. . . . No. His drunken mind shuddered away from the thought of Trunnion. He mustn't think about that. Not now. Not ever.

He saw a brighter flame beneath him, a little to the left—the light of the torch now moving freely in a circle, beckoning him. The grin slipped from his face, replaced by an expression of cautious cunning. This was it. This was the moment when Deevers would show them—the only man to come out of the fore-ends alive. Like a man who knows he is drunk, and also knows he is driving a car, he paused to put his mind, instead of the car, into another gear. He had to take a deep breath, then drop from the ladder, then lunge underwater to the circular hole, then rise up to the surface.

He started to inflate his lungs with the oxygen, and in the middle of the breath he stopped. His mouth open, he narrowed his eyes and wagged his finger in the dark before his face. Breathe out. That was most important. Slowly, regularly, breathe out.

With complete confidence, with no fear whatever mixed into the elation of success, he filled his lungs, dropped from the ladder and kicked himself off towards the torch.

McCook withdrew the light and moved to one side. The rescued man had a long way to go yet, and should not be obstructed on his journey upwards. McCook wondered if he would see Lieutenant Cowan come through the round hole he had cut. In the greenish-white glow made by the burning gases of the torch, he saw a pale hand emerge and grasp the edge, and then another hand. He bent forward. A face came into view, a sleeper's face: the eyes closed, the hair forced flatly back, a nose swooping down above thin lips pressed together, a narrow jaw: not Cowan's face.

Suddenly the sleeper's expression changed into one of alarm and then of terror: he seemed to have entered a nightmare. The two pale hands tightened and tugged ineffectually; the face turned back towards the shoulder; an obscure kicking went on in the water behind. McCook grabbed with his free hand and yanked at the swimmer's sodden shirt. The man came out freely through the hole, and as his body and feet passed up above the diver's helmet, McCook spoke urgently into his telephone.

"He's on the way up! Stop engines!"

He heard Seymour repeat his words and leaned in through the cut-out window to see what had impeded the swimmer's exit. At first he could make out nothing, but as he extended his torch into the dark interior of the submarine, he understood what it had been. A man, foreshortened from McCook's point of view, was floating in there on his back, with outspread arms. McCook saw the top of his head, the glimmering shoulders of his white shirt, the backs of his helpless and peaceful hands.

Lifting one weighted leg over the edge of the round window, McCook lunged forward and seized the floating man by the wrist. He gave a strong heave; but this time there was an equally strong resistance. Cursing, he got his other foot inside and stood up on the deck of the compartment. He moved on, holding the torch higher. Then he saw that the man was dead,

and that his unnatural position—for a drowned man usually
floats face downward, as long as there is more gas in his lungs
than in his stomach· —was due to his being held to the steel ladder
by one leg, which had been forced in between two rungs to a
point above the knee—perhaps by his own weight. McCook
shuddered involuntarily inside his diving-suit.

Outside the submarine again, he began to secure his tools to
the lowering-line. He was very tired, for the water had hindered
his every movement, and he gathered his tools slowly. But he
was pleased with a job well done, even though the man rescued
had not been Cowan. An abrupt grinding noise of steel on steel
brought his helmet up as he sensed danger.

He was so close to *Diana* that at first he could see only her
pressure hull bulging above him. He stepped back awkwardly in
his heavy boots, and at once he saw a great black snake crawling
crosswise over her body. He heard the grinding rasp again and
saw the steel flank tilt towards him. The truth burst upon him in
a flash: *Scourge* had stopped her screws, the gale was forcing
her back, and one of her cables was dragging its weight over
the submarine.

"She's going! Haul up—for God's sake haul up!"

Mr. Seymour, gunner, was an experienced officer. He had not
taken the telephone receiver from his ear since McCook had
reported *Diana's* first movement. He heard the diver's desperate
cry. He snapped his head to the men handling the lifeline, and
his voice, trained in gale and battle, roared out above the big wind.

"Haul! Haul, you bastards—*haul!*"

They hauled. McCook came up, his feet dangling. His eyes,
glaring from the helmet, saw the steel cliff topple slowly towards
him. He reached up and closed his air-escape valve. At once his
suit filled, billowing towards rigidity. He could feel the pressure
of the incoming air stiffening his arm and so pulling his hand
away from the valve. Now he was shooting upwards, and he had
to judge things perfectly: he must rise above the ship, yet must
be able to open his valve again, or else he would fly to the surface
quicker than the man he had rescued. And that, from two hundred
feet, would surely mean the dreaded bends.

Just before the air forced his arm to straighten, he twisted the
valve open. For a moment his rapid ascent continued. *Diana*
turned over slowly, and the guardrail on her casing rapped
McCook's boot as she went.

"Yes, I'm okay," he answered Seymour's urgent query.

"Good. Well done. We've just picked up your bloke. He's all right."

"It wasn't Cowan."

"No, it wasn't Cowan."

CHAPTER FIFTEEN

As soon as he knew that McCook was safely inboard, Brady ordered his engines ahead to take the strain off the cables, and had the cable-party on the fo'c'sle heave in. He already knew that the man for whom he had risked the diver's life was Deevers, and there was some bitterness in his mind as he signalled the squadron to make for home. But it could turn out lucky, he thought after a while. Deevers had no ship now, and would go back to England or Singapore—out of Slocum's life, beyond his own horizon.

Meanwhile, McCook had changed and gone to look for the man he had saved, a man he felt was peculiarly his own. In the sick-bay, which was full of survivors under observation, he learned that the torpedo officer was resting on a settee in the wardroom, and he made his way there. The room was deserted except for Deevers, all the officers being at their stations. The face McCook had last seen two hundred feet down now looked up at him with a drunken leer. No one knew better than he the effects of oxygen —he had experienced them more than once himself—and he smiled back and seated himself on the edge of the couch.

"How do you feel, sir?"

"Fine, my friend, fine. But why do you, of all this company, inquire about my health?"

"I—ah—I was the diver who got you out. I thought I'd see how you were doing."

"A kindly and worthy object, my diving friend." Deevers wagged his finger in the other's face. "I like your approach, my man. Modest. Retiring. Another would have come in here boasting of his prowess, the danger he was in. But you—you realize you were safe in a diving-suit, while I . . . ? I was in my birthday suit—nothing but my birthday suit." He chuckled, seeming to find something especially significant in the phrase. "I'll be in my birthday suit tomorrow night, as well. And so will she—my lovely little darling, so soft, so smooth, so warm, so willing . . . oh, yes."

McCook swallowed, and drew his finger down the side of his

face. Apparently unconscious of his presence, Deevers began to
wave one hand in time and sing in a maudlin monotone:

> *"Oh my cutie, Bondi beauty,*
> *I'll do, I'll do, I'll do*
> *Such a lot of duty*
> *With you!"*

McCook felt a faint disappointment and disgust—elements in
his embarrassment. It made him uneasy to see a man like this so
naked. He stood up, trying to keep his face respectful—you never
knew what the bastard might remember when he was sober again.

"Well, sir, I'd better shove off. Glad to know you're okay."

The man on the couch did not answer him. He had stopped
singing and appeared to be dropping off to sleep. McCook
guessed that he would be stone cold sober in half an hour, and he
left the room quietly.

It was close to an hour later, with North Head gradually
drawing abeam, the squadron astern of *Scourge* burying their
bows to the guardrails in the furious seas, that the coxswain,
relieved of the wheel, found McCook in the gunner's store, super-
vising the stowing of the diving gear. Two of the gunner's party
were with him, and the coxswain said quietly: "See you a
minute, Mac?"

McCook followed him out into the deserted quartermaster's
lobby. "What's up, 'Swain?"

The coxswain stared at him. "I suppose you feel fine, saving
that feller?"

"Eh?" McCook's brown face showed his astonishment.

"I gotta tell someone or I'll bust! You know that bird's the
torpedo officer?" McCook nodded. "You also know he's the
bastard who's been mucking around with Slocum's missus?"

"What!"

"Oh, it's him all right. I seen him with her, remember."

"Does Slocum know?" McCook's voice was hard. Even as he
asked the question he was remembering: birthday suit . . .
Bondi beauty. . . .

"No, not his name, or what he looks like. And he won't
know, from me. I talked to the Old Man. He said there might
be trouble, legal I mean, and scandal. He said I've got to tell
Slocum I was mistaken. I agree with him. I'll do just that as
soon as we get in out of this."

McCook was staring out through the porthole. He said very quietly: "I've got to fix that bastard."

"Now you listen to me," replied the coxswain harshly. "I told you because I had to tell somebody, and you're Ben's go-ashore oppo. But you don't go blabbing all over the ship. And you don't try nothing. Understand?"

"She'll be apples, 'Swain," McCook said, still quietly. He turned to go, and the coxswain grabbed his arm.

"Where you going?"

"Into the store. Where else?"

"You don't tell Ben—got that?"

"Come off it—he'd murder the mongrel if he knew. I got work to do now. See you, cobber."

With the coxswain gone, McCook worked for five minutes in the store, without speaking. His face was lined with thought. Then he got up and went out.

The wardroom was full when he reached it. The navigator saw him at the door and called out cheerily, "Yes, Petty Officer McCook? Can I help you?"

"I was looking for the chap I brought up, sir." The diver had expected this and his answer was easy.

"I imagine you are. Nice work down there. But he's in my cabin now. Sleeping, the last I saw of him. But the doc says he's all right, and I'm sure he'd like to meet the man who saved him. Go ahead."

"Thank you, sir."

McCook let the curtain fall and stepped back into the passage outside the wardroom. His face was composed when he slid the door of the navigator's cabin open and stepped in. The occupant was sleeping on the bunk, covered with a blanket. McCook moved quietly up to him and looked down at his face. This was the man who had seduced Ben's wife; this was the successor to Walshe. A lieutenant, an officer. Frustration put an edge on his dull and aching hatred. But he assumed a smile as he reached out and shook the sleeper's shoulder. He had to shake again, hard, before Deevers opened his eyes. "What d'you want?" Deevers said thickly.

"It's me, sir—the diver."

Deevers wetted his lips and drew the back of his hand across them. He squinted at his visitor. "Well?"

"Don't you remember, sir? You asked me to bring you down some cigarettes."

"Did I? Oh, thanks. Just leave them there."

"Yes, sir. Ah—there's something else."

"What, for heaven's sake!" asked Deevers irritably.

"Well, sir, this is a bit personal, but I want you to remember that I've been oxygen-drunk myself. Nothing of what you said before will go past me."

Deevers lifted himself up on to one elbow. He peered directly and distrustfully into McCook's face. "What's your name?"

"Petty Officer McCook, sir."

"Well, McCook, I don't know what the blazes you're talking about, and frankly I don't care. I've been through a rather nasty experience, remember."

"Don't I know it, sir! I helped you out, you see." McCook felt fairly sure that Deevers had forgotten him. "That's why I think I should warn you of trouble now."

"What the devil are you talking about?" Deevers demanded, and McCook saw with satisfaction a flicker of alarm in his eyes.

"Well, sir, back in the wardroom where I first seen you, you got to talking of a girl out at Bondi." Deevers watched him, his stare intent. "You said her name was Margie, or something like that, and, well"—McCook grinned, man-to-man—"you give me the impression it was on with her tomorrer night."

McCook knew that he was now treading thin ice: Deevers had not spoken the girl's name. But excess oxygen often causes mild amnesia, and Deevers had not contradicted him. He would never have dared to open this conversation with an officer of his own ship, but Deevers could exercise no direct authority aboard the destroyer. Besides, McCook had another reason to feel sure of his footing.

"I want you to understand that I'm only thinking of your own good, sir. What you said about this sheila, and where she lives in that little brick cottage with the veranda—well, you made me certain she's the same one."

He halted in pretended embarrassment.

"The same one?" Deever's voice was curt. He was thinking: God, I must have talked! But what does this fellow know for sure? He felt his anger rising, but held it down, his caution warning him to explore his position before he took action.

"The one we all know, sir," said McCook blandly. He had watched Deevers carefully, following quite accurately what had passed through his mind. "Margie Slocum. You see, sir, there's others been in them waters before you, to use a manner of speaking. To begin with, she's married to a bloke we got aboard, here on *Scourge*."

"Well?"

"Then there's a bookie, Walshe his name is, well known ashore, with an interest to protect as you might say. Nasty bloke, got a gang of razor boys." Correctly judging the moment to follow through, McCook suddenly thrust his small, tough, nut-brown face so close to Deevers that the latter involuntarily started back. "See there, sir? That bruise, and that cut over me eye? Take a good look. That's what Slocum and me got from Walshe the other night. Jealous, he is." He straightened up. "I just thought you'd like to know. He wouldn't want to hear of anyone else around Margie Slocum."

"This is just a friendly warning, eh?"

"That's right, sir."

"This man, Walshe—he isn't a pal of yours, by any chance?"

"Oh no. Didn't I just show you me face? Slocum's my cobber." Retreating an inch, McCook prepared to advance a yard.

"Oh, is he! Right. Now, first of all, what exactly makes you think that I'm so friendly with his wife?"

"Oh, come off it, sir," McCook protested. "After the things you said aloud? Why, they was things that only her Mum should know —or the sort of things you hear in a divorce court."

Deevers gave a short, derisory laugh, but said nothing.

"Well," said McCook reasonably, "that's where Slocum and Margie will end up, ain't it? Slocum's just looking around for someone to pin the case on: adultery. He can't stick Walshe with it, because he wants to go on living in Sydney after. But somebody else, and a witness or two, evidence. . . ." He let his words die away, and surveyed Deevers with hidden relish. He knew very well what would come next.

"You don't think you've got any evidence, do you? Things said in those circumstances, just between the two of us?"

"Between the two of us?" repeated McCook mildly. "'Course, you don't remember how many of us heard you talking. Or who saw you meeting her Friday in the Bondi. Or what they did then. But no need to worry, sir, nothing will go past me, as I said before."

"Then why the hell did you bring the matter up?" snarled Deevers.

"Well, sir, though all that mightn't be real legal evidence in a divorce court, it could make a nasty sort of stink, like. That wouldn't be too good for you, when you get your new berth. It wouldn't be——"

"You're a fool."

"You didn't let me finish, sir. I mean, it wouldn't be too good for you to be in bad odour—again."

"Again?" Deevers was getting jumpy.

"After the inquiry," said McCook grimly.

Only a moment ago Deevers had felt that he was cutting circles round this cocksure little bastard; but at the last words he felt a faint chill, like the memory of water about him, blackness, shortness of breath. . . . McCook was continuing stolidly: "Yes, sir, this inquiry about the cause of the accident. You were in charge of them torpedoes, you'll have to be inquired into. . . ." As the dread closed round him, Deevers rallied for a last defence.

"The cause of the accident will be inquired into, certainly," he said coldly. "I myself will not be the subject of inquiry. Or do you think I will?"

"That's a question, sir," said McCook. "Seems to me, if I knew a bloke had been on that ladder——"

"There wasn't anyone on the ladder with me!" Deevers interrupted too soon.

"Ah, come now, sir," said McCook comfortably. "As I was saying, if I knew that someone had been on that ladder with you, I'd ask why you didn't hold him up, so he could breathe above water same as you did yourself."

Deevers glared at him in silence. Bending forward over the bunk, McCook went on very softly: "You just don't know how much evidence I got, do you, sir? Maybe I brought some up with me; maybe I didn't. Maybe I'm guessing; maybe I'm not. Most of all, sir, maybe my memory is uncertain." Smiling, he began to clench his right fist slowly, to one side of him but within Deever's range of vision. "There'll be a week or so until that inquiry. If I'm not called, I can volunteer to attend it, if I got anything to say. So during the next few days I'll have to try and remember just what I saw in that flooded compartment, won't I? I'll have to knock my brains about a bit, won't I?" And slowly bending down even farther until Deevers was presented with the top of his bullet head, McCook solemnly rapped his skull with his clenched fist, once, twice, thrice. Deevers found this strange gesture so menacing that he would have pushed McCook away, if the gunner had not stood up before he could do so.

"Seems to me, sir, you don't believe I really want to help you out of this nasty situation. There's Walshe, and the razors, there's Slocum, and the divorce court; there's me, but I'm going to shake up me memory for you. So as you don't believe what I say, p'raps we'd better keep apart. P'raps you should keep away—remembering that I usually go about with Slocum, and him with Margie when she ain't with Walshe. Just you keep well away, sir, and maybe I won't be able to remember nothing for that inquiry. You do foller me meaning, don't you, sir?" Deevers did not answer, and McCook leaned above the bunk and repeated: "Don't you, sir?"

Without looking at him, and as if he were looking at something else, Deevers nodded.

"I'm sure you do—and you'll always know my face if you should see it again accidental. Well, sir, got to be off, now." McCook opened the door. "Glad to see you looking so fit, sir," he concluded, and closed the door quietly behind him.

Deevers remained staring into space—a space filled with bad air, black water, a faintly-remembered explosive thus very near the crown of his head, dead arms coming up to close round his legs as he dived for freedom—and suddenly he put his hand over his mouth and lurched out of the bunk. Staggering round the cabin like a drunken man, looking for a basin, he had never felt less like renewing his acquaintance with a woman who had promised so much.

McCook, wiping a cruel grin from his face, made his way to the petty officers' quarters. He had to get to Slocum before the coxswain, to supply his unsuspected corroboration of what the other man would say. He found his friend in the mess, drinking tea, his features grey with tiredness—for Slocum had been with his Asdic set for the whole time of the rescue—and depression.

"Hallo, Stan," Slocum greeted him dully, "seen your bloke yet?"

"Just come from him," the gunner replied cheerfully, and tossed his cap into the hammock-bin. "Nice bloke, real gentleman. Pleasure to fish him out. What's with you?"

"The Old Man sent for me," related Slocum. "I told him about her. I told him the cox'n saw her with that officer from *Diana*. Then this flap started."

"Listen, cobs." McCook seated himself close to his friend. "I been thinking about what the 'swain said to us, and I don't like it at all—I can pick holes through it. First, the 'swain don't know anybody well enough from *Diana* to recognize 'em again, especially in a pub. Second, he said it was an officer—but Ben! look, no offence old feller—officers don't go round tangling with girls like Marge. They don't have to. They got it laid on in Rose Bay, Bellevue Hill, snooty places like that." He saw a flicker of interest lighten Slocum's bleak face, and pressed his advantage. "This officer type would have been in civvies—you know they don't wear uniform ashore. Yet the 'swain says he saw this bird once, then recognized him again in civvies! Not on your life, Ben—he must be mistaken."

"You're sticking up for her?" Slocum said suspiciously.

"For her? Bulldust! You know how I feel about her. But I don't want to see you up a certain creek, which you will be if you take any notice of this evidence. Evidence!" He snorted. "Now, I bet you feel like a nice cool noggin or two after this? We're stepping off tonight."

He was pleased to see some animation in Slocum's face. I've done it, he thought: when the 'swain has put in his bit, old Ben won't worry about that officer any more, at least.

"I'm going home, Stan," Slocum said quietly.

"You're what?"

"I've got to, Stan. I'm going home tonight to her."

"Gawd, what a glutton for punishment!"

"Cut it out, Stan. You don't understand."

McCook looked at him and saw the misery in his face. Maybe I don't—or maybe I do. I'm not married. I don't know what it's like. If it's like this, I don't want to know. But if you feel that way about her, you poor old bludger, then get home to her. Maybe she'll change—yeah, when water runs uphill. Love does funny things to even the nicest blokes. Ah well, nothing I can do about it. That's life. . . .

"All right, Ben," he said slowly, "that's the way you want it, you go ahead." He pushed up from the table and walked to his kit-locker.

"Thanks, Stan," said Slocum.

After a hot shower, Ransome had changed into a suit of Brady's, and joined him on the bridge.

Both men were weary. Brady stood behind the binnacle, swaying to the destroyer's pitch and roll, and he was not thinking of what a fine trouble-free morning it had been, or of what had blown up, or even of his competence in handling the rescue or his foresight in preparing himself for it. He was thinking: thank God I resigned before it happened.

Not that it would really matter, he reflected, if the Press got hold of his resignation and tied it to the disaster, or if the brass in Navy Office and afloat did the same thing. It would have been different if the rescue had not come off so well.

"There'll be a preliminary inquiry?" Ransome asked beside him. "Tonight, I mean?"

"Oh yes, the admiral's waiting now. He'll come aboard as soon as we berth." Brady glanced down at the stocky figure in the outsize clothing. "Will they ever get her up?"

"I can't say. She's pretty deep, and you haven't got the gear out here. No doubt they'll try. Personally, at the moment I couldn't care less."

"Sorry."

"Don't be, Jim. This is my swan-song. Remember young Menotti? The chap who didn't breathe out?"

"I remember."

"I had my eye on him all the time. I thought he might break. Poor little devil." He paused, and Brady wondered what this was leading to. You didn't break, he judged—you stuck to it down there, all the way, and you came through like the man you are.

"I looked at Menotti and I thought—you're not much older than my own boy. Can you imagine what I felt then, down in that stinking hole? Jim—they'll have news of this in London by now. I hope to God they've sent names as well."

"They will have done," Brady nodded definitely. He'd had thoughts like this about Beth and his unborn children—and he had been on a secure bridge. He checked the bearing of North Head for the turn in. "I expect you'll be flying home—soon?"

"Yes, they'll do that. The main inquiry will be at home, of course. They'll want us as soon as possible. There'll be no complaints from me!"

"Eric—there's no chance, is there . . . ?"

"Oh no, no of course not. A faulty tube, faulty engine. . . . No fault of mine, or the crew's. They might even give me a medal for steadiness in the face of disaster. My God . . . !" He grinned at Brady. "You might even collect one yourself."

"Something to show the kids. Hey! You can't fly home. You're my best man!"

"So I was."

"So you are!"

"My dear fellow, they'll shoot me off in a few days, you know that. Unless. . . ."

"Exactly. I've never believed in mucking around. Nor has Beth, I'm sure."

"Time to alter in, sir," the navigator said behind him.

Brady nodded acknowledgment. He looked round for the yeoman, found him waiting, and gave his orders to the squadron. Destroyer *Scourge,* as her hunting-companion of brief acquaintance had done a scant week before, swung under her rudder and placed her slicing bow neatly between the wave-beaten heads of Sydney Harbour.

There was a biology lecture at three-fifteen; but Brady would get off at four, and by five he would be at Whale Beach. There were certain things a woman, a young woman newly in love, had to do before then. Beth skipped the biology lecture.

She was shopping in Sydney in her Morris Minor when she saw a newsboy on the footpath, waving a yellow poster with unusual vehemence. The word SUBSMASH leaped at her like a shout. As abruptly as a taxi-driver she swerved into the kerb. She jumped from the car and gave the newsboy a shilling. He had to fumble the change into her careless hand as she read. Before she had finished the front-page story—it was padded-out with irrelevant technical details of submarines—she was staring about her for a telephone box.

The phone buzzed for almost a minute before she got through. The irritation in the voice came plainly over the wire. "Naval Base Headquarters."

"That submarine," she said quickly. "Where . . . ?"

"Madam," the voice cut in curtly, "are you the Press?"

"No—no, I'm not the Press. I'm. . . ."

"Next of kin?"

"No. That is. . . ."

"I'm sorry, madam, this line is overloaded. The blasted newspapers . . . I'm sorry, I can't tell you anything. Good-bye."

"But listen, don't cut me off. I'm Captain Brady's fiancée."

"Oh."

"Where is he?"

"Where is he?" The tone was only a trifle less curt. "The submarine went down off Barrenjoey."

"I know that." She bit her lip. Keep calm, she told herself. "I know that," she repeated. "What I mean is—where actually is he?

Did he go. . . ." She could not give her fear the reality of words.

"I don't know where he was supposed to go, madam. All I know is that he's in command of the Search Force."

"Then he's on his destroyer?"

"Yes, madam, he's on his destroyer. It is the usual place for a squadron-leader."

Beth at that moment was not conscious of irony. "Thank you," she breathed, "thank you very much."

She was well on her way home, knowing that Jim would telephone her there as soon as he could, when she realized that she had not asked about Ransome. But of course Jim would tell her when he rang. Anxiously she put on more speed, and at the house she left the car outside the garage and ran up the steps. The front door was shut, showing that her father was out. She went straight to his museum, where the big telescope was standing in its corner. Farley's Folly, she had called this room. . . . She took up the telescope and hurried to her bedroom, whose big plate-glass window overlooked the sea, right down to Manly, miles to the south. She pushed the small window at one side wide open and looked out.

Below her the black cliffs, stretching away to right and left, resembled the high side of an indestructible craft riding motionless upon the vengeful and restless sea. But her interest did not lie there. She stared at the point opposite Barrenjoey Lighthouse, but on all that spray-smoking waste nothing moved or waited. She lifted the telescope and rested it against the window-frame.

In the powerful lens the huge seas seemed to roll right at her; she could see them as plainly as if she had been on the beach. Slowly she moved the telescope southward, and in a moment the last ship of the squadron slid into her view. One, two, three— and there was *Scourge,* the big red flag still whipping at the fore-yard, leaning over as she made the turn in through the Heads.

Beth stared at Jim's ship as long as it was in sight. Then she swung the telescope back. Out there, somewhere beneath those wind-driven waves, the submarine lay abandoned. But there was nothing visible on the surface to commemorate *Diana's* swift tragedy—in those rolling seas Beth could not see the marker-buoy, or the dan-buoys Brady had dropped to indicate *Diana's* grave.

She replaced the telescope on its stand, then showered and changed. She sat down to wait. She could not remember the telephone ever having been silent for so long. Not even her father rang—he must be operating, she decided; he had his own problems of life and death. She was in the kitchen preparing dinner when the shrill call rang through the house. It startled her so that she almost dropped her knife. Wiping her hands on her apron, she ran into the living-room.

"Jim?"

"Hello, darling."

"Oh, thank God!"

"I'm all right," he said gently, understanding. "I didn't go down. Ransome's with me now. We got all of them out, except four. I'm at the Island now—there'll be an inquiry right away. Not the real one. I'll be a bit late tonight. You understand?"

"Yes, darling. Eric's all right?"

"Quite all right. He'll probably be flown back home in a few days. D'you see what that means?"

"How lovely for him. Would he like to stay here until then? I could cable his wife for him now, if he's tied up."

"Tied already, but he may take you up on it later. That's not what I meant. I mean about the wedding."

"What a pity, Jim."

"Not at all. Can you be ready the day after tomorrow? I rather want him to be there."

The day after tomorrow? Tonight, she cried silently to him. "Of course, darling. Just as soon as you like."

"Good girl! Look—I must go now, the admiral's coming."

"Give my love to Eric."

"A little bit of it. Good-bye."

"Good-bye, Jim."

She put the receiver back and lowered herself slowly into a chair. Rubbing the tips of her fingers across her temple she tried to think, but her mind was too confused. Later, she knew, she would make reasoned sense of the extraordinary events of the day. Now, thrusting through her thankfulness for Jim's safety, came the precious knowledge that in forty-eight hours she would be married to him.

She closed her eyes and prayed. Then she pushed herself up from the chair and walked quickly into the kitchen.

DEADLY WELCOME

John D. MacDonald

*"Deadly Welcome" is published by
Robert Hale Ltd.*

The Author

John D. MacDonald was born in 1916 in
western Pennsylvania, attended the University
of Pennsylvania, Syracuse University and
Harvard Graduate School of Business
Administration. After a short career in
business he joined the United States Army,
rising to the rank of Lieutenant-Colonel
before being discharged in 1946. Then he at
once turned to writing, having produced forty
novels and some four hundred magazine
stories in the past fifteen years; aside from
his work Mr. MacDonald is interested in
chess, golf, and antique duelling pistols. His
home is in Sarasota, Florida.

CHAPTER ONE

HE had been on special assignment in Montevideo, had been there only a month when, without warning, they had cabled him home. He got Pan Am to Miami and Eastern to Washington. On the April morning after his arrival, he took his written report on his half-completed job to his chief of section at State, and made his verbal report to the chief and two of his aides, carefully concealing his surprise and irritation at being pulled off, and his curiosity at who might be assigned to complete the job. And his greater curiosity at what might be in store for him.

Shoemacher said to him, "Alex, I might say off the record that I do not approve of this sort of thing. I do not believe that any other agency should be entitled to reach down into my section and lift one of my better people. But, because I do not have the facts as to how important or necessary this action is, and because the orders came, quite bluntly, from upstairs, I am in no position to protest. The loan period is indefinite. When they return you, Alex, I will be curious to learn your opinion as to whether this was . . . necessary."

"Who wants me?"

"The name and room number is on this slip. A Colonel Presser. Pentagon. He'll see you at any time."

He taxied to the Pentagon and found Presser's office at eleven thirty. The girl looked blank and aloof until he said he was Alexander Doyle and the colonel was expecting him. Then there was a quickness in her eyes. After a short wait she told him he could go in. The colonel was a pale, meaty man who arose and came round the corner of his bare desk to honour Alex with a heavy handshake.

"So glad to meet you, Mr. Doyle. And this is Captain Derres."

Alex shook the narrower hand of a small rumpled captain with a ferret face. They sat down, Alex across the desk from the colonel, the captain at the colonel's right. The only object on the bare desk was a black-cardboard file-folder. From where he sat Alex could clearly see the title tab of the folder. *Alexander M.*

Doyle. And the never-to-be-forgotten army serial number.

"You are probably very curious as to what this is all about, Mr. Doyle. Let me say that whether our little venture is successful or not, I am most appreciative to State for their co-operation in this matter. And let me say also, Mr. Doyle, that there is no need for us to ask you any questions." He touched the folder with the tip of a thick white finger. "We have here all pertinent data. You will understand, before we are through, just why you are singularly suited for this mission."

"May I make a comment, Colonel? Before you begin?"

"Of course, Mr. Doyle."

"You used the word mission. And there is a sort of . . . cloak and dagger flavour about all this. I want you to understand that even though my work during the past three years has been . . . confidential and investigative, it hasn't been at all . . . dramatic. I mostly juggle a lot of papers. Add bits and pieces together. Sometimes I come up with answers. Usually I don't. What I'm trying to say is that I don't believe I have the . . . talent or training for anything very dramatic."

"There may well be . . . dramatic elements in this, to use your word, Mr. Doyle. But we feel you are perfect for our purposes. To begin then, does the name Colonel Crawford M'Gann mean anything to you?"

"Y-Yes, sir. Something to do with the missile programme. A technical type."

"Age forty-five. West Point graduate. Flyer in World War II. Work at M.I.T. and Cal Tech after the war. A brave and resourceful and . . . rather humourless officer. Cold. Brilliant. Could get to the heart of a technical problem and improvise measures to cure the bugs. A perfect man for these times. A driver. We'll give you a file on all this for your study, Mr. Doyle. I'll tell you the history briefly. Crawford is rather naïve about women. Three years ago he met and fell in love with a woman who was singing some . . . rather questionable songs in a supper club here. In spite of all the subtle pressure his friends could exert, he married her. We thought her a most unsuitable person. But, to our surprise and pleasure, she did a good job of making herself over into an army . . . rather an Air Force wife. Entertained properly. Handled herself well. And Crawford M'Gann's work improved, if anything. A year and a half ago, in November, M'Gann suffered a massive coronary. He did not die. He was given a medical discharge. His wife nursed him. She took him away to a secluded spot. She played the part of the diligent loving wife for a few months, and then it would appear that she became restless. It became necessary for Colonel M'Gann's sister to come and help care for him. November of last year, Mrs. M'Gann was murdered. The case has not been solved. I personally doubt that it ever will be. It is our desire that Colonel M'Gann return to Washington. He is not well enough to be placed on limited service, but he is well enough to operate in a civilian capacity and give us the benefit of his enormous talents. We need the man, Mr. Doyle. The country needs the man, badly. He is too involved with the murder of his wife to consider anything else. We need someone to change his mind. We think you are the man."

Doyle stared at the colonel and wondered if the man was mad. "But this is absurd, sir!"

"Perhaps I've been playing a rather stupid game with you, Mr. Doyle. I've left out certain essential facts. Colonel M'Gann lives with his sister in a rented beach cottage at Ramona Beach, Florida. The maiden name of the woman he married was Larkin. Jenna Larkin."

Alexander Doyle looked down at his hands and saw that he had clenched them into fists, that the knuckles were white with pressure. He felt as if he had been clubbed across the belly. The colonel and the captain seemed far away, and he knew they were watching him. He slowly became aware of the fact that the colonel was speaking.

". . . send other people down there, but it has been an utter failure. They have been strangers. The local officers of the law have chased them out. Celia M'Gann, the sister, has kept them from seeing the colonel. She thinks we . . . want to bring him up here and kill him. I'll be frank. Sustained work might cause his death. But if he were not still under the influence of his dead wife, I know it is a risk he would accept. That town of Ramona seems to . . . unite against anyone from outside. Our research on you shows you were out of the country when the murder occurred, Mr. Doyle. Otherwise you would have known of it. It received a big and unfortunately gaudy play in the papers. And it has made good copy for those magazines who trade on the sensational. There is a complete file of clippings in the folder we will give you."

"I can't go back there," he said simply.

Colonel Presser ignored his statement. "Because you were born and grew up in Ramona, Mr. Doyle, you will be able to fit back into the community with little trouble. And it should not be difficult to devise a reasonable cover story to account for your presence."

"But I. . . ."

"If the murder of Jenna M'Gann were to be solved, I suspect that Crawford M'Gann would come out of his morbid trance, but that is a little too much to hope for. It is hoped that you can . . . penetrate the defences set up by Celia M'Gann and make an opportunity to talk in private to Colonel M'Gann. You will find in your folder the suggested line you should take in talking to him. She intercepts his mail. There is no phone at the cottage. We think that if an intelligent and persuasive man can get to him and talk privately to him, he may listen. And if he will not listen to the . . . call of duty, if I may be so trite as to call it that, he may listen to enough of the unpleasant facts about Jenna M'Gann to . . . weaken his preoccupation. The results of our detailed investigation of her are also in your folder, Mr. Doyle."

"But I don't think you understand."

"What don't we understand, Mr. Doyle?"

"I . . . I was born there, Colonel. Right at the bottom. Swamp cracker, Colonel. Even talking about it, I can hear the accent coming back. Rickets and undernourishment and patched jeans. Side meat and black-eyed peas. A cracker shack on Chaney's Bayou two miles from town. There was me and my brother. Rafe was older. He and my Pa drowned when I was ten. Out netting mackerel by moonlight and nobody knew what happened except they'd both drink when they were out netting. Then Ma and I moved into town, and we had a shed room out in back of the Ramona Hotel and she worked there. She died when I was thirteen, Colonel. In her sleep and I found her. She was just over forty and she was an old, old woman. The Ducklins were distant kin and they took me in and I worked in their store for them all the time I wasn't in school. I don't even think of Ramona any more. Sometimes I find myself remembering, and I make myself stop."

"Are you trying to tell us you are ashamed of your origin, Doyle? And that's why you don't want to go back?"

"No sir. I'm not ashamed. We did as well as we could. It was . . . something else. The way I left. What they'll think of me down there. I was eighteen, sir. Just turned eighteen. That was 1944 and I was about to enlist. I was going on over to Davis, that's the county seat of Ramona County, and enlist on a Monday.

There was a party on Saturday night. Sort of a going away party, sir. And I got drunk for the first time in my life. I passed out. I've thought a lot about the way it must have happened. I had a key to Ducklin's. I think somebody took it out of my pants and went and opened the place up and took the money and a lot of other stuff. Then put the key back in my pants and a little bit of the money. So . . . I ended up over in the county jail in Davis. I kept saying I didn't do it. I knew I didn't do it. I knew what they were saying. That the Ducklins had taken me in and been decent to me, and that was the way I'd paid them back. Like all the rest of the Doyles. Can't trust that trash. And I'd never stolen anything in my life. And it was the first time I'd ever been drunk. And the last time I've ever been that drunk. I was a confused kid, Colonel. They talked to me over there. They said that if I'd promise to enlist, the judge would suspend the sentence. And I should plead guilty. So I did and he suspended sentence and I enlisted and they took me right away and I never went back, even to get my things. Not that there was much to get. I . . . I want you to understand, Colonel. I can't go back. Maybe it's . . . too important in my mind, more important than it should be. But I was . . . proud of myself, I guess. I'd made a good record in Ramona High School. Scholarship and athletics. I was popular with . . . the better class of kids. And then . . . it all went wrong for me. What will they say to me if I go back?"

The colonel stared heavily at him, then slapped the black file-holder with a hard white hand. "I cannot make speeches. I can tell you some facts. You are thirty-three, unmarried. You have no close relatives in Ramona. The incident you speak of took place fifteen years ago. I can appreciate the depth of the . . . psychic scar. You enlisted too late to see action in World War II. From 1946 to 1950 you attended college on the G.I. Bill, after getting the equivalent of your high-school diploma while you were in the service. After college you were in the Korean action. During the two months before you were wounded in the left bicep by a mortar fragment, you were a competent patrol leader. You were given a bronze star. After your discharge, you passed competitive examinations and went to work for State on a civil service basis. You have received regular promotions. Three years ago you were placed on the kind of investigative work you are now doing. They think highly of you over there. We had the Veterans' Administration run a hell of a lot of cards through their I.B.M. sorters to come up with seventy-one possibles from Ramona and the

immediate area on the west coast of Florida. We eliminated
seventy. We are extraordinarily pleased to find you, Mr. Doyle, as
we did not expect to find anyone so curiously well qualified for
what we have in mind. We had to go very high to get permission
to borrow you from State. This is not a make-work project, Mr.
Doyle. I shall wave the flag in your face, sir. There are no indis-
pensable men. But Colonel M'Gann comes as close to that category
as anyone I should care to name. Meagre as is your chance of
success, it is an action we must take. Were this a police state,
the problem would not exist. We would merely go down and get
him in the middle of the night and bring him back. Under this
form of government, he must come willingly. Other methods of
persuasion have failed. This was Captain Derres's idea, to use a
local person. I find it a good idea. And now, Mr. Doyle, you propose that because of an adolescent traumatic experience, we
should salve your tender feelings by giving up the whole idea?"

"Colonel, I. . . ."

"You have security clearance. You have demonstrated that you
have qualities of intelligence and imagination. As a matter of
fact, I should think you would get a certain amount of satisfaction
in showing the people of Ramona what has happened to that
Doyle boy. Have you ever been in touch with anyone down there
since you left?"

"No, sir."

"Have you ever run into anyone from Ramona?"

"No, sir. I've always been afraid I would."

The colonel opened a lower drawer of his desk and took out
a fabricoid zipper folder, thick with papers. He thumped it on to
the desk. "This is the material which has been prepared for you
under the direction of Captain Derres, Mr. Doyle. I suggest you
go through it carefully and come in here to-morrow at two o'clock.
You can give us your answer at that time. If it is yes, and I hope
it will be, you might give some thought to a cover story before
you come in. As one factor you should consider in composing a
cover story, please be informed that you will be supplied with
ample funds out of an appropriation where strict accounting
is not required by the G.A.O."

"Mr. Doyle," Captain Derres said in a soft and humble voice,
"I should not want you to construe this as any sort of threat, you
understand. I merely make a comment for your guidance. After
the extraordinary measures taken to borrow your services, it
would seem most odd to your superiors if you were to return

immediately for reassignment. They would wonder in what way we found you unsuitable. And it would be only human for them to wonder again when considering future assignments and promotions. On the other hand, your efforts for us, regardless of success, will result in a . . . pleasant addition to your file." He smiled thinly. "I am assuming you have your normal share of ambition. Colonel, did you mention his contacting us?"

"I didn't. Thank you for reminding me, Jerry. Mr. Doyle, I am afraid that you will be completely on your own. There are good reasons for that which I cannot go into. As far as official records are concerned, you will be on leave of absence from State. If you get into any sort of trouble, it will be up to you to get out of it. We will be unable to replenish your funds should you run out, but we will be able to reimburse you later for any monies you use out of your own savings. At some point you will either achieve success or become convinced that you cannot accomplish anything. You will then, without delay, telephone this office and talk to either Captain Derres or myself. Whoever answers will make an inquiry as to your health. If you are successful, say that you are feeling good. If not, complain of illness. After we receive the call we will inform State that you will be reporting back to them shortly for reassignment. In the event of failure, we will wish to question you after you have returned. If you succeed, it is unlikely you will see either of us again."

He took the heavy folder back to his hotel. By eight o'clock that evening he had absorbed all of it. He knew how Jenna had died. He knew what they wanted him to say to Crawford M'Gann. With the instinctive caution of long training, he left the folder in the hotel safe and went out into the April evening to walk the sultry streets during the first heat wave of the season.

He had come back a long way, from autumn in Uruguay to spring in Washington. And further than that. Back to the pine and palmetto scrub lands, and the night sounds of that land. The whippoorwill and the mourning dove singing counterpoint to the dirge of the tree toads. Water lapping the pilings of the decaying dock and slapping the old hull of the net boat. The grinding whine of skeeters close to your ear. And often, the muted grunting bray of a gator back in the slough.

He walked steadily, unaware of direction. There had been all the years of painful accretion of the new identity. He had thought it all so sound. He had believed it to be the real Alex Doyle. But now it was all beginning to flake away. Bits falling from a plaster statue to reveal once again that scared, confused and indignant kid.

He wondered what it had been like for Jenna to go back. What special torment it had been for her. Because she had been the first to leave. Six months before he left. They had been but one day apart in age, and he had been the elder. Left with a sailor, a Tampa boy on leave who kept driving all the way down to Ramona in a junk car to see her, and had finally driven away with her and never came back. A town scandal. That Larkin girl. The wild one. And old Spence Larkin had been nearly out of his mind because she had been the eldest child and his favourite. A mean and stingy old devil. Treated the younger two like dirt and was always buying something for Jenna.

The wild one. Talk of the county. They couldn't control her. A little blonde with so much life in her, body turning to perfection at thirteen. All that recklessness and that high yell of silver laughter in the night. Up and down the county, carloads of them, at a hundred miles an hour, heaving the beer cans and the bottles into the ditch. Go way up to a dance in Venice and, the very same night, roar on down to the south, to a dance in Fort Myers.

He remembered how he'd known her without knowing her. Daughter of Spence Larkin. Old devil has more bucks squirrelled away than you'll see in your whole life, Doyle. She'd come in with a gang and sit at the counter at Ducklin's and she'd say, "Hello there, Alex." But they didn't know each other. And he would hear them talking dirty about her, at Ducklin's and at the school. It would give him a feeling of sickness and anger, and he didn't want to hear it and yet he did.

Then, in the Arcadia game in his sophomore year, when Bowers was hurt and they sent him in, he became a personage. He'd had his full height then, one inch over six feet, but he had weighed only a hundred and fifty-five. But it was all hard, fibrous muscle, and there had been a lot to prove, and this was the time. The chance.

And he had become part of the group, running with them when he had time off from the store, accepted. In the group with Jenna, and closer to her. Didn't think she would say yes to a date. Didn't ask for one. She asked him. Spence had given her a fast little runabout. He had taken it in on a trade at the boat yard and put it back in shape. She asked him, in the store, on a Saturday night when they all stopped in. Asked when the others were talking and couldn't hear. "Come to the yard to-morrow morning, Alex. About ten. We'll try out the *Banshee*. Make a picnic out of it."

They took it down the bay, down between the mainland and the south end of Ramona Key, and then out through the tidal chop at Windy Pass, and then, running outside in the Gulf, down most of the deserted length of Kelly Key and anchoring it just off a wide white beach, anchoring it in the shallows and wading ashore with the beer and food and blankets and her little red portable radio. A strange day, unbelievable that he was alone with her. They took turns changing to swim suits behind a screen of sea grapes. Casual talk and some laughter. Swimming and sandwiches and beer. A strange day of mounting tensions, in glance and accidental touch. With the strain mounting between them until, at dusk, she was in his arms whispering that she thought he would never, never try. He had been scared as well as wanting. He hoped they had been wrong—all that talk. He hoped they had been making it all up about her.

But she rolled away and took off the damp green and white swim suit and she was there for a little time to be looked at, and he somehow did not want to look at her but could not look away, until she rolled back to him with a little raw laugh and hungry mouth. He was virgin yet felt he should be gentle and tender because she was such a small girl. But tenderness was not her need. And even as he held her in that ultimate closeness, he had known with a wisdom beyond his years that he still did not know Jenna Larkin, that perhaps no one could know her. And in this union she had contrived, he was but an instrument of her restlessness and protest.

He drove the little *Banshee* home through dark familiar waters, her head on his shoulder while they sang old songs, sleepy with the sun, the swimming, the beer and the love. Very sophisticated. Making no direct reference to what had happened between them. Her car was at the yard, and when she dropped him off at the Ducklin house and responded so completely to his kiss, he asked her when he could have another date, sensing that "date" was now a new word for him.

"I don't know, Alex. Sometime, I guess. You ask me, hear?"

"I'll ask you."

When he was in bed with the lights off that night, it all seemed unreal, and he tried to encompass the enormous realization that It had finally happened to him, and It had happened with Jenna Larkin. He lay in the dark with his eyes wide, and went over each vivid fragment of memory right up to the point where he had not been aware of anything in the world, and beyond that to where he had been aware of her again, watching him with a strange intensity. He tried to think how the next date would be, and he tried to feel anticipation. But he merely felt sleepy and uncomprehending, and subtly soiled.

He tried to date her again, but he had little time off, and when he did, she was busy. And about two months after the picnic trip in the *Banshee* she was gone. With the sailor. The talk about her was worse after she was gone. Once he came close to joining in, letting them know that he hadn't been left out. But at the last moment he had turned away, bitterly ashamed of himself.

Since that time he had often wondered if Spence had found her and brought her back to Ramona. The dossier on Jenna, part of the thick file Colonel Presser had given him, answered the question. She had not come back. It covered the years from when she was eighteen until she was thirty, when M'Gann had met her. Had he read it about some strange woman he would have thought it unsavoury in the extreme. A marriage and divorce. Modelling for life classes and seedy photographers and unsuccessful commercial artists. Singing with third-rate groups and in grubby joints. A police record of sorts. The minor night-time offences for which you can be picked up in Seattle and Biloxi, Buffalo and Scranton. But it was all because she had been so alive . . . and restless.

So how had she felt when she had gone back? As the colonel's lady. Full of an uneasy bravado? Amused, perhaps? Why had she gone back there at all? There had been no need.

CHAPTER TWO

AFTER lunch the next day he got the folder from the hotel manager and went to the Pentagon. He told them he had decided to do it. He did not tell them why. He did not tell them that he had learned in the long and sleepless hours of the night that if he did not go back he would spend the rest of his life in a half-world where neither identity fitted him, neither the old nor the new. He could not say that this was, in a sense, his own search for Alexander Doyle.

When he said he would rather not take the file with him, they both questioned him sharply until they were satisfied that he had retained all the information he needed to know. "And what about a cover story, Mr. Doyle?"

"I've got one that I think is very ordinary and very foolproof, sir. I know South America pretty well. And I know heavy construction equipment. On my last assignment I was working outdoors. And I look it, I guess. A lot of single men take construction jobs abroad for the high pay, and then go back to their home towns. If I had the passport and necessary papers to show I'd been in Venezuela for the last three years. . . ."

"Sounds good enough. Get rolling on that, Jerry. Mr. Doyle, what will be your public reason for going back to Ramona?"

"Tired of knocking around. Got a few bucks saved up. Looking around with the idea of maybe setting myself up in a small business. If it hasn't changed too much, I'll rent a cottage out on Ramona Beach. That will put me closer to Colonel M'Gann. After I get established, I'll have to play it by ear. Maybe I can line up some kind of temporary job that will make it easier to get to the colonel. I'll need mobility, Colonel Presser. I think the best thing would be to fly to Tampa and pick up the right kind of clothes there and a used car. I don't think I was expected to amount to very much. Except for having some cash, I don't think I want to disappoint them."

"You sound bitter, Mr. Doyle."

"A little. Maybe. But I'll be a lot less conspicuous than if I went into town driving a rental sedan and wearing a suit like this one, sir."

"You are absolutely right, Mr. Doyle. I approve the plan. It isn't theatrical. You won't be tripped by the casual question. And you can look and play the part, I'm sure. When can we have his papers ready, Jerry?"

"By to-morrow noon, Colonel."

"We want you to take all the time you need to handle it carefully, Mr. Doyle. I think three thousand dollars would be ample."

"More than enough."

"How would you take it with you? Traveller's cheques?"

"Alex Doyle, construction bum, would wear a money belt, sir. Or he wouldn't have any cash to bring back with him."

Presser laughed his approval. "Come in a little before noon to-morrow."

He bought the three-hundred-dollar Dodge off a Tampa lot

late on Monday afternoon, the thirteenth day of April. He didn't want to arrive in Ramona after dark, so that evening he drove down as far as Sarasota and found a second-class motel south of the city on the Tamiami Trail. Ever since he left Washington he had been trying to fit himself into the part he would play.

That night, when he was ready for bed, he carefully inspected the stranger in the bath-room mirror. The sandy hair had been cropped short and the grey at the temples was now practically invisible. The eyes were a pale grey-blue. It was a long face, subtly stamped with the melancholy of lonely tasks. A big nose and a stubborn shelving of jaw. A sallow facial texture that took a deep tan and kept it. Twisty scar at the left corner of the broad mouth. A flat, hard, rangy body, with big feet and knobbed wrists and big freckled hands.

He studied the stranger and said quite softly, "Banged around here and there. Have driven shovels and Euclids and cats. And some deep-well work."

The face looked back at him, passive, somewhat secretive, with a hidden pride and hint of wildness.

He stretched out in the dark and listened to the trucks go by just beyond his window. There was a band of moonlight in the room. And air scented with diesel fuel and jasmine. This was home land. And different. Sarasota had turned from sleepy village to busy tourist centre. Ramona would be changed too. But not as much. It was miles off Tamiami Trail.

To-morrow he would drive into town, right down Bay Street. His hands were sweaty. He could hear the knocking of his heart. And he was a kid in a cell in Davis, wondering what they were going to do to him.

At ten o'clock on Tuesday morning he turned off Route 41 onto State Road 978, moving slowly through the bright hot morning, through soaring throngs of mosquito hawks, through flat scrub land with occasional oak hammocks and some tall stands of slash pine. The last time he had come over this road he had been going the other way, fast, in a back seat between two deputies, dog-sick and trying not to sniffle. They had stopped to let him be sick at the side of the road while the deputies talked in soft slow voices about the hunting season. He remembered wondering if they were wishing he'd try to run.

About four miles from town he came upon the first change. A huge tract had been cleared and shell roads had been put in, but now the scrub was growing up again. A big faded sign said that it was *Ramona Heights. Florida Living at a Reasonable Price. Big Quarter-Acre Lots at $300. Ten Dollars Down. Title Insurance. See Your Broker.* The roads were named after the states of the union, and the road signs were so faded as to be almost illegible. He could see a few scattered houses, small cinderblock structures painted in brave bright colours.

Farther on he came on new houses where it had all been pasture land, and then some drive-ins and motels and a small shopping section. More houses, and a new school of blond stone and glass, with the yellow buses ranked outside it. And then, ahead of him, he could see where the trees started, the big live oaks, bearded with Spanish moss, that shaded the east end of Bay Street. They were the memorial oaks, planted right after the first World War, and to him they had always marked the edge of town.

He drove along the shade of Bay Street, past the old frame houses and the old stucco houses of the boom of long ago, and he read the forgotten names of the side streets. And then he was back in sunlight again, where the street widened, looking along the three blocks of the business centre towards the blue water of Ramona Bay, bisected by the causeway and old wooden bridge that, as a continuation of Bay Street, provided access to Ramona Key and Ramona Beach.

The old hotel was still there with its broad porches, but the stores across from it had been torn down and replaced by a chain supermarket set well back, a big parking lot, orange parking lines vivid against asphalt, in front of it. Cars dozed in the sun. A pregnant woman walked tiredly towards a dusty station wagon followed by a boy in a soiled white apron pushing a supermarket cart containing two big bags of groceries. A grubby little girl sat on the kerbing in front of the telephone office, solemnly licking a big pink ice-cream cone. Cars were parked diagonally in the sun on either side of Bay Street, noses patient against the kerbing. There was a new bright plastic front on Bolley's Hardware. Where Stimson's Appliance had been there was a big shiny petrol station where two fat red-faced men stood drinking Cokes and watching an attendant check the oil on a Chrysler with Ohio plates.

He read the lawyer names and the doctor names on the second-floor windows of the Gordon Building, and a lot of them were different, but a lot of them could be remembered.

The Castle Theatre was closed, boarded up. There was a new dime store. And now they had parking meters.

He looked at Ducklin's Sundries. It was bigger. It had taken over the feed store, and the whole front was an expanse of cream and crimson plastic and big windows. He parked in front of it. Getting out of the car and walking in was one of the most difficult things he had ever done. It was frigidly air-conditioned. An old man who looked vaguely familiar stood by a big magazine rack mumbling to himself as he read a comic book. Two young women sat at the counter with their packages, eating sundaes. There was a pimpled young girl in a yellow nylon uniform behind the counter, scraping the grill with a spatula, slowly and listlessly. A young man sat on his heels by a centre counter, taking items out of a carton and stacking them on a shelf. Alex Doyle knew no one.

He walked to the counter and slid onto one of the red stools. The pimpled girl glanced at him and dropped the spatula, wiped her hands on her apron and came over.

"Coffee," he said. "Black." When she brought the coffee he said, "Is Joe or Myra around?"

"Joe? Myra? I don't get it."

"Mr. or Mrs. Ducklin," he said.

"They don't own it any more," the girl said. "You want to see the owner, it's Mr. Ellman and he isn't in."

The young housewives had apparently overheard the conversation. "Pardon me, but Joe Ducklin died a long time ago. Oh, ten years anyway. She ran it for a while and then she sold out, a couple years later I guess it was. It's kinda creepy, somebody asking for Joe. Pardon me. I mean it just sounded creepy. You know."

"I used to live here."

She was a heavy young matron, hippy, with a rather coarse face and a dab of chocolate on her chin. "I've been right here my whole life long, so if you lived here I guess maybe I ought to know you." She laughed in a rather disturbingly coy way.

"I used to work in this store," he said.

The other woman peered at him intently. "You wouldn't . . . you couldn't possibly be Alex Doyle? You must be!" She was a sallow blonde with a long upper lip.

"You're right."

"Well, I wouldn't guess you'd know me because I was just a little bit of a thing, but I sure remember you coming over to the house to see Jody. Jody Burch. I'm one of Jody's kid sisters. I'm Junie. Now I'm Junie Hillyard. I don't know if you remember Billy Hillyard. And this here is my best girl friend, Kathy Hubbard, who used to be Kathy King."

"I . . . I don't remember Billy Hillyard, except as a name. But I certainly remember Jody. Does he live here?"

"Jody's dead," she said. "He liked the navy so good he stayed in, and it was just three years ago and he was on a supply ship and they were loading something and something broke and they dropped it on him. It was a terrible thing. He had thirteen years in and he was only going to stay twenty."

"I'm sorry to hear it."

"It just about broke us all up. His wife is married again. She sure didn't wait long, that one. She wasn't local so you wouldn't know her. A Philadelphia girl."

"Does Myra Ducklin still live in town?"

"Why, she surely does! She's right over on Palm Street in that house they always had. I just remembered you're kin to her, somehow, and you used to live there so I guess I don't have to tell you. . . ."

She stopped abruptly and her eyes grew round, and Doyle knew that she had suddenly remembered all the rest of it. She leaned close to her friend and whispered to her, rudely and at length. Then Mrs. Kathy Hubbard turned and stared at him also.

They had finished their sundaes and their money was on the counter. They stood up and Junie cleared her throat and said, "Are you really sure Mrs. Ducklin would want to see you?"

"I wouldn't know."

"Are you on a vacation?"

"I might move back here, Junie. Care to advise me?"

"Maybe you'd feel more at home if you settled down at Bucket Bay, Alex Doyle." They walked out with great dignity. And stared at him through the windows as they walked towards their car with the packages. Junie had the intense look of the confirmed gossip. The self-righteous gossip. That Alex Doyle has come back here, bold as brass, and what are decent people going to do about it? He had the nerve to speak to me. Robbed his kin and they let him run away into the army and here he is right back again after all this time. Cheap sporty shirt and snappy slacks. Tough looking.

He put a dime beside the empty cup and as he got up and turned to go, a big old man, sweaty and slow-moving, came in out of the sidewalk heat, patting his broad forehead with a blue

bandanna. Jeff Ellandon. Perennial mayor of Ramona. Fifteen
years heavier and slower.

He looked at Doyle with shrewd old eyes, stuffed the bandanna
in his pocket and said, in a voice frayed and thin with age, "Guess
I should know you, son. Guess my memory is about to give out on
me. You one of the Bookers?"

"Doyle, Judge. Alex Doyle."

"Well sure now! Bert's boy. There was you and Rafe, and he
was the older one, got drownded with Bert that time. Mother was
Mary Ann Elder from up in Osprey. Come and set, son."

Alex followed the man back to a small booth and sat facing
him. He ordered another cup of coffee and Judge Ellandon had
a double order of chocolate ice cream.

"Been away for some time, I'd say, son. You were the one had
that trouble. You worked right here, come to think of it. Joe
Ducklin was a second cousin of your daddy. I remember Joe
cussin' you almost right up to the time he died. Stingy old rascal.
He and Spence Larkin were the closest men in town. The way
I figured it, you were just collecting back wages, son. I guess you
can see the town ain't changed much."

"I saw a lot of new stuff when I drove in, Judge."

"I guess we must have had maybe fifteen hundred people when
you left and we haven't got more than seventeen eighteen
hundred right now. Everybody else growing up big north and
south of us and we keep poking along. No future here, son. It's
those dang Jansons."

It was a story Alex had long been familiar with, the favourite
gripe of local business men and boosters. At the turn of the
century a wealthy sportsman named Janson had come down from
Chicago to fish. He bought land on the north end of Ramona Key
and built a fishing lodge. When Alex had been little the kids
believed the old corroding structure was haunted. It had burned
down when he had been about nine years old. Janson had been
the one who financed the causeway and bridge to Ramona Key.
And he had so believed in the future of the area that, for a
sickeningly small sum, he had purchased all of Ramona Key
except for a three-quarter-mile strip of Gulf to bay land just
opposite the causeway, all seven miles of Kelly Key, and huge
mainland tracts on either side of the sleepy fishing village. Janson
had died during the first World War, and the estate had been tied
up in litigation for many years. At the time of the Florida boom
there were plans to subdivide and sell off the Janson lands, but

the boom collapsed before any action was taken. Since then any attempt to buy any Janson land had been met with stony indifferent silence.

"They still won't sell any off, Judge?"

He snorted with ancient fury. "Got all the money in the world. Don't want more. Don't give a damn the town is strangled. Can't grow except to the east into the piny woods. Nobody's going to come in here with big money and put up the kind of stuff that'll bring the tourists and make the town grow, not with that little bitty piece of Gulf front that's the only part them Jansons didn't buy."

"Are you mayor now, Judge?"

"Lord, boy, it's been a mighty long time since I was mayor. Or anything else. I was on the County Commissioners a while, but it like to kill me running over to all those meetings in Davis all the time. Seventy-one-mile round trip to argue about if we should buy a two-bit record book. I couldn't get no place political after Spence Larkin died. You know we were close, and just about anything he wanted to happen in this town, it happened. Anybody try to cross Spence and they'd find out he picked up their paper from the bank and he'd start in a-squeezing on them."

"When did he die, Judge?"

"Let me look back now a minute. Yes, that was in nineteen and fifty. Seems he had a gut pain he didn't pay enough attention to, and he finally went up to Tampa and they checked him over and said they wanted to operate. So he come back and he was busy as hell selling stuff and getting all his business stuff straightened away. And he went back up there and they operated and he up and died the next day. There was me and one or two others and his family that felt sorry about it, but the rest of the town went around sort of trying to hide a big grin. He was a man didn't give a damn for making himself popular."

"Did Jenna get down for the funeral?"

"Lordy, no. They never knew how to get hold of her fast. But she found out somehow and she was down here about two weeks later, storming around. Come in a great big car along with some funny-looking people. She'd done her hair red and she wore the tightest pants ever seen around here, son. Didn't even stay over the night. Just found out from her folks that the will said she was to get one dollar, so damn if she didn't go over there across the street to Wilson Willing's office and collect the dollar and take off. Buddy Larkin didn't make the funeral either. He was off there in Korea running up and down them hills with the marines. The only family here was Betty and her Ma. Betty was seventeen then, thereabouts. Well, sir, old Angel Cobey, he was running the boat yard for the heirs, and when Buddy came back home it didn't take him long to find out Angel was stealing the family blind. Buddy brought a marine pal of his back, name of Johnny Geer. So they pitched in and they did fair with it, but they didn't begin to do real good until about fifty-four when Betty come home from college in Gainesville and pitched in too. Buddy is good on the mechanical end, but it's Betty's got more the head for business like Spence had. Of course their Ma, Lila, she's got no more head for business than a water turkey. Spence had left the business awful run down. He wasn't interested in it. Now, Lordy, they get boats in there from all the way from Tarpon Springs to Marathon, boats where people want the work done right and done reasonable. They turned it into a corporation so Johnny Geer could get a piece of it, and they wrote Jenna to see if she wanted in and she said she didn't want no gifts."

"Judge, I'm a little confused on this thing. What for would they want to run that boat yard? After what Mr. Larkin must have left?"

"Well, I'll tell you what Spence left, son. He left that house on Grove Road all free and clear. And a thousand shares of bank stock you can't sell and hasn't paid a dividend in years. And a pretty good new Cadillac. You remember that was about the only thing he ever bought himself, a new car every year and run the living hell out of it. And about eleven thousand in cash. And the boat yard. Oh, and some little pieces of acreage. No-account land."

"Where did it all go anyhow?"

He chuckled. "Good question, son. The tax folks would like to know too. By God, you never saw such digging. Like to tore up half the county looking for Spence's money. Thought they were about to turn up an old coffee can with a million dollars in it. There's some kind of tax action been dragging along in the courts."

"Do you think he hid the money, Judge?"

"I know he had plenty that never showed up. The way I figure it, Spence wasn't quite ready. He counted on some more time. But he got cut off too quick. Son, it was one hell of a funeral. About half of Tallahassee down here, and folks out of county government from all over hell and gone. Ole Spence had put the screws to most of them and the word was they come to make sure he was really dead. When they lowered the box, you could dang near hear the big sigh of relief. Me, I liked old Spence, mean as he was. You just had to understand him. His daddy fished commercial all his life and when they buried him they bought a used suit coat and a new necktie. And borrowed the white shirt. Spence and me were a pair of raggedy-ass kids in those days, and that didn't bother me as much as it did him. It bothered him a lot. And so he spent his life correcting that state of affairs. And he was one hell of a lonely man the whole time. Seems like Jenna was the only thing really meant anything to him outside of the money. But she had that wildness in her. Got it from her grandma, Spence's mother, I'd say. That woman kicked up her heels all over three counties afore work and kids ground her down. And the only kid lived to grow up was Spence."

"And then Jenna came back for the second time." Alex said.

"She surely did. Just about a year and a half ago, with her important husband in such bad shape they had to ambulance him from Tampa airport all the way down here. She'd been down ahead of him and rented the old Proctor cottage out on the beach and fixed it up some, and then went back and got him. It had been in the *Davis Journal* about her marrying him, but you couldn't get folks around here to really believe it. But they believed it all right when she showed up, better than seven years after Spence passed away. Maybe she came back here to prove she'd done good. I don't know. But she come back a lady, son. In dress and talk and manners. You never hear such gabbling and cackling as the women did. Said she looked hard in the face, but I couldn't see it. She looked fine to me. Didn't mix much, not with him so sick, but she saw a lot of Betty and Buddy and her ma. She was nursing that colonel back to health. And she kept it up about six months."

"I saw some of the newspaper stuff when she was killed, Judge. It sort of hinted she'd been living it up."

"Out of the clear blue she shows up one night over there in the Spanish Mackerel on Front Street, Harry Bann's place. The Mack ain't changed since you were here, son. It's rough and tough most of the time, and gets worse when those people down to Bucket Bay come up to town to raise hell. So she had some drinks and she played the jook and the pinball and the bowling and didn't leave until the bar closed and then she didn't leave alone."

The judge winked ponderously and said, "There's a lot of fellas around here in their thirties and early forties that first learned what makes the world go round from Jenna. And the pride in any

man says that if he's once bedded a woman he can do it again. And
if it's been a long time, he gets an itch to prove he's the man he
used to be. So while Jenna was being a lady, they were trying to
edge in on her and getting no place at all. And when she stopped
being a lady, they gathered around pawing the ground something
fierce. It was like she stopped giving a damn. Find her in the
Mack almost any night, sopping it up. Some army friends had
drove their car down, a blue Olds, one of the small ones, and you
could find it parked in front or out in that lot behind the place
any time. Well, sir, after she got picked up for drunk driving, the
colonel's sister come down to take care of him, and I don't guess
Jenna and the sister got along so good. Buddy and Betty and Miz
Larkin were trying to get Jenna straightened out again, but it was
like the old days. She wouldn't listen to nothing. She drove the car
after they took away her licence and she racked it up for fair.
Chopped down a big old cabbage palm with it. Total loss. Then
she took to disappearing two or three days at a stretch. Come back
hung over to rest up and start all over again.

"Well, sir, that went on until last November on the twenty-first
day, a Friday. Better to call it Saturday morning, I guess. She was
in the Mack from maybe eight o'clock on. I stopped in and saw
her. Just happened to see her. Bright yella slacks and a little white
sweater, but both of them looking slept in, and her hair tangly,
and no money so people were buying her drinks for her. There
was always somebody around to buy Jenna a drink. They say
Buddy came in about eleven to get her to go home. She didn't have
transportation. But she bad-mouthed him and he took off and left
her there. But I guess you read all about it, son."

"I can't remember it so good."

"Near as anybody can tell she left the place alone to walk back.
It would be a mile, or a little better. And it would make easier
walking on the beach than on that sand road. She left a little after
two, and the one found her on the beach at daybreak, half-way
home, was that crazy old Darcey woman that goes shelling at dawn
every day of her life no matter what weather it is. Jenna was there,
on her back, her head up the beach slope and her feet in the water.
No rape or anything like that. Somebody had busted her a dandy
on the jaw. It had chipped her teeth. And then they'd took hold
of her by the throat and held on. I tell you it made one hell of a
sight for that Darcey woman to come up on. You know something.
She hasn't acted half as crazy since then, and she hasn't been
shelling one time.

"Well, sir, you never seen such a fuss as we had around here. Sheriff Roy Lawlor, he come over from Davis, and Parnall Lee, the State's Attorney, he was here, and both of them acting like the one in charge. And there was some kind of special investigator down from Tallahassee. And we had reporters from as far off as Atlanta. More questions asked and picture-taking than you ever saw. For once the town was full up. They questioned the colonel's sister and, when she finally let them, the colonel, but they'd both gone to bed early and anyway back then the colonel was still in no shape to go around killing anybody, even a little bit of a thing like Jenna. They questioned everybody lived on the beach which wasn't many, and they locked up just about every customer the Mack had had that night. I guess it was all on account of that Colonel M'Gann being a sort of national figure and Jenna having been, in a manner of speaking, in show business. The papers really struggled keeping that story alive. Some smart fella with a long memory on a Miami paper, he dug around until he got hold of one of those art photography magazines from way back about forty-eight were dang near the whole issue was pictures of Jenna, naked as an egg. And there were a few of them you could just barely print in a family newspaper, like one of her holding a big black cat to kind of cut off the view. So those wire service people picked those up and as you know I guess there wasn't a man in the country didn't find out Jenna was built pretty good. You know, son, back when that magazine came out, while Spence was still alive, somebody from here found a copy on a stand over in Orlando, and he bought all they had and he went around and bought a lot more copies from other stands, and for a time there this town was full up with copies of that magazine. Then somebody sneaked one onto Spence's desk over to the boat yard and why he didn't fall over with a stroke I'll never know.

"Yes, sir, we had us a time last November. Cash registers ringing all over town. It's a wonder the junior chamber didn't try to set up a murder a week to keep things humming. The big shots just elbowed Donnie Capp out of the way. I don't know if you remember him. He got himself a little shot up in the service and got doctored out in forty and three, and when he came back, Sheriff Roy Lawlor he made Donnie a deputy and he's been that ever since. And Donnie takes care of this end of the county all by his own self. Knows every inch of it. He purely loves to beat heads. He had to sit way back while Lawlor and Lee were around here puffing out their chests.

"But they couldn't find out a thing and so it all kind of dwindled away. Jenna is planted right beside Spence. Wonder sometimes if they've had a chance to make up. Before she run off there was an outside chance Spence could have turned into a human being. But that tore the rag off the bush." He sighed. "You get an old man to talking, son, and you've got yourself an all-day listening job. What you been doing all the time you've been gone?"

"A couple of wars, Judge. And knocking around here and there. South America. Construction work. Decided maybe I'd come back and look around. Might settle here."

"Like I said there's no future here. Not in Ramona. The young folks leave fast as they can. Town gets older every year. The waters are about fished out. All the cypress has been logged out. The deer and the turkey are all gone. We got some retireds moving in. Folks that like it quiet and ain't got much to do with. It's quiet all right. Always had the idea I'd like to see some of the world. The furthest away place I ever did get to was Chicago, in nineteen and twenty-six when we made up a committee and went up to dicker with those Janson folks about the land. Scared hell out of me up there."

"Judge, are you still in the real-estate business?"

"Not to strain me none. Got an office just around the corner on Gordon Street. Took a woman in with me, name of Myrtle Loveless. Got a lot of energy, Myrtle has. A Carolina woman that got her divorce down here and stayed on. She does most that has to be done."

"I think I'd like to rent a beach cottage."

"Good time to do it, son. Town folks don't move out there until school's over. Got a pretty good choice right now. You just go see Myrtle. Tell her you're a friend of mine."

"I . . . I guess people are going to remember what happened when I left."

"Sure they'll remember. There isn't enough happens here to cloud up their minds. Most kids do fool things. Some folks will try to nasty things up for you. Do you care?"

"I guess so, Judge."

"Nice to see you back home, son."

As Alex left Ducklin's, turning towards Gordon Street, he saw a young man walking towards him, a slouching, swaggering kid of about twenty-three or four with red hair worn too long, a pinched, insolent face boiled red by the sun, faded jeans patched at the knees, a soiled white sport shirt. When the blue eyes stared at him in reckless, arrogant appraisal, Doyle felt his muscles tighten with ancient angers. And just as suddenly he realized that this could not be Gil Kemmer. He was too young to be Gil. But he was one of the Kemmers. One of the wild breed from Bucket Bay.

The young man stopped in front of Alex and said, "Know you, don't I?" There was a sharp reek of raw corn.

"I used to know Gil pretty well. I'm Alex Doyle."

"I'll be damn. I'm Lee Kemmer. You and Gil used to pound on each other regular. You bust his wrist one time."

"He tried to cut me."

Lee Kemmer swayed in the sunlight, grinning in a knowing way. "Gil didn't get the breaks they give you, Doyle. He drew four at Raiford. He's been out a year, keeping his head down. He draws a little county time now and again on account of they pick on us Kemmers all the time. And need their damn road work done for free. This is a rough place for anybody likes a little fun. Let's you and me go to the Mack and drink up some beer, Doyle."

"Thanks. I've got things to do."

"You still too good for the Kemmers?"

"It isn't that."

"If my brother couldn't whip you, maybe I can. We'll try that some time. I'll tell Gil you're back in town."

Doyle shrugged and stepped around him. When he looked back, Lee was still standing there, grinning at him.

Alex walked to the real-estate office, a small place with a big window, a cluttered bulletin board, a wide hearty woman with black hair cut like a man's sitting on the corner of a desk talking over the phone. She cupped her hand over the phone and said, "Have yourself a chair. Be through here in a minute. Now, Emily Ann, you're jus' not bein' realistic, honey. No, I certainly don't want you to give the lot away, but after all, honey, you've had it on the market three years and this is the first firm offer that's come in, and I think it's better to take it than keep paying taxes on that little old lot. All right, I'll see if he'll come up just a little bitty bit more. And let you know. Bye, honey."

She hung up and said, "Her husband's been dead twenty years and he bought that lot for forty dollars and now she doesn't want to sell it for twelve hundred. I'm Myrtle Loveless. Can I help you?"

"Alex Doyle. The Judge says to see you about renting a beach cottage."

"I've got listings, but they're kinda on the primitive side, Mr. Doyle. They——"

"I used to live here. I know what they're like. I'd want one for a month."

She opened a big key rack. A half-hour later he paid her eighty dollars for a one-month rental, picked up groceries at the supermarket without seeing anyone he knew, and drove back on out to the Carney cottage on the beach. It was of weatherbeaten cypress and sat two feet off the ground on thick piers. There was a small living-room, with rattan furniture and a grass rug, a bedroom, a small and primitive kitchen in the rear with a very noisy refrigerator, an inside bath with tub, and an outside cold-water shower. On the front was a small screened porch with two chairs of corroded aluminium tubing and plastic webbing. The front porch was fifty feet from the high-tide line. He stowed his supplies, took a long swim and a cold shower, and then sat on the screened porch with a cheese sandwich and a bottle of milk, squinting through the white glare of the sand towards the deep blue of the early afternoon Gulf.

The cottage on his left, visible beyond the trees, was empty. Myrtle had told him that the next cottage to the north was also empty. He could not see that one. Beyond that one was the Proctor cottage where Colonel Crawford M'Gann lived with his sister.

He realized that somehow the world had reverted to the dimensions of childhood. This was the known place. So well known. He and Jody Burch had gone gigging along this beach line in Jody's old scow, with a home-made tin reflector around the Coleman lantern, taking turns with the gig. Not two hundred yards from where he sat, but twenty years ago, he had helped work the nets when that unforgettable school of mullet had appeared, a mile and more of mullet, a hundred yards wide and five feet deep, almost solid enough to walk on. Hundreds and hundreds of tons of fish, so that every boat had been out. And he had taken them out of the gil net until his arms had been like lead. But it hadn't done anybody any good. They'd been getting seven cents a pound, but it dropped to five and then three and then a penny, and then you couldn't get rid of them. And they had been buried under fruit trees and rose bushes all over town.

The Sunday School picnics had nearly always been at the Proctor cottage where the colonel was now living. And you showed off by swimming out as far as you dared, pretending not to hear the Reverend Mountainberry bellowing at you to come back.

Up the beach a little farther was where you and Ed Torrance set out all those stone crab traps that year and did so well. And the stone crabs bought that American Flyer bicycle, and Joe Ducklin got so sore because he thought the money should have gone for clothes.

A vivid world, every inch of it known. And now, as in childhood, the rest of the world did not exist, except as coloured maps and faraway names. He had been out into a lot of that world, but now it did not seem real. It was like something he had made up. This was the home place, and the bright borders of it were those farthest places you had been when you were a kid. Beyond the borders was a hazy nothingness.

The Gulf was flat calm, the day strangely still—without thrash of bait fish, or tilting yawp of terns or the busy-legged sandpipers.

He heard, in the stillness, a distant rumbling of the timbers of the old wooden bridge, and the sound of a rough automotive engine, coming closer, running along the sand and shell road between the cottages and the bay shore. He heard it stop directly behind the cottage. He got up and walked back to the kitchen door and looked out through the screen and saw a battered blue jeep parked next to his old grey Dodge. A sign on the side of the jeep said, *The Larkin Boat Yard and Marina—Ramona, Florida.*

A girl had got out of the jeep. She stood for a moment, looking towards the cottage, and then came towards the back door.

CHAPTER THREE

SHE was a girl of good size and considerable prettiness, and she came swinging towards him, moving well in her blue-jean shorts and a sleeveless red blouse with narrow white vertical stripes and battered blue canvas top-siders. She had been endowed with a hefty wilderness of coarse blonde-red hair, now sun-streaked. She was magnificently tanned, but it was the tan of unthinking habitual exposure rather than a pool-side contrivance of oils and careful estimates of basting time.

She stopped at the foot of the two wooden steps and looked up at him through the screen, and smiled in a polite and distant way. There was, he thought, an interesting suggestion of the lioness about her face, the pale eyes spaced wide, a sloping heaviness of cheek structure, a wide and minutely savage mouth.

"I'm sorry to bother you."

"Doesn't bother me a bit. Come on in."

She came into the kitchen, a big, strong, vital-looking woman, and when she was on his level he knew that if she were to wear high heels, she would stand eye to eye with him.

"Myrtle should have remembered this. Mrs. Carney has been letting us use the cottage to change in when it isn't rented. And we left some stuff out here. Maybe you've run across it and wondered about it. Here's the extra key. I don't imagine you want a stranger having a key to your castle."

"Some castle. I haven't found anything. I haven't looked around much."

"Just some swimming gear in that little closet off the living-room. Suits and fins and masks and towels. I ran into Myrtle on Bay Street and she said she'd just rented it. I'll get the stuff if it's all right."

"It isn't going to be in my way. I'm not going to use that closet. As far as I'm concerned, you can leave it right here and come on out with your husband and swim any time you feel like it."

"I come out with my brother. We couldn't impose on you that way, really."

And suddenly he knew the reason why she had seemed so curiously familiar to him. She was Jenna, cut from a bolder pattern. And more forthright than sensuous, more grave than mischievous. He wondered why he had been so slow to recognize the obvious.

"Aren't you Betty Larkin?"

"Yes, and I've seen you before. A long time ago. And I just can't remember. Myrtle didn't tell me your name."

"Doyle. Alex Doyle."

Her eyes widened and she lifted her hand to her throat. "Of course! Of course! And you haven't changed so terribly much. Golly, I had such a horrible crush on you, I don't see how I could have possibly forgotten." Her colour deepened under her tan.

"This isn't flattering, Betty, but I just can't remember you at all. I knew Jenna, of course. And I can remember Buddy a little bit. But you're a blank."

"I used to go into Ducklin's and make a lemon dope last just about forever. But the big football hero wouldn't have had any time for eleven-year-olds. Oh, I was a living doll, Alex. Nearly as tall as I am now, and looked like something made out of broom-sticks. We went to all the home games and some of the out of town ones. Every time they wrote anything about you in the *Davis Journal*, I'd cut it out and paste it in a book. With appropriate comments in my diary. Isn't it crazy the things kids do?"

"It sure is. But I'm flattered anyhow."

"Have you been in town long?"

"Just since mid-morning. Haven't seen anybody to talk to except Judge Ellandon. Sat with him in Ducklin's and got a briefing on the local picture. I can't offer a lemon dope, but the beer I bought ought to have a chill on it by now."

"Sounds good. Right out of the can or bottle, please."

He opened two cans of beer and they took them out on to the small screened porch. She asked him what he'd been doing, and he told her just what he'd told the judge. And then, as though sensing what he'd most want to know, she began to talk of his friends. Who had married and who had died and who had moved away. Who had children and who had been divorced. Having an older brother and sister had given Betty a better working knowledge of his age group than she would otherwise have had. There were only a few names he could recall that she could not tell him about.

He was astonished that so many of them had moved away. When she started to tell him about Jody Burch he said, "I heard about that. Junie was in Ducklin's with a woman named Kathy Hubbard. She told me about Jody. It's a damn shame. And then, all of a sudden, she remembered the dirt about me. And got a little nasty and took off."

"Junie is a terrible pill, Alex. Too bad Billy Hillyard ever married her. She's full of virtue and civic works, but the truth is her home and her kids bore her. That's why she's on so many committees."

He said, into the sudden silence, "Well, when the big hero fell off the pedestal, it sure must have raised hell with your diary."

She grinned at him. It was a good grin that slanted her eyes and wrinkled the tan nose. "It blighted my life. I was your valiant defender, Alex. I got in more darn kicking, scratching, snarling, hair-yanking fights over you. I couldn't *bear* to have anybody call you names."

"But I guess they did."

"They certainly did. You were drinking and you weren't used to drinking, and you'd never been in trouble before. I couldn't understand why people were so . . . vicious about it."

"Don't you know, really?"

"No," she said, frowning.

"I was Bert Doyle's kid. A kid from Chaney's Bayou which was just about a half step better than Bucket Bay. I was from down there where they throw the trash and garbage off the front stoop into the bay, down there where they fish all week and get stinking drunk on Saturday night. My old man and my brother drowned in the Gulf and my old lady scrubbed in the kitchen at the Ramona Hotel until she died, and it was too damn bad Joe Ducklin had such no-account kin, but it wasn't really close kin, and wasn't Joe a hell of a fine man to take me in like he did? They never thought how much wages Joe saved. So I was supposed to be grateful and know my place. And it made them all uneasy when I got better grades than their sons and daughters, and they felt kind of strange about it when I could run harder and faster and carry a ball better than their sons. And get up quicker when I was hurt. And it didn't seem right I should be popular in school and get invited to things, and run around with their kids. I guess they'd look at me and see I was mannerly and knew which fork to use, and they wished they could put a big tag on me, saying I was bayou trash. I was too big for my britches. So then I did just what they wanted. I did it up fine. Got drunk and robbed good old Joe. That proved something, didn't it? You cain't trust that bayou trash. They'll turn on you ever' time. Got that mean shifty streak in 'em."

He turned his head violently away from her and looked blindly south down the afternoon beach, and felt the unexpected sting of tears in his eyes.

"Oh, Alex, Alex," she said softly, and for just a moment she laid her hand on his arm, and took it away. "It was long ago. You were just a kid."

When he was sure of his control he turned back towards her and smiled a crooked smile. "It was so long ago, wasn't it, that there wouldn't be any point in my lying now?"

"I . . . I wouldn't think so. What do you mean?"

"The sad crazy thing about it is I didn't do it."

She was frowning, her eyes moving quickly as she searched his face. "But you pleaded guilty. It was in the papers."

"I pleaded guilty. They talked to me and talked to me and they said if I tried to fight it I'd end up in Raiford sure as hell. So be sensible, kid, and plead guilty and it's all set so the judge'll let it drop if you enlist right off. And I was going to enlist anyway. That was what the party was about. I passed out. Somebody took the store key out of my pocket and they went and they took twenty cartons of cigarettes, and those pens and lighters, and nearly two hundred dollars out of the register. Then they shoved the key and two twenty-dollar bills and three fountain pens in my pockets."

"But you *should* have fought!"

"I know that *now*, Betty. But I was sick and I was scared and I was confused. All I wanted was to get out of that cell and get in the army and never think about Ramona again."

"Why didn't you write Joe later and tell him the truth, Alex? Or write any of your friends."

"I wouldn't have written Joe. I should have written to Myra. I must have started a dozen letters. I couldn't say it right. I tore them up. I told myself when I got out of the service I'd come back and clear things up. I was going to be my own private eye and find out who did it. But I got out and . . . I couldn't make myself come back. I knew I'd never come back."

"And now here you are."

"I got older. And smarter, maybe."

"But it still hurts, doesn't it? You sounded so bitter it made me feel . . . sort of strange. Have you thought of who could have done it?"

"It was a big party, Betty. A beer party and dance, I guess over a hundred of the kids. I kept having to make speeches. It was Willy Reiser brought that raw 'shine and we got to drinking it out of paper cups. They let us have the Legion Hall and when I passed out early, they put me in one of those little back rooms and stuck flowers in my hand and went on with my going-away party. Almost anybody could have done it. It isn't a long walk from Ducklin's to the Hall. They'd need a car, maybe, to carry the cigarettes, but anybody who didn't have a car could borrow one. I'll never know who did it, Betty."

"What a filthy, filthy trick! Worse than the stealing was making it look like it was you. But even so, Joe wouldn't have had to swear out a complaint."

"Hell, he enjoyed it. Do you know something? Outside of trying to tell the county police fifteen years ago and Joe, you're the first person I've ever told this to? It became sort of a point of honour to keep it to myself. I guess I told you because . . . of the clippings and the diary and those scraps you had over me. Now tell me about yourself, Betty. I want to know about my fan club of one."

"I . . . I'm not the dramatic one in my family. I'm just a big healthy uncomplicated horse. After I got out of school in Gainesville I came back here and went to work in the yard. I'm sort of a top sergeant or general manager or something. Buddy bosses all the shop work and I take care of everything else. Buddy and I live with mother at the same old house on Grove Road, Johnny

Geer rents a room from mother, and we pay our share of the board."

"Work, and go swimming?"

"And sailing, Alex. In my little Thistle. Called the *Lady Bird*. And that's about it. It's enough. We're all sort of trying to recover from . . . what happened."

"I'm very sorry about it, Betty."

She shrugged. "I guess something was going to happen to her. Nobody knew what it would be. But I do wish it hadn't been this. Somebody did it. They may be still around. Pretty spooky. Buddy and I have talked about her. I guess we loved her, but not very much. You can't love anybody who doesn't want love, who won't accept it." She looked at her watch. "I've goofed off too long."

"Come back, will you? Any time at all."

"Stop in and look at the yard."

"I will. And leave your gear here. It isn't in my way."

"Well . . . all right."

He walked out to the jeep with her. She turned and shook hands with him. Her hand was solid, her grip strong but feminine. "Hope you'll stay around a while, Alex."

"I hope so too."

"I guess you knew Jenna . . . pretty well."

It was a hesitant question and he saw a look of uneasiness, almost of pain, in her eyes before she looked away.

"We were in the same crowd, but I wasn't somebody special to her. Why?"

"I don't know. I was just talking."

"Did they find her very far from this cottage?"

She slid under the wheel and looked up at him. "You can ask questions, Alex, and they'll be answered because you're from Ramona. But it isn't a very healthy place for strangers who come around prying. It's all over and the town wants it to be forgotten. There was some very . . . strong meat written. At first the town was excited, but now it's kind of ashamed. We kept the worst of it away from mother, thank God. And I guess Celia kept Colonel M'Gann from seeing much of it. It wasn't far from this cottage, Alex. About three hundred yards south. Just opposite that stand of three big Australian pines."

"How is Colonel M'Gann taking it?"

"I wouldn't know. Celia wants no part of the Larkin family, and what Celia wants, Celia gets. Not one of us has seen the colonel since . . . it happened. And I guess that suits Celia perfectly. Her dear brother married so far beneath him. Sorry, but she makes me want to spit. See you later, Alex."

He watched the jeep until it went out of sight around a bend. At the last moment she looked back and waved. He was pleasured by the picture it made, the faded blue jeep and the spume of white shell dust behind it, and her vivid hair and the warm brown of shoulders and arms and the red of the blouse. As he reached the back door he heard the bridge timbers again after she turned on to the causeway.

He took another can of cool beer out on the porch and he wondered why he felt so utterly relaxed, felt such inner peace. And he decided that telling her the truth had been for him a kind of therapy he had not realized he needed so badly. It was like retching away something that had lain sour and heavy on his stomach. And he thought of the tall spindly child fighting so fiercely for him, and it made him smile.

There was such an odd contrast between Jenna and Betty in spite of the elusive resemblance. It had been almost impossible for Jenna to walk or move or speak without making of it an act of provocation. The fabric of her sexual tensions had surrounded her with an unmistakable aura of awareness and surmise.

Betty, in contrast, seemed to handle herself in a way that, through long habit, seemed to negate her bounties, to under-play her charms. She seemed to have no body awareness, no iota of consciousness of self. So there was a bluffness in the way she moved, an asexual indifference. It was a big lovely body, with good shoulders and strong breasts, delicately narrow waist, and long strong shapely legs. Yet when she had sat on the porch she had propped her heels on the railing just inside the screening, and crossed her ankles with neither coyness nor seemingly any awareness that she was good to look upon.

It gave him the feeling that should a man attempt to kiss her, it would surprise her utterly. And she would glare at him and say, with great impatience, "Oh, for heaven's sake!" So it was no wonder that at twenty-six she was unmarried, and seemed perfectly content with that condition.

He finished his beer and put on swim trunks and swam down the beach and came ashore at the stand of three tall pines. There was no mark or footstep on the sand where the tide had gone out. A tan crab ran sideways to its hole and popped in and watched him with stalked eyes. So she had been found just about here. And, with forlorn irony, on her back. In soiled white sweater and soiled yellow slacks, with damaged mouth and staring eyes and darkened face, black tongue parting the swollen lips.

He could remember her so clearly on another beach. Mouth that he had kissed. Eyes and throat that he had kissed.

A drunken little lady in her yellow slacks treading an uncertain path back along the night beach to where the invalid husband slept. Singing her small drunken songs in the night. Saying "Lay di ah" and "Doe di ah" in the parts where she couldn't remember the lyrics. Walking there, with someone coming along behind her, swiftly. Or waiting for her in the black pine shadows, perhaps hearing the drunky song first and then seeing the pallor of the sweater and slacks against the November night.

There was one other memory of Jenna that was especially vivid. There had been a beach picnic and swimming by moonlight, down near Windy Pass. And a big fire that burned down the coals. There was an improvised game, selecting weird, comic futures for each member of the group. Jenna sat in Buddha pose, a boy's jacket around her shoulders, the fire glow red on her face. The game had become more serious, with each person stating what they wanted to be. When it was Jenna's turn she had looked almost broodingly at the dying fire, a strangely quiet Jenna, all vivacity gone for the moment.

"I guess I just want to *be*. I don't want a choice, and be just one thing, one kind of person. I want *all* the choices." She had jumped up, thrown the jacket aside, shoved Willy Reiser over onto his back with her bare foot, then raced for the water, with Willy after her, yelling horrid threats.

Alex looked at the unmarked beach where they had found her, and suddenly he felt a queasy crawling of the skin at the nape of his neck and the backs of his hands. An atavistic warning. He looked up and down the beach, but it was empty. Only the tan crab watched him, wary and patient.

CHAPTER FOUR

THE next morning was sultry and misty, with an oily grey Gulf and a slow gentle swell that curled and slapped the packed sand. At dawn he had heard the rush and thrash of game fish striking bait just off the beach, and so later he had driven over into town to Bolley's Hardware and bought a cheap spinning outfit, and some white and yellow nylon dudes.

He was waited on by Cal Bolley, the son of the owner. Alex remembered Clem Bolley, the father, as a fat, sullen man, driven and harried by a neurotic wife with social ambitions. And he remembered Cal as a fat, shy boy, butt of cruel jokes. The shyness had congealed to sullenness.

"Hello, Cal."

"Hello, Doyle." No smile or offer of hand or flicker of response.

"Glad somebody recognized me."

"Heard you were back in town. Over on the beach."

"How's your father?"

"Had a stroke. Hasn't been out of bed for three years." For the first time there was a flick of expression on the doughy face, a faint shadow of satisfaction, of a smothered glee.

"Sorry to hear it. I want to get a spinning rod."

"Over here. It'll have to be cash, Doyle. I don't run a credit business."

"It will be cash."

He picked out what he wanted. Bolley deftly ran monofilament onto the reel spool, dropped the lures and swivels and leader into a small paper sack. On the other side of the store a clerk was demonstrating a floor fan to an old lady.

As Alex paid and received his change, he said, "You sure as hell give me a big welcome, Cal. Thanks."

Cal Bolley stared at him. "Want I should hire a band? I can't keep you people out of the store. I'll take your money when you've got any. I don't have to stand around and carry on a big conversation."

As Alex walked to the door he was conscious of Bolley standing there, watching him, the piggy little eyes remote and suspicious.

After he got behind the wheel, he knew that there was something he had to do, and the longer he delayed it the more difficult it would become. He forced himself to drive to Palm Street. The old house had been painted not long ago, but it was the same colour, cream with dark brown trim. He glanced up at the window which had been the window to his room, and went on to the porch and pushed the bell, stood looking through the screen into the dim hallway. It could well be like the response he had got from Cal. But this time it would hurt.

"I'm coming, I'm coming," he heard her say, and she came down the hall in a faded print dress, wiping her hands on her apron, a little sparrow of a woman with white hair, sharp features, an air of timeless nervous energy.

"Yes?" she said and looked up at him through the screen, and quite suddenly her face broke, a shattering of delicate ancient glass. And for the first time he realized how lovely a girl Myra Ducklin must have been. She fumbled the screen open and tugged at him and pulled him into the hallway, and hugged him and made broken sounds against his chest that finally turned into an endless saying of his name. She pushed him away and, holding his arms, looked up into his face, trying through tears to smile at him in an accusing and disciplinary way.

"You never wrote!" she said in a shaky voice. "You never did write me one letter, Alex!"

"I tried, Aunt Myra. Honest to God, I tried!"

"Now no cussin' in front of a church lady." She clung to his hands. "You turned into a man, Alex. I guess nobody could call you handsome and I guess you know that. But you've got a good face, Alex. It's a good strong face. Come in the sitting-room. Oh, it's so good to see you! It's been so long, So terrible long."

They went into the small, immaculate, old-fashioned parlour. She sat beside him on the couch and held his hand tightly and said, "There's a big box in the attic. I packed it all up. The old papers and things from your folks and the photographs and all. And your school records and those sports things you won, and the clothes you left behind. I put moth crystals in. Everything is safe, but I guess it wasn't much point, saving the clothes. Joe, he was going to throw everything out he was that mad, but I knew that wouldn't be a Christian act."

"I . . . I didn't have any idea you'd be so glad to see me, Aunt Myra. I guess Joe wouldn't have. I'm sorry about Joe."

"You just don't have much sense, Alex Doyle. That little trouble you had doesn't have anything to do with love, and you should know that. When there's love, the least you can do is give folks a chance to forgive, and you never even gave me a chance to go through the motions. I prayed for so long you'd come back, come to the door just like you did, and then I thought it would never happen and I guess I gave up praying. But there hasn't been a day in all that time I haven't thought about you and where you were and what you were doing. I'll tell you, I loved Joe Ducklin every day of my life, but the way he carried on about you and getting them to arrest you and all, it was pretty hard to keep on loving. Somehow . . . after that happened, it wasn't really ever the same between us. It was almost the same, but there was a little something gone. And that somehow made it worse when he died, Alex. I don't know why but it did."

"You make me ashamed of myself, Aunt Myra."

"Now let's not get carrying on, boy. I can see how you were terrible hurt, the way Joe did you. And a wife has to share the way people think about her husband. You did a real foolish thing and it looked like it was a mean thing, but I knew better on account I knew there was no meanness in you. It was strong drink that did it, and bad company. There was a wild bunch of young folk back then, and I can tell you they seem to get wilder every year, so you don't know what the world is coming to, and sometimes I think it will take one of those terrible bombs to make things clean again, but that is blasphemous talk. You just make it up now by telling me everything you've done in all the years you've been gone, Alex. I got to keep holding onto your hand to keep making sure you're here."

"Aunt Myra, I wasn't going to tell you this. But now I guess I should." She listened intently while he told her, just as he had told Betty Larkin, about the robbery.

When he was through she bobbed her head and she said, "Oh, if I could just be sure Joe Ducklin could know about this!"

"I tried to tell him, Aunt Myra, over in the jail in Davis, but he didn't feel like listening."

She looked surprisingly fierce for a moment. "He wouldn't let me go with him. And he never said a word about that. Not even on his dying bed did he have the . . . common decency to tell me anything about that. All I knew was you said you did it, boy, and they let you pick the army instead of jail. Well, it's all over now, but when you think on it, isn't it a terrible waste, boy? The things folks do to one another. I didn't even ask you if you're married!"

"I'm not married, Aunt Myra."

"That's no kind of life, Alex. Bad hours and bad food, and you turn into a fussy old bachelor. There's some nice girls right here in town."

"Don't go so fast!"

"Now you tell me what you've been doing."

He told her about the two wars, and far places. A young Negro woman, slim and pretty in a white uniform, came to the doorway and said nervously, "Miz Ducklin, I don't want to bust in, but that Miz Stimson, she don't look right to me. She breathing awful funny."

"Excuse me, Alex," Myra Ducklin said. She trotted off and he saw her hurrying up the hall staircase. She came down in a few moments and he heard her on the phone, apparently talking to a Dr. Kearnie, a name Alex did not recognize. She went back upstairs and was gone about ten minutes. The door buzzer sounded and the Negro girl admitted a young man with a medical satchel and a bold, unkempt black moustache.

A little later the doctor came down and used the phone and left. Myra came back into the parlour, looking tired and subdued.

"She died right after Dr. Kearnie got here. Old Mrs. Stimson. Ninety-one, she was. I won't be able to visit now, Alex. I got to phone the family, and then Jeffry Brothers will be sending over to pick her up. And then I'll have to visit with the other people I've got and cheer them up. They get awful low when somebody passes on."

"I don't understand, Aunt Myra. Is this a nursing home?"

"Licensed and everything," she said, and looked slightly ashamed. Ever since he had entered the house he had been subconsciously disturbed by the elusive and unfamiliar odour of medication and that sick sweet undertone of illness.

"When Joe passed on, if I'd had any sense, I'd have sold out the store right away. But I tried to run it myself and I didn't know as much as I thought I knew. So by the time I'd put most of the other money Joe left into it, I ended up having to sell it for less than I could have got in the first place. I like to keep busy. You know that. I've got two full-time girls to help with the cleaning and cooking and all, and one practical nurse, but she's off sick right now." She sighed, lowered her voice. "I know when I look at it square they're here to die, but sometimes it takes a lot of getting used to. Where are you staying, Alex? I can't even offer you a room. I turned that store-room off behind the pantry into my bedroom. You aren't going to take off right soon again, are you?"

He told her he was out on the beach, and he was staying for a time. She kissed him and beamed upon him and patted his shoulder, her eyes shiny. "You came back, finally. I guess I knew you would all along. You'll have to come get that box of your stuff, boy."

Doyle drove slowly back out to the beach. Now that he had seen her, he wondered how he could have been so wrong in his thinking about her for so many years. It had been pride, perhaps, that corrosive disease, which had prevented him from seeing the truth his heart was trying to tell him.

He changed to trunks and assembled the rod and walked out

on to the beach. Something was feeding noisily about two hundred feet out. He waded until the water was above his waist and, after a half-dozen attempts, he was able to put the lure where he wanted it. It was a pearly day with a look of mystery, and he could feel the heat of the hidden sun. It was a school of four-pound jacks, wolfing the demoralized minnows. He beached four and released them before the school broke off feeding. The physical contest eased his emotional turmoil, his deep sense of guilt. It was nearly noon when, after a hundred glances north along the beach, he saw someone on the beach in front of the Proctor cottage. And, in what he hoped was a casual way, he began to move up the beach, casting aimlessly.

The woman squatted on the wet sand, right at the surf line. She had an aluminium pot and she seemed to be grubbing in the sand with her hands. He realized that she was digging up coquinas, those tiny brightly patterned clams that can be found an inch or so beneath the surface of the wet sand on nearly all the Gulf beaches.

She was very sun-browned, a trim-bodied, good-sized woman in a blue two-piece swim suit in batik pattern. She had hair that had greyed almost to white, cropped short. The muscles moved smoothly in her arms and shoulders as she searched for the coquinas, and she sat on her heels without strain.

She seemed to be unaware of him. He moved to within ten feet of her while retrieving a cast, and then said, "Pardon me, ma'am."

She looked up at him with obvious irritation. Her brows were heavy and jet black, her face angular, handsome. "Yes?" The voice was deep and rather husky.

"If you want to get those easy, you get you a piece of screen like they use sifting aggregate for concrete. You get a frame and props for it, and a shovel. And then you shovel that soupy sand against it and you'll get all the coquinas you can use."

"Thank you so much for your advice. I am not terribly interested in efficiency or speed. I prefer doing it this way."

"Okay, ma'am. Sorry. They sure make a wonderful broth, you just simmer 'em long enough. Me, I like it best real cold with a little Worcestershire and tabasco."

She returned to her task and did not answer. He cast again and retrieved the lure. "You must be staying here in the Proctor place, ma'am. Used to come here years back for Sunday School picnics. Miz Proctor, she was in charge of the whole Sunday School."

She looked up at him with exasperation. "That's all mildly interesting, I suppose, but I really don't feel . . . chatty."

"Just being neighbourly. I'm two cottages down. Moved in yesterday. Name is Doyle. Alexander Doyle. Alex. Used to live here and I just came on back to see how the old place looks. Got homesick, I guess. First time in the States in three years. Down in Venezuela on construction jobs."

Her face darkened under the tan. "You don't seem to take a hint, Mr. Doyle. I understand that I can't order you off this beach, at least that area below the high-tide line. I would if I could. I do not feel like talking to you. I do not feel like giving you the opportunity to work the conversation around to the point where you can indulge your idle curiosity by asking dull questions about the colonel."

"Excuse me, ma'am, but I don't know what the hell you're talking about. What colonel? I'm not curious about anything. I wasn't working around to anything, I was just being friendly."

She stood up, facing him. From her face he guessed she was in the middle forties. She had the body of a far younger woman. "This cottage is where Colonel M'Gann lives. I am his sister. Does that name mean anything to you?"

"Why, sure! It does now. I knew Jenna Larkin in high school. I missed the papers, being out of the country like I was, but folks here have told me about it. Honest, I didn't know you people were in the Proctor place."

"In that case, Mr. Doyle, I want you to accept my apology for being rude. We have both had a . . . bellyfull of magazine people and would-be writers and amateur detectives and plain curiosity seekers. So we have become rather . . . antisocial. The traffic has dropped off considerably, but we still get a few—one tiresome little man just last week who had the gall to want to see the colonel to ask him if he could ghost write a book for my brother. I chased him away and he became quite abusive. Horrible teenagers have walked here on the beach, pretending to choke each other and fall dead."

"Then if I was you, I'd move away. You're just renting the place, aren't you? Or did you buy it?"

"We're renting it, and your suggestion is most valid. I would dearly love to move away from here. But the colonel insists on staying."

"I'm not curious. Well, to be honest, I guess I am, a little. Anybody would be, naturally. But I don't care enough about it to come around asking questions. I guess it was a bad thing for you people but the way I look at it, unless that Jenna Larkin changed a hell of a lot since when I knew her, I guess she wasn't what you'd call a big loss. Hope I haven't said the wrong thing."

"You haven't, Mr. Doyle. Indeed you haven't! If any human being could be classified as worthless, Jenna could. And it is a terrible waste for my brother to keep on brooding about her. I hope I wasn't too rude to you."

"I don't mind. I understand how you'd feel about people trying to strike up a conversation. As long as I'll be a neighbour for a while, I just won't talk about it to you at all."

"That will be splendid, Mr. Doyle. You're one of the few sympathetic people I've found in this . . . truly dreadful community. They seem more like animals down here than people, really. I don't mean to offend you, of course."

"I guess it's because there isn't much goes on here, and when something does, they like to make a big thing about it."

Suddenly the grey surface of the water was torn and boiled just fifty feet away, and the small bait fish leaped in panic from predatory jaws. He cast beyond the area, yanked the dude into it, and felt the strike. He brought in a Spanish mackerel of about two and a half pounds. He tossed it up on the beach and caught two more of the same size before the disturbance was over.

"Welcome to two of those if you can use 'em," Alex said. "One will do me. Mackerel. Good eating. They don't so often work in this close."

"You got them so quickly!"

"When they're working, you get them quick."

"Can I see that thing they bit on?" He held the lure so she could inspect it. "I will take the fish, and thank you very much, Mr. Doyle." She looked at him dubiously, uncertainly. "I . . . I wonder if you would do me a great favour, Mr. Doyle."

"Anything I can, ma'am."

"I have been trying to get my brother to take an interest in something. I thought fishing might be good for him. Neither of us know anything about it. I bought a pole and things, and we fished with frozen shrimp, but it was all very boring. We got some nasty little catfish, and one horrible-looking flat thing, and some little things with prickers all over them. But what you were doing looks as if my brother might enjoy it. The pole and reel I bought are much, much heavier than that thing you use. Is it hard to use?"

"No ma'am. It's easy."

"And it wouldn't be a . . . physical strain, I mean to catch something big?"

"Anything too big will just bust loose."

"If I give you the money, could you buy the same sort of outfit for the colonel? How much would it cost?"

"Less than twenty dollars for all he'll need. I can get it and you can pay me later when I bring it around."

"Well . . . all right. And then could you show my brother how to operate it? I don't really know if he *will* take an interest in it, but he does need some hobby. You see, he's never really had a hobby. Except all those model aeroplanes when we were little. I used to help him. We're twins. Then, when he was in school he worked. We both did. He didn't work when he was at the Point, of course. He has always been such a . . . dedicated man. So diligent. There was no room in his life for the things other men did. The fishing and the sports. Oh, he always kept himself in wonderful physical condition through exercise, so he could better accomplish his work. I sometimes wish he'd had more . . . desire and opportunity to play. Then maybe he wouldn't have been so vulnerable when she. . . . Anyway, now that he can't work he has nothing to fill his time. I don't want to trouble you, Mr. Doyle, but I would . . . be most grateful to you."

"Glad to do it," he said.

"If you could find time to come around to-morrow with the fishing things? About this same time. He naps in the afternoon."

She thanked him again and put the two mackerel in the aluminium pot on top of the coquinas, the long slim mackerel tails protruding over the rim, rigid in death. He walked back towards the cottage with the single fish. Thus far it was all too easy. And would continue to be easy, very probably. It sometimes seemed terrifying to him that it was so utterly easy to disarm people by lying to them. People seemed so recklessly anxious to take you at your face value. They would believe what they wanted to believe, and you need only to guide their thinking in a gentle and unobtrusive way. It had worked so many times before, and it would work again. The fishing had been a lucky accident. But if it had not been the fishing, it would be something else. Celia M'Gann was obviously lonely. Once her suspicions had been quieted, she would have responded to casual friendliness. And, inevitably, he would have met the colonel. And, inevitably, made the chance to be alone with him. This fishing gambit did not alter anything. It merely accelerated things.

He cleaned and fried the mackerel and ate it for lunch. He thought of going in to see the Larkin boat yard. And see Betty again. But it seemed too soon. He had accomplished one decisive step in the mission. And now it was waiting time until he could walk up the beach to-morrow with the new tackle.

He stretched out on the bed and wondered who had taken over in Montevideo. He hoped they'd picked Schmidt. He wouldn't mess it up the way some of the new kids might. . . .

He came up out of sleep and heard somebody rapping sharply and insistently on the back door.

CHAPTER FIVE

THERE was a sedan in the back yard, a dark dusty green with bumper aerial for short wave, and a red spot on the roof, and a faded yellow decal on the door that said *Sheriff—Ramona County*.

A man stood on the back steps, a dark silhouette against the white shell glare of the back yard. Doyle had belted on his old seersucker robe. He felt sweaty and fogged by sleep.

"I was sleeping," he said.

"So wake up," the man said, and pulled the door open and came into the kitchen. He was about five seven, with a toughened lean-ness about him, a deeply seamed and sallow face, narrow eyes the colour of spit. He wore bleached khakis, tailored to his body and freshly pressed, a pale, cream-coloured ranch hat. The trouser legs were neatly bloused over black gleaming paratrooper boots in a small and curiously dainty size.

On the pocket of his shirt was pinned one of the most ornate badges Doyle had ever seen, large and golden, with some red enamel and some blue enamel. In a very legible way it said *Sheriff*, and in much smaller letters it said *Deputy*, and it said *Ramona County, State of Florida*, and bore some sort of ornate seal. He wore a black pistol belt with a black speed holster, old leather, shiny and supple with care and age, worn canted to bring the revolver butt-down to the level of "Gunsmoke". A chrome whistle chain disappeared into the other shirt pocket. A black night stick hung from the other side of the pistol belt, white leather thong suspended from a small brass hook.

He brought into the kitchen the slow creak and jingle of petty authority, and a thinly acid edge of sweat, a black-swamp accent and an air of mocking silence. Doyle felt irritated by his own feeling of intense wariness. It was a legacy from the faraway years when there would be trouble and men like this one would come to the bayou and go to Bucket Bay. You let them swagger through the house and poke around as they pleased. You never told them anything. And you never made a fuss because they would put knots on your head.

Yet on another level he sensed his kinship to this man. That light-eyed cracker sallowness, the generations of bad diet and inbreeding behind both of them that had resulted, curiously, in a dogged and enduring toughness, a fibrous talent for survival.

"I've seen you before," Alex said.

"Sure you've seen me before, Doyle. Turkey Kimbroy and I, we tooken you over to Davis long time ago to he'p you get in the army. If'n they'd shot your ass off, you wouldn't be back here giving me problems."

"I'm not making any problems."

"That's what I got to be sure about. Turkey don't have no problems any more. Fool nigger had a razor hung down his back and when Turkey beat on him a little, nigger took one swipe and spilled Turk all over the side of the road. Made me a carefuller man."

Doyle remembered how this Donnie Capp had been on that long-ago ride, a pale slim blond man with a limp, not afraid to be friendly to the boy they were taking in.

"What's that got to do with me, Donnie?"

The thin mouth tightened. "I get called Donnie by my friends. Niggers and thieves, they call me Mister Deputy, sir. You try it."

"Mister Deputy, sir."

"That's nice. Now stand still a minute. Okay. Now you just walk on ahead of me slow while I look around some."

Capp made a leisurely and careful inspection of the cottage. He found the money belt on a hook in the back of the bedroom closet. Doyle made no protest as he took it out and unzipped it, fingered the money.

"Maybe you better come along in and tell Sheriff Roy how come you got all the cash money, Doyle."

"If you think it's necessary, I'd be glad to."

"Then you can tell me how you got it."

"You can look in the top bureau drawer on the left again,

Mister Deputy, sir. Under the shorts. A folder with passport and visas and work papers and pay vouchers."

He opened the folder, looked at the papers, threw folder and papers on the bed.

"But right now you got no job, right?"

"No job. Not yet."

"Where do you figure on working?"

"Some place around here."

"I don't figure that way. I don't figure that way *at* all. Over in Davis we got pictures of you and we got prints and they're in a file. And that there is what you call a dead file. Now I don't want to have to go move that file up into the other file, the one where we keep the records of people living around here. I'm just lazy, I guess. You know, maybe you forgot to stop by and register as a known criminal, Doyle?"

"Would that be necessary? It was a suspended sentence."

"I'm not up on all my law, but maybe it would have been sort of friendly of you to stop by when you come in and not let me find you by accident. And you could have brought us up to date on the police trouble you've had since you been gone."

"There hasn't been any."

"Guess you been clever about it, huh?"

"Can I ask you a queston?"

"Always glad to oblige."

"Why are you on my back? I'm not in any trouble. I don't intend to get into any. I came back here because . . . this is home. That's all. There isn't any law about that, is there?"

"You know, Doyle, the end of this here county is about the cleanest end of any county in the state. Roy likes for me to handle it just the way I do, on account of he doesn't like sending in bad figures on crime up to Tallahassee. And he knows I know this end of the county better than anybody, so he just rides along and he lets me handle it all my own sweet way. You understand?"

"I guess so."

"And one way I do, anybody making for trouble, I just up and run 'em off. Let 'em light some other place. Let 'em go spoil the crime figures in some other county. Now if there's a family or something concerned, then I let 'em stay. But I persuade them to stay out of trouble. You haven't even got a job, so it's no trouble to run you off. Besides, I don't like having you out here on the beach. You stay down in Bucket Bay, I might think on letting you stay 'round."

"I want to stay right here."

"What you want and what you get is two different ends of the rabbit. All this here for miles around is my little ole bait bucket. I keep it nice and clean and throw out the spoiled bait. It isn't good for a fella like you not to have a job. You lay around and get ideas and pretty soon you make me some trouble. But I'll show you I'm not a bad guy, Doyle. You paid a month rent, and it ain't likely you can get it back. So all you got to do is ask me nice if you can stay here, and tell me you won't make trouble."

"I'd like to stay. Please. And I won't make trouble."

Donnie Capp smiled in a thin way and unhooked the night stick, and glided towards Doyle. "Now I'll be quieten you down a little."

Just as Doyle started to back away, raising his arms, the stick smashed down on the point of his left shoulder, bruising the nerves, numbing his arm from shoulder to fingertips. In painful reflex, he struck out at Capp with his right fist. Capp stepped aside and paralysed his right arm with the same cruel and scientific blow, then shouldered him back against the wall beside the bedroom doorway. He could not raise either arm.

Capp jabbed the end of the club into the pit of Doyle's belly, doubling him over. And then, calmly, professionally, he went to work. Through the haze of pain and confusion of impact, Doyle realized that he was getting a scientific head beating. No blow was enough to destroy consciousness. And, in between the rhythms of the blows on his skull, Capp was taking practised strokes at shins and thighs, forearms and biceps, hips and calves. And, in one area of cold and special horror, Doyle realized that the man was crooning softly along with his grunts of exertion. "Now . . . a little of this . . . and some more . . . of that. And a touch here . . . and here."

He was only partially aware of it when Capp straightened him up and belted him across the belly and rib cage. He swung one almost gentle blow into the groin, and Doyle heard his own hoarse yell, coming from an echoing, metallic distance. He doubled, took a harder blow than any of the others, directly over the ear, and tumbled forward, sensing the impact of hitting the floor, but feeling no pain from it. He lay on his side, knees against his chest, in a welcome silence.

With his eyes half open he could see the shiny black boots six inches from his face. Capp was somewhere above him, a thousand feet tall, talking to him in a remote voice.

". . . have the miz'ries for a couple days, Doyle. But you'll keep thinking on this long after you're walking real good. And you'll be nice and tame. On account of you know you make any trouble for Donnie Capp and he'll come back and we'll try it again, with a lot of different tricks I didn't even use. And we'll keep practisin' on it 'til we get it down perfect enough for television. Why, there's niggers I ain't laid this stick on in years, and all I got to do is show it to them and they turn white as a piece of soap. I want every time you think of Donnie Capp, you get sweaty. Then you'll be real good and safe to be around decent folk."

He saw the boots turn, and he heard the footsteps as Donnie went through the cottage. He heard the screen door slap shut, and then a car door, and then the explosive roar of a powerful motor. The motor sound died away.

He sobbed once, more in shame and anger than in pain. After a long time he began to slowly uncoil, straightening his body an inch at a time, enduring the agony. He rolled over on to his face, worked himself up on to his elbows and was wrenchingly ill. And then, like a half-trampled bug, he crawled a hundred miles to his bed. When he had rested long enough, he could pull himself up on to his knees and from that position squirm onto the bed. The effort exhausted him. There was a roaring in his ears. He turned and groaned and at last found the least agonizing position. And knew he could not sleep. And slid away then, sweaty, into sleep. . . .

A moist and wonderful coolness on his forehead awakened him to a world where the face of Betty Larkin was close to his, vast and out of focus, her mouth angry and her eyes concerned as she held the cold cloth against his forehead. He became aware that it was a late afternoon world of slanting sun, and aware that his body was one vast throbbing, shimmering pain.

"I didn't get the licence number," he said in a low and rusty voice.

"Do you feel awful?"

"I've never felt worse. Nobody has ever felt worse."

"I phoned Gil Kearnie to come out here too, and he ought to be along soon. Dr. Kearnie. He's new here and very good."

"How did you know about this?"

"I heard Donnie Capp talking to Buddy near the office. I just caught a few words and Donnie was talking about something he'd done to you. I know Donnie, so I went out and demanded to know. He said it wasn't any business of a nice girl like me, but he had heard you had come back so he'd come out here and got you quieted down. I said I didn't know you were excited. Then Buddy laughed at me and said that Donnie had just given you a little taste of the Ramona massage. So I called Donnie a dirty, sadistic little monster and I drove right out here. You didn't answer so I came in. And you looked so terrible, I hurried back and phoned Gil and came back here. He should be here any minute. I could kill Buddy for acting like he thought it was funny for Donnie to come out here and hit you."

"It's an old southern custom, Miss Betty. Head beating. I can be thankful it was by an expert. It's the amateurs who kill you."

When Dr. Kearnie arrived, Betty let him in and went out into the other room while Dr. Kearnie examined him. Except for the moustache and the tired wise look around his eyes, Kearnie looked eighteen.

After poking and prodding, Kearnie dressed the two places on Alex's skull and the one place on his left shin where the club had split the skin.

"He didn't hit you across the kidneys?"

"Not that I can remember."

"Good. That will save you a lot of pain. And that's dangerous. In some cases he's done some permanent damage."

"You've treated other ... victims, Doctor?"

"A few. He's an expert. He's had years of practice, and he enjoys his work. I don't think there's any need of X-ray in your case. The ribs feel firm. If there's continuing pain, come on in to the office. You're in good shape, Mr. Doyle. If you have to take a beating, it helps to be in condition. I'll leave you something for pain. You'll feel a hundred years old to-morrow. My advice is force yourself to move around. Get out in the sun. Swim. Bake it out."

"And forget it?"

Kearnie raised one eyebrow. "That wouldn't come under the heading of medical advice. But I don't believe it would be ... practical to try to do anything about it. Not without several witnesses who can be kept beyond the reach of the deputy and his club. He's a psychopathic personality."

"How about the bill?"

"Drop in at the office. The nurse will have it. Take one of these every four hours. Two, if the pain is severe." He snapped his bag shut and stood up and for a moment ceased to be the formal and professional young doctor. "The psychological effects of a beating are interesting, Mr. Doyle. The standard result is a great big desire to keep your head down so it won't be whipped again."

"I think that's what he had in mind. Then I'm an exception."

"What's your reaction?"

"I'm going to fix his wagon, Doctor. I don't know how. I just want him one time, without that gun and club."

"I hope you get him. It would be a pleasure to have to patch him up."

After Kearnie left, Betty came back in and said, "Isn't he a lamb?"

"A nice little guy."

"What can I do?"

"I'd like some water so I can take one of those things he left, because I am hurting slightly fierce. And then if I can lean on you, I'd like to make it to the plumbing section. When I'm back in bed you can take off."

"No food?"

"I don't think so."

"And I think you will." She got water and he took the pill. He got his legs over the side of the bed and she pulled him to his feet with slow and gentle strength. He got his left arm around her shoulders. His arm felt like a big sausage roll full of putty. She put her brown right arm around his waist. She walked him slowly to the bath-room, helped him in, closed the door on him. When he came out he opened the door himself and took two teetering steps before she could hurry to him to support him. She told him he was the colour of a sheet of paper, and helped him into bed. She brought his cigarettes, found more pillows and propped him up. He sat and smoked and inventoried his bruised areas, and listened with a certain domestic pleasure to the busy sounds she was making in the kitchen.

And thought, almost with calmness, about Donnie Capp. Those men had their uses. There had been a couple like that, ones he had been glad to take on patrol whenever he could. The catlike, fearless ones, the killing breed, amoral, anti-social, and entirely dangerous.

She had found a tray somewhere and she set it on a table she had placed close to the bed. The servings were abundant and smelled good, and he discovered that he was indeed hungry.

"You knew what you were doing out there, Miss Betty."

"That is one primitive kitchen. I guess I like to cook because

I just live to eat. I eat like a wolf and never gain a pound. Knock wood. I am just not the dainty feminine type, I guess."

"You must have left work early."

"I'm my own boss down there, Alex. I'm pretty well caught up. Some delinquent accounts to needle. The slack season is starting. It will pick up a little in July, and then September will be a graveyard. When we're rushed, I'm one busy kid. I even pitch in on the other end when it's needed. I can clean and adjust a marine carb, adjust spark plugs, do compass compensation. And I can paint hell out of a hull."

"A paragon."

"Irreplaceable. Anyway, I like it. Sails and stinkpots both. The smell of marine varnish. Everything about the water. Buddy is the same way. We're hooked, I guess. We're on the stuff."

"To get back to Donnie Capp."

"Do we want to?"

"That little horror with the black club tried to turn me into a rabbit. The so-called nice people in Ramona don't mind having him around because he never whips their heads. Maybe they even think he's doing a good job. A man like that can be dangerous, Betty. He can get to thinking there's nothing he can't get away with."

"I guess I'm . . . guilty too, Alex. I'd heard how he likes to use that club, but I thought he used it on . . . people who needed it. I didn't know he'd do anything like this. Did you try to . . . throw him out or anything?"

"No. I know the type. He wanted the 'Mister Deputy, sir,' treatment and I gave it to him. To make sure I'd stay humble, he took his little club and went to work like a man felling a tree."

"That's terrible!"

"The worst thing is I can talk rough, but I know damn well I'd better not be fool enough to go after him."

"Well, I'll tell you one thing, Alex Doyle. He's not coming after you again. Even though Daddy's dead, there's still some push behind the name of Larkin. And I'm going to let Donnie know and let Sheriff Lawlor know that if there's anything else like this, Buddy and I are going to make the biggest stink they ever ran into. And I know that doesn't change the fact that he has already hurt you."

"I've been hurt before. I'll get over it. But it would be nice to know it isn't likely to happen again very soon."

She took the tray away and washed the dishes and came back and sat by the bed. It was one of those rare evenings when for a short time all the world is suffused with an orange-yellow glow and all objects are strangely vivid and distinct. The glow from the window by the bed fell softly on her face lighting it so clearly that he could see, in the light grey iris of her eye, little flecks of golden brown close to the pupil. And the strong brown column of her throat with the tender hollow at the base of it, and a heaviness of the level mouth, and a tawny brown of her eyebrows, a shade darker than the sun-struck mane of hair. Here was the special and stirring beauty of the female creature in perfect health, all glow and warmth.

She looked away suddenly and stood up with an awkwardness she had not displayed before. He knew he had stared at her too intently, and had upset her perfectly unconscious poise.

"I guess I'd better go."

"Thanks for everything you've done."

"It doesn't make much of a welcome home."

"I didn't expect too much."

"Alex . . . Just why did you come back?"

"I told you."

She looked down at him, frowning in the fading light. "Something bothers me a little. You don't seem to . . . fit."

"I don't know what you mean."

"Neither do I, exactly. Maybe I shouldn't try to say anything."

"Go ahead."

"You say you've been just wandering, working on construction jobs. The way you talk, it isn't always the same. Sometimes it's real piny woods talk. And then you change and talk as if you had a lot more . . . background and education. I'm not a snob. It just seems strange to me. And there is about you something I can't quite put my finger on. I guess it's sort of an unconscious . . . air of importance. Not importance, maybe. Significance. As if people had been paying attention when you had something to say. And those real sharp bright sports shirts and slacks don't seem to me to be . . . right. They're what you'd buy, I guess, if you are what you say you are. But in some way they're wrong for you."

"I'm bugged by the gay threads, doll."

"I just want to know if you're putting on some kind of an act that I don't understand."

"That's a pretty strange idea, Betty."

"Your nails are well kept, Alex. And your hands aren't calloused."

"Nowadays we sit up there in those big cabs and push the little buttons."

"If it is an act, Alex, has it got anything at all to do with . . . Jenna?"

"Honey, I came back to my home town. With a buck or two saved. Thought I might stay if I found something just right. But the man worked me over good with his little club, and now I'm not so high on sticking around. When the lumps are gone, I might just up and move along in case he gets some more ideas. That's all there is."

She stared at him for a few more moments and then smiled and said, "All right. Good night, Alex."

He lay and listened to the jeep drive away into the dusk. He had a new and special appreciation for her. She was a big healthy blonde and he had been careless. Her intuitions and perceptions were almost frighteningly keen. There was nothing opaque about Miss Betty. And now he could not, when he was with her, revert to a flawless performance of the role he had selected for himself. She was sharp enough to realize that would confirm her guess. And so he would have to maintain the same level of carelessness. It would be easier and safer to avoid her. But he found that prospect surprisingly distasteful.

CHAPTER SIX

BY the time Doyle was up and shaved and dressed on Thursday, he knew that it wasn't going to be one of the best days he had ever spent. His arms were leaden. Each slow movement had to be tested cautiously to see how much it was going to hurt. Even in areas where he could not remember being hit, his muscles felt as though they had been dipped in cement and rolled in broken glass.

It was a day of high, white, scattered clouds that frequently masked the sun, and a fresh north-west wind with a hint of chill in it. After he had breakfast and cleaned up, he hobbled slowly out on to the beach, dragging an ancient grey navy blanket.

After he had baked for nearly an hour, Betty Larkin said, "Good morning! I guess you feel better." She beamed down at him and dropped lithely into a Buddha pose on the corner of his blanket. She wore a pale grey one-piece swim suit with small blue flowers embroidered on it. She carried a white rubber cap and a big towel.

"I feel just fine. I feel just a little bit better than if I was poking myself in the eye with a stick."

"I saw you out here, so I went in and changed. Hope you don't mind?"

"Not a bit. If I don't have to swim too."

"But you do! I heard Gil tell you to."

"I know. But I haven't got any character."

"Come on now! Come on!"

He groaned as he stood up. He followed her to the water. She tucked that bright heavy hair into the rubber cap and dived in and swam out. He paddled very slowly and tentatively, floating often, until, much sooner than he would have thought possible, some of the pain and stiffness began to leave his muscles. And he began to extend himself. He swam beside her, and they swam out to the unexposed sand bar a couple of hundred yards out. He swam with the untutored ease and confidence of any Floridian born and raised near the water. His stroke, he knew, looked clumsy, but it got him through the water quickly and without thrash or great effort. She was a superb swimmer. He knew she had had coaching. She was as sleek and swift and graceful as an otter.

They stood on the bar, facing each other. The water came to her shoulders.

"I talked to Donnie last night. First he tried to laugh it off. Then he got mad. He told me it wasn't any of my business. But I just got twice as mad as he did, and he finally got it through his thick head that I would make trouble for him, all that I possibly could, if he touches you again. And then he pretended that a great light had suddenly dawned on him and he . . ." she paused and looked towards the shore, her face colouring slightly under the deep tan ". . . said he didn't know we were in love. And even if I wasn't showing much taste, he wouldn't beat up any boy-friend of mine. It was just his way of saving face. He knows better than that." She laughed in a bitter and humourless way. "I guess the whole town knows better than that. In his own way, he was being as nasty as he could."

"I don't know what you mean about the whole town."

"It's a long dull story. Anyway, he got the message."

"And thank you. It's a pleasure hiding behind your skirts. I would like to meet him some time outside the State of Florida."

"And I had a scrap with Buddy. No sister of his was going to be buddying around with no sneak thief. I told him you didn't do it, and why you'd said you had. So he said it looked like I'd swallow anything you felt like telling me. I . . . got him straightened out after a while. Now he'd like to see you. But he won't come out here. I would like to have you stop at the yard. Sort of casual-like. I mean, if you're going to settle here, Alex, it's people like Buddy who will make the difference."

"I'll stop by some time, Betty."

"Good."

They swam back in. She towelled herself, pulled off the cap, fluffed her hair, sat on the blanket and took one of his cigarettes. He stretched out near her. She sat looking out towards the water, hugging her knees. She had missed one portion of her back when she had dried herself. The sun-silver droplets of water stood out against the deep warm brown of her shoulder.

"About what I said last night, Alex."

"Yes?"

"About if you were playing a part or something. I guess you thought I was crazy. I guess that ever since . . . Jenna died, the whole town has been a little bit crazy. There were so many people prying. It's terrible the way they flock around. Oh, Donnie Capp had a ball. He really did. Some of them were crackpots and some were free-lance magazine writers and some were amateur detectives. Donnie ran them out just as fast as they came in. The business people weren't too happy about them being run off, but Donnie had the go-ahead from Sheriff Lawlor. There was some trouble about one man, about what they did to him over in Davis in the court house, but Donnie and two of the other deputies swore the man tried to run and fell down a flight of stairs, so nothing came of it. Donnie has said a hundred times that sooner or later, all by himself, he's going to get his hands on the man that killed Jenna. He takes it as a kind of personal insult that it should happen right in his own area. You know, after they locked up just about everybody who'd been in the Mack that night, Donnie, they say, got six or seven confessions before the sheriff pulled him off because there were too many newspaper people in town. Maybe he will find out someday. I hope he does, and on the other hand, I sort of hope he doesn't. Because then it will be the same thing all over again, and maybe worse with a trial and all. And it was very hard on Mother. You know, they'd come and stand in the side yard and stare at the house with their mouths hanging open, like so many morons.

"Anyway, Alex, we've gotten so conditioned to people trying to pry that I got the crazy idea maybe somebody had sent you back here to . . . write it up or something. I guess you could find out . . . personal things that an outsider couldn't. For one of those terrible slander magazines. I guess it was a silly idea."

"You have my word of honour that I'm not here to write up the story of Jenna."

She turned and smiled at him. "I guess it's just an idea that somebody should have thought of. How about me helping you find something to do, Alex? What have you been thinking about doing?"

"Sounds like I'm becoming some sort of a project."

"Maybe. Anyway, to keep the record straight, you don't have to worry that maybe I'm moving in on you in any kind of . . . emotional way. I'd just like . . . to be your friend, Alex. I like to be with you because you don't . . . get sloppy ideas and try to put your hands on me. That is sort of . . . what Donnie was referring to."

"I don't know what you mean."

"This is a small town and it's all public knowledge, and somebody will tell you all about it sooner or later, and they may get it all twisted, so I'll tell you first. So you won't make any . . . mistakes. Now you roll over the other way. It's easier to talk to your back on this topic."

"If it's something that makes you that uncomfortable, I don't have to hear it."

"I think I'd like you to hear it from me so you'll hear it truthfully. I was eleven when you left. And I guess it was all starting at about that time. Or maybe earlier. Jenna was Daddy's favourite. He had no time for me or Buddy. As if he had only just enough love for one of his kids. When we were little, he used to call Sunday Jenna's day. And whenever it was nice weather, they'd go off together on a Sunday picnic, sometimes in the car but almost always in that old skiff of his. I guess Buddy used to think the same way I did that when we got to be older, we'd go too. But it never turned out that way. Even though Jenna was six years older, I tried to be exactly like her. So he'd love me too. And get things for me the way he did for her. Little surprises, special things when he went on trips. And swing me up in his arms and laugh and call me his girl. But no matter how hard I tried to be just like her, it never worked, Alex. And so I began to feel that there was something wrong with me. Something terrible that I didn't know about and nobody would tell me. I used to try to guess what it was.

"And finally, as I kept on growing and growing, I decided that it was because I was so big and ugly. Jenna was so dainty and pretty and little. That was a quality I couldn't duplicate. When I was about eight, Daddy began to have trouble with Jenna. Some kind of trouble I didn't understand. She lost interest in going on picnics with him or anything like that. And he started beating her for the first time, and then buying her presents to make up. Usually he would beat her because she came home so late. And when he'd tell her she couldn't go out, she'd sneak out. I was secretly glad because I knew he was going to stop loving her and begin loving me. And I wouldn't be bad the way Jenna was being bad. I couldn't understand why she wouldn't go on picnics. You remember when Jenna ran away. Daddy was like a crazy man. He spent a lot of money hiring people to find her and bring her home, but nobody could find her. And then he just seemed to pull way back inside of himself, where nobody could reach him.

"About a year later, after I was twelve, I was invited to a party on Saturday afternoon. Daddy was home that day. I had a blue dress, a new one for the party. He was sitting in the living-room, reading some kind of business papers. I remember how Jenna used to go to him and turn around like a model when she was dressed up for a party. And he would call her his girl-friend and tell her how pretty she was. I guess I had some idea of cheering him up. And I did want him to be nice to me. So I went in and held my arms out and started turning around and around. It made me a little dizzy. After a little while he yelled for my mother. 'Lila!' he roared. 'Lila, come get revolving scarecrow out of here'!"

"What a filthy thing to do!"

"I ran upstairs and locked myself in my room. I wouldn't come out. I didn't go to the party. I cut up the blue dress until there wasn't one piece bigger than a postage stamp. And I refused to wear another dress until I went away to Gainesville after Daddy died. I was a big scarecrow, and jeans and shorts and khakis were good enough for scarecrows. That's part of it, part of the reason, I guess.

"Anyway, by the time I was fourteen, I had a pretty good knowledge of what Jenna's local career had been like. I won't mince words, Alex. It was as if she had some strange kind of disease. I don't know when or how it started. Or why. I know she had matured early, and I know I certainly didn't. At fifteen I still looked like a skinny boy. Maybe I wanted to be a boy. I don't know. But in the six months before Daddy died, I suddenly turned into the some approximate shape I still am. Sort of bovine, I guess you could call it.

"And I certainly didn't want to follow in Jenna's footsteps. She'd been gone a long time but they still talked about her. Dirty talk. It offended me. My ideas of romance were highly platonic. I wanted no part of kissing games. I was going to prove that there could be a Miss Larkin who could stay off her back, excuse the expression."

"In my freshman year I came back for Christmas vacation. All my friends were back. There was a big holiday dance at the high school auditorium. I had a date. There was a lot of drinking going on, out in the automobiles. And a rough element was hanging around, quite a few of them from Davis. By the time I realized my date was coming apart at the seams, he was too drunk to drive me home. I didn't want to spoil anybody else's fun by asking for an early ride home. So I started to walk it. It's only about a mile.

"I got about a hundred yards from the auditorium. And suddenly, there in the dark, there were three men around me. They wanted to know where I was going all by myself. They smelled like 'shine. I tried to run and they grabbed me and took me around behind the gym. I kept trying to scream and fight, but they kept clamping their grimy hands over my mouth, and they kept hitting me so that I was dazed. They ripped most of my clothes off, and two of them held me down. I could hear the band playing in the auditorium. If they hadn't been quite so drunk, I wouldn't have had a chance in the world. But I kept kicking and bucking and squirming. I think one of them was trying to knock me out. Then somebody drove in and when they came to that turn in front of the gym, the headlights shone on the little scene and it scared them. Just then the music stopped and I got my mouth free and yelled. And the car backed up so the lights were on us again. They took off. It was Ben Jeffry, coming to get his daughters. He had an old blanket in the car and he wrapped it around me. I was blubbering like a big baby. He took me to the doctor and even though I begged him not to make a fuss, he phoned the sheriff's office and reported it as rape. Sheriff Lawlor

himself come over. By then word had gotten to the dance somehow. Buddy was there, stag, and he came to the doctor's office and
then went home and got me some clothes. I wasn't marked up too
badly. I did develop two dandy black eyes, and I was cut on the
inside of the mouth. I didn't know who the men were, and I
couldn't describe them, and I couldn't have identified them anyway.

"You know this town, Alex. There was more damn talk. I felt
as if I couldn't walk down the street without people running out
of their houses to stare at me. By the time the gossips got through
with it, it was rape instead of attempted rape, and there had been
a whole gang of them, and I was pregnant. And, as I learned later,
there was one contingent that said that after all I was Jenna's
sister and I had been drinking and carrying on, and when I was
caught I'd started screaming to make people believe it was rape,
and I certainly knew who the men were. Very pretty.

"Well, I didn't really stop being shaky until the following
summer. I had a recurrent nightmare that lasted almost until
then. But I had begun to wonder about myself. When a boy at
school put his hand on my shoulder it made my stomach turn
over. And the idea of ever kissing anyone terrified me. I told
myself I'd have to stop being silly. After all, I certainly wanted
a home and kids eventually. And I decided to cure myself. Poor
Billy Hillyard. He'd always been kind of sappy about me. I guess
some men like the big cowy type. So I encouraged him. I didn't
see how Billy could upset me. So I gave him the right chance
to kiss me that summer. And I stood it just as long as I could and
then I had to push him away and jump out of the car and be
terribly, horribly sick. I told Billy it was probably food poisoning.
But, almost a month later, when exactly the same thing happened,
he lost interest.

"In my junior year it seemed to be getting worse instead of
better. I went to a woman doctor in Gainesville. I told her my
sad story. She satisfied herself that I was normal physically in every
respect and sent me to a psychiatrist in Tampa. I told him my
problem. I told him about the attempted rape. He asked a lot
of questions and he seemed much more interested in my childhood, in the father relationship and the sister relationship. I saw
him three times. Then he summarized. My basic instincts were
normal. But I could not react properly because of an extreme
and artificial frigidity that was the direct result of the pattern of
my home life. If I could spend eighteen months to two years in

deep analysis, he might be able to help me. That was impossible, for many reasons. And then the damndest thing happened. When I came home for spring vacation, I found that it was all over town. Just about everybody knew the intriguing fact that I had gone to a psychiatrist because I was scared to death of men. I soon found out how *that* had happened. The Tampa doctor had asked the name of my family doctor. And, I suppose as a professional courtesy, he had sent old Dr. Bormen a detailed report. Maybe you remember that Heeley woman who worked for him. She talked all over town about every treatment Doc Bormen ever gave. And she had spread the news, but good. Talk about invasion of privacy.

"But here is the worst thing about it, Alex. In some crazy way it made me a project for every Don Juan who heard about it. As if I were his personal Sleeping Beauty. And he was just the one to do me the enormous personal favour of waking me up. I was inundated by spooks. And they were all so terribly hurt that I wouldn't even give them a chance. Nobody would have to know a thing about it. I should just co-operate and try not to be afraid.

"They've given up now, most of them. But I'm still one of the town's more notorious crazies. I don't date, and I don't expect to. They watch me. And I suppose it's common knowledge that this is the third time I've been out here. You can understand now how Donnie was being nasty. I like the work at the yard. I like swimming and sailing the *Lady Bird*. I am quite content, thank you, but I do sometimes miss the opportunity of having a normal and uncomplicated friendship with a man. Too much girl talk bores me rigid. So that's it. Don't try to make me your project, Alex. I've filed away those dreams of the joker on the white horse who was always killing a fat dragon who looked like Mr. Bolley. I am resigned to my busy spinsterhood. Even though I think you a very nice guy, Alex, and it's good to see you after all these years, if you were to lay a hand on me in anything but accident or physical assistance, it would chill me to the very marrow of my bones. And as far as being held and kissed by a man, I would much rather stick my head into a bucket of snakes."

"I keep seeing that kid in the blue dress, wanting to be admired."

"So do I, Alex. She was so vulnerable. She can break my heart. You won't mind being a friend of the curious and unnatural Miss Larkin?"

"Not at all. I'm honoured, Miss Larkin."

She grinned at him. "Thanks. Say, is there any bread and anything to put between it?"

She made hefty sandwiches and they ate them on the beach. She went back to work. He baked himself in the sun and thought about her. It seemed curious that she should have such a distorted idea of her own appearance. That was probably part of the quirk. She thought of herself as big, bungling, bovine, cowy. At about five nine and an estimated hundred and thirty-five or forty pounds, she was certainly not tiny. But in the configuration of her body, in the walk and the grace of her, she was superbly feminine.

And, to his own wry amusement, he found himself composing mental charades in which he taught her that she could fulfil her role as a woman. It was a tantalizing situation, and he suspected that any other attitude towards her would be rather less than normal. But it was, of course, impossible. At the very first gesture towards any kind of intimacy, she would be off and running, never to look back.

He swam again, deliberately taxing the sore muscles, getting a certain satisfaction out of feeling the stretching and the pain. The club lumps on his skull were smaller, but still tender to the touch.

He showered and dressed and, at five o'clock, drove over into town. He went to Bolley's Hardware and bought another spinning rig and got a receipted bill to give Celia M'Gann. He had time to pick up some more groceries. He saw Junie Hillyard in the supermarket. As soon as she recognized him, she deliberately turned her back.

He started back towards the beach but, on impulse, just as he reached the foot of Bay Street he turned left on Front Street and drove along the bay shore and parked across from the Spanish Mackerel. As he walked towards the Mack he saw that it had changed very little. It was still a fisherman's bar that managed to look like a seedy lunch-room.

The late afternoon sunlight flooded in through the front windows. It sat in shabby patience looking across the street towards a fishing dock and boats and rotted pilings, and a pelican sitting on a slanting channel marker, and the green jungly growth of Ramona Key beyond the blue bay water.

The walls of the Mack were painted a soiled cream and green, cluttered with calendars, smutty mottoes, dusty mounted fish, pieces of net and old cork floats. There were warped venetian blinds at all the windows. The bar was on his left as he went in, topped with that imitation marble that used to be used on soda fountains. There were a dozen wooden bar stools stained dark. On his right were a dozen round tables with green formica tops in a green that clashed with the green on the walls. Across the back wall was a huge juke box, and two pinball machines, and a bowling game machine, a wall phone, an open door that exposed a narrow dingy area containing a blackened hamburg grill and a big tarnished coffee urn; a closed door that, he remembered, gave access to a back room used for card games, a kitchen, a staircase to the upstairs where Harry Bann lived.

The only customer was a man sitting on the stool farthest from the entrance. He wore a blue work shirt and denim pants, with the shirt sleeves rolled high to expose muscular arms thickly matted with curly black hair. He had an empty beer bottle and an empty glass in front of him. In profile his face looked dark and predatory under a forehead so high and bulging that it gave him something of the look of a surly embryo. The girl behind the bar was leaning on it and talking to the man in a voice so low that Doyle could not distinguish a word. But it all had the flavour of argument. She gave Doyle a casual glance when he took the stool nearest the door and returned to the inaudible wrangle.

He sat and stared at a card of potato chips, a jar of evil-looking pickles, a peanut machine, dusty liquor bottles aligned in front of a long blue panel mirror, a chrome paper-napkin dispenser, a withered menu with a water-ski-ing maiden on the front, a squeeze bottle of catsup and one of mustard, both obviously used often and carelessly, two busy flies on the coffee-spattered rim of a thick china sugar bowl, one poster announcing a dance over in Wellsland that had taken place two months ago, an ancient cash register which sat on a smeared glass case containing cigarettes, cigars, candy and, incongruously, a small plastic Santa Claus with a face of discontent.

He waited patiently, becoming more and more aware of the effluvia of stale grease, spilled beer and elderly nicotine. More subtle were the drifting odours of rancid coffee, perfume, fish scales, armpits, bad plumbing, and the nausea of ten thousand Saturday nights.

The girl finally walked down towards Doyle, a girl in her early twenties he guessed, with carroty red hair, a moon face lightly pocked with old acne scars, small features squeezed together in the middle of an expression of surly petulance, a pinched discontent. She had made her mouth vast and square with a shade of lipstick that did not suit her. She wore tight threadbare red shorts, a faded red halter, a small stained apron. Her figure was heavy, but reasonably good. Her skin had that damp and luminous blue-whiteness of cheap lard and overturned fish. When she walked she set her heels down so heavily she awakened little jinglings among the racked glasses, and her large breasts and heavy thighs joggled most unpleasantly.

He ordered a beer and watched her walk back to the beer cooler, the pulpy buttocks working under the frayed red fabric. From her colouring he guessed she was some kin to Harry Bann's wife. Mrs. Bann had been a meaty carroty woman who had often come to visit Doyle's mother at the hotel, and who had died that same winter Mary Ann Doyle had died. Some kind of kidney trouble.

She banged the beer down in front of him, slapped his change from fifty cents on the bar top and went back to her friend. The old man he had seen reading the comic book in Ducklin's shuffled in, talking gently to himself. He threw down a double shot and trudged out. The hairy embryo stood up and snarled something at the girl.

"So *never* come back!" she yelled. "So who *cares*?"

The man left. The screen-door cylinder hissed wearily as the door swung shut. The girl sighed and began to mop the counter listlessly, working her way down towards Doyle.

"Not much business," he said.

"Friday and Saddy there's more."

"You related to Harry?"

She stopped mopping and stared at him, her eyes small and pale and blue and suspicious. "I'm his niece. Who's asking?"

"My name is Doyle. I used to live here."

Her face brightened. "Hey, you're the one! I hear people talking about you. My brothers were in, talking about you. Lee and Gil. I'm Janie Kemmer. My ma was Mix Bann's sister. Gil says you and him used to fight. How long you been gone?"

"Fifteen years."

"Then I wouldn't remember on account of I was three or four years old."

"I met Lee when I first got back."

"And he was drunk, I bet." She sighed. "They just don't seem to give a damn. They do a little fishing and they hire out on construction sometimes, but most of the work they do is free road work when Donnie Capp picks them up for drunk or fighting. Gil was sent away once for four years. It was just a fight right out behind here in the lot, with a drunk tourist. He was sort of old but he wanted real bad to fight Gil, so that's how come it was only manslaughter. Now Lee is back on road work. Donnie picked him up last night again." She smirked. "Old Lee, he sure is funny sometimes. He didn't have a ride back down to Bucket Bay and he was trying to steal a boat."

"It looked to me like you were having a fuss with your friend sitting up the other end of the bar."

She looked desolate. "That Charlie is a jerk. I been going with him three years; and now I want to get married, he wants to go back in the navy. All the time he says when I'm eighteen we get married and everything is fine. Now he wants to go in the navy. He can damn well go back in the stinking navy." The blue eyes suddenly began to leak tears. "*Damn* him!" she said, and snatched a paper napkin, turned her back and blew her nose.

Doyle sat uncomfortably until she turned back and said, "I didn't mean to pop off. Only he gets me so mad. Only he's twenty-eight, and how long should you wait anyhow? I'm supposed to hang around here and wait or something. Nothing ever happens here. Nothing!"

"From what I've heard since I've been back, a lot has been happening around here, Janie."

"Oh, you mean the murder. Well, that was something, I guess. But how many of those do you get? I mean how often? Every hundred years or something. Oh, I don't mean there hasn't been killings. Knifings and like that. The last time there was a murder-type murder, it was a long time ago, down in Bucket Bay. I guess I was maybe nine or ten. When that old Paul Garnette, him that had all the kids, got caught by that Casey Myers when Paul was fooling around with Casey's fifteen-year-old daughter, the one that wasn't right in the head. Casey grabbed a gaff and yanked him off. Got him right in the throat with the gaff, and then that girl really went nuts. They had to put her away some place. Casey was only in jail overnight and it didn't get into all the big papers like when Jenna was murdered. This little ole town sure was jumping. Harry and I like to work ourselves to death. Those newspaper people drink almost as fast as the commercial fishermen."

"I used to know a lot of the commercial fishermen."

"I guess there was a lot more fifteen years ago, Mr. Doyle. Plenty of them moved further south, and a lot of them got out of the business, they say. There's empty shacks down to Bucket Bay, just standing there rotting. They can still make it on the shrimps, but they got to go to Tampa or Key West to ship out."

She excused herself to go greet two young men in sweaty khakis and serve them beer at the far end of the bar. She talked with them for a little while and then she came back to him. There was just enough coquetry in her walk and manner so that he suspected that he had been considered as a possible substitute for the unco-operative Charlie.

"That's a real pretty sports shirt, Mr. Doyle."

"Thanks."

"What's your line of work?"

"Nothing right now. I'm looking around. Maybe I might pick up a used dozer and see if I can get some land-clearing work."

"There isn't as much of that to do around here as there is other places. But there's some. Don't they cost a lot?"

"I've got a little ahead. I just came back from working in Venezuela."

"I'd like to travel some. I'd like to see me some far-away places. Nothing *ever* happens here."

"Except a murder every once in a while."

"Now you just stop teasing me, Mr. Doyle."

"Alex."

"That's a nice name. I like that name."

"I heard Jenna was in here the night she got killed."

She glanced towards the two boys and lowered her voice. "I've got orders from Harry not to talk about it to strangers. I don't see what difference it makes. It gets talked about a lot in here. And sometimes you wonder if maybe somebody talking or listening is the one did it." She hugged herself with her heavy white arms and gave a little shiver. "That's kind of creepy. Anyhow, I guess it's because Donnie Capp doesn't want any strangers around prying. He runs 'em off. I guess he's maybe afraid somebody might by accident pry around and find out who did it before Donnie finds out. He's got to be the one who gets the killer because it's a matter of pride. The big shots sorta pushed him out of the way last fall when they were investigating. But since you come from here, I guess you aren't a stranger. She was in here all right that night. Friday night. I went off at six on account of Harry doesn't like me working at nights, especially on a Friday or Saddy night when things can get rough around here real fast and a girl can't walk across the room without wise guys grabbing at her. But she was here before I went off and she stayed until closing. And then

she walked right out and got herself strangled. I couldn't hardly
believe it when I heard it the next morning. I wanted to get to
see her at Jeffry Brothers, but that sister of Colonel M'Gann had
fixed it so nobody could get to see her but the family, and they
say the colonel didn't get to see her even. On account of his bad
heart."

"I guess Jenna wasn't much like her kid sister."

"I swear I don't see how those two came out of the same family.
You know, Betty comes in here a lot."

"She does!"

"The boat yard is just down the road another two blocks, you
know. And all the fishermen, they think she's the finest damn
thing on legs. When old Spence Larkin was alive they say he
wouldn't touch a commercial boat unless it was cash on the line.
But she works things out with them so they can get work done
when they have to have it. And she'll stop in here and have a beer
with them. Usually in the afternoon, but sometimes in the
evening. And you don't see anybody making any grabs at her. If
anybody did, all her boatyard customers would tear the poor guy's
head off and use the rest of him for chum. Not that anybody but
some stranger would get fresh with her, him not knowing about
her. There's something wrong with her. She looks like a lot of
woman but she isn't. Something terrible happened to her a long
time ago, and she just isn't any good for anything. I'd hate to be
like that. I guess it just about wouldn't be worth living, wouldn't
you say?"

"I guess so."

"That Jenna was just the other way around. She couldn't get
enough. Funny, isn't it? Right out of the same family. I don't
know if Donnie will ever find who killed her. Some nights people
come from a long way off and drive out to the beach. Me, I think
it was somebody like that, from the other end of the county. It
would be easier if she was raped, because then it could maybe
have been a Negro. But she wasn't, and I guess that just about
every Negro for fifty miles around must know that Donnie checks
that beach every now and then and if he caught any of them out
there, he'd play hell with them for sure. I think it was some
stranger and she got in some kind of drunk argument and got
choked. And they took off. Or maybe somebody beached a boat.
But one thing, I don't think that Donnie will give up looking."

"I guess everybody has their own ideas."

"Some of them are pretty crazy. Some people say it was on

account of the money. They say she got killed because she knew where Spence Larkin hid all the money they never found. So they caught her there on the beach and they killed her and then they went and dug it up. They made her tell where it was. That's plain silly, because the night she was killed she came in here without a dime. Harry'd said not to let her have any more on credit. But there was always somebody to buy her a drink. If she was out of money and knew where it was, she would have gone and dug it up, wouldn't she?"

"Looks like she would."

"Nobody is ever going to find that money except by some kind of accident maybe. And then I bet there won't be much left of it. Not in this climate."

She looked towards the doorway and her face changed in an almost dramatic way, becoming instantaneously blank, almost sleepy. Doyle heard the screen-door cylinder hiss.

He turned and saw Deputy Donnie Capp standing just inside the door. "Hello, Doyle," he said. "Hello, Janie."

"Hello, Mr. Capp," she said faintly.

Capp moved in on Doyle's left and stood at the bar. Doyle could scent the animal sharpness of Capp's perspiration.

"Hear Charlie's going in the navy, Janie."

"I guess that's right."

"Maybe you took off twenty pounds and stopped stuffing that hungry gut of yours, you'd look better than the navy. Harry should have pounded your butt for you the very first time you started sneaking off in the brush with that Charlie. You was so sure of Charlie, Janie, you let yourself get real sloppy. Now what you going to do? Want I should pick you a husband off the road gang? Anything I tell those boys to do, they'll do, no matter how it could ugly up their future."

Tears had started to roll down her white face, but she couldn't seem to look away from Donnie.

"You trot all that beef up the other end of the bar, Janie. I got words with Mr. Doyle here. I got to call him mister now."

She moved away, slowly and heavily. Capp said, "If the slut had a head on her, she'd grab Harry. They aren't blood kin. He's got the asthma and the high-blood pressure, and she'd end up with a good little business instead of it going to his brother."

Doyle lifted his beer glass and drank, and was remotely pleased to see that he could keep his hand from trembling.

"You don't have much to say for yourself, Mr. Doyle."

"I guess not."

"Heard you just as I got near the door. You and Janie talking about Jenna. Guess you knew Jenna before she took off with that sailor boy. That was when you were a big athlete. Before you took up stealing. Knew her, didn't you?"

"Yes."

"Now you're getting to know the sister awful damn fast. Can't see why the Larkins should give a damn what happens to you. Seems real strange to me. And there you are, right out there on the beach near to where she was killed, and near the colonel and his sister. And I've got the word to keep my hands off you. Funny."

"Is there something you want?"

"It don't make much sense, but I find myself wondering if somehow somebody brought you back here to look into the Jenna killing. You got you a oily satisfied look, like an egg-sucking hound dog. I'd hate to find out you were sticking your nose in something that's none of your business. I just might have to naturally take this here club and loosen your insides a little."

"Why?"

"Because you'd be getting in the way of the law. We can handle everything that has to be done our own selves."

Capp moved away, silent in the black boots. The screen-door hissed behind him.

A few minutes later, as Doyle got up to leave, an old man came in, a brown old man with soiled white hair, bleached eyes and a white stubble of beard. He stared at Doyle for a moment and said, "Say, I bet you're Bert Doyle's boy. You look a lot like Bert when he was alive, afore he got drownded that time."

"That's right. I'm Alex Doyle."

"And you don't know me at all?"

"Wait a minute. Arnie Blassit?"

"Dead right, boy. When I was fishing shares with old Lucas Pennyweather, you come along with us a lot of times. You made a good hand, for a kid."

Doyle sat at the bar again and bought a beer for himself and a drink for Blassit. Blassit talked about old times, about the half-remembered people Alex had known before his father died.

"It's not like it used to be, boy. It's getting all fished out. We got no closed season on mullets now, but snook is a game fish and you can't make a catch on trouts any more. I kinda hang on. Too damn old to learn new tricks."

"How about Lucas Pennyweather? Is he still around?"

"No. He was getting pretty crippled up. And last November a grown daughter of his come all the way down from North Carolina and she and her husband, they took Lucas back up to live with them. One day you'd think he was going to be here for ever, and the next day he was gone. It was real sudden. Sold his boat and gear, but sold 'em so fast it was damn near giving them away. I tell you, there was nobody knew these waters any better than Lucas. Some will tell you Spence Larkin knew more, but I say Lucas Pennyweather."

"He liked kids. I can remember going out with him when I couldn't have been more than three or four years old."

And suddenly Doyle remembered a scene that had been buried for years. Old Lucas had taken a half-dozen kids out with him on a Sunday to fish with hand lines in a grouper hole not far outside Windy Pass. And on the way back they had passed a small white skiff with a man at the wheel and a little girl sitting in the bow. The little girl was blonde and wore a pink dress, and to Alex, about six at the time, she was the prettiest thing he had ever seen.

"There goes Spence Larkin and his daughter," Lucas had told them. "He's a big important man there in Ramona, and that's his eldest. He takes her on picnics of a Sunday, down there in those bay islands some place."

Alex remembered that he had turned and watched the small girl until she was lost in the sunny distances of the bay. And later he had seen Spence Larkin many times alone in the same skiff. It was his commonly known eccentricity to leave his office at the boat yard at any time of day and go off down the bay alone. People said that was where he did his thinking. People said he would go out in that skiff with its ancient engine and chug along and plot new meanness, new ways to make a dollar grow from a dime. He always took a fishing rod and a tackle box that he kept in his office, but he didn't do much fishing.

Arnie Blassit chuckled and said, "Just about the last thing old Lucas did in this town was get himself arrested on suspicion of murder. Didn't mean anything. Everybody who'd been right here in the Mack the night Jenna Larkin got choked to death, they got picked up. Me too. But me and Lucas, we could clear each other. We run out of drinking money along about eleven, and we were sharing a shack down to Chaney's Bayou, and we had come up in my boat and tied her right across the road there. So about eleven we went on back down the bay together and the first thing we know about it, them deputies come and took us all the way over to Davis and locked us up. Let us go the next day. Lucas sure was mad. Thing was, he'd spent some time talking to Jenna that night. I thought about that. It was as if the Lord give her one final chance to be nice to somebody and she took it."

"How do you mean?"

"Up to that last night she didn't have any time or any politeness to spare on any old beat-down fishermen. There was a good crowd and after we'd been in a few minutes, standing right over there, she come over to us and was real nice. She wanted to talk about the old days. And after a while she took Lucas right over there to that corner table, and they sat there and talked a long time. And when it finally broke up, some of us were kidding Lucas till he got pretty mad about the whole thing. And then he made it worse for himself by saying that he'd made a date with her to go out in the boat the next day and look around the bay islands. Matter of fact, Alex, when they come and took us to Davis, Lucas was just getting ready to take the boat on up to the yard and pick Jenna up. But she was dead by then. And it sure upset Lucas to hear about it."

"I guess the whole town was upset from what I hear."

Blassit chuckled again. "I see that Donnie Capp leaving as I come down the street a little while ago. Now I guess he was the one most upset. That boy is just as mean as a snake. And he'd been trying to move in on Jenna. Now there's a lot of things people called her, but nobody called her especially choosey when it come to men. But she wouldn't have a thing to do with that Donnie Capp. She just laughed at him. I've heard that Donnie has made some gals real willing by roughing 'em up a little first but he couldn't take a club to Jenna and get away with it. Matter of fact, he was the one broke up Jenna's nice little talk with Lucas. Went right over and sat with them without any invitation, and after a while she got tired of him listening, so she went away. Donnie sat there and talked to Lucas for a while, and then he left. I guess Donnie thought he was getting close to talking Jenna into something, because he sure acted like a crazy man after he found she'd been killed. He put knots on half the heads in the county until the sheriff got him soothed down some."

"Arnie, I've got to run along. It's been good to see you again."

He drove back out to the cottage. After he had unloaded his purchases he took a walk on the beach until the afterglow of the sunset had died to streaks of yellow and green close to the horizon.

He fixed a simple supper, and after he had cleaned up he sat and smoked in the dark on the little screened porch and thought about the days of childhood. The vivid memory of Jenna in the pink dress had aroused other memories. They were memories of the other life that he had tried to forget, telling himself that it had all been bad. But in the re-awakened memories there was much that was good. Later he began to think about Jenna, and to wonder why she had been pleasant to old Lucas. She must have had some reason. There must have been something she wanted.

CHAPTER SEVEN

On Friday morning at eleven, Alex walked up the beach to the Proctor cottage, carrying the two spinning rods. When he was a hundred feet from the porch, Celia M'Gann came out and walked to meet him.

"I expected you yesterday, Mr. Doyle."

"Sure sorry about that, but something came up."

"You didn't have those terrible bruises on your arms and legs. Did you fall?"

"Guess you could say I fell into a deputy sheriff, ma'am. He came out to have a little talk with me. He talked with a club, mostly. That was Wednesday, and I was too stiffened up to get much done yesterday."

"Were you drinking? Why did he hit you?"

"Sort of on general principles, I guess."

"Was it a man named Capp?"

"That's him. Donnie Capp."

"I had difficulty with that man. I don't like him at all. He was determined to bother the colonel. And I was just as determined that he wouldn't. He was very rude."

"Here's the stuff I bought for your brother."

"How much do I owe you?"

"Here's the receipt, ma'am."

She told him to wait and went into the house and came out with the exact amount in cash, and said that the colonel would be out in a few moments.

Colonel M'Gann came out of the cottage and came slowly down the steps. He was a big man, almost uncomfortably thin, but with the look and bearing of someone who had once been much heavier. He had grey hair like his sister, and the same strong planes and structure of face. He wore rope sandals, khaki shorts. He was tanned, but it was tan over an unhealthy skin tone. There was a strange remoteness about him, not coolness or unfriendliness, but merely a vast indifference.

"The mackerel was excellent, Mr. Doyle. My sister and I thank you." As he spoke Alex had the feeling that the colonel was looking through him and beyond him.

The three of them went to the water's edge, and Doyle showed Colonel M'Gann how to handle the spinning tackle. He learned with that special quickness possible only to people who combine manual dexterity with that sort of analytical mind which quickly perceives the purpose of each movement. Yet it seemed a sterile effort. M'Gann obviously had no interest in it, was merely attempting to please his sister.

"No point at all, Colonel, in standing out here and whipping up the water when you don't see any activity. Say, it looks like something going on up the beach there a ways."

Celia tagged along. But when they moved farther, she said she would get lunch started and went back towards the house.

They caught several small jacks and released them. M'Gann said, "Thank you very much for the lesson, Mr. Doyle." He walked up on to the dry sand and sat down. "I think I'll rest for a few moments and then walk back to the house. I still tire easily."

Doyle sat beside him. "You better rinse the rod and reel off in fresh water when you get back."

"Yes, of course."

Doyle turned so he could watch M'Gann's face and said, "They are still having a great deal of trouble with the Henderson circuits, sir. They haven't gotten the bugs out yet."

For long moments the colonel still stared out towards the Gulf, his face impassive. And then he turned and looked at Doyle. The remoteness was gone. And Doyle was aware of the unforgettable impact of a truly strong personality.

"You're clever, Mr. Doyle. If that's your name. Who sent you?"

"Colonel Presser."

"I should have guessed. Austin has always had a taste for intrigue and melodrama."

"The problem was to contact you, sir. The strangers they sent down couldn't make it. Your sister has——"

"Celia has been very diligent about shielding me from all pleas and requests. This little subterfuge will annoy her. She can't seem to understand that I am willing to say no—to Austin Presser or anyone else."

"Can you tell me why you'd say no, Colonel? Is it . . . health?"

The colonel looked out across the Gulf. "I am getting stronger. As a civilian consultant, I could pace myself. But it is as if all that work was done by somebody else. Far away and long ago. I can't go back now, Doyle. I never thought that anything could become more important to me than my sense of duty and obligation. Right now I have a personal problem. Call it an emotional problem. I don't intend to explain it to you. Until it is solved, if it ever can be, I am . . . incapable of considering anything else."

"And if you solve this . . . emotional problem?"

"I can go back to work. And make Austin happy. But you see, Mr. Doyle, one possible solution to my problem would be for me to see how far and fast I can run down this beach."

"I don't understand."

"I don't expect you to understand. Sometimes a man can find himself in a maze that seems insoluble. Laboratory rats, faced with an insoluble maze have been known to give up and lie on their backs and nibble their forepaws. I find that quite touching to contemplate. A man in the process of trying to find a solution to what seems to be an insoluble problem, Mr. Doyle, is not inclined to devote his time and energies to his profession, no matter how vital his work may be. I am sorry. You may tell Austin I am sorry."

Doyle remembered with distaste the next phase of his instructions. "Colonel Presser seems to feel that you are brooding over the death of your wife, Colonel. He has acquired a long and accurate file on her. It isn't pleasant reading. I can give you some of the facts."

"I'm not interested, Doyle. I made a very bad marriage. It took me a long time to become aware of how bad it was. My wife was a reckless, selfish, faithless woman. I met her at a time when she had a yearning for respectability, apparently."

"Then I don't understand."

"There is nothing for you to understand."

"Colonel M'Gann, if your wife's murderer was caught, would you then be willing to go back to work?"

M'Gann looked at him quickly, with an odd expression, as though Doyle had shocked him. Yet, to Doyle, it had seemed a most obvious question.

"I might."

"Here comes your sister. Are you going to tell her about this?"

"I see no point in telling her. I can't see that you have changed anything."

After Celia joined them and they walked back down the beach, M'Gann was again back in his shell. Celia was most friendly. Doyle refused her invitation to lunch. When he glanced back, they were going into the house. She was holding the screen door for the colonel.

Doyle walked slowly back towards his cottage. I might have something to tell you one of these days, Colonel, he thought. I might have a message for you. I'm beginning to see a pattern in things. I might even know why she was killed.

At two o'clock he drove by the Mack and turned in at the Larkin Boat Yard and Marina at the end of Front Street. He had remembered it as a place of clutter and corrosion, with sun-drab, sagging structures and docks, a general air of aimlessness.

But now white posts marked the entrance to a gravelled parking area beside a small white office building. There were a half-dozen cars in the lot in addition to the familiar jeep and a freshly painted pickup with the Larkin name on the door. When he got out of the car he could hear the busy chatter of office equipment and, farther away, the high whine of a wood saw and the roar of a motor under test. As he walked towards the office he could see three wide solid docks built out into the bay, with a T and bright gas pumps at the outer end of the nearest one. He could see a big covered work shed with the open side facing the bay, heavy ways and cradles, some warehouse structures, a boat-storage area with an aluminium roof that was blinding in the sunlight.

When he went into the office Betty was typing and a woman in her middle years was operating an adding machine. The interior was clean and bright and efficient looking.

Betty smiled with obvious pleasure, got up quickly and introduced him to the other woman, a Mrs. West, and then took him on a guided tour. To-day she wore a dark red blouse and a red-and-white-striped skirt. The unruly hair, in all its streaks and shades of umber, toffee and cream, had been pulled back into a pony-tail.

"This is certainly a different place from the one I remember."

"It's been a lot of work, Alex, building it up. And the bank still owns a pretty good hunk of it. But we're doing a good business. Got a total of fifteen on the pay-roll. We do good work and we get a lot of word-of-mouth advertising among boat people. That's the best kind. We can yank stuff out of the water up to seventy feet long. There's Buddy. I guess he's a lot bigger than when you left."

They walked towards a man who had his back turned to them while he scraped at the hull of a small twin-screw cruiser. He was a huge brown man with corn yellow hair worn a quarter of an inch long. He was well over six feet tall. He wore greasy shorts and sneakers. There was hair on his back and shoulders, bleached silvery white by the sun. His calves were like oaken kegs. He was wide and solid from top to bottom, like a tree.

When Betty spoke he turned. He had a brute jaw and small, grey, smouldering eyes under a solid ridge of brow. He could have played a villain part in a Viking movie.

"Glad to see you again, Alex," he said as they shook hands. Just as Alex was considering falling to his knees and howling like a dog, Buddy released his grip. "Hear Donnie welcomed you home."

"In a big way."

"We'll keep him off your back. He goes too damn far lately."

Alex suddenly realized that this prehistoric mammoth was ill at ease, actually quite shy. It amused him.

"I just remembered a phone call I should make," Betty said. "Why don't you show Alex round, Buddy, and introduce him to John Geer. When you've had the rest of the tour, Alex, you come back to the office and you can take me and buy me a beer."

When Betty was out of sight, Buddy said, "This place wouldn't run right without her. I can't handle that office stuff. It drives me nuts. Come meet our partner, John Geer."

John Geer was working on a marine engine. He was grime to the elbows, a shambling man with a remote resemblance to Gary Cooper, but with brown eyes too close together and a pendulous lower lip.

Buddy showed him around the shop area. Alex could sense the man's devotion to good materials and fine workmanship. He showed him the warehouse. As they turned away from the warehouse Alex saw a trim little Thistle on a yellow trailer under a shed roof. The mast was stepped and lashed. He could see the name. The *Lady Bird*.

"Betty's?" he said.

"Her pet. She can really make it get up there and fly. And she'll take it out in the worst weather you ever saw."

"She's quite a gal, Buddy."

Buddy propped one foot on the trailer tyre, lit a cigarette and shook the match out. "She likes you, Alex."

"I'm glad of that."

"I . . . I don't want you should upset her."

"I know the score, Buddy. I got it from her. I've got no intention of upsetting her."

"I had to say it."

"I know."

"Well, I guess there isn't much else around here to see."

"That skiff there, Buddy. Wasn't that your father's?" He gestured towards a small skiff, pointed at both ends, with a centre engine hatch and a horizontal wheel. The paint was fresh and it was up on stubby saw horses.

"That was his. We talk about putting a new engine in it and unloading it. But we never seem to get around to it."

"I want to ask you something, Buddy. You're a little older than Betty, so you might be able to remember more clearly than she could. I haven't asked her. I don't even want you to try to ask me why I'm asking such a question. When you were little, your father used to take Jenna on picnics all alone, didn't he?"

"In that same skiff. All the time."

"And Sunday was Jenna's day, wasn't it?"

"He spoiled her rotten, Alex. The way she turned out, it was his fault."

"Did he take her to a special place?"

"On the picnics? I don't think so."

"Can you remember anything about there being a special place?"

Buddy glared back into the past, motionless for long seconds. "There was a place. It's been a long time. Twenty years. Sure, she used to tease us about it. It was a big secret, she said. She wasn't supposed to tell."

"Can you remember anything she said about it?"

"No. All I can remember is that she used to make up all kinds of stuff. Why are you. . . ." Buddy stopped suddenly and looked beyond Alex with an expression of surprise, almost of consternation, and said, as though speaking to himself, "That's where he could have hid the money."

"That's what I've been thinking."

Buddy turned directly at him, his face changing, growing hard and sceptical. "That's what you've been thinking, is it? Just who the hell are you, Doyle? What's this big fat interest in where the money is? What are all these questions?"

"Now wait a minute."

"Wait for what? I don't know where you came from. You show

up here and sweet-talk Betty. Tell her you never stole a dime. She believes you. You get her to tell me you're such a nice guy."

"I didn't get her to tell you a thing, Larkin."

"What do I know about you? Maybe you've been in the can for years. You were one of Jenna's boy-friends. You'd hear about the murder. The newspapers brought up how the old man's money was never found when they covered the murder. Tried to tie it in somehow, but it wouldn't hold together. How do I know how much Jenna told you and how much you remember? Now you come down here sucking around, asking questions. The hell with you, Doyle."

"Use your head, Buddy. If that was what I was after, why would I give it away talking to you this way?"

"I think you're a clever guy, Doyle. I think you're down here on the make for something. Maybe Donnie does too and that's why he whipped your skull for you."

"Do you want to find out who killed Jenna?"

"Sure, but——"

"Then we should put our heads together and try to figure out if it was tied in with the money your father hid."

"But why should you give a damn who killed Jenna?"

Doyle was momentarily trapped. He could not give his actual reason. And he couldn't think of any other convincing reason.

"You're just meddling," Buddy said. "So get off the place. Keep away from Betty. We can handle our own problems." And he pushed Doyle roughly.

And that push ignited a white flare in the back of the skull of Alex Doyle. He had been physically humiliated by Donnie Capp. He had been conscious of the public disapproval of his return. The emotional tensions and frustrations exploded into a hard overhand right that smacked the shelf of Buddy Larkin's jaw, knocked his mouth open, glazed his eyes, caused him to take two steps back and sit down heavily.

There was no one to see them in that sheltered area near the warehouse. The noise of the marine engine being test-run by Geer obscured any sounds of combat. After a moment of inert surprise, Buddy bounded up with disconcerting agility and lunged towards Doyle, chin on his chest, big fists held low. Doyle ducked and slipped two powerful hooks, looking for a chance to land solidly. Before he had his chance, a solid smash on the chest knocked him backward into the skiff. As Buddy reached for him, he scrambled out the far side and came around the stern. They met there. Doyle got in one solid blow and, without transition, found himself on hands and knees, shaking his head. He got up and, after a moment of blackout, found himself on his back. He wobbled to his feet and swung blindly at the vague shape moving towards him. His fist blazed with pain and with the effort of the blow, he knocked himself sprawling. He got up on to one knee. Buddy Larkin was sitting eight feet away. They stared at each other, sobbing for air. As Buddy got up, Doyle got up and raised his fists.

Buddy stared at him. "Knock it off. Can I whip you?"

"Yes, I guess you can," Doyle said, in a remote, rusty voice.

"But you'll keep trying?"

"As long as I can keep getting up."

"Stubborn devil," Buddy said glumly. He walked over to a hose faucet, bent over, caught water in his cupped hands and sloshed his face thoroughly. When he was through, Doyle knelt by the faucet and stuck his head under the stream.

"Am I marked?" Buddy asked.

"Just a lump on your jaw." Buddy touched the place and winced.

Doyle worked the fingers of his right hand. The knuckles were puffy. Buddy said, "You look okay."

"My mouth is cut on the inside."

They sat on a saw horse, still breathing more deeply than normal. "Damn fools," Buddy said.

"I don't like to be pushed."

"All right. You don't like to be pushed. I'll make a note of it. To get back to the old man. He was always going off by himself. He'd come back from a business trip and almost the first thing, he'd be off in the skiff. He was such a secretive kind of guy. He must have had some place he'd go. Hell, he'd never go there direct. But he'd always head south down the bay, not that that will do us much good. Give me one of those cigarettes."

Doyle lit it for him. He felt sourly amused. The suspicion was gone. Buddy Larkin had made up his mind about him in his own special way. Possibly it was a better way than logic. In Larkin's book a man who kept getting up could be trusted.

"Here's something that might fit, Buddy," he said. "See what you think. The night Jenna was killed, she spent some time talking to old Lucas Pennyweather, and they were going to go out the next day in his boat. That's one of the things that started me thinking. She wouldn't have been nice to him unless she wanted something. You know that as well or better than I do. So maybe she wanted his help in finding the place where her father used to take her. Maybe she could remember enough so there was a good chance of Lucas finding the place she described."

Buddy nodded. "She wouldn't have been able to find it herself. She never had much interest in the water. And you know as well as I do what it's like down there in all those mangrove islands. There must be twenty thousand little islands. If she could remember a little, and anybody could help her, it would be old Lucas."

"And Lucas left shortly after she was killed."

He shook his head slowly. "Not Lucas, if that's what you're thinking. Not that old man. He didn't know his daughter was finally coming after him. She'd been threatening to for a long time. He came around to say good-bye. A decent old guy, Alex."

"So then he didn't know what she was driving at—I mean if we've been making good guesses."

"Lucas was smart as hell about water and weather and fish and children. But he wasn't too bright about people. People like Jenna. He'd take everybody at face value. And you know how he liked to talk. She would never have said anything about the money."

"You're right. Just ask him to take her to the places where her father used to take her. For old times' sake."

Buddy kicked the trailer tyre. "All this is fine, Alex, but it leaves something up in the air. How come Jenna gets that idea all of a sudden?"

"I don't know. As you said, it was a long time ago. Twenty years. Maybe something reminded her. And she started thinking."

"But even if she was right, the money is still there. And she is dead, so even if Lucas wasn't gone, it wouldn't be possible to find it."

"Unless, Buddy, she described the place where she wanted to be taken especially. All she could remember of it. And Lucas said he thought he could find it, and promised to take her there."

"Then we ought to check with Lucas."

"It would be the only way. You've got the shore line of the keys and the shore line of the mainland, and then all those islands, Buddy. It would take years and years to cover the area, even if you had some idea of what you were looking for. You couldn't even look for a place that was kept cleared of brush because it's been nine years since your father made his last trip."

Buddy suddenly grinned in a mirthless way. "If you want any more proof, I've thought of something else. He kept that rod and the tackle box in his office. I went through that stuff after he died. A fair-sized tackle box, with just a couple of lures in it. Damn near empty. I looked around but I couldn't find the rest of the stuff I thought he must have carried in it. And I didn't think anything much about it until now. He liked cash deals. So he'd come back from selling off land with the cash, and he'd transfer it from his brief case to that tackle box, and tell somebody to get the skiff ready. And then he'd take off. Hell, when the big treasure hunt was on after he died, I thought he could have hidden the stuff somewhere down the bay. I guess everybody thought of that. But we just never thought of there being some specific place that he went to that somebody else might know about. We didn't remember about Jenna when she was little and was willing to go on picnics with him."

"Betty told me about Sunday being Jenna's day. I didn't think about there being a special place until Arnie Blassit told me about Jenna being nice to Lucas the night she was killed."

Buddy stared curiously at Alex. "It's the sort of thing the family should have figured out. Not an outsider. Funny you should have come up with a thing like this."

"I've had some practice adding bits and pieces of information together, trying to come up with some kind of pattern. I can tell you about it some time. But right now, we ought to get hold of Lucas. Do you know his address?"

"It's probably at the post office. Or if it isn't, Arnie Blassit would know it."

"Buddy, there's the chance that if we're right, and we get Lucas down here and find the place, it may be gone. If somebody overheard them talking, Jenna and Lucas, and figured they could find it themselves——"

"Then that would be the person who killed Jenna."

Alex made a slow ceremony of lighting a cigarette. He said quietly, "Has anybody thought of Donnie Capp?"

Buddy stared at him blankly. "Donnie?"

"Is there something sacred about him? Look at the facts. He was at the Mack. He sat with Jenna and Lucas during the tail end of their conversation. He patrolled the beach road often enough so it wouldn't mean anything if his car was seen out there. He's put on a hell of an act about finding out who did it. And he's been damned insistent about nobody prying into the case."

"Yes, but——"

"Try this for size, Buddy. He heard enough to know that Lucas

could take him to some spot Jenna had described. He talked to
Lucas after Jenna left the table. And it's possible that Jenna,
drunk, wasn't as subtle as she thought she was being. So he left
and waited for her, thinking about the money. Maybe he tried
to make some kind of deal with her. She wanted no part of Donnie
Capp. And so he killed her. And then he had it made. All he had
to do was wait until it all died down, wait a month or so, and then
get Lucas to take him to the place Jenna had described. Secretly.
And it would have been no trick for him to kill Lucas, sink his
body in a hole and leave his boat adrift. You know what people
would have said. Then all he would have had to do was wait a
little longer, think up some logical reason for quitting, and take
off with the money. But he didn't count on Lucas's daughter
coming after him and taking him away so suddenly. That left
him in a bad spot. He couldn't go bring Lucas back without
attracting a lot of unwelcome attention. And it made the murder
of Jenna meaningless. I think he's under a hell of a strain. He
doesn't know what to do. He's getting damned erratic. The way
he worked me over is maybe an evidence of strain. Take it out on
somebody, anybody."

"Donnie Capp," Buddy said softly. "On the job twenty-four
hours a day, and he's never tried to graft a dime."

"But this is a lot more than a dime."

"Now here is a funny thing," Buddy said slowly. "Donnie has
hunted all his life. He never gave a damn for fishing. About
Christmas he came in and he bought himself a little twelve-foot
aluminium boat and a big rebuilt outboard. Betty made him a
good price, I remember. And we tried to tell him that motor was
too big to troll good, but he said he didn't have much time and
he'd rather run fast to where he was going, even if it did troll a
little rough. And I tell you that most of the winter old Donnie was
the fishingest man you'd ever want to see. He took a lot of kidding
about it on account of he just never could come back in with
much of anything. And finally Roy Lawlor got tired of trying to
get hold of Donnie and not being able to get him, so he clamped
down some. He still goes out a lot but not so often. Keeps the
boat over there the other side of Bay Street, tied up at Garner's
Bait Dock. You see him scoot out under the bridge every so often,
with that big hat on him. He must sleep in that hat."

"So he's been trying to find it by himself."

"You go too damn far, Alex. There's no reason why a man can't
take up fishing. And when a man takes it up, it can get to be a

disease. And Donnie was a hunting fool until he took up fishing.
I know Donnie pretty well. I just can't see him . . . killing my
sister."

Alex thought for a few minutes. "If a man was going out hunting for that money, what would be the thing he'd most likely
take with him?"

"Well, he'd take a shovel. Right after my father died, there was
a run on shovels like you never see before."

"And he wouldn't be likely to carry a shovel to that boat every
time he went out, would he?"

"It would look damn funny. I see what you mean. Let's go."

Buddy stuck his head in the office and told Betty they would
be back in a little while. Buddy drove the blue jeep down Front
Street and across Bay and another three blocks to Garner's. They
walked out on to the dock.

"Here it is," he said. The aluminium boat was tied off, with a
stern line on a piling, the bow line on a cleat on the dock. Buddy
untied the bow line and brought the boat in close to a rotting
step. He stepped into it lithely for a man of his size. Alex held
the bow line and looked down into the boat. Buddy squatted and
reached up under the shallow foredeck. He took out an object
wrapped in a faded green tarp. He unwrapped it. They both
stared at the folded entrenching tool for a few moments. Buddy
wrapped it up again and stowed it. He climbed up on to the dock
and was making the bow line fast when Alex turned and saw
Donnie Capp walking swiftly towards them along the dock, his
sallow face expressionless. "What's goin' on?" he asked.

Buddy looked up at him casually. "Hi, Donnie. Alex here was
thinking on getting a boat for himself. I told him about the rig
we fixed you up with, and he wanted to see it, so I figured you
wouldn't mind if I showed it to him."

"You have to get into it to show it to him?"

"Tell you the truth, Donnie, I forgot what horse motor you got,
so I got in to lift up the motor cover and take a look."

"It's a little big for the boat," Alex said. "I think a ten would
do me."

Buddy stood up and they stood facing Donnie Capp. The
narrow colourless eyes swivelled quickly from face to face. Buddy
said, "I guess it suits you all right, Donnie."

"It's fine."

"Have you got a good used ten-horse around?" Alex asked
Buddy.

"We better go back and check with John Geer."

"If you got a boat like this one, why didn't you show him the one you got instead of mine?" Donnie asked.

Buddy faltered for a moment and said, "Well, we haven't exactly got one, Donnie, but there's a fella has one wants to make a trade. And if we got a sale on the one he wants to trade, we can make him a better price. This time of year you have to get out and move the merchandise."

"How about letting me take it out?" Alex asked quickly.

Donnie stared at him. He turned and spat into the water. "If you was on fire, Doyle, I wouldn't do you the favour to push you off this here dock. And because you sold me the boat, Buddy, it doesn't give you any right to mess with it."

He turned on his heel and walked away. They could see the county car parked beside Garner's shack.

"I need a drink," Buddy said.

They parked the jeep in front of the Mack and went in. Janie was tending bar. They took a table far from the bar, over by the bowling machine. They both ordered beer and, as Janie turned away, Buddy asked her to bring a shot with his.

Buddy threw the shot down, gulped half the glass of beer and said, "I needed that. How did I do, talking to him?" He kept his voice low.

"I don't know. If I'm right, he's going to be suspicious of every damn thing."

"You made a hell of a good guess."

"Will you buy it?"

"I'll buy part of it, Alex. Somebody else could have killed her and all the rest of it could still be the way you say."

"I'll grant that. But suppose we were both sure he did kill her? What would we do next?"

"You couldn't find proof. There wasn't a clue. And I don't think he'd crack. If I was dead sure, Alex, I think I'd just up and kill him with my hands. Ever since I got my growth I've had to be careful about losing my temper. I cleaned this place out one night. Over seven hundred bucks' damages. It was some crack somebody made about Betty. I didn't kill anybody. But I come too damn close for comfort. He was out cold for three days and he didn't get out of Davis General Hospital for nearly three weeks."

"That would be a dandy solution, Buddy. You kill him and the law takes care of you. Nice for Betty and your mother. But you've been the big hero, so it's all right."

"I talk a lot, don't I?"

"The thing to do is get hold of Lucas Pennyweather and get him down here. Pay his way. See if he can take you to the place Jenna described to him, if she did describe a specific place. It's worth the gamble. You've got a legitimate reason. And . . . it might be interesting to see how Capp reacts if Lucas shows up down here."

"Here comes Betty. Let's keep it to ourselves."

She came directly to the table and said, "Well! My spies reported the jeep in front of this place. If a girl wants a beer, she has to come get her own." She sat down. "One brew, Janie, please."

"Who's minding the store?" Buddy asked.

"The capable Mrs. West and the capable Mr. Geer. There was a phone call from Clearwater, Mr. Hitchins. He wants to have that Consolidated of his brought down here for a lot of work and summer storage. I said we could take it."

"Forty-two feet, isn't it?"

"With two Chrysler 275's. I looked it up. His captain will bring it down and turn it over to us. I guess you must have had an intensive tour of inspection, Alex."

"I saw everything. Saw the *Lady Bird*."

"My angel. Can I ask what is the matter with you two? Aren't you getting along? You act odd and strained."

"We're getting along fine, Betty."

She looked at the two of them dubiously. "I hope so." They talked boats for a little while and then went back to the yard. Betty went into the office. Buddy stood by Alex beside the Dodge. "I'll get the address and get the call through. If he's well enough to come down, I'll pay his way. That is, if Jenna told him anything definite. I'll go over town now and find out the address and make the call."

Alex looked at his watch. "It's after four now. I want to stop and see Myra Ducklin. Why don't you bring Betty out for a swim later on and you can tell me how you made out?"

"Okay."

Doyle had a visit with Myra Ducklin. It was a little after five when he drove back towards the key. He thought of his own deductions, not with pride, but with grim and somewhat weary acceptance. A stranger could not have come to Ramona and found such an inevitable way of fitting the pieces together. And the local people had been too close to it all to understand how and why it had happened. It had required the rare combination of great familiarity so that people would talk, plus that special detachment which came from having been away so long. And perhaps one additional factor had been necessary—the sort of training which made you alert to the motives of other human beings, which taught you to turn odd facts this way and that way until a pattern began to form, until you began to sense what you had to look for to complete the pattern and make it so obvious that you began to wonder how it could have been overlooked.

He felt reasonably certain that Capp had killed the woman, had held her by the throat until she was dead. But one portion of the pattern was indistinct. He could not account for the odd reactions of Colonel M'Gann at the time he had talked to him. The curious reference to suicide. The man's insistence on staying here where this thing had happened.

The blue jeep was in his back yard. The house was empty. He changed to trunks and went out on to the beach. They were swimming, a hundred yards off shore. Betty waved to him and he swam out to where they were.

CHAPTER EIGHT

BUDDY made the opportunity to talk privately with Alex by saying: "Any obliging type gal would swim in and open up some cold beer that we brought out and put in your ice box, and be there on the beach to meet us when we come out."

"I just work here," she said, and made a face at them and swam towards the cottage.

Buddy rolled over on his back and floated. "Got the name and the town, but not the address. A Mrs. Trace Annison up in Fayetteville, North Carolina. Ran into Judge Ellandon outside of Ducklin's and he give me the name. So I got change and phoned up there. Got hold of her. Could hear a lot of kids squalling in the background. Funny damn thing, Alex, she thought I was phoning her to say Lucas had showed up down here. Couldn't get it through her head I wasn't phoning from the sheriff's office.

"She cried a little on the phone. Said Lucas had gotten real restless the past few months. Kept saying he was homesick for the sight of water. And about eight or nine days ago he took off. Left her a note saying he was coming back here. She knows he couldn't have had more than ten dollars on him, probably not that much.

Soon as she found the note she phoned the sheriff's office over in Davis. She doesn't think Lucas is right in the head. And he's too old to be beating his way back across country. She asked Lawlor to keep a look-out for him and let her know by collect phone when he arrives so she can come back down and pick him up again."

"Then Lawlor would have told Donnie!"

"Sure he would. So Donnie is waiting for him."

"Where would Lucas head for when he gets back?"

"Depends on the time of day. If it was morning, I guess he'd head for Chaney's Bayou, back to that shack he shared with Arnie Blassit. And if it was afternoon or evening, he'd probably head for the Mack. You know, he must be awful close to eighty years old, Alex."

"I wouldn't want Donnie to get to him before anybody sees him. He might never be seen again."

"Just how the hell do you make sure that won't happen?"

"I don't know, Buddy."

"I know one thing. It isn't natural that if Donnie knew about it from Lawlor, he wouldn't pass the word around. People would get a kick out of it, old Lucas running out on his daughter and heading back here. It's the kind of thing you'd talk about."

"Have you told anybody about it?"

"Just you."

"Then wouldn't it help a little to spread the word? So people would be looking for him?"

Buddy asked then, in a quiet voice, "What if he already got here, Alex? How can we know he didn't make it back here fast? How can we know Donnie hasn't already got the money and Lucas is some place on the bottom of the bay?"

"That could have happened. He could have come in at night, walking over from Davis. Donnie must patrol that road."

"Right often. But, wait a minute—now you've got me doing it —how about that shovel? If Lucas found the place for him, it would be natural to leave that shovel there, wouldn't it? If he got it all, he wouldn't need the shovel. And if he wasn't sure he got it all, he'd leave it there for the next time he got a chance to go back and dig."

"So let's figure that Lucas hasn't gotten here yet. It's about all we can do."

"And I'll spread the word that he's on his way back, that he run away from home like a little kid."

"It will get back to Donnie."

"Sure it will, and it ought to give him the jumps. That is, Alex, if we haven't been going overboard with all this guesswork."

"You saw the shovel."

"I know. I know. And I saw how he acted this afternoon. But we seem to be getting spread so damn thin. I wish there was more to go on."

Alex heard Betty's shout and looked towards the beach. She was standing holding two cans of beer aloft. They swam in, side by side. When they walked up the slant of the beach together, Alex sensed that Buddy's great hard bulk must make him look almost frail in comparison.

Later, when Betty had gone to shower and change, Buddy said, "Got me another idea, Alex."

"Yes?"

"If Lucas comes in and he gets him, he'd use his own boat. Might have to leave Lucas tied up some place along the shore line where nobody would run across him before Donnie came to get him in that boat. So I can fix that boat a little. Easiest way is to plug the cooling system. He wouldn't notice anything wrong. He'd go a couple miles before it quit cold on him. Do that to-night."

"Be careful."

"I can move quiet in the dark."

They left at six-thirty. Doyle sat on his porch and watched the last of the sunset. Just as the light was fading, a figure came into his line of vision, coming from his right, walking hastily along the packed sand at the water's edge, almost running. He recognized Celia M'Gann, and there was such a look of trouble in the way she moved that he got up and went out into the gathering night. The screen door slammed behind him.

She stopped at the sound and took several tentative steps towards the cottage, "Mr. Doyle?" Her voice was shrill and taut, as though she could be close to losing control.

"Yes, Miss M'Gann," he said, walking towards her.

"Have you seen my brother? Have you seen the colonel?"

"No, I haven't."

"Have you been here long?"

"Since a little after five, I guess I would have seen him if he went by on the beach. I wasn't watching the road."

"Could you . . . help me look for him?"

"Sure. What's wrong?"

And suddenly she was crying silently. There was just enough

light in the west so that he could see her face, contorted like a child's, as she stood there with her fists tightly clenched.

"You better try to tell me what's wrong," he said softly. And, to his discomfiture and astonishment, she turned and thrust herself against him, sobbing in a hoarse and rasping way against his throat, her strong body shaking. It did not last long. She wrenched herself away, saying harshly, "How stupid! How damn girlish!"

"Can you tell me what's wrong?"

She stood with her back to him, wearing a pale blouse and a dark skirt, sandalled feet planted strongly on the tide-wet sand. She made a half gesture towards the charcoal Gulf. "He . . . might be out there."

"And he might not be out there. He could have taken a walk."

"Not after what happened."

"What did happen? If you tell me maybe I can be more help to you."

She turned and it was now too dark for him to see her expression. "You seem to be speaking with a good deal more precision, Mr. Doyle. What did you say to him when I left you alone?"

"I don't know what you mean."

"Something changed him. I'm supposed to be an administrator, Mr. Doyle. I am on leave of absence from a large insurance company. I was in charge of a section employing over three hundred women. I'm not a fool. I'm not as brilliant as my brother but I'm no fool. I could handle those women adequately. To-day I said the wrong thing. I said a stupid thing. If he's gone, it's my fault. We're twins. We've always been close. We've always had a curious awareness of what the other is thinking. I do not see how I could have gone six months without knowing what was in his mind and how it was affecting him, holding him back when he should have been improving."

She took a half-step closer to him. "He didn't take his nap to-day. He sat on the porch, almost motionless. I made his highball at five o'clock and took it to him. I sat by him, doing some mending. Without any warning at all, he said, 'Did you kill her, Celia?' What should my reaction have been? I know now. I should have reacted violently, with horror, dismay that he could think such a thing. So, in complete stupidity, I sat there and said in a sort of mild and chiding way, 'What a strange idea, Crawford. Of course not!' And he did not speak again. And about fifteen minutes ago I found he was gone. For six months he's been thinking I killed her. I know that now. It explains how he's acted."

Her fingers suddenly closed around his wrist. They were cold and strong. "So now he must think I did. And what could he do with a conviction like that? Turn me in? Keep on letting me take care of him? Live with that knowledge? An almost insoluble problem for the kind of man he is. I reacted improperly, Mr. Doyle, because you become accustomed to treating invalids as if they were children. And because I am guilty. I came so horribly close to killing her. So desperately close. I should have told him. But I didn't want to risk upsetting him even more than he was already upset when he learned she was dead. He wasn't as strong six months ago as he is now. And after a little while . . . it seemed too late. But he must have heard me leave the cottage that night. And return. And he never let on that he had heard anything. He's always known there wasn't anything in the world I wouldn't do for him. And I almost did him the . . . ultimate favour. Help me, Mr. Doyle. Help me find him."

He went out to the car and got a flashlight out of the glove compartment. He walked up the beach with her. The tide was coming in. The waves had already erased the tracks she had made walking down towards his cottage. He could find no sign of any tracks the colonel might have left.

They walked north. As they walked she said, "I have the feeling it's ended now. All of it. She was such a horror. I was afraid the cumulative strain of her misbehaviour would kill him. Every time she didn't return for two or three nights, I would be hoping she'd never come back. We had a terrible quarrel out on the beach the Wednesday before she was killed. I tried to plead with her, to beg her to be considerate. I couldn't reach her. She told me to live my own life, not hers. I said that I shouldn't have expected more of her. She had come from nothing. And then she started to curse and rant at me, telling me how good her family was, how her father had been a wealthy man, how he had bought her everything. And she brought up that ridiculous myth of hidden money.

"I told her that when a hard, shrewd man lived in a small town and made a fetish of secrecy, rumour always credited him with a fortune he didn't have. Instead of a mythical fortune, it would have been far better, I said, if he had left her a legacy of decency and manners. She started to tell me, violently, how nice her dear daddy had been to her when she was little. And quite suddenly she stopped. She looked as if she had quite forgotten I was there.

When I spoke to her she stared at me as if she didn't know my name, and turned and walked away."

Celia M'Gann was talking tensely and rapidly, with a threat of hysteria in her voice. He sensed that it was compulsive talking, a device she was using to hold herself together.

"I worried about the quarrel, Mr. Doyle. I felt I had handled her wrong. Better if I had tried to bribe her to put less strain on my brother. She was a greedy little thing. I didn't get a chance to try a new tack on Thursday or Friday. I couldn't sleep Friday night. I knew her habits. Many times she had walked back from town alone, along the beach, because the walking was better and there were fewer mosquitoes on the open beach. It was more probable that she would have a date, and then there would be no telling when she would come rolling in. But, because I couldn't sleep with the problem on my mind, it seemed worth taking a chance of meeting her. I got up very quietly, and left the cottage. It was a little after two. Even if I missed her, I thought the walk would help.

"I met her not far beyond the cottage where you are. She was quite unsteady, but she was coherent. She was surprised to see me. There was a little moonlight. We stood there and I tried to reason with her. If all else failed, I was going to offer her all my savings to leave and never come back. It's an . . . adequate amount. She teetered and leered at me there in the moonlight and then in the most foul possible way she hinted at . . . an unspeakable relationship between my brother and myself. She tried to soil the finest thing in my life. I do not know exactly what happened. It was as though I went blind and numb. When sensation came back I was standing over her. She lay unconscious on the sand, and I had a terrible blazing pain in my clenched fist. I had never struck anybody with my fist before. I'm a strong woman. I had noticed the tide was coming in. I bent over her and thought of dragging her into the water. I tried but I could not force myself to touch her. Then I saw that the tide would reach her before very long. I turned and ran, literally ran back to our cottage. I sank exhausted on the sand, trembling, nauseated.

"In a little while I knew it was something I could not do. I could not leave her there. No matter how dangerous she was to my brother, I could not kill. And so I went back. I stopped just about in front of your cottage when I saw, far off in the moonlight, somebody bending over her. I could not tell if it was a man or a woman. I knew she would be all right. It was even possible she

wouldn't remember me striking her. And so I went back to bed
and stayed awake waiting for her to come in. She was always
noisy when she came in. She had no consideration. None. I fell
asleep. And we were both awakened by that Darcey woman,
screaming and gibbering outside the cottage."

"You haven't told anyone this."

"No. What good would it have done to subject myself to a lot
of clumsy interrogation? I couldn't possibly identify the person I
had seen with her. And she had died of strangulation, not drowning. I suppose in a certain sense I did contribute to her death."

"Do you think you were seen by the person who killed her? He
could have been following her, or waiting to intercept her."

"I thought of that. I worried about it. But he could not have
told of seeing me without implicating himself. Unless he were
caught, and then there was the chance he would try to blame it
all on me. That was a risk I had to take. And, you know, I could
not be at all certain I had been seen. When I woke up, my hand
was badly puffed. I pretended to burn it when I fixed breakfast.
It gave me a chance to bandage it so the puffiness did not show. It
did not last long. And now . . . it all ends this way. And all for
nothing. Because I tried to save him."

They were far beyond the Proctor cottage, and beyond where
the road ended at the Janson land.

Doyle had been shining the flashlight on the smooth unmarked
sand. And suddenly he picked up the indentation of a naked foot,
and another, walking away from the water. She clutched his arm.
She looked at the empty beach and towards the blackness of the
brush. "Crawford?" she called, her voice wild and lost in the
emptiness of the night. "Crawford!"

"I'm right here," he said, so close that it startled both of them.
Doyle turned his light towards the shadows. Colonel M'Gann
sat slumped on the sand, his back against the bole of a big
Australian pine that had been brought down by erosion. Celia
ran to him and dropped to her knees in the sand and, with a
strange harsh cry of pain and gladness, put her arms around him.
Doyle turned the light away from them. The woman was sobbing
quietly.

M'Gann said, apparently addressing Doyle, ignoring his sister,
"The survival instinct is a strong and curious thing. I walked up
this way and swam out beyond my limit. I knew it was beyond my
strength to get back. And at the first edge of panic, the brute body
took over, pacing itself, struggling to live. The heart should have

quit, but it didn't. And so I lay in the shallows finally, until I had the strength to get up."

"She has something to tell you, Colonel."

"I know what she has to tell me."

"I don't think you do."

Doyle went up the beach. The murmur of her voice faded away. He waited a long time. Finally Celia called him and he walked back to them.

"I guess I've been a fool," the colonel said.

"We . . . I think I know who killed her."

"Can you tell us? Not that it matters terribly," he said.

"Not yet. If we can't prove it somehow, I'll tell you."

"Mr. Doyle, my sister's protective instinct towards me has always been obsessive. She has had so little emotional release in her own life that her concern has not been entirely . . . healthy. Hush, Celia, please. Jenna's behaviour was hampering my recovery. I heard her go out and I heard her come back, but I lied to the sheriff, as she did. And I let myself believe she had done something I should have known her to be incapable of. I'm ashamed of that. I decided to call it justifiable homicide. Be her judge and jury. But I would find myself looking at her hands and thinking of how Jenna had been when we were first married. I thought I knew what she was keeping from me. Early this evening I finally tested her. From the way she answered, I knew I could no longer afford the small luxury of doubt. And my solution seemed to me to be . . . apt. As I told you, Mr. Doyle, I was faced with an emotional problem. An ethical problem."

"Why would you say that to him?" Celia asked.

"Colonel, what can I tell Colonel Presser now?"

"I don't know yet. I have to adjust to . . . new knowledge. And I will have to find out what damage was done by this . . . asinine little adventure of mine. Heaven help the man who takes himself so seriously, Mr. Doyle."

"What is this talk about Colonel Presser?" Celia demanded. "Has this Mr. Doyle sneaked around my back and . . ."

"Please be still, Celia. Mr. Doyle is a very competent and effective man. Mr. Doyle, it would be inefficient to keep you here while I make one of my slow decisions. Mission accomplished, I would say. There's no more you can do. You can tell Austin that I will be in touch with him in a week or two. If I say yes, and I think I might, he could then send some people down here to bring me up to date."

Celia had jumped to her feet. "I will *not* have it! You are *not* going to go back and let them work you to death. You're a sick man and I will not——"

"Celia!" he roared.

"But . . ." she said in a small voice.

"You will order the lives of those female clerks of yours, but you will not order my life for me. I am grateful for your care. It does not give you the authority you seem to think is yours. My apologies, Mr. Doyle. Family scene."

"Can I help you back to the cottage?"

"No thanks. I'll rest a little longer. And then Celia can help me if necessary. I suppose you'll be going back now?"

"Not yet, Colonel. One mission accomplished. The official one. And now there's a personal one. It seems to be . . . necessary. Miss M'Gann, could I ask you one question?"

"After you lied to me about——"

"My sister will answer your question, Mr. Doyle. She'll remember later she had reasons to be grateful to you, and she'll regret her rudeness."

"You said you were too far to identify the person you saw bending over Jenna."

"That's right."

"Was there any distinguishing thing at all? Light clothing or dark clothing?"

"I was much too far away, in that light. But . . . I got the impression that the figure was wearing a beach hat. One of those straw things, like a coolie hat. It somehow gave me the impression that it was a woman, but it seemed strange for her to be wearing it at night."

"Do you recall Deputy Capp's hat?"

"Of course. That Texas-looking thing. I see what you mean. I couldn't swear to it. But at that distance that cream-coloured hat could have given me that impression. You must realize that had I known I was seeing a murderer, I'd have been more observing."

"Thank you. And good night. If there's anything I can do . . ."

"We're all right now," the colonel said. They both said good night to him. He walked back to his cottage. Now the pattern was more distinct. The blurred area was gone. Donnie Capp had bent over the unconscious woman. Perhaps he, too, had thought of pushing her into the water. And then she had begun to stir. And before she was conscious enough to fight him, he had closed that small, sallow, wiry hand around her throat. Maybe it had not been premeditated. Maybe her very helplessness had triggered a new aspect of that deep sadistic aspect of him.

He knew it was not yet finished here for him. Now that he was free to leave, he could not. It was not revenge against Donnie, or the desire to protect Lucas, or even the strange enchantment of the handsome and unapproachable girl. It was part of being home again. As though, by accomplishing something difficult and perhaps dangerous, he could pay in partial measure for the long years of exile, self-imposed.

As he ate and as he showered and as he lay sleepless in a slant of April moonlight, he thought of Donnie Capp.

CHAPTER NINE

SATURDAY was a strange day. The sun shone through a mist that would not burn away. The Gulf had a silvery, milky look, a shining calm, yet with a swell that lifted slowly, sleekly to break finally after long hesitation against the sand—like long-spaced recurrent sighs. The terns swooped and yelped in an unknown excitement, and Doyle could not see where the sea joined the sky at the distant horizon. He stood on the beach and saw something he had never seen as a child or as a young man.

Five hundred feet from the shore a giant ray—a devil fish—burst up through the pearly surface and seemed to hang for one incredible moment suspended, as black as evil, between sea and sky before falling with its hundreds of pounds of weight, cracking its great wings against the water surface with a sound that had a sharp echoing resonance. The look of it gave him a crawling, shuddering sensation, a special awareness of his own mortality.

At mid-morning he drove over into the town to the boat yard. Buddy said secretively that he had plugged the cooling system on Donnie's motor without being seen, and that he had told enough people about the expected return of Lucas to be assured the news would spread quickly. He had seen Donnie Capp's car parked on Bay Street earlier in the morning, but had not seen Donnie. They stood talking at the far end of the work shed. Buddy said: "I hardly ever dream. But I dreamed last night about Donnie. And today it seems more like he could have done it. Funny, isn't it? But . . . this is the kind of day I guess when it's easier to think of people killing people. Line storms out in the Gulf. We ought to get weather before the day's over."

"Nothing to do now but wait."

"I stopped in the Mack last night. Arnie Blassit came in. Told him that if Lucas showed up to bring him right to me fast as he could make it. He wanted to know why. I told him I'd tell him why later on, that it was important. Told him to keep his mouth shut about it."

Betty came towards them. "Now what's going on? Are you people forming some kind of a secret club? Maybe you should build a nice tree house for meetings. Alex, did you see my watch?"

"No."

"I keep looking at my empty wrist. I left it on that little shelf near your outside shower stall. Very stupid of me. I can see it sitting there, just as plain. I don't want it to get rained on."

"I'll go get it right away."

"Would you, please?" She walked to where she could get a better look at the sky. "On second thoughts, it isn't going to rain right away. John has gone off in the jeep. This whole place is dead as a tomb. And a day like this makes me feel stickier and restlesser than a real hot one. Brother, dear, I think I'll goof off and take a short swim and pick up my watch and let Alex take me to lunch in something air-conditioned. And I will slave like a dog all afternoon to make up. Why don't you come too?"

"I've got to get Marty's boat ready. He's picking it up at twelve-thirty. We can't all goof off around here."

Alex waited a few minutes for Betty in front of the office and then they got into the old Dodge and he drove back towards the beach. She looked slightly wilted. The bridge timbers rumbled under the wheels. After the bridge there was a short stretch of causeway, and then a sharp right-hand turn on to the narrow key road, a turn made almost blind by a big tangle of palmetto and yucca at the corner.

Just as he reached the turn he caught a glimpse of something through the mass of foliage, something big and fast—and heard the hard high roar of a truck moving fast in low gear. He knew at once that if he tried to make the turn, he would turn right into it. If he tried to stop, his momentum would take him across its bows and he would be smashed broadside. With both luck and instinct, he took the only course possible. He swung the wheel hard left and stamped on the gas to swing the rear end around, knowing that if the truck tried to make the turn on to the causeway instead of continuing south on the key road, it would smash into him.

The truck was up on them, and for a frozen moment the blunt
bow of the big dusty GMC seemed to hang over them. But then
the sliding turn pulled his hood away. For one microsecond they
were side by side, both headed in the same direction. And then
his right rear corner, still sliding, slammed into the big rear duals
of the truck, bounced away so violently that the Dodge hung for
a moment on the verge of going over, came down with a force
that burst a tyre, and wobbled crazily into the ditch, the wide and
shallow ditch on the other side of the road, the car aimed back
towards the bridge and the causeway. He turned off the engine;
and they could hear the roar of the truck receding south in the
distance.

They stared at each other. She looked sick under her tan.
"Absolutely insane!" she said.

"Who was it?"

"I haven't the faintest. But he's still on the key, and this is the
only way off. Drunk, I'd say. Alex, you did a perfectly wonderful
job!"

"Thanks." He took out cigarettes, gave her one. When he tried
to light hers, they had difficulty getting the flame and the cigarette
end together until she grinned at him and held his wrist.

"I'd get out," he said. "If I was sure my knees would work."

"You'll have to get out first. It's all bayonets on my side."

He got out on to the sand road and she got out and stood beside
him. Except for the constant metallic song of insects in the brush,
the morning was breathlessly still.

"I'll have to run it forward and up out of the ditch before I
can change that tyre," he said.

"Listen!"

He heard the truck sound again, as faint as the shrilling of the
insects, but growing louder as it came towards them.

"We should flag that maniac down!" she said. "At least we'll
find out who he is so it can be reported."

"Get back in the ditch, Betty, out of the way. We don't know
how drunk he is."

She moved into the ditch behind the car. He stood out beside
the car. In a moment he could see the truck, and he heard the
motor sound change as it slowed to make the turn into town. He
began waving his arm in a big arc, palm down, trying to flag the
truck down. He saw the big hood and a face behind the window
of the cab and, with a feeling of incredulity, he saw the big wheels
cut towards him. He whirled and dived headlong across the left

front fender of the Dodge, banging his right knee sharply on the fender. He hit on his shoulder in the ditch and rolled into a thousand knives. And looked just in time to see the truck bounce high as it hit the crown of the wooden bridge and continue at high speed towards the foot of Bay Street.

He sat and hugged his leg, grimacing with pain. Betty ran to him, her eyes wild and her mouth working.

"Did he hit you?"

Pain made him irritable. "Yes. He hit me square and killed me dead."

"I'm sorry. I couldn't see. He came so close."

"Help me get up so I can walk on this thing."

She took his hand and pulled him up. He limped around in a small circle and felt the pain diminish. In a very few moments he could put all his weight on the leg without wincing. He looked at the dual tracks in the hard sand and shell surface. The truck had barely missed the car, and the duals had run well inside where he had been standing.

"He swerved at you," she said.

"I know."

"Alex, there's spots of blood on the back of your shirt!"

"I rolled into those bayonets."

"You know, it was a County Road Department truck. And it was one of the Kemmer boys driving. I can't remember his name."

"Lee?"

"Yes! That's the one. Did you see him?"

"I was too busy both times he went by."

He started the car and ran it at an angle out of the ditch on the flat right rear. He changed to the bald-headed spare, collapsed the jack, put the burst tyre in the trunk.

"You're so quiet about it," Betty said.

"Right after we got across the bridge I thought I heard a motor start up. I think I know where it could have been. Let's go take a look."

She got in and he got the car turned around. He drove two hundred yards and stopped on the right shoulder and got out. She followed him. He crossed the road and turned and looked towards the bridge. He remembered having noticed that from that spot you could see the crown of the bridge and a segment of the causeway.

A truck had been backed into the brush on the west side of the road at that point where the view was best. He sat on his heels, and when she came up behind him, he pointed with a twig at drops of fresh, shiny, black oil on a green leaf. He guessed where the cab door would have been, and found four fresh cigarette butts near by. A wink of glass in the brush caught his eye. He picked it up. An uncapped and empty pint bottle that had held a cheap blend. He smelled it. The whisky odour was sharp and fresh.

"Do you think he was waiting here? Waiting until you. . . ."

"It's a funny place to park. He was going like hell in a low gear when he hit the corner. And when he came back, he tried again." He threw the bottle aside.

"How about fingerprints on the bottle? It's attempted murder, isn't it?"

"He missed. So it's drunken driving, if you can prove it, or reckless driving, and that would have to be proven too. And if you could grab that Kemmer character and try to beat it out of him, he wouldn't know what the hell you were talking about, because he has first-hand knowledge of just what Donnie can do with that club. Let's get that swim."

"I guess any of those Kemmers would do just what Donnie said. But do you really think Donnie would tell him to kill you?"

"Donnie doesn't like me. Not at all. And you could hardly believe he'd work me over. When a man gets into a habit of thinking he can get away with anything, it isn't much of a jump from a clubbing to a killing."

"There's something going on I don't know about."

"Let's get that swim."

"But if somebody is really trying to kill you, it wouldn't be safe to go and swim, would it?"

"It might not be too safe for me to go swimming alone. I don't know. Lee Kemmer has got to report that it didn't work. Suppose it had worked, and I'd been alone in the car. Donnie could come up with witnesses, some of his tame rabbits willing to swear I'd swerved right into the path of the truck. Too bad. Nobody to get indignant about Alex Doyle, transient."

"I would!"

"But if it hadn't gone sour, he'd have killed both of us, Betty. And that would be more of a stink than Donnie is prepared to face. He can be thankful Lee Kemmer missed. He couldn't have seen there was somebody in the car with me. They'll have to cook up something else, involving me alone. So it's safe to swim. I'm safe when I'm with you. Come on."

They went to the cottage. When he was in his trunks she inspected his back, and went and found the dark dregs of a bottle of iodine and dabbed each puncture. They swam together. A line of green-black had crept up from the south-west horizon, extending all the way across the sky. The swells were heavier and slower, and an infrequent gust of wind would scamper and swirl across the water before dying away.

She sat beside him on the old blanket on the beach, subdued and thoughtful, hugging her knees, while they watched the slow approach of the distant storm. She shuddered suddenly.

"Cold?"

"No. Delayed reaction, I guess. Thinking about how it could have been if you hadn't been so quick. I didn't know what was happening. I would have run right into him."

"It didn't happen."

"Alex?"

"Yes, Miss Betty."

"Everything seems to be changing for me. Since you've come back."

"How?"

"Oh, I had a nice clean tidy little shell. Like a lady hermit crab. I was very comfortable, really. Nothing touched me. Now I'm part way out of my nice shell and I feel sort of . . . soft and naked and defenceless. And uncertain about things."

"My apologies."

"Now don't apologize. I'm more alive, I guess. More aware of the people round me. And their motives. I felt all perfectly adjusted for ever and ever, and pretty smug about myself. And now my tender little psyche is hanging out in the cold cold wind. Maybe it's a kind of discontent. I don't know. I want to back into my shell again, but it doesn't seem to fit." She turned and looked at him. "Have you ever had a bad fever?"

"Yes."

"Do you remember how . . . painful things look? I mean so sharp and clear. And even simple things take on sort of ominous personalities. And sounds are so vivid you want to cover your ears. This is a cousin of that."

"Listen, Betty. Here it comes."

They listened to the oncoming roar of the rain. He folded the blanket and they walked to the cottage. He put the blanket inside and went out on to the porch just as it hit. She stood on white sand thirty feet in front of the cottage in a dark red suit, erect, her brown shoulders back, her face tilted towards the sky, standing in a curious green light, outlined for moments against the onrushing streaming curtain of rain, and the constant flare of lightning beyond it before the rain misted and obscured her. He felt that he had never seen anything quite as primitive and beautiful.

Soon the wind began to slant the cold rain, driving it in on to the porch. The day was darker, the lightning closer, and he could barely hear the thunder above the hammering roar of the rain on the roof. He retreated into the living-room and moments later she came hurrying in, panting and gasping, her riotous hair plastered meekly against the good lines of her skull.

"It's a glorious storm!" she called to him over the rain roar. "It's wonderful!"

She borrowed his bedroom and closed the door and came out a little while later in her yellow blouse and white skirt, barefoot, hair in a white towel turban, her eyes still dancing with the excitement of the storm. The turmoil of the storm seemed to increase. The cottage creaked and stirred as the wind shouldered it. Whips of rain slashed the roof and windows. And between the intensities of rain, all the world was a deep aquarium green. He went in and changed to dry khaki shorts and a T-shirt and then they stood close and looked out at the storm, and spoke loudly above the noise. When there was a rift they could see the Gulf, tilting hills of shining slate, foaming cream-white as it broke.

She turned on the kitchen light and made sandwiches and coffee. Just as they finished the lunch, the storm ended with astonishing abruptness, and went fading, bumbling, grumbling off into the east. And the world stayed dark.

"Come on," she said, and they went out on to the beach where the surf roared. The rain had smashed the sand flat, washed it clean. Their bare feet, male and female, made the first tracks seen on the planet. And, without self-consciousness, she took his hand as they walked.

"Here comes more!" she cried, and they ran back to the cottage just in time. The rain was not as heavy as before, but the wind was strong, the lightning more vivid and continual.

Suddenly there was a vivid and alarming clink of lightning, a white and blinding flash and simultaneous concentrated bang of thunder. The kitchen light went out. He could feel a numbed tingling in his hands and feet and he heard nervousness in her laugh. "I like it, but not that close."

He smiled down at her. Her face changed, illuminated there in the gloom by the dance of lightning, a sudden and solemn heaviness of eyes and lips, a tentative, searching look.

"Before . . . on the beach before the storm . . . I was trying to say something. Trying to hint, I guess. I don't know."

"Are you sure?"

"No, I'm not sure. I'm scared half out of my mind. So hurry, darling, before I turn and run. Try. Quickly."

He took her in his arms and kissed her. He felt the uncompromising rigidity of her lips, the slow stiffening of her body. He released her. She went over and sat on the shabby couch and turned her face away, sitting very still. They heard the last fragment of the storm move away.

"Damn," she said wearily. "All twisted up inside. Emotional cripple. False courage from a little lightning and wind. Sorry I inflicted myself on you. And now I won't be able to be . . . easy with you any more. So that's spoiled too. New element added."

"We'll just make out like it didn't happen."

More light was coming into the world. She looked at him with a strange and frightened defiance. "Maybe I should be forced."

"That's a bad idea."

"How do you know?"

"I don't really. I just have a hunch it would be the worst thing that could happen to you."

She stood up. "The lady is neuter gender." She took off the turban and fluffed her hair. "Better drive it back to work, sir."

He stepped towards her, tilted her chin up, saw the quick alarm in her eyes, and sensed the effort she had to make to keep from twisting away from him. He kissed her very quickly and lightly on the lips.

"That's for affection, Miss Betty."

She smiled a small heartbreak and said: "That one didn't hurt a bit. Very fatherless. I mean fatherly. . . . That was a funny slip of the lip. Probably significant. Without that deep therapy, I'll never know."

"I think one small thing would help. I think it might help a lot if you kept in mind at all times the fact that you are a very, very exciting woman. With a hell of a figure. With considerable loveliness. So walk proud, and think about that once in a while."

There was a red flush under her tan. "You're out of your mind! I'm a big husky horse."

"Ask around. Take a poll. It will check out."

"Jenna was dainty. And lovely."

"With an empty little teasing face and a practised waggle of hips and the soul of a harpy. She was pretty in a shallow and provocative way. No more than that. And no more talk about it. Off we go."

On the way over to town she said: "Buddy will be frantic when he hears about that truck."

"I'd rather you wouldn't tell him."

"But why not!"

He parked in the small lot near her office, turned to face her, lit their cigarettes. "You keep saying, Betty, you think something is going on you don't know about. Something is. It isn't very pretty and there are no definite plans in effect right now. We're just waiting for something to happen. If it works right, you'll be told the whole thing. I'm used to waiting. And watching. Buddy isn't. I want him to be patient. If you tell him about the truck, he may do something impulsive. And dangerous to him."

"Now that I know there *is* something going on, I can get it out of him. He can't keep secrets from me."

"I'd rather you wouldn't try."

"All right. I won't try if you don't want me to. And I won't mention the truck. I will be the helpless female if that's what you want. I'll learn to simper."

"That should be enchanting."

"But for goodness sake, when you can tell me what you two are plotting, don't delay it."

She paused in the office doorway and waved to him and went in. He turned around and drove slowly down Front Street.

Donnie's official car was parked across from the Mack, empty. On impulse, Alex parked and went in. Donnie was at the bar alone, having a beer. Four men were at one table, talking baseball. Two noisy couples were at another table. Two men were playing the bowling machine. Janie was working the bar. It was only two-thirty, but the Mack was getting its usual start on Saturday night. Alex went over and stood beside Donnie and said, "Storm cleared the air."

"Isn't so sticky now."

"Something I wanted to report, Mr. Deputy, sir."

Donnie looked up at him. "Keep talking."

"One of those Kemmer boys was running around drunk in a county truck a couple of hours ago. Came right out at me. He could have run me down and killed me dead the way he was going, but at the last minute he turned the wheel and swerved around me."

"Too bad he missed," Donnie said casually, but Alex saw the little twitch of surprise and anger in the shallow eyes.

"So I've done my duty as a citizen, Mister Deputy, sir."

"If I see him one of these days I'll go out of my way to tell him to take it easy."

"Thank you, Mister Deputy, sir. Now maybe you'd answer a point of law. You remember putting knots on my head, I suppose."

"Enjoyed every minute of it. Hope you did."

"Now suppose while I was there helpless, Mister Deputy, sir, somebody else came in after you left and killed me dead? Would you be guilty of murder too?"

There was no expression on Capp's face, no slight flaw in the utter blankness as the long seconds passed. Alex tried to look casual, but it was becoming a constantly greater effort.

"Now that's a right strange question to ask a man," Capp said.

"I just wondered about it. Idle curiosity, sir."

"It kills cats." Capp stood up. He pushed the club so that it swung on the thong and thumped the front of the bar. "This is the only law I know, Doyle. Only kind I understand. Probably the only kind you understand too, come right down to it."

He pushed by Alex and went out, drove off through the dwindling rain puddles. Alex went out and stood by the car. He felt the familiar tensions of the chase, a taste in the back of his throat of a breathless expectancy. It was, in a sense, a dreadful art, this manipulation of human beings. Discover the area of stress. And then nudge so gently and so carefully. Back up the lions with a kitchen chair. But it had to be done delicately.

He remembered the embassy clerk in Madrid, the wide-faced, smiling fellow whose outgoing reports they had finally intercepted, written in code in a tiny hand on paper of a curious shade of pink. After they had made certain that he would have access to nothing more of any importance, they had searched until they found identical paper. And then, with great care, they had begun to plant strips of it in places where he would come across it. Those who think themselves monstrously clever can best be awed and broken by a phenomenon that can only be the result of greater cleverness. And by something they do not quite understand. It had been the intent to humble the smiling one until, by the time he was interrogated, he would be co-operative.

They watched the changes in him as the weeks went by, the new nervousness of the smile, the increasing intervals of inattention, a suggestion of a stammer, a slight facial tic, a weight loss. They were ready for him if he tried to run. The final strip of pink paper was planted with diabolical efficiency and perfect timing between the inner pages of the newspaper he usually purchased on his way from the embassy to his hotel. In order to guarantee success, slips had to be placed inside a hundred issues of the paper. To other purchasers they would be meaningless. But he could not help but think that his was the only copy containing such a slip, and he could not of course understand how, with such busy traffic at the news stand, it had been managed. Two hours after he entered the hotel, one of those watching him saw him dive from the wide windows to the cobblestones four stories below, and swore later that he had seen a wide, idiot smile in the light of the street lamp as the man fell.

And that had been a mistake, of course. Too strong an attack on the area of strain, so that the subject had broken. A Donnie Capp could resist greater pressure. Now he sensed that he was suspect. He would know of the slow crumbling of his position of strength. The inspection of the boat. The circulation of the gossip about the return of Lucas. And, finally, this unmistakable hint that it was known that the person who had struck Jenna and the person who had strangled her were not the same. Until that moment, Capp would have been certain that only he and the one who struck the blow would have known of that strange division of effort.

Doyle wondered if he had pushed Capp a little too far. The man was capable of murder. He tried to guess what Capp's action would be. He had, perhaps, three choices. He could give up any thought of the money and content himself with the knowledge that the murder could not be proved. Yet he could not be entirely sure it could not be proven. Or he could gamble on being the first to find Lucas and make him lead him to the money and then run with it. Or he could, if bold enough, attempt in some safe way to eliminate the people who now seemed suspicious of him. He would know that included Doyle, Buddy Larkin and perhaps Betty Larkin. But he could not be certain if others had been told, or how much was known—how much they could have been told.

Doyle made his guess based on an appraisal of Capp's nature. The man was direct and brutal, but not essentially clever. Had he been clever he would not have been so impatient. He would have let Lucas help Jenna find the money, or find that there was no money. And if the money had been there, he could have begun his own action from that point. So, considering the factor of impatience, if Lucas had not yet finished his journey, the waiting would be difficult for Capp. And he would feel easier taking some sort of action, no matter how dangerous, than merely waiting. The more he thought of it, the more convinced he became that Capp was now highly dangerous—the lion grown contemptuous of the kitchen chair and the noisy blanks.

And so he drove back through the washed air, under the deep blue afternoon sky, and talked again with Buddy Larkin. He told Buddy that he had every intention of taking care of himself, and he would feel much better if Buddy made it his business to exercise the same care for both himself and Betty.

Buddy was mildly incredulous.

"Listen," Alex said, "your good old familiar Donnie is like a lighted fuse. If Lawlor wasn't the big thick-headed exhibitionist he is, if I could be sure he'd listen, I'd go talk to him. But we've got a hell of an involved chain of deduction. Too many ifs in it. If we had a little more evidence, I'd try to get him locked up."

"It's because he beat you up, Alex. You're jumpy."

"I'll tell you something you don't know, if you promise not to take any action whatsoever—except to be careful."

"What is it?"

"Promise first. It may sound childish, but promise first."

Buddy did. Alex told him of the truck and the narrowness of his and Betty's escape. And he told him why he had told Betty not to tell him. "Because I was afraid you'd turn into a wild man and get yourself in trouble and mess up any chances we have of trapping Capp."

Buddy, with iron face, turned slowly and smacked a stone fist against the shed wall. A pair of nippers ten feet away bounced off a hook and clanged on the slab floor.

"If he had. . . ."

"Settle down! Do you still think it's stupid to use a little care?"

"No! Hell! I think he's gone crazy."

"He hasn't gone crazy, Buddy."

"No?"

"No. He went over the edge six months ago. And this whole town is to blame. You lawful people didn't care if he whipped heads just so long as he whipped the heads on the people who had no way of fighting back. You were even kind of sneaky proud of him. Toughest deputy on the west coast of Florida. And you thought that Old West outfit of his was amusing. You folks grew yourself a paranoid. Nobody has told me, but I can tell you just how he lives. He has a small place somewhere. With a lot of privacy. And he keeps it as bare and neat as a monk's cell. He'll have a gun rack and he'll keep those guns in perfect shape. He'll scrub the floor on his hands and knees. After he makes his bed, you can bounce a coin on it. No books, no television, no hobby except the guns and hunting. Nobody will ever drop in on him. When he wants a woman he'll go after one that's drab and humble and scared, and it will be as close to rape as the law allows."

"You're so damn right, Alex. How do you know about that?"

"I've seen so many of them. In the army, mostly."

"I never thought of it before, but there was a guy like that in my outfit. BAR man. Hell, he kept that thing in shape. He could do a sniper's job with it. Never had a word for anybody. Neatest damn marine I ever saw. Sneak out at night by himself and come back with gook hardware. A killer. Volunteer for every patrol. He finally bought it, but he sure had a lopsided score before he did. He cost them. Donnie has a little cinder-block place he built by himself, off to hell and gone behind the new school."

"Keep an eye on Betty and on yourself."

"I will. Can't he get to you out there on the beach?"

"If he wants to try. And if I happen to stay there. But I won't. I'm going to buy some bug juice and some netting and scoop me a hole in the sand south of the cottage, down under the tree shadows. In case he comes calling."

"I'll stick close to Betty."

"Good deal."

CHAPTER TEN

THE birds woke Doyle in the first grey of dawn. He made a cautious inspection of the cottage and the surrounding area before going in with the blankets. By the time he had washed and shaved, the sun was beginning to cut the morning mist and promise a perfect day. The Gulf had quieted down.

Just as he was pouring a cup of coffee, he heard a racing engine approaching at high speed. He went to the back door. Buddy Larkin skidded to a stop in the pickup and scrambled out and ran heavily towards him, his strong face stamped with panic.

"Come on!" he said. "I'll tell you on the way. I think he's got Lucas and Betty too."

"How the hell did that happen?"

"Mom woke me up about an hour ago," Buddy said, backing the truck around recklessly. "She was worried because Betty hadn't come in."

"I thought you were going. . . ."

"Hell, I did what you said. We all went to bed about eleven I guess it was. He wouldn't come right into the house. Mom said when she woke me up that she heard voices down in the kitchen about two o'clock so she put on a robe and went down. Betty was down there, talking to Lucas Pennyweather. Mom said Lucas looked completely pooped. He said he'd done an awful lot of walking. Seems that Lucas was out in the side yard hollering to me. I sleep like I'm dead. Betty is a light sleeper. She heard him and got up."

They bounced almost clear of the road when they hit the crown of the wooden bridge.

"Lucas said he had come back and gone right to the Mack and run into Arnie Blassit, and Arnie said he was to get hold of me right away. So Lucas walked back to the house and he was calling me. Betty let him into the kitchen. Mom came down in time to hear Lucas telling her he was supposed to see me, but he didn't know what about. Betty told him it must be some kind of a mistake, that Arnie was probably drunk and got confused. By then it was a little after two. Lucas looked so tired Mom asked him to stay in the spare room. But he said no, he thought he'd be getting back to the Mack and get a ride on down with Arnie to the shack and get settled. He'd left his stuff on our back porch. Betty said he might miss Arnie.

"So nothing to do, but Betty decided she'd best drive the old man back to the Mack, and if Arnie had left, she'd drive him on down to Chaney's Bayou to the shack. Mom said Lucas looked pretty grateful. So Betty left in the jeep and I didn't hear a thing, damn it. Mom stayed awake. When Betty wasn't back quick, she figured she had to take the old man down to the shack. Finally she dozed off, and when she woke up again, about an hour ago, she looked out the window and the jeep wasn't there, and Betty wasn't in her bed, so she got nervous and woke me up."

They got out of the truck and hurried to the boat yard office. John Geer was sitting in the office looking unkempt and upset.

"Any luck?"

"He's flying a party over to Clewiston. They got word there for him to call here soon as he gets in. I couldn't get Daniels."

Buddy explained to Alex. "First thing I did was check and found his boat gone. His car is at Garner's. Got the glasses and got up on to the work-shed roof. Couldn't see a thing. Phoned the Coast Guard. But they're running a big air search for an outboard cruiser lost in the Gulf somewhere off Sarasota. I figure a plane search is the answer. Take a look at the chart."

A big chart was open on Betty's desk. Just south of the key bridge, the mainland cut sharply back, so that the bay became very wide. The marked channel hugged the bay shore of Ramona Key and Kelly Key. There was a bay area of ten miles long by an average of four miles wide to search, including the shore line of both keys and the mainland shore line. Forty square miles, so densely packed with islands that a lot of it was like a great salt-water marsh, with winding tidal streams. He saw the oddly shaped indentation of Bucket Bay on the mainland side, eight miles down, opposite Kelly Key.

"Skippy Illman flies charter out of Fort Myers. He's got a good little twin-engined amphib. He's a friend, and once he phones in and gets the pitch, it won't take him long to get on down here. When will he phone in, John?"

"Fifteen or twenty minutes."

"I got hold of Lawlor and I told him just enough so he ought to come roaring over here with some of his people."

"Maybe he didn't take Betty with him."

"Then where the hell is she if he didn't? I found the jeep. In the lot behind the Mack. And then I came over to get you."

"Did you look around that area? Look thoroughly?"

Buddy swallowed with an obvious effort. "See what you mean. Let's go back. Stick by that phone, John."

They turned into the alley and parked beside the empty blue jeep. They looked into it. Buddy pointed at an old canvas duffle bag on the floor. "Didn't see that before. Belongs to Lucas, I guess."

Doyle heard a screen door bang and he turned and saw Janie, pasty and squinting in the morning sun, wearing a shiny green-satin housecoat with a ripped hem, come out with a bulging brown bag and stare at them curiously as she went over to a row of four lidless garbage cans buzzing with flies and drop the bag in.

"What's going on?"

"Did you tend bar last night, Janie?" Buddy asked.

"Just till it got too rough and Harry made me quit. That was maybe nine."

"Is Harry around? I'd like to see him."

"I'll get him."

They quickly searched the brush around the perimeter of the parking lot. Harry came out in his underwear top, baggy cotton slacks, his belly hanging over his belt, the sun shining on the dark spots on his bald head, picking his teeth with a certain amount of daintiness.

"I looked out and saw your jeep earlier and wondered what the hell," Harry said.

"Did you see Lucas last night?"

Harry strolled over and stood by the jeep with them. "Hell, yes. The old basser made it all the way back. He talked to Arnie and then he took off after only one drink, and everybody in the place trying to buy him one."

"I suppose Donnie was in."

"Sure. He's always in and out a half-dozen times on a Saturday night. Wish he'd stay to hell away. He puts a gloom on the place. But he's sure handy when folks get troublesome."

"Harry, see if you can remember. I know how busy you are. How many times did Donnie come in after Lucas was here?"

"That ain't hard, because Lucas was here late. Half an hour before closing. Donnie come in one more time about quarter of, and everybody was still talking about old Lucas. I see him come in but I didn't see him go. He couldn't have stayed more than a minute. One of the times Donnie was in earlier, Gil Kemmer was in jawing at him and I was sure Donnie would take him out back and work him over but he didn't pay any attention to Gil. Seemed funny. Gil was sore on account of Donnie clubbing Lee Kemmer up so bad he had to be took off the road gang and put in the hospital over in Davis. The way I figure——"

"Thanks, Harry."

"Anything I can do, you just let me know." He walked back towards the screen door. He turned and said, "Say. Janie and me are going to get married, Buddy." Doyle saw the girl standing behind the screen and heard her giggle. It was a singularly empty sound. Then, as he turned, something caught his eye. It was a brown smear on the sharp corner of the windshield frame. Adhering to it, and moving slightly in the east wind, was a small swath of hair, perhaps a dozen long glossy strands, ginger and cream, unmistakably hers. Buddy examined it and then the men exchanged quick glances, as though involved in some kind of special shame, a climate of inner revulsion.

"Let's get back to the office," Buddy murmured.

John Geer shook his head dolefully as they walked in. Buddy said: "I'll take it. You go get that Prowler ready to roll. Take the aluminium dink off the Huckins next to it and just dump it in the cockpit. Put that little three-horse of mine on the dink and make sure it's gassed up."

John Geer loped off. As soon as he was gone Buddy said: "This is just as rough on old John as it is on me. He'd follow her around like a dog if she'd let him."

The phone rang and he snatched it up. "Yeah? That's right. Hallo! Skippy? We got trouble. I don't want to take time to explain. Need you for a search. All those bay islands to the south of us here. It's life and death, boy. Can you get over here fast? Good. I'll be out in the bay on a Prowler. White with blue trim. It's got a ship-to-shore, and when you get close enough, you call me on the Coast Guard emergency channel and I'll tell you what to look for. You run that bird flat out, hear?"

He hung up. "It won't take him long."

John Geer had followed orders, and he had the twin engines of the fast little cabin cruiser turning over. They went aboard and Buddy took the controls while John Geer cast off the remaining lines. Doyle noticed that Geer had a pistol shoved into the waistband of his jeans. It looked like a twenty-two, possibly a Woodsman. Once they were clear of the docks, Buddy shoved the throttles forward. The boat came to life, the engines roaring in synchronization, the white bow cutting the blue morning water. They headed down the bay about four miles before Buddy throttled down. He sent John to the bow to throw over the small anchor. When it bit firm and the boat swung to rest in the tidal current at the edge of the channel, Buddy cut the motors, leaned below and turned on the ship-to-shore. From time to time, very faintly, they could pick up the routine reports of the search planes off Sarasota.

Doyle looked at the islands. They were unchanged from the days when the Caloosas had built their mounds there. Jungles of mangrove to the water's edge and, where they were high enough, clumps of cabbage palm, some live oaks on the bigger ones. Sunday fishing traffic passed them; people waved casually.

"If you fixed the motor," Doyle asked, "could he get to where he was going?"

"Running at night it would be cooler. It wouldn't heat up so fast. He might make four miles. He might make ten. Depends on how fast. And at night he'd run slower. He could get where he's going, maybe. He might have gone into the islands and then waited for daylight so old Lucas could guide him the rest of the way. It would have time maybe to cool down so it would start again. But even if it didn't, he had a paddle in there. If he took Betty along, I guess he figured on running. But he won't get out of there fast with that motor. I wish to God I hadn't messed up the motor now. Maybe he would have just left them there. But if he's stuck——"

"Shut up, please, Buddy," John Geer said and turned away.

"*Slow Goose* calling Larkin on the Prowler," a drawling voice came in, startlingly loud and clear. Buddy jumped for the hand mike.

"Larkin on the *Aces Up*, come in, Skippy."

"*Slow Goose* to the *Aces Up*, I'm half-way from Davis, boy, and you should spot me soon. Where are you? Over."

"*Aces Up* to the *Slow Goose*, I'm about a mile north-east of Windy Pass anchored beside the channel. Look for a twelve-foot aluminium boat with a bright red motor on it. Check the islands and the shore lines. If it's pulled up under the trees we may be out of luck, but you might still be able to spot that motor. There can be one person in it or two or three. One is a woman. Betty, if you want to know. And in one hell of a jam, boy. Over."

"Coast Guard to the *Aces Up* and the *Slow Goose*. This is an emergency channel reserved for Coast Guard use. Vacate the emergency channel."

"*Aces Up* to the Coast Guard operator. This is an emergency. Repeat. This is an emergency. We're using a private search plane because you people are busy on something else. This is the only channel we have in common with the search plane. Will continue to use emergency channel, but we'll keep it as short as we can. Over."

"Coast Guard operator to the *Aces Up*. No authority here to grant permission. But no way to stop you. Good luck. Over."

"There he is!" John Geer called. Doyle saw the small amphib coming at them at low altitude, coming from a point just south of Ramona.

The small aircraft gleamed in the morning sun. He buzzed the boat and climbed high.

"*Slow Goose* to the *Aces Up*. I'll take it high first and if no dice,

I'll make a low square search. I'll give you the word. Over."

They stood at the rail and watched the high slow pattern, squinting up against the brightness of the sky. Time passed with a sickening slowness.

"What the hell is he doing?" Buddy snarled. No one answered.

Suddenly the plane tilted and dropped, leaf-lazy in the sun. It swung up again and began a wide slow circle.

"*Slow Goose* to *Aces Up*," the voice drawled. "Got your customer, Buddy boy. He's in the middle of a little round bay right under me. Trying to start the motor apparently. He's stopped now. Paddling towards shore. Fella in khaki with a kind of a cowboy hat on him. What now? Over."

"We've got to get to him, Skippy. Fast as we can. Can you tell us how to get in there? Over."

"*Slow Goose* to *Aces Up*. Damn if I can tell you how, boy. I noticed you got a dinghy. If you run south to the channel marker south of the pass and leave the big boat there, you'll be close as you can get with it. Then you head in between those two bigger islands and turn right and. . . . Damn, boy, it's a mess down there. Tell you what. Once you get going in the dinghy, I'll be Lura, the girl guide. When you got a turn to make, I'll tilt a wing at it, flying right at you or away from you as the case may be. Only way I can see to get you through that mess. And some places you may have to wade. I see deeper water here and there, but I don't know how the cowboy got in there. Over."

"Just get us in there, Skippy. Over and out."

They ran up to the marker. John waited for Buddy to edge the boat into the shallows beyond the channel and then dropped anchor. They dropped the dinghy over the transom and climbed down into it. Three big men badly overcrowded the eight-foot dinghy. John Geer ran the small motor. It started on the first pull, and, at its meagre top speed, it made a sound like a diligent hornet. Buddy knelt forward. Doyle had the middle seat.

As soon as they went between the two islands Skippy had indicated, they were in flats so shallow that Geer had to tilt the motor until the blade was thrashing half out of water for a few moments until it deepened again. The plane shadow swept over them and they followed the tilt of the wing. The guiding system worked. Doyle quickly lost track of the turns. They were in the narrow tidal channels that cut the low land into islands. Needle fish darted away in alarm. Blue herons stared with a fierce amber eye, then flapped slowly away. Doyle saw a water snake swimming near shore. Several times they had to step out and pull the dinghy across shallows and then start it again. As they walked in the shallows they shuffled their feet to minimize the chance of getting hit by a sting ray.

At last they came into an irregular open bay. Skippy flew directly over a dense shore line of mangrove and dipped the port wing. They couldn't believe there was an opening there. They were almost on it before they saw it. The water was deep and sleek and green. The channel was narrow. At places the leaves touched overhead and they were in mottled shadows, ducking under limbs.

Doyle thought of the child who had been brought here long ago, sitting in her pink dress in the bow of the skiff, full of a child's love for secrets and sense of adventure. If this was the place.

The channel writhed and abruptly opened on to an almost circular bay a hundred yards across. Geer throttled down abruptly. The aircraft had climbed high again.

"There's the boat," Buddy said softly, an unnecessary comment. They had all seen it, the gleam of aluminium and the red motor in the shade where it had been drawn up, empty, directly across the bay from the single entrance. With the small motor barely turning over, the dinghy moved very slowly.

"Old shack over there," John Geer murmured. "See it under the trees. Little to the right of the boat."

"I see it," Buddy said. "Cleared off a long time ago but it's grown up. Good high ground. Cabbage palm."

Doyle felt dangerously exposed. Above the muted burbling of the small outboard he heard the sliding click as Geer worked a shell into the chamber of the target pistol.

"Where the hell is he?" Geer whispered. "I don't like this."

"Move it up a little closer," Buddy ordered.

They could see the small shack more distinctly. The warped door had fallen out of the frame and there was a sagging shutter on the single window.

"She used to tell how he'd take her to a stone castle full of jewels and she was a princess," Buddy said.

"Look to the left of the boat," Doyle said. "About fifteen feet from it." The figure was in shadows. It was face down over the mangrove roots, and utterly still. There were sun dollars on the faded back of the blue work shirt. The back of the white head was out of water.

Geer whispered, "If he killed old Lucas like that, we better figure on coming in here with more than just one little——"

The three shots were authoritative, heavy-throated, evenly spaced. They had a flat sound in the stillness, and were harsh in that special way that can happen only when you are in line with the muzzle. Merged with the middle shot, Doyle heard the once-heard-never-forgotten sound of a slug smashing into flesh and bone. He plunged over the side of the dinghy into two feet of shallow water, turned and grasped the dinghy as the slow-turning motor threatened to move it away. Buddy had plunged out of the dinghy too, but stayed on his feet. And, with ponderous strength, ran diagonally towards the shore, angling away from the cabin, head down and knees high. There was a shiny red-black stain on the back of Buddy's right shoulder, spreading as he ran. There was another shot but Buddy kept running. He dived headlong into the mangroves about sixty feet from the shack, and about a hundred feet from the dinghy.

Doyle had turned the dinghy so that it was between him and the shack. He pushed it until he was near the stern, and then pulled down on the near gunwale so as to tip the far side up to give him cover as he reached and turned the motor off. With the dinghy tilted he could see John Geer crumpled in the bottom of it. He could see his face. The slug had entered just above the left eye-brow, hammering a black, round, lethal hole delicately rimmed with a froth of blood.

The aircraft sound grew loud, and the amphib came down so low that Doyle thought for a moment the man was going to attempt a landing in the tiny bay. But it lifted and cleared the trees at the end, and droned away until the sound of it was lost. The bay was still. He heard a sleepy sound of birds, a heat-whine of insects, a crashing in the thick brush where Buddy had disappeared.

"John?" Buddy's call was loud in the stillness.

"He's dead," Doyle called back.

After a long silence Buddy called, with pain and hoarse anger in his voice, "What are you trying to do, Donnie? You crazy devil! You can't kill everybody in the world! Where's Betty?"

There was no answer. "Are you hurt, Alex?"

"No."

"I think I got it bad. I think he smashed hell out of my right shoulder. I'm beginning to feel kind of funny. There's a lot of blood. Where do you think he is?"

"Near the shack. But I'm not sure."

"Maybe he's working his way towards me. I've hunted with him. He can move without a sound. Where's John?"

"In the dinghy."

"Where's his gun?"

"Maybe it's under him. I'll see if I can find it."

"Don't get careless. Don't give him a chance at you."

It was difficult to shift the body. He saw the muzzle under Geer's left thigh. He tilted the dinghy further and worked the gun out. He opened his mouth to call to Buddy that he had it, and then changed his mind. He waited a few minutes longer. Then he called, "Buddy."

"Yes?" The reply was alarmingly weak.

"I can't find it. I guess he dropped it over the side when he was hit."

"Then you . . . better . . . try to get out of here. I . . . can't. . . . Things are fading."

He checked the gun. The safety was off.

"Doyle!" It was Capp's voice, coming from the vicinity of the shack.

"What do you want, Mister Deputy, sir?"

"I want that little boat, Doyle. You shove it into shore nice, and I'll leave you healthy. I have to come get it and you'll be dead as the rest of 'em."

The final phrase made Doyle's heart sink. Up until that moment there had been frail hope. Now there was within him an anger so great that for a moment it blurred his vision.

"You haven't got a damn thing to lose by letting me have it too, Donnie. What guarantee have I got?"

"You took too much time, Doyle. You lost a chance. I'm coming after it."

He knew what the dinghy meant to Capp. With it he could get to the mainland. With his knowledge of the sloughs and swamps, he had a chance to get away. He heard a slow sloshing sound and knew that Donnie was wading out towards him. He could visualize him, the pale watchful eyes, the revolver ready. And he wouldn't want to take a chance on holing the dinghy.

Doyle weighed his chances. They were not good. He knew that he could put at least one hole in Capp, but one little twenty-two slug was not going to prevent Capp firing at least once, and from a range that would make a miss unlikely. And the impact of that slug would make the chance of a second hole in Donnie Capp very unlikely. His only possible chance would be to make Capp lose some of his animal caution. And so, as rapidly as he could without exposing himself in any way, Doyle began to scuttle backward in the deepening water, pulling the dinghy with one hand, holding the target pistol in his right.

Capp gave a grunt of surprise and anger, and, as Doyle continued to pull, he heard the thrashing, splashing sound of Capp running through the shallow water to overtake the boat before Doyle could reach the entrance to the bay.

It was difficult to guess by the sounds when Capp would be at the optimum distance. There would be no time to aim. And if he made his move at a moment when Capp's gun hand was swung forward in the effort of running through the water, one snap shot could end it.

When it seemed that Capp was almost near enough to touch the boat, Doyle got his feet under him, thrust the dinghy violently to one side and came to his feet in water almost to his waist, and saw Capp fifteen feet away plunging towards him. He had no conscious awareness of aiming. He did not hear the snapping of the shots. He merely kept the muzzle centred on Capp's chest and kept pulling the trigger. Donnie Capp blundered to a stop with a look of wild and vacant surprise on his seamed and sallow face. It was that inimitable look, the look a man uses but once in a lifetime. The look of the ultimate surprise.

Still off balance Capp thrust the heavy revolver forward and fired once. He got his balance and lowered the revolver slowly and fired again, down into the water beside his leg. As Doyle fired, he saw the small black spots appearing by magic in the faded khaki shirt. The gaudy deputy shield clinked and whined away.

Capp sat down in the water slowly, as though with deliberate caution. He stared at Doyle and then, suddenly, the look of surprise faded. And he was staring beyond Doyle, looking out into all the limitless space beyond the unknown stars. He toppled over on to his side, straightened out, made a slow half roll on to his face and sank, very slowly, to the bottom. The pale hat floated, right side up.

Doyle looked down at the gun in his hand. He lowered it. He trudged woodenly to the dinghy, dropped the gun in beside John Geer's body, and towed the dinghy ashore and beached it beside Capp's boat. And then he walked along the shore line in the water to the place where Buddy had dived into cover.

Buddy lay on his back, his face wet and grey, his lips blue. Doyle ripped the bloody shirt from the wound. It was blood from shoulder to waist. He took off his own shirt and, ripping long strips and fashioning two pads, he tightly bound the small entrance wound and the great torn hole in the rear. He made the binding tighter by using John Geer's belt. He felt the huge man's pulse. It felt frail and uncertain. There was nothing more he could do for him. He did not dare move him.

He went back to where the boats were. He took Lucas's ankles and dragged him back out of the water. He had seen the crabs hurry away when he pulled the old man out, so he left him face down in the heavy grass. He turned then, slowly, took a deep breath and walked up towards the shack, looking to left and right for the body of the girl.

She lay face down in heavy undergrowth to the left of the shack. He saw the white of her skirt and went over to her. The skirt was rumpled and dirty, and hiked above the brown knees. One foot was bare, a sandal on the other one. She lay, toeing in, one arm under her body. There was a large area behind and above her right ear where the heavy textured hair was matted with dark dried blood. A red ant crawled across the small of her brown back, where the yellow blouse had hiked up out of the waist of the skirt. He looked down at her and knew it was only the greatness of his need that made him think he saw a faint movement, as though she breathed. Suddenly and breathlessly, he dropped to his knees and laid his ear against the back of the yellow blouse. And heard then the slow and vital cadence of her heart, the deep and healthy thudding of the life in her. When he straightened up he was smiling like a fool, and the tears were running down his face.

He rolled her tenderly and carefully on to her back, and smoothed out her skirt and brushed her hair back from her forehead. He tore the pocket out of his trousers and rinsed it in salt water and used that to gently cleanse the grime and bits of twigs from her face. He kissed her unconscious lips.

After what seemed a very long time he heard the aircraft again, moving back and forth, pointing out the channels to someone else. Finally it was close. He could look up and catch glimpses of it through the leaves. It went away then and he heard the sound of motors and the voices of many men. He walked down and watched them come across the bay towards him.

CHAPTER ELEVEN

DOYLE, on the first day of May, walked out of the Davis General Hospital with Betty Larkin. He had driven her over to see Buddy. Buddy had been in a wheel chair on the sun porch, his smashed shoulder in a curious and complicated cast. And he had been restless and in a vile mood, convinced that everything at the yard was going to hell.

They walked across to the parking lot. Betty wore a beige dress with aqua buttons on the pockets. She wore a scarf over her head to hide the place where her hair had been shaved away so that the wound made by Donnie's club could be stitched.

She was subdued, thoughtful. After he had turned on to the road to Ramona, she said, "So you're all packed."

"Just about. Not much to pack."

"And you've got your reservation."

"Tomorrow at ten out of Tampa. I'll have to get a darn early start to unload this heap before I have to be at the airport."

"I could drive up with you, Alex. You could make the title over to me and I could sell it and send you the money."

"I wouldn't want to ask you to go to all that trouble."

"After what you did for us? Good Lord, Alex! And you won't even let us give you a dime of the money."

"What's the word on that, anyway?"

"Oh, you know those fruit jars where the rubber had rotted and water had got in, and the money was just a mass of glop? The lawyer says it will go to Washington where experts work on it, and he thinks we may get an almost hundred per cent recovery. We have no idea how much there is in those jars. And he says that the tax people are prepared to be reasonable. We may be able to keep quite a lot."

"I hope so."

"It would be nice to be out of hock on all the improvements we made. Poor John Geer. He said so many times that when we finally paid off the bank, he was going to get drunk."

"Are you still sore at me for lying to you in the beginning about why I came down?"

"No. I was sort of irritated. But I understand. If you remember, my friend, there were flaws in your performance. And I noticed them, too."

"So you did. Smart gal."

"It's nice to see you relaxed, Alex. You were so strained and nervous-acting."

"Because I was back here, mostly. I didn't want to come back. I felt this place had a hex on me."

"Boy leaves in disgrace. Man comes back and becomes big hero. Gets in all the papers. Becomes public figure."

"All right. I enjoy it, damn it. I enjoy walking down Bay Street and getting the big glad hand from end to end of it."

"You won't take any of the money?"

"How many times are you going to ask? No! Thanks."

She turned sideways in the seat. "I want to tell you something. When I went to the bank and looked at all that money there on that table, something happened to me. Maybe I lost a hex. I'd thought of Daddy as something larger than life. I never saw him in perspective, the way you are supposed to see your parents after you grow up. He kept on being a big, cold, watchful eye looking down at me from up in the clouds somewhere. Making me feel clumsy and guilty and ashamed. And then I saw the money. And I thought of him sneaking away in the skiff and squirrelling that money away in fruit jars in the ground, scared to death somebody would follow him or catch him at it. Something sort of went click. He wasn't big and cold and frightening any more. He was just a scared, greedy twisted little man. The only thing that really mattered in that shrivelled little soul was the money. Not Jenna. She was a pretty toy. And the hex faded. I feel sorry for him. I'm trying to understand him, Alex. He had so very little to start with. And it hurt him. But why should it hurt him? You had almost as little. You've done well. And you aren't all . . . withered up inside the way he was."

"Maybe I am, in some other way."

"Nonsense!"

"I mean it. I avoid emotions. I avoid emotional responsibilities, Betty. They scare me. That's part of why I had to be forced, or I would never have come back." She did not answer.

"Drop you at home?" he asked.

"Please. And if you don't mind, I'll jeep over later for a swim and get that spare key back, and see you haven't left anything around, such as a toothbrush."

She came out and swam, and she seemed particularly gay, joyous in a rather high-keyed way. After they had changed and were having a sunset drink on the porch, she went out to the jeep and came back with a package for him. He opened it, with protests.

"It's from Mom and Buddy and me, but I picked it out. It's the dangdest one I ever saw. It tells time, I think, if you can find the right hands to look at. But see all these little levers? With this you can do anything. But you better read the instructions."

"It's very handsome, and I thank you. Please thank your mother and Buddy for me." He put it on.

"What will you do with this old one?"

"Throw it away, I guess."

She put it in the pocket of her skirt. "I think I'll keep it. I'm a sentimental type. I'll put it with that old diary where you're featured so strongly. Mind?"

"If you want it. I don't know why you should want it. All it does is tell the time, and it doesn't do that very well."

"Which I had noticed and which I remembered." She put her glass on the railing. "Want me to drive up with you to-morrow?"

"I'll manage, thanks."

"So walk me out to the jeep and say good-bye, Alex."

They walked around the cottage to the blue jeep, waiting in patience in the heavy dusk.

"You will come back, won't you? Sometime?"

He looked at her standing there. And the need to say things was strong inside him, trying to break free. I will come back, to see you. Because I don't think I can go very long from here on without seeing you once in a while.

But he heard himself say, too casually, "I suppose I'll be back to look at the town. I don't know when, Betty."

"Oh, Alex!" she said in a choked voice, and he looked quickly at her and saw that there was just enough light to make the tear tracks on her cheeks gleam. She held her arms out towards him shyly, tentatively.

He took her in his arms strongly, with a sound in his throat like a sob, and then he could say the words. Something of how he felt when he thought her dead. How he would come back often, and only to be with her for a little while.

And then he kissed her. He felt again the resistance, her fright, the dead stiffness of her mouth. And just as he was about to release her in despair, her taut body began to relax, and there was a stir and a change in the texture of her mouth. She reached to put her arm awkwardly around his neck. She kissed him back meagrely, and then more firmly, and then suddenly with a great strong overwhelming joy. She pushed away from him and stared at him with her eyes wide and streaming, her lips tremulous.

"Pow!" she said softly, ludicrously. And came back strenuously for more. And backed away again, taking a quick step to regain her balance and said: "I feel dizzy. And I don't feel the least dang bit scared. Or crawly. Or anything like that. I feel like I'd all of a sudden turned into a big pile of warm raspberry Jello."

"I love you."

"Don't be silly! What else could feel like this? I love you too. More, please."

With the next kiss, her warm brown arms were strong and she made a guttural purring sound deep in her throat. And so she went home and she came back, and they walked and talked, with pauses for kisses, until dawn. There was lots of time coming for more than kisses, and this was the time to catch up on all of those that she had missed. She drove to Tampa with him, because he had to go back, at least this time. And by then it had been agreed that because she was a marriageable girl with perhaps plenty of money, he'd be very smart to marry her. He would go up and check on the next assignment and wangle something where a wife could be taken along, and also get enough time off to come down and marry her and take her back with him. And in the meantime she would have a chance to find a very bright girl for the office so Buddy wouldn't miss her too much. Then after she had her taste of far places, and probably enough kids to make travelling a major problem, he would have his twenty years in and they would come back to Ramona and buy on the beach and build there and drive Buddy nuts helping him run the Larkin-Doyle Boat Yard and Marina.

It seemed remarkably easy to organize the rest of your life. No trick at all.

He waved from the top of the ramp as he got on to the plane.

At first, when the stewardess walked down the aisle towards him, she smiled broadly. By the time they were over Georgia he thought she was looking at him rather strangely.

And it was then that he discovered that he was still wearing a big, broad, idiotic smile, fringed with lipstick.